CLUB VAMPYRE

CLUB VAMPYRE

Guilty Pleasures
The Laughing Corpse
Circus of the Damned

Laurell K. Hamilton

GUILDAMERICA
B O O K S®

GUILTY PLEASURES   Copyright © 1993 by Laurell K.
Hamilton

THE LAUGHING CORPSE   Copyright © 1994 by Laurell K.
Hamilton

CIRCUS OF THE DAMNED   Copyright © 1995 by Laurell
K. Hamilton

ISBN 1-56865-529-0

Published by arrangement with Ace Books
A Division of The Berkley Publishing Group
200 Madison Avenue
New York, New York 10016

Contents

GUILTY PLEASURES

To Gary W. Hamilton, my husband,
who doesn't like scary things,
but who read this book anyway.

Acknowledgments

Carl Nassau and Gary Chehowski for introducing me to the wide world of guns. Ricia Mainhardt, my agent, who believed in me. Deborah Millitello for enthusiasm above and beyond the call of duty. M. C. Sumner, new friend and valuable critic. Mary-Dale Amison, who has an eye for the small details that get by the rest of us. And to all the rest of the Alternate Historians who came in too late to critique this book: Janni Lee Simner, Marella Sands, and Robert K. Sheaf. Thanks for the cake, Bob. And to everyone who attended my reading at Archon 14.

1

Willie McCoy had been a jerk before he died. His being dead didn't change that. He sat across from me, wearing a loud plaid sport jacket. The polyester pants were primary Crayola green. His short, black hair was slicked back from a thin, triangular face. He had always reminded me of a bit player in a gangster movie. The kind that sells information, runs errands, and is expendable.

Of course now that Willie was a vampire, the expendable part didn't count anymore. But he was still selling information and running errands. No, death hadn't changed him much. But just in case, I avoided looking directly into his eyes. It was standard policy for dealing with vampires. He was a slime bucket, but now he was an undead slime bucket. It was a new category for me.

We sat in the quiet air-conditioned hush of my office. The powder blue walls, which Bert, my boss, thought would be soothing, made the room feel cold.

"Mind if I smoke?" he asked.

"Yes," I said, "I do."

"Damn, you aren't gonna make this easy, are you?"

I looked directly at him for a moment. His eyes were still brown. He caught me looking, and I looked down at my desk.

Willie laughed, a wheezing snicker of a sound. The laugh hadn't changed. "Geez, I love it. You're afraid of me."

"Not afraid, just cautious."

"You don't have to admit it. I can smell the fear on you, almost like somethin' touching my face, my brain. You're afraid of me, 'cause I'm a vampire."

I shrugged; what could I say? How do you lie to someone who can smell your fear? "Why are you here, Willie?"

"Geez, I wish I had a smoke." The skin began to jump at the corner of his mouth.

"I didn't think vampires had nervous twitches."

His hand went up, almost touched it. He smiled, flashing fangs. "Some things don't change."

I wanted to ask him, what does change? How does it feel to be dead? I knew other vampires, but Willie was the first I had known before and after death. It was a peculiar feeling. "What do you want?"

"Hey, I'm here to give you money. To become a client."

I glanced up at him, avoiding his eyes. His tie tack caught the overhead lights. Real gold. Willie had never had anything like that before. He was doing all right for a dead man. "I raise the dead for a living, no pun intended. Why would a vampire need a zombie raised?"

He shook his head, two quick jerks to either side. "No, no voodoo stuff. I wanna hire you to investigate some murderers."

"I am not a private investigator."

"But you got one of 'em on retainer to your outfit."

I nodded. "You could just hire Ms. Sims directly. You don't have to go through me for that."

Again that jerky head shake. "But she don't know about vampires the way you do."

I sighed. "Can we cut to the chase here, Willie? I have to leave"—I glanced at the wall clock—"in fifteen minutes. I don't like to leave a client waiting alone in a cemetery. They tend to get jumpy."

He laughed. I found the snickery laugh comforting, even with the fangs. Surely vampires should have rich, melodious laughs. "I'll bet they do. I'll just bet they do." His face sobered suddenly, as if a hand had wiped his laughter away.

I felt fear like a jerk in the pit of my stomach. Vampires could change movements like clicking a switch. If he could do that, what else could he do?

"You know about the vampires that are getting wasted over in the District?"

He made it a question, so I answered. "I'm familiar with them." Four vampires had been slaughtered in the new vampire club district. Their hearts had been torn out, their heads cut off.

"You still working with the cops?"

"I am still on retainer with the new task force."

He laughed again. "Yeah, the spook squad. Underbudgeted and undermanned, right."

"You've described most of the police work in this town."

"Maybe, but the cops feel like you do, Anita. What's one more dead vampire? New laws don't change that."

It had only been two years since Addison v. Clark. The court case gave us a revised version of what life was, and what death wasn't. Vampirism was legal in the good ol' U. S. of A. We were one of the few countries to acknowledge them. The immigration people were having fits trying to keep foreign vampires from immigrating in, well, flocks.

All sorts of questions were being fought out in court. Did heirs have to give back their inheritance? Were you widowed if your spouse became undead? Was it murder to slay a vampire? There was even a movement to give them the vote. Times were a-changing.

I stared at the vampire in front of me and shrugged. Did I really believe, what was one more dead vampire? Maybe. "If you believe I feel that way, why come to me at all?"

"Because you're the best at what you do. We need the best."

It was the first time he had said "we." "Who are you working for, Willie?"

He smiled then, a close secretive smile, like he knew something I should know. "Never you mind that. Money's real good. We want somebody who knows the night life to be looking into these murders."

"I've seen the bodies, Willie. I gave my opinions to the police."

"What'd you think?" He leaned forward in the chair, small hands flat on my desk. His fingernails were pale, almost white, bloodless.

"I gave a full report to the police." I stared up at him, almost looking him in the eye.

"Won't even give me that, will ya?"

"I am not at liberty to discuss police business with you."

"I told 'em you wouldn't go for this."

"Go for what? You haven't told me a damn thing."

"We want you to investigate the vampire killings, find out who's, or what's, doing it. We'll pay you three times your normal fee."

I shook my head. That explained why Bert, the greedy son of a gun, had set up this meeting. He knew how I felt about vampires, but my contract forced me to at least meet with any client that had given Bert a retainer. My boss would do anything for money. Problem was he thought I should, too. Bert and I would be having a "talk" very soon.

I stood. "The police are looking into it. I am already giving them all the help I can. In a way I am already working on the case. Save your money."

He sat staring up at me, very still. It was not that lifeless immobility of the long dead, but it was a shadow of it.

Fear ran up my spine and into my throat. I fought an urge to draw my crucifix out of my shirt and drive him from my office. Somehow throwing a client out using a holy item seemed less than professional. So I just stood there, waiting for him to move.

"Why won't you help us?"

"I have clients to meet, Willie. I'm sorry that I can't help you."

"Won't help, you mean."

I nodded. "Have it your way." I walked around the desk to show him to the door.

He moved with a liquid quickness that Willie had never had, but I saw him move and was one step back from his reaching hand. "I'm not just another pretty face to fall for mind tricks."

"You saw me move."

"I heard you move. You're the new dead, Willie. Vampire or not, you've got a lot to learn."

He was frowning at me, hand still half-extended towards me. "Maybe, but no human could a stepped outta reach like that." He stepped up close to me, plaid jacket nearly brushing against me. Pressed together like that, we were nearly the same height—short. His eyes were on a perfect level with mine. I stared as hard as I could at his shoulder.

It took everything I had not to step back from him. But dammit, undead or not, he was Willie McCoy. I wasn't going to give him the satisfaction.

He said, "You ain't human, any more than I am."

I moved to open the door. I hadn't stepped away from him. I had stepped away to open the door. I tried convincing the sweat along my spine that there was a difference. The cold feeling in my stomach wasn't fooled either.

"I really have to be going now. Thank you for thinking of Animators, Inc." I gave him my best professional smile, empty of meaning as a light bulb, but dazzling.

He paused in the open doorway. "Why won't you work for us? I gotta tell 'em something when I go back."

I wasn't sure, but there was something like fear in his voice. Would he get in trouble for failing? I felt sorry for him and knew it was stupid. He was the undead, for heaven's sake, but he stood looking at me, and he was still Willie, with his funny coats and small nervous hands.

"Tell them, whoever they are, that I don't work for vampires."

"A firm rule?" Again he made it sound like a question.

"Concrete."

There was a flash of something on his face, the old Willie peeking through. It was almost pity. "I wish you hadn't said that, Anita. These people don't like anybody telling 'em no."

"I think you've overstayed your welcome. I don't like to be threatened."

"It ain't a threat, Anita. It's the truth." He straightened his tie, fondling the new gold tie tack, squared his thin shoulders and walked out.

I closed the door behind him and leaned against it. My knees felt weak. But there wasn't time for me to sit here and shake. Mrs. Grundick was probably already at the cemetery. She would be standing there with her little black purse and her grown sons, waiting for me to raise her husband from the dead. There was a mystery of two very different wills. It was either years of court costs and arguments, or raise Albert Grundick from the dead and ask.

Everything I needed was in my car, even the chickens. I drew the silver crucifix free of my blouse and let it hang in full view. I have several guns, and I know how to use them. I keep a 9 mm Browning Hi-Power in my desk. The gun weighed a little over two pounds, silver-plated bullets and all. Silver won't kill a vampire, but it can discourage them. It forces them to have to heal the wounds, almost human slow. I wiped my sweaty palms on my skirt and went out.

Craig, our night secretary, was typing furiously at the computer keyboard. His eyes widened as I walked over the thick carpeting. Maybe it was the cross swinging on its long chain. Maybe it was the shoulder rig tight across my back, and the gun out in plain sight. He didn't mention either. Smart man.

I put my nice little corduroy jacket over it all. The jacket didn't lie flat over the gun, but that was okay. I doubted the Grundicks and their lawyers would notice.

2

I had gotten to see the sun rise as I drove home that morning. I hate sunrises. They mean I've overscheduled myself and worked all bloody night. St. Louis has more trees edging its highways than any other city I have driven through. I could almost admit the trees looked nice in the first light of dawn, almost. My apartment always looks depressingly white and cheerful in morning sunlight. The walls are the same vanilla ice cream white as every apartment I've ever seen. The carpeting is a nice shade of grey, preferable to that dog poop brown that is more common.

The apartment is a roomy one-bedroom. I am told it has a nice view of the park next door. You couldn't prove it by me. If I had my choice, there would be no windows. I get by with heavy drapes that turn the brightest day to cool twilight.

I switched the radio on low to drown the small noises of my day-living neighbors. Sleep sucked me under to the soft music of Chopin. A minute later the phone rang.

I lay there for a minute, cursing myself for forgetting to turn on the answering machine. Maybe if I ignored it? Five rings later I gave in. "Hello."

"Oh, I'm sorry. Did I wake you?"

It was a woman I didn't know. If it was a salesperson I was going to become violent. "Who is this?" I blinked at the bedside clock. It was eight. I'd had nearly two hours of sleep. Yippee.

"I'm Monica Vespucci." She said it like it should explain everything. It didn't.

"Yes." I tried to sound helpful, encouraging. I think it came out as a growl.

"Oh, my, uh. I'm the Monica that works with Catherine Maison."

I huddled around the receiver and tried to think. I don't think really well on two hours of sleep. Catherine was a good friend, a name I knew. She had probably mentioned this woman to me, but for the life of me, I couldn't place her. "Sure, Monica, yes. What do you want?" It sounded rude, even to me. "I'm sorry if I don't sound too good. I got off work at six."

"My god, you mean you've only had two hours of sleep. Do you want to shoot me, or what?"

I didn't answer the question. I'm not that rude. "Did you want something, Monica?"

"Sure, yes. I'm throwing a surprise bachelorette party for Catherine. You know she gets married next month."

I nodded, remembered she couldn't see me, and mumbled, "I'm in the wedding."

"Oh, sure, I knew that. Pretty dresses for the bridesmaids, don't you think?"

Actually, the last thing I wanted to spend a hundred and twenty dollars on was a long pink formal with puffy sleeves, but it was Catherine's wedding. "What about the bachelorette party?"

"Oh, I'm rambling, aren't I? And you just desperate for sleep."

I wondered if screaming at her would make her go away any faster. Naw, she'd probably cry. "What do you want, please, Monica?"

"Well, I know it's short notice, but everything just sort of slipped up on me. I meant to call you a week ago, but I just never got around to it."

This I believed. "Go on."

"The bachelorette party is tonight. Catherine says you don't drink, so I was wondering if you could be designated driver."

I just lay there for a minute, wondering how mad to get, and if it would do me any good. Maybe if I'd been more awake, I wouldn't have said what I was thinking. "Don't you think this is awfully short notice, since you want me to drive?"

"I know. I'm so sorry. I'm just so scattered lately. Catherine told me you usually have either Friday or Saturday night off. Is Friday not your night off this week?"

As a matter of fact it was, but I didn't really want to give up my only night off to this airhead on the other end of the phone. "I do have the night off."

"Great! I'll give you directions, and you can pick us up after work. Is that okay?"

It wasn't, but what else could I say. "That's fine."

"Pencil and paper?"

"You said you worked with Catherine, right?" I was actually beginning to remember Monica.

"Why, yes."

"I know where Catherine works. I don't need directions."

"Oh, how silly of me, of course. Then we'll see you about five. Dress up, but no heels. We may be dancing tonight."

I hate to dance. "Sure, see you then."

"See you tonight."

The phone went dead in my ear. I turned on the answering machine and cuddled back under the sheets. Monica worked with Catherine, that made her a lawyer. That was a frightening thought. Maybe she was one of those people who was only organized at work. Naw.

It occurred to me then, when it was too late, that I could just have refused the invitation. Damn. I was quick today. Oh, well, how bad could it be? Watching strangers get blitzed out of their minds. If I was lucky, maybe someone would throw up in my car.

I had the strangest dreams once I got back to sleep. All about this woman I didn't know, a coconut cream pie, and Willie McCoy's funeral.

3

Monica Vespucci was wearing a button that said, "Vampires are People, too." It was not a promising beginning to the evening. Her white blouse was silk with a high, flared collar framing a dark, health-club tan. Her hair was short and expertly cut; her makeup, perfect.

The button should have tipped me off to what kind of bachelorette party she'd planned. Some days I'm just slow to catch on.

I was wearing black jeans, knee-high boots, and a crimson blouse. My hair was made to order for the outfit, black curling just over the shoulders of the red blouse. The solid, nearly black-brown of my eyes matches the hair. Only the skin stands out, too pale, Germanic against the Latin darkness. A very ex-boyfriend once described me as a little china doll. He meant it as a compliment. I didn't take it that way. There are reasons why I don't date much.

The blouse was long-sleeved to hide the knife sheath on my right wrist and the scars on my left arm. I had left my gun locked in the trunk of my car. I didn't think the bachelorette party would get that out of hand.

"I'm so sorry that I put off planning this to the last minute, Catherine. That's why there's only three of us. Everybody else had plans," Monica said.

"Imagine that, people having plans for Friday night," I said.

Monica stared at me as if trying to decide whether I was joking or not.

Catherine gave me a warning glare. I gave them both my best angelic smile. Monica smiled back. Catherine wasn't fooled.

Monica began dancing down the sidewalk, happy as a drunken clam. She had had only two drinks with dinner. It was a bad sign.

"Be nice," Catherine whispered.

"What did I say?"

"Anita." Her voice sounded like my father's used to sound when I'd stayed out too late.

I sighed. "You're just no fun tonight."

"I plan to be a lot of fun tonight." She stretched her arms skyward. She still wore the crumpled remains of her business suit. The wind blew her long, copper-colored hair. I've never been able to decide if Catherine would be prettier if she cut her hair, so you'd notice the face first, or if the hair was what made her pretty.

"If I have to give up one of my few free nights, then I am going to enjoy myself—immensely," she said.

There was a kind of fierceness to the last word. I stared up at her. "You are not planning to get falling-down drunk, are you?"

"Maybe." She looked smug.

Catherine knew I didn't approve of, or rather, didn't understand drinking. I didn't like having my inhibitions lowered. If I was going to cut loose, I wanted to be in control of just how loose I got.

We had left my car in a parking lot two blocks back. The one with the wrought-iron fence around it. There wasn't much parking down by the river. The narrow brick roads and ancient sidewalks had been designed for horses, not automobiles. The streets had been fresh-washed by a summer thunderstorm that had come and gone while we ate dinner. The first stars glittered overhead, like diamonds trapped in velvet.

Monica yelled, "Hurry up, slowpokes."

Catherine looked at me and grinned. The next thing I knew, she was running towards Monica.

"Oh, for heaven's sake," I muttered. Maybe if I'd had drinks with dinner, I'd have run, too, but I doubted it.

"Don't be an old stick in the mud," Catherine called back.

Stick in the mud? I caught up to them walking. Monica was giggling. Somehow I had known she would be. Catherine and she were leaning against each other laughing. I suspected they might be laughing at me.

Monica calmed enough to fake an ominous stage whisper. "Do you know what lies around this corner?"

As a matter of fact, I did. The last vampire killing had been only four blocks from here. We were in what the vampires called "the District." Humans called it the Riverfront, or Blood Square, depending on if they were being rude or not.

"Guilty Pleasures," I said.

"Oh, pooh, you spoiled the surprise."

"What's Guilty Pleasures?" Catherine asked.

Monica giggled. "Oh, goodie, the surprise isn't spoiled after all." She put her arm through Catherine's. "You are going to love this, I promise you."

Maybe Catherine would; I knew I wouldn't, but I followed them around the corner anyway. The sign was a wonderful swirling neon the color of heart blood. The symbolism was not lost on me.

We went up three broad steps, and there was a vampire standing in front of the propped-open door. He had a black crew cut and small, pale eyes. His massive shoulders threatened to rip the tight black t-shirt he wore. Wasn't pumping iron redundant after you died?

Even standing on the threshold I could hear the busy hum of voices, laughter, music. That rich, murmurous sound of many people in a small space, determined to have a good time.

The vampire stood beside the door, very still. There was still a movement to him, an aliveness, for lack of a better term. He couldn't have been dead more than twenty years, if that. In the dark he looked almost human, even to me. He had fed already tonight. His skin was flushed and healthy. He looked damn near rosy-cheeked. A meal of fresh blood will do that to you.

Monica squeezed his arm. "Ooo, feel that muscle."

He grinned, flashing fangs. Catherine gasped. He grinned wider.

"Buzz here is an old friend, aren't you, Buzz?"

Buzz the vampire? Surely not.

But he nodded. "Go on in, Monica. Your table is waiting."

Table? What kind of clout did Monica have? Guilty Pleasures was one of the hottest clubs in the District, and they did not take reservations.

There was a large sign on the door. "No crosses, crucifixes, or other holy items allowed inside." I read the sign and walked past it. I had no intention of getting rid of my cross.

A rich, melodious voice floated around us. "Anita, how good of you to come."

The voice belonged to Jean-Claude, club owner and master vampire. He looked like a vampire was supposed to look. Softly curling hair tangled with the high white lace of an antique shirt. Lace spilled over pale, long-fingered hands. The shirt hung open, giving a glimpse of lean bare chest framed by more frothy lace. Most men couldn't have worn a shirt like that. The vampire made it seem utterly masculine.

"You two know each other?" Monica sounded surprised.

"Oh, yes," Jean-Claude said. "Ms. Blake and I have met before."

"I've been helping the police work cases on the Riverfront."

"She is their vampire expert." He made the last word soft and warm and vaguely obscene.

Monica giggled. Catherine was staring at Jean-Claude, eyes wide and innocent. I touched her arm, and she jerked as if waking from a dream. I didn't bother to whisper because I knew he would have heard me anyway. "Important safety tip—never look a vampire in the eye."

She nodded. The first hint of fear showed in her face.

"I would never harm such a lovely young woman." He took Catherine's hand and raised it to his mouth. A mere brush of lips. Catherine blushed.

He kissed Monica's hand as well. He looked at me and laughed. "Do not worry, my little animator. I will not touch you. That would be cheating."

He moved to stand next to me. I stared fixedly at his chest. There was a burn scar almost hidden in the lace. The burn was in the shape of a cross. How many decades ago had someone shoved a cross into his flesh?

"Just as you having a cross would be an unfair advantage."

What could I say? In a way he was right.

It was a shame that it wasn't merely the shape of a cross that hurt a vampire. Jean-Claude would have been in deep shit. Unfortunately, the cross had to be blessed, and backed up by faith. An atheist waving a cross at a vampire was a truly pitiful sight.

He breathed my name like a whisper against my skin. "Anita, what are you thinking?"

The voice was so damn soothing. I wanted to look up and see what face went with such words. Jean-Claude had been intrigued by my partial immunity to him. That and the cross-shaped burn scar on my arm. He found the scar amusing. Every time we met, he did his best to bespell me, and I did my best to ignore him. I had won up until now.

"You never objected to me carrying a cross before."

"You were on police business then; now you are not."

I stared at his chest and wondered if the lace was as soft as it looked; probably not.

"Are you so insecure in your own powers, little animator? Do you believe that all your resistance to me resides in that piece of silver around your neck?"

I didn't believe that, but I knew it helped. Jean-Claude was a self-admitted two hundred and five years old. A vampire gains a lot of power in two centuries. He was suggesting I was a coward. I was not.

I reached up to unfasten the chain. He stepped away from me and turned his back. The cross spilled silver into my hands. A blonde human woman appeared beside me. She handed me a check stub and took the cross. Nice, a holy item check girl.

I felt suddenly underdressed without my cross. I slept and showered in it.

Jean-Claude stepped close again. "You will not resist the show tonight, Anita. Someone will enthrall you."

"No," I said. But it's hard to be tough when you're staring at someone's chest. You really need eye contact to play tough, but that was a no-no.

He laughed. The sound seemed to rub over my skin, like the brush of fur. Warm and feeling ever so slightly of death.

Monica grabbed my arm. "You're going to love this, I promise you."

"Yes," Jean-Claude said. "It will be a night you will never forget."

"Is that a threat?"

He laughed again, that warm awful sound. "This is a place of pleasure, Anita, not violence."

Monica was pulling at my arm. "Hurry, the entertainment's about to begin."

"Entertainment?" Catherine asked.

I had to smile. "Welcome to the world's only vampire strip club, Catherine."

"You are joking."

"Scout's honor." I glanced back at the door; I don't know why. Jean-Claude stood utterly still, no sense of anything, as if he were not there at all. Then he moved, one pale hand raised to his lips. He blew me a kiss across the room. The night's entertainment had begun.

4

Our table was nearly bumping up against the stage. The room was full of liquor and laughter, and a few faked screams as the vampire waiters moved around the tables. There was an undercurrent of fear. That peculiar terror that you get on roller coasters and at horror movies. Safe terror.

The lights went out. Screams echoed through the room, high and shrill. Real fear for an instant. Jean-Claude's voice came out of the darkness. "Welcome to Guilty Pleasures. We are here to serve you. To make your most evil thought come true."

His voice was silken whispers in the small hours of night. Damn, he was good.

"Have you ever wondered what it would be like to feel my breath upon your skin? My lips along your neck. The hard brush of teeth. The sweet, sharp pain of fangs. Your heart beating frantically against my chest. Your blood flowing into my veins. Sharing yourself. Giving me life. Knowing that I truly could not live without you, all of you."

Perhaps it was the intimacy of darkness; whatever, I felt as if his voice was speaking just for me, to me. I was his chosen, his special one. No, that wasn't right. Every woman in the club felt the same. We were all his chosen. And perhaps there was more truth in that than in anything else.

"Our first gentleman tonight shares your fantasy. He wanted to know how the sweetest of kisses would feel. He has gone before you to tell you that it is wondrous." He let silence fill the darkness, until my own heartbeat sounded loud. "Phillip is with us tonight."

Monica whispered, "Phillip!" A collective gasp ran through the audience, then a soft chanting began. "Phillip, Phillip . . ." The sound rose around us in the dark like a prayer.

The lights began to come up like at the end of a movie. A figure stood in the center of the stage. A white t-shirt hugged his upper body; not a muscleman, but well built. Not too much of a good thing. A black leather jacket, tight jeans and boots completed the outfit. He could have walked off any street. His thick, brown hair was long enough to sweep his shoulders.

Music drifted into the twilit silence. The man swayed to the sounds, hips rotating ever so slightly. He began to slip out of the leather jacket, moving almost in slow motion. The soft music began to have a pulse. A pulse that his body moved with, swaying. The jacket slid to the stage. He stared out at the audience for a minute, letting us see what there was to see. Scars hugged the bend of each arm, until the skin had formed white mounds of scar tissue.

I swallowed hard. I wasn't sure what was about to happen, but I was betting I wasn't going to like it.

He swept back his long hair from his face with both hands. He swayed and strutted around the edge of the stage. He stood near our table, looking down at us. His neck looked like a junkie's arm.

I had to look away. All those neat little bite marks, neat little scars. I glanced up and found Catherine staring at her lap. Monica was leaning forward in her chair, lips half-parted.

He grabbed the t-shirt with strong hands and pulled. It peeled away from his chest, ripping. Screams from the audience. A few of them called his name. He smiled. The smile was dazzling, brilliant, melt-in-your-mouth sexy.

There was scar tissue on his smooth, bare chest: white scars, pinkish scars, new scars, old scars. I just sat staring with my mouth open.

Catherine whispered, "Dear God!"

"He's wonderful, isn't he?" Monica asked.

I glanced at her. Her flared collar had slipped, exposing two neat puncture wounds, fairly old, almost scars. Sweet Jesus.

The music burst into a pulsing violence. He danced, swaying, gyrating, throwing the strength of his body into every move. There was a white mass of scars over his left collarbone, ragged and vicious. My stomach tightened. A vampire had torn through his collarbone, ripped at him like a dog with a piece of meat. I knew, because I had a similar scar. I had a lot of similar scars.

Dollar bills appeared in hands like mushrooms after a rain. Monica was waving her money like a flag. I didn't want Phillip at our table. I had to lean into Monica to be heard over the noise. "Monica, please, don't bring him over here."

Even as she turned to look at me, I knew it was too late. Phillip of the many scars was standing on the stage, looking down at us. I stared up into his very human eyes.

I could see the pulse in Monica's throat. She licked her lips; her eyes were enormous. She stuffed the money down the front of his pants.

Her hands traced his scars like nervous butterflies. She leaned her face close to his stomach and began kissing his scars, leaving red lipstick prints behind. He knelt as she kissed him, forcing her mouth higher and higher up his chest.

He knelt, and she pressed lips to his face. He brushed his hair back from his neck, as if he knew what she wanted. She licked the newest bite scar, tongue small and pink, like a cat. I heard her breath go out in a trembling sigh. She bit him, mouth locking over the wound. Phillip jerked with pain, or just surprise. Her jaws tightened, her throat worked. She was sucking the wound.

I looked across the table at Catherine. She was staring at them, face blank with astonishment.

The crowd was going wild, screaming and waving money. Phillip pulled away from Monica and moved on to another table. Monica slumped forward, head collapsing into her lap, arms limp at her side.

Had she fainted? I reached out to touch her shoulder and realized I didn't want to touch her. I gripped her shoulder gently. She moved, turning her head to look at me. Her eyes held that lazy fullness that sex gives. Her mouth looked pale with most of the lipstick worn away. She hadn't fainted; she was basking in the afterglow.

I drew back from her, rubbing my hand against my jeans. My palms were sweating.

Phillip was back on the stage. He had stopped dancing. He was just standing there. Monica had left a small round mark on his neck.

I felt the first stirrings of an old mind, flowing over the crowd. Catherine asked, "What's happening?"

"It's all right," Monica said. She was sitting upright in her chair, eyes still half-closed. She licked her lips and stretched, hands over her head.

Catherine turned to me. "Anita, what is it?"

"Vampire," I said.

Fear flashed on her face, but it didn't last. I watched the fear fade under the weight of the vampire's mind. She turned slowly to stare at Phillip as he waited on the stage. Catherine was in no danger. This mass hypnosis was not personal, and not permanent.

The vampire wasn't as old as Jean-Claude, nor as good. I sat there feeling the press and flow of over a hundred years of power, and it wasn't enough. I felt him move up through the tables. He had gone to a lot of trouble to make sure the poor humans wouldn't see him come. He would simply appear in their midst, like magic.

You don't get to surprise vampires often. I turned to watch the vampire walk towards the stage. Every human face I saw was enraptured, turned blindly to the stage, waiting. The vampire was tall with high cheekbones, model-perfect, sculpted. He was too masculine to be beautiful, and too perfect to be real.

He strode through the tables wearing a proverbial vampire outfit, black tux and white gloves. He stopped one table away from me, to stare. He held the audience in the palm of his mind, helpless and waiting. But there I sat staring at him, though not at his eyes.

His body stiffened, surprised. There's nothing like ruining the calm of a hundred-year-old vampire to boost a girl's morale.

I looked past him to see Jean-Claude. He was staring at me. I saluted him with my drink. He acknowledged it with a nod of his head.

The tall vampire was standing beside Phillip. Phillip's eyes were as blank as any human's. The spell or whatever drifted away. With a thought he awoke the audience, and they gasped. Magic.

Jean-Claude's voice filled the sudden silence. "This is Robert. Welcome him to our stage."

The crowd went wild, applauding and screaming. Catherine was applauding along with everyone else. Apparently, she was impressed.

The music changed again, pulsing and throbbing in the air, almost painfully loud. Robert the vampire began to dance. He moved with a careful violence, pumping to the music. He threw his white gloves into the audience. One landed at my feet. I left it there.

Monica said, "Pick it up."

I shook my head.

Another woman leaned over from another table. Her breath smelled like whiskey. "You don't want it?"

I shook my head.

She got up, I suppose to get the glove. Monica beat her to it. The woman sat down, looking unhappy.

The vampire had stripped, showing a smooth expanse of chest. He dropped to the stage and did fingertip push-ups. The audience went wild. I wasn't impressed. I knew he could bench press a car, if he wanted to. What's a few push-ups compared to that?

He began to dance around Phillip. Phillip turned to face him, arms outspread, slightly crouched, as if he were ready for an attack. They began circling each other. The music softened until it was only a soft underscoring to the movements on stage.

The vampire began to move closer to Phillip. Phillip moved as if trying to run from the stage. The vampire was suddenly there, blocking his escape.

I hadn't seen him move. The vampire had just appeared in front of the man. I hadn't seen him move. Fear drove all the air from my body in an icy rush. I hadn't felt the mind trick, but it had happened.

Jean-Claude was standing only two tables away. He raised one pale hand in a salute to me. The bastard had been in my mind, and I hadn't known it. The audience gasped, and I looked back to the stage.

They were both kneeling; the vampire had one of Phillip's arms pinned behind his back. One hand gripped Phillip's long hair, pulling his neck back at a painful angle.

Phillip's eyes were wide and terrified. The vampire hadn't put him under. He wasn't under! He was aware and scared. Dear God. He was panting, his chest rising and falling in short gasps.

The vampire looked out at the audience and hissed, fangs flashing in the lights. The hiss turned the beautiful face to something bestial. His hunger rode out over the crowd. His need so intense, it made my stomach cramp.

No, I would not feel this with him. I dug fingernails into the palm of my hand and concentrated. The feeling faded. Pain helped. I opened my shaking fingers and found four half-moons that slowly filled with blood. The hunger beat around me, filling the crowd, but not me, not me.

I pressed a napkin to my hand and tried to look inconspicuous.

The vampire drew back his head.

"No," I whispered.

The vampire struck, teeth sinking into flesh. Phillip shrieked, and it echoed in the club. The music died abruptly. No one moved. You could have dropped a pin.

Soft, moist sucking sounds filled the silence. Phillip began to moan, high in his throat. Over and over again, small helpless sounds.

I looked out at the crowd. They were with the vampire, feeling his hunger, his need, feeling him feed. Maybe sharing Phillip's terror, I didn't know. I was apart from it, and glad.

The vampire stood, letting Phillip fall to the stage, limp, unmoving. I stood without meaning to. The man's scarred back convulsed in a deep, shattering breath, as if he were fighting back from death. And maybe he was.

He was alive. I sat back down. My knees felt weak. Sweat covered my palms and stung the cuts on my hand. He was alive, and he enjoyed it. I wouldn't have believed it if someone had told me. I would have called them a liar.

A vampire junkie. Surely to God, I'd seen everything now.

Jean-Claude whispered, "Who wants a kiss?"

No one moved for a heartbeat; then hands, holding money, raised here and there. Not many, but a few. Most people looked confused, as if they had woken from a bad dream. Monica was holding money up.

Phillip lay where he had been dropped, chest rising and falling.

Robert the vampire came to Monica. She tucked money down his pants. He pressed his bloody, fanged mouth to her lips. The kiss was long and deep, full of probing tongues. They were tasting each other.

The vampire drew away from Monica. Her hands at his neck tried to draw him back, but he pulled away. He turned to me. I shook my head and showed him empty hands. No money here, folks.

He grabbed for me, snake-quick. No time to think. My chair crashed to the floor. I was standing, just out of reach. No ordinary human could have seen him coming. The jig, as they say, was up.

A buzz of voices raised through the audience as they tried to figure out what had happened. Just your friendly neighborhood animator, folks, nothing to get excited about. The vampire was still staring at me.

Jean-Claude was suddenly beside me, and I hadn't seen him come. "Are you all right, Anita?"

His voice held things that the words didn't even hint at. Promises whispered in darkened rooms, under cool sheets. He sucked me under, rolled my mind like a wino after money, and it felt good. Crash—Shrill—Noise thundered through my mind, chased the vampire out, held him at bay.

My beeper had gone off. I blinked and staggered against our table. He reached out to steady me. "Don't touch me," I said.

He smiled. "Of course."

I pushed the button on my beeper to silence it. Thank you God, that I hung the beeper on my waistband instead of stuffing it in a purse. I might never have heard it otherwise. I called from the phone at the bar. The police wanted my expertise at the Hillcrest Cemetery. I had to work on my night off. Yippee, and I meant it.

I offered to take Catherine with me, but she wanted to stay. Whatever else you can say about vampires, they are fascinating. It went with the job description, like drinking blood and working nights. It was her choice.

I promised to come back in time to drive them home. Then I picked up my cross from the holy item check girl and slipped it inside my shirt.

Jean-Claude was standing by the door. He said, "I almost had you, my little animator."

I glanced at his face and quickly down. "Almost doesn't count, you blood-sucking bastard."

Jean-Claude threw back his head and laughed. His laughter followed me out into the night, like velvet rubbing along my spine.

5

The coffin lay on its side. A white scar of claw marks ran down the dark varnish. The pale blue lining, imitation silk, was sliced and gouged. One bloody handprint showed plainly; it could almost have been human. All that was left of the older corpse was a shredded brown suit, a finger bone gnawed clean and a scrap of scalp. The man had been blond.

A second body lay perhaps five feet away. The man's clothes were shredded. His chest had been ripped open, ribs cracked like eggshells. Most of his internal organs were gone, leaving his body cavity like a hollowed-out log. Only his face was untouched. Pale eyes stared impossibly wide up into the summer stars.

I was glad it was dark. My night vision is good, but darkness steals color. All the blood was black. The man's body was lost in the shadows of the trees. I didn't have to see him, unless I walked up to him. I had done that. I had measured the bite marks with my trusty tape measure. With my little plastic gloves I had searched the corpse over, looking for clues. There weren't any.

I could do anything I wanted to the scene of the crime. It had already been videotaped and snapped from every possible angle. I was always the last "expert" called in. The ambulance was waiting to take the bodies away, once I was finished.

I was about finished. I knew what had killed the man. Ghouls. I had narrowed the search down to a particular kind of undead. Bully for me. The coroner could have told them that.

I was beginning to sweat inside the coverall I had put on to protect my clothes. The coverall was originally for vampire stakings, but I had started using it at crime scenes. There were black stains at the knees and down the legs. There had been so much blood in the grass. Thank you, dear God, that I didn't have to see this in broad daylight.

I don't know why seeing something like this in daylight makes it worse, but I'm more likely to dream about a daylight scene. The blood is always so red and brown and thick.

Night softens it, makes it less real. I appreciated that.

I unzipped the front of my coverall, letting it gape open around my clothes. The wind blew against me, amazingly cool. The air smelled of rain. Another thunderstorm was moving this way.

The yellow police tape was wrapped around tree trunks, strung through bushes. One yellow loop went around the stone feet of an angel. The tape flapped and cracked in the growing wind. Sergeant Rudolf Storr lifted the tape and walked towards me.

He was six-eight and built like a wrestler. He had a brisk, striding walk. His close-cropped black hair left his ears bare. Dolph was the head of the newest task force, the spook squad. Officially, it was the Regional Preternatural Investigation Team, R-P-I-T, pronounced rip it. It handled all supernatural-related crime. It wasn't exactly a step up for his career. Willie McCoy had been right; the task force was a half-hearted effort to placate the press and the liberals.

Dolph had pissed somebody off, or he wouldn't have been here. But Dolph, being Dolph, was determined to do the best job he could. He was like a force of nature. He didn't yell, he was just there, and things got done because of it.

"Well," he said.

That's Dolph, a man of many words. "It was a ghoul attack."

"And."

I shrugged. "And there are no ghouls in this cemetery."

He stared down at me, face carefully neutral. He was good at that, didn't like to influence his people. "You just said it was a ghoul attack."

"Yes, but they came from somewhere outside the cemetery."

"So?"

"I have never known of any ghouls to travel this far outside their own cemetery." I stared at him, trying to see if he understood what I was saying.

"Tell me about ghouls, Anita." He had his trusty little notebook out, pen poised and ready.

"This cemetery is still holy ground. Cemeteries that have ghoul infestations are usually very old or have satanic or certain voodoo rites performed in them. The evil sort of uses up the blessing, until the ground becomes unholy. Once that happens, ghouls either move in or rise from the graves. No one's sure exactly which."

"Wait, what do you mean, that no one knows?"

"Basically."

He shook his head, staring at the notes he'd made, frowning. "Explain."

"Vampires are made by other vampires. Zombies are raised from the grave by an animator or voodoo priest. Ghouls, as far as we know, just crawl out of their graves on their own. There are theories that very evil people become ghouls. I don't buy that. There was a theory for a while that people bitten by a supernatural being, wereanimal, vampire, whatever, would be-

come a ghoul. But I've seen whole cemeteries emptied, every corpse a ghoul.
No way they were all attacked by supernatural forces while alive.''

"All right, we don't know where ghouls come from. What do we
know?''

"Ghouls don't rot like zombies. They retain their form more like vampires. They are more than animal intelligent, but not by much. They are
cowards and won't attack a person unless she is hurt or unconscious.''

"They sure as hell attacked the groundskeeper.''

"He could have been knocked unconscious somehow.''

"How?''

"Someone would have had to knock him out.''

"Is that likely?''

"No, ghouls don't work with humans, or any other undead. A zombie
will obey orders, vampires have their own thoughts. Ghouls are like pack
animals, wolves maybe, but a lot more dangerous. They wouldn't be able to
understand working with someone. If you're not a ghoul, you're either meat
or something to hide from.''

"Then what happened here?''

"Dolph, these ghouls traveled quite a distance to reach this cemetery.
There isn't another one for miles. Ghouls don't travel like that. So maybe,
just maybe, they attacked the caretaker when he came to scare them off.
They should have run from him; maybe they didn't.''

"Could it be something, or someone, pretending to be ghouls?''

"Maybe, but I doubt it. Whoever it was, they ate that man. A human
might do that, but a human couldn't tear the body apart like that. They just
don't have the strength.''

"Vampire?''

"Vampires don't eat meat.''

"Zombies?''

"Maybe. There are rare cases where zombies go a little crazy and start
attacking people. They seem to crave flesh. If they don't get it, they'll start
to decay.''

"I thought zombies always decayed.''

"Flesh-eating zombies last a lot longer than normal. There's one case
of a woman who is still human-looking after three years.''

"They let her go around eating people?''

I smiled. "They feed her raw meat. I believe the article said lamb was
preferred.''

"Article?''

"Every career has its professional journal, Dolph.''

"What's it called?''

I shrugged. *The Animator*; what else?''

He actually smiled. "Okay. How likely is it that it's zombies?''

"Not very. Zombies don't run in packs unless they're ordered to.''

"Even''—he checked his notes—"flesh-eating zombies?''

"There have only been three documented cases. All of them were solitary hunters."

"So, flesh-eating zombies, or a new kind of ghoul. That sum it up?"

I nodded. "Yeah."

"Okay, thanks. Sorry to interrupt your night off." He closed his notebook and looked at me. He was almost grinning. "The secretary said you were at a bachelorette party." He wiggled his eyebrows. "Hoochie coochie."

"Don't give me a hard time, Dolph."

"Wouldn't dream of it."

"Riiight," I said. "If you don't need me anymore, I'll be getting back."

"We're finished, for now. Call me if you think of anything else."

"Will do." I walked back to my car. The bloody plastic gloves were shoved into a garbage sack in the trunk. I debated on the coveralls and finally folded them on top of the garbage sack. I might be able to wear them one more time.

Dolph called out, "You be careful tonight, Anita. Wouldn't want you picking up anything."

I glared back at him. The rest of the men waved at me and called in unison, "We loove you."

"Gimme a break."

One called, "If I'd known you liked to see naked men, we could have worked something out."

"The stuff you got, Zerbrowski, I don't want to see."

Laughter, and someone grabbed him around the neck. "She got you, man . . . Give it up, she gets you every time."

I got into my car to the sound of masculine laughter, and one offer to be my "luv" slave. It was probably Zerbrowski.

6

I arrived back at Guilty Pleasures a little after midnight. Jean-Claude was standing at the bottom of the steps. He was leaning against the wall, utterly still. If he was breathing, I couldn't see it. The wind blew the lace on his shirt. A lock of black hair trailed across the smooth paleness of his cheek.

"You smell of other people's blood, ma petite."

I smiled at him, sweetly. "It was no one you knew."

His voice when it came was low and dark, full of a quiet rage. It slithered across my skin, like a cold wind. "Have you been killing vampires, my little animator?"

"No." I whispered it, my voice suddenly hoarse. I had never heard his voice like that.

"They call you The Executioner, did you know that?"

"Yes." He had done nothing to threaten me, yet nothing at that moment would have forced me to pass him. They might as well have barred the door.

"How many kills do you have to your credit?"

I didn't like this conversation. It wasn't going to end anywhere I wanted to be. I knew one master vampire who could smell lies. I didn't understand Jean-Claude's mood, but I wasn't about to lie to him. "Fourteen."

"And you call us murderers."

I just stared at him, not sure what he wanted me to say.

Buzz the vampire came down the steps. He stared from Jean-Claude to me, then took up his post by the door, huge arms crossed over his chest.

Jean-Claude asked, "Did you have a nice break?"

"Yes, thank you, master."

The master vampire smiled. "I've told you before, Buzz, don't call me master."

"Yes, M-M . . . Jean-Claude."

The vampire gave his wondrous, nearly touchable laugh. "Come, Anita, let us go inside where it is warmer."

It was over eighty degrees on the sidewalk. I didn't know what in the world he was talking about. I didn't know what we'd been talking about for the last few minutes.

Jean-Claude walked up the steps. I watched him disappear inside. I stood staring at the door, not wanting to go inside. Something was wrong, and I didn't know what.

"You going inside?" Buzz asked.

"I don't suppose you'd go inside, and ask Monica and the red-haired woman she's with to come outside?"

He smiled, flashing fang. It's the mark of the new dead that they flash their fangs around. They like the shock effect. "Can't leave my post. I just had a break."

"Thought you'd say something like that."

He grinned at me.

I went into the twilit dark of the club. The holy item check girl was waiting for me at the door. I gave her my cross. She gave me a check stub. It wasn't a fair trade. Jean-Claude was nowhere in sight.

Catherine was on the stage. She was standing motionless, eyes wide. Her face had that open, fragile look that faces get when they sleep, like a child's face. Her long, copper-colored hair glistened in the lights. I knew a deep trance when I saw it.

"Catherine." I breathed her name and ran towards her. Monica was sitting at our table, watching me come. There was an awful, knowing smile on her face.

I was almost to the stage when a vampire appeared behind Catherine. He didn't walk out from behind the curtain, he just bloody appeared behind her. For the first time I understood what humans must see. Magic.

The vampire stared at me. His hair was golden silk, his skin ivory, eyes like drowning pools. I closed my eyes and shook my head. This couldn't be happening. No one was that beautiful.

His voice was almost ordinary after the face, but it was a command. "Call her."

I opened my eyes to find the audience staring at me. I glanced at Catherine's blank face and knew what would happen, but like any ignorant client I had to try. "Catherine, Catherine, can you hear me?"

She never moved; only the faintest of movements showed her breathing. She was alive, but for how long? The vampire had gotten to her, deep trance. That meant he could call her anytime, anywhere, and she would come. From this moment on, her life belonged to him. Whenever he wanted it.

"Catherine, please!" There was nothing I could do, the damage was done. Dammit, I should never have left her here, never!

The vampire touched her shoulder. She blinked and stared around, surprised, scared. She gave a nervous laugh. "What happened?"

The vampire raised her hand to his lips. "You are now under my power, my lovely one."

She laughed again, not understanding that he had told her the absolute truth. He led her to the edge of the stage, and two waiters helped her back to her seat. "I feel fuzzy," she said.

Monica patted her hand. "You were great."

"What did I do?"

"I'll tell you later. The show's not over yet." She stared at me when she said the last.

I already knew I was in trouble. The vampire on the stage was staring at me. It was like weight against my skin. His will, force, personality, whatever it was, beat against me. I could feel it like a pulsing wind. The skin on my arms crawled with it.

"I am Aubrey," the vampire said. "Give me your name."

My mouth was suddenly dry, but my name was not important. He could have that. "Anita."

"Anita. How pretty."

My knees sort of buckled and spilled me into a chair. Monica was staring at me, eyes enormous and eager.

"Come, Anita, join me on the stage." His voice wasn't as good as Jean-Claude's, it just wasn't. There was no texture to it, but the mind behind the voice was like nothing I had ever felt. It was ancient, terribly ancient. The force of his mind made my bones ache.

"Come."

I kept shaking my head, over and over. It was all I could do. No words, no real thoughts, but I knew I could not get out of this chair. If I came to him now, he would have power over me just as he did Catherine. Sweat soaked through the back of my blouse.

"Come to me, now!"

I was standing, and I didn't remember doing it. Dear God, help me! "No!" I dug my fingernails into the palm of my hand. I tore my own skin and welcomed the pain. I could breathe again.

His mind receded like the ocean pulling back. I felt light-headed, empty. I slumped against the table. One of the vampire waiters was at my side. "Don't fight him. He gets angry if you fight him."

I pushed him away. "If I don't fight him, he'll own me!"

The waiter looked almost human, one of the new dead. There was a look on his face. It was fear.

I called to the thing on the stage, "I'll come to the stage if you don't force me."

Monica gasped. I ignored her. Nothing mattered but getting through the next few moments.

"Then by all means, come," the vampire said.

I stood away from the table and found I could stand without falling. Point for me. I could even walk. Two points for me. I stared at the hard, polished floor. If I concentrated just on walking I would be all right. The first step of the stage came into view. I glanced up.

Aubrey was standing in the center of the stage. He wasn't trying to call me. He stood perfectly still. It was like he wasn't there at all; he was a terrible nothingness. I could feel his stillness like a pulse in my head. I think he could have stood in plain sight, and unless he wanted me to, I would never have seen him.

"Come." Not a voice, but a sound inside my head. "Come to me."

I tried to move back and couldn't. My pulse thundered into my throat. I couldn't breathe. I was choking! I stood with the force of his mind twisting against me.

"Don't fight me!" He screamed in my head.

Someone was screaming, wordlessly, and it was me. If I stopped fighting, it would be so easy, like drowning after you stop struggling. A peaceful way to die. No, no. "No." My voice sounded strange, even to me.

"What?" he asked. His voice held surprise.

"No," I said, and I looked up at him. I met his eyes with the weight of all those centuries pulsing down. Whatever it was that made me an animator, that helped me raise the dead, it was there now. I met his eyes and stood still.

He smiled then, a slow spreading of lips. "Then I will come to you."

"Please, please, don't." I could not step back. His mind held me like velvet steel. It was everything I could do not to move forward. Not to run to meet him.

He stopped, with our bodies almost touching. His eyes were a solid, perfect brown, bottomless, endless. I looked away from his face. Sweat trickled down my forehead.

"You smell of fear, Anita."

His cool hand traced the edge of my cheek. I started to shake and couldn't stop. His fingers pulled gently through the waves of my hair. "How can you face me this way?"

He breathed along my face, warm as silk. His breath slid to my neck, warm and close. He drew a deep, shuddering breath. His hunger pulsed against my skin. My stomach cramped with his need. He hissed at the audience, and they squealed in terror. He was going to do it.

Terror came in a blinding rush of adrenaline. I pushed away from him. I fell to the stage and scrambled away on hands and knees.

An arm grabbed me around the waist, lifting. I screamed, striking backwards with my elbow. It thudded home, and I heard him gasp, but the arm tightened. Tightened until it was crushing me.

I tore at my sleeve. Cloth ripped. He threw me onto my back. He was crouched over me, face twisted with hunger. His lips curled back from his teeth, fangs glistening.

Someone moved onto the stage, one of the waiters. The vampire hissed at him, spittle running down his chin. There was nothing human left.

It came for me in a blinding rush of speed and hunger. I pressed the silver knife over his heart. A trickle of blood glistened down his chest. He snarled at me, fangs gnashing like a dog on the end of a chain. I screamed.

Terror had washed his power away. There was nothing left but fear. He lunged for me and drove the point of the knife into his skin. Blood began to drip over my hand and onto my blouse. His blood.

Jean-Claude was suddenly there. "Aubrey, let her go."

The vampire growled deep and low in his throat. It was an animal sound.

My voice was high and thin with fear; I sounded like a little girl. "Get him off me, or I'll kill him!"

The vampire reared back, fangs slashing his own lips. "Get him off me!"

Jean-Claude began to speak softly in French. Even when I couldn't understand the language his voice was like velvet, soothing. Jean-Claude knelt by us, speaking softly. The vampire growled and lashed out, grabbing Jean-Claude's wrist.

He gasped, and it sounded like pain.

Should I kill him? Could I plunge the knife home before he tore out my throat? How fast was he? My mind seemed to be working incredibly fast. There was an illusion that I had all the time in the world to decide and act.

I felt the vampire's weight heavier against my legs. His voice sounded hoarse, but calm. "May I get up now?"

His face was human again, pleasant, handsome, but the illusion didn't work anymore. I had seen him unmasked, and that image would always stay with me. "Get off me, slowly."

He smiled then, a slow confident spread of lips. He moved off me, human-slow. Jean-Claude waved him back until he stood near the curtain.

"Are you all right, ma petite?"

I stared at the bloody silver knife and shook my head. "I don't know."

"I did not mean for this to happen." He helped me sit up, and I let him. The room had fallen silent. The audience knew something had gone wrong. They had seen the truth behind the charming mask. There were a lot of pale, frightened faces out there.

My right sleeve hung torn where I ripped it to get the knife.

"Please, put away the knife," Jean-Claude said.

I stared at him, and for the first time I looked him in the eyes and felt nothing. Nothing but emptiness.

"My word of honor that you will leave this place in safety. Put the knife away."

It took me three tries to slide the knife into its sheath, my hands were trembling so badly. Jean-Claude smiled at me, tight-lipped. "Now, we will get off this stage." He helped me stand. I would have fallen if his arm hadn't caught me. He kept a tight grip on my left hand; the lace on his sleeve brushed my skin. The lace wasn't soft at all.

Jean-Claude held his other hand out to Aubrey. I tried to pull away, and he whispered, "No fear, I will protect you, I swear it."

I believed him, I don't know why, maybe because I had no one else to believe. He led Aubrey and me to the front of the stage. His rich voice caressed the crowd. "We hope you enjoyed our little melodrama. It was very realistic, wasn't it?"

The audience shifted uncomfortably, fear plain in their faces.

He smiled out at them and dropped Aubrey's hand. He unbuttoned my sleeve and pushed it back, exposing the burn scar. The cross was dark against my skin. The audience was silent, still not understanding. Jean-Claude pulled the lace away from his chest, exposing his own cross-shaped burn.

There was a moment of stunned silence, then applause thundered around the room. Screams and shouts, and whistles roared around us.

They thought I was a vampire, and it had all been an act. I stared at Jean-Claude's smiling face and the matching scars: his chest, my arm.

Jean-Claude's hand pulled me down into a bow. As the applause finally began to fade, Jean-Claude whispered, "We need to talk, Anita. Your friend Catherine's life depends on your actions."

I met his eyes and said, "I killed the things that gave me this scar."

He smiled broadly, showing just a hint of fang. "What a lovely coincidence. So did I."

7

Jean-Claude led us through the curtains at the back of the stage. Another vampire stripper was waiting to go on. He was dressed like a gladiator, complete with metal breastplate and short sword. "Talk about an act that's hard to follow. Shit." He jerked the curtain open and stalked through.

Catherine came through, her face so pale her freckles stood out like brown ink spots. I wondered if I looked as pale? Naw. I didn't have the skin tone for it.

"My God, are you all right?" she asked.

I stepped carefully over a line of cables that snaked across the backstage floor and leaned against the wall. I began to relearn how to breathe. "I'm fine," I lied.

"Anita, what is going on? What was that stuff on stage? You aren't a vampire any more than I am."

Aubrey made a silent hiss behind her back, fangs straining, making his lips bleed. His shoulders shook with silent laughter.

Catherine gripped my arm. "Anita?"

I hugged her, and she hugged me back. I would not let her die like this. I would not let it happen. She pulled away from me and stared into my face. "Talk to me."

"Shall we talk in my office?" Jean-Claude asked.

"Catherine doesn't need to come."

Aubrey strolled closer. He seemed to glimmer in the twilight dark, like a jewel. "I think she should come. It does concern her—intimately." He licked his bloody lips, tongue pink and quick as a cat's.

"No, I want her out of this, any way I can get her out of it."

"Out of what? What are you talking about?"

Jean-Claude asked, "Is she likely to go to the police?"

"Go to the police about what?" Catherine asked, her voice getting louder with each question.

"If she did?"

"She would die," Jean-Claude said.

"Wait just a minute," Catherine said. "Are you threatening me?"

Catherine's face was gaining a lot of color. Anger did that to her. "She'll go to the police," I said.

"It is your choice."

"I'm sorry, Catherine, but it would be better for us all if you didn't remember any of this."

"That's it! We are leaving, now." She grabbed my hand, and I didn't stop her.

Aubrey moved up behind her. "Look at me, Catherine."

She stiffened. Her fingers dug into my hand; incredible tension vibrated down her muscles. She was fighting it. God, help her. But she didn't have any magic, or crucifixes. Strength of will was not enough, not against something like Aubrey.

Her hand fell away from my arm, fingers going limp all at once. Breath went out of her in a long, shuddering sigh. She stared at something just a little over my head, something I couldn't see.

I whispered, "Catherine, I'm sorry."

"Aubrey can wipe her memory of this night. She will think she drank too much, but that will not undo the damage."

"I know. The only thing that can break Aubrey's hold on her is his death."

"She will be dust in her grave before that happens."

I stared at him, at the blood stain on his shirt. I smiled a very careful smile.

"This little wound was luck and nothing more. Do not let it make you overconfident," Aubrey said.

Overconfident; now that was funny. I barely managed not to laugh. "I understand the threat, Jean-Claude. Either I do what you want or Aubrey finishes what he started with Catherine."

"You have grasped the situation, ma petite."

"Stop calling me that. What is it exactly that you want from me?"

"I believe Willie McCoy told you what we wanted."

"You want to hire me to check into the vampire murders?"

"Exactly."

"This," I motioned to Catherine's blank face, "was hardly necessary. You could have beaten me up, threatened my life, offered me more money. You could have done a lot of things before you did this."

He smiled, lips tight. "All that would have taken time. And let us be truthful. In the end you would still have refused us."

"Maybe."

"This way, you have no choice."

He had a point. "Okay, I'm on the case. Satisfied?"

"Very," Jean-Claude said, his voice very soft. "What of your friend?"

"I want her to go home in a cab. And I want some guarantees that old long-fang isn't going to kill her anyway."

Aubrey laughed, a rich sound that ended in a hysterical hissing. He was bent over, shaking with laughter. "Long-fang, I like that."

Jean-Claude glanced at the laughing vampire and said, "I will give you my word that she will not be harmed if you help us."

"No offense, but that's not enough."

"You doubt my word." His voice growled low and warm, angry.

"No, but you don't hold Aubrey's leash. Unless he answers to you, you can't guarantee his behavior."

Aubrey's laughter had softened to a few faint giggles. I had never heard a vampire giggle before. It wasn't a pleasant sound. The laughter died completely, and he straightened. "No one holds my leash, girl. I am my own master."

"Oh, get real. If you were over five hundred years old, and a master vampire, you'd have cleaned up the stage with me. As it was"—I flattened my hands palms up—"you didn't, which means you're very old but not your own master."

He growled low in his throat, face darkening with anger. "How dare you?"

"Think, Aubrey, she judged your age within fifty years. You are not a master vampire, and she knew that. We need her."

"She needs to learn some humility." He stalked towards me, body rigid with anger, hands clenching and unclenching in the air.

Jean-Claude stepped between us. "Nikolaos is expecting us to bring her, unharmed."

Aubrey hesitated. He snarled; his jaws snapped on empty air. The smack of his teeth biting together was a dull, angry sound.

They stared at each other. I could feel their wills straining through the air, like a distant wind. It made the skin at the back of my neck crawl. It was Aubrey who looked away, with an angry graceful blink. "I will not anger, my master." He emphasized "my," making it clear that Jean-Claude was not "his" master.

I swallowed hard twice, and it sounded loud. If they wanted me scared, they were doing a hell of a job. "Who is Nikolaos?"

Jean-Claude turned to look at me, his face calm and beautiful. "That question is not ours to answer."

"What is that supposed to mean?"

He smiled, lips curling carefully so no fang showed. "Let us put your friend in a cab, out of harm's way."

"What of Monica?"

He grinned then, fangs showing; he looked genuinely amused. "Are you worried for her safety?"

It hit me then—the impromptu bachelorette party, there only being the three of us. "She was the lure to get Catherine and me down here."

He nodded, once down, once up.

I wanted to go back out and smash Monica's face in. The more I thought about the idea, the better it sounded. As if by magic, she parted the curtains and came back. I smiled at her, and it felt good.

She hesitated, glancing from me to Jean-Claude and back. "Is everything going according to plan?"

I walked towards her. Jean-Claude grabbed my arm. "Do not harm her, Anita. She is under our protection."

"I swear to you that I will not lay a finger on her tonight. I just want to tell her something."

He released my arm, slowly, like he wasn't sure it was a good idea. I stepped next to Monica, until our bodies almost touched. I whispered into her face, "If anything happens to Catherine, I will see you dead."

She smirked at me, confident in her protectors. "They will bring me back as one of them."

I felt my head shake, a little to the right, a little to the left, a slow precise movement. "I will cut out your heart." I was still smiling, I couldn't seem to stop. "Then I will burn it and scatter the ashes in the river. Do you understand me?"

She swallowed audibly. Her health-club tan looked a little green. She nodded, staring at me like I was the bogey man.

I think she believed I'd do it. Peachy keen. I hate to waste a really good threat.

8

I watched Catherine's cab vanish around the corner. She never turned, or waved, or spoke. She would wake tomorrow with vague memories. Just a night out with the girls.

I would like to have thought she was out of it, safe, but I knew better. The air smelled thickly of rain. The street lights glistened off the sidewalk. The air was almost too thick to breathe. St. Louis in the summer. Peachy.

"Shall we go?" Jean-Claude asked.

He stood, white shirt gleaming in the dark. If the humidity bothered him, it didn't show. Aubrey stood in the shadows near the door. The only light on him was the crimson neon of the club sign. He grinned at me, face painted red, body lost in shadows.

"It's a little too contrived, Aubrey," I said.

His grin wavered. "What do you mean?"

"You look like a B-movie Dracula."

He flowed down the steps, with that easy perfection that only the really old ones have. The street light showed his face tight, hands balled into fists.

Jean-Claude stepped in front of him and spoke low, voice a soothing whisper. Aubrey turned away with a jerky shrug and began to glide up the street.

Jean-Claude turned to me. "If you continue to taunt him, there will come a point from which I cannot bring him back. And you will die."

"I thought your job was to keep me alive for this Nikolaos."

He frowned. "It is, but I will not die to defend you. Do you understand that?"

"I do now."

"Good. Shall we go?" He gestured down the sidewalk, in the direction Aubrey had gone.

"We're going to walk?"

"It is not far." He held his hand out to me.

I stared at it and shook my head.

"It is necessary, Anita. I would not ask it otherwise."

"How is it necessary?"

"This night must remain secret from the police, Anita. Hold my hand, play the besotted human with her vampire lover. It will explain the blood on your blouse. It will explain where we are going, and why."

His hand hung there, pale and slender. There was no tremor to the fingers, no movement, as if he could stand there offering me his hand forever. And maybe he could.

I took his hand. His long fingers curved over the back of my hand. We began walking, his hand very still in mine. I could feel the pulse in my hand against his skin. His pulse began to speed up to match mine. I could feel his blood flow like a second heart.

"Have you fed tonight?" my voice sounded soft.

"Can you not tell?"

"I can never tell with you."

I saw him smile out of the corner of my eye. "I am flattered."

"You never answered my question."

"No," he said.

"No, you haven't answered me, or no, you haven't fed?"

He turned his head to me, as we walked. Sweat gleamed on his upper lip. "What do you think, ma petite?" His voice was the softest of whispers.

I jerked my hand, tried to get away, even though I knew it was silly, and wouldn't work. His hand convulsed around mine, squeezed until I gasped. He wasn't even trying hard.

"Do not struggle against me, Anita." His tongue slid across his upper lip. "Struggling is—exciting."

"Why didn't you feed earlier?"

"I was ordered not to."

"Why?"

He didn't answer me. Rain began to patter down. Light and cool.

"Why?" I repeated.

"I don't know." His voice was nearly lost in the soft fall of rain. If it had been anyone else I would have said he was afraid.

The hotel was tall and thin, and made of real brick. The sign out front glowed blue and said, "Vacancy." There was no other sign. Nothing to tell you what the place was called, or even what it was. Just vacancy.

Rain glistened in Jean-Claude's hair, like black diamonds. My top was sticking to my body. The blood had begun to wash away. Cold water was just the thing for a fresh blood stain.

A police car eased around the corner. I tensed. Jean-Claude jerked me against him. I put my palm against his chest, to keep our bodies from touching. His heart thudded under my hand.

The police car was going very slowly. A spotlight began to search the shadows. They swept the District regularly. It was bad for tourism if the tourists got wasted by our biggest attractions.

Jean-Claude grabbed my chin and turned me to look at him. I tried to pull away, but his fingers dug into my chin. "Don't fight me!"

"I won't look in your eyes!"

"My word that I will not try to bespell you. For this night you may look into my eyes with safety. I swear it." He glanced at the police car, still moving towards us. "If the police are brought into this, I cannot promise what will happen to your friend."

I forced myself to relax in his arms, letting my body ease against his. My heartbeat sounded loud, as if I had been running. Then I realized it wasn't my heart I was hearing. Jean-Claude's pulse was throbbing through my body. I could hear it, feel it, almost squeeze it in my hand. I stared up at his face. His eyes were the darkest blue I had ever seen, perfect as a midnight sky. They were dark and alive, but there was no sense of drowning, no pull. They were just eyes.

His face leaned towards me. He whispered, "I swear."

He was going to kiss me. I didn't want him to. But I didn't want the police to stop and question us. I didn't want to explain the blood stains, the torn blouse. His lips hesitated over my mouth. His heartbeat was loud in my head, his pulse was racing, and my breathing was ragged with his need.

His lips were silk, his tongue a quick wetness. I tried to pull back and found his hand at the back of my neck, pressing my mouth against his.

The police spotlight swept over us. I relaxed against Jean-Claude, letting him kiss me. Our mouths pressed together. My tongue found the smooth hardness of fangs. I pulled away, and he let me. He pressed my face against his chest, one arm like steel against my back, pressing me against him. He was trembling, and it wasn't from the rain.

His breathing was ragged, his heart jumping under his skin against my cheek. The slick roughness of his burn scar touched my face.

His hunger poured over me in a violent wave, like heat. He had been sheltering me from it, until now. "Jean-Claude!" I didn't try to keep the fear out of my voice.

"Hush." A shudder ran through his body. His breath escaped in a loud sigh. He released me so abruptly, I stumbled.

He walked away from me to lean against a parked car. He raised his face up into the rain. I could still feel his heartbeat. I had never been so aware of my own pulse, the blood flowing through my veins. I hugged myself, shivering in the hot rain.

The police car had vanished into the streetlight darkness. After perhaps five minutes Jean-Claude stood. I could no longer feel his heartbeat. My own pulse was slow and regular. Whatever had happened was over.

He walked past me and called over his shoulder. "Come, Nikolaos awaits us inside."

I followed him through the door. He did not try to take my hand. In fact he stayed out of reach, and I trailed after him through a small square lobby.

A human man sat behind the front desk. He glanced up from the magazine he was reading. His eyes flicked to Jean-Claude and back to me. He leered at me.

I glared back. He shrugged and turned back to his magazine. Jean-Claude moved swiftly up the stairs, not waiting for me. He didn't even look back. Maybe he could hear me walking behind him, or maybe he didn't care if I followed.

I guess we weren't pretending to be lovers anymore. Fancy that. I would almost have said the master vampire didn't trust himself around me.

There was a long hallway with doors on either side. Jean-Claude was halfway through one of those doors. I walked towards it. I refused to hurry. They could damn well wait.

The room held a bed, a nightstand with a lamp, and three vampires: Aubrey, Jean-Claude, and a strange female vampire. Aubrey was standing in the far corner, near the window. He was smiling at me. Jean-Claude stood near the door. The female vampire reclined on the bed. She looked like a vampire should. Long, straight, black hair fell around her shoulders. Her dress was full-skirted and black. She wore high black boots with three-inch heels.

"Look into my eyes," she said.

I glanced at her, before I could stop myself, then stared down at the floor.

She laughed, and it had the same quality of touch that Jean-Claude's did. A sound that you could feel with your hands.

"Close the door, Aubrey," she said. Her r's were thick with some accent that I couldn't place.

Aubrey brushed past me as he closed the door. He stayed in back of me, where I couldn't see him. I moved to stand with my back to the only empty wall, so I could see all of them, for what good it would do me.

"Afraid?" Aubrey asked.

"Still bleeding?" I asked.

He crossed his arms over the blood stain on his shirt. "We shall see who is bleeding come dawn."

"Aubrey, do not be childish." The vampire on the bed stood. Her heels clicked against the bare floor. She stalked around me, and I fought an urge to turn and keep her in sight. She laughed again, as if she knew it.

"You wish me to guarantee your friend's safety?" she asked. She had gone back to sink gracefully onto the bed. The bare, dingy room seemed somehow worse with her sitting there in her two-hundred-dollar leather boots.

"No," I said.

"That is what you asked, Anita," Jean-Claude said.

"I said that I wanted guarantees from Aubrey's master."

"You are speaking with my master, girl."

"No, I am not." The room was suddenly very still. I could hear something scrambling inside the wall. I had to look up to make sure the vampires were still in the room. They were all utterly still, like statues, no sense of movement or breathing, or life. They were all so damn old, but none of them were old enough to be Nikolaos.

"I am Nikolaos," the female said, her voice coaxing and breathing through the room. I wanted to believe her, but I didn't.

"No," I said. "You are not Aubrey's master." I risked a glance into her eyes. They were black and widened in surprise when I looked at them. "You are very old, and very good, but you are not old enough or strong enough to be Aubrey's master."

Jean-Claude said, "I told you she would see through it."

"Silence!"

"The game is over, Theresa. She knows."

"Only because you have told her."

"Tell them how you knew, Anita."

I shrugged. "She feels wrong. She just isn't old enough. There is more of a sense of power from Aubrey than from her. That isn't right."

"Do you still insist on speaking with our master?" the woman asked.

"I still want guarantees on my friend's safety." I glanced through the room, at each of them. "And I am getting tired of stupid little games."

Aubrey was suddenly moving towards me. The world slowed. There was no time for fear. I tried to back away, knowing there was nowhere to go.

Jean-Claude rushed him, hands reaching. He wouldn't make it in time.

Aubrey's hand came out of nowhere and caught me in the shoulder. The blow knocked all the air from my body and sent me flying backwards. My back slammed into the wall. My head hit a moment later, hard. The world went grey. I slid down the wall. I couldn't breathe. Tiny white shapes danced over the greyness. The world began to go black. I slid to the floor. It didn't hurt; nothing hurt. I struggled to breathe until my chest burned, and darkness took everything away.

9

Voices floated through the darkness. Dreams. "We shouldn't have moved her."

"Did you want to disobey Nikolaos?"

"I helped bring her here, did I not?" It was a man's voice.

"Yes," a woman said.

I lay there with my eyes closed. I wasn't dreaming. I remembered Aubrey's hand coming from nowhere. It had been an open backhand slap. If he had closed his fist . . . but he hadn't. I was alive.

"Anita, are you awake?"

I opened my eyes. Light speared into my head. I closed my eyes against the light and the pain, but the pain stayed. I turned my head, and that was a mistake. The pain was a nauseating ache. It felt like the bones in my head were trying to slide off. I raised hands to cover my eyes and groaned.

"Anita, are you all right?"

Why do people always ask you that when the answer is obviously no? I spoke in a whisper, not sure how it would feel to talk. It didn't feel too bad. "Just peachy keen."

"What?" This from the woman.

"I think she is being sarcastic," Jean-Claude said. He sounded relieved. "She can't be hurt too badly if she is making jokes."

I wasn't sure about the hurt too badly part. Nausea flowed in waves, from head to stomach, instead of the other way around. I was betting I had a concussion. The question was, how bad?

"Can you move, Anita?"

"No," I whispered.

"Let me rephrase. If I help you, can you sit up?"

I swallowed, trying to breathe through the pain and nausea. "Maybe."

Hands curved under my shoulders. The bones in my head started sliding forward as he lifted. I gasped and swallowed. "I'm going to be sick."

I rolled over on all fours. The movement was too rapid. The pain was a whirl of light and darkness. My stomach heaved. Vomit burned up my throat. My head was exploding.

Jean-Claude held me around the waist, one cool hand on my forehead, holding the bones of my head in place. His voice held me, a soothing sheet against my skin. He was speaking French, very softly. I didn't understand a word of it, and didn't need to. His voice held me, rocked me, took some of the pain.

He cradled me against his chest, and I was too weak to protest. The pain had been screaming through my head; now it was distant, a throbbing ache. It still felt obscene to turn my head, as if my head were sliding apart, but the pain was different, bearable.

He wiped my face and mouth with a damp cloth. "Do you feel better now?" he asked.

"Yes." I didn't understand where the pain had gone.

Theresa said, "Jean-Claude, what have you done?"

"Nikolaos wishes her to be aware and well for this visit. You saw her. She needs a hospital, not more tormenting."

"So you helped her." The vampire's voice sounded amused. "Nikolaos will not be pleased."

I felt him shrug. "I did what was necessary."

I could open my eyes without squinting or increasing the pain. We were in a dungeon; there was no other word for it. Thick stone walls enclosed a square room, perhaps twenty by twenty feet. Steps led up to a barred, wooden door. There were even chains set in the walls. Torches guttered along the walls. The only thing missing was a rack and a black-hooded torturer, one with big, beefy arms, and a tattoo that said "I love Mom." Yeah, that would have made it perfect.

I was feeling better, much better. I shouldn't have been recovering this quickly. I had been hurt before, badly. It didn't just fade, not like this.

"Can you sit unaided?" Jean-Claude asked.

Surprisingly, the answer was yes. I sat with my back to the wall. The pain was still there, but it just didn't hurt as much. Jean-Claude got a bucket from near the stairs and washed it over the floor. There was a very modern drain in the middle of the floor.

Theresa stood staring at me, hands on hips. "You certainly are recovering quickly." Her voice held amusement, and something else I couldn't define.

"The pain, the nausea, it's almost gone. How?"

She smirked, lips curling. "You'll have to ask Jean-Claude that. It's his doing, not mine."

"Because you could not have done it." There was a warm edge of anger to his voice.

Her face paled. "I would not have, regardless."

"What are you talking about?" I asked.

Jean-Claude looked at me, beautiful face unreadable. His dark eyes stared into mine. They were still just eyes.

"Go on, master vampire, tell her. See how grateful she is."

Jean-Claude stared at me, watching my face. "You are badly hurt, a concussion. But Nikolaos will not let us take you to a hospital until this . . . interview is over with. I feared you would die or be unable to . . . function." I had never heard his voice so uncertain. "So I shared my life-force with you."

I started to shake my head. Big mistake. I pressed hands to my forehead. "I don't understand."

He spread his hands wide. "I do not have the words."

"Oh, allow me," Theresa said. "He has taken the first step to making you a human servant."

"No." I was still having trouble thinking clearly, but I knew that wasn't right. "He didn't try to trick me with his mind, or eyes. He didn't bite me."

"I don't mean one of those pathetic half-creatures that have a few bites and do our bidding. I mean a permanent human servant, one that will never be bitten, never be hurt. One that will age almost as slowly as we do."

I still didn't understand. Perhaps it showed in my face because Jean-Claude said, "I took your pain and gave you some of my . . . stamina."

"Are you experiencing my pain, then?"

"No, the pain is gone. I have made you a little harder to hurt."

I still wasn't taking it all in, or maybe it was just beyond me. "I don't understand."

"Listen, woman, he has shared with you what we consider a great gift to be given only to people who have proven themselves invaluable."

I stared at Jean-Claude. "Does this mean I am in your power somehow?"

"Just the opposite," Theresa said, "you are now immune to his glance, his voice, his mind. You will serve him out of willingness, nothing more. You see what he has done."

I stared into her black eyes. They were just eyes.

She nodded. "Now you begin to understand. As an animator you had partial immunity to our gaze. Now you have almost complete immunity." She gave an abrupt barking laugh. "Nikolaos is going to destroy you both." With that she stalked up the stairs, the heels of her boots smacking against the stone. She left the door open behind her.

Jean-Claude had come to stand over me. His face was unreadable.

"Why?" I asked.

He just stared down at me. His hair had dried in unruly curls around his face. He was still beautiful, but the hair made him seem more real.

"Why?"

He smiled then, and there were tired lines near his eyes. "If you died, our master would have punished us. Aubrey is already suffering for his . . . indiscretion."

He turned and walked up the stairs. He moved up the steps like a cat, all boneless, liquid grace.

He paused at the door and glanced back at me. "Someone will come for you when Nikolaos decides it is time." He closed the door, and I heard it latch and lock. His voice floated through the bars, rich, almost bubbling with laughter, "And perhaps, because I liked you." His laughter was bitter, like broken glass.

10

I had to check the locked door. Rattle it, poke at the lock, as if I knew how to pick locks. See if any bars were loose, though I could never have squeezed through the small window anyway.

I checked the door because I could not resist it. It was the same urge that made you rattle your trunk after you locked your keys inside.

I have been on the wrong side of a lot of locked doors. Not a one of them had just opened for me, but there was always a first time. Yeah, I should live so long. Scratch that; bad phrase.

A sound brought me back to the cell and its seeping, damp walls. A rat scurried against the far wall. Another peered around the edge of the steps, whiskers twitching. I guess you can't have a dungeon without rats, but I would have been willing to give it a try.

Something else pattered around the edge of the steps; in the torchlight I thought it was a dog. It wasn't. A rat the size of a German shepherd sat up on its sleek black haunches. It stared at me, huge paws tucked close to its furry chest. It cocked one large, black button eye at me. Lips drew back from yellowed teeth. The incisors were five inches long, blunt-edged daggers.

I yelled, "Jean-Claude!"

The air filled with high-pitched squeals, echoing, as if they were running up a tunnel. I stepped to the far edge of the stairs. And I saw it. A tunnel cut into the wall, almost man-high. Rats poured out of the tunnel in a thick, furry wave, squealing and biting. They flowed out and began to cover the floor.

"Jean-Claude!" I beat on the door, jerked at the bars, everything I had done before. It was useless. I wasn't getting out. I kicked the door and screamed, "Dammit!" The sound echoed against the stone walls and almost drowned out the sound of thousands of scrambling claws.

"They will not come for you until we are finished."

I froze, hands still on the door. I turned, slowly. The voice had come from inside the cell. The floor writhed and twisted with furry little bodies. High-pitched squeals, the thick brush of fur, the clatter of thousands of tiny claws filled the room. Thousands of them, thousands.

Four giant rats sat like mountains in the writhing furry tide. One of them stared at me with black button eyes. There was nothing ratlike in the stare. I had never seen wererats before, but I was betting that I was seeing them now.

One figure stood, legs half-bent. It was man-size, with a narrow, ratlike face. A huge naked tail curved around its bent legs like thick fleshy rope. It—no, he, definitely he—extended a clawed hand. "Come down and join us, human." The voice sounded thick, almost furry, with an edge of whine to it. Each word precise and a little wrong. Rats' lips are not made for talking.

I was not coming down the steps. No way. I could taste my heart in my throat. I knew a man who survived a werewolf attack, nearly died, and didn't become a werewolf. I know another man who was barely scratched and became a weretiger. Odds were, if I was so much as scratched, in a month's time I would be playing fur-face, complete with black button eyes and yellowish fangs. Dear God.

"Come down, human. Come down and play."

I swallowed hard. It felt like I was trying to swallow my heart. "I don't think so."

It gave a hissing laugh. "We could come up and fetch you." He strode through the lesser rats, and they parted for him frantically, leaping on top of each other to avoid his touch. He stood at the edge of the steps, looking up at me. His fur was almost a honey-brown color, streaked with blond. "If we force you off the steps, you won't like it much."

I swallowed hard. I believed him. I went for my knife and found the sheath empty. Of course, the vampires had taken it. Dammit.

"Come down, human, come down and play."

"If you want me, you're going to have to come get me."

He curled his tail through his hands, stroking it. One clawed hand ran through the fur of his belly, and stroked lower. I stared very hard at his face, and he laughed at me.

"Fetch her."

Two of the dog-size rats moved towards the stairs. A small rat squealed and rolled under their feet. It gave a high, piteous shriek, then nothing. It twitched until the other rats covered it. Tiny bones snapped. Nothing would go to waste.

I pressed against the door, as if I could sink through it. The two rats crept up the steps, sleek well-fed animals. But there was no animal in the eyes. Whatever was there was human, intelligent.

"Wait, wait."

The rats hesitated.

The ratman said, "Yes?"

I swallowed audibly. "What do you want?"

"Nikolaos asked that we entertain you while you wait."

"That doesn't answer my question. What do you want me to do? What do you want?"

Lips curled back from yellowed teeth. It looked like a snarl, but I think it was a smile. "Come down to us, human. Touch us, let us touch you. Let us teach you the joys of fur and teeth." He rubbed claws through the fur of his thighs. It drew my attention to him, between his legs. I looked away, and heat rushed up my skin. I was blushing. Dammit!

My voice came out almost steady. "Is that supposed to be impressive?" I asked.

He froze for an instant, then snarled, "Get her down here!"

Great, Anita, antagonize him. Imply that his equipment is a little under-sized.

His hissing laugh ran up my skin in cold waves. "We are going to have fun tonight. I can tell."

The giant rats came up the steps, muscles working under fur, whiskers thick as wire, wriggling furiously. I pressed my back against the door and began to slide down the wood. "Please, please don't." My voice sounded high and frightened, and I hated it.

"We've broken you so soon; how very sad," the ratman said.

The two giant rats were almost on me. I braced my back against the door, knees tucked up, heels planted, the rest of the foot slightly raised. A claw touched my leg, I flinched, but I waited. It had to be right. Please, God, don't let them draw blood. Whiskers scraped along my face, the weight of fur on top of me.

I kicked out, both feet hitting solidly in the rat. It raised onto its hind legs and toppled backwards. It tittered, tail lashing. I threw myself forward and smashed it in the chest. The rat tumbled over the edge.

The second rat crouched, making a sound low in its throat. I watched its muscles bunch, and I went down to one knee and braced. If it leaped on me standing, I'd go over the edge. I was only inches from the drop.

It leaped. I dropped flat to the floor and rolled. I shoved feet and one hand into the warmth of its body and helped it along. The rat plummeted over me and out of sight. I heard the frightened shrieks as it fell. The sound was a thick "thumpth." Satisfying. I doubted either of them were dead. But it was the best I could do.

I stood, putting my back to the door again. The ratman wasn't smiling anymore. I smiled at him sweetly, my best angelic smile. He didn't seem impressed.

He made a motion like parting air, smooth. The lesser rats flowed forward with his hand. A creeping brown tide of furry little bodies began to boil up the steps.

I might be able to get a few of them, but not all of them. If he wanted them to, they'd eat me alive, one tiny crimson bite at a time.

Rats flowed around my feet, scrambling and arguing. Tiny bodies bumped against my boots. One stretched itself thin, reaching up to grab the edge of my boot. I kicked it off. It fell squealing over the edge.

The giant rats had dragged one of their injured friends off to one side. The rat wasn't moving. The other I had thrown off was limping.

A rat leaped upward, claws hooked in my blouse. It hung there, claws trapped in the cloth. I could feel its weight over my breast. I grabbed it around its middle. Teeth sank into my hand until they met, grinding skin, missing bone. I screamed, jerking the rat away from me. It dangled from my hand like an obscene earring. Blood ran down its fur. Another rat leaped on my blouse.

The ratman was smiling.

A rat was climbing for my face. I grabbed it by the tail and pulled it away. I yelled, "Are you afraid to come yourself? Are you afraid of me?" My voice was thin with panic, but I said it. "Your friends are injured doing something you're afraid to do. Is that it? Is it?"

The giant rats were staring from me to the ratman. He glanced at them. "I am not afraid of a human."

"Then come up, take me yourself, if you can." The rat on my hand dropped away in a spout of blood. The skin between thumb and forefinger was ripped apart.

The lesser rats hesitated, staring wildly around. One was halfway up my jeans. It dropped to the floor.

"I am not afraid."

"Prove it." My voice sounded a little steadier, maybe about nine years old instead of five.

The giant rats were staring at him, intent, judging, waiting. He made that same cutting-air motion in reverse. The rats squeaked and stood on hind legs staring around, as if they couldn't believe it, but they began to pour down the stairs the way they had come.

I leaned into the door, knees weak, cradling the bitten hand against my chest. The ratman began to creep up the stairs. He moved easily on the balls of his elongated feet, strong clawed toes digging into the stone.

Lycanthropes are stronger and faster than humans. No mind tricks, no sleight of hand, they are just better. I would not be able to surprise the wererat, as I had the first. I doubted he would grow angry enough to be stupid, but one could always hope. I was hurt, unarmed, and outmatched. If I couldn't get him to make a mistake, I was in deep shit.

A long, pink tongue curved over his teeth. "Fresh blood," he said. He drew in a loud breath of air. "You stink of fear, human. Blood and fear, smells like dinner to me." The tongue flicked out and he laughed at me.

I slid my uninjured hand behind my back, as if reaching for something. "Come closer, ratman, and we'll see how you like silver."

The ratman hesitated, frozen, half-crouched on the top step. "You have no silver."

"Want to bet your life on it?"

His clawed hands clutched each other. One of the large rats squeaked something. He snarled down at it. "I am not afraid!"

If they egged him on, my bluff wasn't going to work. "You saw what

I did to your friends. That was without a weapon.'' My voice sounded low and sure of itself. Good for me.

He eyed me out of one large patent-leather eye. His fur glistened in the torchlight as if freshly washed. He gave a small jump and was on the landing, just out of reach.

''I've never seen a blond rat before,'' I said. Anything to fill the silence, anything to keep him from taking that one last step. Surely Jean-Claude would come back for me soon. I laughed then, abrupt and half-choked.

The ratman froze, staring at me. ''Why are you laughing?'' His voice held just a hint of unease. Good.

''I was hoping that the vampires would come for me soon and save me. You've got to admit that's funny.''

He didn't seem to think it was funny. A lot of people don't get my jokes. If I was less secure, I'd think my jokes weren't funny. Naw.

I moved my hand behind my back, still pretending that there was a knife in it. One of the giant rats squealed, and even to me it sounded derisive. He would never live it down if I bluffed him. I might not live it down if I didn't.

Most people, when confronted with a wererat, freeze or panic. I'd had time to get used to the idea. I wasn't going to fade away if he touched me. There was one possible solution where I could save myself. If I was wrong, he was going to kill me. My stomach turned a sharp flip-flop, and I had to swallow hard. Better dead than furry. If he attacked me, I'd just as soon he killed me. Rats were not my top choice for being a lycanthrope. If your luck was bad, the smallest scratch could infect you.

If I was quick and lucky, I could go to a hospital and be treated. Sort of like rabies. Of course sometimes the inoculations worked, and sometimes they gave you lycanthropy.

He wrapped his long, naked tail through his clawed hands. ''You ever been had by a were?''

I wasn't sure if he was talking sex or as a meal. Neither sounded pleasant. He was going to work up to it, get himself brave, then he'd come for me, when he was ready. I wanted him to come when I was ready.

I chose sex and said, ''You haven't got what it takes, ratman.''

He stiffened, hand sliding down his body, claws combing fur. ''We'll see who has what, human.''

''Is this the only way you get any sex, forcing yourself on someone? Are you as ugly in human form as you are right now?''

He hissed at me, mouth wide, teeth bared. A sound rose out of his body, deep and high, a whining growl. I'd never heard a sound like it before. It rose up and down and filled the room with violent, hissing echoes. His shoulders crouched.

I held my breath. I had pissed him off. Now we would see if my plan worked, or if he killed me. He leaped forward. I dropped to the floor, but he was ready for it. Incredible speed and he was on me, snarling, claws reaching, screaming in my face.

I bunched my legs against my chest, or he would have been on top of me. He put one claw-hand on my knees and began to push. I tucked arms over my knees, fighting him. It was like fighting steel that moved. He screamed again, high and hissing, spittle raining on me. He went up on his knees to get a better angle at forcing my legs down. I kicked outward, everything I had. He saw it coming and tried to move back, but both feet hit him square between the legs. The impact lifted him off his knees, and he collapsed to the landing, claws scrambling on the stone. He was making a high, whining, breathy sound. He couldn't seem to get enough air.

A second ratman came scrambling through the tunnel, and rats ran everywhere, squeaking and squealing. I just sat there on the landing as far away from the writhing blond ratman as I could get. I stared at the new ratman, feeling tired and angry.

Dammit, it should have worked. The bad guys weren't allowed reinforcements when I was already outnumbered. This one's fur was black, jet absolute black. He wore a pair of jean cutoffs over his slightly bent legs. He motioned, smooth and out from his body.

I swallowed my heart, pulse thudding. My skin crawled with the memory of small bodies sliding over me. My hand throbbed where the rat had bitten me. They'd tear me apart. "Jean-Claude!"

The rats moved, a flowing brownish tide, away from the stairs. The rats ran squeaking and shrilling into the tunnel. All I could do was stare.

The giant rats hissed at him, gesturing with noses and paws at the fallen giant rat. "She was defending herself. What were you doing?" The ratman's voice was low and deep, slurred only around the edges. If I had closed my eyes, I might have said it was human.

I didn't close my eyes. The giant rats left, crouch-dragging their still unconscious friend. He wasn't dead, but he was hurt. One giant rat glanced up at me as the others vanished into the tunnel. Its empty black eye glared at me, promised me painful things if we ever met again.

The blond ratman had stopped writhing and was lying very still, panting, hands cradling himself. The new ratman said, "I told you never to come here."

The first ratman struggled to sit up. The movement seemed to hurt. "The master called and I obeyed."

"I am your king. You obey me." The black-furred rat began to stride up the stairs, tail lashing angrily, almost catlike.

I stood and put the cell door at my back for the umpteenth time that night.

The hurt ratman said, "You are only our king until you die. If you stand against the master, that will be soon. She is powerful, more powerful than you." His voice still sounded weak, thready, but he was recovering. Anger will do that to you.

The rat king leaped, a black blur in motion. He jerked the ratman off his feet, holding him with slightly bent elbows, feet dangling off the ground. He held him close to his face. "I am your king, and you will obey me or I will kill you." Clawed hands dug into the blond ratman's throat, until he scrambled for air. The rat king tossed the ratman down the stairs. He fell tumbling and nearly boneless.

He glared up from the bottom in a painful, gasping heap. The hatred in his eyes would have lit a bonfire.

"Are you all right?" the new ratman asked.

It took me a minute to realize he was speaking to me. I nodded. Apparently I was being rescued, not that I had need of it. Of course not. "Thank you."

"I did not come to save you," he said. "I have forbidden my people to hunt for the vampire. That is why I came."

"Well, I know where I rate, somewhere above a flea. Thank you anyway. Whatever your motives."

He nodded. "You are welcome."

I noticed a burn scar on his left forearm. It was the shape of a crude crown. Someone had branded him. "Wouldn't it be easier just to carry around a crown and scepter?"

He glanced down at his arm, then gave that rat smile, teeth bare. "This leaves my hands free."

I looked up into his eyes to see if he was teasing me, and I couldn't tell. You try reading rat faces.

"What do the vampires want with you?" he asked.

"They want me to work for them."

"Do it. They'll hurt you if you don't."

"Like they'll hurt you if you keep the rats away?"

He shrugged, an awkward motion. "Nikolaos thinks she is queen of the rats because that is her animal to call. We are not merely rats, but men, and we have a choice. I have a choice."

"Do what she wants, and she won't hurt you," I said.

Again that smile. "I give good advice. I do not always take it."

"Me either," I said.

He stared at me out of one black eye, then turned towards the door. "They are coming."

I knew who "they" were. The party was over. The vampires were coming. The rat king sprang down the stairs and scooped up the fallen ratman. He tossed him over his shoulder as if it were no effort, then he was gone, running for the tunnel, fast, fast as a mouse surprised by the kitchen light. A dark blur.

I heard heels clicking down the hallway, and I stepped away from the door. It opened, and Theresa stood on the landing. She stared down at me and the empty room, hands on hips, mouth squeezed tight. "Where are they?"

I held up my wounded hand. "They did their part, then they left."

"They weren't supposed to leave," she said. Theresa made an exasperated sound low in her throat. "It was that rat king of theirs, wasn't it?"

I shrugged. "They left; I don't know why."

"So calm, so unafraid. Didn't the rats frighten you?"

I shrugged again. When something works, stay with it.

"They were not supposed to draw blood." She stared at me. "Are you going to shape shift next full moon?" Her voice held a hint of curiosity. Curiosity killed the vampire. One could always hope.

"No," I said, and I left it at that. No explanation. If she really wanted one, she could just beat me against the wall until I told her what she wanted to hear. She wouldn't even break a sweat. Of course, Aubrey was being punished for hurting me.

Her eyes narrowed as she studied me. "The rats were supposed to frighten you, animator. They don't seem to have done their job."

"Maybe I don't frighten that easily." I met her eyes without any effort. They were just eyes.

Theresa grinned at me suddenly, flashing fang. "Nikolaos will find something that frightens you, animator. For fear is power." She whispered the last as if afraid to say it too loud.

What did vampires fear? Did visions of sharpened stakes and garlic haunt them, or were there worse things? How do you frighten the dead?

"Walk in front of me, animator. Go meet your master."

"Isn't Nikolaos your master as well, Theresa?"

She stared at me, face blank, as if the laughter had been an illusion. Her eyes were cold and dark. The rats' eyes had held more personality. "Before the night is out, animator, Nikolaos will be everyone's master."

I shook my head. "I don't think so."

"Jean-Claude's power has made you foolish."

"No," I said, "it isn't that."

"Then what, mortal?"

"I would rather die than be a vampire's flunky."

Theresa never blinked, only nodded, very slowly. "You may get your wish."

The hair at the back of my neck crawled. I could meet her gaze, but evil has a certain feel to it. A neck-ruffling, throat-tightening feeling that tightens your gut. I have felt it around humans as well. You don't have to be undead to be evil. But it helps.

I walked in front of her. Theresa's boots clicked sharp echoes from the hallway. Maybe it was only my fear talking, but I felt her staring at me, like an ice cube sliding down my spine.

11

The room was huge, like a warehouse, but the walls were solid, massive stone. I kept waiting for Bela Lugosi to sweep around the corner in his cape. What was sitting against one wall was almost as good.

She had been about twelve or thirteen when she died. Small, half-formed breasts showed under a long flimsy dress. It was pale blue and looked warm against the total whiteness of her skin. She had been pale when alive; as a vampire she was ghostly. Her hair was that shining white-blonde that some children have before their hair darkens to brown. This hair would never grow dark.

Nikolaos sat in a carved wooden chair. Her feet did not quite touch the floor.

A male vampire moved to lean on the chair arm. His skin was a strange shade of brownish ivory. He leaned over and whispered in Nikolaos's ear.

She laughed, and it was the sound of chimes or bells. A lovely, calculated sound. Theresa went to the girl in the chair, and stood behind it, hands trailing in the long white-blonde hair.

A human male came to stand to the right of her chair. Back against the wall, hands clasped at his side. He stared straight ahead, face blank, spine rigid. He was nearly perfectly bald, face narrow, eyes dark. Most men don't look good without hair. This one did. He was handsome but had the air of a man who didn't care much about that. I wanted to call him a soldier, though I didn't know why.

Another man came to lean against Theresa. His hair was a sandy blond, cut short. His face was strange, not good-looking, but not ugly, a face you would remember. A face that might become lovely if you looked at it long enough. His eyes were a pale greenish color.

He wasn't a vampire, but I might have been hasty calling him human.

Jean-Claude came last to stand to the left of the chair. He touched no one, and even standing with them, he was apart from them.

"Well," I said, "all we need is the theme from *Dracula, Prince of Darkness*, and we'll be all set."

Her voice was like her laugh, high and harmless. Planned innocence. "You think you are funny, don't you?"

I shrugged. "It comes and goes."

She smiled at me. No fang showed. She looked so human, eyes sparkling with humor, face rounded and pleasant. See how harmless I am, just a pretty child. Right.

The black vampire whispered in her ear again. She laughed, so high and clear you could have bottled it.

"Do you practice the laugh, or is it natural talent? Naw, I'm betting you practice."

Jean-Claude's face twisted. I wasn't sure if he was trying not to laugh, or not to frown. Maybe both. I affected some people that way.

The laughter seeped out of her face, very human, until only her eyes sparkled. There was nothing funny about the look in those twinkling eyes. It was the sort of look that cats give small birds.

Her voice lilted at the end of each word, a Shirley Temple affectation. "You are either very brave, or very stupid."

"You really need at least one dimple to go with the voice."

Jean-Claude said softly, "I'm betting on stupid."

I glanced at him and then back at the ghoulie pack. "What I am is tired, hurt, angry, and scared. I would very much like to get the show over with, and get down to business."

"I am beginning to see why Aubrey lost his temper." Her voice was dry, humorless. The lilting sing-song was dripping away like melting ice.

"Do you know how old I am?"

I stared at her and shook my head.

"I thought you said she was good, Jean-Claude." She said his name like she was angry with him.

"She is good."

"Tell me how old I am." Her voice was cold, an angry grownup's voice.

"I can't. I don't know why, but I can't."

"How old is Theresa?"

I stared at the dark-haired vampire, remembering the weight of her in my mind. She was laughing at me. "A hundred, maybe hundred and fifty, no more."

Her face was unreadable, carved marble, as she asked, "Why, no more?"

"That's how old she feels."

"Feels?"

"In my head, she feels a certain . . . degree of power." I always hated to explain this part aloud. It always sounded mystical. It wasn't. I knew vampires the way some people knew horses, or cars. It was a knack. It was practice. I didn't think Nikolaos would enjoy being compared to a horse, or car, so I kept my mouth shut. See, not stupid after all.

"Look at me, human. Look into my eyes." Her voice was still bland, with none of that commanding power that Jean-Claude had.

Geez, look into my eyes. You'd think the city's master vampire could be more original. But I didn't say it out loud. Her eyes were blue, or grey, or both. Her gaze was like a weight pressing against my skin. If I put my hands up, I almost expected to be able to push something away. I had never felt any vampire's gaze like that.

But I could meet her eyes. Somehow, I knew that wasn't supposed to happen.

The soldier standing to her right was looking at me, as if I'd finally done something interesting.

Nikolaos stood. She moved a little in front of her entourage. She would only come to my collarbone, which made her short. She stood there for a moment, looking ethereal and lovely like a painting. No sense of life but a thing of lovely lines and careful color.

She stood there without moving and opened her mind to me. It felt like she had opened a door that had been locked. Her mind crashed against mine, and I staggered. Thoughts ripped into me like knives, steel-edged dreams. Fleeting bits of her mind danced in my head; where they touched I was numbed, hurt.

I was on my knees, and I didn't remember falling. I was cold, so cold. There was nothing for me. I was an insignificant thing, beside that mind. How could I think to call myself an equal? How could I do anything but crawl to her and beg to be forgiven? My insolence was intolerable.

I began to crawl to her, on hands and knees. It seemed like the right thing to do. I had to beg her forgiveness. I needed to be forgiven. How else did you approach a goddess but on bended knee?

No. Something was wrong. But what? I should ask the goddess to forgive me. I should worship her, do anything she asked. No. No.

"No." I whispered it. "No."

"Come to me, my child." Her voice was like spring after a long winter. It opened me up inside. It made me feel warm and welcome.

She held out pale arms to me. The goddess would let me embrace her. Wondrous. Why was I cowering on the floor? Why didn't I run to her?

"No." I slammed my hands into the stone. It stung, but not enough. "No!" I smashed my fist into the floor. My whole arm tingled and went numb. "NO!" I pounded my fists into the rock over and over until they bled. Pain was sharp, real, mine. I screamed, "Get out of my mind! You bitch!"

I crouched on the floor, panting, cradling my hands against my stomach. My pulse was jumping in my throat. I couldn't breathe past it. Anger washed through me, clean and sharp-edged. It chased the last shadow of Nikolaos's mind away.

I glared up at her. Anger, and behind that terror. Nikolaos had washed over my mind like the ocean in a seashell, filled me up and emptied me out.

She might have to drive me crazy to break me, but she could do it if she wanted to. And there wasn't a damn thing I could do to protect myself.

She stared down at me and laughed, that wondrous wind chime of a laugh. "Oh, we have found something the animator fears. Yes, we have." Her voice was lilting and pleasant. A child bride again.

Nikolaos knelt in front of me, sweeping the sky-blue dress under her knees. Ladylike. She bent at the waist so she could look me in the eyes. "How old am I, animator?"

I was starting to shake with reaction, shock. My teeth chattered like I was freezing to death, and maybe I was. My voice squeezed out between my teeth and the tight jerk of my jaw. "A thousand," I said. "Maybe more."

"You were right, Jean-Claude. She is good." She pressed her face nearly into mine. I wanted to push her away, but more than anything, I didn't want her to touch me.

She laughed again, high and wild, heartrendingly pure. If I hadn't been hurting so badly, I might have cried, or spit in her face.

"Good, animator, we understand each other. You do what we want, or I will peel your mind away like the layers of an onion." She breathed against my face, voice dropping to a whisper. A child's whisper with an edge of giggling to it. "You do believe I can do that, don't you?"

I believed.

12

I wanted to spit in that smooth, pale face, but I was afraid of what she would do to me. A drop of sweat ran slowly down my face. I wanted to promise her anything, anything, if she would never touch me again. Nikolaos didn't have to bespell me; all she had had to do was terrify me. The fear would control me. It was what she was counting on. I could not let that happen.

"Get . . . out . . . of . . . my . . . face," I said.

She laughed. Her breath was warm and smelled like peppermint. Breath mints. But underneath the clean, modern smell, very faint, was the scent of fresh blood. Old death. Recent murder.

I wasn't shivering anymore. I said, "Your breath smells like blood."

She jerked back, a hand going to her lips. It was such a human gesture that I laughed. Her dress brushed my face as she stood. One small, slippered foot kicked me in the chest.

The force tumbled me backwards, sharp pain, no air. For the second time that night, I couldn't breathe. I lay flat on my stomach, gasping, swallowing past the pain. I hadn't heard anything break. Something should have broken.

The voice thudded over me, hot enough to scald. "Get her out of here before I kill her myself."

The pain faded to a sharp ache. Air burned going down. My chest was tight, like I'd swallowed lead.

"Stay where you are, Jean."

Jean-Claude was standing away from the wall, halfway to me. Nikolaos commanded him to stillness with one small, pale hand.

"Can you hear me, animator?"

"Yes." My voice was strangled. I couldn't get enough air to talk.

"Did I break something?" Her voice rose upward like a small bird.

I coughed, trying to clear my throat, but it hurt. I huddled around my chest while the ache faded. "No."

"Pity. But I suppose that would have slowed things down, or made you useless to us.'' She seemed to think about the last as if that had had possibilities. What would they have done to me if something had been broken? I didn't want to know.

"The police are aware of only four vampire murders. There have been six more.''

I breathed in carefully. "Why not tell the police?''

"My dear animator, there are many among us who do not trust the human laws. We know how equal human justice is for the undead.'' She smiled, and again there should have been a dimple. "Jean-Claude was the fifth most powerful vampire in this city. Now he is the third.''

I stared up at her, waiting for her to laugh, to say it was a joke. She continued to smile, the same exact smile, like a piece of wax. Were they playing me for a fool? "Something has killed two master vampires? Stronger than''—I had to swallow before continuing—"Jean-Claude?''

Her smile widened, flashing a distinct glimpse of fang. "You do grasp the situation quickly. I will give you that. And perhaps that will make Jean-Claude's punishment less—severe. He recommended you to us, did you know that?''

I shook my head and glanced at him. He had not moved, not even to breathe. Only his eyes looked at me. Dark blue like midnight skies, almost fever-bright. He hadn't fed yet. Why wouldn't she let him feed?

"Why is he being punished?''

"Are you worried about him?'' Her voice held a mockery of surprise. "My, my, my, aren't you angry that he brought you into this?''

I stared at him for a moment. I knew then what I saw in his eyes. It was fear. He was afraid of Nikolaos. And I knew if I had any ally in this room, it was him. Fear will bind you closer than love, or hate, and it works a hell of a lot quicker. "No,'' I said.

"No, no.'' She minced the word, crying it up and down, a child's imitation. "Fine.'' Her voice was suddenly lower, grown-up, shimmering with heat, angry. "We will give you a gift, animator. We have a witness to the second murder. He saw Lucas die. He will tell you everything he saw, won't he, Zachary?'' She smiled at the sandy-haired man.

Zachary nodded. He stepped from around the chair and swept a low bow towards me. His lips were too thin for his face, his smile crooked. Yet, the ice-green eyes stayed with me. I had seen that face before, but where?

He strode to a small door. I hadn't seen it before. It was hidden in the flickering shadows of the torches, but still I should have noticed. I glanced at Nikolaos, and she nodded at me, a smile curving her lips.

She had hidden the door from me without me knowing it. I tried to stand, pushing myself up with my hands. Mistake. I gasped and stood as quickly as I dared. The hands were already stiff with bruises and scrapes. If I lived until morning, I was going to be one sore puppy.

Zachary opened the door with a flourish, like a magician drawing a curtain. A man stood in the door. He was dressed in the remains of a business suit. A slender figure, a little thick around the middle, too many beers, too little exercise. He was maybe thirty.

"Come," Zachary said.

The man moved out into the room. His eyes were round with fear. A pinkie ring winked in the firelight. He stank of fear and death.

He was still tanned, eyes still full. He could pass for human better than any vampire in the room, but he was more a corpse than any of them. It was just a matter of time. I raised the dead for a living. I knew a zombie when I saw one.

"Do you remember Nikolaos?" Zachary asked.

The zombie's human eyes grew large, and the color drained from his face. Damn, he looked human. "Yes."

"You will answer Nikolaos's questions, do you understand that?"

"I understand." His forehead wrinkled as if he were concentrating on something, something he couldn't quite remember.

"He would not answer our questions before. Would you?" Nikolaos said.

The zombie shook its head, eyes staring at her with a sort of fearful fascination. Birds must look at snakes that way.

"We tortured him, but he was most stubborn. Then before we could continue our work, he hung himself. We really should have taken his belt away." She sounded wistful, pouty.

The zombie was staring at her. "I . . . hung myself. I don't understand. I . . ."

"He doesn't know?" I asked.

Zachary smiled. "No, he doesn't. Isn't it fabulous? You know how hard it is to make one so human, that he forgets he has died."

I knew. It meant somebody had a lot of power. Zachary was staring at the confused undead like he was a work of art. Precious. "You raised him?" I asked.

Nikolaos said, "Did you not recognize a fellow animator?" She laughed, lightly, a breeze of far-off bells.

I glanced at Zachary's face. He was staring at me, eyes memorizing me. Face blank, with a thread of something making the skin under one eye jump. Anger, fear? Then he smiled at me, brilliant, echoing. Again there was that shock of recognition.

"Ask your question, Nikolaos. He has to answer now."

"Is that true?" she asked me.

I hesitated, surprised that she had turned to me. "Yes."

"Who killed the vampire, Lucas?"

He stared at her, face crumbling. His breathing was shallow and too fast.

"Why doesn't he answer me?"

"The question is too complex," Zachary explained. "He may not remember who Lucas is."

"Then you ask him the questions, and I expect him to answer." Her voice was warm with threat.

Zachary turned with a flourish, spreading arms wide. "Ladies and gentlemen, behold, the undead." He grinned at his own joke. No one else even smiled. I didn't get it either.

"Did you see a vampire murdered?"

The zombie nodded. "Yes."

"How was he murdered?"

"Heart torn out, head cut off." His voice was paper-thin with fear.

"Who tore out his heart?"

The zombie started to shake his head over and over, quick, jerky movements. "Don't know, don't know."

"Ask him what killed the vampire," I said.

Zachary shot me a look. His eyes were green glass. Bones stood out in his face. Rage sculpted him into a skeleton with canvas skin.

"This is my zombie, my business!"

"Zachary," Nikolaos said.

He turned to her, movements stiff.

"It is a good question. A reasonable question." Her voice was low, calm. No one was fooled. Hell must be full of voices like that. Deadly, but oh so reasonable.

"Ask her question, Zachary."

He turned back to the zombie, hands balled into fists. I didn't understand where the anger was coming from. "What killed the vampire?"

"Don't understand." The voice held a knife's edge of panic.

"What sort of creature tore out the heart? Was it a human?"

"No."

"Was it another vampire?"

"No."

This was why zombies still didn't do well in court. You had to lead them by the hand, so to speak, to get answers. Lawyers accused you of leading the witness. Which was true, but it didn't mean the zombie was lying.

"Then what killed the vampire?"

Again that head shaking, back and forth, back and forth. He opened his mouth, but no sound came out. He seemed to be choking on the words, as if someone had stuffed paper down his throat. "Can't!"

"What do you mean, can't?" Zachary screamed it at him and slapped him across the face. The zombie threw up its arms to cover its head. "You ... will ... answer ... me." Each word was punctuated with a slap.

The zombie fell to its knees and started to cry. "Can't!"

"Answer me, damn you!" He kicked the zombie, and it collapsed to the ground, rolling into a tight ball.

"Stop it." I walked towards them. "Stop it!"

He kicked the zombie one last time and turned on me. "It's my zombie! I can do what I want with him."

"That used to be a human being. It deserves more respect than this." I knelt by the crying zombie. I felt Zachary looming over me.

Nickolaos said, "Leave her alone, for now."

He stood there like an angry shadow pressing over my back. I touched the zombie's arm. It flinched. "It's all right. I'm not going to hurt you." Not going to hurt you. He had killed himself to escape. But not even the grave was sanctuary enough. Before tonight I would have said no animator would have raised the dead for such a purpose. Sometimes the world is a worse place than I want to know about.

I had to peel the zombie's hands from his face, then turn the face up to stare at me. One look was enough. Dark eyes were incredibly wide, fear, such fear. A thin line of spittle oozed from his mouth.

I shook my head and stood. "You've broken him."

"Damn right. No damn zombie is going to make a fool of me. He'll answer the questions."

I whirled to stare at the man's angry eyes. "Don't you understand? You've broken his mind."

"Zombies don't have minds."

"That's right, they don't. All they have, and for a very short time, is the memory of what they were. If you treat them well, they can retain their personalities for maybe a week, a little more, but this . . ." I pointed at the zombie, then spoke to Nikolaos. "Ill treatment will speed the process. Shock will destroy it."

"What are you saying, animator?"

"This sadist"—I jabbed a thumb at Zachary—"has destroyed the zombie's mind. It won't be answering any more questions. Not for anyone, not ever."

Nikolaos turned like a pale storm. Her eyes were blue glass. Her words filled the room with a soft burning. "You arrogant . . ." A tremor ran through her body, from small, slippered feet to long white-blonde hair. I waited for the wooden chair to catch fire and blaze from the fine heat of her anger.

The anger stripped away the child puppet. Bones stood out against white paper skin. Hands grabbed at the air, clawed and straining. One hand dug into the arm of her chair. The wood whined, then cracked. The sound echoed against the stone walls. Her voice burned along our skin. "Get out of here before I kill you. Take the woman and see her safely back to her car. If you fail me again, large or small, I will tear your throat out, and my children will bathe in a shower of your blood."

Nicely graphic; a little melodramatic, but nicely graphic. I didn't say it out loud. Hell, I wasn't even breathing. Any movement might attract her. All she needed was an excuse.

Zachary seemed to sense it as well. He bowed, eyes never leaving her face. Then without a word he turned and began to walk towards the small door. His movements were unhurried, as if death wasn't staring holes in his back. He paused at the open door and made a motion as if to escort me through the door. I glanced at Jean-Claude, still standing where she had left him. I had not asked about Catherine's safety; there had been no opportunity.

Things were happening too fast. I opened my mouth; maybe Jean-Claude guessed.

He silenced me with a wave of a slender, pale hand. The hand seemed as white as the lace on his shirt. His eye sockets were filled with blue flame. The long, black hair floated around his suddenly death-pale face. His humanity was folding away. His power flared across my skin, raising the hairs on my arms. I hugged myself, staring at the creature that had been Jean-Claude.

"Run!" He screamed it at me, voice slashing into me. I should have been bleeding from it. I hesitated and caught sight of Nikolaos. She was levitating, ever so slowly, upward. Milkweed hair danced around her skeleton head. She raised a clawed hand. Bones and veins were caught in the amber of her skin.

Jean-Claude whirled, claw-hand slashing out at me. Something slammed me into the wall and half out the door. Zachary caught my arm and pulled me through.

I twisted free of him. The door thudded closed in my face. I whispered, "Sweet Jesus."

Zachary was at the foot of a narrow stairway, leading up. He held his hand out to me. His face was slick with sweat. "Please!" He fluttered his hand at me like a trapped bird.

A smell oozed from under the door. It was the smell of rotting corpses. The smell of bloated bodies, of skin cracked and ripening in the sun, of blood slowed and rotting in quiet veins. I gagged and backed away.

"Oh, God," Zachary whispered. He put one hand over his mouth and nose, the other still held out to me.

I ignored his hand but stood beside him on the stairs. He opened his mouth to say something, but the door creaked. The wood shook and hammered, like a giant wind was beating against it. Wind whooshed from under the door. My hair streamed in a tornado wind. We backed up a few steps while the heavy wooden door fluttered and kicked against a wind that couldn't be there. A storm indoors? The sick smell of rotting flesh bled into the wind. We looked at each other. There was that moment of recognition of us against them, or it. We turned and started running like we were attached by wires.

There couldn't be a storm behind that door. There couldn't be a wind chasing us up the narrow stone stairs. There were no rotting corpses in that room. Or were there? God, I didn't want to know. I did not want to know.

13

An explosion ripped up the stairs. The wind smashed us down like toys. The door had blown. I scrambled on all fours trying to get away, just get away. Zachary got to his feet, dragging me up by one arm. We ran.

There was a howling from behind us, out of sight. The wind roared up behind us. My hair streamed over my face, blinding me. Zachary's hand grabbed mine and held on. The walls were smooth, the stairs slick stone, there was nothing to hold on to. We flattened ourselves against the stairs and hung onto each other.

"Anita." Jean-Claude's velvet voice whispered. "Anita." I fought to look up into the wind, blinking to see. There was nothing there. "Anita." The wind was calling my name. "Anita." Something glimmered, blue fire. Two points of blue flame, hung on the wind. Eyes—were those Jean-Claude's eyes? Was he dead?

The blue flames began to float downward. The wind didn't touch them. I screamed, "Zachary!" But the sound was swallowed in the roar of the wind. Did he see it, too, or was I going crazy?

The blue flames came lower and lower, and suddenly I didn't want it to touch me, just as suddenly I knew that was what it was going to do. Something told me that that would be a very bad thing.

I tore loose from Zachary. He screamed something at me, but the wind roared and screeched between the narrow walls like a roller coaster gone mad. There was no other sound. I started to crawl up the stairs, wind beating against me, trying to crush me down. There was one other sound, Jean-Claude's voice in my head. "Forgive me."

The blue lights were suddenly in front of my face. I flattened myself against a wall, hitting at the fire. My hands passed through the burning. It wasn't there.

I screamed, "Leave me alone!"

The fire melted through my hands like they weren't there, and into my eyes. The world was blue glass, silent, nothing, blue ice. A whisper: "Run, run." I was sitting on the stairs again, blinking into the wind. Zachary was staring at me.

The wind stopped like someone had turned a switch. The silence was deafening. My breath was coming in short gasps. I had no pulse. I couldn't feel my heartbeat. All I could hear was my breathing, too loud, too shallow. I finally knew what they meant by breathless with fear.

Zachary's voice was hoarse and too loud in the silence. I think he was whispering, but it came out like a shout. "Your eyes, they glowed blue!"

I whispered, "Hush, shhh." I didn't understand why, but someone must not hear what he had just said, must not know what had happened. My life depended on it. There was no more whispering in my head, but the last bit of advice had been good. Run. Running sounded very good.

The silence was dangerous. It meant the fight was over, and the winner could turn its attention to other things. I did not want to be one of those things.

I stood and offered a hand to Zachary. He looked puzzled but took it, standing. I pulled him up the steps and started running. I had to get away, had to, or I would die in this place, tonight, now. I knew that with a surety that left no room for questions, no time for hesitation. I was running for my life. I would die, if Nikolaos saw me now. I would die.

And I would never know why.

Either Zachary felt the panic too, or he thought I knew something he didn't, because he ran with me. When one of us stumbled, the other pulled him, or her, to their feet, and we ran. We ran until acid burned the muscles in my legs, and my chest squeezed into a hard ache for lack of air.

This was why I jogged, so I could run like hell when something was chasing me. Thinner thighs was not incentive enough. But this was, running when you had to, running for your life. The silence was heavy, almost touchable. It seemed to flow up the stairs, as if searching for something. The silence chased us as surely as the wind had.

The trouble with running up stairs, if you've ever had a knee injury, is that you can't do it forever. Give me a flat surface, and I can run for hours. Put me on an incline, and my knees give me fits. It started as an ache, but it didn't take long to become a sharp, grinding pain. Each step began to scream up my leg, until the entire leg pulsed with it.

The knee began to pop as it moved, an audible sound. That was a bad sign. The knee was threatening to go out on me. If it popped out of joint, I'd be crippled here on the stairs with the silence breathing around me. Nikolaos would find me and kill me. Why was I so sure of that? No answer, but I knew it, knew it with every pull of air. I didn't argue with the feeling.

I slowed and rested on the steps, stretching out the muscles in my legs. Refusing to gasp as the muscles on my bad leg twitched. I would stretch it out and feel better. The pain wouldn't go away, I'd abused it too much for that, but I would be able to walk without the knee betraying me.

Zachary collapsed on the stairs, obviously not a jogger. His muscles would tighten up if he didn't keep moving. Maybe he knew that. Maybe he didn't care.

I stretched my arms against the wall until my shoulders stretched out. Just something familiar to do while I waited for the knee to calm down. Something to do, while I listened for—what? Something heavy and sliding, something ancient, long dead.

Sounds from above, higher up the stairs. I froze pressed against the wall, palms flat against the cool stone. What now? What more? Surely, to God, it would be dawn soon.

Zachary stood and turned to face up the stairs. I stood with my back to the wall, so I could see up as well as down. I didn't want something sneaking up on me from below while I was looking upstairs. I wanted my gun. It was locked in my trunk, where it was doing me a hell of a lot of good.

We were standing just below a landing, a turn in the stairs. There have been times when I wished I could see around corners. This was one of them. The scrape of cloth against stone, the rub of shoes.

The man who walked around the corner was human, surprise, surprise. His neck was even unmarked. Cotton-white hair was shaved close to his head. The muscles in his neck bulged. His biceps were bigger around than my waist. My waist is kinda small, but his arms were still, ah, impressive. He was at least six-three, and there wasn't enough fat on him to grease a cake pan.

His eyes were the crystalline paleness of January skies, a distant, icy, blue. He was also the first bodybuilder I'd ever seen who didn't have a tan. All that rippling muscle was done in white, like Moby Dick. A black mesh tank top showed off every inch of his massive chest. Black jogging shorts flared around the swell of his legs. He had had to cut them up the sides to slip them over the rock bulge of his thighs.

I whispered, "Jesus, how much do you bench press?"

He smiled, close-lipped. He spoke with the barest movement of lips, never giving a glimpse of his incisors. "Four hundred."

I gave a low whistle. And said what he wanted me to say: "Impressive."

He smiled, careful not to show teeth. He was trying to play the vampire. Such a careful act being wasted on me. Should I tell him that he screamed human? Naw, he might break me over his thigh like kindling.

"This is Winter," Zachary said. The name was too perfect to be real, like a 1940s movie star.

"What is happening?" he asked.

"Our master and Jean-Claude are fighting," Zachary said.

He drew a deep, sighing breath. His eyes widened just a bit. "Jean-Claude?" He made it sound like a question.

Zachary nodded and smiled. "Yes, he's been holding out."

"Who are you?" he asked.

I hesitated; Zachary shrugged. "Anita Blake."

He smiled then, flashing nice normal teeth at last. "You're The Executioner?"

"Yes."

He laughed. The sound echoed between the stone walls. The silence seemed to tighten around us. The laughter stopped abruptly, a dew of sweat on his lip. Winter felt it and feared it. His voice came low, almost a whisper, as if he was afraid of being overheard. "You aren't big enough to be The Executioner."

I shrugged. "It disappoints me, too, sometimes."

He smiled, almost laughed again, but swallowed it. His eyes were shiny.

"Let's all get out of here," Zachary said.

I was with him.

"I was sent to check on Nikolaos," Winter said.

The silence pulsed with the name. A bead of sweat dripped down his face. Important safety tip: never say the name of an angry master vampire when they are within "hearing" distance.

"She can take care of herself," Zachary whispered, but the sound echoed anyway.

"Nooo," I said.

Zachary glared at me and I shrugged. Sometimes I just can't help myself.

Winter stared at me, face as impersonal as carved marble; only his eyes trembled. Mr. Macho. "Come," he said. He turned without waiting to see if we would follow. We followed.

I would have followed him anywhere as long as he went upstairs. All I knew was that nothing, absolutely nothing, could get me back down those stairs. Not willingly. Of course, there are always other options. I glanced up at Winter's broad back. Yeah, if you don't want to do it willingly, there are always other options.

14

The stairs opened into a square chamber. An electric bulb dangled from the ceiling. I had never thought one dim electric light could be beautiful, but it was. A sign that we were leaving the underground chamber of horrors behind and approaching the real world. I was ready to go home.

There were two doors leading out of the stone room, one straight ahead and one to the right. Music floated through the one in front of us. High, bright circus music. The door opened, and the music boiled around us. There was a glimpse of bright colors and hundreds of people milling about. A sign flashed, "Fun house." A carnival midway, inside a building. I knew where I was. Circus of the Damned.

The city's most powerful vampires slept under the Circus. It was something to remember.

The door started to shut, dimming the music, cutting off the bright signs. I looked into the eyes of a teenage girl, who was straining to see around the doorway. The door clicked shut.

A man leaned against the door. He was tall and slender, dressed like a riverboat gambler. Royal purple coat, lace at the neck and down the front, straight black pants and boots. A straight-brimmed hat shaded his face, and a gold mask covered everything but his mouth and chin. Dark eyes stared at me through the gold mask.

His tongue danced over his lips and teeth: fangs, a vampire. Why didn't that surprise me?

"I was afraid I would miss you, Executioner." His voice had a Southern thickness.

Winter moved to stand between us. The vampire laughed, a rich barking sound. "The muscle man here thinks he can protect you. Shall I tear him to pieces to prove him wrong?"

"That won't be necessary," I said. Zachary moved up to stand beside me.

"Do you recognize my voice?" the vampire asked.

I shook my head.

"It has been two years. I didn't know until this business came up that you were The Executioner. I thought you died."

"Can we cut to the chase here? Who are you and what do you want?"

"So eager, so impatient, so human." He raised gloved hands and took off his hat. Short, auburn hair framed the gold mask.

"Please don't do this," Zachary said. "The master has ordered me to see the woman safely to her car."

"I don't intend to harm a hair on her head—tonight." The gloves lifted the mask away. The left side of the face was scarred, pitted, melted away. Only his brown eye was still whole and alive, rolling in a circle of pinkish-white scar tissue. Acid burns look like that. Except it hadn't been acid. It had been Holy Water.

I remembered his body pinning me to the ground. His teeth tearing at my arm while I tried to keep him off my throat. The clean sharp snap of bone where he bit through. My screams. His hand forcing my head back. Him rearing to strike. Helpless. He missed the neck; I never knew why. Teeth sank around my collarbone, snapped it. He lapped up my blood like a cat with cream. I lay under his weight listening to him lap up my blood. The broken bones didn't hurt yet; shock. I was beginning not to hurt, not to be afraid. I was beginning to die.

My right hand reached out in the grass and touched something smooth— glass. A vial of Holy Water that had been thrown out of my bag, scattered by the half-human servants. The vampire never looked at me. His face was pressed over the wound. His tongue was exploring the hole he'd made. His teeth grated along the naked bone, and I screamed.

He laughed into my shoulder, laughed while he killed me. I flicked the lid open on the vial and splashed his face. Flesh boiled. His skin popped and bubbled. He knelt over me, clutching his face and shrieking.

I thought he had been trapped in the house when it burned down. I had wanted him dead, wished him dead. I had wished that memory away, pushed it back. Now here he stood, my favorite nightmare come to life.

"What, no scream of horror? No gasp of fright? You disappoint me, Executioner. Don't you admire your own handiwork?"

My voice came out strangled, hushed. "I thought you died."

"Now ya know different. And now I know you're alive, too. How cosy."

He smiled, and the muscles on his scarred cheek pulled the smile to one side, making it a grimace. Even vampires can't heal everything. "Eternity, Executioner, eternity like this." He caressed the scars with a gloved hand.

"What do you want?"

"Be brave, little girl, be brave as you want to be. I can feel your fear. I want to see the scars I gave you, see that you remember me, like I remember you."

"I remember you."

"Scars, girl, show me the scars."

"I show you the scars, then what?"

"Then you go home, or wherever you're going. The master has given strict orders you are not to be harmed until after you do your job for us."

"Then?"

He smiled, a broad glistening expanse of teeth. "Then, I hunt you down, and I pay you back for this." He touched his face. "Come, girl, don't be shy, I seen it all before. I tasted your blood. Show me the scars, and the muscle man won't have to die proving how strong he is."

I glanced at Winter. Massive fists were crossed over his chest. His spine nearly vibrated with readiness. The vampire was right; Winter would die trying. I pushed the ripped sleeve above the elbow. A mound of scar tissue decorated the bend in my arm; scars dribbled down from it, like liquid, crisscrossing and flowing down the outer edge of my arm. The cross-shaped burn took up the only clear space on the inside of my forearm.

"I didn't think you'd ever use that arm again, after the way I tore into it."

"Physical therapy is a wonderful thing."

"Ain't no physical therapy gonna help me."

"No," I said. The first button was missing on my blouse. One more and I spread my shirt back to expose the collarbone. Scars ridged it, crawled over it. It looked real attractive in a bathing suit.

"Good," the vampire said. "You smell like cold sweat when you think of me, little girl. I was hoping I haunted you the way you haunted me."

"There is a difference, you know."

"And what might that be?"

"You were trying to kill me. I was defending myself."

"And why had you come to our house? To put stakes through our hearts. You came to our house to kill us. We didn't go hunting for you."

"But you did go hunting for twenty-three other people. That's a lot of people. Your group had to be stopped."

"Who appointed you God? Who made you our executioner?"

I took a deep breath. It was steady, didn't tremble. Brownie point for me. "The police."

"Bah." He spit on the floor. Very appealing. "You work real hard, girl. You find the murderer, then we'll finish up."

"May I go now?"

"By all means. You're safe tonight, because the master says so, but that will change."

Zachary said, "Out the side door." He walked nearly backwards watching the vampire as we moved away. Winter stayed behind, guarding our backs. Idiot.

Zachary opened the door. The night was hot and sticky. Summer wind slapped against my face, humid, and close, and beautiful.

The vampire called, "Remember the name Valentine, 'cause you'll be hearing from me."

Zachary and I walked out the door. It clanged shut behind us. There was no handle on the outside, no way to open it. A one way ticket, out. Out sounded just fine.

We started to walk. "You got a gun with silver bullets in it?" he asked. "Yes."

"I'd start carrying it if I were you."

"Silver bullets won't kill him."

"But it'll slow him down."

"Yeah." We walked for a few minutes in silence. The warm summer night seemed to slide around us, hold us in sticky, curious hands.

"What I need is a shotgun."

He looked at me. "You going to carry a shotgun with you day after day?"

"Sawed off, it would fit under a coat."

"In the middle of a Missouri summer, you'd melt. Why not a machine gun, or a flamethrower, while you're at it?"

"Machine gun has too wide a spread range. You may hit innocent people. Flamethrower's bulky. Messy, too."

He stopped me with a hand on my shoulder. "You've used a flamethrower on vampires before?"

"No, but I saw it used."

"My god." He stared off into space for a moment, then asked, "Did it work?"

"Like a charm; messy, though. And it burned the house down around us. I thought it was a little extreme."

"I'll bet." We started walking again. "You must hate vampires."

"I don't hate them."

"Then why do you kill them?"

"Because it's my job, and I'm good at it." We turned a corner, and I could see the parking lot where I had left my car. It seemed like I had parked my car days ago. My watch said hours. It was a little like jet lag, but instead of crossing time zones, you crossed events. So many traumatic events and your time sense screws up. Too much happening in too short a space of time.

"I'm your daytime contact. If you need anything, or want to give a message, here's my number." He shoved a matchbook into my hand.

I glanced at the matchbook. It read "Circus of the Damned" bleeding red onto a shiny black background. I shoved it in my jeans pocket.

My gun was lying there in my trunk. I slipped into the shoulder rig, not caring that I had no jacket to cover it. A gun out in plain sight attracts attention, but most people leave you alone. They often even start running, clearing a path before you. It made chases very convenient.

Zachary waited until I was sitting in my car. He leaned into the open door. "It can't just be a job, Anita. There's got to be a better reason than that."

I glanced down at my lap and started the car. I looked up into his pale eyes. "I'm afraid of them. It is a very natural human trait to destroy that which frightens us."

"Most people spend their lives avoiding things they fear. You run after them. That's crazy."

He had a point. I closed the door and left him standing in the hot dark. I raised the dead and laid the undead to rest. It was what I did. Who I was. If I ever started questioning my motives, I would stop killing vampires. Simple as that.

I wasn't questioning my motives tonight, so I was still a vampire slayer, still the name they had given me. I was The Executioner.

15

Dawn slid across the sky like a curtain of light. The morning star glittered like a diamond chip against the easy flow of light.

I had seen two sunrises in as many days. I was beginning to feel grumpy. The trick would be to decide whom to be grumpy at, and what to do about it. Right now all I wanted was to sleep. The rest could wait, would have to wait. I had been running on fear, adrenaline, and stubbornness for hours. In the quiet hush of the car I could feel my body. It was not happy.

It hurt to grip the wheel, hurt to turn it. The bloody scrapes on my hands looked a lot worse than they were, I hoped. My whole body felt stiff. Everybody underrates bruises. They hurt. They would hurt a lot more after I slept on them. There is nothing like waking up the morning after a good beating. It's like a hangover that covers your entire body.

The corridor of my apartment building was hushed. The whir of the air conditioner breathed in the silence. I could almost feel all the people asleep behind the doors. I had an urge to press my ear to one of the doors and see if I could hear my neighbors breathing. So quiet. The hour after dawn is the most private of all. It is a time to be alone and enjoy the silence.

The only hour more hushed is three a.m. and I am not a fan of three a.m.

I had my keys in my hand, had almost touched the door, when I realized it was ajar. A tiny crack, almost closed, but not. I moved to the right of the door and pressed my back against the wall. Had they heard the keys jingling? Who was inside? Adrenaline was flowing like fine champagne. I was alert to every shadow, the way the light fell. My body was in emergency mode, and I hoped to God I didn't need it.

I drew my gun and leaned against the wall. Now what? There was no sound from inside the apartment, nothing. It could be more vampires, but it was nearly true dawn. It wouldn't be vampires. Who else would break into my apartment? I took a deep breath and let it out. I didn't know. Didn't have the faintest idea. You'd think I'd get used to not knowing what the hell is going on, but I never do. It just makes me grumpy, and a little scared.

I had several choices. I could leave and call the police, not a bad choice. But what could they do that I couldn't, except walk in and get killed in my place? That was unacceptable. I could wait in the corridor until whoever it was got curious. That could take a while, and the apartment might be empty. I'd feel pretty stupid standing out here for hours, gun trained on an empty apartment. I was tired, and I wanted to go to bed. Dammit!

I could always just go in, gun blazing. Naw. I could push the door open and be lying on the floor and shoot anyone inside. If they had a gun. If there was anyone inside.

The smart thing would be to outwait them, but I was tired. The adrenaline rush was fading under the frustration of too many choices. There comes a point when you just get tired. I didn't think I could stand out here in the air-conditioned silence and stay alert. I wouldn't fall asleep standing up, but it was a thought. And another hour would see my neighbors up and about, maybe caught in the crossfire. Unacceptable. Whatever was going to happen needed to happen now.

Decision made. Good. Nothing like fear to wash your mind clean. I moved as far from the door as I could and crossed over, gun trained on the door. I moved along the left-hand wall towards the hinge side of the door. It opened in. Just give it a push flat against the wall; simple. Right.

I crouched down on one knee, my shoulders hunched as if I could draw my head down like a turtle. I was betting that any gun would hit above me, chest-high. Crouched down, I was a lot shorter than chest-high.

I shoved the door open with my left hand and hugged the doorsill. It worked like a charm. My gun was pointing at the bad guy's chest. Except his hands were already in the air, and he was smiling at me.

"Don't shoot," he said. "It's Edward."

I knelt there staring at him; anger rose like a warm tide. "You bastard. You knew I was out here."

He steepled his fingers. "I heard the keys."

I stood, eyes searching the room. Edward had moved my white over-stuffed chair to face the door. Nothing else seemed to be moved.

"I assure you, Anita, I am quite alone."

"That I believe. Why didn't you call out to me?"

"I wanted to see if you were still good. I could have blown you away when you hesitated in front of the door, with your keys jingling so nicely."

I shut the door behind me and locked it, though truthfully with Edward inside I might have been safer locking myself out rather than in. He was not an imposing man, not frightening, if you didn't know him. He was five-eight, slender, blond, blue-eyed, charming. But if I was The Executioner, he was Death itself. He was the person I had seen use a flamethrower.

I had worked with him before, and heaven knows you felt safe with him. He carried more firepower than Rambo, but he was a little too careless of innocent bystanders. He began life as a hit man. That much the police knew.

I think humans became too easy so he switched to vampires and lycan-thropes. And I knew that if a time came where it was more expedient to kill me than to be my "friend," he would do it. Edward had no conscience. It made him the perfect killer.

"I've been up all bloody night, Edward. I'm not in the mood for your games."

"How hurt are you?"

I shrugged and winced. "The hands are sore, bruises mostly. I'm all right."

"Your night secretary said you were out at a bachelorette party." He grinned at me, eyes sparkling. "It must have been some party."

"I ran into a vampire you might know."

He raised his yellow eyebrows and made a silent "Oh" with his lips.

"Remember the house you nearly roasted down around us?"

"About two years ago. We killed six vampires, and two human ser-vants."

I walked past him and flopped onto the couch. "We missed one."

"No, we didn't." His voice was very precise. Edward at his most dan-gerous.

I looked at the carefully cut back of his head. "Trust me on this one, Edward. He damn near killed me tonight." Which was a partial truth, also known as a lie. If the vampires didn't want me to tell the police, they cer-tainly didn't want Death to know. Edward was a whole lot more dangerous to them than the police.

"What one?"

"The one who nearly tore me to pieces. He calls himself Valentine. He's still wearing the acid scars I gave him."

"Holy Water?"

"Yeah."

Edward came to sit beside me on the couch. He kept to one end, a careful distance. "Tell me." His eyes were intense on my face.

I looked away. "There isn't much left to tell."

"You're lying, Anita. Why?"

I stared at him, anger coming in a rush. I hate to be caught in a lie. "There have been some vampires murdered down along the river. How long have you been in town, Edward?"

He smiled then, though at what I wasn't sure. "Not long. I heard a rumor that you got to meet the city's head vampire tonight."

I couldn't stop it. My mouth fell open; the surprise was too much to hide. "How the hell do you know that?"

He gave a graceful shrug. "I have my sources."

"No vampire would talk to you, not willingly."

Again that shrug that said everything and nothing at all.

"What have you done tonight, Edward?"

"What have *you* done tonight, Anita?"

Touché, Mexican standoff, whatever. "Why have you come to me then? What do you want?"

"I want the location of the master vampire. The daytime resting place."

I had recovered enough so that my face was bland, no surprise here. "How would I know that?"

"Do you know?"

"No." I stood up. "I'm tired, and I want to go to bed. If there's nothing else?"

He stood, too, still smiling, like he knew I had lied. "I'll be in touch. If you do happen to run across the information I need . . ." He let the sentence trail off and started for the door.

"Edward."

He half-turned to me.

"Do you have a sawed-off shotgun?"

His eyebrows went up again. "I could get one for you."

"I'd pay."

"No, a gift."

"I can't tell you."

"But you do know?"

"Edward . . ."

"How deep are you in, Anita?"

"Eye level and sinking fast."

"I could help you."

"I know."

"Would helping you allow me to kill more vampires?"

"Maybe."

He grinned at me, brilliant, heart-stopping. The grin was his very best harmless good ol' boy smile. I could never decide whether the smile was real or just another mask. Would the real Edward please stand up? Probably not.

"I enjoy hunting vampires. Let me in on it if you can."

"I will."

He paused with a hand on the doorknob. "I hope I have more luck with my other sources than I did with you."

"What happens if you can't find the location from someone else?"

"Why, I come back."

"And?"

"And you will tell me what I want to know. Won't you?" He was still grinning at me, charming, boyish. He was also talking about torturing me if he had to.

I swallowed, hard. "Give me a few days, Edward, and I might have your information."

"Good. I'll bring the shotgun later today. If you're not home, I'll leave it on the kitchen table."

I didn't ask how he'd get inside if I wasn't home. He would only have smiled or laughed. Locks weren't much of a deterrent to Edward. "Thank you. For the shotgun, I mean."

"My pleasure, Anita. Until tomorrow." He stepped out the door, and it closed behind him.

Great. Vampires, now Edward. The day was about fifteen minutes old. Not a very promising beginning. I locked the door, for what good it would do me, and went to bed. The Browning Hi-Power was in its second home, a modified holster strapped to the headboard of my bed. The crucifix was cool metal around my neck. I was as safe as I was going to be and almost too tired to care.

I took one more thing to bed with me, a stuffed toy penguin named Sigmund. I don't sleep with him often, just every once in a while after someone tries to kill me. Everyone has their weaknesses. Some people smoke. I collect stuffed penguins. If you won't tell, I won't.

16

I stood in the huge stone room where Nikolaos had sat. Only the wooden chair remained, empty, alone. A coffin sat on the floor to one side. Torchlight gleamed off the polished wood. A breeze eased through the room. The torches wavered and threw huge black shadows on the walls. The shadows seemed to move independent of the light. The longer I looked at them, the more I was sure the shadows were too dark, too thick.

I could taste my heart in my throat. My pulse was hammering in my head. I couldn't breathe. Then I realized I was hearing a second heartbeat, like an echo. "Jean-Claude?" The shadows cried, "Jean-Claude," in high whining voices.

I knelt by the coffin and gripped the lid. It was all one piece, and raised on smooth oiled hinges. Blood poured down the sides of the coffin. The blood poured over my legs, splashed on my arms. I screamed and stood, covered in blood. It was still warm. "Jean-Claude!"

A pale hand raised out of the blood, spasmed, and collapsed against the side of the coffin. Jean-Claude's face floated to the top. My hand was reaching out. His heart was fluttering in my head, but he was dead. He was dead! His hand was icy wax. His eyes flew open. The dead hand grabbed my wrist.

"No!" I tried to pull my hand free. I went down on my knees in the cooling blood and screamed, "Let me go!"

He sat up. He was covered in blood. The white shirt dripped with it, like a bloody rag.

"No!"

He pulled my arm closer to him, and pulled me with it. I braced one hand on the coffin. I would not go to him. I would not go! He bent over my arm, mouth wide, fangs reaching. His heart beat against the shadows like thunder. "Jean-Claude, no!"

He looked up at me, just before he struck. "I had no choice." Blood began to drip down his face from his hair, until his face was a bloody mask. Fangs sank into my arm. I screamed, and woke sitting straight up in bed.

The doorbell was buzzing. I scrambled out of bed, forgetting. I gasped. I had moved too fast for the beating I'd had last night. I ached all over in places I couldn't possibly be bruised. My hands were stiff with dried blood. They felt arthritic.

The doorbell was buzzing continuously as if someone was leaning against it. Whoever it was, was going to get a hug for waking me up. I was sleeping in an oversized shirt. Pulling last night's jeans on was my version of a robe.

I put Sigmund the stuffed penguin back with all the rest. The stuffed toys sat on a small loveseat against the far wall, under the window. Penguins lined the floor around it like a plump fuzzy tide.

It hurt to move. It even felt tight when I breathed. I yelled, "I'm coming." It occurred to me, halfway to the door, that it might be someone unfriendly. I padded back into the bedroom and got my gun. My hand felt stiff and awkward around it. I should have cleaned and bandaged the hands last night. Oh, well.

I knelt behind the chair Edward had moved in front of the door and called, "Who is it?"

"It's Ronnie, Anita. We're supposed to work out this morning."

It was Saturday. I had forgotten. It was always amazing how ordinary life was, even while people were trying to hurt you. I felt like Ronnie should know about last night. Something so extraordinary should touch all my life, but it didn't work that way. When I'd been in the hospital with my arm in traction and tubes running all through me, my stepmother had complained that I wasn't married yet. She's worried that I will be an old maid at the ripe age of twenty-four. Judith is not what you would call a liberated woman.

My family does not cope well with what I do, the chances I take, the injuries. So they ignore it as best they can. Except for my sixteen-year-old stepbrother. Josh thinks I'm cool, neat, whatever word they're using now.

Veronica Sims is different. She's my friend, and she understands. Ronnie is a private detective. We take turns visiting each other in the hospital.

I opened the door and let her in, gun limp at my side. She took it all in and said, "Shit, you look awful."

I smiled. "Well, at least I look like I feel."

She came in and dropped her gym bag in front of the chair. "Can you tell me what happened?" Not a demand, a question. Ronnie understood that not everything could be shared.

"Sorry that I won't be able to work out today."

"Looks like you had all the workout you can handle. Go soak those hands in the sink. I'll make coffee. Okay?"

I nodded and regretted it. Aspirins, aspirins sounded real good right now. I stopped just before I went into the bathroom. "Ronnie?"

"Yes." She stood there in my small kitchen, a measuring cup of fresh coffee beans in one hand. She was five-nine. Sometimes, I forget how tall that is. It amazes people that we can run together. The trick is I set the pace, and I push myself. It's a very good workout.

"I think I have some bagels in the fridge. Could you pop them in the microwave with some cheese?"

She stared at me. "I've known you for three years, and this is the first time I've ever heard you ask for food before ten o'clock."

"Listen, if it's too much trouble, forget it."

"It isn't that, and you know it."

"Sorry. I'm just tired."

"Go doctor yourself, then you can tell me about it. Okay?"

"Yeah." Soaking the hands did not make them feel better. It felt like I was peeling the skin off my fingers. I patted them dry and rubbed Neosporin ointment over the scrapes. "A topical antibacterial," the label read. By the time I finished all the Band-Aids, I looked like a pinkish-tan version of the mummy's hand.

My back was a mass of dark bruises. My ribs were decorated in putrid purple. There wasn't much I could do about it, except hope the aspirin kicked in. Well, there was one thing I could do—move. Stretching exercises would limber the body and give me movement without pain, sort of. The stretching itself would feel like torture. I'd do it later. I needed to eat first.

I was starving. Usually, the thought of eating before ten made me nauseous. This morning I wanted food, needed food. Very weird. Maybe it was stress.

The smell of bagels and melting cheese made my stomach ripple. The smell of fresh brewed coffee made me want to chew the couch.

I scarfed down two bagels and three cups of coffee while Ronnie sat across from me, sipping her first cup. I looked up and found her watching me. Her grey eyes were staring at me. I'd seen her look at suspects like that. "What?" I asked.

She shrugged. "Nothing. Can you catch your breath and tell me about last night?"

I nodded, and it didn't hurt as much. Aspirin, nature's gift to modern man. I told her, from Monica's call to my meeting with Valentine. I didn't tell her that it all took place at the Circus of the Damned. That was very dangerous information to have right now. And I left out the blue lights on the stairs, the sound of Jean-Claude's voice in my head. Something told me that was dangerous information, too. I've learned to trust my instincts, so I left it out.

Ronnie's good, she looked at me, and said, "Is that everything?"

"Yes." An easy lie, simple, one word. I don't think Ronnie bought it.

"Okay." She took a sip of coffee. "What do you want me to do?"

"Ask around. You have access to the hate groups. Like Humans Against Vampires, The League of Human Voters, the usual. See if any of them might be involved with the murders. I can't go near them." I smiled. "After all, animators are one of the groups they hate."

"But you do kill vampires."

"Yeah, but I also raise zombies. Too weird for the hardcore bigot."

"All right. I'll check out HAV and the rest. Anything else?"

I thought about it and shook my head, almost no pain at all. "Not that I can think of. Just be very careful. I don't want to endanger you the way I did Catherine."

"That wasn't your fault."

"Right."

"It isn't your fault, none of this is."

"Tell that to Catherine and her fiancé if things go bad."

"Anita, dammit, these creatures are using you. They want you discouraged and frightened, so they can control you. If you let the guilt mess with your head, you're going to get killed."

"Well, gee, Ronnie, just what I wanted to hear. If this is your version of a pep talk, I'll skip the rally."

"You don't need cheering up. You need a good shaking."

"Thanks, I already had one last night."

"Anita, listen to me." She was staring at me, eyes intense, her face searching mine, trying to see if I was really hearing her. "You've done all you can for Catherine. I want you to concentrate on keeping yourself alive. You're ass-deep in enemies. Don't get sidetracked."

She was right. Do what you can and move on. Catherine was out of it, for now. It was the best I could do. "Ass-deep in enemies, but ankle-deep in friends."

She grinned. "Maybe it'll even out."

I cradled the coffee in my bandaged hands. Warmth radiated through the cup. "I'm scared."

"Which proves you aren't as stupid as you look."

"Gee, thanks a lot."

"You're welcome." She raised her coffee cup in a salute. "To Anita Blake, animator, vampire slayer, and good friend. Watch your back."

I clinked my cup against hers. "You watch yours, too. Being my friend right now may not be the healthiest of avocations."

"Since when was that a news bulletin?"

Unfortunately, she had a point.

17

I had two choices after Ronnie left: I could go back to sleep, not a bad idea; or I could start solving the case that everyone was so eager for me to work on. I could get by on four hours sleep, for a while. I could not last nearly as long if Aubrey tore my throat out. Guess I would go to work.

It is hard to wear a gun in St. Louis in the summertime. Shoulder or hip holster, you have the same problem. If you wear a jacket to cover the gun, you melt in the heat. If you keep the gun in your purse, you get killed, because no woman can find anything in her purse in under twelve minutes. It is a rule.

No one had been shooting at me yet; I was encouraged by that. But I had also been kidnapped and nearly killed. I did not plan on it happening again without a fight. I could bench press a hundred pounds, not bad, not bad at all. But when you only weigh a hundred and six, it puts you at a disadvantage. I would bet on me against any human bad guy my size. Trouble was, there just weren't many bad guys my size. And vampires, well, unless I could bench press trucks, I was outclassed. So a gun.

I finally settled on a less than professional look. The t-shirt was oversize, hitting me at mid-thigh. It billowed around me. The only thing that saved it was the picture on the front, penguins playing beach volleyball, complete with kiddie penguins making sand castles to one side. I like penguins. I had bought the shirt to sleep in and never planned to wear it where people could see me. As long as the fashion police didn't see me, I was safe.

I looped a belt through a pair of black shorts for my inside-the-pant holster. It was an Uncle Mike's Sidekick and I was very fond of it, but it was not for the Browning. I had a second gun for comfort and concealability: a Firestar, a compact little 9mm with a seven-shot magazine.

White jogging socks, with tasteful blue stripes that matched the blue leather piping on my white Nikes, completed the outfit. It made me look and feel about sixteen, an awkward sixteen, but when I turned to the mirror there was no hint of the gun on my belt. The shirt fell out and around it, invisible.

My upper body is slender, petite if you will, muscular and not bad to look at. Unfortunately, my legs are about five inches too short to ever be America's ideal legs. I will never have skinny thighs, nor anything short of muscular calves. The outfit emphasized my legs and hid everything else, but I had my gun and I wouldn't melt in the heat. Compromise is an imperfect art.

My crucifix hung inside my shirt, but I added a small charm bracelet to my left wrist. Three small crosses dangled from the silver chain. My scars also were in plain sight, but in the summer I try to pretend they aren't there. I cannot face the thought of wearing long sleeves in hundred-degree weather with hundred-percent humidity. My arms would fall off. The scars really aren't the first thing you notice with my arms bare. Really.

Animators, Inc., had new offices. We'd been here only three months. There was a psychologist's office across from us, nothing less than a hundred an hour; a plastic surgeon down the hall; two lawyers; one marriage counselor, and a real estate company. Four years ago Animators, Inc., had worked out of a spare room above a garage. Business was good.

Most of that good luck was due to Bert Vaughn, our boss. He was a businessman, a showman, a moneymaker, a scalawag, and a borderline cheat. Nothing illegal, not really, but . . . Most people choose to think of themselves as white hats, good guys. A few people wear black hats and enjoy it. Grey was Bert's color. Sometimes I think if you cut him, he'd bleed green, fresh-minted money.

He had turned what was an unusual talent, an embarrassing curse, or a religious experience, raising the dead, into a profitable business. We animators had the talent, but Bert knew how to make it pay. It was hard to argue with that. But I was going to try.

The reception room's wallpaper is pale, pale green with small oriental designs done in greens and browns. The carpet is thick and soft green, too pale to be grass, but it tries. Plants are everywhere.

A *Ficus benjium* grows to the right of the door, slender as a willow with small leather green leaves. It nearly curls around the chair in front of its pot. A second tree grows in the far corner, tall and straight with the stiff spiky tops of palm trees—*Dracaena marginta*. Or that's what it says on the tags tied to the spindly trunks. Both trees brush the ceiling. Dozens of smaller plants are pushed and potted in every spare corner of the soft green room.

Bert thinks the pastel green is soothing, and the plants give it that homey touch. I think it looks like an unhappy marriage between a mortuary and a plant shop.

Mary, our day secretary, is over fifty. How much over is her own business. Her hair is short and does not move in the wind. A carton of hair spray sees to that. Mary is not into the natural look. She has two grown sons and four grandchildren. She gave me her best professional smile as I came through the door. "May I help . . . Oh, Anita, I didn't think you were due in until five."

"I'm not, but I need to speak to Bert and get some things from my office."

She frowned down at her appointment book, our appointment book. "Well, Jamison is in your office right now with a client." There are only three offices in our little area. One belongs to Bert, and the other two rotate between the rest of us. Most of our work is done in the field, or rather the graveyard, so we never really need our offices all at the same time. It worked like time-sharing a condo.

"How long will the client be?"

Mary glanced down at her notes. "It's a mother whose son is thinking about joining the Church of Eternal Life."

"Is Jamison trying to talk him into it or out of it?"

"Anita!" Mary scolded me, but it was the truth. The Church of Eternal Life was the vampire church. The first church in history that could guarantee you eternal life, and prove it. No waiting around. No mystery. Just eternity on a silver platter. Most people don't believe in their immortal souls anymore. It isn't popular to worry about Heaven and Hell, and whether you are an absolutely good person. So the Church was gaining followers all over the place. If you didn't believe that it destroyed your soul, what did you have to lose? Daylight. Food. Not much to give up.

It was the soul part that bothered me. My immortal soul is not for sale, not even for eternity. You see, I knew vampires could die. I had proved it. No one seemed curious as to what happened to a vampire's soul when it died. Could you be a good vampire and go to Heaven? Somehow that didn't quite work for me.

"Is Bert with a client, too?"

She glanced once more at the appointment book. "No, he's free." She looked up and smiled, as if she was pleased to be able to help me. Maybe she was.

It is true that Bert took the smallest of the three offices. The walls are a soft pastel blue, the carpet two colors darker. Bert thinks it soothes the clients. I think it's like standing inside a blue ice cube.

Bert didn't match the small blue office. There is nothing small about Bert. Six-four, broad shoulders, a college athlete's figure getting a little soft around the middle. His white hair is close-cut over small ears. A boater's tan forces his pale eyes and hair into sharp contrast. His eyes are a nearly colorless grey, like dirty window glass. You have to work very hard to make dirty grey eyes shine, but they were shining now. Bert was practically beaming at me. It was a bad sign.

"Anita, what a pleasant surprise. Have a sit." He waved a business envelope at me. "We got the check today."

"Check?" I asked.

"For looking into the vampire murders."

I had forgotten. I had forgotten that somewhere in all this I had been promised money. It seemed ridiculous, obscene, that Nikolaos would make everything better with money. From the look on Bert's face, a lot of money.

"How much?"

"Ten thousand dollars." He stretched each word out, making it last.

"It isn't enough."

He laughed. "Anita, getting greedy in your old age. I thought that was my job."

"It isn't enough for Catherine's life, or mine."

His grin wilted slightly. His eyes looked wary, as if I was about to tell him there was no Easter Bunny. I could almost hear him wondering if he would have to return the check.

"What are you talking about, Anita?"

I told him, with a few minor revisions. No "Circus of the Damned." No blue fire. No first vampire mark.

When I got to the part about Aubrey smashing me into the wall, he said, "You are kidding."

"Want to see the bruises?"

I finished the story and watched his solemn, square face. His large, blunt-fingered hands were folded on his desk. The check was lying beside him atop his neat pile of manila folders. His face was attentive, concerned. Empathy never worked well on Bert's face. I could always see the wheels moving. The angles calculating.

"Don't worry, Bert, you can cash the check."

"Now, Anita, that wasn't . . ."

"Save it."

"Anita, truly I would never purposefully endanger you."

I laughed. "Bull."

"Anita!" He looked shocked, small eyes widening, one hand touching his chest. Mr. Sincerity.

"I'm not buying, so save the bullshit for clients. I know you too well."

He smiled then. It was his only genuine smile. The real Bert Vaughn please stand up. His eyes gleamed but not with warmth, more with pleasure. There is something measuring, obscenely knowledgeable, about Bert's smile. As if he knew the darkest thing you had ever done and would gladly keep silent—for a price.

There was something a little frightening about a man who knew he was not a nice person and didn't give a damn. It went against everything America holds dear. We are taught above all else to be nice, to be liked, to be popular. A person who has set aside all that is a maverick and a potentially dangerous human being.

"What can Animators, Inc., do to help?"

"I've already got Ronnie working on some things. I think the fewer people involved, the fewer people in danger."

"You always were a humanitarian."

"Unlike some people I could mention."

"I had no idea what they wanted."

"No, but you knew how I felt about vampires."

He gave me a smile that said, "I know your secret, I know your darkest dreams." That was Bert. Budding blackmailer.

I smiled back at him, friendly. "If you ever send me a vampire client again without running it by me first, I'll quit."

"And go where?"

"I'll take my client list with me, Bert. Who is the one that does the radio interviews? Who did the articles focus on? You made sure it was me, Bert. You thought I was the most marketable of all of us. The most harmless-looking, the most appealing. Like a puppy at the pound. When people call Animators, Inc., who do they ask for?"

His smile was gone, eyes like winter ice. "You wouldn't make it without me."

"The question is, would you make it without me?"

"I'd make it."

"So would I."

We stared at each other for a long space of moments. Neither of us was willing to look away, to blink first. Bert started to smile, still staring into my eyes. The edges of a smile began to tug at my mouth. We laughed together and that was that.

"All right, Anita, no more vampires."

I stood. "Thank you."

"Would you really quit?" His face was all laughing sincerity, a tasteful, pleasant mask.

"I don't believe in idle threats, Bert. You know that."

"Yes," he said, "I know that. I honestly didn't know this job would endanger your life."

"Would it have made a difference?"

He thought about it for a minute, then laughed. "No, but I would have charged more."

"You keep making money, Bert. That's what you're good at."

"Amen."

I left him so he could fondle the check in privacy. Maybe chuckle over it. It was blood money, no pun intended. Somehow, I didn't think that bothered Bert. It bothered me.

18

The door to the other office opened. A tall, blonde woman stepped through. She was somewhere between forty and fifty. Tailored golden pants encircled a slender waist. A sleeveless blouse the color of an eggshell exposed tanned arms, a gold Rolex watch, and a wedding band encircled with diamonds. The rock in the engagement ring must have weighed a pound. I bet she hadn't even blinked when Jamison talked price.

The boy that followed her was also slender and blond. He looked about fifteen, but I knew he had to be at least eighteen. Legally, you cannot join the Church of Eternal Life unless you are of age. He couldn't drink legally yet, but he could choose to die and live forever. Funny, how that didn't make much sense to me.

Jamison brought up the rear, smiling, solicitous. He was talking softly to the boy as he walked them towards the door.

I got a business card out of my purse. I held it out towards the woman. She looked at it, then at me. Her gaze slid over me from top to bottom. She didn't seem impressed; maybe it was the shirt. "Yes," she said.

Breeding. It takes real breeding to make a person feel like shit with one word. Of course, it didn't bother me. No, the great golden goddess did not make me feel small and grubby. Right. "The number on this card is for a man who specializes in vampire cults. He's good."

"I do not want my son brainwashed."

I managed a smile. Raymond Fields was my vampire cult expert, and he didn't do brainwashing. He did do truth, no matter how unpleasant. "Mr. Fields will give you the potential down side of vampirism," I said.

"I believe Mr. Clarke has given us all the information we need."

I raised my arm near her face. "I didn't get these scars playing touch football. Please, take the card. Call him, or not. It's up to you."

She was a little pale under her expert makeup. Her eyes were a little wide, staring at my arm. "Vampires did this?" Her voice was small and breathy, almost human.

"Yes," I said.

Jamison took her elbow. "Mrs. Franks, I see you've met our resident vampire slayer."

She looked at him, then back at me. Her careful face was beginning to crumble. She licked her lips and turned back to me. "Really." She was recovering quickly; she sounded superior again.

I shrugged. What could I say? I pressed the card into her manicured hand, and Jamison tactfully took it from her and pocketed it. But she had let him. What could I do? Nothing. I had tried. Period. Over. But I stared at her son. His face was incredibly young.

I remembered when eighteen was grown-up. I had thought I knew everything. I was about twenty-one when I figured out I knew dip-wad. I still knew nothing, but I tried real hard. Sometimes, that is the best you can do. Maybe the best anyone can do. Boy, Miss Cynical in the morning.

Jamison was ushering them towards the door. I caught a few sentences. "She was trying to kill them. They merely defended themselves."

Yeah, that's me, hit person for the undead. Scourge of the graveyard. Right. I left Jamison to his half-truths and went into the office. I still needed the files. Life goes on, at least for me. I couldn't stop seeing the boy's face, the wide eyes. His face had been all golden tan, baby smooth. Shouldn't you at least have to shave before you can kill yourself?

I shook my head as if I could shake the boy's face away. It almost worked. I was kneeling with the folders in my hands when Jamison came in the office. He shut the door behind him. I had thought he might.

His skin was the color of dark honey, his eyes pale green; long, tight curls framed his face. The hair was almost auburn. Jamison was the first green-eyed, red-haired black man I had ever met. He was slender, lean, not the thinness of exercise but of lucky genetics. Jamison's idea of a workout was lifting shot glasses at a good party.

"Don't ever do that again," he said.

"Do what?" I stood with the files clasped to my chest.

He shook his head and almost smiled, but it was an angry smile, a flash of small white teeth. "Don't be a smart ass."

"Sorry," I said.

"Bullshit, you're not sorry."

"About trying to give Fields's card to the woman, no. I'm not sorry. I'd do it again."

"I don't like to be undermined in front of my clients."

I shrugged.

"I mean it, Anita. Don't ever do that again."

I wanted to ask him, or what, but I didn't. "You aren't qualified to counsel people about whether or not they become the undead."

"Bert thinks I am."

"Bert would take money for a hit on the Pope if he thought he could get away with it."

Jamison smiled, then frowned at me, then couldn't help himself and smiled again. "You do have a way with words."

"Thanks."

"Don't undermine me with clients, okay?"

"I promise never to interfere when you are discussing raising the dead."

"That isn't good enough," he said.

"It's the best you're going to get. You are not qualified to counsel people. It's wrong."

"Little Miss Perfect. You murder people for money. You're nothing but a damned assassin."

I took a deep breath, and let it out. I would not fight with him today. "I execute criminals with the full blessing of the law."

"Yeah, but you enjoy it. You get your jollies by pounding in the stakes. You can't go a fucking week without bathing in someone's blood."

I just stared at him. "Do you really believe that?" I asked.

He wouldn't look at me but finally said, "I don't know."

"Poor little vampires, poor misunderstood creatures. Right? The one who branded me slaughtered twenty-three people before the courts would give me the go-ahead." I yanked my shirt down to expose the collarbone scar. "This vampire had killed ten people. He specialized in little boys, said their meat was most tender. He's not dead, Jamison. He got away. But he found me last night and threatened my life."

"You don't understand them."

"No!" I shoved a finger in his chest. "You don't understand them."

He glared down at me, nostrils flaring, breath coming in warm gasps. I stepped back. I shouldn't have touched him; that was against the rules. You never touch anyone in a fight unless you want violence.

"I'm sorry, Jamison." I don't know if he understood what I was apologizing for. He didn't say anything.

As I walked past him, he asked, "What are the files for?"

I hesitated, but he knew the files as well as I did. He'd know what was missing. "The vampire murders."

We turned towards each other at the same moment. Staring. "You took the money?" he asked.

That stopped me. "You knew about it?"

He nodded. "Bert tried to get them to hire me in your place. They wouldn't go for it."

"And after all the good PR you've given them."

"I told Bert you wouldn't do it. That you wouldn't work for vampires."

His slightly up-tilted eyes were studying my face, searching, trying to squeeze some truth out. I ignored him, my face a pleasant blankness. "Money talks, Jamison, even to me."

"You don't give a damn about money."

"Awful shortsighted of me, isn't it?" I said.

"I always thought so. You didn't do it for money." A statement. "What was it?"

I didn't want Jamison in on this. He thought vampires were fanged people. And they were very careful to keep him on the nice, clean fringes. He never got his hands dirty, so he could afford to pretend or ignore, or even lie to himself. I had gotten dirty once too often. Lying to yourself was a good way to die. "Look, Jamison, we don't agree on vampires, but anything that can kill vampires could make meat pies out of human beings. I want to catch the maniac before he, she, or it, does just that."

It wasn't a bad lie, as lies go. It was even plausible. He blinked at me. Whether he believed me or not would depend on how much he needed to believe me. How much he needed his world to stay safe and clean. He nodded, once, very slowly. "You think you can catch something the master vampires can't catch?"

"They seem to think so." I opened the door and he followed me out. Maybe he would have asked more questions, maybe not, but a voice interrupted.

"Anita, are you ready to go?"

We both turned, and I must have looked as puzzled as Jamison. I wasn't meeting anyone.

There was a man sitting in one of the lobby chairs, half-lost in the jungle plants. I didn't recognize him at first. Thick brown hair, cut short, stretched back from a very nice face. Black sunglasses hid the eyes. He turned his head and spoiled the illusion of short hair. A thick ponytail curled over his collar. He was wearing a blue denim jacket with the collar up. A blood-red tank top set off his tan. He stood slowly, smiled, and removed his glasses.

It was Phillip of the many scars. I hadn't recognized him with his clothes on. There was a bandage on the side of his neck, mostly hidden by the jacket collar. "We need to talk," he said.

I closed my mouth and tried to look reasonably intelligent. "Phillip, I didn't expect to see you so soon."

Jamison was looking from one to the other of us. He was frowning. Suspicious. Mary was sitting, chin leaning on her hands, enjoying the show.

The silence was damn awkward. Phillip put a hand out to Jamison. I mumbled. "Jamison Clarke, this is Phillip . . . a friend." The moment I said it, I wanted to take it back. "Friend" is what people call their lovers. Beats the heck out of significant other.

Jamison smiled broadly. "So, you're Anita's . . . friend." He said the last word slowly, rolling it around on his tongue.

Mary made a hubba-hubba motion with one hand. Phillip saw it and flashed her a dazzling melt-your-libido smile. She blushed.

"Well, we have to go now. Come along, Phillip." I grabbed his arm and began pulling him towards the door.

"Nice to meet you, Phillip," Jamison said. "I'll be sure to mention you to all the rest of the guys who work here. I'm sure they'd love to meet you sometime."

Jamison was really enjoying himself. "We're very busy right now, Jamison. Maybe some other time," I said.

"Sure, sure," he said.

Jamison walked us to the door and held it for us. He grinned at us as we walked down the hallway, arm in arm. Fudge buckets. I had to let the smirking little creep think I had a lover. Good grief. And he would tell everyone. Phillip slid his arm around my waist, and I fought an urge to push him away. We were pretending, right, right. I felt him hesitate as his hand brushed the gun on my belt.

We met one of the real estate agents in the hall. She said hello to me but stared at Phillip. He smiled at her. When we passed her and were waiting for the elevator, I glanced back. Sure enough, she was watching his backside as we walked away.

I had to admit it was a nice backside. She caught me looking at her and hurriedly turned away.

"Defending my honor," Phillip asked.

I pushed away from him and punched the elevator button. "What are you doing here?"

"Jean-Claude didn't come back last night. Do you know why?"

"I didn't do away with him, if that's what you're implying."

The doors opened. Phillip leaned against them, holding them open with his body and one arm. The smile he flashed me was full of potential, a little evil, a lot of sex. Did I really want to be alone in an elevator with him? Probably not, but I was armed. He, as far as I could tell, was not.

I walked under his arm without having to duck. The doors hushed behind us. We were alone. He leaned into one corner, arms crossed over his chest, staring at me from behind black lenses.

"Do you always do that?" I asked.

A slight smile. "Do what?"

"Pose."

He stiffened just a little, then relaxed against the wall. "Natural talent."

I shook my head. "Uh-huh." I stared at the flickering floor numbers.

"Is Jean-Claude all right?"

I glanced at him and didn't know what to say. The elevator stopped. We got out. "You didn't answer me," he said softly.

I sighed. It was too long a story. "It's almost noon. I'll tell you what I can over lunch."

He grinned. "Trying to pick me up, Ms. Blake?"

I smiled before I could stop myself. "You wish."

"Maybe," he said.

"Flirtatious little thing, aren't you?"

"Most women like it."

"I would like it better if I didn't think you'd flirt with my ninety-year-old grandmother the same way you're flirting with me now."

He coughed back a laugh. "You don't have a very high opinion of me."

"I am a very judgmental person. It's one of my faults."

He laughed again, a nice sound. "Maybe I can hear about the rest of your faults after you've told me where Jean-Claude is."

"I don't think so."

"Why not?"

I stopped just in front of the glass doors that led out into the street. "Because I saw you last night. I know what you are, and I know how you get your kicks."

His hand reached out and brushed my shoulder. "I get my kicks a lot of different ways."

I frowned at his hand, and it moved away. "Save it, Phillip. I'm not buying."

"Maybe by the end of lunch you will be."

I sighed. I had met men like Phillip before, handsome men who are accustomed to women drooling over them. He wasn't trying to seduce me; he just wanted me to admit that I found him attractive. If I didn't admit it, he would keep pestering me. "I give up; you win."

"What do I win?" he asked.

"You're wonderful, you're gorgeous. You are one of the best-looking men I have ever seen. From the soles of your boots, the length of your skin-tight jeans, to the flat, rippling plains of your stomach, to the sculpted line of your jaw, you are beautiful. Now can we go to lunch and cut the nonsense?"

He lowered his sunglasses just enough to see over the top of them. He stared at me like that for several minutes, then raised the glasses back in place. "You pick the restaurant." He said it flat, no teasing.

I wondered if I had offended him. I wondered if I cared.

19

The heat outside the doors was solid, a wall of damp warmth that melded to your skin like plastic wrap. "You're going to melt wearing that jacket," I said.

"Most people object to the scars."

I unfolded my arms from around the folders and extended my left arm. The scar glistened in the sunlight, shinier than the other skin. "I won't tell if you won't."

He slipped off his sunglasses and stared at me. I couldn't read his face. All I knew was that something was going on behind those big brown eyes. His voice was soft. "Is that your only bite scar?"

"No," I said.

His hands convulsed into fists, neck jerking, as if he'd had a jolt of electricity. A tremor ran up his arms into his shoulders, along his spine. He rotated his neck, as if to get rid of it. He slipped the black lenses back on his face, his eyes anonymous. The jacket came off. The scars at the bend of his arms were pale against his tan. The collarbone scar peeked from under the edges of the tank top. He had a nice neck, thick but not muscled, a stretch of smooth, tanned skin. I counted four sets of bites on that flawless skin. That was just the right side. The left was hidden by a bandage.

"I can put the jacket back on," he said.

I had been staring at him. "No, it's just . . ."

"What?"

"It's none of my business."

"Ask anyway."

"Why do you do what you do?"

He smiled, but it was twisted, a wry smile. "That is a very personal question."

"You did say ask anyway." I glanced across the street. "I usually go to Mabel's, but we might be seen."

"Ashamed of me?" His voice held a harsh edge to it, like sandpaper. His eyes were hidden, but his jaw muscles were clenched.

"It isn't that," I said. "You are the one who came into the office, pretending to be my 'friend'. If we go some place I'm known, we'll have to continue the charade."

"There are women who would pay to have me escort them."

"I know, I saw them last night at the club."

"True, but the point is still that you're ashamed to be seen with me. Because of this." His hand touched his neck, tentatively, delicate as a bird.

I got the distinct impression I had hurt his feelings. That didn't bother me, not really. But I knew what it was like to be different. I knew what it was like to be an embarrassment to people who should have known better. I knew better. It wasn't Phillip's feelings but the principle of the thing. "Let's go."

"Where to?"

"To Mabel's."

"Thank you," he said. He rewarded me with one of those brilliant smiles. If I had been less professional, it might have melted me into my socks. There was a tinge of evil to it, a lot of sex, but under that was a little boy peeking out, an uncertain little boy. That was it. That was the attraction. Nothing is more appealing than a handsome man who is also uncertain of himself.

It appeals not only to the woman in us all, but the mother. A dangerous combination. Luckily, I was immune. Sure. Besides, I had seen Phillip's idea of sex. He was definitely not my type.

Mabel's is a cafeteria, but the food is wonderful and reasonably priced. On weekdays the place is filled to the brim with suits and business skirts, thin little briefcases, and manila file folders. On Saturdays it was nearly deserted.

Beatrice smiled at me from behind the steaming food. She was tall and plump with brown hair and a tired face. Her pink uniform didn't fit well through the shoulders, and the hairnet made her face look too long. But she always smiled, and we always spoke.

"Hi, Beatrice." And without waiting to be asked, "This is Phillip."

"Hi, Phillip," she said.

He gave her a smile every bit as dazzling as he had given the real estate agent. She flushed, averted her eyes, and giggled. I hadn't known Beatrice could do that. Did she notice the scars? Did it matter to her?

It was too hot for meat loaf, but I ordered it anyway. It was always moist and the catsup sauce just tangy enough. I even got dessert, which I almost never do. I was starving. We managed to pay and find a table without Phillip flirting with anyone else. A major accomplishment.

"What has happened to Jean-Claude?" he asked.

"One more minute." I said grace over my food. He was staring at me when I looked up. We ate, and I told him an edited version of last night. Mostly, I told him about Jean-Claude and Nikolaos and the punishment.

He had stopped eating by the time I finished. He was staring over my head, at nothing that I could see. "Phillip?" I asked.

He shook his head and looked at me. "She could kill him."

"I got the impression she was just going to punish him. Do you know what that would be?"

He nodded, voice soft, saying, "She traps them in coffins and uses crosses to hold them inside. Aubrey disappeared for three months. When I saw him again, he was like he is now. Crazy."

I shivered. Would Jean-Claude go crazy? I picked up my fork and found myself halfway through a piece of blackberry pie. I hate blackberries. Damn, I treat myself to pie and get the wrong kind. What was the matter with me? The taste was still warm and thick in my mouth. I took a big swig of Coke to wash it down. The Coke didn't help much.

"What are you going to do?" he asked.

I pushed the half-eaten pie away and opened one of the folders. The first victim, one Maurice no last name, had lived with a woman named Rebecca Miles. They had cohabited for five years. "Cohabited" sounded better than "shacked up." "I'll talk to friends and lovers of the dead vampires."

"I might know the names."

I stared at him, debating. I didn't want to share information with him because I knew good ol' Phillip was the daytime eyes and ears of the undead. Yet, when I had talked to Rebecca Miles in the company of the police, she had told us zip. I didn't have time to wade through crap. I needed information and fast. Nikolaos wanted results. And what Nikolaos wanted, Nikolaos damn well better get.

"Rebecca Miles," I said.

"I know her. She was Maurice's—property." He shrugged an apology at the word, but he let it stand. And I wondered what he meant by it. "Where do we go first?" he asked.

"Nowhere. I don't want a civilian along while I work."

"I might be able to help."

"No offense, you look strong and maybe even quick, but that isn't enough. Do you know how to fight? Do you carry a gun?"

"No gun, but I can handle myself."

I doubted that. Most people don't react well to violence. It freezes them. There are a handful of seconds where the body hesitates, the mind doesn't understand. Those few seconds can get you killed. The only way to kill the hesitation is practice. Violence has to become a part of your thinking. It makes you cautious, suspicious as hell, and lengthens your life expectancy. Phillip was familiar with violence, but only as the victim. I didn't need a professional victim tagging along. Yet, I needed information from people who wouldn't want to talk to me. They might talk to Phillip.

I didn't expect to run into a gun battle in broad daylight. Nor did I really expect anyone to jump me, at least not today. I've been wrong before but . . . If Phillip could help me, I saw no harm in it. As long as he didn't flash that smile at the wrong time and get molested by nuns, we would be safe.

"If someone threatens me, can you stay out of it and let me do my job, or would you charge in and try to save me?" I asked.

"Oh," he said. He stared down at his drink for a few minutes. "I don't know."

Brownie point for him. Most people would have lied. "Then I'd rather you didn't come."

"How are you going to convince Rebecca you work for the master vampire of this city? The Executioner working for vampires?"

It sounded ridiculous even to me. "I don't know."

He smiled. "Then it's settled. I'll come along and help calm the waters."

"I didn't agree to that."

"You didn't say no, either."

He had a point. I sipped my Coke and looked at his smug face for perhaps a minute. He said nothing, only stared back. His face was neutral, no challenge to it. There was no contest of egos as with Bert. "Let's go," I said.

We stood. I left a tip. We went off in search of clues.

20

Rebecca Miles lived in South City's Dogtown. The streets were all named for states: Texas, Mississippi, Indiana. The building was blind, most of the windows boarded up. The grass was tall as an elephant's eye, but not half so beautiful. A block over were expensive rehabs full of yuppies and politicians. There were no yuppies on Rebecca's block.

Her apartment was on a long, narrow corridor. There was no air conditioning in the hallway, and the heat was like chest-high fur, thick and warm. One dim light bulb gleamed over the threadbare carpeting. In places the off-green walls were patched with white plaster, but it was clean. The smell of pine-scented Lysol was thick and almost nauseating in the small, dark hallway. You could probably have eaten off the carpeting if you had wanted to, but you would have gotten fuzzies in your mouth. No amount of Lysol would get rid of carpet fuzzies.

As we had discussed in the car, Phillip knocked on the door. The idea was that he would calm any misgivings she might have about The Executioner coming into her humble abode. It took fifteen minutes of knocking and waiting before we heard someone moving around behind the door.

The door opened as far as the chain would allow. I couldn't see who answered the door. A woman's voice, thick with sleep, said, "Phillip, what are you doing here?"

"Can I come in for a few minutes?" he asked. I couldn't see his face, but I would have bet everything I owned that he was flashing her one of his infamous smiles.

"Sure; sorry, you woke me up." The door closed, and the chain rattled. The door reopened, wide. I still couldn't see around Phillip. So I guess Rebecca didn't see me either.

Phillip walked in, and I followed behind him before the door could close. The apartment was ovenlike, a gasping, stranded-fish heat. The darkness should have made it cooler, but instead made it claustrophobic. Sweat trickled down my face.

Rebecca Miles stood holding onto the door. She was thin, with lifeless dark hair falling straight to her shoulders. High cheekbones clung to the skin of her face. She was nearly overwhelmed by the white robe she wore. Delicate was the phrase, fragile. Small, dark eyes blinked at me. It was dim in the apartment, thick drapes cutting out the light. She had only seen me once, shortly after Maurice's death.

"Did you bring a friend?" she asked. She shut the door, and we were in near darkness.

"Yes," Phillip said. "This is Anita Blake . . ."

Her voice came out small and choked. "The Executioner?"

"Yes, but . . ."

She opened her small mouth and shrieked. She threw herself at me, hands clawing and slapping. I braced and covered my face with my forearms. She fought like a girl, all open-handed slaps, scratches, and flailing arms. I grabbed her wrist and used her own momentum to pull her past me. She stumbled to her knees with a little help. I had her right arm in a joint lock. It puts pressure on the elbow, it hurts, and a little extra push will snap the arm. Most people don't fight well after you break their arm at the elbow.

I didn't want to break the woman's arm. I didn't want to hurt her at all. There were two bloody scratches on my arm where she had gotten me. I guess I was lucky she hadn't had a gun.

She tried to move, and I pressed on the arm. I felt her tremble. Her breath was coming in huge gasps. "You can't kill him! You can't! Please, please don't." She started to cry, thin shoulders shaking inside the too-big robe. I stood there, holding her arm, causing her pain.

I released her arm, slowly, and stepped back out of reach. I hoped she didn't attack again. I didn't want to hurt her, and I didn't want her to hurt me. The scratches were beginning to sting.

Rebecca Miles wasn't going to try again. She huddled against the door, thin, starved hands locked around her knees. She sobbed, gasping for air, "You . . . can't . . . kill him. Please!" She started to rock back and forth, hugging herself tight as if she might shatter, like weak glass.

Jesus, some days I hate my job. "Talk to her, Phillip. Tell her we didn't come here to hurt anyone."

Phillip knelt beside her. He kept his hands at his sides as he talked to her. I didn't hear what he said. Her shuddering sobs floated after me through a right-hand doorway. It led into the bedroom.

A coffin sat beside the bed, dark wood, maybe cherry, varnished until it gleamed in the twilit dark. She thought I came to kill her lover. Jesus.

The bathroom was small and cluttered. I hit the light switch, and the harsh yellow light was not kind. Her makeup was scattered around the cracked sink like casualties. The tub was nearly rotted with rust. I found what I hoped was a clean washrag and ran cold water over it. The water that trickled out was the color of weak coffee. The pipes shuddered and clanked and whined. The water finally ran clear. It felt good on my hands, but I didn't splash any on my neck or face. It would have been cool, but the bathroom was dirty. I couldn't use the water, not if I didn't have to. I looked up as I squeezed the rag out. The mirror was shattered, a spiderweb of cracks. It gave me my face back in broken pieces.

I didn't look in the mirror again. I walked back past the coffin and hesitated. I had an urge to knock on the smooth wood. Anybody home? I didn't do it. For all I knew, someone might have knocked back.

Phillip had the woman on the couch. She was leaning against him, boneless, panting, but the crying had almost stopped. She flinched when she saw me. I tried not to look menacing, something I'm good at, and handed the rag to Phillip. "Wipe her face and put it against the back of her neck; it'll help."

He did what I asked, and she sat there with the damp rag against her neck, staring at me. Her eyes were wide, a lot of white showing. She shivered.

I found the light switch, and harsh light flooded the room. One look at the room and I wanted to turn the light off again, but I didn't. I thought Rebecca might attack me again if I sat beside her, or maybe she'd have a complete breakdown. Wouldn't that be pretty? The only chair was lopsided and had yellowed stuffing bulging out one side. I decided to stand.

Phillip looked up at me. His sunglasses were hooked over the front of his tank top. His eyes were wide and careful, as if he didn't want me to know what he was thinking. One tanned arm was wrapped around her shoulders, protective. I felt like a bully.

"I told her why we are here. I told her you wouldn't hurt Jack."

"The coffin?" I smiled. I couldn't help it. He was a "jack in the box."

"Yes," Phillip said. He stared at me as if grinning were not appropriate.

It wasn't, so I stopped, but it was something of an effort.

I nodded. If Rebecca wanted to shack up with vampires, that was her business. It certainly wasn't police business.

"Go on, Rebecca. She's trying to help us," Phillip said.

"Why?" she asked.

It was a good question. I had scared her and made her cry. I answered her question. "The master of the city made me an offer I couldn't refuse."

She stared at me, studying my face, like she was committing me to memory. "I don't believe you," she said.

I shrugged. That's what you get for telling the truth. Someone calls you a liar. Most people will accept a likely lie to an unlikely truth. In fact, they prefer it.

"How could any vampire threaten The Executioner?" she asked.

I sighed. "I'm not the bogeyman, Rebecca. Have you ever met the master of the city?"

"No."

"Then you'll have to trust me. I am scared shitless of the master. Anybody in their right mind would be."

She still looked unconvinced, but she started talking. Her small, tight voice told the same story she'd told the police. Bland and useless as a new-minted penny.

"Rebecca, I am trying to catch the person, or thing, that killed your boyfriend. Please help me."

Phillip hugged her. "Tell her what you told me."

She glanced at him, then back at me. She sucked her lower lip in and scraped it with her upper teeth, thoughtful. She took a deep, shaky breath. "We were at a freak party that night."

I blinked, then tried to sound reasonably intelligent. "I know a freak is someone who likes vampires. Is a freak party what I think it is?"

Phillip was the one who nodded. "I go to them a lot." He wouldn't look at me while he said it. "You can have a vampire almost any way you want it. And they can have you." He darted a glance at my face, then down again. Maybe he didn't like what he saw.

I tried to keep my face blank, but I wasn't having much luck. A freak party, dear God. But it was somewhere to start. "Did anything special happen at the party?" I asked.

She blinked at me, face blank, as if she didn't understand. I tried again. "Did anything out of the ordinary happen at the freak party?" When in doubt, change your vocabulary.

She stared down into her lap and shook her head. Long, dark hair trailed over her face like a thin curtain.

"Did Maurice have any enemies that you know of?"

Rebecca shook her head without even looking up. I glimpsed her eyes through her hair like a frightened rabbit staring out from behind a bush. Did she have more information, or had I used her up? If I pushed she'd break, shatter, and maybe a clue would come spilling out, then again, maybe not. Her hands were tangled in her lap, white-knuckled. They trembled ever so slightly. How badly did I want to know? Not that badly. I let it go. Anita Blake, humanitarian.

Phillip tucked Rebecca in bed, while I waited in the living room. I half-expected to hear giggling or some sound that said he was working his charm. There was nothing but the quiet murmur of voices and the cool rustle of sheets. When he came out of the bedroom, his face was serious, solemn. He slipped his glasses back on and hit the light switch. The room was a thick, hot darkness. I heard him move in the ovenlike blackness. A rustle of jeans, a scrape of boot. I fumbled for the doorknob, found it, flung it open.

Pale light spilled in. Phillip was standing, staring at me, eyes hidden. His body was relaxed, easy, but somehow I could feel his hostility. We were no longer playing friends. I wasn't sure if he was angry with me for some reason, or himself, or fate. When you end up with a life like Rebecca's, there should be someone to blame.

"That could have been me," he said.

I looked at him. "But it wasn't."

He spread his arms wide, flexing. "But it could be."

I didn't know what to say to that. What could I say? There but for the grace of God go you? I doubted God had much to do with Phillip's world.

Phillip made sure the door locked behind us, then said, "I know at least two other murdered vampires were regulars on the party circuit."

My stomach tightened, a little flutter of excitement. "Do you think the rest of the . . . victims could be freak aficionados?"

He shrugged. "I can find out." His face was still closed to me, blank. Something had turned off his switch. Maybe it was Rebecca Miles's small, starved hands. I know it hadn't done a lot for me.

Could I trust him to find out? Would he tell me the truth? Would it endanger him? No answers, just more questions, but at least the questions were getting better. Freak parties. A common thread, a real live clue. Hot dog.

21

Inside my car I turned the air conditioning on full blast. Sweat chilled on my skin, jelling in place. I turned the air down before I got a headache from the temperature change.

Phillip sat as far away from me as he could get. His body was half-turned, as much as the seat belt would allow, towards the window. His eyes behind their sunglasses stared out and away. Phillip didn't want to talk about what had just happened. How did I know that? Anita the mind reader. No, just Anita the not so stupid.

His whole body was hunched in upon itself. If I hadn't known better, I'd have said he was in pain. Come to think of it, maybe he was.

I had just bullied a very fragile human being. It hadn't felt very good, but it beat the heck out of knocking her senseless. I had not hurt her physically. Why didn't I believe that? Now, I was going to question Phillip because he had given me a clue. The proverbial lead. I couldn't let it go.

"Phillip?" I asked.

His shoulders tightened, but he continued to stare out the window.

"Phillip, I need to know about the freak parties."

"Drop me at the club."

"Guilty Pleasures?" I asked. Brilliant repartee, that's me.

He nodded, still turned away.

"Don't you need to pick up your car?"

"I don't drive," he said. "Monica dropped me off at your office."

"Did she now?" I felt the anger, instantaneous and warm.

He turned then, stared at me, face blank, eyes hidden. "Why are you so angry at her? She just got you to the club, that's all."

I shrugged.

"Why?" His voice was tired, human, normal.

I wouldn't have answered the teasing flirt, but this person was real. Real people deserve answers. "She's human, and she betrayed other humans to nonhumans," I said.

"And that's a worse crime than Jean-Claude choosing you to be our champion?"

"Jean-Claude is a vampire. You expect treachery from vampires."

"You do. I do not."

"Rebecca Miles looks like a person who's been betrayed."

He flinched.

Great Anita, just great, let's emotionally abuse everyone we meet today. But it was true.

He had turned back to the window, and I had to fill the pained silence. "Vampires are not human. Their loyalty, first and foremost, must be to their own kind. I understand that. Monica betrayed her own kind. She also betrayed a friend. That is unforgivable."

He twisted to look at me. I wished I could see his eyes. "So if someone was your friend, you would do anything for them?"

I thought about that as we drove down 70 East. Anything? That was a tall order. Almost anything? Yes. "Almost anything," I said.

"So loyalty and friendship are very important to you?"

"Yes."

"Because you believe Monica betrayed both of those things, it makes it a worse crime than anything the vampires did?"

I shifted in the seat, not happy with the way the conversation was going. I am not a big one for personal analysis. I know who I am and what I do, and that's usually enough. Not always, but most of the time. "Not anything; I don't believe in many absolutes. But, if you want a short version, yes, that's why I'm angry at Monica."

He nodded, as if that were the answer he wanted. "She's afraid of you; did you know that?"

I smiled, and it wasn't a very nice smile. I could feel the edges curl up with a dark sort of satisfaction. "I hope the little bitch is sweating it out, big time."

"She is," he said. His voice was very quiet.

I glanced at him, then quickly back to the road. I had a feeling he didn't approve of my scaring Monica. Of course, that was his problem. I was quite pleased with the results.

We were getting close to the Riverfront turnoff. He had still not answered my question. In fact, he had very nicely avoided it. "Tell me about freak parties, Phillip."

"Did you really threaten to cut out Monica's heart?"

"Yes. Are you going to tell me about the parties or not?"

"Would you really do it? Cut out her heart, I mean?"

"You answer my question, I'll answer yours." I turned the car onto the narrow brick roads of the Riverfront. Two more blocks and we would be at Guilty Pleasures.

"I told you what the parties are like. I've stopped going the last few months."

I glanced at him again. I wanted to ask why. So I did. "Why?"

"Damn, you do ask personal questions, don't you?"

"I didn't mean it to be."

I thought he wasn't going to answer the question, but he did. "I got tired of being passed around. I didn't want to end up like Rebecca, or worse."

I wanted to ask what was worse, but I let it go. I try not to be cruel, just persistent. There are days when the difference is pretty damn slight. "If you find out that all the vampires went to freak parties, call me."

"Then what?" he asked.

"I need to go to a party." I parked in front of Guilty Pleasures. The neon was quiet, a dim ghost of its nighttime self. The place looked closed.

"You don't want to go to a party, Anita."

"I'm trying to solve a crime, Phillip. If I don't, my friend dies. And I have no illusions about what the master will do to me if I fail. A quick death would be the best I could hope for."

He shivered. "Yeah, yeah." He unbuckled the seat belt and rubbed his hands along his arms, as if he were cold. "You never answered my question about Monica," he said.

"You never really told me about the parties."

He looked down, staring at the tops of his thighs. "There's one tonight. If you have to go, I'll take you." He turned to me, arms still hugging his elbows. "The parties are always at a different location. When I find out where, how do I get in touch with you?"

"Leave a message on my answering machine, my home number." I got a business card out of my purse and wrote my home phone number on the back. He got his jean jacket out of the back seat and stuffed the card into a pocket. He opened the door, and the heat washed into the chill, air-conditioned car like the breath of a dragon.

He leaned into the car, one arm on the roof, one on the door. "Now, answer my question. Would you really cut out Monica's heart, so she couldn't come back as a vampire?"

I stared into the blackness of his sunglasses and said, "Yes."

"Remind me never to piss you off." He took a deep breath. "You'll need to wear something that shows off your scars tonight. Buy something if you don't have it." He hesitated, then asked, "Are you as good at being a friend as you are an enemy?"

I took a deep breath and let it out. What could I say? "You don't want me for an enemy, Phillip. I make a much better friend."

"Yeah, I'll bet you do." He closed the door and walked up to the club door. He knocked, and a few moments later the door opened. I got a glimpse of a pale figure opening the door. It couldn't be a vampire, could it? The door closed before I could see much. Vampires could not come out in daylight. That was a rule. But until last night I had known vampires could not fly. So much for what I knew.

Whoever it was had been expecting Phillip. I pulled away from the curb. Why had they sent him at his flirtatious best? Had he been sent to charm me? Or was he the only human they could get at short notice? The only daytime member of their little club. Except for Monica. And I wasn't real fond of her right now. That was just dandy with me.

I didn't think Phillip was lying about the freak parties, but what did I know about Phillip? He stripped at Guilty Pleasures, not exactly a character reference. He was a vampire junkie, better and better. Was all that pain an act? Was he luring me someplace, just as Monica had?

I didn't know. And I needed to know. There was one place I could go that might have the answers. The only place in the District where I was truly welcome. Dead Dave's, a nice bar that served a mean hamburger. The pro-prietor was an ex-cop who had been kicked off the force for being dead. Picky, picky. Dave liked to help out, but he resented the prejudice of his former comrades. So he talked to me. And I talked to the police. It was a nice little arrangement that let Dave be pissed off at the police and still help them.

It made me nearly invaluable to the police. Since I was on retainer, that pleased Bert to no end.

It being daytime, Dead Dave was tucked in his coffin, but Luther would be there. Luther was the daytime manager and bartender. He was one of the few people in the District who didn't have much to do with vampires, except for the fact that he worked for one. Life is never perfect.

I actually found a parking place not far from Dave's. Daytime parking is a lot more open in the District. When the Riverfront used to be human-owned businesses, there was never any parking on a weekend, day or night. It was one of the few positives of the new vampire laws. That and the tourism.

St. Louis was a real hot spot for vampire watchers. The only place better was New York, but we had a lower crime rate. There was a gang that had gone all vampire in New York. They had spread to Los Angeles and tried to spread here. The police found the first recruits chopped into bite-size pieces.

Our vampire community prides itself on being mainstream. A vampire gang would be bad publicity, so they took care of it. I admired the efficiency of it but wished they had done it differently. I had had nightmares for weeks about walls that bled and dismembered arms that crawled along the floor all by themselves. We never did find the heads.

22

Dead Dave's is all dark glass and glowing beer signs. At night the front windows look like some sort of modern art, featuring brand names. In the daylight everything is muted. Bars are sort of like vampires; they are at their best after dark. There is something tired and wistful about a daytime bar.

The air conditioning was up full blast, like the inside of a freezer. It was almost a physical jolt after the skin-melting heat outside. I stood just inside the door and waited for my eyes to adjust to the twilight interior. Why are all bars so damn dark, like caves, places to hide? The air smelled of stale cigarettes no matter when you came in, as if years of smoke had settled into the upholstery, like aromatic ghosts.

Two guys in business suits were settled at the farthest booth from the door. They were eating and had manila folders spread across the table top. Working on a Saturday. Just like me, well, maybe not just like me. I was betting that no one had threatened to tear their throats out. Of course, I could be wrong, but I doubted it. I was betting the worst threat they had had this week was lack of job security. Ah, the good old days.

There was a man crouched on a bar stool, nursing a tall drink. His face was already slack, his movements very slow and precise, as if he were afraid he'd spill something. Drunk at one-thirty in the afternoon; not a good sign for him. But it wasn't my business. You can't save everybody. In fact, there are days when I think you can't save anyone. Each person has to save himself first, then you can move in and help. I have found this philosophy does not work during a gun battle, or a knife fight either. Outside of that it works just fine.

Luther was polishing glasses with a very clean white towel. He looked up when I slipped up on the bar stool. He nodded, a cigarette dangling from his thick lips. Luther is large, nay, fat. There is no other word for it, but it is hard fat, rock-solid, almost a kind of muscle. His hands are huge-knuckled and as big as my face. Of course, my face is small. He is a very dark black man, nearly purplish black, like mahogany. The creamy chocolate of his eyes is yellow-edged from too much cigarette smoke. I don't think I have ever seen Luther without a cig clasped between his lips. He is overweight, chain-smokes, and the grey in his hair marks him as over fifty, yet he's never sick. Good genetics, I guess.

"What'll it be, Anita?" His voice matched his body, deep and gravelly.
"The usual."

He poured me a short glass of orange juice. Vitamins. We pretended it was a screwdriver, so my penchant for sobriety wouldn't give the bar a bad name. Who wants to get drunk when there are teetotalers in the crowd? And why in the world would I keep coming to a bar if I didn't drink?

I sipped my fake screwdriver and said, "I need some info."

"Figured that. Whatcha need?"

"I need information on a man named Phillip, dances at Guilty Pleasures."

One thick eyebrow raised. "Vamp?"

I shook my head. "Vampire junkie."

He took a big drag on his cig, making the end glow like a live coal. He blew a huge puff of smoke politely away from me. "Whatcha want to know about him?"

"Is he trustworthy?"

He stared at me for a heartbeat, then he grinned. "Trustworthy? Hell, Anita, he's a junkie. Don't matter what he's strung out on, drugs, liquor, sex, vampires, no diff. No junkie is trustworthy, you know that."

I nodded. I did know that, but what could I do? "I have to trust him, Luther. He's all I got."

"Damn, girl, you are moving in the wrong circles."

I smiled. Luther was the only person I let call me girl. All women were "girl," all men "fella." "I need to know if you've heard anything really bad about him," I said.

"What are you up to?" he asked.

"I can't say. I'd share it if I could, or if I thought it would do any good."

He studied me for a moment, cig dribbling ash onto the countertop. He wiped up the ash absentmindedly with his clean white towel. "Okay, Anita, you've earned the right to say no, this once, but next time you better have something to share."

I smiled. "Cross my heart."

He just shook his head and pulled a fresh cigarette out of the pack he always kept behind the bar. He took one last drag of the nearly burned cig, then clasped the fresh one between his lips. He put the glowing orange end of the old cig against the fresh white tip and sucked air. The paper and tobacco caught, flared orange-red, and he stubbed out the old cig in the already full ashtray he carried with him from place to place, like a teddy bear.

"I know they got a dancer down at the club that is a freak. He does the party circuit and is reeeal popular with a certain sort of vamp.'' Luther shrugged, a massive movement like mountains hiccuping. "Don't have no dirt on him, 'cept he's a junkie, and he does the circuit. Shit, Anita, that's bad enough. Sounds like someone to stay away from.''

"I would if I could.'' It was my turn to shrug. "But you haven't heard anything else about him?''

He thought for a moment, sucking on his new cigarette. "No, not a word. He ain't a big player in the district. He's a professional victim. Most of the talk is about the predators down here, not the sheep.'' He frowned. "Just a minute. I got something, an idea.'' He thought very carefully for a few minutes, then smiled broadly. "Yeah, got some news on a predator. Vamp calls himself Valentine, wears a mask. He been bragging that he did ol' Phillip the first time.''

"So,'' I said.

"Not the first time he was a junkie, girl, the first time period. Valentine claims he jumped the boy when he was small, did him good. Claims ol' Phillip liked it so much that's why he's a junkie.''

"Dear God.'' I remembered the nightmares, the reality, of Valentine. What would it have been like to have been small when it happened? What would it have done to me?

"You know Valentine?'' Luther asked.

I nodded. "Yeah. He ever say how old Phillip was when the attack took place?''

He shook his head. "No, but word is anything over twelve is too old for Valentine, 'less it's revenge. He's a real big one for revenge. Word is if the master didn't keep him in line, he'd be damn dangerous.''

"You bet your sweet ass he's dangerous.''

"You know him.'' It wasn't a question.

I looked up at Luther. "I need to know where Valentine stays during the day.''

"That's two bits of information for nuthin'. I don't think so.''

"He wears a mask because I doused him with Holy Water about two years ago. Until last night I thought he was dead, and he thought the same about me. He's going to kill me, if he can.''

"You awful hard to kill, Anita.''

"There's a first time, Luther, and that's all it takes.''

"I hear that.'' He started polishing already clean glasses. "I don't know. Word gets out we giving you daytime resting places, it could go bad for us. They could burn this place to the ground with us inside.''

"You're right. I don't have a right to ask.'' But I sat there on the bar stool, staring at him, willing him to give me what I needed. Risk your life for me old buddy ol' pal, I'd do the same for you. Riiight.

"If you could swear you wouldn't use the info to kill him, I could tell you,'' Luther said.

"It'd be a lie.''

"You got a warrant to kill him?'' he asked.

"Not active, but I could get one."

"Would you wait for it?"

"It's illegal to kill a vampire without a court order of execution," I said.

He stared at me. "That ain't the question. Would you jump the gun to make sure of the kill?"

"Might."

He shook his head. "You gonna be up on charges one of these days, girl. Murder is a serious rap."

I shrugged. "Beats getting your throat torn out."

He blinked. "Well, now." He didn't seem to know what to say, so he polished a sparkling glass over and over in his big hands. "I'll have to ask Dave. If he says it's okay, you can have it."

I finished my orange juice and paid up, a little heavy on the tip to keep things aboveboard. Dave would never admit he helped me because of my tie with the police, so money had to exchange hands, even if it wasn't nearly what the information was worth. "Thanks, Luther."

"Word on the street is that you met the master last night. That true?"

"You know about that before or after the fact?" I asked.

He looked pained. "Anita, we woulda told you if we'd known, gratis."

I nodded. "Sorry, Luther, it's been a rough few nights."

"I'll bet. So the rumor's true?"

What could I say? Deny it? A lot of people seemed to know. I guess you can't even trust the dead to keep a secret. "Maybe." I might as well have said yes, because I didn't say no. Luther understood the game. He nodded. "What did they want with you?"

"Can't say."

"Mmm . . . uh. Okay, Anita, you be damn careful. You might wanta get some help, if there's anybody you can trust."

Trust? It wasn't lack of trust. "There may be only two ways out of this mess, Luther. Death would be my choice. A quick death would be best, but I doubt I'll get the chance if things go bad. What friend am I supposed to drag into that?"

His round, dark face stared at me. "I don't have no answers, girl. I wish I did."

"So do I."

The phone rang. Luther answered it. He looked at me and carried the phone down on its long cord. "For you," he said.

I cradled the phone against my cheek. "Yes."

"It's Ronnie." Her voice was suppressed excitement, a kid on Christmas morning.

My stomach tightened. "You have something?"

"There is a rumor going around Humans Against Vampires. A death squad designed to wipe the vampires off the face of the earth."

"You have proof, a witness?"

"Not yet."

I sighed before I could stop myself.

"Come on, Anita, this is good news."

I cupped my hand over the phone and whispered, "I can't take a rumor about HAV to the master. The vampires would slaughter them. A lot of innocent people would get killed, and we're not even sure that HAV is really behind the murders."

"All right, all right," Ronnie said. "I'll have something more concrete by tomorrow, I promise. Bribe or threat, I'll get the information."

"Thanks, Ronnie."

"What are friends for? Besides, Bert's going to have to pay for overtime and bribes. I always love the look of pain when he has to part with money."

I grinned into the phone. "Me, too."

"What are you doing tonight?"

"Going to a party."

"What?"

I explained as briefly as I could. After a long silence she said, "That is very freaky."

I agreed with her. "You keep working your end, I'll try from this side. Maybe we'll meet in the middle."

"It'd be nice to think so." Her voice sounded warm, almost angry.

"What's wrong?"

"You're going in without backup, aren't you?" she asked.

"You're alone," I said.

"But I'm not surrounded by vampires and freakazoids."

"If you're at HAV headquarters, that last is debatable."

"Don't be cute. You know what I mean."

"Yes, Ronnie, I know what you mean. You are the only friend I have who can handle herself." I shrugged, realized she couldn't see it, and said, "Anybody else would be like Catherine, sheep among wolves, and you know it."

"What about another animator?"

"Who? Jamison thinks vampires are nifty. Bert talks a good game, but he doesn't endanger his lily white ass. Charles is a good enough corpse-raiser, but he's squeamish, and he's got a four-year-old kid. Manny doesn't hunt vampires anymore. He spent four months in the hospital being put back together after his last hunt."

"If I remember correctly, you were in the hospital, too," she said.

"A broken arm and a busted collarbone were my worst injuries, Ronnie. Manny almost died. Besides, he's got a wife and four kids."

Manny had been the animator who trained me. He taught me how to raise the dead, and how to slay vampires. Though admittedly I had expanded on Manny's teachings. He was a traditionalist, a stake-and-garlic man. He had carried a gun, but as backup, not as a primary tool. If modern technology will allow me to take out a vampire from a distance, rather than straddling its waist and pounding a stake through its heart, heh, why not?

Two years ago, Rosita, Manny's wife, had come to me and begged me not to endanger her husband anymore. Fifty-two was too old to hunt vampires, she had said. What would happen to her and the children? Somehow I had gotten all the blame, like a mother whose favorite child had been led astray by the neighborhood ruffians. She had made me swear before God that I would never again ask Manny to join me on a hunt. If she hadn't cried, I would have held out, refused. Crying was damned unfair in a fight. Once a person started to cry, you couldn't talk anymore. You suddenly just wanted them to stop crying, stop hurting, stop making you feel like the biggest scum-bucket in the world. Anything to stop the tears.

Ronnie was quiet on the other end of the phone. "All right, but you be careful."

"Careful as a virgin on her wedding night, I promise."

She laughed. "You are incorrigible."

"Everybody tells me that," I said.

"Watch your back."

"You do the same."

"I will." She hung up. The phone buzzed dead in my hands.

"Good news?" Luther asked.

"Yeah." Humans Against Vampires had a death squad. Maybe. But maybe was better than what I'd had before. Look, folks, nothing up my sleeves, nothing in my pockets, no idea in hell what I was doing. Just blundering around trying to track down a killer that has taken out two master vampires. If I was on the right track, I'd attract attention soon. Which meant someone might try to kill me. Wouldn't that be fun?

I would need clothes that showed off my vampire scars and allowed me to hide weapons. It would not be an easy combination to find.

I would have to spend the afternoon shopping. I hate to shop. I consider it one of life's necessary evils, like brussels sprouts and high-heeled shoes. Of course, it beat the heck out of having my life threatened by vampires. But wait; we could go shopping now and be threatened by vampires in the evening. A perfect way to spend a Saturday night.

23

I transferred all the smaller bags into one big bag, to leave one hand free for my gun. You'd be amazed what a nice target you make juggling two armloads of shopping bags. First drop the bags—that is, if one of the handles isn't tangled over your wrist—then reach for your gun, pull, aim, fire. By the time you do all that, the bad guy has shot you twice and is walking away humming Dixie between his teeth.

I had been downright paranoid all afternoon, aware of everyone near me. Was I being followed? Had that man looked too long at me? Was that woman wearing a scarf around her neck because she had bite marks?

By the time I went for the car, my neck and shoulders were knotted into one painful ache. The most frightening thing I'd seen all afternoon had been the prices on the designer clothing.

The world was still bright blue and heat-soaked when I went for my car. It's easy to forget the passage of time in a mall. It is air conditioned, climate controlled, a private world where nothing real touches you. Disneyland for shopaholics.

I shut my packages in the trunk and watched the sky darken. I knew what fear felt like, a leaden balloon in the pit of your gut. A nice, quiet dread.

I shrugged to loosen my shoulders. Rotated my neck until it popped. Better, but still tight. I needed some aspirin. I had eaten in the mall, something I almost never did. The moment I smelled the food stalls, I had gone for them, starved.

The pizza had tasted like thin cardboard with imitation tomato paste spread over it. The cheese had been rubbery and tasteless. Yum, yum, mall food. Truth is, I love Corn Dog on a Stick and Mrs. Field's Cookies.

I got one piece of pizza with just cheese, the way I like it, but one piece with everything. I hate mushrooms and green peppers. Sausage belongs on the breakfast table, not on pizza. I didn't know which bothered me more;

that I ordered it in the first place, or that I had eaten half of it before I realized what I was doing. I was craving food that I normally hated. Why? One more question without an answer. Why did this one scare me?

My neighbor, Mrs. Pringle, was walking her dog back and forth on the grass in front of our apartment building. I parked and unloaded my one overstuffed bag from the trunk.

Mrs. Pringle is over sixty, nearly six feet tall, stretched too thin with age. Her faded blue eyes are bright and curious behind silver-rimmed glasses. Her dog Custard is a Pomeranian. He looks like a golden dandelion fluff with cat feet.

Mrs. Pringle waved at me, and I was trapped. I smiled and walked over to them. Custard began jumping up on me, like he had springs in his tiny legs. He looked like a wind-up toy. His yapping was frequent and insistent, joyous.

Custard knows I don't like him, and in his twisted doggy mind he is determined to win me over. Or maybe he just knows it irritates me. Whatever.

"Anita, you naughty girl, why didn't you tell me you had a beau?" Mrs. Pringle asked.

I frowned. "A beau?"

"A boyfriend," she said.

I didn't know what in the world she was talking about. "What do you mean?"

"Be coy if you wish, but when a young woman gives her apartment key to a man, it means something."

That lead balloon in my gut floated up a few inches. "Did you see someone going in my apartment today?" I worked very hard at keeping my face and voice casual.

"Yes, your nice young man. Very handsome."

I wanted to ask what he looked like, but if he was my boyfriend with a key to my apartment, I should know. I couldn't ask. Very handsome—could it be Phillip? But why? "When did he stop by?"

"Oh, around two this afternoon. I was just coming out to walk Custard as he was going in."

"Did you see him leave?"

She was staring at me a little too hard. "No. Anita, was he not supposed to be in your home? Did I let a burglar get away?"

"No." I managed a smile and almost a whole laugh. "I just didn't expect him today, that's all. If you see anyone going into my apartment, just let them. I'll have friends going in and out for a few days."

Her eyes had narrowed; her delicate-boned hands were very still. Even Custard was sitting in the grass, panting up at me. "Anita Blake," she said, and I was reminded that she was a retired schoolteacher, it was that kind of voice. "What are you up to?"

"Nothing, really. I've just never given my key to a man before, and I'm a little unsure about it. Jittery." I gave her my best wide-eyed innocent look. I resisted the urge to bat my eyes, but everything else was working.

She crossed her arms over her stomach. I don't think she believed me. "If you are that nervous about this young man, then he is not the right one for you. If he was, you wouldn't be jittery."

I felt light with relief. She believed. "You're probably right. Thank you for the advice. I may even take it." I felt so good, I patted Custard on top of his furry little head.

I heard Mrs. Pringle say as I walked away, "Now, Custard, do your business and let's go upstairs."

For the second time in the same day I might have an intruder in my apartment. I walked down the hushed corridor and drew my gun. A door opened. A man and two children walked out. I slipped my gun and my hand in the shopping bag, pretending to search for something. I listened to their footsteps echo down the stairs.

I couldn't just sit out here with a gun. Someone would call the police. Everybody was home from work, eating dinner, reading the paper, playing with the kids. Suburban America was awake and alert. You could not walk through it with a gun drawn.

I carried the shopping bag in my left hand in front of me, gun and right hand still inside it. If worse came to worse, I'd shoot through the bag. I walked two doors past my apartment and dug my keys out of my purse. I sat the shopping bag against the wall and transferred the gun to my left hand. I could shoot left-handed, not as well, but it would have to do. I held the gun parallel to my thigh and hoped nobody would come the wrong way down the hall and see it. I knelt by the door, keys cupped in my right hand, quiet, not jingling this time. I learn fast.

I held the gun in front of my chest and inserted the keys. The lock clicked. I flinched and waited for gunshots or noise, or something. Nothing. I slipped the keys into my pocket and switched the gun back to my right hand. With just my wrist and part of my arm in front of the door, I turned the knob and pushed, hard.

The door swung back and banged against the far wall, nobody there. No gunshots at the door. Silence.

I was crouched by the doorjamb, gun straight out, scanning the room. There was no one to see. The chair, still facing the door, was empty this time. I would almost have been relieved to see Edward.

Footsteps pounded up the stairs at the end of the hall. I had to make a decision. I reached my left hand back and got the shopping bag, never taking eyes or gun from the apartment. I scrambled inside, shoving the bag ahead of me. I shoved the door closed, still crouched by the floor.

The aquarium heater clicked, then whirred, and I jumped. Sweat was oozing down my spine. The brave vampire slayer. If they could only see me now. The apartment felt empty. There was no one here but me, but just in case, I searched in closets, under beds. Playing Dirty Harry as I slammed doors and flattened myself against walls. I felt like a fool, but I would have been a bigger fool to have trusted the apartment was empty and been wrong.

There was a shotgun on the kitchen table, along with two boxes of ammo. A sheet of white typing paper lay under it. In neat, black letters, it said, "Anita, you have twenty-four hours."

I stared at the note, reread it. Edward had been here. I don't think I breathed for a minute. I was picturing my neighbor chatting with Edward. If Mrs. Pringle had hesitated at his lie, showed fear, would he have killed her?

I didn't know. I just didn't know. Dammit! I was like a plague. Everyone around me was in danger, but what could I do?

When in doubt, take a deep breath and keep moving. A philosophy I have lived by for years. I've heard worse, really.

The note meant I had twenty-four hours before Edward came for the location of Nikolaos' daytime retreat. If I didn't give it to him, I would have to kill him. I might not be able to do that.

I told Ronnie we were professionals, but if Edward was a professional, then I was an amateur. And so was Ronnie.

Heavy damn sigh. I had to get dressed for the party. There just wasn't time to worry about Edward. I had other problems tonight.

My answering machine was blinking, and I switched it on. Ronnie's voice first, telling me what she had already told me about HAV. Evidently, she had called here first before contacting me at Dave's bar. Then, "Anita, this is Phillip. I know the location for the party. Pick me up in front of Guilty Pleasures at six-thirty. Bye."

The machine clicked, whirred, and was silent. I had two hours to dress and be there. Plenty of time. My average time for makeup is fifteen minutes. Hair takes less, because all I do is run a brush through it. Presto, I'm presentable.

I don't wear makeup often, so when I do, I always feel like it's too dark, too fake. But I always get compliments on it, like, "Why don't you wear eye shadow more often? It really brings out your eyes," or my favorite, "You look so much better in makeup." All the above implies that without makeup, you look like a candidate for the spinster farm.

One piece of makeup I don't use is base. I can't imagine smearing cake over my whole face. I own one bottle of clear nail polish, but it isn't for my fingers, it's for my panty hose. If I wear a pair of hose once without snagging them, I have had a very good day.

I stood in front of the full-length mirror in the bedroom. The top slipped over my head with one thin strap. There was no back; it tied across the small of my back in a cute little bow. I could have done without the bow, but otherwise it wasn't too bad. The top slipped into the black skirt, complete, dresslike without a break. The tan bandages on my hands clashed with the dress. Oh, well. The skirt was full and swirled when I moved. It had pockets.

Through those pockets were two thigh sheaths complete with silver knives. All I had to do was slip my hands in and come out with a weapon. Neat. Sweat is an interesting thing when you're wearing a thigh sheath. I had not been able to figure out how to hide a gun on me. I don't care how many times you've seen women carry guns on a thigh holster on television, it is damn awkward. You walk like a duck with a wet diaper on.

Hose and high-heeled black satin pumps completed the outfit. I had owned the shoes and the weapons; everything else was new.

One other new item was a cute black purse with a thin strap that would hang across my shoulders, leaving my hands free. I stuffed my smaller gun, the Firestar, into it. I know, I know, by the time I dug the gun from the depths of the purse, the bad guys would be feasting on my flesh, but it was better than not having it at all.

I slipped my cross on, and the silver looked good against the black top. Unfortunately, I doubted the vampires would let me into the party wearing a blessed crucifix. Oh, well. I'd leave it in the car, along with the shotgun and ammo.

Edward had kindly left a box near the table. What I assumed he had brought the gun up in. What had he told Mrs. Pringle, that it was a present for me?

Edward had said twenty-four hours, but twenty-four hours from when? Would he be here at dawn, bright and early, to torture the information out of me? Naw, Edward didn't strike me as a morning person. I was safe until at least afternoon. Probably.

24

I slid into a no-parking zone in front of Guilty Pleasures. Phillip was leaning against the building, arms loose at his sides. He wore black leather pants. The thought of leather in this heat made my knees break out in heat rash. His shirt was black fishnet, which showed off both scars and tan. I don't know if it was the leather or the fishnet, but the word "sleazy" came to mind. He had passed over some invisible line, from flirt to hustler.

I tried to picture him at twelve. It didn't work. Whatever had been done to him, he was what he was, and that was what I had to deal with. I wasn't a psychiatrist who could afford to feel sorry for the poor unfortunate. Pity is an emotion that can get you killed. The only thing more dangerous is blind hate, and maybe love.

Phillip pushed away from the wall and walked towards the car. I unlocked his door, and he slid inside. He smelled of leather, expensive cologne, and faintly of sweat.

I pulled away from the curb. "Aggressive little outfit there, Phillip."

He turned to stare at me, face immobile, eyes hidden behind the same sunglasses he had worn earlier. He lounged in the seat, one leg bent and pressed against the door, the other spread wide, knee tucked up on the seat. "Take Seventy West." His voice was rough, almost hoarse.

There is that moment when you are alone with a man and you both realize it. Alone together, there are always possibilities in that. There is a nearly painful awareness of each other. It can lead to awkwardness, to sex, or to fear, depending on the man and the situation.

Well, we weren't having sex, you could make book on that. I glanced at Phillip, and he was still turned towards me, lips slightly parted. He'd taken off the sunglasses. His eyes were very brown and very close. What the hell was going on?

We were on the highway and up to speed. I concentrated on the cars around me, on driving, and tried to ignore him. But I could feel the weight of his gaze along my skin. It was almost a warmth.

He began to slide along the seat towards me. I was suddenly very aware of the sound of leather rubbing along the upholstery. A warm, animal sound. His arm slid across my shoulders, his chest leaning into me.

"What do you think you're doing, Phillip!"

"What's wrong?" He breathed along my neck. "Isn't this aggressive enough for you?"

I laughed; I couldn't help it. He stiffened beside me. "I didn't mean to insult you, Phillip. I just didn't picture fishnet and leather for tonight."

He stayed too close to me, pressing, warm, his voice still strange and rough. "What do you like then?"

I glanced at him, but he was too close. I was suddenly staring into his eyes from two inches away. His nearness ran through me like an electric shock. I turned back to the road. "Get on your side of the car, Phillip."

"What turns you," he whispered in my ear, "on?"

I'd had enough. "How old were you the first time Valentine attacked you?"

His whole body jerked, and he scooted away from me. "Damn you!" He sounded like he meant it.

"I'll make you a deal, Phillip. You don't have to answer my question, and I won't answer yours."

His voice came out choked and breathy. "When did you see Valentine? Is he going to be here tonight? They promised me he wouldn't be here tonight." His voice held a thick edge of panic. I had never heard such instant terror.

I didn't want to see Phillip afraid. I might start feeling sorry for him, and I couldn't afford that. Anita Blake, hard as nails, sure of herself, unaffected by crying men. Riiight. "I did not talk to Valentine about you, Phillip, I swear."

"Then how . . ." He stopped, and I glanced at him. He'd slid the sunglasses back in place. His face looked very tight and still behind his dark glasses. Fragile. Sort of ruined the image.

I couldn't stand it. "How did I find out what he did to you?"

He nodded.

"I paid money to find out about your background. It came up. I needed to know if I could trust you."

"Can you?"

"I don't know yet," I said.

He took several deep breaths. The first two trembled, but each breath was a little more solid, until finally he had it under control, for now. I thought of Rebecca Miles and her small, starved-looking hands.

"You can trust me, Anita. I won't betray you. I won't." His voice sounded lost, a little boy with all his illusions stripped away.

I couldn't stomp all over that lost child voice. But I knew and he knew that he would do anything the vampires wanted, anything, including betraying me. A bridge was rising over the highway, a tall latticework of grey metal. Trees hugged the road on either side. The summer sky was pale watery blue, washed out by the heat and the bright summer sun. The car bumped up on the bridge, and the Missouri River stretched away on either side. The air seemed open and distant over the rolling water. A pigeon fluttered onto the bridge, settling beside maybe a dozen others, all strutting and burring over the bridge.

I had actually seen seagulls on the river before, but you never saw one near the bridge, just pigeons. Maybe seagulls didn't like cars.

"Where are we going, Phillip?"

"What?"

I wanted to say, "Question too hard for you?" but I resisted. It would have been like picking on him. "We're across the river. What is our destination?"

"Take the Zumbehl exit and turn right."

I did what he said. Zumbehl veers to the right and spills you automatically to a turn lane. I sat at the light and turned on red when it was clear. There is a small gathering of stores to the left, then an apartment complex, then trees, almost a woods, houses tucked back in them. A nursing home is next and then a rather large cemetery. I always wondered what the people in the nursing home thought of living next door to a cemetery. Was it a ghoulish reminder, no pun intended? A convenience, just in case?

The cemetery had been there a lot longer than the nursing home. Some of the stones went back to the early 1800s. I always thought the developer must have been a closet sadist to put the windows staring out over the rolling tombstoned hills. Old age is enough of a reminder of what comes next. No visual aids are needed.

Zumbehl is lined with other things—video store, kids clothing boutique, a place that sold stained glass, gas stations, and a huge apartment complex proclaiming, "Sun Valley Lake." There actually was a lake large enough to sail on if you were very careful.

A few more blocks and we were in suburbia. Houses with tiny yards stuffed with huge trees lined the road. There was a hill that sloped downward. The speed limit was thirty. It was impossible to keep the car to thirty going down the hill without using brakes. Would there be a policeman at the bottom of the hill?

If he stopped us with Phillip in his little fishnet shirt, all nicely scarred, would he be suspicious? Where are you going, miss? I'm sorry, officer, we have this illegal party to go to, and we're running late. I used my brakes going down the hill. Of course, there was no policeman. If I had been speeding, he'd have been there. Murphy's law is the only true dependable in my life most of the time.

"It's the big house on the left. Just pull into the driveway," Phillip said.

The house was dark red brick, two, maybe three stories, lots of windows, at least two porches. Victorian American does still exist. The yard was large with a private forest of tall, ancient trees. The grass was too high, giving the place a deserted look. The drive was gravel and wound through the trees to a modern garage that had been designed to match the house and almost succeeded.

There were only two other cars here. I couldn't see into the garage; maybe there were more inside.

"Don't leave the main room with anyone but me. If you do, I can't help you," he said.

"Help me how?" I asked.

"This is our cover story. You are the reason I have missed so many meetings. I left hints that not only are we lovers, but I've been . . ." He spread his hands wide as if searching for a word. ". . . cultivating you, until I felt you were ready for a party."

"Cultivating me?" I turned off the car, and the silence settled between us. He was staring at me. Even behind the glasses I felt the weight of his gaze. The skin between my shoulders crawled.

"You are a reluctant survivor of a real attack, not a freak, or a junkie, but I've talked you into a party. That's the story."

"Have you ever done this for real?" I asked.

"You mean given them someone?"

"Yes," I said.

He gave a rough snort. "You don't think much of me, do you?"

What was I supposed to say, no? "If we're lovers, that means we have to play lovers all evening."

He smiled. This smile was different, anticipatory.

"You bastard."

He shrugged and rotated his neck as if his shoulders were tight. "I'm not going to throw you down on the floor and ravish you, if that's what you're worried about."

"I knew you wouldn't be doing that tonight." I was glad he didn't know I had weapons. Maybe I could surprise him tonight.

He frowned at me. "Follow my lead. If anything I do makes you uncomfortable, we'll discuss it." He smiled, dazzling, teeth white and even against his tan.

"No discussion. You'll just stop."

He shrugged. "You might blow our cover and get us killed."

The car was filling with heat. A bead of sweat dripped down his face. I opened my door and got out. The heat was like a second skin. Cicadas droned, a high, buzzing song far up in the trees. Cicadas and heat, ah, summer.

Phillip walked around the car, his boots crunching on the gravel. "You might want to leave the cross in the car," he said.

I had expected it, but I didn't have to like it. I put the crucifix into the glove compartment, crawling over the seat to do so. When I closed the door, my hand went to my neck. I wore the chain so much it only felt odd when I wasn't wearing it.

Phillip held out his hand, and after a moment I took it. The palm of his hand was cupped heat, slightly moist in the center.

The back door was shaded by a white lattice arch. A clematis vine grew thick on one side. Flowers as big as my hand spread purple to the tree-filtered sun. A woman was standing in the shadow of the door, hidden from neighbors and passing cars. She wore sheer black stockings held up by garter belts. A bra and matching panties, both royal purple, left most of her body pale and naked. She was wearing five-inch spikes that forced her legs to look long and slender.

"I'm overdressed," I whispered to Phillip.

"Maybe not for long," he breathed into my hair.

"Don't bet your life on it." I stared up at him as I said it and watched his face crumble into confusion. It didn't last long. The smile came, a soft curl of lips. The serpent must have smiled at Eve like that. I have this nice, shiny apple for you. Want some candy, little girl?

Whatever Phillip thought he was selling, I wasn't buying. He hugged me around the waist, one hand playing along the scars on my arm, fingers digging into the scar tissue just a little. His breath went out in a quick sigh. Jesus, what had I gotten myself into?

The woman was smiling at me, but her large brown eyes were fixed on Phillip's hand where it played with my scar. Her tongue darted out to wet her lips. I saw her chest rise and fall.

"Come into my parlor, said the spider to the fly."

"What did you say?" Phillip asked.

I shook my head. He probably didn't know the poem anyway. I couldn't remember how it ended. I couldn't remember if the fly got away. My stomach was tight. When Phillip's hand brushed my naked back, I jumped.

The woman laughed, high and maybe a little drunk. I whispered the fly's words as I went up the steps, "Oh, no, no, to ask me is in vain for whoever goes up your winding stairs can ne'er come down again."

Ne'er come down again. It had a bad ring to it.

25

The woman pressed against the wall, so we could pass, and shut the door behind us. I kept waiting for her to lock it so we couldn't get away, but she didn't. I shoved Phillip's hand off my scars, and he wrapped himself around my waist and led me down a long narrow hall. The house was cool, air conditioning purring against the heat. A square archway opened into a room.

It was a living room with all that implies—a couch, love seat, two chairs, plants hanging in front of a bay window, afternoon shadows snaking across the carpeting. Homey. A man stood in the center of the room, a drink in his hand. He looked like he had just come from Leather 'R' Us. Leather bands crisscrossed his chest and arms, like Hollywood's idea of an oversexed gladiator.

I owed Phillip an apology. He'd dressed downright conservatively. The happy homemaker came up behind us in her royal purple lingerie and laid a hand on Phillip's arm. Her fingernails were painted dark purple, almost black. The nails scratched along his arm, leaving faint reddish tracks behind.

Phillip shivered beside me, his arm tightening around my waist. Was this his idea of fun? I hoped not.

A tall, black woman rose from the couch. Her rather plentiful breasts threatened to squeeze out of a black wire bra. A crimson skirt with more holes than cloth hung from the bra and moved as she walked, giving glimpses of dark flesh. I was betting she was naked under the skirt.

There were pinkish scars on one wrist and her neck. A baby junkie, new, almost fresh. She stalked around us, like we were for sale and she wanted to get a good look. Her hand brushed my back, and I stood away from Phillip, facing the woman.

"That scar on your back; what is it? It isn't vampire bites." Her voice was low for a woman, an alto tenor maybe.

"A sharp piece of wood was slammed into my back by a human servant." I didn't add that the sharp piece of wood had been one of the stakes

I brought with me, or that I had killed the human servant later that same night.

"My name's Rochelle," she said.

"Anita."

The happy homemaker stepped up next to me, hand stroking over my arm. I stepped away from her, her fingers sliding over my skin. Her nails left little red lines on my arm. I resisted the urge to rub them. I was a tough-as-nails vampire slayer; scratches didn't bother me. The look in the woman's eyes did. She looked like she wondered what flavor I was and how long I'd last. I had never been looked at that way by another woman. I didn't like it much.

"I'm Madge. That's my husband Harvey," she said, pointing to Mr. Leather, who had moved to stand beside Rochelle. "Welcome to our home. Phillip has told us so much about you, Anita."

Harvey tried to come up behind me, but I stepped back towards the couch, so I could face him. They were trying to circle like sharks. Phillip was staring at me, hard. Right; I was supposed to be enjoying myself, not acting like they all had communicable diseases.

Which was the lesser evil? A sixty-four-thousand-dollar question if ever I heard one. Madge licked her lips, slowly, suggestively. Her eyes said she was thinking naughty things about me, and her. No way. Rochelle swished her skirt, exposing far too much thigh. I had been right. She was naked under the skirt. I'd die first.

That left Harvey. His small, blunt-fingered hands were playing with the leather-and-metal studding of the little kilt he wore. Fingers rubbing over and over the leather. Shit.

I flashed him my best professional smile, not seductive, but it was better than a frown. His eyes widened and he took a step towards me, hand reaching out towards my left arm. I took a deep breath and held it, smile freezing in place.

His fingers barely traced over the bend of my arm, tickling down the skin, until I shivered. Harvey took the shiver for an invitation and moved in closer, bodies almost touching. I put a hand on his chest to keep him from coming any closer. The hair on his chest was coarse and thick, black. I've never been a fan of hairy chests. Give me smooth any day. His arm began to encircle my back. I wasn't sure what to do. If I took a step back I was going to sit down on the couch, not a good idea. If I stepped forward I'd be stepping into him, pressed against all that leather and skin.

He smiled at me. "I've been dying to meet you."

He said "dying" like it was a dirty word, or an inside joke. The others laughed, all except Phillip. He took my arm and pulled me away from Harvey. I leaned into Phillip, even put my arms around his waist. I had never hugged anyone in a fishnet shirt before. It was an interesting sensation.

Phillip said, "Remember what I said."

"Sure, sure," Madge said. "She's yours, all yours, no sharing, no half-sies." She stalked over to him, swaying in her tight lace panties. With the heels on she could look him in the eye. "You can keep her safe from us for now, but when the big boys get here, you'll share. They'll make you share."

He stared at her until she looked away. "I brought her here, and I'll take her home," he said.

Madge raised an eyebrow. "You're going to fight them? Phillip, my boy, she must be a sweet piece of tail, but no bedwarmer is worth pissing off the big guys."

I stepped away from Phillip and put a hand flat against her stomach and pushed, just enough to make her back up. The heels made her balance bad, and she almost fell. "Let's get something straight," I said. "I am not a piece of anything, nor am I a bedwarmer."

Phillip said, "Anita . . ."

"My, my, she's got a temper. Wherever did you find her, Phillip?" Madge asked.

If there is anything I hate, it is being found amusing when I'm angry. I stepped up close to her, and she smiled down at me. "Did you know," I said, "that when you smile, you get deep wrinkles on either side of your mouth? You are over forty, aren't you?"

She drew a deep, gasping breath and stepped back from me. "You little bitch."

"Don't ever call me a piece of tail again, Madge, darling."

Rochelle was laughing silently, her considerable bosom shaking like dark brown jello. Harvey stood straight-faced. If he had so much as smiled, I think Madge would have hurt him. His eyes were very shiny, but there was no hint of a smile.

A door opened and closed down the hall, farther into the house. A woman stepped into the room. She was around fifty, or maybe a hard forty. Very blonde hair framed a plump face. Even money the blonde came out of a bottle. Plump little hands glittered with rings, real stones. A long, black negligee swept the floor, complete with an open lace robe. The flat black of the negligee was kind to her figure, but not kind enough. She was overweight and there was no hiding it. She looked like a PTA member, a Girl Scout leader, a cookie baker, someone's mother. And there she stood in the doorway, staring at Phillip.

She let out a little squeal and came running towards him. I got out of the way before I was crushed in the stampede. Phillip had just enough time to brace himself before she flung her considerable weight into his arms. For a minute I thought he was going to fall backwards into the floor with her on top, but his back straightened, his legs tensed, and he righted them both.

Strong Phillip, able to lift overweight nymphomaniacs with both hands.

Harvey said, "This is Crystal."

Crystal was kissing Phillip's chest, chubby, homey little hands trying to pull his shirt out of his pants so she could touch his bare flesh. She was like a cheerful little puppy in heat.

Phillip was trying to discourage her without much success. He gave me a long glance. And I remembered what he had said, that he had stopped coming to these parties. Was this why? Crystal and her like? Madge of the sharp fingernails? I had forced him to bring me, but in doing so, I had forced him to bring himself.

If you thought of it that way, it was my fault Phillip was here. Damn, I owed him.

I patted the woman's cheek, softly. She blinked at me, and I wondered if she was nearsighted. "Crystal," I said. I smiled my best angelic smile. "Crystal, I don't mean to be rude, but you're pawing my date."

Her mouth fell open; her pale eyes bugged out. "Date," she squeaked. "No one has dates at a party."

"Well, I'm new to the parties. I don't know the rules yet. But where I come from, one woman does not grope another woman's date. At least wait until I turn my back, okay?"

Crystal's lower lip trembled. Her eyes began to fill with tears. I had been gentle, kind even, and she was still going to cry. What was she doing here with these people?

Madge came and put her arm around Crystal and led the woman away. Madge was making soothing noises and patting her black silken arms.

Rochelle said, "Very cold." She walked away from me towards a liquor cabinet that was against one wall.

Harvey had also left, following Madge and Crystal without so much as a backwards glance.

You'd think I'd kicked a puppy. Phillip let out a long breath and set down on the couch. He clasped his hands in front of him, between his knees. I sat down next to him, tucking my skirt down over my legs.

"I don't think I can do this," he whispered.

I touched his arm. He was trembling, a constant shaking that I didn't like at all. I hadn't realized what it would cost him to come tonight, but I was beginning to find out.

"We can go," I said.

He turned very slowly and stared at me. "What do you mean?"

"I mean we can go."

"You'd leave now without finding out anything because I'm having problems?" he asked.

"Let's just say I like you better as the overconfident flirt. You keep acting like a real person, and you'll have me all confused. We can go if you can't handle it."

He took a deep breath and let it out, then shook himself like a dog coming out of water. "I can do it. If I have a choice, I can do it."

It was my turn to stare. "Why didn't you have a choice before?"

He looked away. "I just felt like I had to bring you if you wanted to come."

"No, dammit, that wasn't what you meant at all." I touched his face and forced him to look at me. "Someone gave you orders to come see me the other day, didn't they? It wasn't just to find out about Jean-Claude, was it?"

His eyes were wide, and I could feel his pulse under my fingers. "What are you afraid of, Phillip? Who's giving you orders?"

"Anita, please, I can't."

My hand dropped to my lap. "What are your orders, Phillip?"

He swallowed, and I watched his throat work. "I'm to keep you safe here, that's all." His pulse was jumping under the bruised bite in his neck. He licked his lips, not seductive, nervous. He was lying to me. The trick was, how much of a lie and what about?

I heard Madge's voice coming up the hall, all cheerful seduction. Such a good hostess. She escorted two people into the room. One was a woman with short auburn hair and too much eye makeup, like green chalk smeared above her eyes. The second was Edward, smiling, at his charming best, with his arm around Madge's bare waist. She gave a rich, throaty laugh as he whispered something to her.

I froze, for a second. It was so unexpected that I just froze. If he had pulled out a gun, he could have killed me while I sat with my mouth hanging open. What the hell was he doing here?

Madge led him and the woman towards the bar. He glanced back at me over her shoulder and gave me a delicate smile that left his blue eyes empty as a doll's.

I knew my twenty-four hours were not up. I knew that. Edward had decided to come looking for Nikolaos. Had he followed us? Had he listened to Phillip's message on my machine?

"What's wrong?" Phillip asked.

"What's wrong?" I said. "You are taking orders from somebody, probably a vampire . . ." I finished the statement silently in my head: And Death has just waltzed in the door to play freak while he searches for Nikolaos. There was only one reason Edward searched for a particular vampire. He meant to kill her, if he could.

The assassin might finally have met his match. I had thought I wanted to be around when Edward finally lost. I wanted to see what prey was too large for Death to conquer. I had seen this prey, up close and personal. If Edward and Nikolaos met and she even suspected that I had a hand in it . . . shit. Shit, shit, shit!

I should turn Edward in. He had threatened me, and he would carry it out. He would torture me to get information. What did I owe him? But I couldn't do it, wouldn't do it. A human being does not turn another human being over to the monsters. Not for any reason.

Monica had broken that rule, and I despised her for it. I think I was the closest thing Edward had to a real friend. A person who knows who and what you are and likes you anyway. I did like him, despite or because of what he was. Even though I knew he'd kill me if it worked out that way? Yes, even though. It didn't make much sense when you looked at it that way. But I couldn't worry about Edward's morality. The only person I had to face in the mirror was me. The only moral dilemma I could solve was my own.

I watched Edward play kissy-face with Madge. He was much better at role-playing than I was. He was also a much better liar.

I would not tell, and Edward had known I would not tell. In his own way, he knew me, too. He had bet his life on my integrity, and that pissed me off. I hate to be used. My virtue had become its own punishment.

But maybe, I didn't know how yet, I could use Edward the way he was using me. Perhaps I could use his lack of honor as he used my honor now.

It had possibilities.

26

The auburn-haired woman with Edward came over to the couch and slid into Phillip's lap. She giggled and wrapped her arms around his neck with a little kick of her feet. Her hands didn't wander lower, and she didn't try to undress him. The night was looking up. Edward followed behind the woman like a blond shadow. There was a drink in his hand and a suitably harmless smile on his face.

If I hadn't known him, I would never have looked at him and said, there, there is a dangerous man. Edward the Chameleon. He balanced on the couch arm at the woman's back, one hand rubbing her shoulder.

"Anita, this is Darlene," Phillip said.

I nodded. She giggled and kicked her little feet.

"This is Teddy. Isn't he scrumptious?"

Teddy? Scrumptious? I managed a smile, and Edward kissed the side of her neck. She snuggled against his chest, managing to wiggle in Phillip's lap at the same time. Coordination.

"Let me have a taste." Darlene sucked her lower lip under her teeth and drew it out slowly.

Phillip's breath trembled. He whispered, "Yes."

I didn't think I was going to like this.

Darlene cupped his arm in her hands and raised it to her mouth. She bestowed a delicate kiss over one of his scars, then she slid her legs down between his until she was kneeling at his feet, still holding his arm. The full skirt of her dress was bunched up around her waist, caught on his legs. She was wearing red lace panties and matching garters. Color coordination.

Phillip's face had gone slack. He was staring at her as she brought his arm towards her mouth. A small pink tongue licked his arm, quick, out, wet, gone. She glanced up at Phillip, eyes dark and full. She must have liked what she saw because she began to lick his scars, one by one, delicate, a cat with cream. Her eyes never left his face.

Phillip shuddered; his spine spasmed. He closed his eyes and leaned his head back against the couch. Her hands went to his stomach. She gripped the fishnet and pulled. It slid out of his pants, and her hands stroked up bare chest.

He jerked, eyes wide, and caught her arms. He shook his head. "No, no." His voice sounded hoarse, too deep.

"You want me to stop?" Darlene asked. Her eyes were nearly closed, breath deep, lips full and waiting.

He was struggling to talk and make sense at the same time. "If we do this . . . that leaves Anita alone. Fair game. Her first party."

Darlene looked at me, maybe for the first time. "With scars like that?"

"Scars are from a real attack. I talked her into the party." He brought her hands out from under his shirt. "I can't desert her." His eyes seemed to be focusing again. "She doesn't know the rules."

Darlene leaned her head on his thigh. "Phillip, please, I've missed you."

"You know what they'd do to her."

"Teddy will keep her safe. He knows the rules."

I asked, "You've been to other parties?"

"Yes," Edward said. He held my gaze for several seconds while I tried to picture him at other parties. So this was where he got his information about the vampire world, through the freaks.

"No," Phillip said. He stood, bringing Darlene to her feet, still holding her forearms. "No," he said, and his voice sounded certain, confident. He released her and held out his hand to me. I took it. What else could I do?

His hand was sweating and warm. He strode out of the room, and I was forced to half-run in my heels to catch up with my hand.

He led me down the hall to the bathroom and we went in. He locked the door and leaned against it, sweat beaded on his face, eyes closed. I took back my hand, and he didn't fight me.

I looked around at the available seating and finally chose to sit on the edge of the bathtub. It wasn't comfortable, but it seemed the lesser of two evils. Phillip drew in great gulps of air and finally turned to the sink. He ran water loud and splashing, dipped his hands in, and covered his face again and again until he stood, water dripping down his face. Droplets caught in his eyelashes and hair. He blinked at himself in the mirror over the basin. He looked startled, wide-eyed.

The water was dripping down his neck and chest. I stood and handed him a towel from the rack. He didn't respond. I mopped up his chest with the soft, clean-smelling folds of the towel.

He finally took the towel and finished drying off. His hair was dark and wet around his face. There was no way to dry it out. "I did it," he said.

"Yes," I said, "you did it."

"I almost let her."

"But you didn't, Phillip. That's what counts."

He nodded, rapidly, head bobbing. "I guess so." He still seemed out of breath.

"We better be getting back to the party."

He nodded. But he stayed where he was, breathing too deep, like he couldn't get enough oxygen.

"Phillip, are you all right?" It was a stupid question, but I couldn't think of what else to say.

He nodded. Mr. Conversation.

"Do you want to leave?" I asked.

He looked at me then. "That's the second time you've offered that. Why?"

"Why what?"

"Why would you offer to let me out of my promise?"

I shrugged and rubbed my hands over my arms. "Because . . . because you seem to be in some kind of pain. Because you're a junkie trying to kick the habit, sort of, and I don't want to screw that up for you."

"That's a very . . . decent thing to offer." He said decent like he wasn't used to the word.

"Do you want to leave?"

"Yes," he said, "but we can't."

"You said that before. Why can't we?"

"I can't, Anita, I can't."

"Yes, you can. Who are you taking orders from, Phillip? Tell me. What is going on?" I was standing nearly touching him, spitting each word into his chest, looking up at his face. It is always hard to be tough when you have to look up to see someone's eyes. But I've been short all my life, and practice makes perfect.

His hand slid around my shoulders. I pushed away from him, and his hands locked behind my back. "Phillip, stop it."

I had my hands flat on his chest to keep our bodies from pressing together. His shirt was wet and cold. His heart was hammering in his chest. I swallowed hard and said, "Your shirt's wet."

He released me so suddenly, I stumbled back from him. He drew the shirt over his head in one fluid motion. Of course, he had a lot of practice in undressing himself. It would have been such a nice chest without the scars.

He took one step towards me. "Stop, right where you are," I said. "What is this sudden change of mood?"

"I like you; isn't that enough?"

I shook my head. "No, it isn't."

He dropped the shirt to the floor. I watched it fall like it was important. Two steps and he was beside me. Bathrooms are so small. I did the only thing I could think of—I stepped into the bathtub. Not very dignified in high heels, but I wasn't pressed up against Phillip's chest. Anything was an improvement.

"Somebody is watching us," he said.

I turned, slowly, like a bad horror movie. Twilight hung against the sheer drapes, and a face peered out of the coming dark. It was Harvey, Mr. Leather. The windows were too high for him to be standing on the ground. Was he standing on a box? Or maybe they had little platforms at all the windows, so you could watch the show.

I let Phillip help me out of the bathtub. I whispered, "Could he hear us?"

Phillip shook his head. His arms slid around my back again. "We are supposed to be lovers. Do you want Harvey to stop believing that?"

"This is blackmail."

He smiled, dazzling, hold it in your hand and stroke it, sexy. My stomach tightened. He bent down, and I didn't stop him. The kiss was everything advertised, full soft lips, a press of skin, a heated weight. His hands tightened across my bare back, fingers kneading the muscles along the spine until I relaxed against him.

He kissed the lobe of my ear, breath warm. Tongue flicked along the edge of my jaw. His mouth found the pulse in my throat, his tongue searching for it, as if he were melting through the skin. Teeth scraped over the beating of my neck. Teeth clamped down, tight, hurting.

I shoved him back, away. "Shit! You bit me."

His eyes were unfocused, dazed. A crimson drop stained his lower lip.

I touched a hand to my neck and came away with blood. "Damn you!"

He licked my blood off his mouth. "I think Harvey believes the performance. Now you're marked. You've got the proof of what you are and why you came." He took a deep, shaking breath. "I won't have to touch you again tonight. I'll see that no one else does either. I swear."

My neck was throbbing; a bite, a freaking bite! "Do you know how many germs are in the human mouth?"

He smiled at me, still a little unfocused. "No," he said.

I shoved him out of the way and dabbed water on the cut. It looked like what it was, human teeth. It wasn't a perfect set of bite marks, but it was close. "Damn you."

"We need to go out so you can hunt for clues." He had picked his shirt up from the floor and stood there, holding it at his side. Bare tanned chest, leather pants, lips full like he'd been sucking on something. Me. "You look like an ad for Rent A Gigolo," I said.

He shrugged. "Ready to go out?"

I was still touching the wound. I tried to be angry and couldn't. I was scared. Scared of Phillip and what he was, or wasn't. I hadn't expected it. Was he right? Would I be safe for the rest of the night? Or had he just wanted to see what I tasted like?

He opened the door and waited for me. I went out. As we walked back to the living room, I realized Phillip had distracted me from my question. Who was he working for? I still didn't know.

It was damn embarrassing that every time he took his shirt off, my brain went out to lunch. But no more; I had had my first and last kiss from Phillip of the many scars. From now on I would remain the tough-as-nails vampire slayer, not to be distracted by rippling muscles or nice eyes.

My fingers touched the bite mark. It hurt. No more Ms. Nice Guy. If Phillip came near me again, I was going to hurt him. Of course, knowing Phillip, he'd probably enjoy it.

27

Madge stopped us in the hall. Her hand started to go up to my throat. I grabbed her wrist. "Touchy, touchy," she said. "Didn't you like it? Don't tell me you've been with Phillip a month and he hasn't tasted you before?"

She pulled down the silky bra to expose the upper mound of her breast. There was a perfect set of bite marks in the pale flesh. "It's Phillip's trademark, didn't you know?"

"No," I said. I pushed past her and started to turn into the living room. A man I did not know fell at my feet. Crystal was on top of him, pinning him to the floor. He looked young and a little frightened. His eyes looked up past Crystal, to me. I thought he was going to ask for help, but she kissed him, sloppy and deep, like she was drinking him from the mouth down. His hands began to lift the silk folds of her skirt. Her thighs were incredibly white, like beached whales.

I turned abruptly and went for the door. My heels made an important-sounding clack on the hardwood floor. If I hadn't known better, I would have said it sounded like I was running. I was not running. I was just walking very fast.

Phillip caught up with me at the door. His hand pressed flat against it to keep me from opening it. I took a deep, steadying breath. I would not lose my temper, not yet.

"I'm sorry, Anita, but it's better this way. You're safe now, from the humans."

I looked up at him and shook my head. "You just don't get it. I need some air, Phillip. I'm not leaving for the night, if that's what you're afraid of."

"I'll go out with you."

"No. That would defeat the purpose, Phillip. Since you are one of the things I want to get away from."

He stepped back then, hand at his side. His eyes shut down, guarded, hiding. Why had that hurt his feelings? I didn't know, and I didn't want to know.

I opened the door, and the heat fell around me like fur.

"It's dark," he said. "They'll be here soon. I can't help you if I'm not with you."

I stepped close to him and said in a near whisper, "Let's be honest, Phillip. I'm a whole lot better at protecting myself than you are. The first vampire that crooks its finger will have you for lunch."

His face started to crumble, and I didn't want to see it. "Dammit, Phillip, pull yourself together." I walked out onto the trellis-covered porch and resisted an urge to slam the door behind me. That would have been childish. I was feeling a little childish about now, but I'd save it. You never know when some childish rage may come in handy.

The cicadas and crickets filled the night. There was a wind pulling at the tops of the tall trees, but it never touched the ground. The air down here was as stale and close as plastic.

The heat felt good after the air-conditioned house. It was real and somehow cleansing. I touched the bite on my neck. I felt dirty, used, abused, angry, pissed off. I wasn't going to find anything out here. If someone or something was killing off vampires who did the freak circuit, it didn't seem to be such a bad idea.

Of course, whether I sympathized with the murderer was not the point. Nikolaos expected me to solve the crimes, and I damn well better do it.

I took a deep breath of the stiff air and felt the first stirrings of . . . power. It oozed through the trees like wind, but the touch of it didn't cool the skin. The hair at the back of my neck was trying to crawl down my spine. Whoever it was, they were powerful. And they were trying to raise the dead.

Despite the heat, we'd had a lot of rain, and my heels sank into the grass immediately. I ended up walking in a sort of tiptoe crouch, trying not to flounder in the soft earth.

The ground was littered with acorns. It was like walking on marbles. I fell against a tree trunk, catching myself painfully against the shoulder Aubrey had bruised so nicely.

A sharp bleating, high and panic-stricken, sounded. It was close. Was it a trick of the still air or was it really a goat bleating? The cry ended in a wet gurgle of sound, thick and bubbling. The trees ended, and the ground was clear and moon-silvered.

I slipped off one shoe and tried the ground. Damp, cool, but not too bad. I slipped off the other shoe, tucked them in one hand, and ran.

The back yard was huge, stretching out into the silvered dark. It spread empty, except for a wall of overgrown hedges, like small trees in the distance. I ran for the hedges. The grave had to be there; there was no other place for it to hide.

The actual ritual for raising the dead is a short one, as rituals go. The power poured out into the night and into the grave. It built in a slow, steady rise, a warm "magic." It tugged at my stomach and brought me to the hedges. They towered up, black in the moonlight, hopelessly overgrown. There was no way I was squeezing through them.

A man cried out. Then a woman: "Where is it? Where is the zombie you promised us?"

"It was too old!" The man's voice was thin with fear.

"You said chickens weren't enough, so we got you a goat to kill. But no zombie. I thought you were good at this."

I found a gate in the opposite side of the hedges. Metal, rusted, and crooked in its frame. It groaned, a metal scream, as I pushed it open. More than a dozen pairs of eyes turned to me. Pale faces, the utter stillness of the undead. Vampires. They stood among the ancient grave markers of the small family cemetery, waiting. Nothing waits as patiently as the dead.

One of the vampires nearest me was the black male from Nikolaos's lair. My pulse quickened, and I did a quick scan of the crowd. She wasn't here. Thank you, God.

The vampire smiled and said, "Did you come to watch . . . animator?" Had he almost said, "Executioner"? Was it a secret?

Whatever, he motioned the others back and let me see the show. Zachary lay on the ground. His shirt was damp with blood. You can't slit anything's throat without getting a little messy. Theresa was standing over him, hands on hips. She was dressed in black. The only skin showing was a strip of flesh down the middle, pale and almost luminous in the starlight. Theresa, Mistress of the Dark.

Her eyes flicked to me, a moment, then back to the man. "Well, Zach-a-ri, where is our zombie?"

He swallowed audibly. "It's too old. There isn't enough left."

"Only a hundred years old, animator. Are you so weak?"

He looked down at the ground. His fingers dug into the soft earth. He glanced up at me, then quickly down. I didn't know what he was trying to tell me with that one glance. Fear? For me to run? A plea for help? What?

"What good is an animator who can't raise the dead?" Theresa asked. She dropped to her knees, suddenly beside him, hands touching his shoulders. Zachary flinched but didn't try to get away.

A ripple of almost-movement ran through the other vampires. I could feel the whole circle at my back tense. They were going to kill him. The fact that he couldn't raise the zombie was just an excuse, part of the game.

Theresa ripped his shirt down the back. It fluttered around his lower arms, still tucked into his waist. A collective sigh ran through the vampires.

There was a woven rope band around his right upper arm. Beads were worked into it. It was a gris-gris, a voodoo charm, but it wouldn't help him now. No matter what it was supposed to do, it wouldn't be enough.

Theresa did a stage whisper. "Maybe you're just fresh meat?"

The vampires began to move in, silent as wind in the grass.

I couldn't just watch. He was a fellow animator and a human being. I couldn't just let him die, not like this, not in front of me. "Wait," I said.

No one seemed to hear me. The vampires moved in, and I was losing sight of Zachary. If one bit him, the feeding frenzy would be on. I had seen that happen once. I would never get rid of the nightmares if I saw it again.

I raised my voice and hoped they listened. ''Wait! Didn't he belong to Nikolaos? Didn't he call Nikolaos master?''

They hesitated, then parted for Theresa to stride through them until she faced me. ''This is not your business.'' She stared at me, and I didn't avoid her gaze. One less thing to worry about.

''I'm making it my business,'' I said.

''Do you wish to join him?''

The vampires began to spread out from Zachary to encircle me as well. I let them. There wasn't much I could do about it anyway. Either I'd get us both out alive or I'd die, too, maybe, probably. Oh, well.

''I wish to speak with him, one professional to another,'' I said.

''Why?'' she asked.

I stepped close to her, almost touching. Her anger was nearly palpable. I was making her look bad in front of the others, and I knew it, and she knew I knew it. I whispered, though some of the others would hear me, ''Nikolaos gave orders for the man to die, but she wants me alive, Theresa. What would she do to you if I accidentally died here tonight?'' I breathed the last words into her face. ''Do you want to spend eternity locked in a cross-wrapped coffin?''

She snarled and jerked away from me as if I had scalded her. ''Damn you, mortal, damn you to hell!'' Her black hair crackled around her face, her hands gripped into claws. ''Talk to him, for what good it will do you. He must raise this zombie, this zombie, or he is ours. So says Nikolaos.''

''If he raises the zombie, then he goes free, unharmed?'' I asked.

''Yes, but he cannot do it; he isn't strong enough.''

''Which was what Nikolaos was counting on,'' I said.

Theresa smiled, a fierce tug of lips exposing fangs. ''Yesss.'' She turned her back on me and strode through the other vampires. They parted for her like frightened pigeons. And I was standing up to her. Sometimes bravery and stupidity are almost interchangeable.

I knelt by Zachary. ''Are you hurt?''

He shook his head. ''I appreciate the gesture, but they're going to try to kill me tonight.'' He looked up at me, pale eyes searching my face. ''There isn't anything you can do to stop them.'' He gave a thin smile. ''Even you have your limits.''

''We can raise this zombie if you'll trust me.''

He frowned, then stared at me. I couldn't read his expression—puzzlement and something else. ''Why?''

What could I say, that I couldn't just watch him die? He had watched a man be tortured and hadn't lifted a hand. I opted for the short reason. ''Because I can't let them have you, if I can stop it.''

''I don't understand you, Anita, I don't understand you at all.''

''That makes two of us. Can you stand?''

He nodded. ''What are you planning?''

"We're going to share our talent."

His eyes widened. "Shit, you can act as a focus?"

"I've done it twice before." Twice before with the same person. Twice before with someone who had trained me as an animator. Never with a stranger.

His voice dropped to a bare whisper. "Are you sure you want to do this?"

"Save you?" I asked.

"Share your power," he said.

Theresa strode over to us in a swish of cloth. "Enough of this, animator. He can't do it, so he pays the price. Either leave now, or join us at our . . . feast."

"Are you having rare Who-roast-beast?" I asked.

"What are you talking about?"

"It's from Dr. Seuss, *How the Grinch Stole Christmas*. You know the part, 'And they'd Feast! Feast! Feast! Feast! They would feast on Who-pudding, and rare Who-roast-beast.' "

"You are crazy."

"So I've been told."

"Do you want to die?" she asked.

I stood up, very slowly, and felt something build in me. A sureness, an absolute certainty that she was not a danger to me. Stupid, but it was there, solid and real. "Someone may kill me before all this is over, Theresa"—I stepped into her, and she gave ground—"but it won't be you."

I could almost taste her pulse in my mouth. Was she afraid of me? Was I going crazy? I had just stood up to a hundred-year-old vampire, and she had backed down. I felt disoriented, almost dizzy, as if reality had moved and no one had warned me.

Theresa turned her back on me, hands balled into fists. "Raise the dead, animators, or by all the blood ever spilled, I'll kill you both."

I think she meant it. I shook myself like a dog coming out of deep water. I had a baker's dozen worth of vampires to pacify and a one-hundred-year-old corpse to raise. I could only handle a zillion problems at a time. A zillion and one was beyond me.

"Get up, Zachary," I said. "Time to go to work."

He stood. "I've never worked with a focus before. You'll have to tell me what to do."

"No problem," I said.

28

The goat lay on its side. The bare white of its spine glimmered in the moonlight. Blood still seeped into the ground from the gaping wound. Eyes were rolled and glazed, tongue lolling out of its mouth.

The older the zombie, the bigger the death needed. I knew that, and that was why I avoided older zombies when I could. At a hundred years the corpse was just so much dust. Maybe a few bone fragments if you were lucky. They re-formed to rise from the grave. If you had the power to do it.

Problem was, most animators couldn't raise the long-dead, a century and over. I could. I just didn't want to. Bert and I had had long discussions about my preferences. The older the zombie, the more we can charge. This was at least a twenty-thousand-dollar job. I doubted I'd get paid tonight, unless living 'til morning was payment enough. Yeah, I guess it was. Here's to seeing another dawn.

Zachary came to stand beside me. He had torn the remnants of his shirt off. He stood thin and pale beside me. His face was all shadows and white flesh, high cheekbones almost cavernous. "What next?" he asked.

The goat carcass was inside the blood circle he had traced earlier; good. "Bring everything we need into the circle."

He brought a long hunting knife and a pint jar full of pale faintly luminous ointment. I preferred a machete myself, but the knife was huge, with one jagged edge and a gleaming point. The knife was clean and sharp. He took good care of his tools. Brownie point for him.

"We can't kill the goat twice," he said. "What are we going to use?"

"Us," I said.

"What are you talking about?"

"We'll cut ourselves; fresh, live blood, as much as we're willing to give."

"The blood loss would leave you too weak to go on."

I shook my head. "We already have a blood circle, Zachary. We're just going to rewalk, not redraw it."

"I don't understand."

"I don't have time to explain metaphysics to you. Every injury is a small death. We'll give the circle a lesser death, and reactivate it."

He shook his head. "I still don't get it."

I took a deep breath, and then realized I couldn't explain it to him. It was like trying to explain the mechanics of breathing. You could break it down into steps, but that didn't tell you what it felt like to breathe. "I'll show you what I mean." If he didn't feel this part of the ritual, understand it without words, the rest wouldn't work anyway.

I held out my hand for the knife. He hesitated, then handed it to me, hilt first. The thing felt top-heavy, but then it wasn't designed for throwing. I took a deep breath and pressed the blade edge against my left arm, just below the cross burn. A quick down stroke, and blood welled up, dark and dripping. It stung, sharp and immediate. I let out the breath I'd been holding and handed the knife to Zachary.

He was staring from me to the knife.

"Do it, right arm, so we'll mirror each other," I said.

He nodded and made a quick slash across his right upper arm. His breath hissed, almost a gasp.

"Kneel with me." I knelt, and he followed me down, mirroring me as I asked. A man who could follow directions; not bad.

I bent my left arm at the elbow and raised it so the fingertips were head-high, elbow shoulder-high. He did the same. "We clasp hands and press the cuts together."

He hesitated, immobile.

"What's the matter?" I asked.

He shook his head, two quick shakes, and his hand wrapped around mine. His arm was longer than mine, but we managed.

His skin felt uncomfortably cool against mine. I glanced up at his face, but I couldn't read it. I had no idea what he was thinking. I took a deep, cleansing breath and began. "We give our blood to the earth. Life for death, death for life. Raise the dead to drink our blood. Let us feed them as they obey us."

His eyes did widen then; he understood. One hurdle down. I stood and drew him with me. I led him along the blood circle. I could feel it, like an electric current up my spine. I stared straight into his eyes. They were almost silver in the moonlight. We walked the circle and ended where we had begun, by the sacrifice.

We sat in the blood-soaked grass. I dabbed my right hand in the still-oozing blood of the goat's wound. I was forced to kneel to reach Zachary's face. I smeared blood over his forehead, down his cheeks. Smooth skin, the rub of new beard. I left a dark handprint over his heart.

The woven band was like a ring of darkness on his arm. I smeared blood along the beads, fingertips finding the soft brush of feathers worked into the string. The gris-gris needed blood, I could feel that, but not goat blood. I shrugged it away. Time to worry about Zachary's personal magic later.

He smeared blood on my face. Fingertips only, as if afraid to touch me. I could feel his hand shake as he traced my cheek. The blood was a cool wetness over my breast. Heart blood.

Zachary unscrewed the jar of homemade ointment. It was a pale off-white color with flecks of greenish light in it. The glowing flecks were grave-yard mold.

I rubbed ointment over the blood smears. The skin soaked it up.

He brushed the cream on my face. It felt waxy, thick. I could smell the pine scent of rosemary for memory, cinnamon and cloves for preservation, sage for wisdom, and some sharp herb, maybe thyme, to bind it all together. There was too much cinnamon in it. The night suddenly smelled like apple pie.

We went together to smear ointment and blood on the tombstone. The name was only soft grooves in the marble. I traced them with my fingertips. Estelle Hewitt. Born 18 something, died 1866. There had been more writing below the date and name, but it was gone, beyond reading. Who had she been? I had never raised a zombie that I knew nothing about. It wasn't always a good idea, but then this whole thing wasn't a good idea.

Zachary stood at the foot of the grave. I stayed by the tombstone. It felt like an invisible cord was stretched between Zachary and me. We started the chant together, no questions needed. "Hear us, Estelle Hewitt. We call you from the grave. By blood, magic, and steel, we call you. Arise, Estelle, come to us, come to us."

His eyes met mine, and I felt a tug along the invisible line that bound us. He was powerful. Why hadn't he been able to do it alone?

"Estelle, Estelle, come to us. Waken, Estelle, arise and come to us." We called her name in ever-rising voices.

The earth shuddered. The goat slid to one side as the ground erupted, and a hand clutched for air. A second hand grabbed at nothing, and the earth began to pour the dead woman out.

It was then, only then, that I realized what was wrong, why he hadn't been able to raise her on his own. I now knew where I had seen him before. I had been at his funeral. There were so few animators that if anyone died, you went, period. Professional courtesy. I had glimpsed that angular face, rouged and painted. Somebody had done a bad job of making him up, I remembered thinking that at the time.

The zombie had almost pulled itself from the grave. It sat panting, legs still trapped in the ground.

Zachary and I stared at each other over the grave. All I could do was stare at him like an idiot. He was dead, but not a zombie, not anything I'd ever heard of. I would have bet my life he was human, and I may have done just that.

The woven band on his arm. The spell that hadn't been satisfied with goat's blood. What was he doing to stay "alive"?

I had heard rumors of gris-gris that could cheat death. Rumors, legends, fairy tales. But then again, maybe not.

Estelle Hewitt may have been pretty once, but a hundred years in the grave takes a lot out of a person. Her skin was an ugly greyish white, waxy, nearly expressionless, fake-looking. White gloves hid the hands, stained with grave dirt. The dress was white and lace-covered. I was betting on wedding finery. Dear God.

Black hair clung to her head in a bun, wisps of it tracing her nearly skeletal face. All the bones showed, as if the skin were clay molded over a framework. Her eyes were wild, dark, showing too much white. At least they hadn't dried out like shriveled grapes. I hated that.

Estelle sat by her grave and tried to gather her thoughts. It would take a while. Even the recently dead took a few minutes to orient themselves. A hundred years was a damn long time to be dead.

I walked around the grave, careful to stay within the circle. Zachary watched me come without a word. He hadn't been able to raise the corpse because he was a corpse. The recently dead he could still handle, but not long-dead. The dead calling the dead from the grave; there was something really wrong with that.

I stared up at him, watching him grip the knife. I knew his secret. Did Nikolaos? Did anyone? Yes, whoever had made the gris-gris knew, but who else? I squeezed the skin around the cut on my arm. I reached bloody fingers towards the gris-gris.

He caught my wrist, eyes wide. His breathing had quickened. "Not you."

"Then who?"

"People who won't be missed."

The zombie we had raised moved in a rustle of petticoats and hoops. It began crawling towards us.

"I should have let them kill you," I said.

He smiled then. "Can you kill the dead?"

I jerked my wrist free. "I do it all the time."

The zombie was scrambling at my legs. It felt like sticks digging at me. "Feed it yourself, you son of a bitch," I said.

He held his wrist down to it. The zombie grabbed for it, clumsy, eager. It sniffed his skin but released him untouched. "I don't think I can feed it, Anita."

Of course not; fresh, live blood was needed to close the ritual. Zachary was dead. He didn't qualify anymore. But I did.

"Damn you, Zachary, damn you."

He just stared at me.

The zombie was making a mewling sound low in her throat. Dear God. I offered her my bleeding left arm. Her stick-hands dug into my skin. Her mouth fastened over the wound, sucking. I fought the urge to jerk away. I had made the bargain, had chosen the ritual. I had no choice. I stared at

Zachary while the thing fed on my blood. Our zombie, a joint venture. Dammit.

"How many people have you killed to keep yourself alive?" I asked.

"You don't want to know."

"How many!"

"Enough," he said.

I tensed, raising my arm, nearly lifting the zombie to her feet. She cried, a soft sound, like a newborn kitten. She released my arm so suddenly, she fell backwards. Blood dripped down her bony chin. Her teeth were stained with it. I couldn't look at it, any of it.

Zachary said, "The circle is open. The zombie is yours."

For a minute I thought he was talking to me; then I remembered the vampires. They had been huddled in the dark, so still and unmoving I had forgotten them. I was the only live thing in the whole damn place. I had to get out of there.

I picked up my shoes and walked out of the circle. The vampires made way for me. Theresa stopped me, blocking my path. "Why did you let it suck your blood? Zombies don't do that."

I shook my head. Why did I think it would be faster to explain than to fight about it? "The ritual had already gone wrong. We couldn't start over without another sacrifice. So I offered myself as the sacrifice."

She stared. "Yourself?"

"It was the best I could do, Theresa. Now get out of my way." I was tired and sick. I had to get out of there, now. Maybe she heard it in my voice. Maybe she was too eager to get to the zombie to mess with me. I don't know, but she moved aside. She was just gone, like the wind had swept her away. Let them play their mind games. I was going home.

There was a small scream from behind me. A short, strangled sound, as if the voice wasn't used to talking. I kept walking. The zombie screamed, human memories still there, enough for fear. I heard a rich laugh, a faint echo of Jean-Claude's. Where are you, Jean-Claude?

I glanced back once. The vampires were closing in. The zombie was stumbling from one side to the other, trying to run. But there was nowhere to go.

I stumbled through the crooked gate. A wind had finally come down out of the trees. Another scream sounded from behind the hedges. I ran, and I didn't look back.

29

I slipped on the damp grass. Hose are not made for running in. I sat there, breathing, trying not to think. I had raised a zombie to save another human being, who wasn't a human being. Now the zombie I had raised was being tortured by vampires. Shit. The night wasn't even half-over. I whispered, "What next?"

A voice answered, light as music. "Greetings, animator. You seem to be having a full night."

Nikolaos was standing in the shadows of the trees. Willie McCoy was with her, a little to one side, not quite beside her, like a bodyguard or a servant. I was betting on servant.

"You seem agitated. What ever is the matter?" Her voice rose in a lilting sing-song. The dangerous little girl had returned.

"Zachary raised the zombie. You can't use that as an excuse to kill him." I laughed then, and it sounded abrupt and harsh even to me. He was already dead. I didn't think she knew. She couldn't read minds, only force the truth from them. I bet Nikolaos had never thought to ask, "Are you alive, Zachary, or a walking corpse?" I laughed and couldn't seem to stop.

"Anita, you all right?" Willie's voice was like his voice had always been.

I nodded, trying to catch my breath. "I'm fine."

"I do not see the humor in the situation, animator." The child voice was slipping, like a mask sliding down. "You helped Zachary raise the zombie." She made it sound like an accusation.

"Yes."

I heard movement over the grass. Willie's footsteps, and nothing else. I glanced up and saw Nikolaos moving towards me, noiseless as a cat. She was smiling, a cute, harmless, model, beautiful child. No. Her face was a little long. The perfect child bride wasn't perfect anymore. The closer she came, the more flaws I could pick out. Was I seeing her the way she really looked? Was I?

"You are staring at me, animator." She laughed, high and wild, wind chimes in a storm. "As if you'd seen a ghost." She knelt, smoothing her slacks over her knees, as if they were a skirt. "Have you seen a ghost, animator? Have you seen something that frightened you? Or is it something else?" Her face was only an arm's length away.

I was holding my breath, fingers digging into the ground. Fear washed over me like a cool second skin. The face was so pleasant, smiling, encouraging. She really needed a dimple to go with it all. My voice was hoarse, and I had to cough to clear it. "I raised the zombie. I don't want it hurt."

"But it is only a zombie, animator. They have no real minds."

I just stared at that thin, pleasant face, afraid to look away from her, afraid to look at her. My chest was tight with the urge to run. "It was a human being. I don't want it tortured."

"They won't hurt it much. My little vampires will be disappointed. The dead cannot feed off the dead."

"Ghouls can. They feed off the dead."

"But what is a ghoul, animator? Is it truly dead?"

"Yes."

"Am I dead?" she asked.

"Yes."

"Are you sure?" She had a small scar near her upper lip. She must have gotten it before she died.

"I'm sure," I said.

She laughed then, a sound to bring a smile to your face and a song to your heart. My stomach jerked at the noise. I might never enjoy Shirley Temple movies again.

"I don't think you are sure in the least." She stood, one smooth motion. A thousand years of practice makes perfect.

"I want the zombie put back, now, tonight," I said.

"You are not in a position to want anything." The voice was cold, very adult. Children didn't know how to strip skin with their voice.

"I raised it. I don't want it tortured."

"Isn't that too bad?"

What else could I say? "Please."

She stared down at me. "Why is it so important to you?"

I didn't think I could explain it to her. "It just is."

"How important?" she asked.

"I don't know what you mean."

"What would you be willing to endure for your zombie?"

Fear settled into a cold lump in the pit of my gut. "I don't know what you mean."

"Yes, you do," she said.

I stood then, not that it would help. I was actually taller than she was. She was tiny, a delicate fairy of a child. Right. "What do you want?"

"Don't do it, Anita." Willie was standing away from us, as if afraid to come too close. He was smarter dead than he had been alive.

"Quiet, Willie." Her voice was conversational when she said it, no yelling, no threat. But Willie fell silent instantly, like a well-trained dog.

Maybe she caught my look. Whatever, she said, "I had Willie punished for failing to hire you that first time."

"Punished?"

"Surely, Phillip has told you about our methods?"

I nodded. "A cross-wrapped coffin."

She smiled, brilliant, cheery. The shadows leeched it into a leer. "Willie was very afraid that I would leave him in there for months, or even years."

"Vampires can't starve to death. I understand the principle." I added silently in my head: You bitch. I can only be terrified so long before I get angry. Anger feels better.

"You smell of fresh blood. Let me taste you, and I will see your zombie safe."

"Does taste mean bite?" I asked.

She laughed, sweet, heartrending. Bitch. "Yes, human, it means bite." She was suddenly beside me. I jerked back without thinking. She laughed again. "It seems Phillip has beaten me to it."

For a minute I couldn't think what she meant; then my hand went to the bite mark on my neck. I felt suddenly uneasy, like she'd caught me naked.

The laugh floated on the summer air. It was really beginning to get on my nerves.

"No tasting," I said.

"Then let me enter your mind again. That's a type of feeding."

I shook my head, too rapid, too many times. I'd die before I'd let her in my mind again. If I had the choice.

A scream sounded in the not so far distance. Estelle was finding her voice. I winced like I'd been slapped.

"Let me taste your blood, animator. No teeth." She flashed fang as she said the last. "You stand and make no move to stop me. I will taste the fresh wound on your neck. I won't feed on you."

"It's not bleeding anymore. It's clotted."

She smiled, oh so sweetly. "I'll lick it clean."

I swallowed hard. I didn't know if I could do it. Another scream sounded, high and lost. God.

Willie said, "Anita . . ."

"Silence, or risk my anger." Her voice growled low and dark.

Willie seemed to shrink in upon himself. His face was a white triangle under his black hair.

"It's all right, Willie. Don't get hurt on my account," I said.

He stared at me across the distance, a few yards; it might as well have been miles. Only the lost look on his face helped. Poor Willie. Poor me.

"What good is it going to do you if you're not feeding off me?" I asked.

"No good at all." She reached a small, pale hand towards me. "Of course, fear is a kind of substance." Cool fingers slid around my wrist. I flinched but didn't pull back. I was going to let her do this, wasn't I?

"Call it shadow feeding, human. Blood and fear are always precious, no matter how one obtains them." She stepped up to me. She exhaled against my skin, and I backed away. Only her hand on my wrist kept me close.

"Wait. I want the zombie freed now, first."

She just stared at me, then nodded slowly. "Very well." She stared past me, pale eyes seeing things that weren't there or that I couldn't see. I felt a tension through her hand, almost a jerk of electricity. "Theresa will chase them off and have the animator lay the zombie to rest."

"You did all that, just then?"

"Theresa is mine to command; didn't you know that?"

"Yeah, I guessed that." I had not known that any vampire could do telepathy. Of course, before last night I hadn't thought they could fly either. Oh, I was just learning all sorts of new things.

"How do I know you're not just telling me that?" I asked.

"You will just have to trust me."

Now that was almost funny. If she had a sense of humor, maybe we could work something out. Naw.

She pulled my wrist closer to her body and me with it. Her hand was like fleshy steel. I couldn't pry her hand off, not with anything short of a blowtorch. And I was all out of blowtorches.

The top of her head fitted under my chin. She had to rise on tiptoe to breathe on my neck. It should have ruined the menace. It didn't. Soft lips touched my neck. I jerked. She laughed against my skin, face pressed against me. I shivered and couldn't stop.

"I promise to be gentle." She laughed again, and I fought an urge to shove her away. I would have given almost anything to hit her, just once, hard. But I didn't want to die tonight. Besides, I'd made a deal.

"Poor darling, you're shaking." She laid a hand on my shoulder to steady herself. She brushed lips along the hollow of my neck. "Are you cold?"

"Cut the crap. Just do it!"

She stiffened against me. "Don't you want me to touch you?"

"No," I said. Was she crazy? Rhetorical question.

Her voice was very still. "Where is the scar on my face?"

I answered without thinking. "Near your mouth."

"And how," she hissed, "did you know that?"

My heart leaped into my throat. Oops. I had let her know her mind tricks weren't working, and they should have been.

Her hand dug into my shoulder. I made a small sound, but I didn't cry out. "What have you been doing, animator?"

I didn't have the faintest idea. Somehow, I doubted she'd believe that.

"Leave her alone!" Phillip came half-running through the trees. "You promised me you wouldn't hurt her tonight."

Nikolaos didn't even turn around. "Willie." Just his name, but like all good servants he knew what was wanted.

He stepped in front of Phillip, one arm straight out from his body. He was going to stiff-arm him. Phillip sidestepped the arm, brushing past.

Willie never had been much of a fighter. Strength wasn't enough if you had shit for balance.

Nikolaos touched my chin and turned my face back to hers. "Do not force me to hold your attention, animator. You wouldn't like the methods I would choose."

I swallowed audibly. She was probably right. "You have my full attention, honest." My voice came out as a hoarse whisper, fear squeezing it down. If I coughed to clear it, I'd cough in her face. Not a good idea.

I heard the rush of feet swishing through the grass. I fought the urge to look up and away from the vampire.

Nikolaos spun from me to face the footsteps. I saw her move, but it was still blurring speed. She was just suddenly facing the other way. Phillip was standing in front of her. Willie caught up to him and grabbed an arm, but didn't seem to know what to do with it.

Would it occur to Willie that he could just crush the man's arm? I doubted it.

It had occurred to Nikolaos. "Release him. If he wants to keep coming, let him." Her voice promised a great deal of pain.

Willie stepped back. Phillip just stood there, staring past her at me. "Are you all right, Anita?"

"Go back inside, Phillip. I appreciate the concern, but I made a bargain. She isn't going to bite me."

He shook his head. "You promised she wouldn't be harmed. You promised." He was talking to Nikolaos again, carefully not looking directly at her.

"And so she shall not be harmed. I keep my word, Phillip, most of the time."

"I'm all right, Phillip. Don't get hurt because of me," I said.

His face crumbled with confusion. He didn't seem to know what to do. His courage seemed to have spilled out on the grass. But he didn't back off. Big point for him. I would have backed off, maybe. Probably. Oh, hell, Phillip was being brave, and I didn't want to see him die because of it.

"Just go back, Phillip, please!"

"No," Nikolaos said. "If the little man is feeling brave, let him try."

Phillip's hands flexed, as if trying to grab on to something.

Nikolaos was suddenly beside him. I hadn't seen her move. Phillip still hadn't. He was staring where she had been. She kicked his legs out from under him. He fell to the grass, blinking up at her like she'd just appeared.

"Don't hurt him!" I said.

A pale little hand shot out, the barest touch. His whole body jerked backwards. He rolled on one side, blood staining his face.

"Nikolaos, please!" I said. I had actually taken two steps towards her.

Voluntarily. I could always try for my gun. It wouldn't kill her, but it might give Phillip time to run away. If he would run.

Screams sounded from the direction of the house. A man's voice yelled, "Perverts!"

"What is it?" I asked.

Nikolaos answered, "The Church of Eternal Life has sent its congregation." She sounded mildly amused. "I must leave this little get-together." She whirled to me, leaving Phillip dazed on the grass. "How did you see my scar?" she asked.

"I don't know."

"Little liar. We will finish this later." And she was gone, running like a pale shadow under the trees. At least she hadn't flown away. I didn't think my wits could handle that tonight.

I knelt by Phillip. He was bleeding where she had hit him. "Can you hear me?"

"Yes." He managed to sit up. "We have to get out of here. The church-goers are always armed."

I helped him to stand. "Do they invade the freak parties often?"

"Whenever they can," he said.

He seemed steady on his feet. Good, I could never have carried him far.

Willie said, "I know I don't have a right to ask, but I'll help you get to your car." He wiped his hands down his pants. "Can I catch a ride?"

I couldn't help it. I laughed. "Can't you just disappear like the rest of them?"

He shrugged. "Don't know how yet."

"Oh, Willie." I sighed. "Come on, let's get out of here."

He grinned at me. Being able to look him in the eyes made him seem almost human. Phillip didn't object to the vampire joining us. Why had I thought he would?

There were screams from the house. "Somebody's gonna call the cops," Willie said.

He was right. I'd never be able to explain it. I grabbed Phillip's hand and steadied myself while I put the high heels back on. "If I'd known we'd be running from crazed fanatics tonight, I'd have worn lower heels," I said.

I kept a grip on Phillip's arm to steady myself through the minefield of acorns. This was not the time to twist an ankle.

We were almost to the gravel drive when three figures spilled out of the house. One held a club. The others were vampires. They didn't need a weapon. I opened my purse and got my gun out, held down at my side, hidden against my skirt. I gave Phillip the car keys. "Start the car; I'll cover our backs."

"I don't know how to drive," he said.

I had forgotten. "Shit!"

"I'll do it." Willie took the keys, and I let him.

One of the vampires rushed us, arms wide, hissing. Maybe he meant to scare us; maybe he meant to do us harm. I'd had enough for one night. I clicked off the safety, chambered a round and fired into the ground at his feet.

He hesitated, almost stumbled. "Bullets can't hurt me, human."

There was more movement under the trees. I didn't know if it was friend or foe, or if it made a hell of a lot of difference. The vampire kept coming. It was a residential neighborhood. Bullets can travel a great distance before they hit something. I couldn't take the chance.

I raised my arm, aimed, and fired. The bullet took him in the stomach. He jerked and sort of crumpled over the wound. His face held astonishment.

"Silver-plated bullets, fang-face."

Willie went for the car. Phillip hesitated between helping me and going. "Go, Phillip, now."

The second vampire was trying to circle around. "Stop right where you are," I said. The vampire froze. "Anybody makes a threatening gesture, I'm going to put a bullet in their brain."

"It won't kill us," the second vampire said.

"No, but it won't do you a hell of a lot of good, either."

The human with the club inched forward. "Don't," I told him.

The car started. I didn't dare glance back at it. I stepped backwards, hoping I wouldn't trip in the damn high heels. If I fell, they'd rush me. If they rushed me, somebody was going to die.

"Come on, Anita, get in." It was Phillip, leaning out of the passenger side door.

"Scoot over." He did, and I slid into the seat. The human rushed us. "Drive, now!"

Willie spun gravel, and I slammed the door shut. I really didn't want to kill anyone tonight. The human was shielding his face from the gravel as we rushed down the driveway.

The car bounced wildly, nearly colliding with a tree. "Slow down; we're safe," I said.

Willie eased back on the gas. He grinned at me. "We made it."

"Yeah." I smiled back at him, but I wasn't so sure.

Blood was dripping down Phillip's face in a nice steady flow. He voiced my thoughts. "Safe, but for how long?" He sounded as tired as I felt.

I patted his arm. "Everything will be all right, Phillip."

He looked at me. His face seemed older than it had, tired. "You don't believe that any more than I do."

What could I say? He was right.

30

I clicked on the safety of my gun and struggled into a seat belt. Phillip slumped down into the seat, long legs spreadeagled on either side of the floorboard hump. His eyes were closed.

"Where to?" Willie asked.

Good question. I wanted to go home and go to sleep, but . . . "Phillip's face needs patching up."

"You wanna take him to a hospital?"

"I'm all right," Phillip said. His voice was low and strange.

"You aren't all right," I said.

He opened his eyes and turned to look at me. The blood had run down his neck, a dark, glistening stream that shone in the flashes of the streetlights. "You were hurt a lot worse last night," he said.

I looked away from him, out the window. I didn't know what to say. "I'm all right now."

"I'll be all right, too."

I looked back at him. He was staring at me. I couldn't read the expression on his face, and wanted to. "What are you thinking, Phillip?"

He turned his head to stare straight ahead. His face was all silhouette and shadows. "That I stood up to the master. I did it. I did it!" His voice held a fierce warmth with the last. Fierce pride.

"You were very brave," I said.

"I was, wasn't I?"

I smiled and nodded. "Yes."

"I hate ta interrupt you two, but I need ta know where to drive this thing," Willie said.

"Drop me back at Guilty Pleasures," Phillip said.

"You should see a doc."

"They'll take care of me at the club."

"Ya sure?"

He nodded, then winced and turned to me. "You wanted to know who was giving me orders. It was Nikolaos. You were right. That first day. She wanted me to seduce you." He smiled. It didn't look right with the blood. "Guess I wasn't up to the job."

"Phillip . . ." I said.

"No, it's all right. You were right about me. I'm sick. No wonder you didn't want me."

I glanced over at Willie. He was concentrating on his driving as if his life depended on it. Damn, he was smarter dead than alive.

I took a deep breath and tried to decide what to say. "Phillip . . . The kiss before you . . . bit me." God, how did I say this? "It was nice."

He glanced at me, quick, then away. "You mean that?"

"Yes."

An awkward silence stretched through the car. No sound but the rush of pavement under the wheels. The night flashes of lights, and the isolating darkness.

"Standing up to Nikolaos tonight was one of the bravest things I've ever seen anybody do. Also one of the stupidest," I said.

He laughed, abrupt and surprised.

"Don't ever do it again. I don't want your death on my hands."

"It was my choice," he said.

"No more heroics, okay?"

He glanced at me. "Would you be sorry if I died?"

"Yes."

"I guess that's something."

What did he want me to say? To confess undying love, or something silly like that? How about undying lust? Either one would be a lie. What did he want from me? I almost asked him, but I didn't. I wasn't that brave.

31

It was nearly three by the time I walked up the stairs to my apartment. All the bruises were aching. My knees, feet, and lower back were a nearly burning grind of pain from the high heels. I wanted a long, hot shower and bed. Maybe if I were lucky I could actually get eight uninterrupted hours of sleep. Of course, I wouldn't bet on it.

I got my keys in one hand and gun in the other. I held the gun at my side, just in case a neighbor should open his or her door unexpectedly. Nothing to fear, folks, just your friendly neighborhood animator. Right.

For the first time in far too long my door was just the way I left it: locked. Thank you, God. I was not in the mood to play cops and robbers this very early morning.

I kicked off my shoes just inside the door, then stumbled to the bedroom. The message light was blinking on my answering machine. I laid my gun on the bed, hit the play button, and started undressing.

"Hi, Anita, this is Ronnie. I got a meeting set up for tomorrow with the guy from HAV. My office, eleven o'clock. If the time is bad, leave a message on my machine, and I'll get back to you. Be careful."

Click, whirr, and Edward's voice came out of the machine. "The clock is ticking, Anita." Click.

Damn. "You like your little games, don't you, you son of a bitch?" I was getting grumpy, and I didn't know what I was going to do about Edward. Or Nikolaos, or Zachary, or Valentine, or Aubrey. I did know I wanted a shower. I could start there. Maybe I'd have a brilliant idea while I was scrubbing goat blood off my skin.

I locked the door to the bathroom and laid my gun on the top of the toilet. I was beginning to get a little paranoid. Or maybe realistic was a better word.

I turned the water on until it steamed, then stepped into it. I was no closer to solving the vampire murders now than I had been twenty-four hours ago.

Even if I solved the case, I still had problems. Aubrey and Valentine were going to kill me once Nikolaos removed her protection from me. Peachy. I wasn't even sure that Nikolaos herself didn't have ideas in that direction. Now, Zachary, he was killing people to feed his voodoo charm. I had heard of charms that demanded human sacrifice. Charms that gave you a whole lot less than immortality. Wealth, power, sex—the age-old wants. It was very specific blood—children, or virgins, or preadolescent boys, or little old ladies with blue hair and one wooden leg. All right, not that specific, but there had to be a pattern to it. A string of disappearances with similar victims. If Zachary had been simply leaving the bodies to be found, the newspapers would have picked up on it by now. Maybe.

He had to be stopped. If I hadn't interfered tonight, he would have been stopped. No good deed goes unpunished.

I leaned palms against the bathroom tile, letting the water wash down my back in nearly scalding rivulets. Okay, I had to kill Valentine before he killed me. I had a warrant for his death. It had never been revoked. Of course, I had to find him first.

Aubrey was dangerous, but at least he was out of the way until Nikolaos let him out of his trapped coffin.

I could just turn Zachary over to the police. Dolph would listen to me, but I didn't have a shred of proof. Hell, the magic was even something I'd never heard of. If I couldn't understand what Zachary was, how was I going to explain it to the police?

Nikolaos. Would she let me live if I solved the case? Or not? I didn't know.

Edward was coming to get me tomorrow evening. I either gave him Nikolaos or he took a piece of my hide. Knowing Edward, it would be a painful piece to lose. Maybe I could just give him the vampire. Just tell him what he wanted to know. And he fails to kill her, and she comes and gets me. The one thing I wanted to avoid, almost more than anything else, was Nikolaos coming to get me.

I dried off, ran a brush through my hair, and had to get something to eat. I tried to tell myself I was too tired to eat. My stomach didn't believe me.

It was four before I fell into bed. My cross was safely around my neck. The gun in its holster behind the head board. And, just for pure panic's sake, I slipped a knife between the mattress and box springs. I'd never get to it in time to do any good, but . . . Well, you never know.

I dreamed about Jean-Claude again. He was sitting at a table eating blackberries.

"Vampires don't eat solid food," I said.

"Exactly." He smiled and pushed the bowl of fruit towards me.

"I hate blackberries," I said.

"They were always my favorite. I hadn't tasted them in centuries." His face looked wistful.

I picked up the bowl. It was cool, almost cold. The blackberries were floating in blood. The bowl fell from my hands, slow, spilling blood on the table, more than it could ever have held. Blood dripped down the tabletop, onto the floor.

Jean-Claude stared at me over the bleeding table. His words came like a warm wind. "Nikolaos will kill us both. We must strike first, ma petite."

"What's this 'we' crap?"

He cupped pale hands in the flowing blood and held them out to me, like a cup. Blood dripped out from between his fingers. "Drink. It will make you strong."

I woke staring up into the darkness. "Damn you, Jean-Claude," I whispered. "What have you done to me?"

There was no answer from the dark, empty room. Thank goodness for small favors. The clock read six-oh-three a.m. I rolled over and snuggled back into the covers. The whir of air conditioning couldn't hide the sounds of one of my neighbors running water. I switched on the radio. Mozart's piano concerto in E flat filled the darkened room. It was really too lively to sleep to, but I wanted noise. My choice of noise.

I don't know if it was Mozart or I was just too tired; whatever, I went back to sleep. If I dreamed, I didn't remember it.

32

The alarm shrieked through my sleep. It sounded like a car alarm, hideously loud. I smashed my palm on the buttons. Mercifully, it shut off. I blinked at the clock through half-slit eyes. Nine a.m. Damn. I had forgotten to unset the alarm. I had time to get dressed and make church. I did not want to get up. I did not want to go to church. Surely, God would forgive me just this once.

Of course, I did need all the help I could get right now. Maybe I'd even have a revelation, and everything would fall into place. Don't laugh; it had happened before. Divine aid is not something I rely on, but every once in a while I think better at church.

When the world is full of vampires and bad guys, and a blessed cross may be all that stands between you and death, it puts church in a different light. So to speak.

I crawled out of bed, groaning. The phone rang. I sat on the edge of the bed, waiting for the answering machine to pick up. It did. "Anita, this is Sergeant Storr. We got another vampire murder."

I picked up the receiver. "Hi, Dolph."

"Good. Glad I caught you before church."

"Is it another dead vampire?"

"Mmhuh."

"Just like the others?" I asked.

"Seems to be. Need you to come down and take a look."

I nodded, realized he couldn't see it, and said, "Sure, when?"

"Right now."

I sighed. So much for church. They couldn't hold the body until noon, or after, just for little ol' me. "Give me the location. Wait, let me get a pen that works." I kept a notepad by the bed, but the pen had died without my knowing it. "Okay, shoot."

The location was only about a block from Circus of the Damned. "That's

on the fringe of the District. None of the other murders have been that far
away from the Riverfront."

"True," he said.

"What else is different about this one?"

"You'll see it when you get here."

Mr. Information. "Fine, I'll be there in half an hour."

"See you then." The phone went dead.

"Well, good morning to you too, Dolph," I said to the receiver. Maybe
he wasn't a morning person either.

My hands were healing. I had taken the Band-Aids off last night because
they were covered with goat blood. The scrapes were scabbing nicely, so I
didn't bother with more Band-Aids.

One fat bandage covered the knife wound on my arm. I couldn't hurt
my left arm anymore. I had run out of room. The bite mark on my neck was
beginning to bruise. It looked like the world's worst hicky. If Zerbrowski
saw it, I would never live it down. I put a Band-Aid on it. Now it looked
like I was covering a vampire bite. Damn. I left it. Let people wonder. None
of their business anyway.

I put a red polo shirt on, tucked into jeans. My Nikes, and a shoulder
harness for my gun, and I was all set. My shoulder rig has a little pouch for
extra ammo. I put fresh clips in it. Twenty-six bullets. Watch out, bad guys.
Truth was, most firefights were finished before the first eight shots were gone.
But there was always a first time.

I carried a bright yellow windbreaker over my arm. I'd put it on just in
case the gun started making people nervous. I would be working with the
police. They'd have their guns out in plain sight. Why couldn't I? Besides,
I was tired of games. Let the bastards know I was armed and willing.

There are always too many people at a murder scene. Not the gawkers,
the people who come to watch; you expect that. There is always something
fascinating about someone else's death. But the place always swarms with
police, mostly detectives with a sprinkling of uniforms. So many cops for
one little murder.

There was even a news van, with a huge satellite antenna sticking out
of its back like a giant ray gun from some 1940s science fiction movie. There
would be more news vans, I was betting on that. I don't know how the police
kept it quiet this long.

Vampire murders, gee whiz, sensationalism at its best. You don't even
have to add anything to make it bizarre.

I kept the crowd between myself and the cameraman. A reporter with
short blond hair and a stylish business suit was shoving a microphone in
Dolph's face. As long as I stayed near the gruesome remains, I was safe.
They might get me on film, but they wouldn't be able to show it on television. Good taste and all, you know.

I had a little plastic-enclosed card, complete with picture, that gave me access to police areas. I always felt like a junior G-man when I clipped it to my collar.

I was stopped at the yellow police banner by a vigilant uniform. He stared at my I. D. for several seconds, as if trying to decide whether I was kosher or not. Would he let me through the line, or would he call a detective over first?

I stood, hands at my sides, trying to look harmless. I'm actually very good at that. I can look downright cute. The uniform raised the tape and let me through. I resisted an urge to say, "Atta boy." I did say, "Thank you."

The body lay near a lamp pole. Legs were spreadeagled. One arm twisted under the body, probably broken. The center of the back was missing, as if someone had shoved a hand through the body and just scooped out the center. The heart would be gone, just like all the others.

Detective Clive Perry was standing by the body. He was a tall, slender, black man, and most recent member of the spook squad. He always seemed so soft-spoken and pleasant. I could never imagine Perry doing anything rude enough to piss someone off, but you didn't get assigned to the squad without a reason.

He looked up from his notebook. "Hi, Ms. Blake."

"Hello, Detective Perry."

He smiled. "Sergeant Storr said you'd be coming down."

"Is everyone else finished with the body?"

He nodded. "It's all yours."

A dark brown puddle of blood spread out from under the body. I knelt beside it. The blood had congealed to a tacky, gluelike consistency. Rigor mortis had come and gone, if there had been rigor mortis. Vampires didn't always react to "death" the way a human body did. It made judging the time of death harder. But that was the coroner's job, not mine.

The bright summer sun pressed down over the body. From the shape and the black pants suit, I was betting it was female. It was sort of hard to tell, lying on its stomach, chest caved in, and the head missing. The spine showed white and glistening. Blood had poured out of the neck like a broken bottle of red wine. The skin was torn, twisted. It looked like somebody had ripped the freaking head off.

I swallowed very hard. I hadn't thrown up on a murder victim in months. I stood up and put a little distance between myself and the body.

Could this have been done by a human being? No; maybe. Hell. If it was a human being, then they were trying very hard to make it look otherwise. No matter what a surface look revealed, the coroner always found knife marks on the body. The question was, did the knife marks come before or after death? Was it a human trying to look like a monster, or a monster trying to look like a human?

"Where's the head?" I asked.

"You sure you feel all right?"

I looked up at him. Did I look pale? "I'll be fine." Me, big, tough vampire slayer, no throw up at the sight of decapitated heads. Right.

Perry raised his eyebrows but was too polite to push the issue. He led me about eight feet down the sidewalk. Someone had thrown a plastic cover over the head. A second smaller pool of congealing blood oozed out from under the plastic.

Perry bent over and grasped the plastic. "You ready?"

I nodded, not trusting my voice. He lifted the plastic, like a curtain backdrop to what lay on the sidewalk.

Long, black hair flowed around a pale face. The hair was matted and sticky with blood. The face had been attractive but no more. The features were slack, almost doll-like in their unreality. My eyes saw it, but it took my brain a few seconds to register. "Shit!"

"What is it?"

I stood up, fast, and took two steps out into the street. Perry came to stand beside me. "Are you all right?"

I glanced back at the plastic with its grisly little lump. Was I all right? Good question. I could identify this body.

It was Theresa.

33

I arrived at Ronnie's office a few minutes before eleven. I paused with my hand on the doorknob. I couldn't shake the image of Theresa's head on the sidewalk. She had been cruel and had probably killed hundreds of humans. Why did I feel pity for her? Stupidity, I suppose. I took a deep breath and pushed the door inward.

Ronnie's office is full of windows. Light glares in from two sides, south and west. Which means in the afternoon the room is like a solar heater. No amount of air conditioning is going to overcome that much sunshine.

You can see the District from Ronnie's sunshiny windows. If you care to look.

Ronnie waved me through the door into the almost blinding glare of her office.

A delicate-looking woman was sitting in a chair across from the desk. She was Asian with shiny, black hair styled carefully back from her face. A royal purple jacket, which matched her tailored skirt, was folded neatly on the chair arm. A shiny, lavender blouse brought attention to the up-tilted eyes and the faint lavender shading on the lids and brow. Her ankles were crossed, hands folded in her lap. She looked cool in her lavender blouse, even in the sweltering sunshine.

It caught me off guard for a minute, seeing her like that, after all these years. Finally, I closed my gaping mouth and walked forward, hand extended. "Beverly, it has been a long time."

She stood neatly and put a cool hand in mine. "Three years." Precise, that was Beverly all over.

"You two know each other?" Ronnie asked.

I turned back to her. "Bev didn't mention that she knew me?"

Ronnie shook her head.

I stared at the new woman. "Why didn't you mention it to Ronnie?"

"I did not think it necessary." Bev had to raise her chin to look me in the eye. Not many people have to do that. It's rare enough that I always find it an odd sensation, as if I should stoop down so we can be at eye level.

"Is someone going to tell me where you two know each other from?" Ronnie asked.

Ronnie moved past us to sit behind her desk. She tilted the chair slightly back on its swivel, crossed hands over stomach, and waited. Her pure grey eyes, soft as kitten fur, stared at me.

"Do you mind if I tell her, Bev?"

Bev had sat down again, smooth and ladylike. She had real dignity and had always impressed me as being a lady, in the best sense of the word. "If you feel it necessary, I do not object," she said.

Not exactly a rousing go-ahead, but it would do. I flopped down in the other chair, very aware of my jeans and jogging shoes. Beside Bev I looked like an ill-dressed child. For just a moment I felt it; then it was gone. Remember, no one can make you feel inferior without your consent. Eleanor Roosevelt said that. It is a quote I try to live by. Most of the time I succeed.

"Bev's family were the victims of a vampire pack. Only Beverly survived. I was one of the people who helped destroy the vampires." Brief, to the point, a hell of a lot left out. Mostly the painful parts.

Bev spoke in that quiet, precise voice of hers. "What Anita has left out is that she saved my life at risk of her own." She glanced down at her hands where they lay in her lap.

I remembered my first glimpse of Beverly Chin. One pale leg thrashing against the floor. The flash of fangs as the vampire reared to strike. A glimpse of pale, screaming face, and dark hair. The pure terror as she screamed. My hand throwing a silver-bladed knife and hitting the vampire's shoulder. Not a killing blow; there had been no time. The creature had sprung to its feet, roaring at me. I stood facing the thing with the last knife I had, gun long since emptied, alone.

And I remembered Beverly Chin beating the vampire's head in with a silver candlestick, while he crouched over me, breath warm on my neck. Her shrieks echoed through my dreams for weeks, as she beat the thing's head to pieces until blood and brain seeped out onto the floor.

All that passed between us without words. We had saved each other's lives; it is a bond that sticks with you. Friendships may fade, but there is always that obligation, that knowledge forged of terror and blood and shared violence, that never really leaves. It was there between us after three long years, straining and touchable.

Ronnie is a smart lady. She caught on to the awkward silence. "Would anybody like a drink?"

"Nonalcoholic," Bev and I said together. We laughed at each other, and the strain faded. We would never be true friends, but perhaps we could stop being ghosts to each other.

Ronnie brought us two diet Cokes. I made a face but took it anyway. I knew that was all she had in the office's little fridge. We had had discussions about diet drinks, but she swore she liked the taste. Liked the taste, garg!

Bev took hers graciously; perhaps that was what she drank at home. Give me something fattening with a little taste to it any day.

"Ronnie mentioned on the phone that there might be a death squad attached to HAV. Is that true?" I said.

Bev stared down at the can, which she held with one hand cupped underneath so it wouldn't stain her skirt. "I do not know positively that it is true, but I believe it to be."

"Tell me what you've heard?" I asked.

"There was talk for a while of forming a squad to hunt the vampires. To kill them as they have killed our . . . families. The president of course vetoed the idea. We work within the system. We are not vigilantes." She said it almost as a question, as if trying to convince herself more than us. She was shaken by what might have happened. Her neat little world collapsing again.

"But lately I have heard talk. People in our organization bragging of slaying vampires."

"How were they supposedly killed?" I asked.

She looked at me, hesitated. "I do not know."

"No hint?"

She shook her head. "I believe I could find out for you. Is it important?"

"The police have hidden certain details from the general public. Things only the murderer would know."

"I see." She glanced down at the can in her hands, then up at me. "I do not believe it is murder even if my people have done what the papers say. Killing dangerous animals should not be a crime."

In part I agreed with her. Once I had agreed with her wholeheartedly. "Then why tell us?" I asked.

She looked directly at me, dark, nearly black eyes staring into my face. "I owe you."

"You saved my life as well. You owe me nothing."

"There will always be a debt between us, always."

I looked into her face and understood. Bev had begged me not to tell anyone that she had beaten the vampire's head in. I think it horrified her that she was capable of such violence, regardless of motive.

I had told the police that she distracted the vampire so I could kill it. She had been disproportionately grateful for that small white lie. Maybe if no one else knew, she could pretend it had never happened. Maybe.

She stood, smoothing her skirt down in back. She sat her soda can carefully on the edge of the desk. "I will leave a message with Ms. Sims when I find out more."

I nodded. "I appreciate what you're doing." She might be betraying her cause for me.

She laid her purple jacket over her arm, small purse clasped in her hands. "Violence is not the answer. We must work within the system. Humans Against Vampires stands for law and order, not vigilantism." It sounded like a prerecorded speech. But I let it go. Everyone needs something to believe in.

She shook hands with both of us. Her hand was cool and dry. She left, slender shoulders very straight. The door closed firmly but quietly behind her. To look at her you would never know that she had been touched by extreme violence. Maybe that's the way she wanted it. Who was I to argue?

Ronnie said, "Okay, now you fill me in. What have you found out?"

"How do you know I've found out anything?" I asked.

"Because you looked a little green around the gills when you came through the door."

"Great. And I thought I was hiding it."

She patted my arm. "Don't worry. I just know you too well, that's all."

I nodded, taking the explanation for what it was, comforting crap. But I took it anyway. I told her about Theresa's death. I told her everything, except the dreams with Jean-Claude in them. That was private.

She let out a low whistle. "Damn, you have been busy. Do you think a human death squad is doing it?"

"You mean HAV?"

She nodded.

I took a deep breath and let it out. "I don't know. If it's humans, I don't have the faintest idea how they're doing it. It would take superhuman strength to rip a head off."

"A very strong human?" she asked.

The image of Winter's bulging arms flashed into my mind. "Maybe, but that kind of strength . . . "

"Under pressure, little old grannies have lifted entire cars."

She had a point. "How would you like to visit the Church of Eternal Life?" I asked.

"Thinking about joining up?"

I frowned at her.

She laughed. "Okay, okay, stop glowering at me. Why are we going?"

"Last night they raided the party with clubs. I'm not saying they meant to kill anyone, but when you start beating on people"—I shrugged—"accidents happen."

"You think the Church is behind it?"

"Don't know, but if they hate the freaks enough to storm their parties, maybe they hate them enough to kill them."

"Most of the Church's members are vampires," she said.

"Exactly. Superhuman strength and the ability to get close to the victims."

Ronnie smiled. "Not bad, Blake, not bad."

I bowed my head modestly. "Now all we got to do is prove it."

Her eyes were still shiny with humor when she said, "Unless of course they didn't do it."

"Oh, shut up. It's a place to start."

She spread her hands wide. "Hey, I'm not complaining. My father always told me, 'Never criticize, unless you can do a better job.' "

"You don't know what's going on either, huh?" I asked.

Her face sobered. "Wish I did."

So did I.

34

The Church of Eternal Life, main building, is just off Page Avenue, far from the District. The Church doesn't like to be associated with the riffraff. Vampire strip club, Circus of the Damned, tsk-tsk. How shocking. No, they think of themselves as mainstream undead.

The church itself is set in an expanse of naked ground. Small trees struggled to grow into big trees and shade the startling white of the church. It seemed to glow in the hot July sunshine, like a land-bound moon.

I pulled into the parking lot and parked on the shiny new black asphalt. Only the ground looked normal, bare reddish earth churned to mud. The grass had never had a chance.

"Pretty," Ronnie said. She nodded in the building's direction.

I shrugged. "If you say so. Frankly, I never get used to the generic effect."

"Generic effect?" she asked.

"The stained glass is all abstract color. No scenes of Christ, no saints, no holy symbols. Clean and pure as a wedding gown fresh out of plastic."

She got out of the car, sunglasses sliding into place. She stared at the church, arms crossed over her stomach. "It looks like they just unwrapped it and haven't put the trimmings on yet."

"Yeah, a church without God. What is wrong with this picture?"

She didn't laugh. "Will anybody be up this time of day?"

"Oh, yes, they recruit during the day."

"Recruit?"

"You know, go door to door, like the Mormons and the Jehovah's Witnesses."

She stared at me. "You've got to be kidding?"

"Do I look like I'm kidding?"

She shook her head. "Door-to-door vampires. How"—she wiggled her hands back and forth—"convenient."

"Yep," I said. "Let's go see who's minding the office."

Broad white steps led up to huge double doors. One of the doors was open; the other had a sign that read, "Enter Friend and be at Peace." I fought an urge to tear down the sign and stomp on it.

They were preying on one of the most basic fears of man—death. Everyone fears death. People who don't believe in God have a hard time with death being it. Die and you cease to exist. Poof. But at the Church of Eternal Life, they promise just what the name says. And they can prove it. No leap of faith. No waiting around. No questions left unanswered. How does it feel to be dead? Just ask a fellow church member.

Oh, and you'll never grow old either. No face-lifts, no tummy tucks, just eternal youth. Not a bad deal, as long as you don't believe in the soul.

As long as you don't believe the soul becomes trapped in the vampire's body and can never reach Heaven. Or worse yet, that vampires are inherently evil and you are condemned to Hell. The Catholic Church sees voluntary vampirism as a kind of suicide. I tend to agree. Though the Pope also excommunicated all animators, unless we ceased raising the dead. Fine; I became Episcopalian.

Polished wooden pews ran in two wide rows up towards what would have been an altar. There was a pulpit, but I couldn't call it an altar. It was just a blank blue wall surrounded by more white upsweeping walls.

The windows were red and blue stained glass. The sunlight sparkled through them, making delicate colored patterns on the white floor.

"Peaceful," Ronnie said.

"So are graveyards."

She smiled at me. "I'd thought you'd say that."

I frowned at her. "No teasing; we're here on business."

"What exactly do you want me to do?"

"Just back me up; look menacing if you can manage it. Look for clues."

"Clues?" she asked.

"Yeah, you know, clues, ticket stubs, half-burned notes, leads."

"Oh, those."

"Quit grinning at me, Ronnie."

She adjusted her sunglasses and did her best "cold" look. She's pretty good at it. Thugs have been known to shrivel at twenty paces. We would see how it worked on church members.

There was a small door to one side of the "altar." It led into a carpeted hallway. The air-conditioned hush enveloped us. There were bathrooms to the left, and an open room to the right. Perhaps this is where they had ... coffee after services. No, probably not coffee. A rousing sermon followed by a little blood, perhaps?

The offices were marked with a little sign that said "Office." How clever. There was an outer office, the proverbial secretarial desk and etc. ... A young man sat behind the desk. Slender, short brown hair carefully cut. Wire-frame glasses decorated a pair of really lovely brown eyes. There was a healing bite mark on his throat.

He rose and came around the desk, hand extended, smiling at us. "Greetings, friends, I'm Bruce. How may I help you today?"

The handshake was firm but not too firm, strong but not overbearing, a friendly lingering touch, but not sexual. Really good car salesmen shake hands like that. Real estate brokers, too. I have this nice little soul, hardly used at all. The price is right. Trust me. If his big brown eyes had looked any more sincere, I would have given him a doggie biscuit and patted his head.

"I would like to set up an appointment to speak with Malcolm," I said.

He blinked once. "Have a seat."

I sat. Ronnie leaned against the wall, to one side of the door. Hands folded, looking cool and bodyguardish.

Bruce went back around his desk, after offering us coffee, and sat with folded hands. "Now, Miss . . ."

"Ms. Blake."

He didn't flinch; he hadn't heard of me. How fleeting fame. "Ms. Blake, why do you wish to meet with the head of our church? We have many competent and understanding counselors that will help you make your decision."

I smiled at him. I'll just bet you do, you little pipsqueak. "I think Malcolm will want to speak with me. I have information about the vampire murders."

His smile slipped. "If you have such information, then go to the police."

"Even if I have proof that certain members of your church are doing the murders?" A small bluff, otherwise known as a lie.

He swallowed, fingers pressing the top of his desk until the fingertips turned white. "I don't understand. I mean . . ."

I smiled at him. "Let's just face it, Bruce. You are not equipped to handle murder. It isn't in your training, now is it?"

"Well, no, but . . ."

"Then just give me a time to come back tonight and see Malcolm."

"I don't know. I . . ."

"Don't worry about it. Malcolm is the head of the church. He'll take care of it."

He was nodding, too rapidly. His eyes flicked to Ronnie, then back to me. He flipped through a leatherbound day planner on his desk. "Nine, tonight." He picked up a pen, poised and ready. "If you'll give me your full name, I'll pencil you in."

I started to point out that he wasn't using a pencil, but decided to let it slide. "Anita Blake."

He still didn't recognize the name. So much for me being the terror of vampireland. "And this is pertaining to?" He was regaining his professionalism.

I stood up. "Murder, it's pertaining to murder."

"Oh, yes, I . . ." He scribbled something down. "Nine tonight, Anita

Blake, murder.'' He frowned down at the note as if there were something wrong with it.

I decided to help him out. "Don't frown so. You've got the message right.''

He stared up at me. He looked a little pale.

"I'll be back. Make sure he gets the message.''

Bruce nodded again, too fast, eyes large behind his glasses.

Ronnie opened the door, and I preceded her out. She brought up the rear like a bad-movie bodyguard. When we were out into the main church again, she laughed. "I think we scared him.''

"Bruce scares easy.''

She nodded, eyes shining.

The barest mention of violence, murder, and he had fallen apart. When he "grew up,'' he was going to be a vampire. Sure.

The sunshine was nearly blinding after the dimness of the church. I squinted, putting a hand over my eyes. I caught movement from the corner of my eye.

Ronnie screamed, "Anita!''

Everything slowed down. I had plenty of time to stare at the man and the gun in his hands. Ronnie smashed into me, carrying us both down and back through the church door. Bullets thunked into the door where I'd been.

Ronnie scrambled behind me, near the wall. I had my gun out and lay on my side pressed against the door. My heart was thundering in my ears. Yet I could hear everything. The wrinkle of my windbreaker was like static. I heard the man walk up the steps. The son of a bitch was gonna keep coming.

I inched forward. He walked up the steps. His shadow fell inside the door. He wasn't even trying to hide. Maybe he thought I wasn't armed. He was about to learn different.

Bruce called, "What's going on here?''

Ronnie yelled, "Get back inside.''

I kept my eyes on the door. I would not get shot because ol' Bruce distracted me. Nothing was important but that shadow in the door, the halting footsteps. Nothing.

The man walked right into it. Gun in his hand, eyes searching the church. Amateur.

I could have touched him with the barrel of my gun. "Don't move.'' "Freeze'' always sounds so melodramatic. Don't move, short, to the point. "Don't move,'' I said.

He turned just his head, slow, towards me. "You're The Executioner.'' His voice was soft, hesitant.

Was I supposed to deny it? Maybe. If he had come here to kill The Executioner, definitely. "No,'' I said.

He started to turn. "Then it must be her.'' He was turning towards Ronnie. Shit.

He raised his arm and started to point.

"Don't!" Ronnie screamed.

Too late. I fired, point-blank into his chest. Ronnie's shot echoed mine. The impact raised him off his feet and sent him staggering backwards. Blood blossomed on his shirt. He slammed into the half-opened door and fell flat on his back through it. All I could see were his legs.

I hesitated, listening. I couldn't hear any movement. I eased around the door. He wasn't moving, but the gun was still clutched in his hand. I pointed my gun at him and stalked to him. If he had so much as twitched, I would have hit him again.

I kicked the gun out of his hand and checked the pulse in his neck. Nada, zip. Dead.

I use ammunition that can take out vampires, if I get a lucky shot, and if they're not ancient. The bullet had made a small hole on the side it went in, but the other side of his chest was gone. The bullet had done what it was supposed to do; expand, and make a very big exit hole.

His neck lolled to one side. Two bite marks decorated his neck. Dammit! Bite marks or not, he was dead. There wasn't enough left of his heart to thread a needle. A lucky shot. A stupid amateur with a gun.

Ronnie was leaning in the doorway, looking pale. Her gun was pointed at the dead man. Her arms trembled ever so slightly.

She almost smiled. "I don't usually carry a gun during the day, but I knew I'd be with you."

"Is that an insult?" I asked.

"No," she said, "reality."

I couldn't argue with that. I sat down on the cool stone steps; my knees felt weak. The adrenaline was draining out of me, like water from a broken cup.

Bruce was in the doorway, ice pale. "He . . . he tried to kill you." His voice cracked with fear.

"Do you recognize him?" I asked.

He shook his head over and over again, rapid jerky movements.

"Are you sure?"

"We . . . we do not . . . condone violence." He swallowed hard, his voice a cracking whisper. "I don't know him."

The fear seemed genuine. Maybe he didn't know him, but that didn't mean the dead man wasn't a member of the church. "Call the police, Bruce."

He just stood there, staring at the corpse.

"Call the cops, okay?"

He stared at me, eyes glazed. I wasn't sure if he heard me or not, but he went back inside.

Ronnie sat down beside me, staring out at the parking lot. Blood was running down the white steps in tiny rivulets of scarlet.

"Jesus," she whispered.

"Yeah." I still held my gun loose-gripped in my hand. The danger seemed to be over. Guess I could put away the gun. "Thanks for pushing me out of the way," I said.

"You're welcome." She took a deep, shaky breath. "Thanks for shooting him before he shot me."

"Don't mention it. Besides, you got a piece of him, too."

"Don't remind me."

I stared at her. "You all right?"

"No, I'm well and truly scared."

"Yeah." Of course, all Ronnie had to do was stay away from me. I seemed to be the free-fire zone. A walking, talking menace to my friends and coworkers. Ronnie could have died today, and it would have been my fault. She had been a few seconds slower to shoot than I was. Those few seconds could have cost her her life. Of course, if she hadn't been here today, I might have died. One bullet in the chest, and my gun wouldn't have done me a hell of a lot of good.

I heard the distant whoop-whoop of police sirens. They must have been damn close, or maybe it was another killing. Possible. Would the police believe he was just a fanatic trying to kill The Executioner? Maybe. Dolph wouldn't buy it.

The sunshine pressed down around us like bright yellow plastic. Neither of us said a word. Maybe there was nothing left to say. Thank you for saving my life. You're welcome. What else was there?

I felt light and empty, almost peaceful. Numb. I must be getting close to the truth, whatever that was. People were trying to kill me. It was a good sign. Sort of. It meant I knew something important. Important enough to kill for. The trouble was, I didn't know what it was I was supposed to know.

35

I was back at the church at 8:45 that night. The sky was a rich purple. Pink clouds were stretched across it like cotton candy pulled apart by eager kids and left to melt. True dark was only minutes away. Ghouls would already be out and about. But the vampires had a few heartbeats of waiting left.

I stood on the steps of the church, admiring the sunset. There was no blood left. The white steps were as shiny and new as if this afternoon had never happened. But I remembered. I had decided to sweat in the July heat so I could carry an arsenal. The windbreaker hid not only the shoulder rig and 9mm, plus extra ammo, but a knife on each forearm. The Firestar was snug in the inner pant holster, set for a right-hand cross draw. There was even a knife strapped to my ankle.

Of course, nothing I was carrying would stop Malcolm. He was one of the most powerful master vampires in the city. After seeing Nikolaos and Jean-Claude, I'd say he ranked third. In the company I was judging him against, third wasn't bad. So why confront him? Because I couldn't think of what else to do.

I had left a letter detailing my suspicions about the church and everybody else in a safe deposit box. Doesn't everybody have one? Ronnie knew about it, and there was a letter on the secretary's desk at Animators, Inc. It would go out Monday morning to Dolph, unless I called up to stop it.

One attempt on my life and I was getting all paranoid. Fancy that.

The parking lot was full. People were drifting inside the church in small groups. A few had simply walked up, no cars. I stared hard at them, Vampires, before full dark? But no, just humans.

I zipped the windbreaker partway up. Didn't want to disturb services by flashing a gun.

A young woman, brown hair style-gelled into an artificial wave over one eye, was handing out pamphlets just inside the door. A guide to the service, I supposed. She smiled and said, "Welcome. Is this your first time?"

I smiled back at her, pleasant, as if I wasn't carrying enough weaponry to take out half the congregation. "I have an appointment to see Malcolm."

Her smile didn't change. If anything it deepened, flashing a dimple to one side of her lipsticked mouth. Somehow, I didn't think she knew I'd killed someone today. People don't generally smile at me when they know things like that.

"Just a minute; let me get someone to handle the door." She walked away to tap a young man on the shoulder. She whispered against his cheek and shoved the pamphlets into his hands.

She came back to me, hands smoothing along the burgundy dress she wore. "If you'll follow me?"

She made it a question. What would she do if I said no? Probably look puzzled. The young man was greeting a couple that had just entered the church. The man wore a suit; the woman the proverbial dress, hose, and sandals. They could have been coming to my church, any church. As I followed the woman down the side aisle towards the door, I glanced at a couple dressed in postmodern punk. Or whatever phrase is common now. The girl's hair looked like Frankenstein's Bride done in pink and green. A second glance and I wasn't sure; maybe the pink and green was a guy. If so, his girlfriend's hair was a buzz so close to her head, it looked like stubble.

The Church of Eternal Life attracted a wide following. Diversity, that's the ticket. They appealed to the agnostic, the atheist, the disillusioned mainstreamer, and some who had never decided what they were. The church was nearly full, and it wasn't dark yet. The vampires had yet to show. It had been a long time since I'd seen a church this full, except at Easter, or Christmas. Holiday Christians. A chill tiptoed along my spine.

This was the fullest church I'd been to in years. The vampire church. Maybe the real danger wasn't the murderer. Maybe the real danger was right here in this building.

I shook my head and followed my guide through the door, out of the church, and past the coffee klatch area. There really was coffee percolating on a white-draped table. There was also a bowl of reddish punch that looked a little too viscous to be punch at all.

The woman said, "Would you like some coffee?"

"No, thank you."

She smiled pleasantly and opened the door marked "Office" for me. I went in. No one was there.

"Malcolm will be with you as soon as he wakens. If you like, I can wait with you." She glanced at the door as she said it.

"I wouldn't want you to miss the service. I'll be fine alone."

Her smile flashed into dimple again. "Thank you; I'm sure it will be a short wait." With that she was gone, and I was alone. Alone with the secretary's desk and the leatherbound day planner for the Church of Eternal Life. Life was good.

I opened the planner to the week before the first vampire murder. Bruce, the secretary, had very neat handwriting, each entry very precise. Time, name, and a one-sentence description of the meeting. 10:00, Jason MacDonald, Magazine interview. 9:00, Meeting with Mayor, Zoning problems. Normal stuff for the Billy Graham of Vampirism. Then two days before the first murder there was a notation that was in a different handwriting. Smaller, no less neat. 3:00, Ned. That was all, no last name, no reason for the meeting. And Bruce didn't make the appointment. Methinks we have a clue. Be still, my heart.

Ned was a short form of Edward, just like Teddy. Had Malcolm had a meeting with the hit man of the undead? Maybe. Maybe not. It could be a clandestine meeting with a different Ned. Or maybe Bruce had been away from the desk and someone else had just filled in? I went through the rest of the planner as quickly as I could. Nothing else seemed out of the ordinary. Every other entry was in Bruce's large, rolling hand.

Malcolm had met with Edward, if it had been Edward, two days before the first death. If that was true, where did that leave things? With Edward a murderer and Malcolm paying him to do it. There was one problem with that. If Edward had wanted me dead, he'd have done it himself. Maybe Malcolm panicked and sent one of his followers to do it? Could be.

I was sitting in a chair against the wall, leafing through a magazine, when the door opened. Malcolm was tall and almost painfully thin, with large, bony hands that belonged to a more muscular man. His short, curly hair was the shocking yellow of goldfinch feathers. This was what blond hair looked like after nearly three hundred years in the dark.

The last time I had seen Malcolm, he had seemed beautiful, perfect. Now he was almost ordinary, like Nikolaos and her scar. Had Jean-Claude given me the ability to see master vampires' true forms?

Malcolm's presence filled the small room like invisible water, chilling and pricking along my skin, knee-deep and rising. Give him another nine hundred years, and he might rival Nikolaos. Of course, I wouldn't be around to test my little theory.

I stood, and he swept into the room. He was dressed modestly in a dark blue suit, pale blue shirt, and blue silk tie. The pale shirt made his eyes look like robin's eggs. He smiled, angular face, beaming at me. He wasn't trying to cloud my mind. Malcolm was very good at resisting the urge. His entire credibility rested on the fact that he didn't cheat.

"Miss Blake, how good to see you." He didn't offer to shake hands; he knew better. "Bruce left me a very confused message. Something about the vampire murders?" His voice was deep and soothing, like the ocean.

"I told Bruce I have proof that your church is involved with the vampire murders."

"And do you?"

"Yes." I believed it. If he had met with Edward, I had my murderer.

"Hmmm, you are telling the truth. Yet, I know that it is not true." His voice rolled around me, warm and thick, powerful.

I shook my head. "Cheating, Malcolm, using your powers to probe my mind. Tsk, tsk."

He shrugged, hands open at his sides. "I control my church, Miss Blake. They would not do what you have accused them of."

"They raided a freak party last night with clubs. They hurt people." I was guessing on that part.

He frowned. "There is a small faction of our followers who persist in violence. The freak party, as you call it, is an abomination and must be stopped, but through legal channels. I have told my followers this."

"But do you punish them when they disobey you?" I asked.

"I am not a policeman, or a priest, to mete out punishment. They are not children. They have their own minds."

"I'll bet they do."

"And what is that supposed to mean?" he asked.

"It means, Malcolm, that you are a master vampire. None of them can stand against you. They'll do anything you want them to."

"I do not use mind powers on my congregation."

I shook my head. His power oozed over my arms like a cold wave. He wasn't even trying. It was just spillover. Did he realize what he was doing? Could it actually be an accident?

"You had a meeting two days before the first murder."

He smiled, careful not to show fangs. "I have many meetings."

"I know, you are real popular, but you'll remember this meeting. You hired a hit man to kill vampires." I watched his face, but he was too good. There was a flicker in his eyes, unease maybe; then it was gone, replaced by that shining blue-eyed confidence.

"Miss Blake, why are you looking me in the eyes?"

I shrugged. "If you don't try to bespell me, it's safe."

"I have tried to convince you of that on several occasions, but you always played it . . . safe. Now you are staring at me; why?" He strode towards me, quick, nearly a blur of motion. My gun was in my hand, no thinking needed. Instinct.

"My," he said.

I just stared at him, quite willing to put a bullet through his chest if he came one step closer.

"You carry at least the first mark, Miss Blake. Some master vampire has touched you. Who?"

I let out my breath in one long sigh. I hadn't even realized I'd been holding it. "It's a long story."

"I believe you." He was suddenly standing near the door again, as if he had never moved. Damn, he was good.

"You hired a man to slay the freak vampires," I said.

"No," he said, "I did not."

It is always unnerving when a person looks so damn blasé while I point a gun at them. "You did hire an assassin."

He shrugged. Smiled. "You do not really expect me to do anything but deny that, do you?"

"Guess not." What the heck, might as well ask. "Are you or your church connected in any way to the vampire murders?"

He almost laughed. I didn't blame him. No one in their right mind would just say yes, but sometimes you can learn things from the way a person denies something. The choice of lies can be almost as helpful as the truth.

"No, Miss Blake."

"You did hire an assassin." I made it a statement.

The smile drained from his face, poof. He stared at me, his presence crawling along my skin like insects. "Miss Blake, I believe it is time for you to leave."

"A man tried to kill me today."

"That is hardly my fault."

"He had two vampire bites in his neck."

Again that flicker in the eyes. Unease? Maybe.

"He was waiting for me outside your church. I was forced to kill him on your steps." A small lie, but I didn't want Ronnie further involved.

He was frowning now, a thread of anger like heat oozing through the room. "I am unaware of this, Miss Blake. I will look into it."

I lowered my gun but didn't put it away. You can only hold a person at gunpoint so long. If they aren't afraid, and they aren't going to hurt you, and you aren't going to shoot them, it gets rather silly. "Don't be too hard on Bruce. He doesn't do well around violence."

Malcolm straightened, pulling at his suit jacket. A nervous gesture? Oh, boy. I'd hit a nerve.

"I will look into it, Miss Blake. If he was a member of our church, we owe you an extreme apology."

I stared at him for a minute. What could I say to that? Thank you? It didn't seem appropriate. "I know you hired a hit man, Malcolm. Not exactly good press for your church. I think you are behind the vampire murders. Your hands may not have spilled the blood, but it was done with your approval."

"Please, go now, Miss Blake." He opened the door as he said it.

I walked through, gun still in my hand. "Sure, I'll go, but I won't go away."

He stared down at me, eyes angry. "Do you know what it means to be marked by a master vampire?"

I thought a minute and wasn't sure how to answer it. Truth. "No."

He smiled, and it was cold enough to freeze your heart. "You will learn, Miss Blake. If it becomes too much for you, remember our church is here to help." He closed the door in my face. Softly.

I stared at the door. "And what is that supposed to mean?" I whispered. No one answered me.

I put away my gun and spotted a small door marked "Exit." I took it. The church was softly lit, candles maybe. Voices rose on the night air, singing. I didn't recognize the words. The tune was *Bringing in the Sheaves*. I caught one phrase: "We will live forever, never more to die."

I hurried to my car and tried not to listen to the song. There was something frightening about all those voices raised skyward, worshipping . . . what? Themselves? Eternal youth? Blood? What? Another question that I didn't have an answer to.

Edward was my murderer. The question was, could I turn him over to Nikolaos? Could I turn over a human being to the monsters, even to save myself? Another question that I didn't have an answer for. Two days ago I would have said no. Now I just didn't know.

36

I didn't want to go back to my apartment. Edward would be coming tonight. Tell him where Nikolaos slept in daylight or he'd force the information from me. Complicated enough. Now, I thought he was my murderer. Very complicated.

The best thing I could think of was to avoid him. That wouldn't work forever, but maybe I'd have a brainstorm and figure it all out. All right, there wasn't much chance of that, but one could always hope.

Maybe Ronnie would have a message for me. Something helpful. God knows I needed all the help I could get. I pulled the car into a service station that had a pay phone out front. I had one of those high-tech answering machines that allowed me to read my messages without having to go home for them. Maybe I could avoid Edward all night, if I slept in a hotel. Sigh. If I'd had any solid proof at all right that minute, I'd have called the police.

I heard the tape whir and click; then, "Anita, it's Willie, they got Phillip. The guy you was with. They're hurtin' him, bad! You gotta come—" The phone went dead, abruptly. Like he'd been cut off.

My stomach tightened. A second message came up. "This is you know who. You've heard Willie's message. Come and get it, animator. I don't really have to threaten your pretty lover, do I?" Nikolaos's laughter filled the phone, scratchy and distant with tape.

There was a loud click and Edward's voice came over the phone. "Anita, tell me where you are. I can help you."

"They'll kill Phillip," I said. "Besides, you aren't on my side, remember."

"I'm the closest thing you've got to an ally."

"God help me, then." I hung up on him, hard. Phillip had tried to defend me last night. Now he was paying for it. I yelled, "Dammit!"

A man pumping gas stared at me.

"What are you looking at?" I nearly yelled that, too. He dropped his eyes and concentrated very hard on filling his tank with gas.

I got behind the wheel of my car and sat there for a few minutes. I was so angry, I was shaking. I could feel the tension in my teeth. Dammit. Dammit! I was too angry to drive. It wouldn't help Phillip if I got in a car accident on the way.

I tried breathing deep gulps of air. It didn't help. I turned the key in the ignition. "No speeding, can't afford to get stopped by the cops. Easy does it, Anita, easy does it." I talk to myself every once in a while. Give myself very good advice. Sometimes I even take it.

I put the car in gear and drove out onto the road—carefully. Anger rode up my back and into my shoulders and neck. I gripped the steering wheel too hard and found that my hands weren't quite healed. Sharp little jabs of pain, but not enough. There wasn't enough pain in the whole world to get rid of the anger.

Phillip was being hurt because of me. Just like Catherine and Ronnie. No more. No freaking more. I was going to get Phillip, save him any way I could; then I was turning the whole blasted thing over to the police. Without proof, yeah, without anything to back it up. I was bailing out before more people got hurt.

The anger was almost enough to hide the fear behind it. If Nikolaos was tormenting Phillip for last night, she might not be too happy with me either. I was going back down those stairs into the master's lair, at night. Didn't seem real bright when you put it that way.

The anger was fading in a wash of cold, skin-shivering fear. "No!" I would not go in there afraid. I held onto my anger with everything I had. This was the closest I'd come to hate in a long time. Hatred; now there's an emotion that'll spread warmth through your body.

Most hatred is based on fear, one way or another. Yeah. I wrapped myself in anger, with a dash of hate, and at the bottom of it all was an icy center of pure terror.

37

The Circus of the Damned is housed in an old warehouse. Its name is emblazoned across the roof in colored lights. Giant clown figurines dance around the words in frozen pantomime. If you look very closely at the clowns, you notice they have fangs. But only if you look very closely.

The sides of the building are strung with huge plastic cloth signs, like an old-fashioned sideshow. One banner showed a man being hung; "The Death Defying Count Alcourt," it said. Zombies crawled from a graveyard in one picture; "Watch the Dead Rise from the Grave." A very bad drawing showed a man halfway between wolf and man shape; Fabian, the Werewolf. There were other signs. Other attractions. None of them looked very wholesome.

Guilty Pleasures treads a thin line between entertainment and the sadistic. The Circus goes over the edge and down into the abyss.

And here I go inside. Oh, joy in the morning.

Noise hits you at the door. A blast of carnival sound, the push and shove of the crowd, the rustling of hundreds of people. The lights spill and scream in a hundred different colors, all eye-searing, all guaranteed to attract attention, or make you lose your lunch. Of course, maybe that was just my nerves.

The smell is formed of cotton candy, corn dogs, the cinnamon smell of elephant ears, snow cones, sweat, and under it all a neck-ruffling smell. Blood smells like sweet copper pennies, and that smell mingles over everything. Most people don't recognize it. But there is another scent on the air, not just blood, but violence. Of course, violence has no smell. Yet, always here, there is—something. The barest hint of long-closed rooms and rotting cloth.

I had never come here before, except on police business. What I wouldn't have given for a few uniforms right now.

The crowd parted like water in front of a ship. Winter, Mr. Muscles, moved through the people, and instinctively they moved out of his way. I'd have moved out of his way, too, but I didn't think I'd get the chance.

Winter was wearing a proverbial strongman's outfit. It had fake zebra stripes on a white background and left most of his upper body exposed. His legs in the striped leotard rippled and corded, like it was a second skin. His bicep, unflexed, was bigger around than both my arms. He stopped in front of me, towering over me, and knowing it.

"Is your entire family obscenely tall, or is it just you?" I asked.

He frowned, eyes narrowing. I don't think he got it. Oh, well. "Follow me," he said. With that he turned and walked back through the crowd.

I guess I was supposed to follow like a good little girl. Shit. A large blue tent took up one corner of the warehouse. People were lining up, showing tickets. A man was calling out in a booming voice, "Almost show time, folks. Present your tickets and enter. See the hanging man. Count Alcourt will be executed before your very eyes."

I had paused to listen. Winter was not waiting. Luckily, his broad, white back didn't blend with the crowd. I had to trot to catch up with him. I hate having to do that. It makes me feel like a child running after an adult. If a little running was the worst thing I experienced tonight, things would be just hunky-dory.

There was a full-size Ferris wheel, its glowing top nearly brushing the ceiling. A man held a baseball out to me. "Try your luck, little lady."

I ignored him. I hate being called little lady. I glanced at the prizes to be won. It ran long on stuffed animals and ugly dolls. The stuffed toys were mostly predators: soft plush panthers, toddler-size bears, spotted snakes, and giant fuzzy-toothed bats.

There was a bald man in white clown makeup selling tickets to the mirror maze. He stared at the children as they went inside his glass house. I could almost feel the weight of his eyes on their backs, like he would memorize every line of their small bodies. Nothing would have gotten me past him into that sparkling river of glass.

The Funhouse was next, more clowns and screams, the shooting whoosh of air. The metal sidewalk leading into its depths buckled and twisted. A little boy nearly fell. His mother dragged him to his feet. Why would any parent bring their child here, to this frightening place?

There was even a haunted house; it was almost funny. Sort of redundant, if you ask me. The whole freaking place was a house of horrors.

Winter had paused before the little door leading into the back areas. He was frowning at me, massive arms almost crossed over equally massive chest. The arms didn't quite fold right, too much muscle for that, but he was trying.

He opened the door. I went inside. The tall, bald man who had been with Nikolaos that first time was standing against the wall, at attention. His handsome, narrow face, the eyes very prominent because there was no hair, nothing much else to stare at, looked at me the way elementary school teachers look at troublemaking children. You must be punished, young lady. But what had I done wrong?

The man's voice was deep, faintly British, cultured, but human. "Search her for weapons before we go down."

Winter nodded. Why talk when gestures will do? His big hands lifted my jacket and took the gun. He shoved one shoulder so that I spun around. He found the second gun, too. Had I really thought they'd let me keep the weapons? Yes, I guess I had. Stupid me.

"Check her arms for knives."

Damn.

Winter gripped my jacket sleeves like he meant to tear them. "Wait, please. I'll just take the jacket off. You can search it, too, if you like."

Winter took the knives on my arms. The bald-headed man searched the yellow windbreaker for concealed weapons. He didn't find any. Winter patted my legs down, but not well. He missed the knife at my ankle. I had one weapon, and they didn't know it. Bully for me.

Down the long stairs and into the empty throne room. Maybe it showed on my face because the man said, "The master waits for us, with your friend."

The man led the way as he had down the stairs. Winter brought up the rear. Perhaps they thought I would make a break for it. Right. Where would I go?

They stopped at the dungeon. How had I known they would? The bald-headed man knocked on the door twice, not too hard, not too soft.

There was silence; then bright, high laughter drifted from inside. My skin crawled with the sound. I did not want to see Nikolaos again. I did not want to be in a cell again. I wanted to go home.

The door opened. Valentine made a hand-sweeping motion. "Come in, come in." He was wearing a silver mask this time. A strand of his auburn hair was stuck to the forehead of the mask, sticky with blood.

My heart thudded into my throat. Phillip, are you alive? It was all I could do not to yell out.

Valentine stepped against the door as if waiting for me to pass. I glanced at the nameless bald man. His face was unreadable. He motioned me ahead of him. What could I do? I went.

What I saw stopped me at the top of the steps. I couldn't go farther. I couldn't. Aubrey stood against the far wall, grinning at me. His hair was still golden; his face, bestial. Nikolaos stood in a dress of flowing white that made her skin look like chalk, her hair cotton-white. She was sprinkled with blood, like someone had taken a red ink pen and splattered her.

Her grey-blue eyes stared up at me. She laughed again, rich and pure and wicked. I had no other word for it. Wicked. She caressed a white, blood-spattered hand against Phillip's bare chest. She rolled her fingertip over his nipple, and laughed.

He was chained to the wall at wrist and ankle. His long, brown hair had fallen forward, hiding one eye. His muscular body was covered in bites. Blood rained down his tan skin in thin crimson lines. He stared up at me from that one brown eye, the other hidden in his hair. Despair. He knew he had been brought here to die, like this, and there wasn't a damn thing he could do about it. But there was something I could do. There had to be. God, please let there be!

The man touched my shoulder, and I jumped. The vampires laughed. The man did not. I walked down the steps to stand a few feet in front of Phillip. He wouldn't look at me.

Nikolaos touched his naked thigh and ran her fingers up it. His body tightened, hands clenching into fists.

"Oh, we have been having a fine time with your lover here," Nikolaos said. Her voice was sweet as ever. The child bride incarnate. Bitch.

"He isn't my lover."

She pouted out her lower lip. "Now, Anita, no lying. That's no fun." She stalked towards me, slender hips swaying to some inner dance. She reached for me, and I backed up, bumping into Winter. "Animator, animator," she said. "When will you learn that you cannot fight me?"

I don't think she wanted me to argue, so I didn't.

She reached for me again, with one bloody, dainty hand. "Winter can hold you, if you like."

Stay still, or we hold you down. Great choices. I stayed still. I watched those pale fingers glide towards my face. I ground my fingernails into the palms of my hands. I would not move away from her. I would not move. Her fingers touched my forehead, and I felt the cool wetness of blood. She brushed it down my temple to my cheek and traced her fingers over my lower lip. I think I stopped breathing.

"Lick your lips," she said.

"No," I said.

"Oh, you are a stubborn one. Has Jean-Claude given you this courage?"

"What the hell are you talking about?"

Her eyes darkened, face clouding over. "Don't be coy, Anita. It does not become you." Her voice was suddenly adult, hot enough to scald. "I know your little secret."

"I don't know what you are talking about," I said, and I meant it. I didn't understand the anger.

"If you like, we can play games for a little while longer." She was suddenly standing beside Phillip, and I hadn't seen her move. "Did that surprise you, Anita? I am still master of this city. I have powers that you and your master have never even dreamed of."

My master? What the hell was she talking about? I didn't have a master.

She rubbed her hands along the side of his chest, over his rib cage. Her hand wiped away the blood to show the skin smooth and untouched. She stood in front of him and didn't come to his collarbone. Phillip had closed his eyes. Her head arched backwards, a glimpse of fangs, lips drawn back in a snarl.

"No." I stepped towards them. Winter's hands descended on my shoulders. He shook his head, slow and careful. I was not to interfere.

She drove her fangs into his side. His whole body stiffened, neck arching, arms jerking at the chains.

"Leave him alone!" I drove an elbow into Winter's stomach. He grunted, and his fingers dug into my shoulders until I wanted to scream. His arms enveloped me, tight to his chest, no movement allowed.

She raised her face from Phillip's skin. Blood trickled down her chin. She licked her lips with a tiny pink tongue. "Ironic," she said in a voice years older than the body would ever be. "I sent Phillip to seduce you. Instead, you seduced him."

"We are not lovers." I felt ridiculous with Winter's arms crushing me to his chest.

"Denial will not help either of you," she said.

"What will help us?" I asked.

She motioned, and Winter released me. I stepped away from him, out of reach. It put me closer to Nikolaos, perhaps not an improvement.

"Let us discuss your future, Anita." She began to walk up the steps. "And your lover's future."

I assumed she meant Phillip, and I didn't correct her. The nameless man motioned for me to follow her up the stairs. Aubrey was moving closer to Phillip. They would be alone together. Unacceptable.

"Nikolaos, please."

Maybe it was the "please." She turned. "Yes," she said.

"May I ask two things?"

She was smiling at me, amused with me. An adult's amusement with a child who had used a new word. I didn't care what she thought of me as long as she did what I wanted. "You may ask," she said.

"That when we go, all the vampires leave this room." She was still staring at me, smiling, so far so good. "And that I be allowed to speak with Phillip privately."

She laughed, high and wild, chimes in a storm wind. "You are bold, mortal. I give you that. I begin to see what Jean-Claude sees in you."

I let the comment go because I felt like I was missing part of the meaning. "May I have what I ask, please?"

"Call me master, and you will have it."

I swallowed and it was loud in the sudden stillness. "Please . . . master." See, I didn't choke on the word after all.

"Very good, animator, very good indeed." Without her needing to say anything, Valentine and Aubrey went up the steps and out the door. They didn't even argue. That was frightening all on its own.

"I will leave Burchard at the top of the steps. He has human hearing. If you whisper, he won't be able to hear you at all."

"Burchard?" I asked.

"Yes, animator, Burchard, my human servant." She stared at me as if that was significant. My expression didn't seem to please her. She frowned. Then she turned abruptly in a swing of white skirts. Winter followed her like an obedient puppy on steroids.

Burchard, the once nameless man, took up a post in front of the closed door. He stared straight ahead, not at us. Privacy, or as close as we were getting to it.

I went to Phillip, and he still wouldn't look at me. His thick, brown hair acted like a kind of curtain between us. "Phillip, what happened?"

His voice was an abused whisper; screaming will do that to you. I had to stand on tiptoe and nearly press my body against his to hear him. "Guilty Pleasures; they took me from there."

"Didn't Robert try to stop them?" For some reason that seemed important. I had only met Robert once, but part of me was angry that he had not protected Phillip. He was in charge of things while Jean-Claude was away. Phillip was one of those things.

"Wasn't strong enough."

I lost my balance and was forced to catch myself, hands flat against his ruined chest. I jerked back, hands held out from me, bloody.

Phillip closed his eyes and leaned back into the wall. His throat worked hard at swallowing. There were two fresh bites on his neck. They were going to bleed him to death if someone didn't get carried away first.

He lowered his head and tried to look at me, but his hair had spilled into both eyes. I wiped the blood on my jeans and went back to stand almost on tiptoe next to him. I brushed the hair back from his eyes, but it spilled forward again. It was beginning to bug me. I combed my fingers through his hair until it stayed out of his face. His hair was softer than it looked, thick and warm with the heat of his body.

He almost smiled. His voice breaking as he whispered, "Few months back, I'd have paid money for this."

I stared at him, then realized he was trying to make a joke. God. My throat felt tight.

Burchard said, "It is time to go."

I stared into Phillip's eyes, perfect brown, torchlight dancing in them like black mirrors. "I won't leave you here, Phillip."

His eyes flickered to the man on the stairs and back to me. Fear turned his face young, helpless. "See you later," he said.

I stepped back from him. "You can count on it."

"It is not wise to keep her waiting," Burchard said.

He was probably right. Phillip and I stared at each other for a handful of moments. The pulse in his throat jumped under his skin like it was trying to escape. My throat ached; my chest was tight. The torchlight flickered in my vision for just a second. I turned away and walked to the steps. We tough-as-nails vampire slayers don't cry. At least, never in public. At least, never when we can help it.

Burchard held the door open for me. I glanced back at Phillip and waved, like an idiot. He watched me go, his eyes too large for his face suddenly, like a child who watches its parent leave the room before all the monsters are gone.

I had to leave him like that—alone, helpless. God help me.

38

Nikolaos sat in her carved wooden chair, tiny feet swinging off the ground. Charming.

Aubrey leaned against the wall, tongue running over his lips, getting the last bit of blood off them. Valentine stood very still beside him, staring at me.

Winter stood beside me. The prison guard.

Burchard went to stand by Nikolaos, one hand on the back of her chair.

"What, animator, no jokes?" Nikolaos asked. Her voice was still the grown-up version. It was like she had two voices and could change them with a push of a button.

I shook my head. I didn't feel very funny.

"Have we broken your spirit? Taken the fight out of you?"

I stared at her. Anger flared through me like a wave of heat. "What do you want, Nikolaos?"

"Oh, that's much better." Her voice rose and fell, a little-girl giggle at the end of each word. I might never like children again.

"Jean-Claude should be growing weak inside his coffin. Starving, but instead he is strong and well fed. How can this be?"

I didn't have the faintest idea, so I kept quiet. Maybe it was rhetorical?

It wasn't. "Answer me, A-n-i-t-a." She stretched my name out, biting off each syllable.

"I don't know."

"Oh, but you do."

I didn't, but she wasn't going to believe me. "Why are you hurting Phillip?"

"He needed to be taught a lesson, after last night."

"Because he stood up to you?" I asked.

"Yes," she said, "because he stood up to me." She scooted out of the chair and pattered towards me. She did a little turn so the white dress billowed around her. She freaking skipped over to me, smiling. "And because I was angry with you. I torture your lover, and maybe I won't torture you. And perhaps, this demonstration will give you fresh incentive to find the vampire murderer." Her pretty little face was turned up to me, pale eyes gleaming with humor. She was good.

I swallowed hard, and I asked the question I had to ask, "Why were you angry with me?"

She cocked her head to one side. If she hadn't been blood-spattered, it would have been cute. "Could it be that you do not know?" She turned back to Burchard. "What think you, my friend? Is she ignorant?"

He straightened his shoulders and said, "I believe that it is possible."

"Oh, Jean-Claude has been a very naughty boy. Giving the second mark to an unsuspecting mortal."

I stood very still. I was remembering blue, fiery eyes on the stairs, and Jean-Claude's voice in my head. All right, I had suspected it, but I still didn't understand what it meant. "What does the second mark mean?"

She licked her lips, soft like a kitten. "Shall we explain, Burchard? Shall we tell her what we know?"

"If she truly does not know, mistress, we must enlighten her," he said.

"Yes," she said and glided back to the chair. "Burchard, tell her how old you are."

"I am six hundred and three years of age."

I stared at his smooth face and shook my head. "But you're human, not a vampire."

"I have been given the fourth mark and will live as long as my mistress needs me."

"No, Jean-Claude wouldn't do that to me," I said.

Nikolaos made a small shrugging motion with her hands. "I had pressed him very hard. I knew of the first mark to heal you. I suppose he was desperate to save himself."

I remembered the echo of his voice in my head. "I'm sorry. I had no choice." Damn him, there were always choices. "He's been in my dreams every night. What does that mean?"

"He is communicating with you, animator. With the third mark will come more direct mind contact."

I shook my head. "No."

"No what, animator? No third mark, or no you don't believe us?" she asked.

"I don't want to be anyone's servant."

"Have you been eating more than usual?" she asked.

The question was so odd, I just stared for a minute, then I remembered. "Yes. Is that important?"

Nikolaos frowned. "He is siphoning energy from you, Anita. He is feeding through your body. He should be growing weak by now, but you will keep him strong."

"I didn't mean to."

"I believe you," she said. "Last night when I realized what he had done, I was beside myself with anger. So I took your lover."

"Please believe me, he is not my lover."

"Then why did he risk my anger to save you last night? Friendship? Decency? I think not."

All right, let her believe it. Just get us out alive, that was the goal. Nothing else mattered. "What can Phillip and I do to make amends?"

"Oh, so polite, I like that." She put a hand on Burchard's waist, a casual gesture like petting a dog. "Shall we show her what she has to look forward to?"

His whole body tensed as if an electric current had run through it. "If my mistress wishes."

"I do," she said.

Burchard knelt in front of her, face about chest level. Nikolaos looked over his head at me. "This," she said, "is the fourth mark." Her hands went to the small pearl buttons that decorated the front of the white dress. She spread the cloth wide, baring small breasts. They were a child's breasts, small and half-formed. She drew a fingernail beside her left breast. The skin opened like earth behind a plow, spilling blood in a red line down her chest and stomach.

I could not see Burchard's face as he leaned forward. His hands slid around her waist. His face buried between her breasts. She tensed, back arching. Soft, sucking sounds filled the room's stillness.

I looked away, staring at anything but them, as if I had found them having sex but couldn't leave. Valentine was staring at me. I stared back. He tipped an imaginary hat at me and flashed fangs. I ignored him.

Burchard was sitting beside the chair, half-leaning against it. His face was slack and flushed, his chest rising and falling in deep gasps. He wiped blood from his mouth with a shaking hand. Nikolaos sat very still, head back, eyes closed. Perhaps sex wasn't such a bad analogy after all.

Nikolaos spoke with her eyes closed, head thrown back, voice thick. "Your friend, Willie, is back in a coffin. He felt sorry for Phillip. We will have to cure him of such instincts."

She raised her head abruptly, eyes bright, almost glittering, as if they had a light all their own. "Can you see my scar today?"

I shook my head. She was the beautiful child, complete and whole. No imperfections. "You look perfect again, why?"

"Because I am expending energy to make it so. I am having to work at it." Her voice was low and warm, a building heat like thunderstorms in the distance.

The hair at the back of my neck crawled. Something bad was about to happen.

"Jean-Claude has his followers, Anita. If I kill him, they will make him a martyr. But if I prove him weak, powerless, they just fall away and follow me, or follow no one."

She stood, dress buttoned to her neck once more. Her cotton-white hair seemed to move as if a wind stirred it, but there was no wind. "I will destroy something Jean-Claude has given his protection to."

How fast could I get to the knife on my leg? And what good would it do me?

"I will prove to all that Jean-Claude can protect nothing. I am master of all."

Egocentric bitch. Winter grabbed my arm before I could do anything. Too busy watching the vampires to notice the humans.

"Go," she said. "Kill him."

Aubrey and Valentine stood away from the wall and bowed. Then they were gone, as if they had vanished. I turned to Nikolaos.

She smiled. "Yes, I clouded your mind, and you did not see them go."

"Where are they going?" My stomach was tight. I think I already knew the answer.

"Jean-Claude has given Phillip his protection; thus he must die."

"No."

Nikolaos smiled. "Oh, but yes."

A scream ripped through the hallway. A man's scream. Phillip's scream.

"No!" I half-fell to my knees; only Winter's hand kept me from falling to the floor. I pretended to faint, sagging in his grip. He released me. I grabbed the knife from its ankle sheath. Winter and I were close to the hallway, far away from Nikolaos and her human. Maybe far enough.

Winter was staring at her as if waiting for orders. I came up off the ground and drove the knife into his groin. The knife sank in, and blood poured out as I drew the blade free and raced for the hallway.

I was at the door when the first trickle of wind oozed down my back. I didn't look back. I opened the door.

Phillip sagged in the chains. Blood poured in a bright red flood down his chest. It splattered onto the floor, like rain. Torchlight glittered on the wet bone of his spine. Someone had ripped his throat out.

I staggered against the wall as if someone had hit me. I couldn't get enough air. Someone kept whispering, "Oh, God, oh, God," over and over, and it was me. I walked down the steps with my back pressed against the wall. I couldn't take my eyes from him. Couldn't look away. Couldn't breathe. Couldn't cry.

The torchlight reflected in his eyes, giving the illusion of movement. A scream built in my gut and spilled out my throat. "Phillip!"

Aubrey stepped between me and Phillip. He was covered in blood. "I look forward to visiting your lovely friend, Catherine."

I wanted to run at him, screaming. Instead, I leaned against the wall, knife held down at my side, unnoticed. The goal was no longer to get out alive. The goal was to kill Aubrey. "You son of a bitch, you fucking son of a bitch." My voice sounded utterly calm, no emotion whatsoever. I wasn't afraid. I didn't feel anything.

Aubrey's face frowned at me through a mask of Phillip's blood. "Do not say such things to me."

"You ugly, stinking, mother-fucking bastard."

He glided to me, just like I wanted him to. He put a hand on my shoulder. I screamed in his face as loud as I could. He hesitated for just a heartbeat. I shoved the knife blade between his ribs. It was sharp and thin, and I shoved it hilt deep. His body stiffened, leaning into me. Eyes wide and surprised. His mouth opened and closed, but no sound came out. He toppled to the floor, fingers grabbing at air.

Valentine was instantly there, kneeling by the body. "What have you done?" He couldn't see the knife. It was shielded by Aubrey's body.

"I killed him, you son of a bitch, just like I'm going to kill you."

Valentine jerked to his feet, started to say something, and all hell broke loose. The cell door crashed inward and smashed to bits against the far wall. A tornado wind blasted into the room.

Valentine dropped to his knees, head touching the floor. He was bowing. I flattened myself against the wall. The wind clawed at my face, tangling my hair in front of my eyes.

The noise grew less, and I squinted up at the door. Nikolaos floated just above the top step. Her hair crackled around her head, like spider silk. Her skin had shrunken against her bones, until she was skeletal. Her eyes glowed, pale blue fire. She started floating down the steps, hands outstretched.

I could see her veins like blue lights under her skin. I ran. Ran for the far wall, and the tunnel the ratmen had used.

The wind threw me against the wall, and I scrambled on hands and feet towards the tunnel. The hole was large, and black, cool air brushed my face, and something grabbed my ankle.

I screamed. The thing that was Nikolaos dragged me back. It slammed me against the wall and pinned my wrists in one clawed hand. The body leaned into my legs, bone under cloth.

The lips had receded, exposing the fangs and teeth. The skeletal head hissed, "You will learn obedience, to me!" It screamed in my face, and I screamed back. Wordlessly, an animal screaming in a trap.

My heart was thudding in my throat. I couldn't breathe. "Nooo!"

The thing shrieked, "Look at me!"

And I did. I fell into the blue fire that was her eyes. The fire burrowed into my brain, pain. Her thoughts cut me up like knives, slicing away parts of me. Her rage scalded and burned until I thought the skin was peeling away from my face. Claws scraped the inside of my skull, grinding bone into dust.

When I could see again, I was huddled by the wall, and she was standing over me, not touching, not needing to. I was shaking, shaking so badly my teeth chattered. I was cold, so cold.

"Eventually, animator, you will call me master, and you will mean it." She was suddenly kneeling over me. She pressed her slender body over mine, hands pinning my shoulders to the floor. I couldn't move.

The beautiful little girl leaned her face against my cheek and whispered,

"I am going to sink fangs into your neck, and there is nothing you can do to stop me."

Her delicate shell of an ear was brushing my lips. I sank teeth into it until I tasted blood. She shrieked and jerked away, blood running down the side of her neck.

Bright razor claws tore through my brain. Her pain, her rage, turning my brain into silly putty. I think I was screaming again, but I couldn't hear it. After a while I couldn't hear anything. Darkness came. It swallowed up Nikolaos and left me alone, floating in the dark.

39

I woke up, which was a pleasant surprise all on its own. I was blinking up into an electric light set in a ceiling. I was alive, and I wasn't in the dungeon. Good things to know.

Why should it surprise me that I was alive? My fingers caressed the rough, knobby fabric of the couch I was lying on. There was a picture hanging over the couch. A river scene with flatboats, mules, people. Someone came to stand over me, long yellow hair, square-jawed, handsome face. Not as inhumanly beautiful as he had been to me before, but still handsome. I guess you had to be handsome to be a stripper.

My voice came out in a harsh croak. "Robert."

He knelt beside me. "I was afraid you wouldn't wake up before dawn. Are you hurt?"

"Where . . ." I cleared my throat and that helped a little. "Where am I?"

"Jean-Claude's office at Guilty Pleasures."

"How did I get here?"

"Nikolaos brought you. She said, 'Here's your master's whore.'" I watched his throat work as he swallowed. It reminded me of something, but I couldn't think what.

"You know what Jean-Claude has done?" I asked.

Robert nodded. "My master has marked you twice. When I speak to you, I am speaking to him."

Did he mean that figuratively or literally? I really didn't want to know.

"How do you feel?" he asked.

There was something in the way he asked it that meant I shouldn't feel all right. My throat hurt. I raised a hand and touched it. Dried blood. On my neck.

I closed my eyes, but that didn't help. A small sound escaped my throat, very like a whimper. Phillip's image was burned on my mind. The blood pouring from his throat, torn pink meat. I shook my head and tried to breathe deep and slow. It was no good. "Bathroom," I said.

Robert showed me where it was. I went inside, knelt on the cool floor, and threw up in the toilet, until I was empty and nothing but bile came up. Then I walked to the sink and splashed cold water in my mouth and on my face. I stared at myself in the mirror above the sink. My eyes looked black, not brown, my skin sickly. I looked like shit and felt worse.

And there on the right side of my neck was the real thing. Not Phillip's healing bite marks, but fang marks. Tiny, diminutive, fang marks. Nikolaos had . . . contaminated me. To prove she could harm Jean-Claude's human servant. She had proved how tough she was, oh, yeah. Real tough.

Phillip was dead. Dead. Try the word over in your mind, but could I say it out loud? I decided to try. "Phillip is dead," I told my reflection.

I crumbled the brown paper towel and stuffed it in the metal trash can. It wasn't enough. I screamed, "Ahhh!" I kicked the trash can, over and over until it toppled to the floor, spilling its contents.

Robert came through the door. "Are you all right?"

"Does it look like I'm all right?" I yelled.

He hesitated in the doorway. "Is there anything I can do to help?"

"You couldn't even keep them from taking Phillip!"

He winced as if I had hit him. "I did my best."

"Well, it wasn't good enough, was it?" I was still screaming like a mad person. I sank to my knees, and all that rage choked up my throat and spilled out my eyes. "Get out!"

He hesitated. "Are you sure?"

"Get out of here!"

He closed the door behind him. And I sat in the floor and rocked and cried and screamed. When my heart felt as empty as my stomach, I felt leaden, used up.

Nikolaos had killed Phillip and bitten me to prove how powerful she was. I bet she thought I'd be scared absolutely shitless of her. She was right on that. But I spend most of my waking hours confronting and destroying things that I fear. A thousand-year-old master vampire was a tall order, but a girl's got to have a goal.

40

The club was quiet and dark. There was no one there but me. It must have been after dawn. The club was hushed and full of that waiting silence that all buildings get after the people go home. As if once we leave, the building has a life of its own, if only we would leave it in peace. I shook my head and tried to concentrate. To feel something. All I wanted was to go home and try to sleep. And pray I didn't dream.

There was a yellow Post-it note on the door. It read, "Your weapons are behind the bar. The master brought those, too. Robert."

I put both guns in place and the knives. The one I had used on Winter and Aubrey was missing. Was Winter dead? Maybe. Was Aubrey dead? Hopefully. Usually it took a master vampire to survive a blow to the heart, but I'd never tried it on a five-hundred-year-old walking corpse. If they took the knife out, he might be tough enough to survive it. I had to call Catherine. And tell her what? Get out of town, a vampire is after you. Didn't sound like something she'd buy. Shit.

I walked out into the soft white light of dawn. The street was empty and awash in that gentle morning air. The heat hadn't had time to creep in. It was almost cool. Where was my car? I heard footsteps a second before the voice said, "Don't move. I have a gun pointed at your back."

I clasped my hands atop my head without being asked. "Good morning, Edward," I said.

"Good morning, Anita," he said. "Stand very still, please." He stood just behind me, gun pressing against my spine. He frisked me completely, top to bottom. Nothing haphazard about Edward; that's one of the reasons he's still alive. He stepped back from me, and said, "You may turn around now."

He had my Firestar tucked into his belt, the Browning loose in his left hand. I don't know what he did with the knives.

He smiled, boyish and charming, gun very steadily pointed at my chest. "No more hiding. Where is this Nikolaos?" he asked.

I took a deep breath and let it out. I thought about accusing him of being the vampire murderer, but now didn't seem to be a good time. Maybe later, when he wasn't pointing a gun at me. "May I lower my arms?" I asked.

He gave a slight nod.

I lowered my arms slowly. "I want one thing clear between us, Edward. I'll give you the information, but not because I'm afraid of you. I want her dead. And I want a piece of it."

His smile widened, eyes glittering with pleasure. "What happened last night?"

I glanced down at the sidewalk, then up. I stared into his blue eyes and said, "She had Phillip killed."

He was watching my face very closely. "Go on."

"She bit me. I think she plans on making me a personal servant."

He put his gun back in his shoulder holster and came to stand next to me. He turned my head to one side to see the bite mark better. "You need to clean this bite. It's going to hurt like hell."

"I know. Will you help me?"

"Sure." His smile softened. "Here I was going to cause you pain to get information. Now you ask me to help you pour acid on a wound."

"Holy Water," I said.

"It's going to feel the same," he said.

Unfortunately, he was right.

41

I sat with my back pressed against the cool porcelain of the bathtub. The front and side of my shirt was clinging to me, water-soaked. Edward knelt beside me, a half-empty bottle of Holy Water in one hand. We were on the third bottle. I had thrown up only once. Bully for me.

We had started with me sitting on the edge of the sink. I had not stayed there long. I had jumped, yelled, and whimpered. I had also called Edward a son of a bitch. He didn't hold it against me.

"How do you feel?" he asked. His face was utterly blank. I couldn't tell if he was enjoying himself or hating it.

I glared up at him. "Like someone's been shoving a red-hot knife against my throat."

"I mean, do you want to stop and rest awhile?"

I took a deep breath. "No. I want it clean, Edward. All the way."

He shook his head, almost smiled. "It is customary to do this over a matter of days, you know."

"Yes," I said.

"But you want it all in one marathon session?" His gaze was very steady, as if the question were more important than it seemed.

I looked away from the intensity of his eyes. I didn't want to be stared at right now. "I don't have a few days. I need this wound clean before nightfall."

"Because Nikolaos will come visit you again," he said.

"Yes," I said.

"And unless this first wound is purified, she'll have a hold on you."

I took a deep breath and it trembled. "Yes."

"Even if we clean the bite, she may still be able to call you. If she's as powerful as you say she is."

"She's that powerful and more." I rubbed my hands along my jeans.

"You think Nikolaos can turn me against you, even if we clean the bite?" I looked up at him then, hoping to be able to read his face.

He stared down at me. "We vampire slayers take our chances."

"That wasn't a no," I said.

He gave a flash of smile. "It wasn't a yes, either."

Oh, goody, Edward didn't know either. "Pour some more on, before I lose my nerve."

He did smile then, eyes gleaming. "You will never lose your nerve. Your life, probably, but never your nerve."

It was a compliment and meant as one. "Thank you."

He put a hand on my shoulder, and I turned my face away. My heart was thudding in my throat until all I could hear was my blood pulsing inside my head. I wanted to run, to lash out, to scream, but I had to sit there and let him hurt me. I hate that. It had always taken at least two people to give me injections when I was a child. One person to man the needle and one to hold me down.

Now I held myself down. If Nikolaos bit me twice, I would probably do anything she wanted me to. Even kill. I had seen it happen before, and that vampire had been child's play compared to the master.

The water trickled down my skin and hit the bite mark like molten gold, scalding through my body. It was eating through my skin and bone. Destroying me. Killing me.

I shrieked. I couldn't hold it. Too much pain. Couldn't run away. Had to scream.

I was lying on the floor, my cheek pressed against the coolness of it, breathing in short, hungry gasps.

"Slow your breathing, Anita. You're hyperventilating. Breathe, slow and easy, or you're going to pass out."

I opened my mouth and took in a deep breath; it wheezed and screamed down my throat. I was choking on air. I coughed and fought to breathe. I was light-headed and a little sick by the time I could take a deep breath, but I hadn't passed out. A zillion brownie points for me.

Edward almost had to lie on the floor to put his face near mine. "Can you hear me?"

I managed, "Yes."

"Good. I want to try to put the cross against the bite. Do you agree or do you think it's too soon?"

If we hadn't cleansed the wound with enough Holy Water, the cross would burn me, and I'd have a fresh scar. I had been brave above and beyond the call of duty. I didn't want to play anymore. I opened my mouth to say, "No," but it wasn't what came out. "Do it," I said. Shit. I was going to be brave.

He brushed my hair away from my neck. I lay on the floor and pressed my hands into fists, trying to prepare myself. There is no real way to prepare yourself for somebody shoving a branding iron into your neck.

The chain rustled and slithered through Edward's hands. "Are you ready?"

No. "Just do it, dammit."

He did. The cross pressed against my skin, cool metal, no burning, no smoke, no seared flesh, no pain. I was pure, or as pure as I started out.

He dangled the crucifix in front of my face. I grabbed it with one hand and squeezed until my hand shook. It didn't take long. Tears seeped from the corners of my eyes. I wasn't crying, not really. I was exhausted.

"Can you sit up?" he asked.

I nodded and forced myself to sit, leaning against the bathtub.

"Can you stand up?" he asked.

I thought about it, and decided no, I didn't think I could. My whole body was weak, shaky, nauseous. "Not without help."

Edward knelt beside me, put an arm behind my shoulders and one under my knees, and lifted me in his arms. He stood in one smooth motion, no strain.

"Put me down," I said.

He looked at me. "What?"

"I am not a child. I don't want to be carried."

He drew a loud breath, then said, "All right." He lowered me to my feet and let go. I staggered against the wall and slid to the floor. The tears were back, dammit. I sat in the floor, crying, too weak to walk from my bathroom to my bed. God!

Edward just stood there, looking down at me, face neutral and unreadable as a cat.

My voice came out almost normal, no hint of crying. "I hate being helpless. I hate it!"

"You are one of the least helpless people I know," Edward said. He knelt beside me again, draped my right arm over his shoulders, grabbed my right wrist with his hand. His other arm encircled my waist. The height difference made it a little awkward, but he managed to give me the illusion that I walked to the bed.

The stuffed penguins sat against the wall. Edward hadn't said anything about them. If he wouldn't mention it, I wouldn't. Who knows, maybe Death slept with a teddy bear? Naw.

The heavy drapes were still closed, leaving the room in permanent twilight. "Rest. I'll stand guard and see that none of the bogeys sneak up on you."

I believed him.

Edward brought the white chair from the living room and sat it against the bedroom wall, near the door. He slipped his shoulder holster back on, gun ready at hand. He had brought a gym bag up from the car with us. He unzipped it and drew out what looked like a miniature machine gun. I didn't know much about machine guns, and all I could think of was an Uzi.

"What kind of gun is that?" I asked.

"A Mini-Uzi."

What do you know? I had been right. He popped the clip and showed me how to load it, where the safety was, all the finer points, like it was a new car. He sat down in the chair with the machine gun on his knees.

My eyes kept fluttering shut, but I said, "Don't shoot any of my neighbors, okay?"

I think he smiled. "I'll try not to."

I nodded. "Are you the vampire murderer?"

He smiled then, bright, charming. "Go to sleep, Anita."

I was on the edge of sleep when his voice called me back, soft and faraway. "Where is Nikolaos's daytime retreat?"

I opened my eyes and tried to focus on him. He was still sitting in the chair, motionless. "I'm tired, Edward, not stupid." His laughter bubbled up around me as I fell asleep.

42

Jean-Claude sat in the carved throne. He smiled at me and extended one long-fingered hand. "Come," he said.

I was wearing a long, white dress that had lace of its own. I had never dreamed of myself in anything like it. I glanced up at Jean-Claude. It was his choice, not mine. Fear tightened my throat. "It's my dream," I said.

He held out both hands and said, "Come."

And I went to him. The dress whispered and scraped on the stones, a continuous rustling noise. It grated on my nerves. I was suddenly standing in front of him. I raised my hands towards his slowly. I shouldn't do it. Bad idea, but I couldn't seem to stop myself.

His hands wrapped around mine, and I knelt before him. He drew my hands to the lace that spilled down the front of his shirt, forced my fingers to take two handfuls of it.

He cupped his hands over mine, holding them tight; then he ripped his shirt open using my hands.

His chest was smooth and pale with black hair curling in a line down the middle. The hair thickened over the flatness of his stomach, incredibly black against the white of his belly. The burn scar was firm and shiny and out of place against the perfection of his body.

He gripped my chin in one hand, raising my face towards him. His other hand touched his chest, just below his right nipple. He drew blood on his pale skin. It trickled down his chest in a bright, crimson line.

I tried to pull away, but his fingers dug into my jaw like a vise. I shouted, "No!"

I hit at him with my left hand. He caught my wrist and held it. I used my right hand to grip the floor and shoved with my knees. He held me at jaw and wrist like a butterfly on a pin. You can move, but you can't get away. I dropped to a sitting position, forcing him to strangle me or lower me to the ground. He lowered me.

I kicked out with everything I had. Both feet connected with his knee. Vampires can feel pain. He dropped my jaw so suddenly, I fell backwards. He grabbed both my wrists and jerked me to my knees, body pinned on either side by his legs. He sat in the chair, knees controlling my lower body, hands like chains on my wrists.

A high, tinkling laughter filled the room. Nikolaos stood to one side, watching us. Her laughter echoed through the room, growing louder and louder, like music gone mad.

Jean-Claude transferred both my wrists to one hand, and I could not stop him. His free hand stroked my cheek, smoothing down the line of my neck. His fingers tightened at the base of my skull and began to push.

"Jean-Claude, please, don't do this!"

He pressed my face closer and closer to the wound on his chest. I struggled, but his fingers were welded to my skull, a part of me. "NO!"

Nikolaos's laughter changed to words. "Scratch the surface, and we are all much alike, animator."

I screamed, "Jean-Claude!"

His voice came like velvet, warm and dark, sliding through my mind. "Blood of my blood, flesh of my flesh, two minds with but one body, two souls wedded as one." For one bright, shining moment, I saw it, felt it. Eternity with Jean-Claude. His touch . . . forever. His lips. His blood.

I blinked and found my lips almost touching the wound in his chest. I could have reached out and licked it. "Jean-Claude, no! Jean-Claude!" I screamed it. "God help me!" I screamed that, too.

Darkness and someone gripping my shoulder. I didn't even think about it. Instinct took over. The gun from the headboard was in my hand and turning to point.

A hand trapped my arm under the pillow, pointing the gun at the wall, a body pressing against mine. "Anita, Anita, it's Edward. Look at me!"

I blinked up at Edward, who was pinning my arms. His breathing was coming a little fast.

I stared at the gun in my hand and back at Edward. He was still holding my arms. I guess I didn't blame him.

"Are you all right?" he asked.

I nodded.

"Say something, Anita."

"I had a nightmare," I said.

He shook his head. "No shit." He released me slowly.

I slid the gun back in its holster.

"Who's Jean-Claude?" he asked.

"Why?"

"You were calling his name."

I brushed a hand over my forehead, and it came away slick with sweat. The clothes I'd slept in and the sheet were drenched with it. These nightmares were beginning to get on my nerves.

"What time is it?" The room looked too dark, as if the sun had gone down. My stomach tightened. If it was near dark, Catherine wouldn't have a chance.

"Don't panic; it's just clouds. You've got about four hours until dusk."

I took a deep breath and staggered into the bathroom. I splashed cold water on my face and neck. I looked ghost-pale in the mirror. Had the dream been Jean-Claude's doing or Nikolaos's? If it had been Nikolaos, did she already control me? No answers. No answers to anything.

Edward was sitting in the white chair when I came back out. He watched me like I was an interesting species of insect that he had never seen before.

I ignored him and called Catherine's office. "Hi, Betty, this is Anita Blake. Is Catherine in?"

"Hello, Ms. Blake. I thought you knew that Ms. Maison is going to be out of town from the thirteenth until the twentieth on a deposition."

Catherine had told me, but I forgot. I finally lucked out. It was about time. "I forgot, Betty. Thanks a lot. Thanks more than you'll ever know."

"Glad to be of help. Ms. Maison has scheduled the first fitting for the bridesmaid dresses on the twenty-third." She said it like it should make me feel better. It didn't.

"I won't forget. Bye."

"Have a nice day."

I hung up and phoned Irving Griswold. He was a reporter for the *Saint Louis Post-Dispatch*. He was also a werewolf. Irving the werewolf. It didn't quite work, but then what did? Charles the werewolf, naw. Justin, Oliver, Wilbur, Brent? Nope.

Irving answered on the third ring.

"It's Anita Blake."

"Well, hi, what's up?" He sounded suspicious, as if I never called him unless I wanted something.

"Do you know any wererats?"

He was quiet for almost too long; then, "Why do you want to know?"

"I can't tell you."

"You mean you want my help, but I don't get a story out of it."

I sighed. "That's about it."

"Then why should I help you?"

"Don't give me a hard time, Irving. I've given you plenty of exclusives. My information is what got you your first front page byline. So don't give me grief."

"A little grouchy today, aren't you?"

"Do you know a wererat or don't you?"

"I do."

"I need to get a message to the Rat King."

He gave a low whistle that was piercing over the phone. "You don't ask for much, do you? I might be able to get you a meeting with the wererat I know, but not their king."

"Give the Rat King this message; got a pencil?"

"Always," he said.

"The vampires didn't get me, and I didn't do what they wanted."

Irving read it back to me. When I confirmed it, he said, "You're involved with vampires and wererats, and I don't get an exclusive."

"No one's going to get this one, Irving. It's going to be too messy for that."

He was silent a moment. "Okay. I'll try to set up a meeting. I should know sometime tonight."

"Thanks, Irving."

"You be careful, Blake. I'd hate to lose my best source of front page bylines."

"Me, too," I said.

I had no sooner hung up the phone when it rang again. I picked it up without thinking. A phone rings, you pick it up, years of training. I haven't had my answering machine long enough to shake it completely.

"Anita, this is Bert."

"Hi, Bert." I sighed, quietly.

"I know you are working on the vampire case, but I have something you might be interested in."

"Bert, I am way over my head already. Anything else and I may never see daylight." You'd think Bert would ask if I was all right. How I was doing. But no, not my boss.

"Thomas Jensen called today."

My spine straightened. "Jensen called?"

"That's right."

"He's going to let us do it?"

"Not us, you. He specifically asked for you. I tried to get him to take someone else, but he wouldn't do it. And it has to be tonight. He's afraid he'll chicken out."

"Damn," I said softly.

"Do I call him back and cancel, or can you give me a time to have him meet you?"

Why did everything have to come at once? One of life's rhetorical questions. "Have him meet me at full dark tonight."

"That's my girl. I knew you wouldn't let me down."

"I'm not your girl, Bert. How much is he paying you?"

"Thirty thousand dollars. The five-thousand-dollar down payment has already arrived by special messenger."

"You are an evil man, Bert."

"Yes," he said, "and it pays very well, thank you." He hung up without saying good-bye. Mr. Charm.

Edward was staring at me. "Did you just take a job raising the dead, for tonight?"

"Laying the dead to rest actually, but yes."

"Does raising the dead take it out of you?"

"It?" I asked.

He shrugged. "Energy, stamina, strength."

"Sometimes."

"How about this job? Is it an energy drain?"

I smiled. "Yes."

He shook his head. "You can't afford to be used up, Anita."

"I won't be used up," I said. I took a deep breath and tried to think how to explain things to Edward. "Thomas Jensen lost his daughter twenty years ago. Seven years ago he had her raised as a zombie."

"So?"

"She committed suicide. No one knew why at the time. It was later learned that Mr. Jensen had sexually abused his daughter and that was why she had killed herself."

"And he raised her from the dead." Edward grimaced. "You don't mean . . ."

I waved my hands as if I could erase the sudden vivid image. "No, no, not that. He felt remorseful and raised her to say he was sorry."

"And?"

"She wouldn't forgive him."

He shook his head. "I don't understand."

"He raised her to make amends, but she had died hating him, fearing him. The zombie wouldn't forgive him, so he wouldn't put her back. As her mind deteriorated and her body, too, he kept her with him as a sort of punishment."

"Jesus."

"Yeah," I said. I walked to the closet and got out my gym bag. Edward carried guns in his; I carried my animator paraphernalia in it. Sometimes, I carried my vampire-slaying kit in it. The matchbook Zachary gave me was in the bottom of the bag. I stuffed it in my pants pocket. I don't think Edward saw me. He does catch on if a clue sits up and barks. "Jensen finally agreed to put her in the ground if I'll do it. I can't say no. He's sort of a legend among animators. The closest we come to a ghost story."

"Why tonight? If it's waited seven years, why not a few more nights?"

I kept putting things in the gym bag. "He insisted. He's afraid he'll lose his nerve if he has to wait. Besides, I may not be alive a few nights from now. He might not let anybody else do it."

"That is not your problem. You didn't raise his zombie."

"No, but I am an animator first. Vampire slaying is . . . a sideline. I am an animator. It isn't just a job."

He was still staring at me. "I don't understand why, but I understand you have to do it."

"Thanks."

He smiled. "Your show. Mind if I come along to make sure no one offs you while you're gone?"

I glanced at him. "Ever see a zombie raising?"

"No."

"You're not squeamish, are you?" I smiled when I said it.

He stared at me, blue eyes gone suddenly cold. His whole face became different. There was nothing there, no expression, except that awful coldness. Emptiness. I'd had a leopard look at me like that once, through the cage bars, no emotion I understood, thoughts so alien it might as well have inhabited a different planet. Something that could kill me, skillfully, efficiently, because that was what it was meant to do, if it was hungry, or if I annoyed it.

I didn't faint from fear or run screaming from the room, but it was something of an effort. "You've proved your point, Edward. Can the perfect-killer routine, and let's go."

His eyes didn't revert to normal instantly but had to warm up, like dawn easing through the sky.

I hoped Edward never turned that look on me for real. If he did, one of us would die. Odds are it would be me.

43

The night was almost perfectly black. Thick clouds hid the sky. A wind rushed along the ground and smelled of rain.

Iris Jensen's grave marker was smooth, white marble. It was a nearly life-size angel, wings outspread, arms open, welcoming. You could still read the lettering by flashlight: "Beloved daughter. Sadly missed." The same man who had had the angel carved, who sadly missed her, had been molesting her. She had killed herself to escape him, and he had brought her back. That was why I was out here in the dark, waiting for the Jensens, not him, but her. Even though I knew her mind was gone by now, I wanted Iris Jensen in the ground and at peace.

I couldn't explain that to Edward, so I hadn't tried. A huge oak stood sentinel over the empty grave. The wind rushed through the leaves and sent them skittering and whispering overhead. It sounded too dry, like autumn leaves instead of summer. The air felt cool and damp, rain almost upon us. It wasn't unbearably hot for once.

I had picked up a pair of chickens. They clucked softly from inside their crate where they sat near the grave. Edward leaned against my car, ankles crossed, arms loose at his sides. The gym bag was open by me on the ground. The machete I used gleamed from inside.

"Where is he?" Edward asked.

I shook my head. "I don't know." It had been almost an hour since full dark. The cemetery grounds were mostly bare; only a few trees dotted the soft roll of hills. We should have been seeing car lights on the gravel road. Where was Jensen? Had he chickened out?

Edward stepped away from the car and walked to stand beside me. "I don't like it, Anita."

I wasn't too thrilled either, but . . . "We'll give it another fifteen minutes. If he's not here by then, we'll leave."

Edward glanced around the open ground. "Not much cover around here."

"I don't think we have to worry about snipers."

"You said someone shot at you, right?"

I nodded. He had a point. Goosebumps marched up my arms. The wind blew a hole in the clouds and moonlight streamed down. Off in the distance a small building gleamed silver-grey in the light.

"What's that?" Edward asked.

"The maintenance shed," I said. "You think the grass cuts itself?"

"Never thought about it," he said.

The clouds rolled in again and plunged the cemetery into blackness. Everything became soft shapes; the white marble seemed to glow with its own light.

There was the sound of scrabbling claws on metal. I whirled. A ghoul sat on top of my car. It was naked and looked as if a human being had been stripped and dipped into silver-grey paint, almost metallic. But the teeth and claws on its hands and feet were long and black, curved talons. The eyes glowed crimson.

Edward moved up beside me, gun in his hand.

I had my gun out, too. Practice, practice, and you don't have to think about it.

"What's it doing up there?" he asked.

"Don't know." I waved my free hand at it and said, "Scat!"

It crouched, staring at me. Ghouls are cowards; they don't attack healthy human beings. I took two steps, waving my gun at it. "Go away, shoo!" Any show of force sends them scuttling away. This one just sat there. I backed away.

"Edward," I said, softly.

"Yes."

"I didn't sense any ghouls in this cemetery."

"So? You missed one."

"There's no such thing as just one ghoul. They travel in packs. And you don't miss them. They leave a sort of psychic stench behind. Evil."

"Anita." His voice was soft, normal, but not normal. I glanced where he was looking and saw two more ghouls creeping up behind us.

We stood almost back to back, guns pointing out. "I saw a ghoul attack earlier this week. Healthy man killed, a cemetery where there were no ghouls."

"Sounds familiar," he said.

"Yeah. Bullets won't kill them."

"I know. What are they waiting for?" he asked.

"Courage, I think."

"They're waiting for me," a voice said. Zachary stepped around the trunk of the tree. He was smiling.

I think my mouth dropped to the ground. Maybe that was what he was smiling at. I knew then. He wasn't killing human beings to feed his gris-

gris. He was killing vampires. Theresa had tormented him, so she had been the next victim. There were still some questions though, big ones.

Edward glanced at me, then back at Zachary. "Who is this?" he asked.

"The vampire murderer, I presume," I said.

Zachary gave a little bow. A ghoul leaned against his leg, and he stroked its nearly bald head. "When did you guess?"

"Just now. I'm a little slow this year."

He frowned then. "I thought you'd figure it out eventually."

"That's why you destroyed the zombie witness's mind. To save yourself."

"It was fortunate that Nikolaos left me in charge of questioning the man." He smiled when he said it.

"I'll bet," I said. "How did you get the two-biter to shoot me at the church?"

"That was easy. I told him the orders came from Nikolaos."

Of course. "How are you getting the ghouls out of their cemetery? How come they obey your orders?"

"You know the theory that if you bury an animator in a cemetery, you get ghouls."

"Yeah."

"When I came out of the grave, they came with me, and they were mine. Mine."

I glanced at the creatures and found that there were more of them. At least twenty, a big pack. "So you're saying that's where ghouls come from." I shook my head. "There aren't enough animators in the world to account for all the ghouls."

"I've been thinking about that," he said. "I think that the more zombies you raise in a cemetery, the greater your chances for ghouls."

"You mean like a cumulative effect?"

"Exactly. I've been wanting to talk this over with another animator, but you see the problem."

"Yes," I said, "I do. Can't talk shop without admitting what you are and what you've done."

Edward fired without warning. The bullet took Zachary in the chest and twisted him around. He lay face down, the ghouls frozen; then Zachary raised himself up on his elbows. He stood with a little help from an anxious ghoul. "Sticks and stones may break my bones, but bullets will never hurt me."

"Great, a comedian," I said.

Edward fired again, but Zachary darted behind the tree trunk.

He called, hidden from sight. "Now, now, no hitting the head. I'm not sure what would happen if you put a bullet in my brain."

"Let's find out," Edward said.

"Good-bye, Anita. I won't stay around to watch." He walked away with a troop of ghouls surrounding him. He was crouched in the middle of them, hiding I supposed from a bullet in the brain, but for a minute I couldn't pick him out.

Two more ghouls appeared around the car, crouched low on the gravel drive. One was female with the tatters of a dress still clinging to her.

"Let's give them something to be afraid of," Edward said. I felt him move, and his gun fired twice. A high-pitched squealing filled the night. The ghoul on my car leaped to the ground and hid. But there were more of them moving in from all sides. At least fifteen of them had been left behind for us to play with.

I fired and hit one of them. It fell to its side and rolled in the gravel, making that same high-pitched noise, like a wounded rabbit. Piteous and animal.

"Is there anyplace we can run to?" Edward asked.

"The maintenance shed," I said.

"Is it wood?"

"Yes."

"It won't stop them."

"No," I said, "but it will get us out of the open."

"Okay, any advice before we start to move?"

"Don't run until we are very close to the shed. If you run, they'll chase you. They'll think you're scared."

"Anything else?" he asked.

"You don't smoke, do you?"

"No, why?"

"They're afraid of fire."

"Great; we're going to be eaten alive because neither one of us smokes."

I almost laughed. He sounded so thoroughly disgusted, but a ghoul was crouching to leap at me, and I had to shoot it between the eyes. No time for laughter.

"Let's go, slow and easy," I said.

"I wish the machine gun wasn't in the car."

"Me, too."

Edward fired three shots, and the night filled with squeals and animal screams. We started walking towards the distant shed. I'd say maybe a quarter of a mile away. It was going to be a long walk.

A ghoul charged us. I dropped it, and it spilled to the grass, but it was like shooting targets, no blood, just empty holes. It hurt, but not enough. Not nearly enough.

I was walking nearly backwards, one hand back feeling Edward's forward movement. There were too many of them. We were not going to make it to the shed. No way. One of the chickens made a soft, questioning cluck. I had an idea.

I shot one of the chickens. It flopped, and the other bird panicked, beating its wings against the wooden crate. The ghouls froze, then one put its face into the air and sniffed.

Fresh blood, boys, come and get it. Fresh meat. Two ghouls were suddenly racing for the chickens. The rest followed, scrambling over each other to crack the wood and get to the juicy morsels inside.

"Keep walking, Edward, don't run, but walk a little faster. The chickens won't hold them long."

We walked a little faster. The sounds of scrambling claws, cracking bone, the splatter of blood, the squabbling howls of the ghouls—it was an unwelcome preview.

Halfway to the shed, a howl went up through the night, long and hostile. No dog ever sounded like that. I glanced back, and the ghouls were rushing over the ground on all fours.

"Run!" I said.

We ran.

We crashed against the shed door and found the damn thing padlocked. Edward shot the lock off; no time to pick it. The ghouls were close, howling as they came.

We scrambled inside, closing the door, for what good it would do us. There was one small window high up near the ceiling; moonlight suddenly spilled through it. There was a herd of lawnmowers against one wall, some of them hanging from hooks. Gardening shears, hedge trimmers, trowels, a curl of garden hose. The whole shed smelled of gasoline and oily rags.

Edward said, "There's nothing to put against the door, Anita."

He was right. We'd blown the lock off. Where was a heavy object when you needed it? "Roll a lawnmower against it."

"That won't hold them long."

"It's better than nothing," I said. He didn't move, so I rolled a lawnmower against the door.

"I won't die, eaten alive," he said. He put a fresh clip in his gun. "I'll do you first if you want, or you can do it yourself."

I remembered then that I had shoved the matchbook Zachary had given me in my pocket. Matches, we had matches!

"Anita, they're almost here. Do you want to do it yourself?"

I pulled the matchbook out of my pocket. Thank you, God. "Save your bullets, Edward." I lifted a can of gasoline in one hand.

"What are you planning?" he asked.

The howls were crashing around us; they were almost here.

"I'm going to set the shed on fire." I splashed gasoline on the door. The smell was sharp and tugged at the back of my throat.

"With us inside?" he asked.

"Yes."

"I'd rather shoot myself, if it's all the same to you."

"I don't plan to die tonight, Edward."

A claw smashed through the door, talons raking the wood, tearing it apart. I lit a match and threw it on the gasoline-soaked door. It went up with a blue-white whoosh of flame. The ghoul screamed, covered in fire, stumbling back from the ruined door.

The stench of burning flesh mingled with gasoline. Burnt hair. I coughed, putting a hand over my mouth. The fire was eating up the wood of the shed, spreading to the roof. We didn't need more gasoline; the damn thing was a fire trap. With us inside. I hadn't thought it would spread this fast.

Edward was standing near the back wall, hand over his mouth. His voice came muffled. "You did have a plan to get us out, right?"

A hand crashed through the wood, clawing at him. He backed away from it. The ghoul began to tear through the wood, leering at us. Edward shot it between the eyes, and it disappeared from sight.

I grabbed a rake from the far wall. Cinders were beginning to float down on us. If the smoke didn't get us first, the shed was going to collapse on top of us. "Take off your shirt," I said.

He didn't even ask why. Practical to the end. He stripped the shoulder rig off and pulled his shirt over his head, tossed it to me, and slipped the gun over his bare chest.

I wrapped the shirt over the tines of the rake and soaked it with gasoline. I set it on fire from the walls; no need for matches. The front of the shed was raining fire on us. Tiny burning stings like wasps on my skin.

Edward had caught on. He found an axe and started chopping at the hole the ghoul had made. I carried the improvised torch and a can of gasoline in my hands. The thought occurred to me that the heat was going to set the gasoline off. We weren't going to suffocate from smoke; we were going to blow up.

"Hurry!" I said.

Edward squeezed through the opening, and I followed, nearly burning him with the torch. There wasn't a ghoul for a hundred yards. They were smarter than they looked. We ran, and the explosion slammed into my back like a huge wind. I tumbled over into the grass, all the air knocked out of me. Bits of burning wood clattered to the ground on either side of me. I covered my head and prayed. My luck, I'd get caught by a flying nail.

Silence, or no more explosions. I raised my head cautiously. The shed was gone, nothing left. Bits of wood burned in the grass around me. Edward was lying on the ground, nearly touching distance from me. He stared at me. Did my face look as surprised as his did? Probably.

Our improvised torch was slowly setting the grass on fire. He knelt and raised it up.

I found the gasoline can unharmed and got to my feet. Edward followed, carrying the torch. The ghouls seemed to have fled, smart ghouls, but just in case . . . We didn't even have to discuss it. Paranoia, we had that in common.

We walked towards the car. The adrenaline was gone, and I was tireder than before. A person only has so much adrenaline; then you start running on numb.

The chicken crate was history; nameless bits and pieces were scattered around the grave. I didn't look any closer. I stopped to pick up my gym bag. It was untouched, just lying there. Edward moved ahead of me and tossed the torch on the gravel driveway. The wind rustled through the trees; then Edward yelled, "Anita!"

I rolled. Edward's gun fired, and something fell squealing on the grass. I stared at the ghoul while Edward pumped bullets into it. When I swallowed my heart back down into my chest, I crawled to the gasoline can and unscrewed it.

The ghoul screamed. Edward was driving the ghoul with the burning torch. I splashed gasoline on the cringing thing, dropped to my knees, and said, "Light it."

Edward shoved the torch home. Fire whooshed over the ghoul, and it started screaming. The night stank of burning meat and hair. And gasoline.

It rolled over and over on the ground trying to put out the fire, but it wouldn't go out.

I whispered, "You're next, Zachary baby. You are next."

The shirt had burned away, and Edward tossed the rake to the ground. "Let's get out of here," he said.

I agreed wholeheartedly. I unlocked the car, tossed my gym bag in the back seat, and started the car. The ghoul was lying on the grass, not moving, burning.

Edward was in the passenger seat with the machine gun in his lap. For the first time since I'd met him, Edward looked shaken. Scared, even.

"You going to sleep with that machine gun?" I asked.

He glanced at me. "You going to sleep with your gun?" he asked.

Point for Edward. I took the narrow gravel turns as quick as I dared. My Nova wasn't built for speed maneuvering. Having a wreck here in the cemetery didn't seem like a real good idea tonight. The headlights bounced over the tombstones, but nothing moved. No ghouls in sight.

I took a deep breath and let it out. This was the second attempt on my life in as many days. Frankly, I'd rather be shot at.

44

We drove in silence for a long time. It was Edward who finally spoke into the wheel-rushing quiet. "I don't think we should go back to your apartment," he said.

"Agreed."

"I'll take you to my hotel. Unless you have someplace else you'd rather go?"

Where could I go? Ronnie's? I didn't want her endangered anymore. Who else could I endanger? No one. No one but Edward, and he could handle it. Maybe better than I could.

My beeper trembled against my waist, sending shock waves all along my rib cage. I hated putting the beeper on silent mode. The damn thing always scared me when it went off.

Edward said, "What the hell happened? You jumped like something bit you."

I hit the button on the beeper, to shut it off and see who had called. The number lit up briefly. "My beeper went off on silent mode. No noise, just vibration."

He glanced at me. "You are not going to call work." He made it sound like a statement or an order.

"Look, Edward, I'm not feeling so hot, so don't argue with me."

I heard his breath ease out, but what could he say? I was driving. Short of drawing his gun and hijacking me, he was along for the ride. I took the next exit and located a pay phone at a convenience store. The store lot was fully lit and made me a wonderful target, but after the ghouls I wanted light.

Edward watched me get out of the car with my billfold gripped in my hand. He did not get out to watch my back. Fine, I had my gun. If he wanted to pout, let him.

I called work. Craig, our night secretary, answered. "Animators, Inc. May I help you?"

"Hi, Craig, this is Anita. What's up?"

"Irving Griswold called, says to call him back ASAP or the meeting's off. He said you'd know what that meant. Do you?"

"Yes. Thanks, Craig."

"You sound awful."

"Good night, Craig." I hung up on him. I felt tired and sluggish, and my throat hurt. I wanted to curl up somewhere dark and quiet for about a week. Instead, I called Irving. "It's me," I said.

"Well, it's about time. Do you know the trouble I've gone through to set this up? You almost missed it."

"If you don't quit talking, I may still miss it. Tell me where and when."

He did. If we hurried, we'd make it. "Why is everyone so hot to do everything tonight?" I said.

"Hey, if you don't want to meet, that's fine."

"Irving, I've had a very, very long night, so stop bitching at me."

"Are you all right?"

What a stupid question. "Not really, but I'll live."

"If you're hurt, I'll try to get the meeting postponed, but I can't promise anything, Anita. It was your message that got him this far."

I leaned my forehead against the metal of the booth. "I'll be there, Irving."

"I won't be." He sounded thoroughly disgusted. "One of the conditions was no reporters and no police."

I had to smile. Poor Irving; he was getting left out of everything. He hadn't been attacked by ghouls and almost blown up, though. Maybe I should save my pity for myself.

"Thanks, Irving, I owe you one."

"You owe me several," he said. "Be careful. I don't know what you're into this time, but it sounds bad."

He was fishing, and I knew it. "Good night, Irving." I hung up before he could ask any more questions.

I called Dolph's home phone number. I don't know why it couldn't wait until morning, but I had almost died tonight. If I did die, I wanted someone to hunt Zachary down.

Dolph answered on the sixth ring. His voice sounded gruff with sleep. "Yes."

"This is Anita Blake, Dolph."

"What's wrong?" His voice sounded almost alert.

"I know who the murderer is."

"Tell me."

I told him. He took notes and asked questions. The biggest question came at the end. "Can you prove any of this?"

"I can prove he wears a gris-gris. I can testify that he confessed to me. He tried to kill me; that I witnessed personally."

"It's going to be a tough sell to a jury or a judge."

"I know."

"I'll see what I can find out."

"We've almost got a solid case on him, Dolph."

"True, but it all hinges on you being alive to testify."

"Yeah, I'll be careful."

"You come down tomorrow and get all this information recorded officially."

"I will."

"Good work."

"Thanks," I said.

"Good night, Anita."

"Good night, Dolph."

I eased back into the car. "We have a meeting with the wererats in forty-five minutes."

"Why is it so important?" he asked.

"Because I think they can show us a back way into Nikolaos's lair. If we come in the front door, we'll never make it." I started the car and pulled out into the road.

"Who else did you call?" he asked.

So he had been paying attention. "The police."

"What?"

Edward never likes dealing with the police. Fancy that. "If Zachary manages to kill me, I want someone else to be looking into it."

He was silent for a little while. Then he asked, "Tell me about Nikolaos."

I shrugged. "She's a sadistic monster, and she's over a thousand years old."

"I look forward to meeting her."

"Don't," I said.

"We've killed master vampires before, Anita. She's just one more."

"No. Nikolaos is at least a thousand years old. I don't think I've ever been so frightened of anything in my life."

He was silent, face unreadable.

"What are you thinking?" I asked.

"That I love a challenge." Then he smiled, a beautiful, spreading smile. Shit. Death had seen his ultimate goal. The biggest catch of all. He wasn't afraid of her, and he should have been.

There aren't that many places open at one-thirty A.M., but Denny's is. There was something wrong with meeting wererats in Denny's over coffee and donuts. Shouldn't we have been meeting in some dark alley? I wasn't complaining, mind you. It just struck me as . . . funny.

Edward went in first to make sure it wasn't another setup. If he took a table, it was safe. If he came back out, it wasn't safe. Simple. No one knew what he looked like yet. As long as he wasn't with me, he could go anywhere and no one would try to kill him. Amazing. I was beginning to feel like Typhoid Mary.

Edward took a table. Safe. I walked into the bright lights and artificial comfort of the restaurant. The waitress had dark circles under her eyes, cleverly disguised by thick base, which made the circles look sort of pinkish. I looked past her. A man was motioning to me. Hand straight up, finger crooked like he was calling the waitress, or some other subservient.

"I see my party, now. Thanks anyway," I said.

The restaurant was mostly empty in the wee hours of Monday, or rather Tuesday morning. Two men sat at a table in front of the first man. They looked normal enough, but there was a sense of contained energy that seemed to spark in the air around them. Lycanthropes. I would have bet my life on it, and maybe I was.

There was a couple, male and female, sitting catty-corner from the first two. I would have bet money they were lycanthropes, too.

Edward had taken a table near them, but not too near. He had hunted lycanthropes before; he knew what to look for as well.

As I passed the table, one of the men looked up. Pure brown eyes, so dark they were almost black, stared into mine. His face was square, body slender, small build, muscles worked in his arms as he folded his hands under his chin and looked at me. I stared back; then I was past him and to the booth where the Rat King sat.

He was tall, at least six feet, dark brown skin, with thick, short-cut black hair, brown eyes. His face was thin, arrogant, lips almost too soft for the haughty expression he gave me. He was darkly handsome, strongly Mexican, and his suspicion rode the air like lightning.

I eased into the booth. I took a deep, steadying breath and looked across the counter at him.

"I got your message. What do you want?" His voice was soft but deep, without a trace of accent.

"I want you to lead myself and at least one man into the tunnels beneath the Circus of the Damned."

His frown deepened, forming faint wrinkles between his eyes. "Why should I do this for you?"

"Do you want your people free of the master's influence?"

He nodded. Still frowning.

I was really winning him over. "Guide us in through the dungeon entrance, and I'll take care of it."

He clasped his hands together on the table. "How can I trust you?"

"I am not a bounty hunter. I have never harmed a lycanthrope."

"We cannot fight beside you if you go against her. Even I cannot fight her. She calls to me. I don't answer, but I feel it. I can keep the small rats and my people from helping her against you, but that is all."

"Just get us inside. We'll do the rest."

"Are you so confident?"

"I'm willing to bet my life on it," I said.

He steepled his fingers against his lips, elbows on the table. The burn scar in his forearm was still there even in human form, a rough, four-pointed crown. "I'll get you inside," he said.

I smiled. "Thank you."

He stared at me. "When you come back out alive, then you can thank me."

"It's a deal." I held my hand out. After a moment's hesitation, he took it. We shook on it.

"You wish to wait a few days?" he asked.

"No," I said. "I want to go in tomorrow."

He cocked his head to one side. "Are you sure?"

"Why? Is that a problem?"

"You are hurt. I thought you might wish to heal."

I was a little bruised, and my throat hurt, but . . . "How did you know?"

"You smell like death has brushed you close tonight."

I stared at him. Irving never does this to me, the supernatural powers bit. I'm not saying he can't, but he works hard at being human. This man did not.

I took a deep breath. "That is my business."

He nodded. "We will call you and give you the place and time."

I stood up. He remained sitting. There didn't seem to be anything else to say, so I left.

About ten minutes later Edward got into the car with me. "What now?" he asked.

"You mentioned your hotel room. I'm going to sleep while I can."

"And tomorrow?"

"You take me out and show me how the shotgun works."

"Then?" he asked.

"Then we go after Nikolaos," I said.

He gave a shaky breath, almost a laugh. "Oh, boy."

Oh, boy? "Glad to see someone is enjoying all this."

He grinned at me. "I love my work," he said.

I had to smile. Truth was, I loved my work, too.

45

During the day I learned how to use a shotgun. That night I went caving with wererats.

The cave was dark. I stood in absolute blackness, gripping my flashlight. I touched my hand to my forehead and couldn't see a damn thing but the funny white images your eyes make when there is no light. I was wearing a hard hat with a light on it, turned off at present. The wererats had insisted on it. All around me were sounds. Cries, moans, the popping of bone, a curious sliding sound like a knife drawing out of flesh. The wererats were changing from human to animal. It sounded like it hurt—a lot. They had made me swear not to turn on a light until they told me to.

I had never wanted to see so badly in my life. It couldn't be so horrible. Could it? But a promise is a promise. I sounded like Horton the Elephant. "A person is a person no matter how small." What the hell was I doing standing in the middle of a cave, in the dark, surrounded by wererats, quoting Dr. Seuss, and trying to kill a one-thousand-year-old vampire?

It had been one of my stranger weeks.

Rafael, the Rat King, said, "You may turn on your lights."

I did, instantly. My eyes seemed to leech on the light, eager to see. The ratmen stood in small groups in the wide, flat-roofed tunnel. There were ten of them. I had counted them in human form. Now the seven males were fur-covered and wearing jean cutoffs. Two wore loose t-shirts. The three women wore loose dresses, like maternity clothes. Their black button eyes glittered in the light. Everybody was furry.

Edward came to stand near me. He was staring at the weres, face distant, unreadable. I touched his arm. I had told Rafael that I was not a bounty hunter, but Edward was, sometimes. I hoped I had not endangered these people.

"Are you ready?" Rafael asked. He was the same sleek black ratman I remembered.

"Yes," I said.

Edward nodded.

The wererats scattered to either side of us, scrambling over low, weathered flowstone. I said to no one in particular, "I thought caves were damp."

A smaller ratman in a t-shirt said, "Cherokee Caverns is dead cave."

"I don't understand."

"Live cave has water and growing formations. A dry cave where none of the formations are growing is called dead cave."

"Oh," I said.

He drew lips back from huge teeth, a smile, I think. "More than you wanted to know, huh?"

Rafael hissed back, "We are not here to give guided tours, Louie. Now be quiet, both of you."

Louie shrugged and scrambled ahead of me. He was the same human that had been with Rafael in the restaurant, the one with the dark eyes.

One of the females was nearly grey-furred. Her name was Lillian, and she was a doctor. She carried a backpack full of medical supplies. They seemed to be planning on us getting hurt. At least that meant they thought we would come out alive. I was beginning to wonder about that part myself.

Two hours later the ceiling dropped to a point where I couldn't stand upright. And I learned what the hard hats they had given Edward and me were for. I scraped my head on the rock at least a thousand times. I'd have knocked myself unconscious long before we saw Nikolaos.

The rats seemed designed for the tunnel, sliding along, flattening their bodies in a strange, scrambling grace. Edward and I could not match it. Not even close.

He cursed softly behind me. His five inches of extra height were causing him pain. My lower back was an aching burn. He had to be in worse shape. There were pockets where the ceiling opened up and we could stand. I started looking very forward to them, like air pockets to a diver.

The quality of darkness changed. Light—there was light up ahead, not much, but it was there. It flickered at the far end of the tunnel like a mirage.

Rafael crouched beside us. Edward sat flat on the dry rock. I joined him. "There is your dungeon. We will wait here until near dark. If you have not come out, we will leave. After Nikolaos is dead, if we can, we will help you."

I nodded; the light on my hard hat nodded with me. "Thank you for helping us."

He shook his narrow, ratty face. "I have delivered you to the devil's door. Do not thank me for that."

I glanced at Edward. His face was still distant, unreadable. If he was interested in what the ratman had just said, I couldn't tell it. We might as well have been talking about a grocery list.

Edward and I knelt before the opening into the dungeon. Torchlight flickered, incredibly bright after the darkness. Edward was cradling his Uzi that hung on a strap across his chest. I had the shotgun. I was also carrying my two pistols, two knives, and a derringer stuffed in the pocket of my jacket. It was a present from Edward. He had handed it to me with this advice: "It kicks like a sonofabitch, but press it under someone's chin, and it will blow their fucking head off." Nice to know.

It was daylight outside. There shouldn't be a vampire stirring, but Burchard would be there. And if he saw us, Nikolaos would know. Somehow, she'd know. Goosebumps marched up my arms.

We scrambled inside, ready to kill and maim. The room was empty. All that adrenaline sort of sat in my body, making my breathing too quick and my heart pound for no reason. The spot where Phillip had been chained was clean. Someone had scrubbed it down real good.

I fought an urge to touch the wall where he'd been.

Edward called softly, "Anita." He was at the door.

I hurried up to him.

"What's wrong?" he asked.

"She killed Phillip in here."

"Keep your mind on business. I don't want to die because you're daydreaming."

I started to get angry and swallowed it. He was right.

Edward tried the door, and it opened. No prisoners, no need to lock it. I took the left side of the door, and he took the right. The corridor was empty.

My hands were sweating on the shotgun. Edward led off down the right hand side of the corridor. I followed him into the dragon's lair. I didn't feel much like a knight. I was fresh out of shiny steeds, or was that shiny armor?

Whatever. We were here. This was it. I could taste my heart in my throat.

46

The dragon didn't come out and eat us right away. In fact, the place was quiet. As the cliché goes, too quiet.

I stepped close to Edward and whispered, "I don't mean to complain, but where is everybody?"

He leaned his back against the wall and said, "Maybe you killed Winter. That just leaves Burchard. Maybe he's on an errand."

I shook my head. "This is too easy."

"Don't worry. Something will go wrong soon." He continued down the corridor, and I followed. It took me three steps to realize Edward had made a joke.

The corridor opened into a huge room like Nikolaos's throne room, but there was no chair here. There were coffins. Five of them spaced around the room on raised platforms, so they didn't have to sit on the floor in the draft. Tall, iron candelabra burned in the room, one at the foot and head of each coffin.

Most vampires made some effort to hide their coffins, but not Nikolaos. "Arrogant," Edward whispered.

"Yes," I whispered back. You always whispered around the coffins, at first, as if it were a funeral and they could hear you.

There was a neck-ruffling smell to the room, stale. It caught at the back of my throat and was almost a taste, faintly metallic. It was like the smell of snakes kept in cages. You knew there was nothing warm and furry in this room just by smell. And that really doesn't do it justice. It was the smell of vampires.

The first coffin was dark, well-varnished wood, with golden handles. It was wider at the shoulder area and then narrowed, following the contour of the human body. Older coffins did that sometimes.

"We start here," I said.

Edward didn't argue. He let the machine gun hang by its strap and drew his pistol. "You're covered," he said.

I laid the shotgun on the floor in front of the coffin, gripped the edge of the lid, said a quick prayer, and lifted. Valentine lay in the coffin. His scarred face was bare. He was still dressed as a riverboat gambler but this time in black. His frilly shirt was crimson. The colors didn't look good against his auburn hair. One hand was half-curled over his thigh, a careless sleeper's gesture. A very human gesture.

Edward peered into the coffin, gun pointed ceilingward. "This the one you threw Holy Water on?"

I nodded.

"Did a bang-up job," Edward said.

Valentine never moved. I couldn't even see him breathe. I wiped my sweating palms on my jeans and felt for a pulse in his wrist. Nothing. His skin was cool to the touch. He was dead. It wasn't murder, no matter what the new laws said. You can't kill a corpse.

The wrist pulsed. I jerked back like he'd burned me.

"What's wrong?" Edward asked.

"I got a pulse."

"It happens sometimes."

I nodded. Yeah, it happened sometimes. If you waited long enough, the heart did beat, blood did flow, but so slow that it was painful to watch. Dead. I was beginning to think I didn't know what that meant.

I knew one thing. If night fell with us here, we would die, or wish we had. Valentine had helped kill over twenty people. He had nearly killed me. When Nikolaos withdrew her protection, he'd finish the job if he could. We had come to kill Nikolaos. I think she would withdraw her protection ASAP. As the old saying goes, it was him or me. I preferred him.

I shook off the shoulder straps of the backpack.

"What are you looking for?" Edward asked.

"Stake and hammer," I said without looking up.

"Not going to use the shotgun?"

I glanced up at him. "Oh, right. Why not rent a marching band while we're at it?"

"If you just want to be quiet, there is another way." He had a slight smile on his face.

I had the sharpened stake in my hand, but I was willing to listen. I've staked most of the vampires that I've killed, but it never gets easier. It is hard, messy work, though I don't throw up anymore. I am a professional, after all.

He took a small case out of his own backpack. It held syringes. He drew out an ampule of some greyish liquid. "Silver nitrate," he said.

Silver. Bane of the undead. Scourge of the supernatural. And all nicely modernized. "Does it work?" I asked.

"It works." He filled one syringe and asked, "How old is this one?"

"A little over a hundred," I said.

"Two ought to do it." He shoved the needle into the big vein in Valentine's neck. Before he had filled the syringe a second time, the body shivered. He shoved the second dose into the neck. Valentine's body arched against the walls of the coffin. His mouth opened and closed. He gasped for air as if he were drowning.

Edward filled up another syringe and handed it towards me. I stared at it.

"It isn't going to bite," he said.

I took it gingerly between my thumb and the first two fingers on my right hand.

"What's the matter with you?" he asked.

"I'm not a big fan of needles."

He grinned. "You're afraid of needles?"

I scowled at him. "Not exactly."

Valentine's body shook and bucked, hands thumping against the wooden walls. It made a small, helpless noise. His eyes never opened. He was going to sleep through his own death.

He gave one last shuddering jump, then collapsed against the side of the coffin like a broken rag doll.

"He doesn't look very dead," I said.

"They never do."

"Stake their heart and chop off their heads, and you know they're dead."

"This isn't staking," he said.

I didn't like it. Valentine lay there looking very whole and nearly human. I wanted to see some rotting flesh and bones turning to dust. I wanted to know he was dead.

"No one has ever gotten up out of their coffin after a syringe full of silver nitrate, Anita."

I nodded but remained unconvinced.

"You check the other side. Go on."

I went, but I kept glancing back at Valentine. He had haunted my nightmares for years, nearly killed me. He just didn't look dead enough for me.

I opened the first coffin on my side, one-handed, holding the syringe carefully. An injection of silver nitrate probably wouldn't do me much good either. The coffin was empty. The white imitation silk lining had conformed to the body like a mattress, but the body wasn't there.

I flinched and stared around the room, but there was nothing there. I stared slowly upward, hoping that there was nothing floating above me. There wasn't. Thank you, God.

I remembered to breathe finally. It was probably Theresa's coffin. Yeah, that was it. I left it open and went to the next one. It was a newer model, probably fake wood, but nice and polished. The black male was in it. I had never gotten his name. Now I never would. I knew what it meant, coming in here. Not just defending yourself but taking out the vampires while they lay helpless. As far as I knew, this vampire had never hurt anyone. I laughed then; he was Nikolaos's protege. Did I really think he'd never tasted human blood? No. I pressed the needle against his neck and swallowed hard. I hated needles. No particular reason.

I shoved it in and closed my eyes while I depressed the plunger. I could have pounded a stake through his heart, but sticking a needle in him put cold chills down my spine.

Edward called, "Anita!"

I whirled and found Aubrey sitting up in his coffin. He had Edward by the throat and was slowly lifting him off his feet.

The shotgun was still by Valentine's coffin. Damn! I drew the 9mm and fired at Aubrey's forehead. The bullet tossed his head back, but he just smiled and raised Edward straight-armed, legs dangling.

I ran for the shotgun.

Edward was having to use both hands to keep himself from being strangled by his own weight. He dropped one hand, fumbling for the machine gun.

Aubrey caught his wrist.

I picked up the shotgun, took two steps towards them and fired from three feet away. Aubrey's head exploded; blood and brains spattered over the wall. The hands lowered Edward to the floor but didn't let go. Edward drew a ragged breath. The right hand convulsed around his throat, fingers digging for his windpipe.

I had to step around Edward to fire at the chest. The blast took out the heart and most of the left side of the chest. The left arm sort of hung there by strands of tissue and bone. The corpse flopped back into its coffin.

Edward dropped to his knees, breath wheezing and choking through his throat.

"Nod if you can breathe, Edward," I said. Though if Aubrey had crushed his windpipe I don't know what I could have done. Run back and gotten Lillian the doctor rat, maybe.

Edward nodded. His face was a mottled reddish purple, but he was breathing.

My ears were ringing with the sound of the shotgun inside the stone walls. So much for surprise. So much for silver nitrate. I pumped another round into the gun and went to Valentine's coffin. I blew him apart. Now, he was dead.

Edward staggered to his feet. He croaked, "How old was that thing?"

"Over five hundred," I said.

He swallowed, and it looked like it hurt. "Shit."

"I wouldn't try sticking any needles into Nikolaos."

He managed to glare at me, still half-leaning against Aubrey's coffin.

I turned to the fifth coffin. The one we had saved until last without any talk between us. It was set against the far wall. A dainty white coffin, too small for an adult. Candlelight gleamed on the carvings in the lid.

I was tempted to just blow a hole in the coffin, but I had to see her. I had to see what I was shooting at. My heart started thudding in my throat; my chest was tight. She was a master vampire. Killing them, even in daylight, is a chancy thing. Their gaze can trap you until nightfall. Their minds. Their voices. So much power. And Nikolaos was the most powerful I'd ever seen. I had my blessed cross. I would be all right. I had had too many crosses taken from me to feel completely safe. Oh, well. I tried to raise the lid one-handed, but it was heavy and not balanced for easy opening like modern coffins. "Can you back me on this, Edward? Or are you still relearning how to breathe?"

Edward came to stand beside me. His face looked almost its normal color. He took hold of the lid and I readied the shotgun. He lifted and the whole lid slid off. It wasn't hinged on.

I said, "Shiiit!"

The coffin was empty.

"Are you looking for me?" A high, musical voice called from the doorway. "Freeze; I believe that is the word. We have the drop on you."

"I wouldn't advise going for your gun," Burchard said.

I glanced at Edward and found his hands close to the machine gun but not close enough. His face was unreadable, calm, normal. Just a Sunday drive. I was so scared I could taste bile at the back of my throat. We looked at each other and raised our hands.

"Turn around slowly," Burchard said.

We did.

He was holding a semiautomatic rifle of some kind. I'm not the gun freak Edward is, so I didn't know the make and model, but I knew it'd make a big hole. There was also a sword hilt sticking over his back. A sword, an honest-to-god sword.

Zachary was standing beside him, holding a pistol. He held it two-handed, arms stiff. He didn't seem happy.

Burchard held the rifle like he was born with it. "Drop your weapons, please, and lace your fingers on top of your heads."

We did what he asked. Edward dropped the machine gun, and I lost the shotgun. We had plenty more guns.

Nikolaos stood to one side. Her face was cold, angry. Her voice, when it came, echoed through the room. "I am older then anything you have ever imagined. Did you think daylight holds me prisoner? After a thousand years?" She walked out into the room, careful not to cross in front of Burchard and Zachary. She glanced at the remains in the coffins. "You will pay for this, animator." She smiled then, and I had never seen anything more evil. "Strip them of the rest of their weaponry, Burchard; then we will give the animator a treat."

They stood in front of us but not too close. "Up against the wall, animator," Burchard said. "If the man moves, Zachary, shoot him."

Burchard shoved me into the wall and frisked me very thoroughly. He didn't check my teeth or have me drop my pants, but that was about it. He found everything I was carrying. Even the derringer. He shoved my cross into his pocket. Maybe I could tattoo one on my arm? Probably wouldn't work.

I went out to stand with Zachary, and Edward got his turn. I stared at Zachary. "Does she know?" I asked.

"Shut up."

I smiled. "She doesn't, does she?"

"Shut up!"

Edward came back, and we stood there with our hands on top of our heads, weapons gone. It was not a pretty sight.

Adrenaline was bubbling like champagne, and my pulse was threatening to jump out of my throat. I wasn't afraid of the guns, not really. I was afraid of Nikolaos. What would she do to us? To me? If I had a choice, I'd force them to shoot me. It had to be better than anything Nikolaos had in her evil little mind.

"They are unarmed, Mistress," Burchard said.

"Good," she said. "Do you know what we were doing while you destroyed my people?"

I didn't think she wanted an answer, so I didn't give her one.

"We were preparing a friend of yours, animator."

My stomach jerked. I had a wild image of Catherine, but she was out of town. My god, Ronnie. Did they have Ronnie?

It must have showed on my face because Nikolaos laughed, high and wild, an excited tittering.

"I really hate that laugh," I said.

"Silence," Burchard said.

"Oh, Anita, you are so amusing. I will enjoy making you one of my people." Her voice started high and childlike and ended low enough to crawl down my spine.

She called out in a clear voice, "Enter this room now."

I heard shuffling footsteps; then Phillip walked into the room. The horrible wound at his throat was thick, white scar tissue. He stared around the room as if he didn't really see it.

I whispered, "Dear God."

They had raised him from the dead.

47

Nikolaos danced around him. The skirt of her pastel pink dress swirled around her. The large, pink bow in her hair bobbed as she twirled, arms outstretched. Her slender legs were covered in white tights. The shoes were white with pink bows.

She stopped, laughing and breathless. A healthy pink flush on her cheeks, eyes sparkling. How did she do that?

"He looks very alive, doesn't he?" She stalked around him, hand brushing his arm. He drew away from her, eyes following her every move, afraid. He remembered her. God help us. He remembered her.

"Do you want to see him put through his paces?" she asked.

I hoped I didn't understand her. I fought to keep my face blank. I must have succeeded because she stomped over to me, hands on hips.

"Well," she said, "do you want to watch your lover perform?"

I swallowed bile, hard. Maybe I should just throw up on her. That would teach her. "With you?" I asked.

She sidled up to me, hands clasped behind her back. "It could be you. Your choice."

Her face was almost touching mine. Eyes so damned wide and innocent that it seemed sacrilegious. "Neither sounds very appealing," I said.

"Pity." She half-skipped back to Phillip. He was naked, and his tanned body was still handsome. What were a few more scars?

"You didn't know I was going to be here, so why raise Phillip from the dead?" I asked.

She turned on the heels of her little shoes. "We raised him so he could try to kill Aubrey. Murdered zombies can be so much fun, while they try to kill their murderers. We thought we'd give him a chance while Aubrey was asleep. Aubrey can move if you disturb him." She glanced at Edward. "But then you know that."

"You were going to let Aubrey kill him again," I said.

She nodded, head bobbing. "Mmm-uh."

"You bitch," I said.

Burchard shoved the rifle butt into my stomach, and I dropped to my knees. I panted, trying to breathe. It didn't help much.

Edward was staring very fixedly at Zachary, who was holding the pistol square on his chest. You didn't have to be good at that range or even lucky. Just squeeze the trigger and kill someone. Poof.

"I can make you do whatever I please," Nikolaos said.

A fresh spurt of adrenaline rushed through me. It was too much. I threw up in the corner. Nerves and being hit very hard in the stomach with a rifle. Nerves I'd had before; the rifle butt was a new experience.

"Tsk, tsk," Nikolaos said. "Do I frighten you that much?"

I managed to stand up at last. "Yes," I said. Why deny it?

She clapped her hands together. "Oh, goody." Her face shifted gears, instant switch. The little girl was gone, and no amount of pink, frilly dresses would bring her back. Nikolaos's face was thinner, alien. The eyes were great drowning pools. "Hear me, Anita. Feel my power in your veins."

I stood there, staring at the floor, fear like a cold rush on my skin. I waited for something to tug at my soul. Her power to roll me under and away. Nothing happened.

Nikolaos frowned. The little girl was back. "I bit you, animator. You should crawl if I ask it. What did you do?"

I breathed a small, heartfelt prayer, and answered her. "Holy Water."

She snarled. "This time we will keep you with us until after the third bite. You will take Theresa's place. Perhaps then you will be more eager to find out who is murdering vampires."

I fought with everything in me not to glance at Zachary. Not because I didn't want to give him away, I would do that, but I was waiting for the moment when it would help us. It might get Zachary killed, but it wouldn't take out Burchard or Nikolaos. Zachary was the least dangerous person in this whole room.

"I don't think so," I said.

"Oh, but I do, animator."

"I would rather die."

She spread her arms wide. "But I want you to die, Anita, I want you to die."

"That makes us even," I said.

She giggled. The sound made my teeth hurt. If she really wanted to torture me, all she had to do was lock me in a room and laugh at me. Now that would be hell.

"Come on, boys and girls, let's go play in the dungeon." Nikolaos led the way. Burchard motioned for us to follow. We did. Zachary and he brought up the rear, guns in hand. Phillip stood uncertainly in the middle of the room, watching us go.

Nikolaos called back, "Have him follow us, Zachary."

Zachary called, "Come, Phillip, follow me."

He turned and walked after us, his eyes still uncertain and not really focused.

"Go on," Burchard said. He half-raised the rifle, and I went.

Nikolaos called back, "Gazing at your lover; how nice."

It wasn't a long enough walk to the dungeon door. If they tried to chain me to the wall, I'd rush them. I'd force them to kill me. Which meant I'd better rush Zachary. Burchard might wound me or knock me unconscious, and that would be very, very bad.

Nikolaos led us down the steps and out into the floor. What a day for a parade. Phillip followed, but he was looking around now, really seeing things. He froze, staring at the place where Aubrey had killed him. His hand reached out to touch the wall. He flexed his hand, rubbing fingers into his palm as if he was feeling something. A hand went to his neck and found the scar. He screamed. It echoed against the walls.

"Phillip," I said.

Burchard held me back with the rifle. Phillip crouched in the corner, face hidden, arms locked around his knees. He was making a high, keening noise.

Nikolaos laughed.

"Stop it, stop it!" I walked towards Phillip, and Burchard shoved the gun against my chest. I yelled into his face, "Shoot me, shoot me, dammit! It's got to be better than this."

"Enough," Nikolaos said. She stalked over to me, and I gave ground. bShe kept walking, forcing me to back up until I bumped against the wall. "I don't want you shot, Anita, but I want you hurt. You killed Winter with your little knife. Let's see how good you really are." She strode away from me. "Burchard, give her back her knives."

He never even hesitated or asked why. He just walked over to me and handed them to me, hilt first. I didn't question it either. I took them.

Nikolaos was suddenly beside Edward. He started to move away. "Kill him if he moves again, Zachary."

Zachary came to stand close, gun out.

"Kneel, mortal," she said.

Edward didn't do it. He glanced at me. Nikolaos kicked him in the bend of the knee hard enough to make him grunt. He dropped to one knee, and she grabbed his right arm and tugged it behind his back. One slender hand grabbed his throat.

"I'll tear out your throat if you move, human. I can feel your pulse like a butterfly beating against my hand." She laughed and filled the room with warm, jostling horror. "Now, Burchard, show her what it means to use a knife."

Burchard went to the far wall, with the door above him at the top of the steps. He laid the rifle on the floor, and unbuckled his sword harness, and laid that beside the rifle. Then he drew a long knife with a nearly triangular blade.

He did some quick stretches to limber his muscles, and I stood staring at him.

I know how to use a knife. I can throw well; I practice that. Most people are afraid of knives. If you show yourself willing to carve someone up, they tend to be afraid of you. Burchard was not most people. He went down into a slight crouch, knife held loose but firm in his right hand.

"Fight Burchard, animator, or this one dies." She pulled his arm, sharp, but he didn't cry out. She could dislocate his shoulder, and Edward wouldn't cry out.

I put the knife back in its right wrist sheath. Fighting with a knife in each hand may look nifty, but I've never really mastered it. A lot of people don't. Hey, Burchard didn't have two knives either. "Is this to the death?" I asked.

"You will not be able to kill Burchard, Anita. So silly. Burchard is only going to cut you. Let you taste the blade, nothing too serious. I don't want you to lose too much blood." There was an undercurrent of laughter in her voice, then it was gone. Her voice crawled through the room like a fire-wind. "I want to see you bleed."

Great.

Burchard began to circle me, and I kept the wall at my back. He rushed me, knife flashing. I held my ground, dodging his blade, and slashing at him as he darted in. My knife hit empty air. He was standing out of reach, staring at me. He had had six hundred years of practice, give or take. I couldn't top that. I couldn't even come close.

He smiled. I gave him a slight nod. He nodded back. A sign of respect between two warriors, maybe. Either that, or he was playing with me. Guess which way I voted?

His knife was suddenly there, slicing my arm open. I slashed outward and caught him across the stomach. He darted into me, not away. I dodged the knife and stumbled away from the wall. He smiled. Dammit, he'd wanted to get me out in the open. His reach was twice mine.

The pain in my arm was sharp and immediate. But there was a thin line of crimson on his flat stomach. I smiled at him. His eyes flinched, just a little. Was the mighty warrior uneasy? I hoped so.

I backed away from him. This was ridiculous. We were going to die, piece by piece, both of us. What the hell. I charged Burchard, slashing. It caught him by surprise, and he backpedaled. I mirrored his crouch, and we began to circle the floor.

And I said, "I know who the murderer is."

Burchard's eyebrows raised.

Nikolaos said, "What did you say?"

"I know who is killing vampires."

Burchard was suddenly inside my arm, slicing my shirt. It didn't hurt. He was playing with me.

"Who?" Nikolaos said. "Tell me, or I will kill this human."

"Sure," I said.

Zachary screamed, "No!" He turned to fire at me. The bullet whined overhead. Burchard and I both sank to the floor.

Edward screamed. I half-rose to run to him. His arm was twisted at a funny angle, but he was alive.

Zachary's gun went off twice, and Nikolaos took it away from him, tossing it to the floor. She grabbed him and forced him against her body, bending him at the waist, cradling him. Her head darted downward. Zachary shrieked.

Burchard was on his knees, watching the show. I stabbed my knife into his back. It thunked solid and hilt-deep. His spine stiffened, one hand trying to tear out the blade. I didn't wait to see if he could do it. I drew my other knife and plunged it into the side of his throat. Blood poured down my hand when I took the knife out. I stabbed him again, and he fell slowly forward, face down on the floor.

Nikolaos let Zachary drop to the floor and turned, face bloodstained, the front of her pink dress crimson. Blood spattered on her white tights. Zachary's throat was torn out. He lay gasping on the floor but still moving, alive.

She stared at Burchard's body, then screamed, a wild banshee sound that wailed and echoed. She rushed me, hands outstretched. I threw the knife, and she batted it away. She hit me, the force of her body slamming me into the floor, her scrambling on top of me. She was still screaming, over and over. She held my head to one side. No mind tricks, brute strength.

I screamed, "Nooo!"

A gun fired, and Nikolaos jerked, once, twice. She rose off me, and I felt the wind. It was creeping through the room like the beginnings of a storm.

Edward leaned against the wall, holding Zachary's dropped gun.

Nikolaos went for him, and he emptied the gun into her frail body. She didn't even hesitate.

I sat up and watched her stalk towards Edward. He threw the empty gun at her. She was suddenly on him, forcing him back into the floor.

The sword lay on the floor, nearly as tall as I was. I drew it out of its sheath. Heavy, awkward, drawing my arm down. I raised it over my head, flat of the blade half resting on my shoulder, and ran for Nikolaos.

She was talking again in a high, sing-song voice. "I will make you mine, mortal. Mine!"

Edward screamed. I couldn't see why. I raised the sword, and its weight carried it down and across, like it was meant to. It bit into her neck with a great wet thunk. The sword grated on bone, and I drew it out. The tip fell to scrape on the floor.

Nikolaos turned to me and started to stand. I raised the sword, and it cut outward, swinging my body with it. Bone cracked, and I fell to the floor as Nikolaos tumbled to her knees. Her head still hung by strips of meat and skin. She blinked at me and tried to stand up.

I screamed and drove the blade upward with everything I had. It took her between the breasts, and I stood running with it, shoving it in. Blood poured. I pinned her against the wall. The blade shoved out her back, scraping along the wall as she slid downward.

I dropped to my knees beside the body. Yes, the body. She was dead!

I looked back at Edward. There was blood on his neck. "She bit me," he said.

I was gasping for air, having trouble breathing, but it was wonderful. I was alive and she wasn't. She fucking wasn't. "Don't worry, Edward, I'll help you. Plenty of Holy Water left." I smiled.

He stared at me a minute, then laughed, and I laughed with him. We were still laughing when the wererats crept in from the tunnel. Rafael, the Rat King, stared at the carnage with black-button eyes. "She is dead."

"Ding dong, the witch is dead," I said.

Edward picked it up, half-singing, "The wicked old witch."

We collapsed into laughter again, and Lillian the doctor, all covered with fur, tended our hurts, Edward first.

Zachary was still lying on the ground. The wound at his throat was beginning to close up, skin knitting together. He would live, if that was the right word.

I picked my knife up off the floor and staggered to him. The rats watched me. No one interfered. I dropped to my knees beside him and ripped the sleeve of his shirt. I laid the gris-gris bare. He still couldn't talk, but his eyes widened.

"Remember when I tried to touch this with my own blood? You stopped me. You seemed afraid, and I didn't understand why." I sat beside him and watched him heal. "Every gris-gris has a thing you must do for it, vampire blood for this one, and one thing you must never do, or the magic stops. Poof." I held up my arm, dripping blood quite nicely. "Human blood, Zachary; is that bad?"

He managed a noise like, "Don't."

Blood dripped down my elbow and hung, thick and trembling over his arm. He sort of shook his head, no, no. The blood dripped down and splatted on his arm, but it didn't touch the gris-gris.

His whole body relaxed.

"I've got no patience today, Zachary." I rubbed blood along the woven band.

His eyes flared, showing white. He made a strangling noise in his throat. His hands scrabbled at the floor. His chest jerked as if he couldn't breathe. A sigh ran out of his body, a long whoosh of breath, and he was quiet.

I checked for a pulse; nothing. I cut the gris-gris off with my knife, balled it in my hand, and shoved it in my pocket. Evil piece of work.

Lillian came to bind my arm up. "This is just temporary. You'll need stitches."

I nodded and got to my feet.

Edward called, "Where are you going?"

"To get the rest of our guns." To find Jean-Claude. I didn't say that part out loud. I didn't think Edward would understand.

Two of the ratmen went with me. That was fine. They could come as long as they didn't interfere. Phillip was still huddled in the corner. I left him there.

I did get the guns. I strung the machine gun over my shoulders and kept the shotgun in my hands. Loaded for bear. I had killed a one-thousand-year-old vampire. Naw, not me. Surely not.

The ratmen and I found the punishment room. There were six coffins in it. Each had a blessed cross on its lid and silver chains to hold the lid down. The third coffin held Willie, so deeply asleep that he seemed like he would never wake. I left him like that, to wake with the night. To go on about his business. Willie wasn't a bad person. And for a vampire he was excellent.

All the other coffins were empty, only the last one still unopened. I undid the chains and laid the cross on the ground. Jean-Claude stared up at me. His eyes were midnight fire, his smile gentle. I flashed on the first dream and the coffin filled with blood, him reaching for me. I stepped back, and he rose from the coffin.

The ratmen stepped back, hissing.

"It's all right," I said. "He's sort of on our side."

He stepped from the coffin like he'd had a good nap. He smiled and extended a hand. "I knew you would do it, ma petite."

"You arrogant son of a bitch." I smashed the shotgun butt into his stomach. He doubled over just enough. I hit him in the jaw. He rocked back. "Get out of my mind!"

He rubbed his face and came away with blood. "The marks are permanent, Anita. I cannot take them back."

I gripped the shotgun until my hands ached. Blood began to trickle down my arm from the wound. I thought about it. For one moment, I considered blowing his perfect face away. I didn't do it. I would probably regret it later.

"Can you stay out of my dreams, at least?" I asked.

"That, I can do. I am sorry, ma petite."

"Stop calling me that."

He shrugged. His black hair had nearly crimson highlights in the torch-light. Breathtaking. "Stop playing with my mind, Jean-Claude."

"Whatever do you mean?" he asked.

"I know that the otherworldly beauty is a trick. So stop it."

"I am not doing it," he said.

"What is that supposed to mean?"

"When you have the answer, Anita, come back to me, and we will talk."

I was too tired for riddles. "Who do you think you are? Using people like this."

"I am the new master of the city," he said. He was suddenly next to me, fingers touching my cheek. "And you put me upon the throne."

I jerked away from him. "You stay away from me for a while, Jean-Claude, or I swear . . ."

"You'll kill me?" he said. He was smiling, laughing at me.

I didn't shoot him. And some people say I have no sense of humor.

*   *   *

I found a room with a dirt floor and several shallow graves. Phillip let me lead him to the room. It was only when we stood staring down at the fresh-turned earth that he turned to me. "Anita?"

"Hush," I said.

"Anita, what's happening?"

He was beginning to remember. He would become more alive in a few hours, up to a point. It would almost be the real Phillip for a day, or two.

"Anita?" His voice was high and uncertain. A little boy afraid of the dark. He grabbed my arm, and his hand felt very real. His eyes were still that perfect brown. "What's going on?"

I stood on tiptoe and kissed his cheek. His skin was warm. "You need to rest, Phillip. You're tired."

He nodded. "Tired," he said.

I led him to the soft dirt. He lay down on it, then sat up, eyes wild, grabbing for me. "Aubrey! He . . . "

"Aubrey's dead. He can't hurt you anymore."

"Dead?" He stared down the length of his body as if just seeing it. "Aubrey killed me."

I nodded. "Yes, Phillip."

"I'm scared."

I held him, rubbing his back in smooth, useless circles. His arms hugged me like he would never let go.

"Anita!"

"Hush, hush. It's all right. It's all right."

"You're going to put me back, aren't you?" He drew back so he could see my face.

"Yes," I said.

"I don't want to die."

"You're already dead."

He stared down at his hands, flexing them. "Dead?" he whispered. "Dead?" He lay down on the fresh-turned earth. "Put me back," he said.

And I did.

At the end his eyes closed and his face went slack, dead. He sank into the grave and was gone.

I dropped to my knees beside Phillip's grave, and wept.

48

Edward had a dislocated shoulder and two broken bones in his arm, plus one vampire bite. I had fourteen stitches. We both healed. Phillip's body was moved to a local cemetery. Every time I work in it, I have to go by and say hello. Even though I know Phillip is dead and doesn't care. Graves are for the living, not the dead. It gives us something to concentrate on instead of the fact that our loved one is rotting under the ground. The dead don't care about pretty flowers and carved marble statues.

Jean-Claude sent me a dozen pure white, long-stemmed roses. The card read, "If you have answered the question truthfully, come dancing with me."

I wrote "No" on the back of the card and slipped it under the door at Guilty Pleasures, during daylight hours. I had been attracted to Jean-Claude. Maybe I still was. So what? He thought it changed things. It didn't. All I had to do was visit Phillip's grave to know that. Oh, hell, I didn't even have to go that far. I know who and what I am. I am The Executioner, and I don't date vampires. I kill them.

THE
LAUGHING
CORPSE

To Ricia Mainhardt, my agent:
beautiful, intelligent, confident, and honest.
What more could any writer ask for?

Acknowledgments

As always, for my husband, Gary, who after nearly nine years is still my sweetie. Ginjer Buchanan, our editor, who believed in Anita and me from the start. Carolyn Caughey, our British editor, who is taking Anita and me across the seas. Marcia Woolsey, who read the first Anita short story and pronounced it good. (Marcia, please contact my publisher, I would love to talk to you.) Richard A. Knaak, good friend and honorary alternate historian. You finally get to read the rest of the book. Janni Lee Simner, Marella Sands, and Robert K. Sheaf, who made sure this book stood alone. Good luck in Arizona, Janni. We'll miss you. Deborah Millitello for holding my hand when I needed it. M. C. Sumner, neighbor and friend. Alternate historians forever. Thanks to everyone who attended my readings at Windycon and Capricon.

1

Harold Gaynor's house sat in the middle of intense green lawn and the graceful sweep of trees. The house gleamed in the hot August sunshine. Bert Vaughn, my boss, parked the car on the crushed gravel of the driveway. The gravel was so white, it looked like handpicked rock salt. Somewhere out of sight the soft whir of sprinklers pattered. The grass was absolutely perfect in the middle of one of the worst droughts Missouri has had in over twenty years. Oh, well. I wasn't here to talk with Mr. Gaynor about water management. I was here to talk about raising the dead.

Not resurrection. I'm not that good. I mean zombies. The shambling dead. Rotting corpses. Night of the living dead. That kind of zombie. Though certainly less dramatic than Hollywood would ever put up on the screen. I am an animator. It's a job, that's all, like selling.

Animating had only been a licensed business for about five years. Before that it had just been an embarrassing curse, a religious experience, or a tourist attraction. It still is in parts of New Orleans, but here in St. Louis it's a business. A profitable one, thanks in large part to my boss. He's a rascal, a scalawag, a rogue, but damn if he doesn't know how to make money. It's a good trait for a business manager.

Bert was six-three, a broad-shouldered, ex–college football player with the beginnings of a beer gut. The dark blue suit he wore was tailored so that the gut didn't show. For eight hundred dollars the suit should have hidden a herd of elephants. His white-blond hair was trimmed in a crew cut, back in style after all these years. A boater's tan made his pale hair and eyes dramatic with contrast.

Bert adjusted his blue and red striped tie, mopping a bead of sweat off his tanned forehead. "I heard on the news there's a movement there to use zombies in pesticide-contaminated fields. It would save lives."

"Zombies rot, Bert, there's no way to prevent that, and they don't stay smart enough long enough to be used as field labor."

"It was just a thought. The dead have no rights under law, Anita."

"Not yet."

It was wrong to raise the dead so they could slave for us. It was just wrong, but no one listens to me. The government finally had to get into the act. There was a nationwide committee being formed of animators and other experts. We were supposed to look into the working conditions of local zombies.

Working conditions. They didn't understand. You can't give a corpse nice working conditions. They don't appreciate it anyway. Zombies may walk, even talk, but they are very, very dead.

Bert smiled indulgently at me. I fought an urge to pop him one right in his smug face. "I know you and Charles are working on that committee," Bert said. "Going around to all the businesses and checking up on the zombies. It makes great press for Animators, Inc."

"I don't do it for good press," I said.

"I know. You believe in your little cause."

"You're a condescending bastard," I said, smiling sweetly up at him.

He grinned at me. "I know."

I just shook my head; with Bert you can't really win an insult match. He doesn't give a damn what I think of him, as long as I work for him.

My navy blue suit jacket was supposed to be summer weight but it was a lie. Sweat trickled down my spine as soon as I stepped out of the car.

Bert turned to me, small eyes narrowing. His eyes lend themselves to suspicious squints. "You're still wearing your gun," he said.

"The jacket hides it, Bert. Mr. Gaynor will never know." Sweat started collecting under the straps of my shoulder holster. I could feel the silk blouse beginning to melt. I try not to wear silk and a shoulder rig at the same time. The silk starts to look indented, wrinkling where the straps cross. The gun was a Browning Hi-Power 9mm, and I liked having it near at hand.

"Come on, Anita. I don't think you'll need a gun in the middle of the afternoon, while visiting a client." Bert's voice held that patronizing tone that people use on children. Now, little girl, you know this is for your own good.

Bert didn't care about my well-being. He just didn't want to spook Gaynor. The man had already given us a check for five thousand dollars. And that was just to drive out and talk to him. The implication was that there was more money if we agreed to take his case. A lot of money. Bert was all excited about that part. I was skeptical. After all, Bert didn't have to raise the corpse. I did.

The trouble was, Bert was probably right. I wouldn't need the gun in broad daylight. Probably. "All right, open the trunk."

Bert opened the trunk of his nearly brand-new Volvo. I was already taking off the jacket. He stood in front of me, hiding me from the house. God forbid that they should see me hiding a gun in the trunk. What would they do, lock the doors and scream for help?

I folded the holster straps around the gun and laid it in the clean trunk.

It smelled like new car, plastic and faintly unreal. Bert shut the trunk, and I stared at it as if I could still see the gun.

"Are you coming?" he asked.

"Yeah," I said. I didn't like leaving my gun behind, for any reason. Was that a bad sign? Bert motioned for me to come on.

I did, walking carefully over the gravel in my high-heeled black pumps. Women may get to wear lots of pretty colors, but men get the comfortable shoes.

Bert was staring at the door, smile already set on his face. It was his best professional smile, dripping with sincerity. His pale grey eyes sparkled with good cheer. It was a mask. He could put it on and off like a light switch. He'd wear the same smile if you confessed to killing your own mother. As long as you wanted to pay to have her raised from the dead.

The door opened, and I knew Bert had been wrong about me not needing a gun. The man was maybe five-eight, but the orange polo shirt he wore strained over his chest. The black sport jacket seemed too small, as if when he moved the seams would split, like an insect's skin that had been outgrown. Black acid-washed jeans showed off a small waist, so he looked like someone had pinched him in the middle while the clay was still wet. His hair was very blond. He looked at us silently. His eyes were empty, dead as a doll's. I caught a glimpse of shoulder holster under the sport jacket and resisted an urge to kick Bert in the shins.

Either my boss didn't notice the gun or he ignored it. "Hello, I'm Bert Vaughn and this is my associate, Anita Blake. I believe Mr. Gaynor is expecting us." Bert smiled at him charmingly.

The bodyguard—what else could he be—moved away from the door. Bert took that for an invitation and walked inside. I followed, not at all sure I wanted to. Harold Gaynor was a very rich man. Maybe he needed a bodyguard. Maybe people had threatened him. Or maybe he was one of those men who have enough money to keep hired muscle around whether they need it or not.

Or maybe something else was going on. Something that needed guns and muscle, and men with dead, emotionless eyes. Not a cheery thought.

The air-conditioning was on too high and the sweat gelled instantly. We followed the bodyguard down a long central hall that was paneled in dark, expensive-looking wood. The hall runner looked oriental and was probably handmade.

Heavy wooden doors were set in the right-hand wall. The bodyguard opened the doors and again stood to one side while we walked through. The room was a library, but I was betting no one ever read any of the books. The place was ceiling to floor in dark wood bookcases. There was even a second level of books and shelves reached by an elegant sweep of narrow staircase. All the books were hardcover, all the same size, colors muted and collected together like a collage. The furniture was, of course, red leather with brass buttons worked into it.

A man sat near the far wall. He smiled when we came in. He was a large man with a pleasant round face, double-chinned. He was sitting in an electric wheelchair, with a small plaid blanket over his lap, hiding his legs.

"Mr. Vaughn and Ms. Blake, how nice of you to drive out." His voice went with his face, pleasant, damn near amiable.

A slender black man sat in one of the leather chairs. He was over six feet tall, exactly how much over was hard to tell. He was slumped down, long legs stretched out in front of him with the ankles crossed. His legs were taller than I was. His brown eyes watched me as if he were trying to memorize me and would be graded later.

The blond bodyguard went to lean against the bookcases. He couldn't quite cross his arms, jacket too tight, muscles too big. You really shouldn't lean against a wall and try to look tough unless you can cross your arms. Ruins the effect.

Mr. Gaynor said, "You've met Tommy." He motioned towards the sitting bodyguard. "That's Bruno."

"Is that your real name or just a nickname?" I asked, looking straight into Bruno's eyes.

He shifted just a little in his chair. "Real name."

I smiled.

"Why?" he asked.

"I've just never met a bodyguard who was really named Bruno."

"Is that supposed to be funny?" he asked.

I shook my head. Bruno. He never had a chance. It was like naming a girl Venus. All Brunos had to be bodyguards. It was a rule. Maybe a cop? Naw, it was a bad guy's name. I smiled.

Bruno sat up in his chair, one smooth, muscular motion. He wasn't wearing a gun that I could see, but there was a presence to him. Dangerous, it said, watch out.

Guess I shouldn't have smiled.

Bert interrupted, "Anita, please. I do apologize, Mr. Gaynor . . . Mr. Bruno. Ms. Blake has a rather peculiar sense of humor."

"Don't apologize for me, Bert. I don't like it." I don't know what he was so sore about anyway. I hadn't said the really insulting stuff out loud.

"Now, now," Mr. Gaynor said. "No hard feelings. Right, Bruno?"

Bruno shook his head and frowned at me, not angry, sort of perplexed.

Bert flashed me an angry look, then turned smiling to the man in the wheelchair. "Now, Mr. Gaynor, I know you must be a busy man. So, exactly how old is the zombie you want raised?"

"A man who gets right down to business. I like that." Gaynor hesitated, staring at the door. A woman entered.

She was tall, leggy, blond, with cornflower-blue eyes. The dress, if it was a dress, was rose-colored and silky. It clung to her body the way it was supposed to, hiding what decency demanded, but leaving very little to the imagination. Long pale legs were stuffed into pink spike heels, no hose. She stalked across the carpet, and every man in the room watched her. And she knew it.

She threw back her head and laughed, but no sound came out. Her face brightened, her lips moved, eyes sparkled, but in absolute silence, like someone had turned the sound off. She leaned one hip against Harold Gaynor, one hand on his shoulder. He encircled her waist, and the movement raised the already short dress another inch.

Could she sit down in the dress without flashing the room? Naw.

"This is Cicely," he said. She smiled brilliantly at Bert, that little soundless laugh making her eyes sparkle. She looked at me and her eyes faltered, the smile slipped. For a second uncertainty filled her eyes. Gaynor patted her hip. The smile flamed back into place. She nodded graciously to both of us.

"I want you to raise a two-hundred-and-eighty-three-year-old corpse."

I just stared at him and wondered if he understood what he was asking.

"Well," Bert said, "that is nearly three hundred years old. Very old to raise as a zombie. Most animators couldn't do it at all."

"I am aware of that," Gaynor said. "That is why I asked for Ms. Blake. She can do it."

Bert glanced at me. I had never raised anything that old. "Anita?"

"I could do it," I said.

He smiled back at Gaynor, pleased.

"But I won't do it."

Bert turned slowly back to me, smile gone.

Gaynor was still smiling. The bodyguards were immobile. Cicely looked pleasantly at me, eyes blank of any meaning.

"A million dollars, Ms. Blake," Gaynor said in his soft pleasant voice.

I saw Bert swallow. His hands convulsed on the chair arms. Bert's idea of sex was money. He probably had the biggest hard-on of his life.

"Do you understand what you're asking, Mr. Gaynor?" I asked.

He nodded. "I will supply the white goat." His voice was still pleasant as he said it, still smiling. Only his eyes had gone dark; eager, anticipatory.

I stood up. "Come on, Bert, it's time to leave."

Bert grabbed my arm. "Anita, sit down, please."

I stared at his hand until he let go of me. His charming mask slipped, showing me the anger underneath, then he was all pleasant business again. "Anita. It is a generous payment."

"The white goat is a euphemism, Bert. It means a human sacrifice."

My boss glanced at Gaynor, then back to me. He knew me well enough to believe me, but he didn't want to. "I don't understand," he said.

"The older the zombie the bigger the death needed to raise it. After a few centuries the only death 'big enough' is a human sacrifice," I said.

Gaynor wasn't smiling anymore. He was watching me out of dark eyes. Cicely was still looking pleasant, almost smiling. Was there anyone home behind those so blue eyes? "Do you really want to talk about murder in front of Cicely?" I asked.

Gaynor beamed at me, always a bad sign. "She can't understand a word we say. Cicely's deaf."

I stared at him, and he nodded. She looked at me with pleasant eyes. We were talking of human sacrifice and she didn't even know it. If she could read lips, she was hiding it very well. I guess even the handicapped, um, physically challenged, can fall into bad company, but it seemed wrong.

"I hate a woman who talks constantly," Gaynor said.

I shook my head. "All the money in the world wouldn't be enough to get me to work for you."

"Couldn't you just kill lots of animals, instead of just one?" Bert asked. Bert is a very good business manager. He knows shit about raising the dead.

I stared down at him. "No."

Bert sat very still in his chair. The prospect of losing a million dollars must have been real physical pain for him, but he hid it. Mr. Corporate Negotiator. "There has to be a way to work this out," he said. His voice was calm. A professional smile curled his lips. He was still trying to do business. My boss did not understand what was happening.

"Do you know of another animator that could raise a zombie this old?" Gaynor asked.

Bert glanced up at me, then down at the floor, then at Gaynor. The professional smile had faded. He understood now that it was murder we were talking about. Would that make a difference?

I had always wondered where Bert drew the line. I was about to find out. The fact that I didn't know whether he would refuse the contract told you a lot about my boss. "No," Bert said softly, "no, I guess I can't help you either, Mr. Gaynor."

"If it's the money, Ms. Blake, I can raise the offer."

A tremor ran through Bert's shoulders. Poor Bert, but he hid it well. Brownie point for him.

"I'm not an assassin, Gaynor," I said.

"That ain't what I heard," Tommy of the blond hair said.

I glanced at him. His eyes were still as empty as a doll's. "I don't kill people for money."

"You kill vampires for money," he said.

"Legal execution, and I don't do it for the money," I said.

Tommy shook his head and moved away from the wall. "I hear you like staking vampires. And you aren't too careful about who you have to kill to get to 'em."

"My informants tell me you have killed humans before, Ms. Blake," Gaynor said.

"Only in self-defense, Gaynor. I don't do murder."

Bert was standing now. "I think it is time to leave."

Bruno stood in one fluid movement, big dark hands loose and half-cupped at his sides. I was betting on some kind of martial arts.

Tommy was standing away from the wall. His sport jacket was pushed back to expose his gun, like an old-time gunfighter. It was a .357 Magnum. It would make a very big hole.

I just stood there, staring at them. What else could I do? I might be able to do something with Bruno, but Tommy had a gun. I didn't. It sort of ended the argument.

They were treating me like I was a very dangerous person. At five-three I am not imposing. Raise the dead, kill a few vampires, and people start considering you one of the monsters. Sometimes it hurt. But now . . . it had possibilities. "Do you really think I came in here unarmed?" I asked. My voice sounded very matter-of-fact.

Bruno looked at Tommy. He sort of shrugged. "I didn't pat her down." Bruno snorted.

"She ain't wearing a gun, though," Tommy said.

"Want to bet your life on it?" I said. I smiled when I said it, and slid my hand, very slowly, towards my back. Make them think I had a hip holster at the small of my back. Tommy shifted, flexing his hand near his gun. If he went for it, we were going to die. I was going to come back and haunt Bert.

Gaynor said, "No. No need for anyone to die here today, Ms. Blake."

"No," I said, "no need at all." I swallowed my pulse back into my throat and eased my hand away from my imaginary gun. Tommy eased away from his real one. Goody for us.

Gaynor smiled again, like a pleasant beardless Santa. "You of course understand that telling the police would be useless."

I nodded. "We have no proof. You didn't even tell us who you wanted raised from the dead, or why."

"It would be your word against mine," he said.

"And I'm sure you have friends in high places." I smiled when I said it.

His smile widened, dimpling his fat little cheeks. "Of course."

I turned my back on Tommy and his gun. Bert followed. We walked outside into the blistering summer heat. Bert looked a little shaken. I felt almost friendly towards him. It was nice to know that Bert had limits, something he wouldn't do, even for a million dollars.

"Would they really have shot us?" he asked. His voice sounded matter-of-fact, firmer than the slightly glassy look in his eyes. Tough Bert. He unlocked the trunk without being asked.

"With Harold Gaynor's name in our appointment book and in the computer?" I got my gun out and slipped on the holster rig. "Not knowing who we'd mentioned this trip to?" I shook my head. "Too risky."

"Then why did you pretend to have a gun?" He looked me straight in the eyes as he asked, and for the first time I saw uncertainty in his face. Ol' money bags needed a comforting word, but I was fresh out.

"Because, Bert, I could have been wrong."

2

The bridal shop was just off 70 West in St. Peters. It was called The Maiden Voyage. Cute. There was a pizza place on one side of it and a beauty salon on the other. It was called Full Dark Beauty Salon. The windows were blacked out, outlined in bloodred neon. You could get your hair and nails done by a vampire, if you wanted to.

Vampirism had only been legal for two years in the United States of America. We were still the only country in the world where it was legal. Don't ask me; I didn't vote for it. There was even a movement to give the vamps the vote. Taxation without representation and all that.

Two years ago if a vampire bothered someone I just went out and staked the son of a bitch. Now I had to get a court order of execution. Without it, I was up on murder charges, if I was caught. I longed for the good ol' days.

There was a blond mannequin in the wedding shop window wearing enough white lace to drown in. I am not a big fan of lace, or seed pearls, or sequins. Especially not sequins. I had gone out with Catherine twice to help her look for a wedding gown. It didn't take long to realize I was no help. I didn't like any of them.

Catherine was a very good friend or I wouldn't have been here at all. She told me if I ever got married I'd change my mind. Surely being in love doesn't cause you to lose your sense of good taste. If I ever buy a gown with sequins on it, someone just shoot me.

I also wouldn't have chosen the bridal dresses Catherine picked out, but it was my own fault that I hadn't been around when the vote was taken. I worked too much and I hated to shop. So, I ended up plunking down $120 plus tax on a pink taffeta evening gown. It looked like it had run away from a junior high prom.

I walked into the air-conditioned hush of the bridal shop, high heels sinking into a carpet so pale grey it was nearly white. Mrs. Cassidy, the manager, saw me come in. Her smile faltered for just a moment before she got it under control. She smiled at me, brave Mrs. Cassidy.

I smiled back, not looking forward to the next hour.

Mrs. Cassidy was somewhere between forty and fifty, trim figure, red hair so dark it was almost brown. The hair was tied in a French knot like Grace Kelly used to wear. She pushed her gold wire-framed glasses more securely on her nose and said, "Ms. Blake, here for the final fitting, I see."

"I hope it's the final fitting," I said.

"Well, we have been working on the . . . problem. I think we've come up with something." There was a small room in back of the desk. It was filled with racks of plastic-covered dresses. Mrs. Cassidy pulled mine out from between two identical pink dresses.

She led the way to the dressing rooms with the dress draped over her arms. Her spine was very straight. She was gearing for another battle. I didn't have to gear up, I was always ready for battle. But arguing with Mrs. Cassidy about alterations to a formal beat the heck out of arguing with Tommy and Bruno. It could have gone very badly, but it hadn't. Gaynor had called them off, for today, he had said.

What did that mean exactly? It was probably self-explanatory. I had left Bert at the office still shaken from his close encounter. He didn't deal with the messy end of the business. The violent end. No, I did that, or Manny, or Jamison, or Charles. We, the animators of Animators, Inc., we did the dirty work. Bert stayed in his nice safe office and sent clients and trouble our way. Until today.

Mrs. Cassidy hung the dress on a hook inside one of the dressing stalls and went away. Before I could go inside, another stall opened, and Kasey, Catherine's flower girl, stepped out. She was eight, and she was glowering. Her mother followed behind her, still in her business suit. Elizabeth (call me Elsie) Markowitz was tall, slender, black-haired, olive-skinned, and a lawyer. She worked with Catherine and was also in the wedding.

Kasey looked like a smaller, softer version of her mother. The child spotted me first and said, "Hi, Anita. Isn't this dress dumb-looking?"

"Now, Kasey," Elsie said, "it's a beautiful dress. All those nice pink ruffles."

The dress looked like a petunia on steroids to me. I stripped off my jacket and started moving into my own dressing room before I had to give my opinion out loud.

"Is that a real gun?" Kasey asked.

I had forgotten I was still wearing it. "Yes," I said.

"Are you a policewoman?"

"No."

"Kasey Markowitz, you ask too many questions." Her mother herded her past me with a harried smile. "Sorry about that, Anita."

"I don't mind," I said. Sometime later I was standing on a little raised platform in front of a nearly perfect circle of mirrors. With the matching pink high heels the dress was the right length at least. It also had little puff sleeves and was an off-the-shoulder look. The dress showed almost every scar I had.

The newest scar was still pink and healing on my right forearm. But it was just a knife wound. They're neat, clean things compared to my other scars. My collarbone and left arm have both been broken. A vampire bit through them, tore at me like a dog with a piece of meat. There's also the cross-shaped burn mark on my left forearm. Some inventive human vampire slaves thought it was amusing. I didn't.

I looked like Frankenstein's bride goes to the prom. Okay, maybe it wasn't that bad, but Mrs. Cassidy thought it was. She thought the scars would distract people from the dress, the wedding party, the bride. But Catherine, the bride herself, didn't agree. She thought I deserved to be in the wedding, because we were such good friends. I was paying good money to be publicly humiliated. We must be good friends.

Mrs. Cassidy handed me a pair of long pink satin gloves. I pulled them on, wiggling my fingers deep into the tiny holes. I've never liked gloves. They make me feel like I'm touching the world through a curtain. But the bright pink things did hide my arms. Scars all gone. What a good girl. Right.

The woman fluffed out the satiny skirt, glancing into the mirror. "It will do, I think." She stood, tapping one long, painted fingernail against her lipsticked mouth. "I believe I have come up with something to hide that, uh . . . well . . ." She made vague hand motions towards me.

"My collarbone scar?" I said.

"Yes." She sounded relieved.

It occurred to me for the first time that Mrs. Cassidy had never once said the word "scar." As if it were dirty, or rude. I smiled at myself in the ring of mirrors. Laughter caught at the back of my throat.

Mrs. Cassidy held up something made of pink ribbon and fake orange blossoms. The laughter died. "What is that?" I asked.

"This," she said, stepping towards me, "is the solution to our problem."

"All right, but what is it?"

"Well, it is a collar, a decoration."

"It goes around my neck?"

"Yes."

I shook my head. "I don't think so."

"Ms. Blake, I have tried everything to hide that, that . . . mark. Hats, hairdos, simple ribbons, corsages . . ." She literally threw up her hands. "I am at my wit's end."

This I could believe. I took a deep breath. "I sympathize with you, Mrs. Cassidy, really I do. I've been a royal pain in the ass."

"I would never say such a thing."

"I know, so I said it for you. But that is the ugliest piece of frou-frou I've ever laid eyes on."

"If you, Ms. Blake, have any better suggestions, then I am all ears." She half crossed her arms over her chest. The offending piece of "decoration" trailed nearly to her waist.

"It's huge," I protested.

"It will hide your"—she set her mouth tight—"scar."

I felt like applauding. She'd said the dirty word. Did I have any better suggestions? No. I did not. I sighed. "Put it on me. The least I can do is look at it."

She smiled. "Please lift your hair."

I did as I was told. She fastened it around my neck. The lace itched, the ribbons tickled, and I didn't even want to look in the mirror. I raised my eyes, slowly, and just stared.

"Thank goodness you have long hair. I'll style it myself the day of the wedding so it helps the camouflage."

The thing around my neck looked like a cross between a dog collar and the world's biggest wrist corsage. My neck had sprouted pink ribbons like mushrooms after a rain. It was hideous, and no amount of hairstyling was going to change that. But it hid the scar completely, perfectly. Ta-da.

I just shook my head. What could I say? Mrs. Cassidy took my silence for assent. She should have known better. The phone rang and saved us both. "I'll be just a minute, Ms. Blake." She stalked off, high-heels silent on the thick carpet.

I just stared at myself in the mirrors. My hair and eyes match, black hair, eyes so dark brown they look black. They are my mother's Latin darkness. But my skin is pale, my father's Germanic blood. Put some makeup on me and I look not unlike a china doll. Put me in a puffy pink dress and I look delicate, dainty, petite. Dammit.

The rest of the women in the wedding party were all five-five or above. Maybe some of them would actually look good in the dress. I doubted it.

Insult to injury, we all had to wear hoop skirts underneath. I looked like a reject from *Gone With the Wind*.

"There, don't you look lovely." Mrs. Cassidy had returned. She was beaming at me.

"I look like I've been dipped in Pepto-Bismol," I said.

Her smile faded around the edges. She swallowed. "You don't like this last idea." Her voice was very stiff.

Elsie Markowitz came out of the dressing rooms. Kasey was trailing behind, scowling. I knew how she felt. "Oh, Anita," Elsie said, "you look adorable."

Great. Adorable, just what I wanted to hear. "Thanks."

"I especially like the ribbons at your throat. We'll all be wearing them, you know."

"Sorry about that," I said.

She frowned at me. "I think they just set off the dress."

It was my turn to frown. "You're serious, aren't you?"

Elsie looked puzzled. "Well, of course I am. Don't you like the dresses?"

I decided not to answer on the grounds that it might piss someone off.

I guess, what can you expect from a woman who has a perfectly good name like Elizabeth, but prefers to be named after a cow?

"Is this the absolutely last thing we can use for camouflage, Mrs. Cassidy?" I asked.

She nodded, once, very firmly.

I sighed, and she smiled. Victory was hers, and she knew it. I knew I was beaten the moment I saw the dress, but if I'm going to lose, I'm going to make someone pay for it. "All right. It's done. This is it. I'll wear it."

Mrs. Cassidy beamed at me. Elsie smiled. Kasey smirked. I hiked the hoop skirt up to my knees and stepped off the platform. The hoop swung like a bell with me as the clapper.

The phone rang. Mrs. Cassidy went to answer it, a lift in her step, a song in her heart, and me out of her shop. Joy in the afternoon.

I was struggling to get the wide skirt through the narrow little door that led to the changing rooms when she called, "Ms. Blake, it's for you. A Detective Sergeant Storr."

"See, Mommy, I told you she was a policewoman," Kasey said.

I didn't explain because Elsie had asked me not to, weeks ago. She thought Kasey was too young to know about animators and zombies and vampire slayings. Not that any child of eight could not know what a vampire was. They were pretty much the media event of the decade.

I tried to put the phone to my left ear, but the damned flowers got in the way. Pressing the receiver in the bend of my neck and shoulder, I reached back to undo the collar. "Hi, Dolph, what's up?"

"Murder scene." His voice was pleasant, like he should sing tenor.

"What kind of murder scene?"

"Messy."

I finally pulled the collar free and dropped the phone.

"Anita, you there?"

"Yeah, having some wardrobe trouble."

"What?"

"It's not important. Why do you want me to come down to the scene?"

"Whatever did this wasn't human."

"Vampire?"

"You're the undead expert. That's why I want you to come take a look."

"Okay, give me the address, and I'll be right there." There was a notepad of pale pink paper with little hearts on it. The pen had a plastic cupid on the end of it. "St. Charles, I'm not more than fifteen minutes from you."

"Good." He hung up.

"Good-bye to you, too, Dolph." I said it to empty air just to feel superior. I went back into the little room to change.

I had been offered a million dollars today, just to kill someone and raise a zombie. Then off to the bridal shop for a final fitting. Now a murder scene. Messy, Dolph had said. It was turning out to be a very busy afternoon.

3

Messy, Dolph had called it. A master of understatement. Blood was every-where, splattered over the white walls like someone had taken a can of paint and thrown it. There was an off-white couch with brown and gold patterned flowers on it. Most of the couch was hidden under a sheet. The sheet was crimson. A bright square of afternoon sunlight came through the clean, spar-kling windows. The sunlight made the blood cherry-red, shiny.

Fresh blood is really brighter than you see it on television and the mov-ies. In large quantities. Real blood is screaming fire-engine red, in large quantities, but darker red shows up on the screen better. So much for realism.

Only fresh blood is red, true red. This blood was old and should have faded, but some trick of the summer sunshine kept it shiny and new.

I swallowed very hard and took a deep breath.

"You look a little green, Blake," a voice said almost at my elbow.

I jumped, and Zerbrowski laughed. "Did I scare ya?"

"No," I lied.

Detective Zerbrowski was about five-seven, curly black hair going grey, dark-rimmed glasses framed brown eyes. His brown suit was rumpled; his yellow and maroon tie had a smudge on it, probably from lunch. He was grinning at me. He was always grinning at me.

"I gotcha, Blake, admit it. Is our fierce vampire slayer gonna upchuck on the victims?"

"Putting on a little weight there, aren't you, Zerbrowski?"

"Ooh, I'm hurt," he said. He clutched hands to his chest, swaying a little. "Don't tell me you don't want my body, the way I want yours."

"Lay off, Zerbrowski. Where's Dolph?"

"In the master bedroom." Zerbrowski gazed up at the vaulted ceiling with its skylight. "Wish Katie and I could afford something like this."

"Yeah," I said. "It's nice." I glanced at the sheet-covered couch. The sheet clung to whatever was underneath, like a napkin thrown over spilled juice. There was something wrong with the way it looked. Then it hit me, there weren't enough bumps to make a whole human body. Whatever was under there was missing some parts.

The room sort of swam. I looked away, swallowing convulsively. It had been months since I had actually gotten sick at a murder scene. At least the air-conditioning was on. That was good. Heat always makes the smell worse.

"Hey, Blake, do you really need to step outside?" Zerbrowski took my arm as if to lead me towards the door.

"Thanks, but I'm fine." I looked him straight in his baby-browns and lied. He knew I was lying. I wasn't all right, but I'd make it.

He released my arm, stepped back, and gave me a mock salute. "I love a tough broad."

I smiled before I could stop it. "Go away, Zerbrowski."

"End of the hall, last door on the left. You'll find Dolph there." He walked away into the crowd of men. There are always more people than you need at a murder scene, not the gawkers outside but uniforms, plainclothes, technicians, the guy with the video camera. A murder scene was like a bee swarm, full of frenzied movement and damn crowded.

I threaded my way through the crowd. My plastic-coated ID badge was clipped to the collar of my navy-blue jacket. It was so the police would know I was on their side and hadn't just snuck in. It also made carrying a gun into a crowd of policemen safer.

I squeezed past a crowd that was gathered like a traffic jam beside a door in the middle of the hall. Voices came, disjointed, "Jesus, look at the blood . . . Have they found the body yet? . . . You mean what's left of it? . . . No."

I pushed between two uniforms. One said, "Hey!" I found a cleared space just in front of the last door on the left-hand side. I don't know how Dolph had done it but he was alone in the room. Maybe they were just finished in here.

He knelt in the middle of the pale brown carpet. His thick hands, encased in surgical gloves, were on his thighs. His black hair was cut so short it left his ears sort of stranded on either side of a large blunt face. He saw me and stood. He was six-eight, built big like a wrestler. The canopied bed behind him suddenly looked small.

Dolph was head of the police's newest task force, the spook squad. Official title was the Regional Preternatural Investigation Team, R-P-I-T, pronounced "rip it." It handled all supernatural crime. It was a place to dump the troublemakers. I never wondered what Zerbrowski had done to get on the spook squad. His sense of humor was too strange and absolutely merciless. But Dolph. He was the perfect policeman. I had always sort of figured he had offended someone high up, offended them by being too good at his job. Now that I could believe.

There was another sheet-covered bundle on the carpet beside him.

"Anita." He always talks like that, one word at a time.

"Dolph," I said.

He knelt between the canopy bed and the blood-soaked sheet. "You ready?"

"I know you're the silent type, Dolph, but could you tell me what I'm supposed to be looking for?"

"I want to know what you see, not what I tell you you're supposed to see."

For Dolph it was a speech. "Okay," I said, "let's do it."

He pulled back the sheet. It peeled away from the bloody thing underneath. I stood and I stared and all I could see was a lump of bloody meat. It could have been from anything: a cow, horse, deer. But human? Surely not.

My eyes saw it, but my brain refused what it was being shown. I squatted beside it, tucking my skirt under my thighs. The carpeting squeezed underfoot like rain had gotten to it, but it wasn't rain.

"Do you have a pair of gloves I can borrow? I left my crime scene gear at the office."

"Right jacket pocket." He lifted his hands in the air. There were blood marks on the gloves. "Help yourself. The wife hates me to get blood on the dry cleaning."

I smiled. Amazing. A sense of humor is mandatory at times. I had to reach across the remains. I pulled out two surgical gloves; one size fits all. The gloves always felt like they had powder in them. They didn't feel like gloves at all, more like condoms for your hands.

"Can I touch it without damaging evidence?"

"Yes."

I poked the side of it with two fingers. It was like poking a side of fresh beef. A nice, solid feel to it. My fingers traced the bumps of bone, ribs under the flesh. Ribs. Suddenly I knew what I was looking at. Part of the rib cage of a human being. There was the shoulder, white bone sticking out where the arm had been torn away. That was all. All there was. I stood too quickly and stumbled. The carpet squeeshed underfoot.

The room was suddenly very hot. I turned away from the body and found myself staring at the bureau. Its mirror was splattered so heavily with blood, it looked like someone had covered it in layers of red fingernail polish. Cherry Blossom Red, Carnival Crimson, Candy Apple.

I closed my eyes and counted very slowly to ten. When I opened them the room seemed cooler. I noticed for the first time that a ceiling fan was slowly turning. I was fine. Heap big vampire slayer. Ri-ight.

Dolph didn't comment as I knelt by the body again. He didn't even look at me. Good man. I tried to be objective and see whatever there was to see. But it was hard. I liked the remains better when I couldn't figure out what part of the body they were. Now all I could see was the bloody remains. All I could think of was this used to be a human body. "Used to be" was the operative phrase.

"No signs of a weapon that I can see, but the coroner will be able to tell you that." I reached out to touch it again, then stopped. "Can you help me raise it up so I can see inside the chest cavity? What's left of the chest cavity.''

Dolph dropped the sheet and helped me lift the remains. It was lighter than it looked. Raised on its side there was nothing underneath. All the vital organs that the ribs protect were gone. It looked for all the world like a side of beef ribs, except for the bones where the arm should have connected. Part of the collarbone was still attached.

"Okay,'' I said. My voice sounded breathy. I stood, holding my blood-spattered hands out to my sides. "Cover it, please.''

He did, and stood. "Impressions?''

"Violence, extreme violence. More than human strength. The body's been ripped apart by hand.''

"Why by hand?''

"No knife marks.'' I laughed, but it choked me. "Hell, I'd think some-one had used a saw on the body like butchering a cow, but the bones . . .'' I shook my head. "Nothing mechanical was used to do this.''

"Anything else?''

"Yeah, where is the rest of the fucking body?''

"Down the hall, second door on the left.''

"The rest of the body?'' The room was getting hot again.

"Just go look. Tell me what you see.''

"Dammit, Dolph, I know you don't like to influence your experts, but I don't like walking in there blind.''

He just stared at me.

"At least answer one question.''

"Maybe, what?''

"Is it worse than this?''

He seemed to think about that for a moment. "No, and yes.''

"Damn you.''

"You'll understand after you've seen it.''

I didn't want to understand. Bert had been thrilled that the police wanted to put me on retainer. He had told me I would gain valuable experience working with the police. All I had gained so far was a wider variety of nightmares.

Dolph walked ahead of me to the next chamber of horrors. I didn't really want to find the rest of the body. I wanted to go home. He hesitated in front of the closed door until I stood beside him. There was a cardboard cutout of a rabbit on the door like for Easter. A needlework sign hung just below the bunny. Baby's Room.

"Dolph,'' my voice sounded very quiet. The noise from the living room was muted.

"Yes.''

"Nothing, nothing.'' I took a deep breath and let it out. I could do this. I could do this. Oh, God, I didn't want to do this. I whispered a prayer under my breath as the door swung inward. There are moments in life when the only way to get through is with a little grace from on high. I was betting this was going to be one of them.

Sunlight streamed through a small window. The curtains were white with little duckies and bunnies stitched around the edges. Animal cutouts danced around the pale blue walls. There was no crib, only one of those beds with handrails halfway down. A big boy bed, wasn't that what they were called?

There wasn't as much blood in here. Thank you, dear God. Who says prayers never get answered? But in a square of bright August sunshine sat a stuffed teddy bear. The teddy bear was candy-coated with blood. One glassy eye stared round and surprised out of the spiky fake fur.

I knelt beside it. The carpet didn't squeeze, no blood soaked in. Why was the damn bear sitting here covered in congealing blood? There was no other blood in the entire room that I could see.

Did someone just set it here? I looked up and found myself staring at a small white chest of drawers with bunnies painted on it. When you have a motif, I guess you stick with it. On the white paint was one small, perfect handprint. I crawled towards it and held up my hand near it comparing size. My hands aren't big, small even for a woman's, but this handprint was tiny. Two, three, maybe four. Blue walls, probably a boy.

"How old was the child?"

"Picture in the living room has Benjamin Reynolds, age three, written on the back."

"Benjamin," I whispered it, and stared at the bloody handprint. "There's no body in this room. No one was killed here."

"No."

"Why did you want me to see it?" I looked up at him, still kneeling.

"Your opinion isn't worth anything if you don't see everything."

"That damn bear is going to haunt me."

"Me, too," he said.

I stood, resisting the urge to smooth my skirt down in back. It was amazing how many times I touched my clothing without thinking and smeared blood on myself. But not today.

"Is it the boy's body under the sheet in the living room?" As I said it, I prayed that it wasn't.

"No," he said.

Thank God. "Mother's body?"

"Yes."

"Where is the boy's body?"

"We can't find it." He hesitated, then asked, "Could the thing have eaten the child's body completely?"

"You mean so there wouldn't be anything left to find?"

"Yes," he said. His face looked just the tiniest bit pale. Mine probably did, too.

"Possible, but even the undead have a limit to what they can eat." I took a deep breath. "Did you find any signs of—regurgitation."

"Regurgitation." He smiled. "Nice word. No, the creature didn't eat and then vomit. At least we haven't found it."

"Then the boy's probably still around somewhere."

"Could he be alive?" Dolph asked.

I looked up at him. I wanted to say yes, but I knew the answer was probably no. I compromised. "I don't know."

Dolph nodded.

"The living room next?" I asked.

"No." He walked out of the room without another word. I followed. What else could I do? But I didn't hurry. If he wanted to play tough, silent policeman, he could damn well wait for me to catch up.

I followed his broad back around the corner through the living room into the kitchen. A sliding glass door led out onto a deck. Glass was everywhere. Shiny slivers of it sparkled in the light from yet another skylight. The kitchen was spotless, like a magazine ad, done in blue tile and rich light-colored wood. "Nice kitchen," I said.

I could see men moving around the yard. The party had moved outside. The privacy fence hid them from the curious neighbors, as it had hidden the killer last night. There was just one detective standing beside the shiny sink. He was scribbling something in a notebook.

Dolph motioned me to have a closer look. "Okay," I said. "Something crashed through the sliding glass door. It must have made a hell of a lot of noise. This much glass breaking even with the air-conditioning on . . . You'd hear it."

"You think so?" he asked.

"Did any of the neighbors hear anything?" I asked.

"No one will admit to it," he said.

I nodded. "Glass breaks, someone comes to check it out, probably the man. Some sexist stereotypes die hard."

"What do you mean?" Dolph asked.

"The brave hunter protecting his family," I said.

"Okay, say it was the man, what next?"

"Man comes in, sees whatever crashed through the window, yells for his wife. Probably tells her to get out. Take the kid and run."

"Why not call the police?" he asked.

"I didn't see a phone in the master bedroom." I nodded towards the phone on the kitchen wall. "This is probably the only phone. You have to get past the bogeyman to reach the phone."

"Go on."

I glanced behind me into the living room. The sheet-covered couch was just visible. "The thing, whatever it was, took out the man. Quick, disabled him, knocked him out, but didn't kill him."

"Why not kill?"

"Don't test me, Dolph. There isn't enough blood in the kitchen. He was eaten in the bedroom. Whatever did it wouldn't have dragged a dead man off to the bedroom. It chased the man into the bedroom and killed him there.''

"Not bad, want to take a shot at the living room next?''

Not really, but I didn't say it out loud. There was more left of the woman. Her upper body was almost intact. Paper bags enveloped her hands. We had samples of something under her fingernails. I hoped it helped. Her wide brown eyes stared up at the ceiling. The pajama top clung wetly to where her waist used to be. I swallowed hard and used my index finger and thumb to raise the pajama top.

Her spine glistened in the hard sunshine, wet and white and dangling, like a cord that had been ripped out of its socket.

Okay. "Something tore her apart, just like the . . . man in the bedroom.''

"How do you know it's a man?''

"Unless they had company, it has to be the man. They didn't have a visitor, did they?''

Dolph shook his head. "Not as far as we know.''

"Then it has to be the man. Because she still has all her ribs, and both arms.'' I tried to swallow the anger in my voice. It wasn't Dolph's fault. "I'm not one of your cops. I wish you'd stop asking me questions that you already have the answers to.''

He nodded. "Fair enough. Sometimes I forget you're not one of the boys.''

"Thank you for that.''

"You know what I mean.''

"I do, and I even know you mean it as a compliment, but can we finish discussing this outside, please?''

"Sure.'' He slipped off his bloody gloves and put them in a garbage sack that was sitting open in the kitchen. I did the same.

The heat fastened round me like melting plastic, but it felt good, clean somehow. I breathed in great lungfuls of hot, sweating air. Ah, summer.

"I was right though, it wasn't human?'' he asked.

There were two uniformed police officers keeping the crowd off the lawn and in the street. Children, parents, kids on bikes. It looked like a freaking circus.

"No, it wasn't human. There was no blood on the glass that it came through.''

"I noticed. What's the significance?''

"Most dead don't bleed, except for vampires.''

"Most?''

"Freshly dead zombies can bleed, but vampires bleed almost like a person.''

"You don't think it was a vampire then?''

"If it was, then it ate human flesh. Vampires can't digest solid food.''

"Ghoul?''

"Too far from a cemetery, and there'd be more destruction of the house. Ghouls would tear up furniture like wild animals.''

"Zombie?"

I shook my head. "I honestly don't know. There are such things as flesh-eating zombies. They're rare, but it happens."

"You told me that there have been three reported cases. Each time the zombies stay human longer and don't rot."

I smiled. "Good memory. That's right. Flesh-eating zombies don't rot, as long as you feed them. Or at least don't rot as quickly."

"Are they violent?"

"Not so far," I said.

"Are zombies violent?" Dolph asked.

"Only if told to be."

"What does that mean?" he asked.

"You can order a zombie to kill people if you're powerful enough."

"A zombie as a murder weapon?"

I nodded. "Something like that, yes."

"Who could do something like that?"

"I'm not sure that's what happened here," I said.

"I know. But who could do it?"

"Well, hell, I could, but I wouldn't. And nobody I know that could do it would do it."

"Let us decide that," he said. He had gotten his little notebook out.

"You really want me to give you names of friends so you can ask them if they happened to have raised a zombie and sent it to kill these people?"

"Please."

I sighed. "I don't believe this. All right, me, Manny Rodriguez, Peter Burke, and . . ." I stopped words already forming a third name.

"What is it?"

"Nothing. I just remembered that I've got Burke's funeral to go to this week. He's dead so I don't think he's a suspect."

Dolph was looking at me hard, suspicion plain on his face. "You sure this is all the names you want to give me?"

"If I think of anyone else, I'll let you know," I said. I was at my wide-eyed most sincere. See, nothing up my sleeve.

"You do that, Anita."

"Sure thing."

He smiled and shook his head. "Who are you protecting?"

"Me," I said. He looked puzzled. "Let's just say I don't want to get someone mad at me."

"Who?"

I looked up into the clear August sky. "You think we'll get rain?"

"Dammit, Anita, I need your help."

"I've given you my help," I said.

"The name."

"Not yet. I'll check it out, and if it looks suspicious, I promise to share it with you."

"Well, isn't that just generous of you?" A flush was creeping up his neck. I had never seen Dolph angry before. I feared I was about to.

"The first death was a homeless man. We thought he'd passed out from liquor and ghouls got him. We found him right next to a cemetery. Open and shut, right?" His voice was rising just a bit with each word.

"Next we find this couple, teenagers caught necking in the boy's car. Dead, still not too far from the cemetery. We called in an exterminator and a priest. Case closed." He lowered his voice, but it was like he had swallowed the yelling. His voice was strained and almost touchable with its anger.

"Now this. It's the same beastie, whatever the hell it is. But we are miles from the nearest frigging cemetery. It isn't a ghoul, and maybe if I had called you in with the first or even the second case, this wouldn't have happened. But I figure I'm getting good at this supernatural crap. I've had some experience now, but it isn't enough. It isn't nearly enough." His big hands were crushing his notebook.

"That's the longest speech I've ever heard you make," I said.

He half laughed. "I need the name, Anita."

"Dominga Salvador. She's the voodoo priest for the entire Midwest. But if you send police down there she won't talk to you. None of them will."

"But they'll talk to you?"

"Yes," I said.

"Okay, but I better hear something from you by tomorrow."

"I don't know if I can set up a meeting that soon."

"Either you do it, or I do it," he said.

"Okay, okay, I'll do it, somehow."

"Thanks, Anita. At least now we have someplace to start."

"It might not be a zombie at all, Dolph. I'm just guessing."

"What else could it be?"

"Well, if there had been blood on the glass, I'd say maybe a lycanthrope."

"Oh, great, just what I need—a rampaging shapeshifter."

"But there was no blood on the glass."

"So probably some kind of undead," he said.

"Exactly."

"You talk to this Dominga Salvador and give me a report ASAP."

"Aye, aye, Sergeant."

He made a face at me and walked back inside the house. Better him than me. All I had to do was go home, change clothes, and prepare to raise the dead. At full dark tonight I had three clients lined up or would that be lying down?

Ellen Grisholm's therapist thought it would be therapeutic for Ellen to confront her child-molesting father. The trouble was the father had been dead for several months. So I was going to raise Mr. Grisholm from the dead and let his daughter tell him what a son of a bitch he was. The therapist said it would be cleansing. I guess if you have a doctorate, you're allowed to say things like that.

The other two raisings were more usual; a contested will, and a prosecution's star witness that had had the bad taste to have a heart attack before testifying in court. They still weren't sure if the testimony of a zombie was admissible in court, but they were desperate enough to try, and to pay for the privilege.

I stood there in the greenish-brown grass. Glad to see the family hadn't been addicted to sprinklers. A waste of water. Maybe they had even recycled their pop cans, newspapers. Maybe they had been decent earth-loving citizens. Maybe not.

One of the uniforms lifted the yellow Do-Not-Cross tape and let me out. I ignored all the staring people and got in my car. It was a late-model Nova. I could have afforded something better but why bother? It ran.

The steering wheel was too hot to touch. I turned on the air-conditioning and let the car cool down. What I had told Dolph about Dominga Salvador had been true. She wouldn't talk to the police, but that hadn't been the reason I tried to keep her name out of it.

If the police came knocking on Señora Dominga's door, she'd want to know who sent them. And she'd find out. The Señora was the most powerful vaudun priest I had ever met. Raising a murderous zombie was just one of many things she could do, if she wanted to.

Frankly, there were things worse than zombies that could come crawling through your window some dark night. I knew as little about that side of the business as I could get away with. The Señora had invented most of it.

No, I did not want Dominga Salvador angry with me. So it looked like I was going to have to talk with her tomorrow. It was sort of like getting an appointment to see the godfather of voodoo. Or in this case the godmother. The trouble was this godmother was unhappy with me. Dominga had sent me invitations to her home. To her ceremonies. I had politely declined. I think my being a Christian disappointed her. So I had managed to avoid a face to face, until now.

I was going to ask the most powerful vaudun priest in the United States, maybe in all of North America, if she just happened to raise a zombie. And if that zombie just happened to be going around killing people, on her orders? Was I crazy? Maybe. It looked like tomorrow was going to be another busy day.

4

The alarm screamed. I rolled over swatting at the buttons on top of the digital clock. Surely to God, I'd hit the snooze button soon. I finally had to prop myself up on one elbow and actually open my eyes. I turned off the alarm and stared at the glowing numbers. 6:00 A.M. Shit. I'd only gotten home at three.

Why had I set the alarm for six? I couldn't remember. I am not at my best after only three hours of sleep. I lay back down in the still warm nest of sheets. My eyes were fluttering shut when I remembered. Dominga Salvador.

She had agreed to meet me at 7:00 A.M. today. Talk about a breakfast meeting. I struggled out of the sheet, and just sat on the side of the bed for a minute. The apartment was absolutely still. The only sound was the hush-hush of the air-conditioning. Quiet as a funeral.

I got up then, thoughts of blood-coated teddy bears dancing in my head.

Fifteen minutes later I was dressed. I always showered after coming in from work no matter how late it was. I couldn't stand the thought of going to bed between nice clean sheets smeared with dried chicken blood. Sometimes it's goat blood, but more often chicken.

I had compromised on the outfit, caught between showing respect and not melting in the heat. It would have been easy if I hadn't planned to carry a gun with me. Call me paranoid, but I don't leave home without it.

The acid washed jeans, jogging socks, and Nikes were easy. An Uncle Mike's inter-pants holster complete with a Firestar 9mm completed the outfit. The Firestar was my backup piece to the Browning Hi-Power. The Browning was far too bulky to put down an inter-pants holster, but the Firestar fit nicely.

Now all I needed was a shirt that would hide the gun, but leave it accessible to grab and shoot. This was harder than it sounded. I finally settled on a short, almost midriff top that just barely fell over my waistband. I turned in front of the mirror.

The gun was invisible as long as I didn't forget and raise my arms too high. The top, unfortunately, was a pale, pale pink. What had possessed me to buy this top, I really didn't remember. Maybe it had been a gift? I hoped so. The thought that I had actually spent money on anything pink was more than I could bear.

I hadn't opened the drapes at all yet. The entire apartment was in twilight. I had special-ordered very heavy drapes. I rarely saw sunlight, and I didn't miss it much. I turned on the light over my fish tank. The angelfish rose towards the top, mouths moving in slow-motion begging.

Fish are my idea of pets. You don't walk them, pick up after them, or have to housebreak them. Clean the tank occasionally, feed them, and they don't give a damn how many hours of overtime you work.

The smell of strong brewed coffee wafted through the apartment from my Mr. Coffee. I sat at my little two-seater kitchen table sipping hot, black Colombian vintage. Beans fresh from my freezer, ground on the spot. There was no other way to drink coffee. Though in a pinch I'll take it just about any way I can get it.

The doorbell chimed. I jumped, spilling coffee onto the table. Nervous? Me? I left my Firestar on the kitchen table instead of taking it to the door with me. See, I'm not paranoid. Just very, very careful.

I checked the peephole and opened the door. Manny Rodriguez stood in the doorway. He's about two inches taller than I am. His coal-black hair is streaked with grey and white. Thick waves of it frame his thin face and black mustache. He's fifty-two, and with one exception, I would still rather have him backing me in a dangerous situation than anyone else I know.

We shook hands, we always do that. His grip was firm and dry. He grinned at me, flashing very white teeth in his brown face. "I smell coffee."

I grinned back. "You know it's all I have for breakfast." He walked in, and I locked the door behind him, habit.

"Rosita thinks you don't take care of yourself." He dropped into a near-perfect imitation of his wife's scolding voice, a much thicker Mexican accent than his own. "She doesn't eat right, so thin. Poor Anita, no husband, not even a boyfriend." He grinned.

"Rosita sounds like my stepmother. Judith is sick with worry that I'll be an old maid."

"You're what, twenty-four?"

"Mm-uh."

He just shook his head. "Sometimes I do not understand women."

It was my turn to grin. "What am I, chopped liver?"

"Anita, you know I didn't mean . . ."

"I know, I'm one of the boys. I understand."

"You are better than any of the boys at work."

"Sit down. Let me pour coffee in your mouth before your foot fits in again."

"You are being difficult. You know what I meant." He stared at me out of his solid brown eyes, face very serious.

I smiled. "Yeah, I know what you meant."

I picked one of the dozen or so mugs from my kitchen cabinet. My favorite mugs dangled from a mug-tree on the countertop.

Manny sat down, sipping coffee, glancing at his cup. It was red with black letters that said, "I'm a coldhearted bitch but I'm good at it." He laughed coffee up his nose.

I sipped my own coffee from a mug decorated with fluffy baby penguins. I'd never admit it, but it is my favorite mug.

"Why don't you bring your penguin mug to work?" he asked.

Bert's latest brainstorm was that we all use personalized coffee cups at work. He thought it would add a homey note to the office. I had brought in a grey on grey cup that said, "It's a dirty job and I get to do it." Bert had made me take it home.

"I enjoy yanking Bert's chain."

"So you're going to keep bringing in unacceptable cups."

I smiled. "Mm-uh."

He just shook his head.

"I really appreciate you coming to see Dominga with me."

He shrugged. "I couldn't let you go see the devil woman alone, could I?"

I frowned at the nickname, or was it an insult? "That's what your wife calls Dominga, not what I call her."

He glanced down at the gun still lying on the tabletop. "But you'll take a gun with you, just in case."

I looked at him over the top of my cup. "Just in case."

"If it comes to shooting our way out, Anita, it will be too late. She has bodyguards all over the place."

"I don't plan to shoot anybody. We are just going to ask a few questions. That's all."

He smirked. "*Por favor*, Señora Salvador, did you raise a killer zombie recently?"

"Knock it off, Manny. I know it's awkward."

"Awkward?" He shook his head. "Awkward, she says. If you piss off Dominga Salvador, it's a hell of a lot more than just awkward."

"You don't have to come."

"You called me for backup." He smiled that brilliant teeth-flashing smile that lit up his entire face. "You didn't call Charles or Jamison. You called me, and, Anita, that is the best compliment you could give an old man."

"You're not an old man." And I meant it.

"That is not what my wife keeps telling me. Rosita has forbidden me to go vampire hunting with you, but she can't curtail my zombie-related activities, not yet anyway."

The surprise must have shone on my face, because he said, "I know she talked to you two years back, when I was in the hospital."

"You almost died," I said.

"And you had how many broken bones?"

"Rosita made a reasonable request, Manny. You have four children to think of."

"And I'm too old to be slaying vampires." His voice held irony, and almost bitterness.

"You'll never be too old," I said.

"A nice thought." He drained his coffee mug. "We better go. Don't want to keep the Señora waiting."

"God forbid," I said.

"Amen," he said.

I stared at him as he rinsed his mug out in the sink. "Do you know something you're not telling me?"

"No," he said.

I rinsed my own cup, still staring at him. I could feel a suspicious frown between my eyes. "Manny?"

"Honest Mexican, I don't know nuthin'."

"Then what's wrong?"

"You know I was vaudun before Rosita converted me to pure Christianity."

"Yeah, so?"

"Dominga Salvador was not just my priestess. She was my lover."

I stared at him for a few heartbeats. "You're kidding?"

His face was very serious as he said, "I wouldn't joke about something like that."

I shrugged. People's choices of lovers never failed to amaze me. "That's why you could get me a meeting with her on such short notice."

He nodded.

"Why didn't you tell me before?"

"Because you might have tried to sneak over there without me."

"Would that have been so bad?"

He just stared at me, brown eyes very serious. "Maybe."

I got my gun from the table and fitted it to the inter-pants holster. Eight bullets. The Browning could hold fourteen. But let's get real; if I needed more than eight bullets, I was dead. And so was Manny.

"Shit," I whispered.

"What?"

"I feel like I'm going to visit the bogeyman."

Manny made a back and forth motion with his head. "Not a bad analogy."

Great, just freaking, bloody great. Why was I doing this? The image of Benjamin Reynolds's blood-coated teddy bear flashed into my mind. All right, I knew why I was doing it. If there was even a remote chance that the boy could still be alive, I'd go into hell itself—if I stood a chance of coming back out. I didn't mention this out loud. I did not want to know if hell was a good analogy, too.

5

The neighborhood was older houses; fifties, forties. The lawns were dying to brown for lack of water. No sprinklers here. Flowers struggled to survive in beds close to the houses. Mostly petunias, geraniums, a few rosebushes. The streets were clean, neat, and one block over you could get yourself shot for wearing the wrong color of jacket.

Gang activity stopped at Señora Salvador's neighborhood. Even teenagers with automatic pistols fear things you can't stop with bullets no matter how good a shot you are. Silver-plated bullets will harm a vampire, but not kill it. It will kill a lycanthrope, but not a zombie. You can hack the damn things to pieces, and the disconnected body parts will crawl after you. I've seen it. It ain't pretty. The gangs leave the Señora's turf alone. No violence. It is a place of permanent truce.

There are stories of one Hispanic gang that thought it had protection against gris-gris. Some people say that the gang's ex-leader is still down in Dominga's basement, obeying an occasional order. He was great show-and-tell to any juvenile delinquents who got out of hand.

Personally, I had never seen her raise a zombie. But then I'd never seen her call the snakes either. I'd just as soon keep it that way.

Señora Salvador's two-story house is on about a half acre of land. A nice roomy yard. Bright red geraniums flamed against the whitewashed walls. Red and white, blood and bone. I was sure the symbolism was not lost on casual passersby. It certainly wasn't lost on me.

Manny parked his car in the driveway behind a cream-colored Impala. The two-car garage was painted white to match the house. There was a little girl of about five riding a tricycle furiously up and down the sidewalk. A slightly older pair of boys were sitting on the steps that led up to the porch. They stopped playing and looked at us.

A man stood on the porch behind them. He was wearing a shoulder holster over a sleeveless blue T-shirt. Sort of blatant. All he needed was a flashing neon sign that said "Bad Ass."

There were chalk markings on the sidewalk. Pastel crosses and unreadable diagrams. It looked like a children's game, but it wasn't. Some devoted fans of the Señora had chalked designs of worship in front of her house. Stubs of candles had melted to lumps around the designs. The girl on the tricycle peddled back and forth over the designs. Normal, right?

I followed Manny over the sun-scorched lawn. The little girl on the tricycle was watching us now, small brown face unreadable.

Manny removed his sunglasses and smiled up at the man. "*Buenos días,* Antonio. It has been a long time."

"*Sí,*" Antonio said. His voice was low and sullen. His deeply tanned arms were crossed loosely over his chest. It put his right hand right next to his gun butt.

I used Manny's body to shield me from sight and casually put my hands close to my own gun. The Boy Scout motto, "Always be prepared." Or was that the Marines?

"You've become a strong, handsome man," Manny said.

"My grandmother says I must let you in," Antonio said.

"She is a wise woman," Manny said.

Antonio shrugged. "She is the Señora." He peered around Manny at me. "Who is this?"

"Señorita Anita Blake." Manny stepped back so I could move forward. I did, right hand loose on my waist like I had an attitude, but it was the closest I could stay to my gun.

Antonio looked down at me. His dark eyes were angry, but that was all. He didn't have near the gaze of Harold Gaynor's bodyguards. I smiled. "Nice to meet you."

He squinted at me suspiciously for a moment, then nodded. I continued to smile at him, and a slow smile spread over his face. He thought I was flirting with him. I let him think it.

He said something in Spanish. All I could do was smile and shake my head. He spoke softly, and there was a look in his dark eyes, a curve to his mouth. I didn't have to speak the language to know I was being propositioned. Or insulted.

Manny's neck was stiff, his face flushed. He said something from between clenched teeth.

It was Antonio's turn to flush. His hand started to go for his gun. I stepped up two steps, touching his wrist as if I didn't know what was going on. The tension in his arm was like a wire, straining.

I beamed up at him as I held his wrist. His eyes flicked from Manny to me, then the tension eased, but I didn't let go of his wrist until his arm fell to his side. He raised my hand to his lips, kissing it. His mouth lingered on the back of my hand, but his eyes stayed on Manny. Angry, rage-filled.

Antonio carried a gun, but he was an amateur. Amateurs with guns eventually get themselves killed. I wondered if Dominga Salvador knew that?

She may have been a whiz at voodoo but I bet she didn't know much about guns, and what it took to use one on a regular basis. Whatever it took, Antonio didn't have it. He'd kill you all right. No sweat. But for the wrong reasons. Amateur's reasons. Of course, you'll be just as dead.

He guided me up on the porch beside him, still holding my hand. It was my left hand. He could hold that all day. "I must check you for weapons, Manuel."

"I understand," Manny said. He stepped up on the porch and Antonio stepped back, keeping room between them in case Manny jumped him. That left me with a clear shot of Antonio's back. Careless; under different circumstances, deadly.

He made Manny lean against the porch railing like a police frisk. Antonio knew what he was doing, but it was an angry search, lots of quick jerky hand movements, as if just touching Manny's body enraged him. A lot of hate in old Tony.

It never occurred to him to pat me down for weapons. Tsk-tsk.

A second man came to the screen door. He was in his late forties, maybe. He was wearing a white undershirt with a plaid shirt unbuttoned over it. The sleeves were folded back as far as they'd go. Sweat stood out on his forehead. I was betting there was a gun at the small of his back. His black hair had a pure white streak just over the forehead. "What is taking so long, Antonio?" His voice was thick and held an accent.

"I searched him for weapons."

The older man nodded. "She is ready to see you both."

Antonio stood to one side, taking up his post on the porch once more. He made a kissing noise as I walked past. I felt Manny stiffen, but we made it into the living room without anyone getting shot. We were on a roll.

The living room was spacious, with a dining-room set taking up the left-hand side. There was a wall piano in the living room. I wondered who played. Antonio? Naw.

We followed the man through a short hallway into a roomy kitchen. Golden oblongs of sunshine lay heavy on a black and white tiled floor. The floor and kitchen were old, but the appliances were new. One of those deluxe refrigerators with an ice maker and water dispenser took up a hunk of the back wall. All the appliances were done in a pale yellow: Harvest Gold, Autumn Bronze.

Sitting at the kitchen table was a woman in her early sixties. Her thin brown face was seamed with a lot of smile lines. Pure white hair was done in a bun at the nape of her neck. She sat very straight in her chair, thin-boned hands folded on the tabletop. She looked terribly harmless. A nice old granny. If a quarter of what I'd heard about her was true, it was the greatest camouflage I'd ever seen.

She smiled and held out her hands. Manny stepped forward and took the offering, brushing his lips on her knuckles. "It is good to see you, Manuel." Her voice was rich, a contralto with the velvet brush of an accent.

"And you, Dominga." He released her hands and sat across from her.

Her quick black eyes flicked to me, still standing in the doorway. "So, Anita Blake, you have come to me at last."

It was a strange thing to say. I glanced at Manny. He gave a shrug with his eyes. He didn't know what she meant either. Great. "I didn't know you were eagerly awaiting me, Señora."

"I have heard stories of you, *chica*. Wondrous stories." There was a hint in those black eyes, that smiling face, that was not harmless.

"Manny?" I asked.

"It wasn't me."

"No, Manuel does not talk to me anymore. His little wife forbids it." That last sentence was angry, bitter.

Oh, God. The most powerful voodoo priestess in the Midwest was acting like a scorned lover. Shit.

She turned those angry black eyes to me. "All who deal in vaudun come to Señora Salvador eventually."

"I do not deal in vaudun."

She laughed at that. All the lines in her face flowed into the laughter. "You raise the dead, the zombie, and you do not deal in vaudun. Oh, *chica,* that is funny." Her voice sparkled with genuine amusement. So glad I could make her day.

"Dominga, I told you why we wished this meeting. I made it very clear . . ." Manny said.

She waved him to silence. "Oh, you were very careful on the phone, Manuel." She leaned towards me. "He made it very clear that you were not here to participate in any of my pagan rituals." The bitterness in her voice was sharp enough to choke on.

"Come here, *chica,*" she said. She held out one hand to me, not both. Was I supposed to kiss it as Manny had done. I didn't think I'd come to see the pope.

I realized then that I didn't want to touch her. She had done nothing wrong. Yet, the muscles in my shoulders were screaming with tension. I was afraid, and I didn't know why.

I stepped forward and took her hand, uncertain what to do with it. Her skin was warm and dry. She sort of lowered me to the chair closest to her, still holding my hand. She said something in her soft, deep voice.

I shook my head. "I'm sorry, I don't understand Spanish."

She touched my hair with her free hand. "Black hair like the wing of a crow. It does not come from any pale skin."

"My mother was Mexican."

"Yet you do not speak her tongue."

She was still holding my hand, and I wanted it back. "She died when I was young. I was raised by my father's people."

"I see."

I pulled my hand free and instantly felt better. She had done nothing to me. Nothing. Why was I so damn jumpy? The man with the streaked hair had taken up a post behind the Señora. I could see him clearly. His hands were in plain sight. I could see the back door and the entrance to the kitchen. No one was sneaking up behind me. But the hair at the base of my skull was standing at attention.

I glanced at Manny, but he was staring at Dominga. His hands were gripped together on the tabletop so tightly that his knuckles were mottled.

I felt like someone at a foreign film festival without subtitles. I could sort of guess what was going on, but I wasn't sure I was right. The creeping skin on my neck told me some hocus-pocus was going on. Manny's reaction said that just maybe the hocus-pocus was meant for him.

Manny's shoulders slumped. His hands relaxed their awful tension. It was a visible release of some kind. Dominga smiled, a brilliant flash of teeth. "You could have been so powerful, *mi corazón*."

"I did not want the power, Dominga," he said.

I stared from one to the other, not exactly sure what had just happened. I wasn't sure I wanted to know. I was willing to believe that ignorance was bliss. It so often is.

She turned her quick black eyes to me. "And you, *chica,* do you want power?" The creeping sensation at the base of my skull spread over my body. It felt like insects marching on my skin. Shit.

"No." A nice simple answer. Maybe I should try those more often.

"Perhaps not, but you will."

I didn't like the way she said that. It was ridiculous to be sitting in a sunny kitchen at 7:28 in the morning, and be scared. But there it was. My gut was twitching with it.

She stared at me. Her eyes were just eyes. There was none of that seductive power of a vampire. They were just eyes, and yet . . . The hair on my neck tried to crawl down my spine. Goose bumps broke out on my body, a rush of prickling warmth. I licked my lips and stared at Dominga Salvador.

It was a slap of magic. She was testing me. I'd had it done before. People are so fascinated with what I do. Convinced that I know magic. I don't. I have an affinity with the dead. It's not the same.

I stared into her nearly black eyes and felt myself sway forward. It was like falling without movement. The world sort of swung for a moment, then steadied. Warmth burst out of my body, like a twisting rope of heat. It went outward to the old woman. It hit her solid, and I felt it like a jolt of electricity.

I stood up, gasping for air. "Shit!"

"Anita, are you all right?" Manny was standing now, too. He touched my arm gently.

"I'm not sure. What the hell did she do to me?"

"It is what you have done to me, *chica,*" Dominga said. She looked a little pale around the edges. Sweat beaded on her forehead.

The man stood away from the wall, his hands loose and ready. "No," Dominga said, "Enzo, I am all right." Her voice was breathy as if she had been running.

I stayed standing. I wanted to go home now, please.

"We did not come here for games, Dominga," Manny said. His voice had deepened with anger and, I think, fear. I agreed with that last emotion.

"It is not a game, Manuel. Have you forgotten everything I taught you. Everything you were?"

"I have forgotten nothing, but I did not bring her here to be harmed."

"Whether she is harmed or not is up to her, *mi corazón.*"

I didn't much like that last part. "You're not going to help us. You're just going to play cat and mouse. Well, this mouse is leaving." I turned to leave, keeping a watchful eye on Enzo. He wasn't an amateur.

"Don't you wish to find the little boy that Manny said was taken? Three years old, very young to be in the hands of the bokor."

It stopped me. She knew it would. Damn her. "What is a bokor?"

She smiled. "You really don't know, do you?"

I shook my head.

The smile widened, all surprised pleasure. "Place your right hand palm up on the table, *por favor.*"

"If you know something about the boy, just tell me. Please."

"Endure my little tests, and I will help you."

"What sort of tests?" I hoped I sounded as suspicious as I felt.

Dominga laughed, an abrupt and cheery sound. It went with all the smile lines in her face. Her eyes were practically sparkling with mirth. Why did I feel like she was laughing at me?

"Come, *chica,* I will not hurt you," she said.

"Manny?"

"If she does anything that may harm you, I will say so."

Dominga gazed up at me, a sort of puzzled wonder on her face. "I have heard that you can raise three zombies in a night, night after night. Yet, you truly are a novice."

"Ignorance is bliss," I said.

"Sit, *chica.* This will not hurt, I promise."

This will not hurt. It promised more painful things later. I sat. "Any delay could cost the boy his life." Try to appeal to her good side.

She leaned towards me. "Do you really think the child is still alive?" Guess she didn't have a good side.

I leaned back from her. I couldn't help it, and I couldn't lie to her. "No."

"Then we have time, don't we?"

"Time for what?"

"Your hand, *chica, por favor*, then I will answer your questions."

I took a deep breath and placed my right hand on the table, palm up. She was being mysterious. I hated people who were mysterious.

She brought a small black bag from under the table, as if it had been sitting in her lap the whole time. Like she'd planned this.

Manny was staring at the bag like something noisome was about to crawl out. Close. Dominga Salvador pulled something noisome out of it.

It was a charm, a gris-gris made of black feathers, bits of bone, a mummified bird's foot. I thought at first it was a chicken until I saw the thick black talons. There was a hawk or eagle out there somewhere with a peg leg.

I had visions of her digging the talons into my flesh, and was all tensed to pull away. But she simply placed the gris-gris on my open palm. Feathers, bits of bone, the dried hawk foot. It wasn't slimy. It didn't hurt. In fact, I felt a little silly.

Then I felt it, warmth. The thing was warm, sitting there in my hand. It hadn't been warm a second ago. "What are you doing to it?"

Dominga didn't answer. I glanced up at her, but her eyes were staring at my hand, intent. Like a cat about to pounce.

I glanced back down. The talons flexed, then spread, then flexed. It was moving in my hand. "Shiiit!" I wanted to stand up. To fling the vile thing to the floor. But I didn't. I sat there with every hair on my body tingling, my pulse thudding in my throat, and let the thing move in my hand. "All right," my voice sounded breathy, "I've passed your little test. Now get this thing the hell out of my hand."

Dominga lifted the claw gently from my hand. She was careful not to touch my skin. I didn't know why, but it was a noticeable effort.

"Dammit, dammit!" I whispered under my breath. I rubbed my hand against my stomach, touching the gun hidden there. It was comforting to know that if worse came to worst, I could just shoot her. Before she scared me to death. "Can we get down to business now?" My voice sounded almost steady. Bully for me.

Dominga was cradling the claw in her hands. "You made the claw move. You were frightened, but not surprised. Why?"

What could I say? Nothing I wanted her to know. "I have an affinity with the dead. It responds to me like some people can read thoughts."

She smiled. "Do you really believe that your ability to raise the dead is like mind reading? Parlor tricks?"

Dominga had obviously never met a really good telepath. If she had, she wouldn't have been scornful. In their own way, they were just as scary as she was.

"I raise the dead, Señora. It is just a job."

"You do not believe that any more than I do."

"I try real hard," I said.

"You've been tested before by someone." She made it a statement.

"My grandmother on my mother's side tested me, but not with that." I pointed to the still flexing foot. It looked like one of those fake hands that you can buy at Spencer's. Now that I wasn't holding it, I could pretend it just had tiny little batteries in it somewhere. Right.

"She was vaudun?"

I nodded.

"Why did you not study with her?"

"I have an inborn gift for raising the dead. That doesn't dictate my religious preferences."

"You are Christian." She made the word sound like something bad.

"That's it." I stood. "I wish I could say it's been a pleasure, but it hasn't."

"Ask your questions, *chica*."

"What?" The change of subject was too fast for me.

"Ask whatever you came here to ask," she said.

I glanced at Manny. "If she says she will answer, she will answer." He didn't look completely happy about it.

I sat down, again. The next insult and I'm outta here. But if she could really help . . . oh, hell, she was dangling that thin little thread of hope. And after what I'd seen at the Reynolds' house, I was grabbing for it.

I had planned to be as polite as possible on the wording of the question, now I didn't give a shit. "Have you raised a zombie in the last few weeks?"

"Some," she said.

Okay. I hesitated over the next question. The feel of that thing moving in my hand flashed back on me. I rubbed my hand against my pants leg as if I could rub the sensation away. What was the worst she could do to me if I offended her? Don't ask. "Have you sent any zombies out on errands . . . of revenge?" There; that was polite, amazing.

"None."

"Are you sure?" I asked.

She smiled. "I'd remember if I loosed murderers from the grave."

"Killer zombies don't have to be murderers," I said.

"Oh?" Her pale eyebrows raised. "Are you so very familiar with raising 'killer' zombies?"

I fought the urge to squirm like a schoolchild caught at a lie. "Only one."

"Tell me."

"No." My voice was very firm. "No, that is a private matter." A private nightmare that I was not going to share with the voodoo lady.

I decided to change the subject just a little. "I've raised murderers before. They weren't more violent than regular undead."

"How many dead have you called from the grave?" she asked.

I shrugged. "I don't know."

"Give me an"—she seemed to be groping for a word—"estimation."

"I can't. It must have been hundreds."

"A thousand?" she asked.

"Maybe, I haven't kept count," I said.

"Has your boss at Animators, Incorporated, kept count?"

"I would assume that all my clients are on file, yes," I said.

She smiled. "I would be interested in knowing the exact number."

What could it hurt? "I'll find out if I can."

"Such an obedient girl." She stood. "I did not raise this 'killer' zombie of yours. If that is what is eating citizens." She smiled, almost laughed, as if it were funny. "But I know people that would never speak to you. People that could do this horrible deed. I will question them, and they will answer me. I will have truth from them, and I will pass this truth on to you, Anita."

She said my name like it was meant to be said, Ahneetah. Made it sound exotic.

"Thank you very much, Señora Salvador."

"But there is one favor I will ask in return for this information," she said.

Something unpleasant was about to be said, I'd have bet on it. "What would that favor be, Señora?"

"I want you to pass one more test for me."

I stared at her, waiting for her to go on, but she didn't. "What sort of test?" I asked.

"Come downstairs, and I will show you." Her voice was mild as honey.

"No, Dominga," Manny said. He was standing now. "Anita, nothing the Señora could tell you would be worth what she wants."

"I can talk to people and things that will not talk to you, either of you. Good Christians that you are."

"Come on, Anita, we don't need her help." He had started for the door. I didn't follow him. Manny hadn't seen the slaughtered family. He hadn't dreamed about blood-coated teddy bears last night. I had. I couldn't leave if she could help me. Whether Benjamin Reynolds was dead or not wasn't the point. The thing, whatever it was, would kill again. And I was betting it had something to do with voodoo. It wasn't my area. I needed help, and I needed it fast.

"Anita, come on." He touched my arm, pulling me a little towards the door.

"Tell me about the test."

Dominga smiled triumphantly. She knew she had me. She knew I wasn't leaving until I had her promised help. Damn.

"Let us retire to the basement. I will explain the test there."

Manny's grip on my arm tightened. "Anita, you don't know what you're doing."

He was right, but . . . "Just stay with me, Manny, back me up. Don't let me do anything that will really hurt. Okay?"

"Anita, anything she wants you to do down there will hurt. Maybe not physically, but it will hurt."

"I have to do this, Manny." I patted his hand and smiled. "It'll be all right."

"No," he said, "it won't be."

I didn't know what to say to that, except that he was probably right. But it didn't matter. I was going to do it. Whatever she asked, within reason, if it would stop the killings. If it would fix it so that I never had to see another half-eaten body.

Dominga smiled. "Let us go downstairs."

"May I speak with Anita alone, Señora, *por favor*," Manny said. His hand was still on my arm. I could feel the tension in his hand.

"You will have the rest of this beautiful day to talk to her, Manuel. But

I have only this short time. If she does this test for me now, I promise to aid her in any way I can to catch this killer.''

It was a powerful offer. A lot of people would talk to her just out of pure terror. The police can't inspire that. All they can do is arrest you. It wasn't enough of a deterrent. Having the undead crawl through your window . . . that was a deterrent.

Four, maybe five people were already dead. It was a bad way to die. ''I've already said I'd do it. Let's go.''

She walked around the table and took Manny's arm. He jumped like she'd struck him. She pulled him away from me. ''No harm will come to her, Manuel. I swear.''

''I do not trust you, Dominga.''

She laughed. ''But it is her choice, Manuel. I have not forced her.''

''You have blackmailed her, Dominga. Blackmailed her with the safety of others.''

She looked back over her shoulder. ''Have I blackmailed you, *chica*?''

''Yes,'' I said.

''Oh, she is your student, *corazón*. She has your honesty. And your bravery.''

''She is brave, but she has not seen what lies below.''

I wanted to ask what exactly was in the basement, but I didn't. I really didn't want to know. I've had people warn me about supernatural shit before. Don't go in that room; the monster will get you. There usually is a monster, and it usually tries to get me. But up till now I've been faster or luckier than the monsters. Here's to my luck holding.

I wished that I could heed Manny's warning. Going home sounded very good about now, but duty reared its ugly head. Duty and a whisper of nightmares. I didn't want to see another butchered family.

Dominga led Manny from the room. I followed with Enzo bringing up the rear. What a day for a parade.

6

The basement stairs were steep, wooden slats. You could feel the vibrations in the stairs as we tromped down them. It was not comforting. The bright sunlight from the door spilled into absolute darkness. The sunlight faltered, seemed to fade as if it had no power in this cavelike place. I stopped on the grey edge of daylight, staring down into the night-dark of the room. I couldn't even make out Dominga and Manny. They had to be just in front of me, didn't they?

Enzo the bodyguard waited at my back like some patient mountain. He made no move to hurry me. Was it my decision then? Could I just pack up my toys and go home?

"Manny," I called.

A voice came distantly. Too far away. Maybe it was an acoustic trick of the room. Maybe not. "I'm here, Anita."

I strained to see where the voice was coming from, but there was nothing to see. I took two steps farther down into the inky dark and stopped like I'd hit a wall. There was the damp rock smell of most basements, but under that something stale, sour, sweet. That almost indescribable smell of corpses. It was faint here at the head of the stairs. I was betting it would get worse the farther down I went.

My grandmother had been a priestess of vaudun. Her Humfo had not smelled like corpses. The line between good and evil wasn't as clear cut in voodoo as in Wicca or Christianity and satanism, but it was there. Dominga Salvador was on the wrong side of the line. I had known that when I came. It still bothered me.

Grandmother Flores had told me that I was a necromancer. It was more than being a voodoo priestess, and less. I had a sympathy with the dead, all dead. It was hard to be vaudun and a necromancer and not be evil. Too tempting, Grandma said. She had encouraged my being Christian. Encouraged my father to cut me off from her side of the family. Encouraged it for love of me and fear for my soul.

And here I was going down the steps into the jaws of temptation. What would Grandma Flores say to that? Probably, go home. Which was good advice. The tight feeling in my stomach was saying the same thing.

The lights came on. I blinked on the stairs. The one dim bulb at the foot of the staircase seemed as bright as a star. Dominga and Manny stood just under the bulb, looking up at me.

Light. Why did I feel instantly better? Silly, but true. Enzo let the door swing shut behind us. The shadows were thick, but down a narrow bricked hallway more bare light bulbs dangled.

I was almost at the bottom of the stairs. That sweet, sour smell was stronger. I tried breathing through my mouth, but that only made it clog the back of my throat. The smell of rotting flesh clings to the tongue.

Dominga led the way between the narrow walls. There were regular patches in the walls. Places where it looked like cement had been put over— doors. Paint had been smoothed over the cement, but there had been doors, rooms, at regular intervals. Why wall them up? Why cover the doors in cement? What was behind them?

I rubbed fingertips across the rough cement. The surface was bumpy and cool. The paint wasn't very old. It would have flaked in this dampness. It hadn't. What was behind this blocked up door?

The skin just between my shoulder blades started to itch. I fought an urge to glance back at Enzo. I was betting he was behaving himself. I was betting that being shot was the least of my worries.

The air was cool and damp. A very basement of a basement. There were three doors, two to the right, one to the left that were just doors. One door had a shiny new padlock on it. As we walked past it, I heard the door sigh as if something large had leaned against it.

I stopped. "What's in there?"

Enzo had stopped when I stopped. Dominga and Manny had rounded a corner, and we were alone. I touched the door. The wood creaked, rattling against its hinges. Like some giant cat had rubbed against the door. A smell rolled out from under the door. I gagged and backed away. The stench clung to my mouth and throat. I swallowed convulsively and tasted it all the way down.

The thing behind the door made a mewling sound. I couldn't tell if it was human or animal. It was bigger than a person, whatever it was. And it was dead. Very, very dead.

I covered my nose and mouth with my left hand. The right was free just in case. In case that thing should come crashing out. Bullets against the walking dead. I knew better, but the gun was still a comfort. In a pinch I could shoot Enzo. But somehow I knew that if the thing rattling the door got out, Enzo would be in as much danger as I was.

"We must go on, now," he said.

I couldn't tell anything from his face. We might have been walking down the street to the corner store. He seemed impervious, and I hated him for it. If I'm terrified, by God, everyone else should be, too.

I eyed the supposedly unlocked door to my left. I had to know. I yanked it open. The room was maybe eight by four, like a cell. The cement floor and whitewashed walls were clean, empty. It looked like a cell waiting for its next occupant. Enzo slammed the door shut. I didn't fight him. It wasn't worth it. If I was going to go one on one with someone who outweighed me by over a hundred pounds, I was going to be picky about where I drew the line. An empty room wasn't worth it.

Enzo leaned against the door. Sweat glimmered across his face in the harsh light. "Do not try any other doors, señorita. It could be very bad."

I nodded. "Sure, no problem." An empty room and he was sweating. Nice to know something frightened him. But why this room and not the one with the mewling stench behind it? I didn't have a clue.

"We must catch up with the Señora." He made a gracious motion like a maître d' showing me to a chair. I went where he pointed. Where else was I going to go?

The hallway fed into a large rectangular chamber. It was painted the same startling white as the cell had been. The whitewashed floor was covered in brilliant red and black designs. Verve it was called. Symbols drawn in the voodoo sanctuary to summon the lao, the gods of vaudun.

The symbols acted as walls bordering a path. They led to the altar. If you stepped off the path you messed up all those carefully formed symbols. I didn't know if that would be good or bad. Rule number three hundred sixty-nine when dealing with unfamiliar magic: when in doubt, leave it alone.

I left it alone.

The end of the room gleamed with candles. The warm, rich light flickered and filled the white walls with heat and light. Dominga stood in the midst of that light, that whiteness, and gleamed with evil. There was no other word for it. She wasn't just bad, she was evil. It gleamed around her like darkness made liquid and touchable. The smiling old woman was gone. She was a creature of power.

Manny stood off to one side. He was staring at her. He glanced at me. His eyes were showing a lot of white. The altar was directly behind Dominga's straight back. Dead animals spilled off the top of it to form a pool on the floor. Chickens, dogs, a small pig, two goats. Lumps of fur and dried blood that I couldn't identify. The altar looked like a fountain where dead things flowed out of the center, sluggish and thick.

The sacrifices were fresh. No smell of decay. The glazed eyes of a goat stared at me. I hated killing goats. They always seemed so much more intelligent than chickens. Or maybe I just thought they were cuter.

A tall woman stood to the right of the altar. Her skin gleamed nearly black in the candlelight as if she had been carved of some heavy, gleaming wood. Her hair was short and neat, falling to her shoulders. Wide cheekbones, full lips, expert makeup. She wore a long silky dress, the bright scarlet of fresh blood. It matched her lipstick.

To the right of the altar stood a zombie. It had once been a woman. Long, pale brown hair fell nearly to her waist. Someone had brushed it until it gleamed. It was the only thing about the corpse that looked alive. The skin had turned a greyish color. The flesh had narrowed down around the bones like shrink wrap. Muscles moved under the thin, rotting skin, stringy and shrunken. The nose was almost gone, giving it a half-finished look. A crimson gown hung loose and flapping on the skeletal remains.

There was even an attempt at makeup. Lipstick had been abandoned when the lips shriveled up but a dusting of mauve eye shadow outlined the bulging eyes. I swallowed very hard and turned to stare at the first woman.

She was a zombie. One of the best preserved and most lifelike I had ever seen, but no matter how luscious she looked, she was dead. The woman, the zombie, stared back at me. There was something in her perfect brown eyes that no zombie has for long. The memory of who and what they were fades within a few days, sometimes hours. But this zombie was afraid. The fear was like a shiny, bright pain in her eyes. Zombies didn't have eyes like that.

I turned back to the more decayed zombie and found her staring at me, too. The bulging eyes were staring at me. With most of the flesh holding the eyes in the socket gone, her facial expressions weren't as good, but she managed. It managed to be afraid. Shit.

Dominga nodded, and Enzo motioned me farther into the circle. I didn't want to go.

"What the hell is going on here, Dominga?"

She smiled, almost a laugh. "I am not accustomed to such rudeness."

"Get used to it," I said. Enzo sort of breathed down my back. I did my best to ignore him. My right hand was sort of casually near my gun, without looking like I was reaching for my gun. It wasn't easy. Reaching for a gun usually looks like reaching for a gun. No one seemed to notice though. Goody for our side.

"What have you done to the two zombies?"

"Inspect them yourself, *chica*. If you are as powerful as the stories say, you will answer your own question."

"And if I can't figure it out?" I asked.

She smiled, but her eyes were as flat and black as a shark's. "Then you are not as powerful as the stories."

"Is this the test?"

"Perhaps."

I sighed. The voodoo lady wanted to see how tough I really was. Why? Maybe there wasn't a reason. Maybe she was just a sadistic power-hungry bitch. Yeah, I could believe that. Then again, maybe there was a purpose to the theatrics. If so, I still didn't know what it was.

I glanced at Manny. He gave a barely perceivable shrug. He didn't know what was going on either. Great.

I didn't like playing Dominga's games, especially when I didn't know the rules. The zombies were still staring at me. There was something in their eyes. It was fear, and something worse—hope. Shit. Zombies didn't have hope. They didn't have anything. They were dead. These weren't dead. I had to know. Here's hoping that curiosity didn't kill the animator.

I stepped around Dominga carefully, watching her out of the corner of my eye. Enzo stayed behind blocking the path between the verve. He looked big and solid standing there, but I could get past him, if I wanted it bad enough. Bad enough to kill him. I hoped I wouldn't want it that bad.

The decayed zombie stared down at me. She was tall, almost six feet. Skeletal feet peeked out from underneath the red gown. A tall, slender woman, probably beautiful, once. Bulging eyes rolled in the nearly bare sockets. A wet, sucking sound accompanied the movements.

I'd thrown up the first time I heard that sound. The sound of eyeballs rolling in rotting sockets. But that was four years ago, when I was new at this. Decaying flesh didn't make me flinch anymore or throw up. As a general rule.

The eyes were pale brown with a lot of green in them. The smell of some expensive perfume floated around her. Powdery and fine, like talcum powder in your nose, sweet, flowery. Underneath was the stink of rotting flesh. It wrinkled my nose, caught at the back of my throat. The next time I smelled this delicate, expensive perfume, I would think of rotting flesh. Oh, well, it smelled too expensive to buy, anyway.

She was staring at me. She, not it, she. There was the force of personality in her eyes. I call most zombies "it" because it fits. They may come from the grave very alive-looking, but it doesn't last. They rot. Personality and intelligence goes first, then the body. It's always that order. God is not cruel enough to force anyone to be aware while their body decays around them. Something had gone very wrong with this one.

I stepped around Dominga Salvador. For no reason that I could name, I stayed out of reach. She had no weapon, I was almost sure of that. The danger she represented had nothing to do with knives or guns. I simply didn't want her to touch me, not even by accident.

The zombie on the left was perfect. Not a sign of decay. The look in her eyes was alert, alive. God help us. She could have gone anywhere and passed for human. How had I known she wasn't alive? I wasn't even sure. None of the usual signs were there, but I knew dead when I felt it. Yet . . . I stared up at the second woman. Her lovely, dark face stared back. Fear screamed out of her eyes.

Whatever power let me raise the dead told me this was a zombie, but my eyes couldn't tell. It was amazing. If Dominga could raise zombies like this, she had me beat hands down.

I have to wait three days before I raise a corpse. It gives the soul time to leave the area. Souls usually hover around for a while. Three days is average. I can't call shit from the grave if the soul's still present. It has been theorized that if an animator could keep the soul intact while raising the body, we'd get resurrection. You know, resurrection, the real thing, like in Jesus and Lazarus. I didn't believe that. Or maybe I just know my limitations.

I stared up at this zombie and knew what was different. The soul was still there. The soul was still inside both bodies. How? How in Jesus' name did she do it?

"The souls. The souls are still in the bodies." My voice held the distaste I felt. Why bother to hide it?

"Very good, *chica.*"

I went to stand to her left, keeping Enzo in sight. "How did you do it?"

"The soul was captured at the moment it took flight from the body."

I shook my head. "That doesn't explain anything."

"Don't you know how to capture souls in a bottle?"

Souls in a bottle? Was she kidding? No, she wasn't. "No, I don't." I tried not to sound superior as I said it.

"I could teach you so much, Anita, so very much."

"No, thanks," I said. "You captured their souls, then you raised the body, and put the soul back in." I was guessing, but it sounded right.

"Very, very good. That is it exactly." She was staring at me so hard that it was uncomfortable. Her empty, black eyes were memorizing me.

"But why is the second zombie rotting? The theory is with the soul intact, the zombie won't decay?"

"It is no longer a theory. I have proved it," she said.

I stared at the rotted corpse, and it stared back. "Then why is that one rotting, and this one isn't?" Just two necromancers talking shop. Tell me, do you raise your zombies only during the dark of the moon?

"The soul may be put into the body, then removed again, as often as I wish."

I stared at Dominga Salvador now. I stared and tried not to let my jaw drop, not to let the dawning horror slip across my face. She would enjoy shocking me. I didn't want her taking pleasure from me, for any reason.

"Let me test my understanding here," I said in my best executive trainee voice. "You put the soul into the body and it didn't rot. Then you took the soul out of the body, making it an ordinary zombie, and it did rot."

"Exactly," she said.

"Then you put the soul back in the rotted corpse, and the zombie was aware and alive again. Did the rotting stop when the soul went back in?"

"Yes."

Shit. "So you could keep the zombie over there rotted just that much forever?"

"Yes."

Double shit. "And this one?" I pointed this time, like I was doing a lecture.

"Many people would pay dearly for her."

"Wait a minute, you mean sell her as a sex slave?"

"Perhaps."

"But . . ." The idea was too horrible. She was a zombie, which meant she didn't need to eat or sleep or anything. You could keep her in a closet and take her out like a toy. A perfectly obedient slave.

"Are they as obedient as normal zombies, or does the soul give them free will?"

"They seem to be very obedient."

"Maybe they're just scared of you," I said.

She smiled. "Perhaps."

"You can't just keep the soul imprisoned forever."

"I can't," she said.

"The soul needs to go on."

"To your Christian heaven or hell?"

"Yes," I said.

"These were wicked women, *chica*. Their own families gave them to me. Paid me to punish them."

"You took money for this?"

"It is illegal to tamper with dead bodies without permission of the family," she said.

I don't know if she had planned to horrify me. Maybe not. But with that one sentence she let me know that what she was doing was perfectly legal. The dead had no rights. This was the reason we needed some laws to protect zombies. Shit.

"No one deserves to spend eternity locked in a corpse," I said.

"We could do this to criminals on death row, *chica*. They could be made to serve society after death."

I shook my head. "No, it's wrong."

"I have created a nonrotting zombie, *chica*. Animators, I believe you call yourselves, have been searching for the secret for years. I have it, and people will pay for it."

"It's wrong. I may not know much about voodoo, but even among your own people, it's wrong. How can you keep the souls prisoner and not allow them to go on and join with the lao?"

She shrugged and sighed. She suddenly looked tired. "I was hoping, *chica,* that you would help me. With two of us working, we could create more zombies much faster. We could be wealthy beyond our dreams."

"You've asked the wrong girl."

"I see that now. I had hoped that since you were not vaudun, you would not see it as wrong."

"Christian, Buddhist, Moslem, you name it, Dominga, no one's going to think it's all right."

"Perhaps, perhaps not. It does not hurt to ask."

I glanced at the rotted zombie. "At least put your first experiment out of its misery."

Dominga glanced at the zombie. "She makes a powerful demonstration, does she not?"

"You've created a nonrotting zombie, great. Don't be sadistic."

"You think I am being cruel?"

"Yeah," I said.

"Manuel, am I being cruel?"

Manny stared at me while he answered. His eyes were trying to tell me something. I couldn't tell what. "Yes, Señora, you are being cruel."

She glanced over at him then, surprise in the movement of her body, her face. "Do you really think I am cruel, Manuel? Your beloved *amante*?"

He nodded slowly. "Yes."

"You were not so quick to judge a few years back, Manuel. You slew the white goat for me, more than once."

I turned towards Manny. It was like that moment in a movie where the main character has a revelation about someone. There should be music and camera angles when you learn one of your best friends participated in human sacrifice. More than once she had said. More than once.

"Manny?" My voice was a hoarse whisper. This, for me, was worse than the zombies. The hell with strangers. This was Manny, and it couldn't be true.

"Manny?" I said it again. He wouldn't look at me. Bad sign.

"You didn't know, *chica*? Didn't your Manny tell you of his past?"

"Shut up," I said.

"He was my most treasured helper. He would have done anything for me."

"Shut up!" I screamed it at her. She stopped, her face thinning with anger. Enzo took two steps into the altar area. "Don't." I wasn't even sure who I was saying it to. "I need to hear from him, not from you."

The anger was still in her face. Enzo loomed like an avalanche about to be unleashed. Dominga gave one sharp nod. "Ask him then, *chica*."

"Manny, is she telling the truth? Did you perform human sacrifices?" My voice sounded so normal. It shouldn't have. My stomach was so tight, it hurt. I wasn't afraid anymore, or at least not of Dominga. The truth; I was afraid of the truth.

He looked up. His hair fell across his face framing his eyes. A lot of pain in those eyes. Almost flinching.

"It's the truth, isn't it?" My skin felt cold. "Answer me, dammit." My voice still sounded ordinary, calm.

"Yes," he said.

"Yes, you committed human sacrifice?"

He glared at me now, anger helping him meet my eyes. "Yes, yes!"

It was my turn to look away. "God, Manny, how could you?" My voice was soft now, not ordinary. If I didn't know better, I'd say it sounded like I was on the verge of tears.

"It was nearly twenty years ago, Anita. I was vaudun and a necromancer. I believed. I loved the Señora. Thought I did."

I stared up at him. The look on his face made my throat tight. "Manny, dammit."

He didn't say anything. He just stood there looking miserable. And I couldn't reconcile the two images. Manny Rodriguez and someone who would slaughter the hornless goat in a ritual. He had taught me right from wrong in this business. He had refused to do so many things. Things not half as bad as this. It made no sense.

I shook my head. "I can't deal with this right now." I heard myself say it out loud, and hadn't really meant to. "Fine, you've dropped your little bombshell, Señora Salvador. You said you'd help us, if I passed your test. Did I pass?" When in doubt, concentrate on one disaster at a time.

"I wanted to offer you a chance to help me with my new business venture."

"We both know I'm not going to do that," I said.

"It is a pity, Anita. With training you could rival my powers."

Be just like her when I grew up. No thanks. "Thanks anyway, but I'm happy where I am."

Her eyes flicked to Manny, back to me. "Happy?"

"Manny and I will deal with it, Señora. Now will you help me?"

"If I help you without you helping me in some way, you will owe me a favor."

I didn't want to owe her a favor. "I would rather just trade information."

"What could you possibly know that would be worth all the effort I will expend hunting for your killer zombie?"

I thought about that for a moment. "I know that legislation is being written right now, about zombies. Zombies are going to have rights, and laws protecting them soon." I hoped it was soon. No need to tell her how early in the process the legislation was.

"So, I must sell a few nonrotting zombies soon, before it becomes illegal."

"I wouldn't think illegal would bother you much. Human sacrifice is illegal, too."

She gave a tiny smile. "I do not do such things anymore, Anita. I have given up my wicked ways."

I didn't believe that, and she knew I didn't believe it. Her smile widened. "When Manuel left, I stopped such evil practices. Without his urgings, I became a respectable bokar."

She was lying, but I couldn't prove it. And she knew that, too. "I gave you valuable information. Now will you help me?"

She nodded graciously. "I will search among my followers to see if any knows of your killer zombie." I had the sense that she was quietly laughing at me.

"Manny, will she help us?"

"If the Señora says she will do a thing, it will be done. She is good that way."

"I will find your killer if it has anything to do with vaudun," she said.

"Great." I didn't say thank you, because it seemed wrong. I wanted to call her a bitch and shoot her between the eyes, but then I would have had to shoot Enzo, too. And how would I explain that to the police? She was breaking no laws. Dammit.

"I don't suppose appealing to your better nature would make you forget this mad scheme to use your new improved zombies for slaves?"

She smiled. "*Chica, chica,* I will be rich beyond your wildest dreams. You can refuse to join me, but you cannot stop me."

"Don't bet on it," I said.

"What will you do, go to the police? I am breaking no laws. The only way to stop me is to kill me." She looked directly at me while she said it.

"Don't tempt me."

Manny moved up beside me. "Don't, Anita, don't challenge her."

I was sort of mad at him, too, so what the hell. "I will stop you, Señora Salvador. Whatever it takes."

"You call death magic against me, Anita, and it is you who will die."

I didn't know death magic from frijoles. I shrugged. "I was thinking something more down to earth, like a bullet."

Enzo surged into the altar area, moving to stand between his boss-lady and me. Dominga stopped him. "No, Enzo, she is angry this morning, and shocked." Her eyes were still laughing at me. "She knows nothing of the deeper magics. She cannot harm me, and she is too morally superior to commit cold-blooded murder."

The worst part about it was that she was right. I couldn't just put a bullet between her eyes, not unless she threatened me. I glanced at the waiting zombies, patient as the dead, but underneath that endless patience was fear, and hope, and . . . God, the line between life and death was getting thinner all the time.

"At least lay to rest your first experiment. You've proved you can put the soul in and out multiple times. Don't make her watch."

"But, Anita, I already have a buyer for her."

"Oh, Jesus, you don't mean . . . Oh, God, a necrophiliac."

"Those that love the dead better than you or I ever will, will pay extraordinary amounts for such as her."

Maybe I could just shoot her. "You are a cold-hearted, amoral bitch."

"And you, *chica,* need to learn respect for your elders."

"Respect has to be earned," I said.

"I think, Anita Blake, that you need to remember why people fear the dark. I will see that very soon you have a visitor to your window. Some dark night when you are fast asleep in your warm, safe bed. Something evil will creep into your room. I will earn your respect, if that is the way you want it."

I should have been afraid, but I wasn't. I was angry and wanted to go home. "You can force people to be afraid of you, Señora, but you can't force them to respect you."

"We shall see, Anita. Call me after you have gotten my gift. It will be soon."

"Will you still help locate the killer zombie?"

"I said I would, and I will."

"Good," I said. "May we go now?"

She waved Enzo back beside her. "By all means run out into the daylight where you can be brave."

I walked to the pathway. Manny stayed right with me. We were careful not to look at each other. We were too busy watching the Señora and her pets. I stopped just inside the path. Manny touched my arm lightly, as if he knew what I was about to say. I ignored him.

"I may not be willing to kill you in cold blood, but hurt me first, and I'll put a bullet in you some bright, sunshiny day."

"Threats will not save you, *chica*," she said.

I smiled sweetly. "You either, bitch."

Her face went all thin and angry. I smiled wider.

"She does not mean it, Señora," Manny said. "She will not kill you."

"Is this true, *chica*?" Her voice was a rich growl of sound, pleasant and frightening at the same time.

I gave Manny a quick dirty look. It was a good threat. I didn't like weakening it with common sense, or truth. "I said, I'd shoot you. I didn't say I'd kill you. Now did I?"

"No, you did not."

Manny grabbed my arm and started pulling me backwards towards the stairs. He was pulling on my left arm, leaving my right free for my gun. Just in case.

Dominga never moved. Her black, angry eyes stared at me until we rounded the corner. Manny pulled me into the hallway with its cement covered doors. I pulled free of him. We stared at each other for a heartbeat.

"What's behind the doors?"

"I don't know."

Doubt must have shown on my face because he said, "God as my witness, Anita, I don't know. It wasn't like this twenty years ago."

I just stared at him as if looking would change things. I wish Dominga Salvador had kept Manny's secret to herself. I had not wanted to know.

"Anita, we have to get out of here, now." The light bulb over our head went out, like someone had snuffed it. We both looked up. There was nothing to see. My arms broke out in goose bumps. The bulb just ahead of us dimmed, then blinked off.

Manny was right. We needed to leave now. I broke into a half jog towards the stairs. Manny stayed with me. The door with its shiny padlock rattled and thumped as if the thing were trying to get out. Another light bulb flashed off. The darkness was snapping at our heels. We were at a full run by the time we hit the stairs. There were two bulbs left.

We were halfway up the stairs when the last light vanished. The world went black. I froze on the stairs unwilling to move without being able to see. Manny's arm brushed mine, but I couldn't see him. The darkness was complete. I could have touched my eyeballs and not seen my finger. We grabbed hands and held on. His hand wasn't much bigger than mine. It was warm and familiar, and damn comforting.

The cracking of wood was loud as a shotgun blast in the dark. The stench of rotting meat filled the stairwell. "Shit!" The word echoed and bounced in the blackness. I wished I hadn't said it. Something large pulled itself into the corridor. It couldn't be as big as it sounded. The wet, slithering sounds moved towards the stairs. Or sounded like they did.

I stumbled up two steps. Manny didn't need any urging. We stumbled through the darkness, and the sounds below hurried. The light under the door was so bright, it almost hurt. Manny flung open the door. The sunlight blazed against my eyes. We were both momentarily blinded.

Something screamed behind us, caught in the edge of daylight. The scream was almost human. I started to turn, to look. Manny slammed the door. He shook his head. "You don't want to see. I don't want to see."

He was right. So why did I have this urge to yank the door open, to stare down into the dark until I saw something pale and shapeless? A screaming nightmare of a sight. I stared at the closed door, and I let it go.

"Do you think it will come out after us?" I asked.

"Into the daylight?" Manny asked.

"Yeah," I said.

"I don't think so. Let's leave without finding out."

I agreed. The August sunlight streamed into the living room. Warm and real. The scream, the darkness, the zombies, all of it seemed wrong for the sunlight. Things that go bump in the morning. It didn't sound quite right.

I opened the screen door calmly, slowly. Panicked, me? But I was listening so hard I could hear blood rush in my ears. Listening for slithery sounds of pursuit. Nothing.

Antonio was still on guard outside. Should we warn him about the possibility of a Lovecraftian horror nipping at our heels?

"Did you fuck the zombie downstairs?" Antonio asked.

So much for warning old Tony.

Manny ignored him.

"Go fuck yourself," I said.

He said, "Heh!"

I kept walking down the porch steps. Manny stayed with me. Antonio didn't draw his gun and shoot us. The day was looking up.

The little girl on the tricycle had stopped by Manny's car. She stared up at me as I got in the passenger side door. I stared back into huge brown eyes. Her face was darkly tanned. She couldn't have been more than five.

Manny got in the driver's side door. He put the car in gear, and we pulled away. The little girl and I stared at each other. Just before we turned the corner she started pedaling up and down the sidewalk again.

7

The air conditioner blasted cold air into the car. Manny drove through the residential streets. Most of the driveways were empty. People off to work. Small children playing in the yards. A few moms out on the front steps. I didn't see any daddies at home with the kids. Things change, but not that much. The silence stretched out between us. It was not a comfortable silence.

Manny glanced at me furtively out of the corner of his eye.

I slumped in the passenger seat, the seat belt digging across my gun. "So," I said, "you used to perform human sacrifice."

I think he flinched. "Do you want me to lie?"

"No, I want to not know. I want to live in blessed ignorance."

"It doesn't work that way, Anita," he said.

"I guess it doesn't," I said. I adjusted the lap strap so it didn't press over my gun. Ah, comfort. If only everything else were that easy to fix. "What are we going to do about it?"

"About you knowing?" he asked. He glanced at me as he asked. I nodded.

"You aren't going to rant and rave? Tell me what an evil bastard I am?"

"Doesn't seem much point in it," I said.

He looked at me a little longer this time. "Thanks."

"I didn't say it was all right, Manny. I'm just not going to yell at you. Not yet, anyway."

He passed a large white car full of dark-skinned teenagers. Their car stereo was up so loud, my teeth rattled. The driver had one of those high-boned, flat faces, straight off of an Aztec carving. Our eyes met as we moved by them. He made kissing motions with his mouth. The others laughed up-roariously. I resisted the urge to flip them off. Mustn't encourage the little tykes.

They turned right. We went straight. Relief.

Manny stopped two cars back from a light. Just beyond the light was the turnoff 40 West. We'd take 270 up to Olive and then a short jaunt to my apartment. We had forty-five minutes to an hour of travel time. Not a problem normally. Today I wanted away from Manny. I wanted some time to digest. To decide how to feel.

"Talk to me, Anita, please."

"Honest to God, Manny, I don't know what to say." Truth, try to stick to the truth between friends. Yeah.

"I've known you for four years, Manny. You are a good man. You love your wife, your kids. You've saved my life. I've saved yours. I thought I knew you."

"I haven't changed."

"Yes," I looked at him as I said it, "you have. Manny Rodriguez would never under any circumstance take part in human sacrifice."

"It's been twenty years."

"There's no statute of limitations on murder."

"You going to the cops?" His voice was very quiet.

The light changed. We waited our turn and merged into the morning traffic. It was as heavy as it ever got in St. Louis. It's not the gridlock of L.A., but stop and jerk is still pretty darn annoying. Especially this morning.

"I don't have any proof. Just Dominga Salvador's word. I wouldn't exactly call her a reliable witness."

"If you had proof?"

"Don't push me on this, Manny." I stared out the window. There was a silver Miada with the top down. The driver was white-haired, male, and wore a jaunty little cap, plus racing gloves. Middle-age crisis.

"Does Rosita know?" I asked.

"She suspects, but she doesn't know for sure."

"Doesn't want to know," I said.

"Probably not." He turned and stared at me then.

A red Ford truck was nearly in front of us. I yelled, "Manny!"

He slammed on the brakes, and only the seat belt kept me from kissing the dashboard.

"Jesus, Manny, watch your driving!"

He concentrated on traffic for a few seconds, then without looking at me this time, "Are you going to tell Rosita?"

I thought about that for about a second. I shook my head, realized he couldn't see it, and said, "I don't think so. Ignorance is bliss on this one, Manny. I don't think your wife could deal with it."

"She'd leave me and take the kids."

I believed she would. Rosita was a very religious person. She took all the commandments very seriously.

"She already thinks I'm risking my eternal soul by raising the dead," Manny said.

"She didn't have a problem until the pope threatened to excommunicate all animators unless they stopped raising the dead."

"The Church is very important to Rosita."

"Me, too, but I'm a happy little Episcopalian now. Switch churches."

"It's not that easy," he said.

It wasn't. I knew that. But, hey, you do what you can, or what you have to. "Can you explain why you would do human sacrifice? I mean, something that will make sense to me?"

"No," he said. He pulled into the far lane. It seemed to be going a little faster. It slowed down as soon as we pulled in. Murphy's law of traffic.

"You won't even try to explain?"

"It's indefensible, Anita. I live with what I did. I can't do anything else."

He had a point. "This has to change the way I think about you, Manny."

"In what way?"

"I don't know yet." Honesty. If we were very careful, we could still be honest with each other. "Is there anything else you think I should know? Anything that Dominga might spill later on?"

He shook his head. "Nothing worse."

"Okay," I said.

"Okay," he said. "That's it, no interrogation?"

"Not now, maybe not ever." I was tired all at once. It was 9:23 in the morning, and I needed a nap. Emotionally drained. "I don't know how to feel about this, Manny. I don't know how it changes our friendship, or our working relationship, or even if it does. I think it does. Oh, hell, I don't know."

"Fair enough," he said. "Let's move on to something we aren't confused about."

"And what would that be?" I asked.

"The Señora will send something bad to your window, just like she said she would."

"I figured that."

"Why did you threaten her?"

"I didn't like her."

"Oh, great, just great," he said. "Why didn't I think of that?"

"I am going to stop her, Manny. I figured she should know."

"Never give the bad guys a head start, Anita. I taught you that."

"You also taught me that human sacrifice is murder."

"That hurt," he said.

"Yes," I said, "it did."

"You need to be prepared, Anita. She will send something after you. Just to scare you, I think, not to really harm."

"Because you made me 'fess up to not killing her," I said.

"No, because she doesn't really believe you'll kill her. She's intrigued with your powers. I think she'd rather convert you than kill you."

"Have me as part of her zombie-making factory."

"Yes."

"Not in this lifetime."

"The Señora is not used to people saying no, Anita."

"Her problem, not mine."

He glanced at me, then back to the traffic. "She'll make it your problem."

"I'll deal with it."

"You can't be that confident."

"I'm not, but what do you want me to do, break down and cry. I'll deal with it when, and if, something noisome drags itself through my window."

"You can't deal with the Señora, Anita. She is powerful, more powerful than you can ever imagine."

"She scared me, Manny. I am suitably impressed. If she sends something I can't handle, I'll run. Okay?"

"Not okay. You don't know, you just don't know."

"I heard the thing in the hallway. I smelled it. I'm scared, but she's just human, Manny. All the mumbo jumbo won't keep her safe from a bullet."

"A bullet may take her out, but not down."

"What does that mean?"

"If she were shot, say in the head or heart, and seemed dead, I'd treat her like a vampire. Head and heart taken out. Body burned." He glanced at me sort of sideways.

I didn't say anything. We were talking about killing Dominga Salvador. She was capturing souls and putting them into corpses. It was an abomination. She would probably attack me first. Some supernatural goodie come creeping into my home. She was evil and would attack me first. Would it be murder to ambush her? Yeah. Would I do it anyway? I let the thought take shape in my head. Rolled it over like a piece of candy, tasting the idea. Yeah, I could do it.

I should have felt bad that I could plan a murder, for any reason, and not flinch. I didn't feel bad. It was sort of comforting to know if she pushed me, I could push back. Who was I to cast stones at Manny for twenty-year-old crimes? Yeah, who indeed.

8

It was early afternoon. Manny had dropped me off without a word. He hadn't asked to come up, and I hadn't offered. I still didn't know what to think about him, Dominga Salvador, and nonrotting zombies, complete with souls. I decided not to think. What I needed was good physical activity. As luck would have it, I had judo class this afternoon.

I have a black belt, which sounds a lot more impressive than it really is. In the dojo with referees and rules, I do okay. Out in the real world where most bad guys outweigh me by a hundred pounds, I trust a gun.

I was actually reaching for the doorknob when the bell chimed. I put the overstuffed gym bag by the door and used the little peephole. I always had to stand on tiptoe to see out of it.

The distorted image was blond, fair-eyed, and barely familiar. It was Tommy, Harold Gaynor's muscle-bound bodyguard. This day was just getting better and better.

I don't usually take a gun to judo class. It's in the afternoon. In the summer that means daylight. The really dangerous stuff doesn't come out until after dark. I untucked the red polo shirt I was wearing and clipped my inter-pants holster back in place. The pocket-size 9mm dug in just a little. If I had known I was going to need it, I would have worn looser jeans.

The doorbell rang again. I hadn't called out to let him know I was in here. He didn't seem discouraged. He rang the doorbell a third time, leaning on it.

I took a deep breath and opened the door. I looked up into Tommy's pale blue eyes. They were still empty, dead. A perfect blankness. Were you born with a stare like that, or did you have to practice?

"What do you want?" I asked.

His lips twitched. "Aren't you going to invite me in?"

"I don't think so."

He shrugged massive shoulders. I could see the straps of his shoulder holster imprinted on his suit jacket. He needed a better tailor.

A door opened to my left. A woman came out with a toddler in her arms. She locked the door before turning and seeing us. "Oh, hi." She smiled brightly.

"Hello," I said.

Tommy nodded.

The woman turned and walked towards the stairs. She was murmuring something nonsensical and high-pitched to the toddler.

Tommy looked back at me. "You really want to do this in the hallway?"

"What are we doing?"

"Business. Money."

I looked at his face, and it told me nothing. The only comfort I had was that if Tommy meant to do me harm he probably wouldn't have come to my apartment to do it. Probably.

I stepped back, holding the door very wide. I stayed out of arm's reach as he walked into my apartment. He looked around. "Nice, clean."

"Cleaning service," I said. "Talk to me about business, Tommy. I've got an appointment."

He glanced at the gym bag by the door. "Work or pleasure?" he asked.

"None of your business," I said.

Again that bare twist of lips. I realized it was his version of a smile. "Down in the car I got a case full of money. A million five, half now, half after you raise the zombie."

I shook my head. "I gave Gaynor my answer."

"But that was in front of your boss. This is just you and me. No one'll know if you take it. No one."

"I didn't say no because there were witnesses. I said no because I don't do human sacrifice." I could feel myself smiling. This was ridiculous. I thought about Manny then. Alright, maybe it wasn't ridiculous. But I wasn't doing it.

"Everyone has their price, Anita. Name it. We can meet it."

He had never once mentioned Gaynor's name. Only I had. He was being so bloody careful, too careful. "I don't have a price, Tommy-boy. Go back to Mr. Harold Gaynor and tell him that."

His face clouded up then. A wrinkling between his eyes. "I don't know that name."

"Oh, give me a break. I'm not wearing a wire."

"Name your price. We can meet it," he said.

"There is no price."

"Two million, tax-free," he said.

"What zombie could be worth two million dollars, Tommy?" I stared at his softly frowning face. "What could Gaynor hope to gain that would allow him to make a profit on that kind of expenditure?"

Tommy just stared at me. "You don't need to know that."

"I thought you'd say that. Go away, Tommy. I'm not for sale." I stepped back towards the door, planning to escort him out. He moved forward suddenly, faster than he looked. Muscled arms wide to grab me.

I pulled the Firestar and pointed it at his chest. He froze. Dead eyes, blinking at me. His large hands balled into fists. A nearly purple flush crept up his neck into his face. Rage.

"Don't do it," I said, my voice sounded soft.

"Bitch," he wheezed it at me.

"Now, now, Tommy, don't get nasty. Ease down, and we can all live to see another glorious day."

His pale eyes flicked from the gun to my face, then back to the gun. "You wouldn't be so tough without that piece."

If he wanted me to offer to arm wrestle him, he was in for a disappointment. "Back off, Tommy, or I'll drop you here and now. All the muscle in the world won't help you."

I watched something move behind his dead eyes, then his whole body relaxed. He took a deep breath through his nose. "Okay, you got the drop on me today. But if you keep disappointing my boss, I'm gonna find you without that gun." His lips twitched. "And we'll see how tough you really are."

A little voice in my head said, "Shoot him now." I knew as surely as I knew anything that dear Tommy would be at my back someday. I didn't want him there, but . . . I couldn't just kill him because I thought he might come after me someday. It wasn't a good enough reason. And how would I ever have explained it to the police?

"Get out, Tommy." I opened the door without taking either my gaze or the gun off the man. "Get out and tell Gaynor that if he keeps annoying me, I'll start sending his bodyguards home in boxes."

Tommy's nostrils flared just a bit at that, veins straining in his neck. He walked very stiffly past me and out into the hall. I held the gun at my side and watched him, listening to his footsteps retreat down the stairs. When I was as sure as I could be that he was gone, I put my gun back in its holster, grabbed my gym bag, and headed for judo class. Mustn't let these little interruptions spoil my exercise program. Tomorrow I would miss my workout for sure. I had a funeral to attend. Besides, if Tommy really did challenge me to arm wrestling, I was going to need all the help I could get.

9

I hate funerals. At least this one wasn't for anyone I had particularly liked. Cold, but true. Peter Burke had been an unscrupulous SOB when alive. I didn't see why death should automatically grant him sainthood. Death, especially violent death, will turn the meanest bastard in the world into a nice guy. Why is that?

I stood there in the bright August sunlight in my little black dress and dark sunglasses, watching the mourners. They had set up a canopy over the coffin, flowers, and chairs for the family. Why was I here, you might ask, if I had not been a friend? Because Peter Burke had been an animator. Not a very good one, but we are a small, exclusive club. If one of us dies, we all come. It's a rule. There are no exceptions. Maybe your own death, but then again being that we raise the dead, maybe not.

There are things you can do to a corpse so it won't rise again as a vampire, but a zombie is a different beast. Short of cremation, an animator can bring you back. Fire was about the only thing a zombie respected or feared.

We could have raised Peter and asked him who put a gun to his head. But they had put a 357 Magnum with an expanding point just behind his ear. There wasn't enough left of his head to fill a plastic bag. You could raise him as a zombie, but he couldn't talk. Even the dead need mouths.

Manny stood beside me, uncomfortable in his dark suit. Rosita, his wife, stood spine absolutely straight. Thick brown hands gripping her black patent leather purse. She is what my stepmother used to call large-boned. Her black hair was cut just below the ears and loosely permed. The hair needed to be longer. It emphasized how perfectly round her face was.

Charles Montgomery stood just behind me like a tall dark mountain. Charles looks like he played football somewhere. He has the ability to frown and make people run for cover. He just looks like a hard ass. Truth is, Charles faints at the sight of anything but animal blood. It's lucky for him he looks like such a big black dude. He has almost no tolerance for pain. He cries at Walt Disney movies, like when Bambi's mother dies. It's endearing as hell.

His wife, Caroline, was working. She hadn't been able to switch shifts with anyone. I wondered how hard she had tried. Caroline is okay but she sort of looks down on what we do. Mumbo jumbo she calls it. She's a registered nurse. I guess after dealing with doctors all day, she has to look down on someone.

Up near the front of the crowd was Jamison Clarke. He was tall, thin, and the only red-haired, green-eyed black man I've ever met. He nodded at me across the grave. I nodded back.

We were all here; the animators of Animators, Incorporated. Bert and Mary, our daytime secretary, were holding down the fort. I hoped Bert didn't book us in anything we couldn't handle. Or would refuse to handle. He did that if you didn't watch him.

The sun slapped my back like a hot metal hand. The men kept pulling at their ties and high collars. The smell of chrysanthemums was thick like wax at the back of my throat. No one ever gives you football mums unless you die. Carnations, roses, snapdragons, they all have happier lives, but mums, and glads—they're the funeral flowers. At least the tall spires of gladiolus had no scent.

A woman sat in the front line of chairs under the canopy. She was leaning over her knees like a broken doll. Her sobs were loud enough to drown out the words of the priest. Only his quiet, soothing rhythm reached me as I stood near the back.

Two small children were gripping the hands of an older man. Grampa? The children were pale, hollow-eyed. Fear vied with tears on their faces. They watched their mother break down completely, useless to them. Her grief was more important than theirs. Her loss greater. Bullshit.

My own mother had died when I was eight. You never really filled in the hole. It was like a piece of you gone missing. An ache that never quite goes away. You deal with it. You go on, but it's there.

A man sat beside her, rubbing her back in endless circles. His hair was nearly black, cut short and neat. Broad-shouldered. From the back he looked eerily like Peter Burke. Ghosts in sunlight.

The cemetery was dotted with trees. The shade rustled and flickered pale grey in the sunlight. On the other side of the gravel driveway that twined through the cemetery were two men. They stood quietly, waiting. Grave diggers. Waiting to finish the job.

I looked back at the coffin under its blanket of pink carnations. There was a bulky mound just behind it, covered in bright green fake grass. Underneath was the fresh dug earth waiting to go back in the hole.

Mustn't let the loved ones think about red-clay soil pouring down on the gleaming coffin. Clods of dirt hitting the wood, covering your husband, father. Trapping them forever inside a lead-lined box. A good coffin will keep the water and worms out, but it doesn't stop decay.

I knew what would be happening to Peter Burke's body. Cover it in satin, wrap a tie round its neck, rouge the cheeks, close the eyes; it's still a corpse.

The funeral ended while I wasn't looking. The people rose gratefully in one mass movement. The dark-haired man helped the grieving widow to stand. She nearly fell. Another man rushed forward and supported her other side. She sagged between them, feet dragging on the ground.

She looked back over her shoulder, head almost lolling on her neck. She screamed, loud and ragged, then flung herself on the coffin. The woman collapsed against the flowers, digging at the wood. Fingers scrambling for the locks on the coffin. The ones that held the lid down.

Everyone just froze for a moment, staring. I saw the two children through the crowd still standing, wide-eyed. Shit. "Stop her," I said it too loud. People turned to stare. I didn't care.

I pushed my way through the vanishing crowd and the aisles of chairs. The dark-haired man was holding the widow's hands while she screamed and struggled. She had collapsed to the ground, and her black dress had worked up high on her thighs. She was wearing a white slip. Her mascara had run like black blood down her face.

I stood in front of the man and the two children. He was staring at the woman like he would never move again. "Sir," I said. He didn't react. "Sir?"

He blinked, staring down at me like I had just appeared in front of him. "Sir, do you really think the children need to see all this?"

"She's my daughter," he said. His voice was deep and thick. Drugged or just grief?

"I sympathize, sir, but the children should go to the car now."

The widow had begun to wail, loud and wordless, raw pain. The girl was beginning to shake. "You're her father, but you're their grandfather. Act like it. Get them out of here."

Anger flickered in his eyes then. "How dare you?"

He wasn't going to listen to me. I was just an intrusion on their grief. The oldest, a boy of about five, was staring up at me. His brown eyes were huge, his thin face so pale it looked ghostly.

"I think it is you who should go," the grandfather said.

"You're right. You are so right," I said. I walked around them out into the grass and the summer heat. I couldn't help the children. I couldn't help them, just as no one had been there to help me. I had survived. So would they, maybe.

Manny and Rosita were waiting for me. Rosita hugged me. "You must come to Sunday dinner after church."

I smiled. "I don't think I can make it, but thanks for asking."

"My cousin Albert will be there," she said. "He is an engineer. He will be a good provider."

"I don't need a good provider, Rosita."

She sighed. "You make too much money for a woman. It makes you not need a man."

I shrugged. If I ever did marry, which I'd begun to doubt, it wouldn't be for money. Love. Shit, was I waiting for love? Naw, not me.

"We have to pick up Tomas at kindergarten," Manny said. He was smiling at me apologetically around Rosita's shoulder. She was nearly a foot taller than he. She towered over me, too.

"Sure, tell the little guy hi for me."

"You should come to dinner," Rosita said, "Albert is a very handsome man."

"Thanks for thinking of me, Rosita, but I'll skip it."

"Come on, wife," Manny said. "Our son is waiting for us."

She let him pull her towards the car, but her brown face was set in disapproval. It offended some deep part of Rosita that I was twenty-four and had no prospects of marriage. Her and my stepmother.

Charles was nowhere to be seen. Hurrying back to the office to see clients. I thought Jamison had, too, but he stood in the grass, waiting for me.

He was dressed impeccably, crossed-lapels, narrow red tie with small dark dots on it. His tie clip was onyx and silver. He smiled at me, always a bad sign.

His greenish eyes looked hollow, like someone had erased part of the skin. If you cry enough, the skin goes from puffy red to hollow white. "I'm glad so many of us showed up," he said.

"I know he was a friend of yours, Jamison. I'm sorry."

He nodded and looked down at his hands. He was holding a pair of sunglasses loosely. He looked up at me, eyes staring straight into mine. All serious.

"The police won't tell the family anything," he said. "Peter gets blown away, and they don't have a clue who did it."

I wanted to tell him the police were doing their best, because they were. But there are a hell of a lot of murders in St. Louis over a year. We were giving Washington, D.C. a run for their money as murder capital of the United States. "They're doing their best, Jamison."

"Then why won't they tell us anything?" His hands convulsed. The sound of breaking plastic was a crumbling sharp sound. He didn't seem to notice.

"I don't know," I said.

"Anita, you're in good with the police. Could you ask?" His eyes were naked, full of such real pain. Most of the time I could ignore, or even dislike, Jamison. He was a tease, a flirt, a bleeding-heart liberal who thought that vampires were just people with fangs. But today . . . today he was real.

"What do you want me to ask?"

"Are they making any progress? Do they have any suspects? That sort of thing."

They were vague questions, but important ones. "I'll see what I can find out."

He gave a watery smile. "Thanks, Anita, really, thanks." He held out his hand. I took it. We shook. He noticed his broken sunglasses. "Damn, ninety-five dollars down the tubes."

Ninety-five dollars for sunglasses? He had to be kidding. A group of mourners were taking the family away at last. The mother was smothered in well-meaning male relatives. They were literally carrying her away from the grave. The children and Grampa brought up the rear. No one listens to good advice.

A man stepped away from the crowd and walked towards us. He was the one who reminded me of Peter Burke from the back. He was around six feet, dark-complected, a black mustache, and thin almost goateelike beard framing a handsome face. It was handsome, a dark movie-star face, but there was something about the way he moved. Maybe it was the white streak in his black hair just over the forehead. Whatever, you knew that he would always play the villain.

"Is she going to help us?" he asked, no preamble, no hello.

"Yes," Jamison said. "Anita Blake, this is John Burke, Peter's brother."

John Burke, *the* John Burke, I wanted to ask. New Orleans's greatest animator and vampire slayer? A kindred spirit. We shook hands. His grip was strong, almost painfully so, as if he wanted to see if I would flinch. I didn't. He let go. Maybe he just didn't know his own strength? But I doubted it.

"I am truly sorry about your brother," I said. I meant it. I was glad I meant it.

He nodded. "Thank you for talking to the police about him."

"I'm surprised you couldn't get the New Orleans police to give you some juice with our local police," I said.

He had the grace to look uncomfortable. "The New Orleans police and I have had a disagreement."

"Really?" I said, eyes wide. I had heard the rumors, but I wanted to hear the truth. Truth is always stranger than fiction.

"John was accused of participating in some ritual murders," Jamison said. "Just because he's a practicing vaudun priest."

"Oh," I said. Those were the rumors. "How long have you been in town, John?"

"Almost a week."

"Really?"

"Peter had been missing for two days before they found the . . . body." He licked his lips. His dark brown eyes flicked to the scene behind me. Were the grave diggers moving in? I glanced back, but the grave looked just the same to me.

"Anything you could find out would be most appreciated," he said.

"I'll do what I can."

"I have to get back to the house." He shrugged, as if to loosen the shoulder muscles. "My sister-in-law isn't taking it well."

I let it go. I deserved brownie points for that. One thing I didn't let go. "Can you look after your niece and nephew?"

He looked at me, a puzzled frown between his black eyebrows.

"I mean, keep them out of the really dramatic stuff if you can."

He nodded. "It was rough for me to watch her throw herself on the coffin. God, what must the kids be thinking?" Tears glittered in his eyes like silver. He kept them open very wide so the tears wouldn't spill out.

I didn't know what to say. I did not want to see him cry. "I'll talk to the police, find out what I can. I'll tell Jamison when I have anything."

John Burke nodded, carefully. His eyes were like a glass where only the surface tension kept the water from spilling over.

I nodded to Jamison and left. I turned on the air-conditioning in my car and let it run full blast. The two men were still standing in the hot sunshine in the middle of summer brown grass when I put the car in gear and drove away.

I would talk to the police and find out what I could. I also had another name for Dolph. John Burke, biggest animator in New Orleans, voodoo priest. Sounded like a suspect to me.

10

The phone was ringing as I shoved the key into my apartment door. I yelled at it, "I'm coming, I'm coming!" Why do people do that? Yell at the phone as if the other person can hear you and will wait?

I shoved the door open and scooped up the phone on the fourth ring. "Hello."

"Anita?"

"Dolph," I said. My stomach tightened. "What's up?"

"We think we found the boy." His voice was quiet, neutral.

"Think," I said. "What do you mean, think?"

"You know what I mean, Anita," he said. He sounded tired.

"Like his parents?" It wasn't a question.

"Yeah."

"God, Dolph, is there much left?"

"Come and see. We're at the Burrell Cemetery. Do you know it?"

"Sure, I've done work there."

"Be here as soon as you can. I want to go home and hug my wife."

"Sure, Dolph, I understand." I was talking to myself. The phone had gone dead. I stared at the receiver for a moment. My skin felt cold. I did not want to go and view the remains of Benjamin Reynolds. I did not want to know. I pulled a lot of air in through my nose and let it out slowly.

I stared down at the dark hose, high heels, dress. It wasn't my usual crime scene attire, but it would take too long to change. I was usually the last expert called in. Once I was through, they could cover the body. And everyone could go home. I grabbed a pair of black Nikes for walking over grass and through blood. Once you got bloodstains on dress shoes, they never come clean.

I had the Browning Hi-Power, complete with holster, sort of draped atop my little black clutch purse. The gun had been in my car during the funeral. I couldn't figure out a way to carry a gun of any kind while wearing a dress.

I know you see thigh holsters on television, but does the word "chafing" mean anything to you?

I hesitated on getting my backup gun and shoving it in my purse, but didn't. My purse, like all purses, seems to have a traveling black hole in it. I'd never get the gun out in time if I really needed it.

I did have a silver knife in a thigh sheath under the short black skirt. I felt like Kit Carson in drag, but after Tommy's little visit, I didn't want to be unarmed. I had no illusions what would happen if Tommy did catch me with no gun. Knives weren't as good, but they beat the hell out of kicking my little feet and screaming.

I had never yet had to try to fast draw a knife from a thigh sheath. It was probably going to look vaguely obscene, but if it kept me alive . . . hey, I can take a little embarrassment.

Burrell Cemetery is at the crest of a hill. Some of the gravestones go back centuries. The soft, weathered limestone is almost unreadable, like hard candy that's been sucked clean. The grass is waist tall, luxuriant with only the headstones standing like tired sentinels.

There is a house on the edge of the cemetery where the caretaker lives, but he doesn't have to take care of much. The graveyard is full and has been for years. The last person buried here could remember the 1904 World's Fair.

There is no road into the graveyard anymore. There is a ghost of one, like a wagon track where the grass doesn't grow quite so high. The caretaker's house was surrounded by police cars and the coroner's van. My Nova seemed underdressed. Maybe I should get some buggy whip antennae, or plaster Zombies "R" Us on the side of the car. Bert would probably get mad.

I got a pair of coveralls from the trunk and slipped into them. They covered me from neck to ankle. Like most coveralls the crotch hit at knee level, I never understood why, but it meant my skirt didn't bunch up. I bought them originally for vampire stakings, but blood is blood. Besides, the weeds would play hell with my panty hose. I got a pair of surgical gloves from the little Kleenex-like box in the trunk. Nikes instead of dress shoes, and I was ready to view the remains.

Remains. Nice word.

Dolph stood like some ancient sentinel, towering over everyone else in the field. I worked my way towards him, trying not to trip over broken bits of headstone. A wind hot enough to scald rustled the grass. I was sweating inside the overalls.

Detective Clive Perry came to meet me, as if I needed an escort. Detective Perry was one of the most polite people I had ever met. He had an old-world courtliness to him. A gentleman in the best sense of the word. I always wanted to ask what he had done to end up on the spook squad.

His slender black face was beaded with sweat. He still wore his suit jacket even though it had to be over a hundred degrees. "Ms. Blake."

"Detective Perry," I said. I glanced up at the crest of the hill. Dolph and a handful of men were standing around like they didn't know what to do. No one was looking at the ground.

"How bad is it, Detective Perry?" I asked.

He shook his head. "Depends on what you compare it to."

"Did you see the tapes and pictures of the Reynolds' house?"

"I did."

"Is it worse than that?" It was my new "worst thing I ever saw" measurement. Before this it had been a vampire gang that had tried to move in from Los Angeles. The respectable vampire community had chopped them up with axes. The parts were still crawling around the room when we found them. Maybe this wasn't worse. Maybe time had just dimmed the memory.

"It isn't bloodier," he said, then he hesitated, "but it was a child. A little boy."

I nodded. He didn't need to explain. It was always worse when it was a child. I never knew exactly why. Maybe it was some primal instinct to protect the young. Some deep hormonal thing. Whatever, kids were always worse. I stared down at a white tombstone. It looked like dull, melted ice. I didn't want to go up the hill. I didn't want to see.

I went up the hill. Detective Perry followed. Brave detective. Brave me.

A sheet rested on the grass like a tent. Dolph stood closest to it. "Dolph," I said.

"Anita."

No one offered to pull back the sheet. "Is this it?"

"Yeah."

Dolph seemed to shake himself, or maybe it was a shiver. He reached down and grabbed the edge of the sheet. "Ready?" he asked.

No, I wasn't ready. Don't make me look. Please don't make me look. My mouth was dry. I could taste my pulse in my throat. I nodded.

The sheet flew back, caught by a gust of wind like a white kite. The grass was trampled down. Struggles? Had Benjamin Reynolds been alive when he was pulled down into the long grass? No, surely not. God, I hoped not.

The footed pajamas had tiny cartoon figures on them. The pajamas had been pulled back like the skin of a banana. One small arm was flung up over his head like he was sleeping. Long-lashed eyelids helped the illusion. His skin was pale and flawless, small cupid-bow mouth half open. He should have looked worse, much worse.

There was a dirty brown stain on his pajamas, the cloth covering his lower body. I did not want to see what had killed him. But that was why I was here. I hesitated, fingers hovering over the torn cloth. I took a deep breath, and that was a mistake. Hunkered over the body in the windy August heat the smell was fresh. New death smells like an outhouse, especially if the stomach or bowels have been ripped open. I knew what I'd find when I lifted the bloody cloth. The smell told me.

I knelt with a sleeve over my mouth and nose for a few minutes, breathing shallow and through my mouth, but it didn't really help. Once you caught a whiff of it, your nose remembered. The smell crawled down my throat and wouldn't let go.

Quick or slow? Did I jerk the cloth back or pull it? Quick. I jerked on the cloth, but it stuck, dried blood catching. The cloth peeled back with a wet, sucking sound.

It looked like someone had taken a giant ice cream scoop and gutted him. Stomach, intestines, upper bowels, gone. The sunshine swam around me, and I had to put a hand on the ground to keep from falling.

I glanced up at the face. His hair was pale brown like his mother's. Damp curls traced his cheeks. My gaze was pulled back to the gaping ruin that was his abdomen. There was some dark, heavy fluid leaking out of the end of his small intestine.

I stumbled away from the crime scene, using the tombstones to help me stand. I would have run if I hadn't known I would fall. The sky was spinning to meet the ground. I collapsed in the smothering grass and vomited.

I threw up until I was empty and the world stopped spinning. I wiped my mouth on my sleeve and stood up using a crooked headstone for support.

No one said a word as I walked back to them. The sheet was covering the body. The body. Had to think of it that way. Couldn't dwell on the fact that it had been a small child. Couldn't. I'd go mad.

"Well?" Dolph asked.

"He hasn't been dead long. Dammit to hell, Dolph, it was late morning, maybe just before dawn. He was alive, alive when that thing took him!" I stared up at him and felt the hot beginnings of tears. I would not cry. I had already disgraced myself enough for one day. I took a deep careful breath and let it out. I would not cry.

"I gave you twenty-four hours to talk to this Dominga Salvador. Did you find out anything?"

"She says she knows nothing of it. I believe her."

"Why?"

"Because if she wanted to kill people she wouldn't have to do anything this dramatic."

"What do you mean?" he asked.

"She could wish them to death," I said.

He widened his eyes. "You believe that?"

I shrugged. "Maybe. Yes. Hell, I don't know. She scares me."

He raised one thick eyebrow. "I'll remember that."

"I have another name to add to your list though," I said.

"Who?"

"John Burke. He's up from New Orleans for his brother's funeral."

He wrote the name in his little notebook. "If he's just visiting, would he have time?"

"I can't think of a motive, but he could do it if he wanted to. Check him out with the New Orleans police. I think he's under suspicion down there for murder."

"What's he doing traveling out of state?"

"I don't think they have any proof," I said. "Dominga Salvador said she'd help me. She's promised to ask around and tell me anything she turns up."

"I've been asking around since you gave me her name. She doesn't help anyone outside her own people. How did you get her to cooperate?"

I shrugged. "My winning personality."

He shook his head.

"It wasn't illegal, Dolph. Beyond that I don't want to talk about it."

He let it go. Smart man. "Tell me as soon as you hear anything, Anita. We've got to stop this thing before it kills again."

"Agreed." I turned and looked out over the rolling grass. "Is this the cemetery near where you found the first three victims?"

"Yes."

"Maybe part of the answer's here then," I said.

"What do you mean?"

"Most vampires have to return to their coffins before dawn. Ghouls stay in underground tunnels, like giant moles. If it was either of those I'd say the creature was out here somewhere waiting for nightfall."

"But," he said.

"But if it's a zombie it isn't harmed by sunlight and it doesn't need to rest in a coffin. It could be anywhere, but I think it originally came from this cemetery. If they used voodoo there will be signs of the ritual."

"Like what?"

"A chalk verve, drawn symbols around the grave, dried blood, maybe a fire." I stared off at the rustling grass. "Though I wouldn't want to start an open fire in this place."

"If it wasn't voodoo?" he asked.

"Then it was an animator. Again you look for dried blood, maybe a dead animal. There won't be as many signs and it's easier to clean up."

"Are you sure it's some kind of a zombie?" he asked.

"I don't know what else it could be. I think we should act like that's what it is. It gives us someplace to look, and something to look for."

"If it's not a zombie we don't have a clue," he said.

"Exactly."

He smiled, but it wasn't pleasant. "I hope you're right, Anita."

"Me, too," I said.

"If it did come from here, can you find what grave it came from?"

"Maybe."

"Maybe?" he said.

"Maybe. Raising the dead isn't a science, Dolph. Sometimes I can feel the dead under the ground. Restlessness. How old without looking at the tombstone. Sometimes I can't." I shrugged.

"We'll give you any help you need."

"I have to wait until full dark. My . . . powers are better after dark."

"That's hours away. Can you do anything now?"

I thought about that for a moment. "No. I'm sorry but no."

"Okay, you'll come back tonight then?"

"Yeah," I said.

"What time? I'll send some men out."

"I don't know what time. And I don't know how long it will take. I could be wandering out here for hours and find nothing."

"Or?"

"Or I could find the beastie itself."

"You'll need backup for that, just in case."

I nodded. "Agreed, but guns, even silver bullets, won't hurt it."

"What will?"

"Flamethrowers, napalm like the exterminators use on ghoul tunnels," I said.

"Those aren't standard issue."

"Have an exterminator team standing by," I said.

"Good idea." He made a note.

"I need a favor," I said.

He looked up. "What?"

"Peter Burke was murdered, shot to death. His brother asked me to find out what progress the police are making."

"You know we can't give out information like that."

"I know, but if you can get the facts I can feed just enough to John Burke to keep in touch with him."

"You seem to be getting along well with all our suspects," he said.

"Yeah."

"I'll find out what I can from homicide. Do you know what jurisdiction he was found in?"

I shook my head. "I could find out. It would give me an excuse to talk to Burke again."

"You say he's suspected of murder in New Orleans."

"Mm-huh," I said.

"And he may have done this." He motioned at the sheet.

"Yep."

"You watch your back, Anita."

"I always do," I said.

"You call me as early tonight as you can. I don't want all my people sitting around twiddling their thumbs on overtime."

"As soon as I can. I've got to cancel three clients just to make it." Bert was not going to be pleased. The day was looking up.

"Why didn't it eat more of the boy?" Dolph asked.

"I don't know," I said.

He nodded. "Okay, I'll see you tonight then."

"Say hello to Lucille for me. How's she coming with her master's degree?"

"Almost done. She'll have it before our youngest gets his engineering degree."

"Great."

The sheet flapped in the hot wind. A trickle of sweat trailed down my forehead. I was out of small talk. "See you later," I said, and started down the hill. I stopped and turned back. "Dolph?"

"Yes?" he said.

"I've never heard of a zombie exactly like this one. Maybe it does rise from its grave more like a vampire. If you kept that exterminator team and backup hanging around until after dark, you might catch it rising from the grave and be able to bag it."

"Is that likely?"

"No, but it's possible," I said.

"I don't know how I'll explain the overtime, but I'll do it."

"I'll be here as soon as I can."

"What else could be more important than this?" he asked.

I smiled. "Nothing you'd like to hear about."

"Try me," he said.

I shook my head.

He nodded. "Tonight, early as you can."

"Early as I can," I said.

Detective Perry escorted me back. Maybe politeness, maybe he just wanted to get away from the corpus delicti. I didn't blame him. "How's your wife, Detective?"

"We're expecting our first baby in a month."

I smiled up at him. "I didn't know. Congratulations."

"Thank you." His face clouded over, a frown puckering between his dark eyes. "Do you think we can find this creature before it kills again?"

"I hope so," I said.

"What are our chances?"

Did he want reassurance or the truth. Truth. "I haven't the faintest idea."

"I was hoping you wouldn't say that," he said.

"So was I, Detective. So was I."

11

What was more important than bagging the critter that had eviscerated an entire family? Nothing, absolutely nothing. But it was a while until full dark, and I had other problems. Would Tommy go back to Gaynor and tell him what I said? Yes. Would Gaynor let it go? Probably not. I needed information. I needed to know how far he would go. A reporter, I needed a reporter. Irving Griswold to the rescue.

Irving had one of those pastel cubicles that passes for an office. No roof, no door, but you got walls. Irving is five-three. I'd like him for that reason if nothing else. You don't meet many men exactly my height. Frizzy brown hair framed his bald spot like petals on a flower. He wore a white dress shirt, sleeves rolled up to the elbow, tie at half-mast. His face was round, pink-cheeked. He looked like a bald cherub. He did not look like a werewolf, but he was one. Even lycanthropy can't cure baldness.

No one on the St. Louis *Post-Dispatch* knew Irving was a shapeshifter. It is a disease, and it's illegal to discriminate against lycanthropes, just like people with AIDS, but people do it anyway. Maybe the paper's management would have been broad-minded, liberal, but I was with Irving. Caution was better.

Irving sat in his desk chair. I leaned in the doorway of his cubicle. "How's tricks?" Irving said.

"Do you really think you're funny, or is this just an annoying habit?" I asked.

He grinned. "I'm hilarious. Ask my girlfriend."

"I'll bet," I said.

"What's up, Blake? And please tell me whatever it is is on the record, not off."

"How would you like to do an article on the new zombie legislation that's being cooked up?"

"Maybe," he said. His eyes narrowed, suspicion gleamed forth. "What do you want in return?"

"This part is off the record, Irving, for now."

"It figures." He frowned at me. "Go on."

"I need all the information you have on Harold Gaynor."

"Name doesn't ring any bells," he said. "Should it?" His eyes had gone from cheerful to steady. His concentration was nearly perfect when he smelled a story.

"Not necessarily," I said. Cautious. "Can you get the information for me?"

"In exchange for the zombie story?"

"I'll take you to all the businesses that use zombies. You can bring a photographer and snap pictures of corpses."

His eyes lit up. "A series of articles with lots of semigruesome pictures. You center stage in a suit. Beauty and the Beast. My editor would probably go for it."

"I thought he might, but I don't know about the center stage stuff."

"Hey, your boss will love it. Publicity means more business."

"And sells more papers," I said.

"Sure," Irving said. He looked at me for maybe a minute. The room was almost silent. Most had gone home. Irving's little pool of light was one of just a few. He'd been waiting on me. So much for the press never sleeps. The quiet breath of the air conditioner filled the early evening stillness.

"I'll see if Harold Gaynor's in the computer," Irving said at last.

I smiled at him. "Remembered the name after me mentioning it just once, pretty good."

"I am, after all, a trained reporter," he said. He swiveled his chair back to his computer keyboard with exaggerated movements. He pulled imaginary gloves on and adjusted the long tails of a tux.

"Oh, get on with it." I smiled a little wider.

"Do not rush the maestro." He typed a few words and the screen came to life. "He's on file," Irving said. "A big file. It'd take forever to print it all up." He swiveled the chair back to look at me. It was a bad sign.

"I'll tell you what," he said. "I'll get the file together, complete with pictures if we have any. I'll deliver it to your sweet hands."

"What's the catch?"

He put his fingers to his chest. "*Moi,* no catch. The goodness of my heart."

"All right, bring it by my apartment."

"Why don't we meet at Dead Dave's, instead?" he said.

"Dead Dave's is down in the vampire district. What are you doing hanging around out there?"

His sweet cherubic face was watching me very steadily. "Rumor has it that there's a new Master Vampire of the City. I want the story."

I just shook my head. "So you're hanging around Dead Dave's to get information?"

"Exactly."

"The vamps won't talk to you. You look human."

"Thanks for the compliment," he said. "The vamps do talk to you, Anita. Do you know who the new Master is? Can I meet him, or her? Can I do an interview?"

"Jesus, Irving, don't you have enough troubles without messing with the king vampire?"

"It's a him then," he said.

"It's a figure of speech," I said.

"You know something. I know you do."

"What I know is that you don't want to come to the attention of a master vampire. They're mean, Irving."

"The vampires are trying to mainstream themselves. They want positive attention. An interview about what he wants to do with the vampire community. His vision of the future. It would be very up-and-coming. No corpse jokes. No sensationalism. Straight journalism."

"Yeah, right. On page one a tasteful little headline: THE MASTER VAMPIRE OF ST. LOUIS SPEAKS OUT."

"Yeah, it'll be great."

"You've been sniffing newsprint again, Irving."

"I'll give you everything we have on Gaynor. Pictures."

"How do you know you have pictures?" I said.

He stared up at me, his round, pleasant face cheerfully blank.

"You recognized the name, you little son of . . ."

"Tsk, tsk, Anita. Help me get an interview with the Master of the City. I'll give you anything you want."

"I'll give you a series of articles about zombies. Full-color pictures of rotting corpses, Irving. It'll sell papers."

"No interview with the Master?" he said.

"If you're lucky, no," I said.

"Shoot."

"Can I have the file on Gaynor?"

He nodded. "I'll get it together." He looked up at me. "I still want you to meet me at Dead Dave's. Maybe a vamp will talk to me with you around."

"Irving, being seen with a legal executioner of vampires is not going to endear you to the vamps."

"They still call you the Executioner?"

"Among other things."

"Okay, the Gaynor file for going along on your next vampire execution?"

"No," I said.

"Ah, Anita . . ."

"No."

He spread his hands wide. "Okay, just an idea. It'd be a great article."

"I don't need the publicity, Irving, not that kind anyway."

He nodded. "Yeah, yeah. I'll meet you at Dead Dave's in about two hours."

"Make it an hour. I'd like to be out of the District before full dark."

"Is anybody gunning for you down there? I mean I don't want to endanger you, Blake." He grinned. "You've given me too many lead stories. I wouldn't want to lose you."

"Thanks for the concern. No, no one's after me. Far as I know."

"You don't sound real certain."

I stared at him. I thought about telling him that the new Master of the City had sent me a dozen white roses and an invitation to go dancing. I had turned him down. There had been a message on my machine and an invitation to a black tie affair. I ignored it all. So far the Master was behaving like the courtly gentleman he had been a few centuries back. It couldn't last. Jean-Claude was not a person who took defeat easily.

I didn't tell Irving. He didn't need to know. "I'll see you at Dead Dave's in an hour. I'm gonna run home and change."

"Now that you mention it, I've never seen you in a dress before."

"I had a funeral today."

"Business or personal?"

"Personal," I said.

"Then I'm sorry."

I shrugged. "I've got to go if I'm going to have time to change and then meet you. Thanks, Irving."

"It's not a favor, Blake. I'll make you pay for those zombie articles."

I sighed. I had images of him making me embrace the poor corpse. But the new legislation needed attention. The more people who understood the horror of it, the better chance it had to pass. In truth, Irving was still doing me a favor. No need to let him know that, though.

I walked away into the dimness of the darkened office. I waved over my shoulder without looking back. I wanted to get out of this dress and into something I could hide a gun on. If I was going into Blood Square, I might need it.

12

Dead Dave's is in the part of St. Louis that has two names. Polite: the Riverfront. Rude: the Blood Quarter. It is our town's hottest vampire commercial district. Big tourist attraction. Vampires have really put St. Louis on the vacation maps. You'd think that the Ozark Mountains, some of the best fishing in the country, the symphony, Broadway level musicals, or maybe the Botanical Gardens would be enough, but no. I guess it's hard to compete with the undead. I know I find it difficult.

Dead Dave's is all dark glass and beer signs in the windows. The afternoon sunlight was fading into twilight. Vamps wouldn't be out until full dark. I had a little under two hours. Get in, look over the file, get out. Easy. Ri-ight.

I had changed into black shorts, royal-blue polo shirt, black Nikes with a matching blue swish, black and white jogging socks, and a black leather belt. The belt was there so the shoulder holster had something to hang on. My Browning Hi-Power was secure under my left arm. I had thrown on a short-sleeved dress shirt to hide the gun. The dress shirt was in a modest black and royal-blue print. The outfit looked great. Sweat trickled down my spine. Too hot for the shirt, but the Browning gave me thirteen bullets. Fourteen if you're animal enough to shove the magazine full and carry one in the chamber.

I didn't think things were that bad, yet. I did have an extra magazine shoved into the pocket of my shorts. I know it picks up pocket lint, but where else was I going to carry it? One of these days I promise to get a deluxe holster with spaces for extra magazines. But all the models I'd seen had to be cut down to my size and made me feel like the Frito Bandito.

I almost never carry an extra clip when I've got the Browning. Let's face it, if you need more than thirteen bullets, it's over. The really sad part was the extra ammo wasn't for Tommy, or Gaynor. It was for Jean-Claude.

The Master Vampire of the City. Not that silver-plated bullets would kill him. But they would hurt him, make him heal almost human slow.

I wanted out of the District before dark. I did not want to run into Jean-Claude. He wouldn't attack me. In fact, his intentions were good, if not exactly honorable. He had offered me immortality without the messy part of becoming a vampire. There was some implication that I got him along with eternity. He was tall, pale, and handsome. Sexier than a silk teddy.

He wanted me to be his human servant. I wasn't anyone's servant. Not even for eternal life, eternal youth, and a little compromise of the soul. The price was too steep. Jean-Claude didn't believe that. The Browning was in case I had to make him believe it.

I stepped into the bar and was momentarily blind, waiting for my eyes to adjust to the dimness. Like one of those old westerns where the good guy hesitates at the front of the bar and views the crowd. I suspected he wasn't looking for the bad guy at all. He had just come out of the sun and couldn't see shit. No one ever shoots you while you're waiting for your eyes to adjust. I wonder why?

It was after five on a Thursday. Most of the bar stools and all the tables were taken. The place was cheek to jowl with business suits, male and female. A spattering of work boots and tans that ended at the elbow, but mostly upwardly mobile types. Dead Dave's had become trendy despite efforts to keep it at bay.

It looked like happy hour was in high gear. Shit. All the yuppies were here to catch a nice safe glimpse of a vampire. They would be slightly sloshed when it happened. Increase the thrill I guess.

Irving was sitting at the rounded corner of the bar. He saw me and waved. I waved back and started pushing my way towards him.

I squeezed between two gentlemen in suits. It took some maneuvering, and a very uncool-looking hop to mount the bar stool.

Irving grinned broadly at me. There was a nearly solid hum of conversation in the air. Words translated into pure noise like the ocean. Irving had to lean into me to be heard over the murmuring sound.

"I hope you appreciate how many dragons I had to slay to save that seat for you," he said. The faint smell of whiskey breathed along my cheek as he spoke.

"Dragons are easy, try vampires sometimes," I said.

His eyes widened. Before his mouth could form the question, I said, "I'm kidding, Irving." Sheesh, some people just don't have a sense of humor. "Besides, dragons were never native to North America," I said.

"I knew that."

"Sure," I said.

He sipped whiskey from a faceted glass. The amber liquid shimmered in the subdued light.

Luther, daytime manager and bartender, was down at the far end of the bar dealing with a group of very happy people. If they had been any happier they'd have been passed out on the floor.

Luther is large, not tall, fat. But it is solid fat, almost a kind of muscle. His skin is so black, it has purple highlights. The cigarette between his lips flared orange as he took a breath. He could talk around a cig better than anyone I'd ever met.

Irving picked up a scuffed leather briefcase from off the floor near his feet. He fished out a file over three inches thick. A large rubber band wrapped it together.

"Jesus, Irving. Can I take it home with me?"

He shook his head. "A sister reporter is doing a feature on local upstanding businessmen who are not what they seem. I had to promise her dibs on my firstborn to borrow it for the night."

I looked at the stack of papers. I sighed. The man on my right nearly rammed an elbow in my face. He turned. "Sorry, little lady, sorry. No harm done." Little came out liddle, and sorry slushed around the edges.

"No harm," I said.

He smiled and turned back to his friend. Another business type who laughed uproariously at something. Get drunk enough and everything is funny.

"I can't possibly read the file here," I said.

He grinned. "I'll follow you anywhere."

Luther stood in front of me. He pulled a cigarette from the pack he always carried with him. He put the tip of his still burning stub against the fresh cigarette. The end flared red like a live coal. Smoke trickled up his nose and out his mouth. Like a dragon.

He crushed the old cig in the clear glass ashtray he carried with him from place to place like a teddy bear. He chain smokes, is grossly overweight, and his grey hair puts him over fifty. He's never sick. He should be the national poster child for the Tobacco Institute.

"A refill?" he asked Irving.

"Yeah, thanks."

Luther took the glass, refilled it from a bottle under the bar, and set it back down on a fresh napkin.

"What can I get for ya, Anita?" he asked.

"The usual, Luther."

He poured me a glass of orange juice. We pretend it is a screwdriver. I'm a teetotaler, but why would I come to a bar if I didn't drink?

He wiped the bar with a spotless white towel. "Gotta message for you from the Master."

"The Master Vampire of the City?" Irving asked. His voice had that excited lilt to it. He smelled news.

"What?" There was no excited lilt to my voice.

"He wants to see you, bad."

I glanced at Irving, then back at Luther. I tried to telepathically send the message, not in front of the reporter. It didn't work.

"The Master's put the word out. Anybody who sees you gives you the message."

Irving was looking back and forth between us like an eager puppy. "What does the Master of the City want with you, Anita?"

"Consider it given," I said.

Luther shook his head. "You ain't going to talk to him, are you?"

"No," I said.

"Why not?" Irving asked.

"None of your business."

"Off the record," he said.

"No."

Luther stared at me. "Listen to me, girl, you talk to the Master. Right now all the vamps and freaks are just supposed to tell you the Master wants a powwow. The next order will be to detain you and take ya to him."

Detain, it was a nice word for kidnap. "I don't have anything to say to the Master."

"Don't let this get outta hand, Anita," Luther said. "Just talk to him, no harm."

That's what he thought. "Maybe I will." Luther was right. It was talk to him now or later. Later would probably be a lot less friendly.

"Why does the Master want to talk to you?" Irving asked. He was like some curious, bright-eyed bird that had spied a worm.

I ignored the question, and thought up a new one. "Did your sister reporter give you any highlights from this file? I don't really have time to read *War and Peace* before morning."

"Tell me what you know about the Master, and I'll give you the highlights."

"Thanks a lot, Luther."

"I didn't mean to sic him on you," he said. His cig bobbed up and down as he spoke. I never understood how he did that. Lip dexterity. Years of practice.

"Would everybody stop treating me like the bubonic fucking plague," Irving said. "I'm just trying to do my job."

I sipped my orange juice and looked at him. "Irving, you're messing with things you don't understand. I cannot give you info on the Master. I can't."

"Won't," he said.

I shrugged. "Won't, but the reason I won't is because I can't."

"That's a circular argument," he said.

"Sue me." I finished the juice. I didn't want it anyway. "Listen, Irving, we had a deal. The file info for the zombie articles. If you're going to break your word, deal's off. But tell me it's off. I don't have time to sit here and play twenty damn questions."

"I won't go back on the deal. My word is my bond," he said in as stagy a voice as he could manage in the murmurous noise of the bar.

"Then give me the highlights and let me get the hell out of the District before the Master hunts me up."

His face was suddenly solemn. "You're in trouble, aren't you?"

"Maybe. Help me out, Irving. Please."

"Help her out," Luther said.

Maybe it was the please. Maybe it was Luther's looming presence. Whatever, Irving nodded. "According to my sister reporter, he's crippled in a
wheelchair."

I nodded. Nondirective, that's me.

"He likes his women crippled."

"What do you mean?" I remembered Cicely of the empty eyes.

"Blind, wheelchair, amputee, whatever, old Harry'll go for it."

"Deaf," I said.

"Up his alley."

"Why?" I asked. Clever questions are us.

Irving shrugged. "Maybe it makes him feel better since he's trapped in
a chair himself. My fellow reporter didn't know why he was a deviant, just
that he was."

"What else did she tell you?"

"He's never even been charged with a crime, but the rumors are real
ugly. Suspected mob connections, but no proof. Just rumors."

"Tell me," I said.

"An old girlfriend tried to sue him for palimony. She disappeared."

"Disappeared as in probably dead," I said.

"Bingo."

I believed it. So he'd used Tommy and Bruno to kill before. Meant it
would be easier to give the order a second time. Or maybe Gaynor'd given
the order lots of times, and just never gotten caught.

"What does he do for the mob that earns him his two bodyguards?"

"Oh, so you've met his security specialist."

I nodded.

"My fellow reporter would love to talk to you."

"You didn't tell her about me, did you?"

"Do I look like a stoolie?" He grinned at me.

I let that go. "What's he do for the mob?"

"Helps them clean money, or that's what we suspect."

"No evidence?" I said.

"None." He didn't look happy about it.

Luther shook his head, tapping his cig into the ashtray. Some ash spilled
onto the bar. He wiped it with his spotless towel. "He sounds like bad news,
Anita. Free advice, leave him the hell alone."

Good advice. Unfortunately. "I don't think he'll leave me alone."

"I won't ask, I don't want to know." Someone else was frantically
signaling for a refill. Luther drifted over to them. I could watch the entire
bar in the full-length mirror that took up the wall behind the bar. I could
even see the door without turning around. It was convenient and comforting.

"I will ask," Irving said, "I do want to know."

I just shook my head.

"I know something you don't know," he said.

"And I want to know it?"

He nodded vigorously enough to make his frizzy hair bob.

I sighed. "Tell me."

"You first."

I had about enough. "I have shared all I am going to tonight, Irving. I've got the file. I'll look through it. You're just saving me a little time. Right now, a little time could be very important to me."

"Oh, shucks, you take all the fun out of being a hard-core reporter." He looked like he was going to pout.

"Just tell me, Irving, or I'm going to do something violent."

He half laughed. I don't think he believed me. He should have. "All right, all right." He brought out a picture from behind his back with a flourish like a magician.

It was a black and white photo of a woman. She was in her twenties, long brown hair down in a modern style, just enough mousse to make it look spiky. She was pretty. I didn't recognize her. The photo was obviously not posed. It was too casual and there was a look to the face of someone who didn't know she was being photographed.

"Who is she?"

"She was his girlfriend until about five months ago," Irving said.

"So she's ... handicapped?" I stared down at the pretty, candid face. You couldn't tell by the picture.

"Wheelchair Wanda."

I stared at him. I could feel my eyes going wide. "You can't be serious."

He grinned. "Wheelchair Wanda cruises the streets in her chair. She's very popular with a certain crowd."

A prostitute in a wheelchair. Naw, it was too weird. I shook my head. "Okay, where do I find her?"

"I and my sister reporter want in on this."

"That's why you kept her picture out of the file."

He didn't even have the grace to look embarrassed. "Wanda won't talk to you alone, Anita."

"Has she talked to your reporter friend?"

He frowned, the light of conquest dimming in his eyes. I knew what that meant. "She won't talk to reporters will she, Irving?"

"She's afraid of Gaynor."

"She should be," I said.

"Why would she talk to you and not us?"

"My winning personality," I said.

"Come on, Blake."

"Where does she hang out, Irving?"

"Oh, hell." He finished his dwindling drink in one angry swallow. "She stays near a club called The Grey Cat."

The Grey Cat, like that old joke, all cats are grey in the dark. Cute. "Where's the club?"

Luther answered. I hadn't seen him come back. "On the main drag in the Tenderloin, corner of Twentieth and Grand. But I wouldn't go down there alone, Anita.''

"I can take care of myself.''

"Yeah, but you don't look like you can. You don't want to have to shoot some dumb shmuck just because he copped a feel, or worse. Take someone who looks mean, save yourself the aggravation.''

Irving shrugged. "I wouldn't go down there alone.''

I hated to admit it, but they were right. I may be heap big vampire slayer but it doesn't show much on the outside. "Okay, I'll get Charles. He looks tough enough to take on the Green Bay Packers, but his heart is oh so gentle.''

Luther laughed, puffing smoke. "Don't let ol' Charlie see too much. He might faint.''

Faint once in public and people never let you forget.

"I'll keep Charles safe.'' I put more money down on the bar than was needed. Luther hadn't really given me much information this time, but usually he did. Good information. I never paid full price for it. I got a discount because I was connected with the police. Dead Dave had been a cop before they kicked him off the force for being undead. Shortsighted of them. He was still pissed about that, but he liked to help. So he fed me information, and I fed the police selected bits of it.

Dead Dave came out of the door behind the bar. I glanced at the dark glass windows. It looked the same, but if Dave was up, it was full dark. Shit. It was a walk back to my car surrounded by vampires. At least I had my gun. Comforting that.

Dave is tall, wide, short brown hair that had been balding when he died. He lost no more hair but it didn't grow back either. He smiled at me wide enough to flash fangs. An excited wiggle ran through the crowd, as if the same nerve had been touched in all of them. The whispers spread like rings in a pool. Vampire. The show was on.

Dave and I shook hands. His hand was warm, firm, and dry. Have you fed tonight, Dave? He looked like he had, all rosy and cheerful. What did you feed on, Dave? And was it willing? Probably. Dave was a good guy for a dead man.

"Luther keeps telling me you stopped by but it's always in daylight. Nice to see you're slumming after dark.''

"Truthfully, I planned to be out of the District before full dark.''

He frowned. "You packing?''

I gave him a discreet glimpse of my gun.

Irving's eyes widened. "You're carrying a gun.'' It only sounded like he shouted it.

The noise level had died down to a waiting murmur. Quiet enough for people to overhear. But then, that's why they had come, to listen to the vampire. To tell their troubles to the dead. I lowered my voice and said, "Announce it to the world, Irving.''

He shrugged. "Sorry.''

"How do you know newsboy over here?" Dave asked.

"He helps me sometimes with research."

"Research, well la-de-da." He smiled without showing any fang. A trick you learn after a few years. "Luther give you the message?"

"Yeah."

"You going to be smart or dumb?"

Dave is sorta blunt, but I like him anyway. "Dumb probably," I said.

"Just because you got a special relationship with the new Master, don't let it fool you. He's still a master vampire. They are freaking bad news. Don't fuck with him."

"I'm trying to avoid it."

Dave smiled broad enough to show fang. "Shit, you mean . . . Naw, he wants you for more than good tail."

It was nice to know he thought I'd be good tail. I guess. "Yeah," I said.

Irving was practically bouncing in his seat. "What the hell is going on, Anita?"

Very good question. "My business, not yours."

"Anita . . ."

"Stop pestering me, Irving. I mean it."

"Pestering? I haven't heard that word since my grandmother."

I looked him straight in the eyes and said, carefully, "Leave me the fuck alone. That better?"

He put his hands out in an I-give-up gesture. "Heh, just trying to do my job."

"Well, do it somewhere else."

I slid off the bar stool.

"The word's out to find you, Anita," Dave said. "Some of the other vampires might get overzealous."

"You mean try to take me?"

He nodded.

"I'm armed, cross and all. I'll be okay."

"You want me to walk you to your car?" Dave asked.

I stared into his brown eyes and smiled. "Thanks, Dave, I'll remember the offer, but I'm a big girl." Truth was a lot of the vampires didn't like Dave feeding information to the enemy. I was the Executioner. If a vampire stepped over the line, they sent for me. There was no such thing as a life sentence for a vamp. Death or nothing. No prison can hold a vampire.

California tried, but one master vampire got loose. He killed twenty-five people in a one-night bloodbath. He didn't feed, he just killed. Guess he was pissed about being locked up. They'd put crosses over the doors and on the guards. Crosses don't work unless you believe in them. And they certainly don't work once a master vampire has convinced you to take them off.

I was the vampire's equivalent of an electric chair. They didn't like me much. Surprise, surprise.

"I'll be with her," Irving said. He put money down on the bar and stood up. I had the bulky file under my arm. I guess he wasn't going to let it out of his sight. Great.

"She'll probably have to protect you, too," Dave said.

Irving started to say something, then thought better of it. He could say, but I'm a lycanthrope, except he didn't want people to know. He worked very, very hard at appearing human.

"You sure you'll be okay?" he asked. One more chance for a vampire guard to my car.

He was offering to protect me from the Master. Dave hadn't been dead ten years. He wasn't good enough. "Nice to know you care, Dave."

"Go on, get outta here," he said.

"Watch yourself, girl," Luther said.

I smiled brightly at both of them, then turned and walked out of the near silent bar. The crowd couldn't have overheard much, if any, of the conversation, but I could feel them staring at my back. I resisted an urge to whirl around and go "boo." I bet somebody would have screamed.

It's the cross-shaped scar on my arm. Only vampires have them, right? A cross shoved into unclean flesh. Mine had been a branding iron specially made. A now dead master vampire had ordered it. Thought it would be funny. Hardy-har.

Or maybe it was just Dave. Maybe they hadn't noticed the scar. Maybe I was overly sensitive. Make friendly with a nice law-abiding vampire, and people get suspicious. Have a few funny scars and people wonder if you're human. But that's okay. Suspicion is healthy. It'll keep you alive.

13

The sweltering darkness closed around me like a hot, sticky fist. A streetlight formed a puddle of brilliance on the sidewalk, as if the light had melted. All the streetlights are reproductions of turn-of-the-century gas lamps. They rise black and graceful, but not quite authentic. Like a Halloween costume. It looks good but is too comfortable to be real.

The night sky was like a dark presence over the tall brick buildings, but the streetlights held the darkness back. Like a black tent held up by sticks of light. You had the sense of darkness without the reality.

I started walking for the parking garage just off First Street. Parking on the Riverfront is damn near impossible. The tourists have only made the problem worse.

The hard soles of Irving's dress shoes made a loud, echoing noise on the stone of the street. Real cobblestones. Streets meant for horses, not cars. It made parking a bitch, but it was . . . charming.

My Nike Airs made almost no sound on the street. Irving was like a clattery puppy beside me. Most lycanthropes I've met have been stealthy. Irving may have been a werewolf but he was more dog. A big, fun-loving dog.

Couples and small groups passed us, laughing, talking, voices too shrill. They had come to see vampires. Real-live vampires, or was that real-dead vampires? Tourists, all of them. Amateurs. Voyeurs. I had seen more undead than any of them. I'd lay money on that. The fascination escaped me.

It was full dark now. Dolph and the gang would be awaiting me at Burrell Cemetery. I needed to get over there. What about the file on Gaynor? And what was I going to do with Irving? Sometimes my life is too full.

A figure detached itself from the darkened buildings. I couldn't tell if he had been waiting or had simply appeared. Magic. I froze, like a rabbit caught in headlights, staring.

"What's wrong, Blake?" Irving asked.

I handed him the file and he took it, looking puzzled. I wanted my hands free in case I had to go for my gun. It probably wouldn't come to that. Probably.

Jean-Claude, Master Vampire of the City, walked towards us. He moved like a dancer, or a cat, a smooth, gliding walk. Energy and grace contained, waiting to explode into violence.

He wasn't that tall, maybe five-eleven. His shirt was so white, it gleamed. The shirt was loose, long, full sleeves made tight at the wrist by three-buttoned cuffs. The front of the shirt had only a string to close the throat. He'd left it untied, and the white cloth framed the pale smoothness of his chest. The shirt was tucked into tight black jeans, and only that kept it from billowing around him like a cape.

His hair was perfectly black, curling softly around his face. The eyes, if you dared to look into them, were a blue so dark it was almost black. Glittering, dark jewels.

He stopped about six feet in front of us. Close enough to see the dark cross-shaped scar on his chest. It was the only thing that marred the perfection of his body. Or what I'd seen of his body.

My scar had been a bad joke. His had been some poor sod's last attempt to stave off death. I wondered if the poor sod had escaped? Would Jean-Claude tell me if I asked? Maybe. But if the answer was no, I didn't want to hear it.

"Hello, Jean-Claude," I said.

"Greetings, *ma petite,*" he said. His voice was like fur, rich, soft, vaguely obscene, as if just talking to him was something dirty. Maybe it was.

"Don't call me *ma petite,*" I said.

He smiled slightly, not a hint of fang. "As you like." He looked at Irving. Irving looked away, careful not to meet Jean-Claude's eyes. You never looked directly into a vampire's eyes. Never. So why was I doing it with impunity. Why indeed?

"Who is your friend?" The last word was very soft and somehow threatening.

"This is Irving Griswold. He's a reporter for the *Post-Dispatch.* He's helping me with a little research."

"Ah," he said. He walked around Irving as if he were something for sale, and Jean-Claude wanted to see all of him.

Irving gave nervous little glances so that he could keep the vampire in view. He glanced at me, widening his eyes. "What's going on?"

"What indeed, Irving?" Jean-Claude said.

"Leave him alone, Jean-Claude."

"Why have you not come to see me, my little animator?"

Little animator wasn't much of an improvement over *ma petite,* but I'd take it. "I've been busy."

The look that crossed his face was almost anger. I didn't really want him mad at me. "I was going to come see you," I said.

"When?"

"Tomorrow night."

"Tonight." It was not a suggestion.

"I can't."

"Yes, *ma petite,* you can." His voice was like a warm wind in my head.

"You are so damn demanding," I said.

He laughed then. Pleasant and resonating like expensive perfume that lingers in the room after the wearer has gone. His laughter was like that, lingering in the ears like distant music. He had the best voice of any master vampire I'd ever met. Everyone has their talents.

"You are so exasperating," he said, the edge of laughter still in his voice. "What am I to do with you?"

"Leave me alone," I said. I was utterly serious. It was one of my biggest wishes.

His face sobered completely, like someone had flipped a switch. On, happy, off, unreadable. "Too many of my followers know you are my human servant, *ma petite.* Bringing you under control is part of consolidating my power." He sounded almost regretful. A lot of help that did me.

"What do you mean, bringing me under control?" My stomach was tight with the beginnings of fear. If Jean-Claude didn't scare me to death, he was going to give me an ulcer.

"You are my human servant. You must start acting like one."

"I am not your servant."

"Yes, *ma petite,* you are."

"Dammit, Jean-Claude, leave me alone."

He was suddenly standing next to me. I hadn't seen him move. He had clouded my mind without me even blinking. I could taste my pulse at the back of my throat. I tried to step back, but one pale slender hand grabbed my right arm, just above the elbow. I shouldn't have stepped back. I should have gone for my gun. I hoped I would live through the mistake.

My voice came out flat, normal. At least I'd die brave. "I thought having two of your vampire marks meant you couldn't control my mind."

"I cannot bewitch you with my eyes, and it is harder to cloud your mind, but it can be done." His fingers encircled my arm. Not hurting. I didn't try to pull away. I knew better. He could crush my arm without breaking a sweat, or tear it from its socket, or bench press a Toyota. If I couldn't arm wrestle Tommy, I sure as hell couldn't match Jean-Claude.

"He's the new Master of the City, isn't he?" It was Irving. I think we had forgotten about him. It would have been better for Irving if we had.

Jean-Claude's grip tightened slightly on my right arm. He turned to look at Irving. "You are the reporter that has been asking to interview me."

"Yes, I am." Irving sounded just the tiniest bit nervous, not much, just the hint of tightness in his voice. He looked brave and resolute. Good for Irving.

"Perhaps after I have spoken with this lovely young woman, I will grant you your interview."

"Really?" Astonishment was plain in his voice. He grinned widely at me. "That would be great. I'll do it any way you want. It . . ."

"Silence." The word hissed and floated. Irving fell quiet as if it were a spell.

"Irving, are you all right?" Funny me asking. I was the one cheek to jowl with a vampire, but I asked anyway.

"Yeah," Irving said. That one word was squeezed small with fear. "I've just never felt anything like him."

I glanced up at Jean-Claude. "He is sort of one of a kind."

Jean-Claude turned his attention back to me. Oh, goody. "Still making jokes, *ma petite.*"

I stared up into his beautiful eyes, but they were just eyes. He had given me the power to resist them. "It's a way to pass the time. What do you want, Jean-Claude?"

"So brave, even now."

"You aren't going to do me on the street, in front of witnesses. You may be the new Master, but you're also a businessman. You're mainstream vampire. It limits what you can do."

"Only in public," he said, so soft that only I heard him.

"Fine, but we both agree you aren't going to do violence here and now." I stared up at him. "So cut the theatrics and tell me what the bloody hell you want."

He smiled then, a bare movement of lips, but he released my arm and stepped back. "Just as you will not shoot me down in the street without provocation."

I thought I had provocation, but nothing I could explain to the police. "I don't want to be up on murder charges, that's true."

His smile widened, still not fangs. He did that better than any living vampire I knew. Was living vampire an oxymoron? I wasn't sure anymore.

"So, we will not harm each other in public," he said.

"Probably not," I said. "What do you want? I'm late for an appointment."

"Are you raising zombies or slaying vampires tonight?"

"Neither," I said.

He looked at me, waiting for me to say more. I didn't. He shrugged and it was graceful. "You are my human servant, Anita."

He'd used my real name, I knew I was in trouble now. "Am not," I said.

He gave a long sigh. "You bear two of my marks."

"Not by choice," I said.

"You would have died if I had not shared my strength with you."

"Don't give me crap about how you saved my life. You forced two marks on me. You didn't ask or explain. The first mark may have saved my life, great. The second mark saved yours. I didn't have a choice either time."

"Two more marks and you will have immortality. You will not age because I do not age. You will remain human, alive, able to wear your crucifix. Able to enter a church. It does not compromise your soul. Why do you fight me?''

"How do you know what compromises my soul? You don't have one anymore. You traded your immortal soul for earthly eternity. But I know that vampires can die, Jean-Claude. What happens when you die? Where do you go? Do you just go poof? No, you go to hell where you belong.''

"And you think by being my human servant you will go with me?''

"I don't know, and I don't want to find out.''

"By fighting me, you make me appear weak. I cannot afford that, *ma petite*. One way or another, we must resolve this.''

"Just leave me alone.''

"I cannot. You are my human servant, and you must begin to act like one.''

"Don't press me on this, Jean-Claude.''

"Or what, will you kill me? Could you kill me?''

I stared at his beautiful face and said, ''Yes.''

"I feel your desire for me, *ma petite,* as I desire you.''

I shrugged. What could I say? "It's just a little lust, Jean-Claude, nothing special.'' That was a lie. I knew it even as I said it.

"No, *ma petite,* I mean more to you than that.''

We were attracting a crowd, at a safe distance. "Do you really want to discuss this in the street?''

He took a deep breath and let it out in a sigh. "Very true. You make me forget myself, *ma petite.*''

Great. "I really am late, Jean-Claude. The police are waiting for me.''

"We must finish this discussion, *ma petite,*'' he said.

I nodded. He was right. I'd been trying to ignore it, and him. Master vampires are not easy to ignore. "Tomorrow night.''

"Where?'' he asked.

Polite of him not to order me to his lair. I thought about where best to do it. I wanted Charles to go down to the Tenderloin with me. Charles was going to be checking the zombie working conditions at a new comedy club. Good a place as any. "Do you know The Laughing Corpse?''

He smiled, a glimpse of fang touching his lips. A woman in the small crowd gasped. "Yes.''

"Meet me there at, say, eleven o'clock.''

"My pleasure.'' The words caressed my skin like a promise. Shit.

"I will await you in my office, tomorrow night.''

"Wait a minute. What do you mean, your office?'' I had a bad feeling about this.

His smile widened into a grin, fangs glistening in the streetlights. "Why, I own The Laughing Corpse. I thought you knew.''

"The hell you did.''

"I will await you.''

I'd picked the place. I'd stand by it. Dammit. "Come on, Irving.''

"No, let the reporter stay. He has not had his interview.''

"Leave him alone, Jean-Claude, please."

"I will give him what he desires, nothing more."

I didn't like the way he said desires. "What are you up to?"

"Me, *ma petite,* up to something?" He smiled.

"Anita, I want to stay," Irving said.

I turned to him. "You don't know what you're saying."

"I'm a reporter. I'm doing my job."

"Swear to me, swear to me you won't harm him."

"You have my word," Jean-Claude said.

"That you will not harm him in any way."

"That I will not harm him in any way." His face was expressionless, as if all the smiles had been illusions. His face had that immobility of the long dead. Lovely to look at, but empty of life as a painting.

I looked into his blank eyes and shivered. Shit. "Are you sure you want to stay here?"

Irving nodded. "I want the interview."

I shook my head. "You're a fool."

"I'm a good reporter," he said.

"You're still a fool."

"I can take care of myself, Anita."

We looked at each other for a space of heartbeats. "Fine, have fun. May I have the file?"

He looked down at his arms as if he had forgotten he was holding it. "Drop it by tomorrow morning or Madeline is going to have a fit."

"Sure. No problem." I tucked the bulky file under my left arm as loosely as I could manage it. It hampered my being able to draw my gun, but life's imperfect.

I had information on Gaynor. I had the name of a recent ex-girlfriend. A woman scorned. Maybe she'd talk to me. Maybe she'd help me find clues. Maybe she'd tell me to go to hell. Wouldn't be the first time.

Jean-Claude was watching me with his still eyes. I took a deep breath through my nose and let it out through my mouth. Enough for one night. "See you both tomorrow." I turned and walked away. There was a group of tourists with cameras. One was sort of tentatively raised in my direction.

"If you snap my picture, I will take the camera away from you and break it." I smiled while I said it.

The man lowered his camera uncertainly. "Geez, just a little picture."

"You've seen enough," I said. "Move on, the show's over." The tourists drifted away like smoke when the wind blows through it. I walked down the street towards the parking garage. I glanced back and found the tourists had drifted back to surround Jean-Claude and Irving. The tourists were right. The show wasn't over yet.

Irving was a big boy. He wanted the interview. Who was I to play nursemaid on a grown werewolf? Would Jean-Claude find out Irving's secret? If he did, would it make a difference? Not my problem. My problem was Harold Gaynor, Dominga Salvador, and a monster that was eating the good citizens of St. Louis, Missouri. Let Irving take care of his own problems. I had enough of my own.

14

The night sky was a curving bowl of liquid black. Stars like pinprick diamonds gave a cold, hard light. The moon was a glowing patchwork of greys and goldish-silver. The city makes you forget how dark the night, how bright the moon, how very many stars.

Burrell Cemetery didn't have any streetlights. There was nothing but the distant yellow gleam of a house's windows. I stood at the top of the hill in my coveralls and Nikes, sweating.

The boy's body was gone. It was in the morgue waiting for the coroner's attentions. I was finished with it. Never had to look at it again. Except in my dreams.

Dolph stood beside me. He didn't say a word, just looked out over the grass and broken tombstones, waiting. Waiting for me to do my magic. To pull the rabbit out of the hat. The best that could happen was the rabbit to be in and to destroy it. Next best thing was finding the hole it had come from. That could tell us something. And something was better than what we had right now.

The exterminators followed a few paces behind. The man was short, beefy, grey hair cut in a butch. He looked like a retired football coach, but he handled the flamethrower strapped to his back like it was something alive. Thick hands caressing it.

The woman was young, no more than twenty. Thin blond hair tied back in a ponytail. She was a little taller than me, small. Wisps of hair trailed across her face. Her eyes were wide and searched the tall grass, side to side. Like a gunner on point.

I hoped she didn't have an itchy trigger finger. I didn't want to be eaten by a killer zombie, but I didn't want to be plastered with napalm either. Burned alive or eaten alive? Is there anything else on the menu?

The grass rustled and whispered like dry autumn leaves. If we did use the flamethrowers in here, it'd be a grass fire. We'd be lucky to outrun it.

But fire was the only thing that could stop a zombie. If it was a zombie and not something else altogether.

I shook my head and started walking. Doubts would get us nowhere. Act like you know what you're doing; it was a rule I lived by.

I am sure that Señora Salvador would have had a specific rite or sacrifice to find a zombie's grave. Her way of doing all this had more rules than my way. Of course her way enabled her to trap souls in rotting corpses. I had never hated anyone enough to do that to them. Kill them, yes, but entrap their soul and make it sit and wait and feel its body rotting. No, that was worse than wicked. It was evil. She needed to be stopped, and only death would do that. I sighed. Another problem for another night.

It bothered me to hear Dolph's footsteps echoing mine. I glanced back at the two exterminators. They killed everything from termites to ghouls, but ghouls are cowards, scavengers mostly. Whatever we were after wasn't a scavenger.

I could feel the three of them at my back. Their footsteps seemed louder than mine. I tried to clear my mind and start the search, but all I could hear was their footsteps. All I could sense was the woman's fear. They were messing up my concentration.

I stopped. "Dolph, I need more room."

"What does that mean?"

"Hang back a little. You're ruining my concentration."

"We might be too far away to help."

"If the zombie rises out of the ground and leeches on me ..." I shrugged. "What are you going to do, shoot it with napalm and crispy-critter me, too?"

"You said fire was the only weapon," he said.

"It is, but if the zombie actually grapples with anyone, tell the exterminators not to fry the victim."

"If the zombie grabs one of us, we can't use the napalm?" he said.

"Bingo."

"You could have said this sooner."

"I just thought of it."

"Great," he said.

I shrugged. "I'll take point. My oversight. Just hang back and let me do my job." I stepped in close to him to whisper, "And watch the woman. She looks scared enough to start shooting shadows."

"They're exterminators, Anita, not police or vampire slayers."

"For tonight, our lives could depend on them, so keep an eye on her, okay?"

He nodded and glanced back at the two exterminators. The man smiled and nodded. The girl just stared. I could almost smell her fear.

She was entitled to it. Why did it bother me so much? Because she and I were the only women here, and we had to be better than the men. Braver, quicker, whatever. It was a rule for playing with the big boys.

I walked out into the grass alone. I waited until the only thing I could hear was the grass; soft, dry, whispering. Like it was trying to tell me some- thing in a scratchy, frantic voice. Frantic, fearful. The grass sounded afraid. That was stupid. Grass didn't feel shit. But I did, and there was sweat on every inch of my body. Was it here? Was the thing that had reduced a man to so much raw meat, here in the grass, hiding, waiting?

No. Zombies weren't smart enough for that, but of course, it had been smart enough to hide from the police. That was smart for a corpse. Too smart. Maybe it wasn't a zombie at all. I had finally found something that scared me more than vampires. Death didn't bother me much. Strong Chris- tian and all that. Method of death did. Being eaten alive. One of my top three ways not to go out.

Who would ever have thought I'd be afraid of a zombie, any kind of zombie? Nicely ironic that. I'd laugh later when my mouth wasn't so damn dry.

There was that quiet waiting that all cemeteries have. As if the dead held their collective breath, waiting, but for what? The resurrection? Maybe. But I've dealt with the dead too long to believe in just one answer. The dead are like the living. They do different things.

Most people die and go to heaven or hell, and that's that. But a few, for whatever reason, don't work that way. Ghosts, restless spirits, violence, evil, or simple confusion; all of these can trap a spirit on earth. I'm not saying that it traps the soul. I don't believe that, but some memory of the soul, the essence, lingers.

Was I expecting some specter to rise from the grass and rush screaming towards me? No. I had never seen a ghost yet that could cause actual physical harm. If it causes physical damage, it isn't a ghost; demon maybe, or the spirit of some sorcerer, black magic, but ghosts don't hurt.

That was almost a comforting thought.

The ground sloped out from under my feet. I stumbled and caught myself on one of the leaning headstones. Sunken earth, a grave without a marker. A tingling shock ran up my leg, a whisper of ghostly electricity. I jerked back and sat down hard on the ground.

"Anita, you all right?" Dolph yelled.

I glanced back at him and found the grass completely hid me from view. "I'm fine," I yelled. I got to my feet careful to avoid stepping on the old grave. Whatever person lay under the earth, he, or she, was not a happy camper. It was a hot spot, not a ghost, or even a haunt, but something. It had probably been a full-blown ghost once, but time had worn it away. Ghosts wear out like old clothes and go on to wherever old ghosts go.

The sunken grave would fade away, probably in my lifetime. If I could avoid killer zombies for a few years. And vampires. And gun-toting humans. Oh, hell, the hot spot would probably outlast me.

I looked back to find Dolph and the exterminators maybe twenty yards back. Twenty yards, wasn't that awfully far? I had told them to hang back, but I hadn't meant for them to leave me hanging in the wind. I was just never satisfied.

If I called them to come closer, you think they'd get mad? Probably. I started walking again, trying not to step on any more graves. But it was hard with most of the stones hidden in the long grass. So many unmarked graves, so much neglect.

I could wander aimlessly all bloody night. Had I really thought that I could just accidentally walk over the right grave? Yes. Hope springs eternal, especially when the alternative isn't very human.

Vampires were once ordinary human beings; zombies, too. Most lycanthropes start out human, though there are a few rare inherited curses. All the monsters start out normal except me. Raising the dead wasn't a career choice. I didn't sit down in the guidance counselor's office one day and say, "I'd like to raise the dead for a living." No, it wasn't that neat or clean.

I have always had an affinity for the dead. Always. Not the newly dead. No, I don't mess with souls, but once the soul departs, I know it. I can feel it. Laugh all you want. It's the truth.

I had a dog when I was little. Just like most kids. And like most kids' dogs, she died. I was thirteen. We buried Jenny in the backyard. I woke up a week after Jenny died and found her curled up beside me. Thick black fur coated with grave dirt. Dead brown eyes following my every move, just like when she was alive.

I thought for one wild moment she was alive. It had been a mistake, but I know dead when I see it. Feel it. Call it from the grave. I wonder what Dominga Salvador would think about that story. Calling an animal zombie. How shocking. Raising the dead by accident. How frightening. How sick.

My stepmother, Judith, never quite recovered from the shock. She rarely tells people what I do for a living. Dad? Well, Dad ignores it, too. I tried ignoring it, but couldn't. I won't go into details, but does the term "road kill" have any significance for you? It did for Judith. I looked like a nightmare version of the Pied Piper.

My father finally took me to meet my maternal grandmother. She's not as scary as Dominga Salvador, but she's ... interesting. Grandma Flores agreed with Dad. I should not be trained in voodoo, only in enough control to stop the ... problems. "Just teach her to control it," Dad said.

She did. I did. Dad took me back home. It was never mentioned again. At least not in front of me. I always wondered what dear stepmother said behind closed doors. For that matter Dad wasn't pleased either. Hell, I wasn't pleased.

Bert recruited me straight out of college. I never knew how he heard about me. I refused him at first, but he waved money at me. Maybe I was rebelling against parental expectations? Or maybe I had finally realized that there is damn little employment opportunity for a B.S. in biology with an emphasis on the supernatural. I minored in creatures of legend. That was real helpful on my résumé.

It was like having a degree in ancient Greek or the Romantic Poets, interesting, enjoyable, but then what the hell can you do with it? I had planned to go on to grad school and teach college. But Bert came along and showed me a way to turn my natural talent into a job. At least I can say I use my degree every day.

I never puzzled about how I came to do what I do. There was no mystery. It was in the blood.

I stood in the graveyard and took a deep breath. A bead of sweat trickled down my face. I wiped it with the back of my hand. I was sweating like a pig, and I still felt cold. Fear, but not of the bogeyman, of what I was about to do.

If it were a muscle, I would move it. If it were a thought, I would think it. If it were a magic word, I could say it. It is nothing like that. It is like my skin becomes cool even under cloth. I can feel all my nerve endings naked to the wind. And even in this hot, sweating August night, my skin felt cool. It is almost like a tiny, cool wind emanates from my skin. But it isn't wind, no one else can feel it. It doesn't blow through a room like a Hollywood horror movie. It isn't flashy. It's quiet. Private. Mine.

The cool fingers of "wind" searched outward. Within a ten-to-fifteen-foot circle I would be able to search the graves. As I moved, the circle would move with me, searching.

How does it feel to search through the hard-packed earth for dead bodies? Like nothing human. The closest I can come to describing it is like phantom fingers rifling through the dirt, searching for the dead. But, of course, that isn't quite what it feels like either. Close but no cigar.

The coffin nearest me had been water-ruined years ago. Bits of warped wood, shreds of bone, nothing whole. Bone and old wood, dirt, clean and dead. The hot spot flared almost like a burning sensation. I couldn't read its coffin. The hot spot could keep its secrets. It wasn't worth forcing the issue. It was a life force of sorts, trapped to a dead grave until it faded. That is bound to make you grumpy.

I walked slowly forward. The circle moved with me. I touched bones, intact coffins, bits of cloth in newer graves. This was an old cemetery. There were no decaying corpses. Death had progressed to the nice neat stage.

Something grabbed my ankle. I jumped and walked forward without looking down. Never look down. It's a rule. I got a brief glimpse just behind my eyes of something pale and mistlike with wide screaming eyes.

A ghost, a real-live ghost. I had walked over its grave and it had let me know it didn't like it. A ghost had grabbed me round the ankles. Big deal. If you ignored them, the spectral hands would fade. If you noticed them, you gave them substance, and you could be in deep shit.

Important safety tip with most of the spiritual world: if you ignore it, it has less power. This does not work with demons or other demi-beings. Other exceptions to the rule are vampires, zombies, ghouls, lycanthropes, witches . . . Oh, hell, ignoring only works for ghosts. But it does work.

Phantom hands tugged at my pants leg. I could feel skeletal fingers pulling upwards, as if it would use me to pull itself from the grave. Shit! I was eating my pulse between my teeth. Just keep walking. Ignore it. It will go away. Dammit to hell.

The fingers slipped away, reluctantly. Some types of ghost seem to bear a grudge against the living. A sort of jealousy. They cannot harm you, but they scare the bejesus out of you and laugh while they're doing it.

I found an empty grave. Bits of wood decaying into the earth, but no trace of bone. No body. Empty. The earth above it was thick with grass and weeds. The earth was hard-packed and dry from the drought. The grass and weeds had been disturbed. Bare roots were showing, almost as if someone had tried to pull the grass up. Or something had come up underneath the grass and left a trail.

I knelt on all fours above the dying grass. My hands stayed on top of the hard, reddish dirt, but I could feel the inside of the grave like rolling your tongue around your teeth. You can't see it, but you can feel it.

The corpse was gone. The coffin was undisturbed. A zombie had come from here. Was it the zombie we were looking for? No guarantees. But it was the only zombie raising I could sense.

I stared out away from the grave. It was hard using just my eyes to search the grass. I could almost see what lay under the dirt. But the grave showed behind my eyes in my head somewhere where there were no optic nerves. The graveyard that I could see with my eyes ended at a fence maybe five yards away. Had I walked it all? Was this the only grave that was empty?

I stood and looked out over the graves. Dolph and the two exterminators were still with me about thirty yards back. Thirty yards? Some backup.

I had walked it all. There was the grabby ghost. The hot spot was there. The newest grave over there. It was mine now. I knew this cemetery. And everything that was restless. Everything that wasn't quite dead was dancing above its grave. White misty phantoms. Sparkling angry lights. Agitated. There was more than one way to wake the dead.

But they would quiet down and sleep, if that was the word. No permanent damage. I glanced back down at the empty grave. No permanent damage.

I waved Dolph and the others over. I got a Ziploc bag out of the coverall pocket and scooped some grave dirt into it.

The moonlight suddenly seemed dimmer. Dolph was standing over me. He did sort of loom.

"Well?" he asked.

"A zombie came out of this grave," I said.

"Is it the killer zombie?"

"I don't know for sure."

"You don't know?"

"Not yet."

"When will you know?"

"I'll take it to Evans and let him do his touchie-feelie routine on it."

"Evans, the clairvoyant," Dolph said.

"Yep."

"He's a flake."

"True, but he's good."

"The department doesn't use him anymore."

"Bully for the department," I said. "He's still on retainer at Animators, Inc."

Dolph shook his head. "I don't trust Evans."

"I don't trust anybody," I said. "So what's the problem?"

Dolph smiled. "Point taken."

I had rolled some of the grass and weeds, roots carefully intact, inside a second bag. I crawled to the head of the grave and spread the weeds. There was no marker. Dammit! The pale limestone had been chipped away at the base. Shattered. Carried away. Shit.

"Why would they destroy the headstone?" Dolph asked.

"The name and date could have given us some clue to why the zombie was raised and to what went wrong."

"Wrong, how?"

"You might raise a zombie to kill one or two people but not wholesale slaughter. Nobody would do that."

"Unless they're crazy," he said.

I stared up at him. "That's not funny."

"No, it isn't."

A madman that could raise the dead. A murderous zombie corpse controlled by a psychotic. Great. And if he, or she, could do it once . . .

"Dolph, if we have a crazy man running around, there could be more than one zombie."

"And if it is crazy, then there won't be a pattern," he said.

"Shit."

"Exactly."

No pattern meant no motive. No motive meant we might not be able to figure this out. "No, I don't believe that."

"Why not?" he asked.

"Because if I do believe it, it leaves us no place to go." I took out a pocketknife that I brought for the occasion and started to chip at the remains of the tombstone.

"Defacing a gravemarker is against the law," Dolph said.

"Isn't it though." I scraped a few smaller pieces into a third bag, and finally got a sizable chunk of marble, big as my thumb.

I stuffed all the bags into the pockets of my coveralls, along with the pocketknife.

"You really think Evans will be able to read anything from those bits and pieces?"

"I don't know." I stood and looked down at the grave. The two exterminators were standing just a short distance away. Giving us privacy. How very polite. "You know, Dolph, they may have destroyed the tombstone, but the grave is still here."

"But the corpse is gone," he said.

"True, but the coffin might be able to tell us something. Anything might help."

He nodded. "Alright, I'll get an exhumation order."

"Can't we just dig it up now, tonight?"

"No," he said. "I have to play by the rules." He stared at me very hard. "And I don't want to come back out here and find the grave dug up. The evidence won't mean shit if you tamper with it."

"Evidence? You really think this case will go to court?"

"Yes."

"Dolph, we just need to destroy the zombie."

"I want the bastards that raised it, Anita. I want them up on murder charges."

I nodded. I agreed with him, but I thought it unlikely. Dolph was a policeman, he had to worry about the law. I worried about simpler things, like survival.

"I'll let you know if Evans has anything useful to say," I said.

"You do that."

"Wherever the beastie is, Dolph, it isn't here."

"It's out there, isn't it?"

"Yeah," I said.

"Killing someone else while we sit here and chase our tails."

I wanted to touch him. To let him know it was all right, but it wasn't all right. I knew how he felt. We were chasing our tails. Even if this was the grave of the killer zombie, it didn't get us any closer to finding the zombie. And we had to find it. Find it, trap it, and destroy it. The sixty-four-thousand-dollar question was, could we do all that before it needed to feed again? I didn't have an answer. That was a lie. I had an answer. I just didn't like it. Out there somewhere, the zombie was feeding again.

15

The trailer park where Evans lives is in St. Charles just off Highway 94. Acres of mobile homes roll out in every direction. Of course, there's nothing mobile about them. When I was a kid, trailers could be hooked to the back of a car and moved. Simple. It was one of their appeals. Some of these mobile homes had three and four bedrooms, multiple baths. The only thing moving these puppies was a semitruck, or a tornado.

Evans's trailer is an older model. I think, if he had to, he could chain it to the back of a pickup and move. Easier than hiring a moving van, I guess. But I doubt Evans will ever move. Hell, he hasn't left the trailer in nearly a year.

The windows were golden with light. There was a little makeshift porch complete with an awning, guarding the door. I knew he would be up. Evans was always up. Insomnia sounded so harmless. Evans had made it a disease.

I was back in my black shorts outfit. The three bags of goodies were stuffed in a fanny pack. If I went in there waving them around, Evans would freak. I needed to work up to it, be subtle. Just thought I'd drop by to see my old buddy. No ulterior motives here. Right.

I opened the screen door and knocked. Silence. No movement. Nothing. I raised my hand to knock again, then hesitated. Had Evans finally gotten to sleep? His first decent night's sleep since I'd known him. Drat. I was still standing there with my hand half-raised when I felt him staring at me.

I looked up at the little window in the door. A slice of pale face was staring out from between the curtains. Evans's blue eye blinked at me.

I waved.

His face disappeared. The door unlocked, then opened. There was no sight of Evans, just the open door. I walked in. Evans was standing behind the door, hiding.

He closed the door by leaning against it. His breathing was fast and shallow as if he'd been running. Stringy yellow hair trailed over a dark blue bathrobe. His face was covered in bristly reddish beard.

"How are you doing, Evans?"

He leaned against the door, eyes too wide. His breathing was still too fast. Was he on something?

"Evans, you all right?" When in doubt, reverse your word order.

He nodded. "What do you want?" His voice was breathy.

I didn't think he was going to believe I had just stopped by. Call it an instinct. "I need your help."

He shook his head. "No."

"You don't even know what I want."

He shook his head. "Doesn't matter."

"May I sit down?" I asked. If directness wouldn't work, maybe politeness would.

He nodded. "Sure."

I glanced around the small living-room area. I was sure there was a couch under the newspapers, paper plates, half-full cups, old clothes. There was a box of petrified pizza on the coffee table. The room smelled stale.

Would he freak if I moved stuff? Could I sit on the pile that I thought was the couch without everything collapsing? I decided to try. I'd sit in the freaking moldy pizza box if Evans would agree to help me.

I perched on a pile of papers. There was definitely something large and solid under the newspapers. Maybe the couch. "May I have a cup of coffee?"

He shook his head. "No clean cups."

This I could believe. He was still pressed against the door as if afraid to come any closer. His hands were plunged into the pockets of his bathrobe.

"Can we just talk?" I asked.

He shook his head. I shook my head with him. He frowned at that. Maybe somebody was home.

"What do you want?" he asked.

"I told you, your help."

"I don't do that anymore."

"What?" I asked.

"You know," he said.

"No, Evans, I don't know. Tell me."

"I don't touch things anymore."

I blinked. It was an odd way to phrase it. I stared around at the piles of dirty dishes, the clothes. It did look untouched. "Evans, let me see your hands."

He shook his head. I didn't imitate him this time. "Evans, show me your hands."

"No," it was loud, clear.

I stood up and started walking towards him. It didn't take long. He backed away into the corner by the door and the doorway into the bedroom. "Show me your hands."

Tears welled in his eyes. He blinked, and the tears slid down his cheeks. "Leave me alone," he said.

My chest was tight. What had he done? God, what had he done? "Evans, either you show me your hands voluntarily, or I make you do it." I fought an urge to touch his arm, but that was not allowed.

He was crying harder now, small hiccupy sobs. He pulled his left hand out of the robe pocket. It was pale, bony, whole. I took a deep breath. Thank you, dear God.

"What did you think I'd done?" he asked.

I shook my head. "Don't ask."

He was looking at me now, really looking at me. I did have his attention. "I'm not that crazy," he said.

I started to say, "I never thought you were," but obviously I had. I had thought he had cut his hands off so he wouldn't have to touch anymore. God, that was crazy. Seriously crazy. And I was here to ask him to help me with a murder. Which of us was crazier? Don't answer that.

He shook his head. "What are you doing here, Anita?" The tears weren't even dry on his face, but his voice was calm, ordinary.

"I need your help with a murder."

"I don't do that anymore. I told you."

"You told me once that you couldn't not have visions. Your clairvoyance isn't something you can just turn off."

"That's why I stay in here. If I don't go out, I don't see anybody. I don't have visions anymore."

"I don't believe you," I said.

He took a clean white handkerchief out of his pocket and wrapped it around the doorknob. "Get out."

"I saw a three-year-old boy today. He'd been eaten alive."

He leaned his forehead into the door. "Don't do this to me, please."

"I know other psychics, Evans, but no one with your success rate. I need the best. I need you."

He rubbed his forehead against the door. "Please don't."

I should have gone then, left, done what he said, but I didn't. I stood behind him and waited. Come on, old buddy, old pal, risk your sanity for me. I was the ruthless zombie raiser. I didn't feel guilt. Results were all that mattered. Ri-ight.

But in a way, results *were* all that mattered. "Other people are going to die unless we can stop it," I said.

"I don't care," he said.

"I don't believe you."

He stuffed the handkerchief back into his pocket and whirled around. "The little boy, you're not lying about that, are you?"

"I wouldn't lie to you."

He nodded. "Yeah, yeah." He licked his lips. "Give me what ya got."

I got the bags out of my purse and opened the one with the gravestone fragments in it. Had to start somewhere.

He didn't ask what it was, that would be cheating. I wouldn't even have mentioned the boy except I needed the leverage. Guilt is a wonderful tool.

His hand shook as I dropped the largest rock fragment into his palm. I was very careful that my fingers did not brush his hand. I didn't want Evans inside my secrets. It might scare him off.

His hand clenched around the stone. A shock ran up his spine. He jerked, eyes closed. And he was gone.

"Graveyard, grave." His head jerked to the side like he was listening to something. "Tall grass. Hot. Blood, he's wiping blood on the tombstone." He looked around the room with his closed eyes. Would he have seen the room if his eyes had been open?

"Where does the blood come from?" he asked that. Was I supposed to answer? "No, no!" He stumbled backwards, back smacking into the door. "Woman screaming, screaming, no, no!"

His eyes flew open wide. He threw the rock fragment across the room. "They killed her, they killed her!" He pressed his fists into his eyes. "Oh, God, they slit her throat."

"Who is they?"

He shook his head, fists still shoved against his face. "I don't know."

"Evans, what did you see?"

"Blood." He stared at me between his arms, shielding his face. "Blood everywhere. They slit her throat. They smeared the blood on the tombstone."

I had two more items for him. Dare I ask? Asking didn't hurt. Did it? "I have two more items for you to touch."

"No fucking way," he said. He backed away from me towards the short hall that led to the bedroom. "Get out, get out, get the fuck out of my house. Now!"

"Evans, what else did you see?"

"Get out!"

"Describe one thing about the woman. Help me, Evans!"

He leaned in the doorway and slid to sit on the floor. "A bracelet. She wore a bracelet on her left wrist. Little dangling charms, hearts, bow and arrow, music." He shook his head and buried his head against his eyes. "Go away now."

I started to say thank you, but that didn't cut it. I picked my way over the floor searching for the rock fragment. I found it in a coffee cup. There was something green and growing in the bottom of it. I picked up the stone and wiped it on a pair of jeans on the floor. I put it back in the bag and shoved all of it inside the purse.

I stared around at the filth and didn't want to leave him here. Maybe I was just feeling guilty for having abused him. Maybe. "Evans, thanks."

He didn't look up.

"If I had a cleaning person drop by, would you let her in to clean?"

"I don't want anybody in here."

"Animators, Inc., could pick up the tab. We owe you for this one."

He looked up then. Anger, pure anger was all that was in his face. "Evans, get some help. You're tearing yourself apart."

"Get-the-fuck-out-of-my-house." Each word was hot enough to scald. I had never seen Evans angry. Scared, yes, but not like this. What could I say? It was his house.

I got out. I stood on the shaky porch until I heard the door lock behind me. I had what I wanted, information. So why did I feel so bad? Because I had bullied a seriously disturbed man. Okay, that was it. Guilt, guilt, guilt.

An image flashed into my head, the blood-soaked sheet on the brown patterned couch. Mrs. Reynolds's spine dangling wet and glistening in the sunlight.

I walked to my car and got in. If abusing Evans could save one family, then it was worth it. If it would keep me from having to see another three-year-old boy with his intestines ripped out, I'd beat Evans with a padded club. Or let him beat me.

Come to think of it, wasn't that what we'd just done?

16

I was small in the dream. A child. The car was crushed in front where it had been broadsided by another car. It looked like it was made of shiny paper that had been crushed by hand. The door was open. I crawled inside on the familiar upholstery, so pale it was almost white. There was a dark liquid stain on the seat. It wasn't all that large. I touched it, tentatively.

My fingers came away smeared with crimson. It was the first blood I'd ever seen. I stared up at the windshield. It was broken in a spiderweb of cracks, bowed outward where my mother's face had smashed into it. She had been thrown out the door to die in a field beside the road. That's why there wasn't a lot of blood on the seat.

I stared at the fresh blood on my fingers. In real life the blood had been dry, just a stain. When I dreamed about it, it was always fresh.

There was a smell this time. The smell of rotten flesh. That wasn't right. I stared up in the dream and realized it was a dream. And the smell wasn't part of it. It was real.

I woke instantly, staring into the dark. My heart thudding in my throat. My hand went for the Browning in its second home, a sheath attached to the headboard of my bed. It was firm and solid, and comforting. I stayed on the bed, back pressed against the headboard, gun held in a teacup grip.

Through a tiny crack in the drapes moonlight spilled. The meager light outlined a man's shape. The shape didn't react to the gun or my movement. It shuffled forward, dragging its feet through the carpet. It had stumbled into my collection of toy penguins that spilled like a fuzzy tide under my bedroom window. It had knocked some of them over, and it didn't seem able to pick its feet up and walk over them. The figure was wading through the fluffy penguins, dragging its feet as if wading in water.

I kept the gun pointed one-handed at the thing and reached without looking to turn on my bedside lamp. The light seemed harsh after the darkness. I blinked rapidly willing my pupils to contract, to adjust. When they did, and I could see, it was a zombie.

He had been a big man in life. Shoulders broad as a barn door filled with muscle. His huge hands were very strong-looking. One eye had dehydrated and was shriveled like a prune. The remaining eye stared at me. There was nothing in that stare, no anticipation, no excitement, no cruelty, nothing but a blankness. A blankness that Dominga Salvador had filled with purpose. Kill she had said. I would have bet on it.

It was her zombie. I couldn't turn it. I couldn't order it to do anything until it fulfilled Dominga's orders. Once it killed me, it would be docile as a dead puppy. Once it killed me.

I didn't think I'd wait for that.

The Browning was loaded with Glazer Safety Rounds, silver-coated. Glazer Safety Rounds will kill a man if you hit him anywhere near the center of the body. The hole will be too big for salvage. A hole in its chest wouldn't bother the zombie. It would keep coming, heart or no heart. If you hit a person in the arm or leg with Safety Rounds, it will take off that arm or leg. Instant amputee. If you hit it right.

The zombie seemed in no hurry. He shuffled through the fallen stuffed toys with that single-minded determination of the dead. Zombies are not inhumanly strong. But they can use every ounce of strength; they don't save anything. Almost any human being could do a superhuman feat, once. Pop muscles, tear cartilage, snap your spine, but you can lift the car. Only inhibitors in the brain prevent us all from destroying ourselves. Zombies don't have inhibitors. The corpse could literally tear me apart while it tore itself apart. But if Dominga had really wanted to kill me, she would have sent a less-decayed zombie. This one was so far gone I might have been able to dodge around it, and make the door. Maybe. But then again . . .

I cupped the butt of the gun in my left, the right where it was supposed to be, my finger on the trigger. I pulled the trigger and the explosion was incredibly loud in the small room. The zombie jerked, stumbled. Its right arm flew off in a welter of flesh and bone. No blood, it had been dead too long for that.

The zombie kept coming.

I sighted on the other arm. Hold your breath, squee-eeze. I was aiming for the elbow. I hit it. The two arms lay on the carpet and began to worm their way towards the bed. I could chop the thing to pieces, and all the pieces would keep trying to kill me.

The right leg at the knee. The leg didn't come loose completely, but the zombie toppled to one side, listing. It fell on its side, then rolled onto its stomach and began pushing with its remaining leg. Some dark liquid was leaking out of the shattered leg. The smell was worse.

I swallowed, and it was thick. God. I got off the bed on the far side away from the thing. I walked around the bed coming in behind the thing. It knew instantly that I had moved. It tried to turn and come at me, pushing with that last leg. The crawling arms turned faster, fingers scrambling on the carpet. I stood over it and blasted the other leg from less than two feet away. Bits and pieces of it splattered onto my penguins. Damn.

The arms were almost at my bare feet. I fired two quick shots and the hand shattered, exploding on the white carpet. The handless arms flopped and struggled. They were still trying to reach me.

There was a brush of cloth, a sense of movement just behind me, in the darkened living room. I was standing with my back to the open door. I turned and knew it was too late.

Arms grabbed me, clutching me to a very solid chest. Fingers dug into my right arm, pinning the gun against my body. I turned my head away, using my hair to shield my face and neck. Teeth sank into my shoulder. I screamed.

My face was pressed against the thing's shoulder. The fingers were digging in. It was going to crush my arm. The gun barrel was pressed against its shoulder. Teeth tore at the flesh of my shoulder, but it wasn't fangs. It only had human teeth to work with. It hurt like hell, but it would be all right, if I could get away.

I turned my face forward away from the shoulder and pulled the trigger. The entire body jerked backwards. The left arm crumbled. I rolled out of its grip. The arm dangled from my forearm, fingers hanging on.

I was standing in the doorway of my bedroom staring at the thing that had almost got me. It had been a white male, about six-one, built like a football player. It was fresh from the farm. Blood spattered where the shoulder had torn away. The fingers on my arm tightened. It couldn't crush my arm, but I couldn't make it let go either. I didn't have the time.

The zombie charged, one arm wide to grab me. I seemed to have all the time in the world to lift the gun, two-handed. The arm struggled and fought me as if it were still connected to the zombie's brain. I got off two quick shots. The zombie stumbled, its left leg collapsing, but it was too late. It was too close. As it fell, it took me with it.

We landed on the floor with me on the bottom. I managed to keep the Browning up, so that my arms were free and so was the gun. His weight pinned my body, nothing I could do about it. Blood glistened on his lips. I fired point-blank, closing my eyes as I pulled the trigger. Not just because I didn't want to see, but to save my eyes from bone shards.

When I looked, the head was gone except for a thin line of naked jawbone and a fragment of skull. The remaining hand scrambled for my throat. The hand still attached to my arm was helping its body. I couldn't get the gun around to shoot the arm. The angle was wrong.

A sound of something heavy sliding behind me. I risked a glance, craning my neck backwards to see the first zombie coming towards me. Its mouth, all that it had left to hurt me with, was open wide.

I screamed and turned back to the one on top of me. The attached hand fluttered at my neck. I pulled it away and gave it its own arm to hold. It grabbed it. With the brain gone, it wasn't as smart. I felt the fingers on my arm loosen. A shudder ran through the dangling arm. Blood burst out of it like a ripe melon. The fingers spasmed, releasing my arm. The zombie crushed its own arm until it spattered and bones snapped.

The scrambling sounds behind me were closer. "God!"

"Police! Come out with your hands up!" The voice was male and loud from the hallway.

The hell with being cool and self-sufficient. "Help me!"

"Miss, what's happening in there?"

The scrambling sounds were right next to me. I craned my neck and found myself almost nose to nose with the first zombie. I shoved the Browning in its open mouth. Its teeth scraped on the barrel, and I pulled the trigger.

A policeman was suddenly in the doorway framed against the darkness. From my angle he was huge. Curly brown hair, going gray, mustache, gun in hand. "Jesus," he said.

The second zombie dropped its crushed arm and reached for me again. The policeman took a firm grip of the zombie's belt and pulled him upward with one hand. "Get her out of here," he said.

His partner moved in, but I didn't give him time. I scrambled out from under the half-raised body, scuttling on all fours into the living room. You didn't have to ask me twice. The partner lifted me to my feet by one arm. It was my right and the Browning came up with it.

Normally, a cop will make you drop your gun before anything else. There is usually no way to tell who the bad guy is. If you have a gun, you are a bad guy unless proven otherwise. Innocent until proven guilty does not work in the field.

He scooped the gun from my hand. I let him. I knew the drill.

A gunshot exploded behind us. I jumped, and the cop did, too. He was about my age, but right then I felt about a million years old. We turned and found the first cop shooting into the zombie. The thing had struggled free of his hand. It was on its feet, staggered by the bullets but not stopped.

"Get over here, Brady," the first cop said. The younger cop drew his gun and moved forward. He hesitated, glancing at me.

"Help him," I said.

He nodded and started firing into the zombie. The sound of gunfire was like thunder. It filled the room until my ears were ringing and the reek of gunpowder was almost overpowering. Bullet holes blossomed in the walls. The zombie kept staggering forward. They were just annoying it.

The problem for police is that they can't load up with Glazer Safety Rounds. Most cops don't run into the supernatural as much as I do. Most of the time they're chasing human crooks. The powers that be frown on taking off the leg of John Q. Public just 'cause he fired at you. You're not really supposed to kill people just because they're trying to kill you. Right?

So they had normal rounds, maybe a little silver coating to make the medicine go down, but nothing that could stop a zombie. They were being backed up. One reloaded while the other fired. The thing staggered forward. Its remaining arm sweeping in front of it, searching. For me. Shit.

"My gun's loaded with Glazer Safety Rounds," I said. "Use it."

The first cop said, "Brady, I told you to get her out of here."

"You needed help," Brady said.

"Get the civilian the fuck out of here."

Civilian, me?

Brady didn't question again. He just backed towards me, gun out but not firing. "Come on, miss, we gotta get out of here."

"Give me my gun."

He glanced at me, shook his head.

"I'm with the Regional Preternatural Investigation Team." Which was true. I was hoping he would assume I was a cop, which wasn't true.

He was young. He assumed. He handed me back the Browning. "Thanks."

I moved up with the older cop. "I'm with the Spook Squad."

He glanced at me, gun still trained on the advancing corpse. "Then do something."

Someone had turned on the living-room light. Now that no one was shooting it, the zombie was moving out. It walked like a man striding down the street, except it had no head and only one arm. There was a spring in its step. Maybe it sensed I was close.

The body was in better condition than the first zombie's had been. I could cripple it but not incapacitate it. I'd settle for crippled. I fired a third round into the left leg that I had wounded earlier. I had more time to aim, and my aim was true.

The leg collapsed under it. It pulled itself forward with the one arm, leg pushing against the rug. He was on his last leg. I started to smile, then to laugh, but it choked in my throat. I walked around the far side of the couch. I didn't want any accidents after what I'd seen it do to its own body. I didn't want any crushed limbs.

I came in behind it, and it scrambled quicker than it should have to try to face me. It took two shots for the other leg. I couldn't remember how many bullets I'd used. Did I have one more left, or two, or none?

I felt like Dirty Harry, except that this punk didn't give a damn how many bullets I had left. The dead don't scare easy.

It was still pulling itself and its damaged legs along. That one hand. I fired nearly point-blank, and the hand exploded like a crimson flower on the white carpet. It kept coming, using the wrist stump to push along.

I pulled the trigger, and it clicked empty. Shit. "I'm out," I said. I stepped back away from it. It followed me.

The older cop moved in and grabbed it by both ankles. He pulled it backwards. One leg slid slowly out of the pants and twisted free in his hand. "Fuck!" He dropped the leg. It wiggled like a broken-backed snake.

I stared down at the still determined corpse. It was struggling towards me. It wasn't making much progress. The policeman was holding it one-legged sort of in the air. But the zombie kept trying. It would keep trying until it was incinerated or Dominga Salvador changed her orders.

More uniformed cops came in the door. They fell on the butchered zombie like vultures on a wildebeest. It bucked and struggled. Fought to get away, to finish its mission. To kill me. There were enough cops to subdue it. They would hold it until the lab boys arrived. The lab boys would do what they could on-site. Then the zombie would be incinerated by an exterminator team. They had tried taking zombies down to the morgue and holding them for tests, but little pieces kept escaping and hiding out in the strangest places.

The medical examiner had decreed that all zombies were to be truly dead before shipping. The ambulance crew and lab techs agreed with her. I sympathized but knew that most evidence disappears in a fire. Choices, choices.

I stood to one side of my living room. They had forgotten me in the melee. Fine, I didn't feel like wrestling any more zombies tonight. I realized for the first time that I was wearing nothing but an oversize T-shirt and panties. The T-shirt clung wetly to my body, thick with blood. I started towards the bedroom. I think I meant to get a pair of pants. The sight on the floor stopped me.

The first zombie was like a legless insect. It couldn't move, but it was trying. The bloody stump of a body was still trying to carry out its orders. To kill me.

Dominga Salvador had meant to kill me. Two zombies, one almost new. She had meant to kill me. That one thought chased round my head like a piece of song. We had threatened each other, but why this level of violence? Why kill me? I couldn't stop her legally. She knew that. So why make such a damned serious attempt to kill me?

Maybe because she had something to hide? Dominga had given her word that she hadn't raised the killer zombie, but maybe her word didn't mean anything. It was the only answer. She had something to do with the killer zombie. Had she raised it? Or did she know who had? No. She'd raised the beast or why kill me the night after I talked to her? It was too big a coincidence. Dominga Salvador had raised a zombie, and it had gotten away from her. That was it. Evil as she was, she wasn't psychotic. She wouldn't just raise a killer zombie and let it loose. The great voodoo queen had screwed up royally. That, more than anything else, more than the deaths, or the possible murder charge, would piss her off. She couldn't afford her reputation to be trashed like that.

I stared past the bloody, stinking remnants in the bedroom. My stuffed penguins were covered in blood and worse. Could my long suffering dry cleaner get them clean? He did pretty good with my suits.

Glazer Safety Rounds didn't go through walls. It was another reason I liked them. My neighbors didn't get shot up. The police bullets had pierced the bedroom walls. Neat round holes were everywhere.

No one had ever attacked me at home before, not like this. It should have been against the rules. You should be safe in your own bed. I know, I know. Bad guys don't have rules. It's one of the reasons they're bad guys.

I knew who had raised the zombie. All I had to do was prove it. There was blood everywhere. Blood and worse things. I was actually getting used to the smell. God. But it stank. The whole apartment stank. Almost everything in my apartment is white; walls, carpet, couch, chair. It made the stains show up nicely, like fresh wounds. The bullet holes and cracked plaster board set off the blood nicely.

The apartment was trashed. I would prove Dominga had done this, then, if I was lucky, I'd get to return the favor.

"Sweets to the sweet," I whispered to no one in particular. Tears started to burn at the back of my throat. I didn't want to cry, but a scream was sort of tickling around in my throat, too. Crying or screaming. Crying seemed better.

The paramedics came. One was a short black woman about my own age. "Come on, honey, we got to take a look at you." Her voice was gentle, her hands sort of leading me away from the carnage. I didn't even mind her calling me honey.

I wanted very much to crawl up into someone's lap about now and be comforted. I needed that badly. I wasn't going to get it.

"Honey, we need to see how bad you're bleeding before we take you down to the ambulance."

I shook my head. My voice sounded far away, detached. "It's not my blood."

"What?"

I looked at her, fighting to focus and not drift. Shock was setting in. I'm usually better than this, but hey, we all have our nights.

"It's not my blood. I've got a bite on the shoulder, that's it."

She looked like she didn't believe me. I didn't blame her. Most people see you covered in blood, they just assume part of it has to be yours. They do not take into account that they are dealing with a tough-as-nails vampire slayer and corpse raiser.

The tears were back, stinging just behind my eyes. There was blood all over my penguins. I didn't give a damn about the walls and carpet. They could be replaced, but I'd collected those damned stuffed toys over years. I let the paramedic lead me away. Tears trickling down my cheeks. I wasn't crying, my eyes were running. My eyes were running because there were pieces of zombie all over my toys. Jesus.

17

I'd seen enough crime scenes to know what to expect. It was like a play I'd seen too many times. I could tell you all the entrances, the exits, most of the lines. But this was different. This was my place.

It was silly to be offended that Dominga Salvador had attacked me in my own home. It was stupid, but there it was. She had broken a rule. One I hadn't even known I had. Thou shalt not attack the good guy in his, or her, own home. Shit.

I was going to nail her hide to a tree for it. Yeah, me and what army? Maybe, me and the police.

The living-room curtains billowed in the hot breeze. The glass had been shattered in the firefight. I was glad I had just signed a two-year lease. At least they couldn't kick me out.

Dolph sat across from me in my little kitchen area. The breakfast table with its two straight-backed chairs seemed tiny with him sitting at it. He sort of filled my kitchen. Or maybe I was just feeling small tonight. Or was it morning?

I glanced at my watch. There was a dark, slick smear obscuring the face. Couldn't read it. Would have to chip the damn thing clean. I tucked my arm back inside the blanket the paramedic had given me. My skin was colder than it should have been. Even thoughts of vengeance couldn't warm me. Later, later I would be warm. Later I would be pissed. Right now I was glad to be alive.

"Okay, Anita, what happened?"

I glanced at the living room. It was nearly empty. The zombies had been carried away. Incinerated on the street no less. Entertainment for the entire neighborhood. Family fun.

"Could I change clothes before I give a statement, please?"

He looked at me for maybe a second, then nodded.

"Great." I got up gripping the blanket around me, edges folded carefully. Didn't want to accidentally trip on the ends. I'd embarrassed myself enough for one night.

"Save the T-shirt for evidence," Dolph called.

I said, "Sure thing," without turning around.

They had thrown sheets over the worst of the stains so they didn't track blood all over the apartment building. Nice. The bedroom stank of rotted corpse, stale blood, old death. God. I'd never be able to sleep in here tonight. Even I had my limits.

What I wanted was a shower, but I didn't think Dolph would wait that long. I settled for jeans, socks, and a clean T-shirt. I carried all of it into the bathroom. With the door closed, the smell was very faint. It looked like my bathroom. No disasters here.

I dropped the blanket on the floor with the T-shirt. There was a bulky bandage over my shoulder where the zombie had bitten me. I was lucky it hadn't taken a hunk of flesh. The paramedic warned me to get a tetanus booster. Zombies don't make more zombies by biting, but the dead have nasty mouths. Infection is more of a danger but a tetanus booster is a precaution.

Blood had dried in flaking patches on my legs and arms. I didn't bother washing my hands. I'd shower later. Get everything clean at once.

The T-shirt hung almost to my knees. A huge caricature of Arthur Conan Doyle was on the front. He was peering through a huge magnifying glass, one eye comically large. I gazed into the mirror over the sink, looking at the shirt. It was soft and warm and comforting. Comforting was good right now.

The old T-shirt was ruined. No saving it. But maybe I could save some of the penguins. I ran cold water into the bathtub. If it was a shirt, I'd soak it in cold water. Maybe it worked with toys.

I got a pair of jogging shoes out from under the bed. I didn't really want to walk over the drying stains in only socks. Shoes were made for such occasions. All right, so the creator of Nike Airs never foresaw walking over drying zombie blood. It's hard to prepare for everything.

Two of the penguins were turning brown as the blood dried. I carried them gingerly into the bathroom and laid them in the water. I pushed them under until they soaked up enough water to stay partially submerged, then I turned the water off. My hands were cleaner. The water wasn't. Blood trailed out of the two soft toys like water squeezed out of a sponge. If these two came clean, I could save them all.

I dried my hands on the blanket. No sense getting blood on anything else.

Sigmund, the penguin I occasionally slept with, was barely spattered. Just a few specks across his fuzzy white belly. Small blessings. I almost tucked him under my arm to hold while I gave a statement. Dolph probably wouldn't tell. I put Sigmund a little farther from the worst stains, as if that would help. Seeing the stupid toy tucked safely in a corner did make me feel better. Great.

Zerbrowski was peering at the aquarium. He glanced my way. "These are the biggest freaking angelfish I've ever seen. You could fry some of 'em up in a pan.''

"Leave the fish alone, Zerbrowski," I said.

He grinned. "Sure, just a thought."

Back in the kitchen Dolph sat with his hands folded on the tabletop. His face unreadable. If he was upset that I'd almost cashed it in tonight, he didn't show it. But then Dolph didn't show much of anything, ever. The most emotion I'd ever seen him display was about this case. The killer zombie. Butchered civilians.

"You want some coffee?" I asked.

"Sure."

"Me, too," Zerbrowski said.

"Only if you say please."

He leaned against the wall just outside the kitchen. "Please."

I got a bag of coffee out of the freezer.

"You keep the coffee in the freezer?" Zerbrowski said.

"Hasn't anyone ever fixed real coffee for you?" I asked.

"My idea of gourmet coffee is Taster's Choice."

I shook my head. "Barbarian."

"If you two are finished with clever repartee," Dolph said, "could we start the statement now?" His voice was softer than his words.

I smiled at him and at Zerbrowski. Damned if it wasn't nice to see both of them. I must have been hurt worse than I knew to be happy to see Zerbrowski.

"I was asleep minding my own business when I woke up to find a zombie standing over me." I measured beans and poured them into the little black coffee grinder that I'd bought because it matched the coffee maker.

"What woke you?" Dolph asked.

I pressed the button on the grinder and the rich smell of fresh ground coffee filled the kitchen. Ah, heaven.

"I smelled corpses," I said.

"Explain."

"I was dreaming, and I smelled rotting corpses. It didn't match the dream. It woke me."

"Then what?" He had his ever present notebook out. Pen poised.

I concentrated on each small step to making the coffee and told Dolph everything, including my suspicions about Señora Salvador. The coffee was beginning to perk and fill the apartment with that wonderful smell that coffee always has by the time I finished.

"So you think Dominga Salvador is our zombie raiser?" Dolph said.

"Yes."

He stared at me across the small table. His eyes were very serious. "Can you prove it?"

"No."

He took a deep breath, closing his eyes for a moment. "Great, just great."

"The coffee smells done," Zerbrowski said. He was sitting on the floor, back propped against the kitchen doorway.

I got up and poured the coffee. "If you want sugar or cream, help yourself." I put the cream, real cream, out on the kitchen counter along with the sugar bowl. Zerbrowski took a lot of sugar and a dab of cream. Dolph went for black. It was the way I took it most of the time. Tonight I added cream and sweetened it. Real cream in real coffee. Yum, yum.

"If we could get you inside Dominga's house, could you find proof?" Dolph asked.

"Proof of something, sure, but of raising the killer zombie . . ." I shook my head. "If she did raise it and it got away, then she won't want to be tied to it. She'll have destroyed all the proof, just to save face."

"I want her for this," Dolph said.

"Me, too."

"She might also try and kill you again," Zerbrowski said from the doorway. He was blowing on his coffee to cool it.

"No joke," I said.

"You think she'll try again?" Dolph asked.

"Probably. How the hell did two zombies get inside my apartment?"

"Someone picked the lock," Dolph said. "Could the zombie . . ."

"No, a zombie would rip a door off its hinges, but it wouldn't take the time to pick a lock. Even if it had the fine motor skill to do it."

"So someone with skill opened the door and let them in," Dolph said.

"Appears so," I said.

"Any ideas on that?"

"I would bet one of her bodyguards. Her grandson Antonio or maybe Enzo. A big guy in his forties who seems to be her personal protection. I don't know if either of them have the skill, but they'd do it. Enzo, but not Antonio."

"Why cross him off?"

"If Tony had let the zombies in, he'd have stayed and watched."

"You sure?"

I shrugged. "He's that kind of guy. Enzo would do business and leave. He'd follow orders. The grandson wouldn't."

Dolph nodded. "There's a lot of heat from upstairs to solve this case. I think I can get us a search warrant in forty-eight hours."

"Two days is a long time, Dolph."

"Two days without one piece of proof, Anita. Except for your word. I'm going out on a limb for this one."

"She's in it, Dolph, somehow. I don't know why, and I don't know what could have caused her to lose control of the zombie, but she's in it."

"I'll get the warrant," he said.

"One of the brothers in blue said you told him you were a cop," Zerbrowski said.

"I told him I was with your squad. I never said I was a cop."

Zerbrowski grinned. "Mmm-huh."

"Will you be safe here tonight?" Dolph asked.

"I think so. The Señora doesn't want to get on the bad side of the law. They treat renegade witches sort of like renegade vampires. It's an automatic death sentence."

"Because people are too scared of them," Dolph said.

"Because some witches can slip through the fucking bars."

"How about voodoo queens?" Zerbrowski said.

I shook my head. "I don't want to know."

"We better go, leave you to get some sleep," Dolph said. He left his empty coffee cup on the table. Zerbrowski hadn't finished his, but he put it on the counter and followed Dolph out.

I walked them to the door.

"I'll let you know when we get the warrant," Dolph said.

"Could you arrange for me to see Peter Burke's personal effects?"

"Why?"

"There are only two ways to lose control of a zombie this badly. One, you are strong enough to raise it, but not to control it. Dominga can control anything she can raise. Second, someone of near equal power interferes, sort of a challenge." I stared up at Dolph. "John Burke might just be strong enough to have done it. Maybe if I'm helpful enough to take John down to go over his brother's effects—you know, does any of this look out of place, that type of thing—maybe this Burke will let something slip."

"You've already got Dominga Salvador pissed at you, Anita. Isn't that enough for one week?"

"For one lifetime," I said. "But it's something we can do while we wait for the warrant."

Dolph nodded. "Yeah. I'll arrange it. Call Mr. Burke tomorrow morning and set up a time. Then call me."

"Will do."

Dolph hesitated in the doorway for a moment. "Watch your back."

"Always," I said.

Zerbrowski leaned into me and said, "Nice penguins." He followed Dolph down the hallway. I knew the next time I saw the rest of the spook squad they'd all know I collected toy penguins. My secret was out. Zerbrowski would spread it far and wide. At least, he was consistent.

It was nice to know something was.

18

Stuffed animals are not meant to be submerged in water. The two in the bathtub were ruined. Maybe spot remover? The smell was thick and seemed permanent. I put an emergency message on my cleaning service's answering machine. I didn't give a lot of details. Didn't want to frighten them off.

I packed an overnight bag. Two changes of clothes and one penguin with his tummy freshly scrubbed, Harold Gaynor's file, and I was set. I also packed both guns: the Firestar in its inner pants holster; the Browning under my arm. A windbreaker hid the Browning from view. I had extra ammo in the jacket pockets. Between both guns I had twenty-two bullets. Twenty-two bullets. Why didn't I feel safe?

Unlike most walking dead, zombies can bear the touch of sunlight. They don't like it, but they can exist with it. Dominga could order a zombie to kill me in daylight just as easily as moonlight. She wouldn't be able to raise the dead during daylight, but if she planned it right, she could raise the dead the night before and send it out to get me the next day. A voodoo priestess with executive planning skills. It would be just my luck.

I didn't really believe that Dominga had backup zombies waiting to jump me. But somehow I was feeling paranoid this morning. Paranoia is just another word for longevity.

I stepped out into the quiet hallway, glancing both ways as if it were a street. Nothing. No walking corpses hiding in the shadows. No one but us fraidy-cats. The only sound was the hush of the air-conditioning. The hallway had that feel to it. I came home often enough at dawn to know the quality of silence. I thought about that for a minute. I knew it was almost dawn. Not by clock or window, but on some level deeper than that. Some instinct that an ancestor had found while hiding in a dark cave, praying for light.

Most people fear the dark in a vague way. They fear what might be out there. I raise the dead. I've slain over a dozen vampires. I know what's out there in the dark. And I am terrified of it. People are supposed to fear the unknown, but ignorance is bliss when knowledge is so damn frightening.

I knew what would have happened to me if I had failed last night. If I had been slower or a worse shot. Two years ago there had been three murders. Nothing connected them except the method of death. They had been torn apart by zombies. They had not been eaten. Normal zombies don't eat anything. They may bite a time or two, but that's the worst of it. There had been the man whose throat was crushed, but that had been accidental. The zombie just bit down on the nearest body part. It happened to be a killing blow. Blind luck.

A zombie will normally just wrestle you to pieces. Like a small boy tearing pieces off of a fly.

Raising a zombie for the purposes of being a murder weapon is an automatic death sentence. The court system has gotten rather quick on the draw the last few years. A death sentence meant what it said these days. Especially if your crime was supernatural in some way. You didn't burn witches anymore. You electrocuted them.

If we could get proof, the state would kill Dominga Salvador for me. John Burke, too, if we could prove he had knowingly caused the zombie to go ape-shit. The trouble with supernatural crimes is proving them in court. Most juries aren't up on the latest spells and incantations. Heck, neither am I. But I've tried explaining zombies and vampires in court before. I've learned to keep it simple and to add any gory details the defense will allow me. A jury appreciates a little vicarious adventure. Most testimony is terribly boring or heartbreaking. I try to be interesting. It's a change of pace.

The parking area was dark. Stars still glimmered overhead. But they were fading like candles in a steady wind. I could taste dawn on the air. Roll it around on my tongue. Maybe it's all the vampire hunting I do, but I was more attuned to the passage of light and dark than I had been four years ago. I hadn't been able to taste the dawn.

Of course my nightmares were a lot less interesting four years ago. You gain something, you lose something else. It's the way life works.

It was after 5:00 A.M. when I got in my car and headed out for the nearest hotel. I wouldn't be able to stand my apartment until the cleaning crew got the smell out. If they could get the smell out. My landlord was not going to be pleased if they couldn't.

He was going to be even less pleased with the bullet holes and shattered window. Replace the window. Replaster the walls, maybe? I really didn't know what you did to repair bullet holes? Here I was hoping my lease couldn't be challenged in court.

The first hint of dawn was slipping over the eastern sky. A pure white light that spread like ice over the darkness. Most people think dawn is as colorful as sunset but the first color of dawn is white, a pure not-color, that is almost an absence of night.

There was a motel, but all its rooms were on one or two stories, some of them awfully isolated. I wanted a crowd. I settled on The Stouffer Concourse which wasn't terribly cheap but it would force zombies to ride up in elevators. People tended to notice the smell in an elevator. The Stouffer Concourse also had room service at this ungodly hour of dawn. I needed room service. Coffee, give me coffee.

The clerk gave me that wide-eyed-I'm-too-polite-to-say-it-out-loud look. The elevators were mirrored, and I had nothing to do for several floors but look at my reflection. Blood had dried in a stiff darkness in my hair. A stain went down the right side of my face just below the hairline and trailed down my neck. I hadn't noticed it in the mirror at home. Shock will make you forget things.

It wasn't the bloodstains that had made the clerk look askance. Unless you knew what to look for, you wouldn't know it was blood. No, the problem was that my skin was deathly pale, like clean paper. My eyes that are perfectly brown looked black. They were huge and dark and . . . strange. Startled, I looked startled. Surprised to be alive. Maybe. I was still fighting off the edge of shock. No matter how together I felt, my face told a different story. When the shock wore off, I'd be able to sleep. Until then, I'd read Gaynor's file.

The room had two double beds. More room than I needed, but what the heck. I got out clean clothes, put the Firestar in the drawer of the nightstand, and took the Browning into the bathroom with me. If I was careful and didn't turn the shower on full blast, I could fasten the shoulder holster to the towel rack in the back of the stall. It wouldn't even get wet. Though truthfully with most modern guns, wet doesn't hurt them. As long as you clean them afterwards. Most guns will shoot underwater.

I called room service wearing nothing but a towel. I'd almost forgotten. I ordered a pot of coffee, sugar, and cream. They asked if I wanted decaf. I said no thank you. Pushy. Like waiters asking if I wanted a diet Coke when I didn't ask for it. They never ask men, even portly men, if they want diet Cokes.

I could drink a pot of caffeine and sleep like a baby. It doesn't keep me awake or make me jumpy. It just tastes better.

Yes, they would leave the cart outside the door. No, they wouldn't knock. They would add the coffee to my bill. That was fine, I said. They had a credit card number. When they have plastic, people are always eager to add on to your bill. As long as the limit holds.

I propped the straight-backed chair under the doorknob to the hallway. If someone forced the door, I'd hear it. Maybe. I locked the bathroom door and had a gun in the shower with me. I was as secure as I was going to get.

There is something about being naked that makes me feel vulnerable. I would much rather face bad guys with my clothes on than off. I guess everyone's like that.

The bite on my shoulder with its thick bandage was a problem when I wanted to wash my hair. I had to get the blood out, bandage or no bandage.

I used their little bottles of shampoo and conditioner. They smelled like flowers are supposed to smell but never do. Blood had dried in patches on my body. I looked spotted. The water that washed down the drain was pink-ish.

It took the entire bottle of shampoo before my hair was squeaky clean. The last rinse water soaked through the bandage on my right shoulder. The pain was sharp and persistent. I'd have to remember to get that tetanus booster.

I scrubbed my body with a washcloth and the munchkin bar of soap. When I had washed and soaked every inch of myself, and was as clean as I was going to get, I stood under the hot needling spray. I let the water pour over my back, down my body. The bandage had soaked through long ago.

What if we couldn't tie Dominga to the zombies? What if we couldn't find proof? She'd try again. Her pride was at stake now. She had set two zombies on me, and I had wasted them both. With a little help from the police. Dominga Salvador would see it as a personal challenge.

She had raised a zombie and it had escaped her control completely. She would rather have innocent people slaughtered than to admit her mistake. And she would rather kill me than have me prove it. Vindictive bitch.

Señora Salvador had to be stopped. If the warrant didn't help, then I'd have to be more practical. She'd made it clear that it was her or me. I preferred it to be her. And if necessary, I'd make sure of it.

I opened my eyes and turned off the water. I didn't want to think about it anymore. I was talking about murder. I saw it as self-defense, but I doubted a jury would. It'd be damn hard to prove. I wanted several things. Dominga out of the picture, dead or in jail. To stay alive. Not to be in jail on a murder charge. To catch the killer zombie before it killed again. Fat chance that. To figure out how John Burke fit into this mess.

Oh, and to keep Harold Gaynor from forcing me to perform human sacrifice. Yeah, I almost forgot that one.

It had been a busy week.

The coffee was outside the door on a little tray. I set it inside on the floor, locked the door, and put the chair against the doorknob again. Only then did I set the coffee tray on a small table by the curtained windows. The Browning was already sitting on the table, naked. The shoulder holster was on the bed.

I opened the drapes. Normally, I would have kept the drapes closed, but today I wanted to see the light. Morning had spread like a soft haze of light. The heat hadn't had time to creep up and strangle that first gentle touch of morning.

The coffee wasn't bad, but it wasn't great either. Of course, the worst coffee I've ever had was still wonderful. Well, maybe not the coffee at police headquarters. But even that was better than nothing. Coffee was my comfort drink. Better than alcohol, I guess.

I spread Gaynor's file on the table and started to read. By eight that morning, earlier than I usually get up, I had read every scribbled note, gazed at every blurry picture. I knew more about Mr. Harold Gaynor than I wanted to, none of it particularly helpful.

Gaynor was mob-connected, but it couldn't be proven. He was a self-made multimillionaire. Bully for him. He could afford the million five that Tommy had offered me. Nice to know a man can pay his bills.

His only family had been a mother who died ten years ago. His father was supposed to have died before he was born. There was no record of the father's death. In fact, the father didn't seem to exist.

An illegitimate birth, carefully disguised? Maybe. So Gaynor was a bastard in the original definition of the word. So what? I'd already known he was one in spirit.

I propped Wheelchair Wanda's picture against the coffeepot. She was smiling, almost like she'd known the picture was being taken. Maybe she was just photogenic. There were two pictures with her and Gaynor together. In one they were smiling, holding hands as Tommy pushed Gaynor's wheelchair and Bruno pushed Wanda. She was gazing at Gaynor with a look I had seen in other women. Adoration, love. I'd even experienced it myself for a brief time in college. You get over it.

The second picture was almost identical to the first. Bruno and Tommy pushing them. But they weren't holding hands. Gaynor was smiling. Wanda wasn't. She looked angry. Cicely of the blond hair and empty eyes was walking on the other side of Gaynor. They were holding hands. Ah-ha.

So Gaynor had kept both of them around for a while. Why had Wanda left? Jealousy? Had Cicely arranged it? Had Gaynor tired of her? The only way to know was to ask.

I stared at the picture with Cicely in it. I put it beside the laughing close-up of Wanda's face. An unhappy young woman, a scorned lover. If she hated Gaynor more than she feared him, Wanda would talk to me. She would be a fool to talk to the papers, but I didn't want to publish her secrets. I wanted Gaynor's secrets, so I could keep him from hurting me. Barring that, I wanted something to take to the police.

Mr. Gaynor would have other things to worry about if I could get him in jail. He might forget all about one reluctant animator. Unless, of course, he found out I'd had something to do with him being arrested. That would be bad. Gaynor struck me as vengeful. I had Dominga Salvador mad at me. I didn't need anyone else.

I closed the drapes and left a wake-up call for noon. Irving would just have to wait for his file. I had unintentionally given him the interview with the new Master of the City. Surely that cut me a little slack. If not, to hell with it. I was going to bed.

The last thing I did before going to bed was call Peter Burke's house. I figured that John would be staying there. It rang five times before the machine kicked on. "This is Anita Blake, I may have some information for John Burke on a matter we discussed Thursday." The message was a little vague, but I didn't want to leave a message saying, "Call me about your brother's murder." It would have seemed melodramatic and cruel.

I left the hotel's number as well as my own. Just in case. They probably had the ringers turned off. I would. The story had been front page because

Peter was, had been, an animator. Animators don't get murdered much in the run-of-the-mill muggings. It's usually something more unusual.

I would drop off Gaynor's file on the way home. I wanted to drop it off at the receptionist desk. I didn't feel like talking to Irving about his big interview. I didn't want to hear that Jean-Claude was charming or had great plans for the city. He'd be very careful what he told a reporter. It would look good in print. But I knew the truth. Vampires are as much a monster as any zombie, maybe worse. Vamps usually volunteer for the process, zombies don't.

Just like Irving volunteered to go off with Jean-Claude. Of course, if Irving hadn't been with me the Master would have left him alone. Probably. So it was my fault, even if it had been his choice. I was achingly tired, but I knew I'd never be able to sleep until I heard Irving's voice. I could pretend I'd called to tell him I was dropping the file off late.

I wasn't sure if Irving would be on his way to work or not. I tried home first. He answered on the first ring.

"Hello."

Something tight in my stomach relaxed. "Hi, Irving, it's me."

"Ms. Blake, to what do I owe this early morning pleasure?" His voice sounded so ordinary.

"I had a bit of excitement at my apartment last night. I was hoping I could drop the file off later in the day."

"What sort of excitement?" His voice had that "tell me" lilt to it.

"The kind that's police business and not yours," I said.

"I thought you'd say that," he said. "You just getting to bed?"

"Yeah."

"I guess I can let a hardworking animator sleep in a little. My sister reporter may even understand."

"Thanks, Irving."

"You all right, Anita?"

No, I wanted to say, but I didn't. I ignored the question. "Did Jean-Claude behave himself?"

"He was great!" Irving's enthusiasm was genuine, all bubbly excitement. "He's a great interview." He was quiet for a moment. "Hey, you called to check up on me. To make sure I was okay."

"Did not," I said.

"Thanks, Anita, that means a lot. But really, he was very civilized."

"Great. I'll let you go then. Have a good day."

"Oh, I will, my editor is doing cartwheels about the exclusive interview with the Master of the City."

I had to laugh at the way he rolled the title off his tongue. "Good night, Irving."

"Get some sleep, Blake. I'll be calling you in a day or two about those zombie articles."

"Talk to you then," I said. We hung up.

Irving was fine. I should worry more about myself and less about everyone else.

I turned off the lights and cuddled under the sheets. My penguin was cradled in my arms. The Browning Hi-Power was under my pillow. It wasn't as easy to get to as the bed holster at home, but it was better than nothing.

I wasn't sure which was more comforting, the penguin or the gun. I guess both were equally comforting, for very different reasons.

I said my prayers like a good little girl. I asked very sincerely that I not dream.

19

The cleaning crew had a cancellation and moved my emergency into the slot. By afternoon my apartment was clean and smelled like spring cleaning. Apartment maintenance had replaced the shattered window. The bullet holes had been smeared with white paint. The holes looked like little dimples in the wall. All in all, the place looked great.

John Burke had not returned my call. Maybe I'd been too clever. I'd try a more blunt message later. But right at this moment I had more pleasant things to worry about.

I was dressed for jogging. Dark blue shorts with white piping, white Nikes with pale blue swishes, cute little jogging socks, and tank top. The shorts were the kind with one of those inside pockets that shut with Velcro. Inside the pocket was a derringer. An American derringer to be exact; 6.5 ounces, .38 Special, 4.82 total length. At 6.5 ounces, it felt like a lumpy feather.

A Velcro pocket was not conducive to a fast draw. Two shots and spitting would be more accurate at a distance, but then Gaynor's men didn't want to kill me. Hurt me, but not kill me. They had to get in close to hurt me. Close enough to use the derringer. Of course, that was just two shots. After that, I was in trouble.

I had tried to figure out a way to carry one of my 9mms, but there was no way. I could not jog and tote around that much firepower. Choices, choices.

Veronica Sims was standing in my living room. Ronnie is five-nine, blond hair, grey eyes. She is a private investigator on retainer to Animators, Inc. We also work out together at least twice a week unless one of us is out of town, injured, or up to our necks in vampires. Those last two happen more often than I would like.

She was wearing French-cut purple shorts, and a T-shirt that said, "Outside of a dog, a book is man's best friend. Inside of a dog, it's too dark to read.'' There are reasons why Ronnie and I are friends.

"I missed you Thursday at the health club," she said. "Was the funeral awful?"

"Yeah."

She didn't ask me to elaborate. She knows funerals are not my best thing. Most people hate funerals because of the dead. I hate all the emotional shit.

She was stretching long legs parallel to her body, low on the floor. In a sort of stretching crouch. We always warm up in the apartment. Most leg stretches were never meant to be done while wearing short shorts.

I mirrored her movement. The muscles in my upper thighs moved and protested. The derringer was an uncomfortable but endurable lump.

"Just out of curiosity," Ronnie said, "why do you feel it necessary to take a gun with you?"

"I always carry a gun," I said.

She just looked at me, disgust plain in her eyes. "If you don't want to tell me, then don't, but don't bullshit me."

"All right, all right," I said. "Strangely enough, no one's told me not to tell anyone."

"What, no threats about not going to the police?" she asked.

"Nope."

"My, how terribly friendly."

"Not friendly," I said, sitting flat on the floor, legs out at angles. Ronnie mirrored me. It looked like we were going to roll a ball across the floor. "Not friendly at all." I leaned my upper body over my left leg until my cheek touched my thigh.

"Tell me about it," she said.

I did. When I was done, we were limbered and ready to run.

"Shit, Anita. Zombies in your apartment and a mad millionaire after you to perform human sacrifices." Her grey eyes searched my face. "You're the only person I know who has weirder problems than I do."

"Thanks a lot," I said. I locked my door behind us and put my keys in the pocket along with the derringer. I know it would scratch hell out of it, but what was I supposed to do, run with the keys in my hand?

"Harold Gaynor. I could do some checking on him for you."

"Aren't you on a case?" We clattered down the stairs.

"I'm doing about three different insurance scams. Mostly surveillance and photography. If I have to eat one more fast-food dinner, I'm going to start singing jingles."

I smiled. "Shower and change at my place. We'll go out for a real dinner."

"Sounds great, but you don't want to keep Jean-Claude waiting."

"Cut it out, Ronnie," I said.

She shrugged. "You should stay as far away from that . . . creature as you can, Anita."

"I know it." It was my turn to shrug. "Agreeing to meet him seemed the lesser of evils."

"What were your choices?"

"Meeting him voluntarily or being kidnapped and taken to him."

"Great choices."

"Yeah."

I opened the double doors that led outside. The heat smacked me in the face. It was staggeringly hot, like stepping into an oven. And we were going to jog in this?

I looked up at Ronnie. She is six inches taller than I am, and most of that is leg. We can run together, but I have to set the pace and I have to push myself. It is a very good workout. "It has to be over a hundred today," I said.

"No pain, no gain," Ronnie said. She was carrying a sport water bottle in her left hand. We were as prepared as we were going to get.

"Four miles in hell," I said. "Let's do it." We set off at a slow pace, but it was steady. We usually finished the run in a half hour or less.

The air was solid with heat. It felt like we were running through semi-solid walls of scalding air. The humidity in St. Louis is almost always around a hundred percent. Combine the humidity with hundred-plus temperatures and you get a small, damp slice of hell. St. Louis in the summertime, yippee.

I do not enjoy exercise. Slim hips and muscular calves are not incentive enough for this kind of abuse. Being able to outrun the bad guys is incentive. Sometimes it all comes down to who is faster, stronger, quicker. I am in the wrong business. Oh, I'm not complaining. But 106 pounds is not a lot of muscle to throw around.

Of course, when it comes to vampires, I could be two-hundred-plus of pure human muscles and it wouldn't do me a damn bit of good. Even the newly dead can bench press cars with one hand. So I'm outclassed. I've gotten used to it.

The first mile was behind us. It always hurts the worst. My body takes about two miles to be convinced it can't talk me out of this insanity.

We were moving through an older neighborhood. Lots of small fenced yards and houses dating to the fifties, or even the 1800s. There was the smooth brick wall of a warehouse that dated to pre-Civil War. It was our halfway point. Two miles. I was feeling loose and muscled, like I could run forever, if I didn't have to do it very fast. I was concentrating on moving my body through the heat, keeping the rhythm. It was Ronnie who spotted the man.

"I don't mean to be an alarmist," she said, "but why is that man just standing there?"

I squinted ahead of us. Maybe fifteen feet ahead of us the brick wall ended and there was a tall elm tree. A man was standing near the trunk of the tree. He wasn't trying to conceal himself. But he was wearing a jean jacket. It was much too hot for that, unless you had a gun under it.

"How long's he been there?"

"Just stepped out from around the tree," she said.

Paranoia reigns supreme. "Let's turn back. It's two miles either way." Ronnie nodded.

We pivoted and started jogging back the other way. The man behind us did not cry out or say stop. Paranoia, it was a vicious disease.

A second man stepped out from the far corner of the brick wall. We jogged towards him a few more steps. I glanced back. Mr. Jean Jacket was casually walking towards us. The jacket was unbuttoned, and his hand was reaching under his arm. So much for paranoia.

"Run," I said.

The second man pulled a gun from his jacket pocket.

We stopped running. It seemed like a good idea at the time.

"Un-uh," the man said, "I don't feel like chasing anyone in this heat. All ya gotta be is alive, chickie, anything else is gravy." The gun was a .22 caliber automatic. Not much stopping power, but it was perfect for wounding. They'd thought this out. That was scary.

Ronnie was standing very stiff beside me. I fought the urge to grab her hand and squeeze it, but that wouldn't be very tough-as-nails vampire slayer, would it? "What do you want?"

"That's better," he said. A pale blue T-shirt gapped where his beer gut spilled over his belt. But his arms had a beefy look to them. He may have been overweight, but I bet it hurt when he hit you. I hoped I didn't have to test the theory.

I backed up so the brick wall was to my back. Ronnie moved with me. Mr. Jean Jacket was almost with us now. He had a Beretta 9mm loose in his right hand. It was not meant for wounding.

I glanced at Ronnie, then at Fatty who was nearly right beside her. I glanced at Mr. Jean Jacket, who was nearly beside me. I glanced back at Ronnie. Her eyes widened just a bit. She licked her lips once, then turned back to stare at Fatty. The guy with the Beretta was mine. Ronnie got the .22. Delegation at its best.

"What do you want?" I said again. I hate repeating myself.

"You to come take a little ride with us, that's all." Fatty smiled as he said it.

I smiled back, then turned to Jean Jacket, and his tame Beretta. "Don't you talk?"

"I talk," he said. He took two steps closer to me, but his gun was very steadily pointed at my chest. "I talk real good." He touched my hair, lightly, with his fingertips. The Beretta was damn near pressed against me. If he pulled the trigger now, it was all over. The dull black barrel of the gun was getting bigger. Illusion, but the longer you stare at a gun, the more important it gets to be. When you're on the wrong end of it.

"None of that, Seymour," Fatty said. "No pussy and we can't kill her, those are the rules."

"Shit, Pete."

Pete, alias Fatty, said, "You can have the blonde. No one said we couldn't have fun with her."

I did not look at Ronnie. I stared at Seymour. I had to be ready if I got that one second chance. Glancing at my friend to see how she was taking the news of her impending rape was not going to help. Really.

"Phallic power, Ronnie. It always goes to the gonads," I said.

Seymour frowned. "What the hell does that mean?"

"It means, Seymour, that I think you're stupid and what brains you have are in your balls." I smiled pleasantly while I said it.

He hit me with the flat of his hand, hard. I staggered but didn't go down. The gun was still steady, unwavering. Shit. He made a sound deep in his throat and hit me, closed fist. I went down. For a moment I lay on the gritty sidewalk, listening to the blood pound in my ears. The slap had stung. The closed fist hurt.

Someone kicked me in the ribs. "Leave her alone!" Ronnie screamed.

I lay on my stomach and pretended to be hurt. It wasn't hard. I groped for the Velcro pocket. Seymour was waving the Beretta in Ronnie's face. She was screaming at him. Pete had grabbed Ronnie's arms and was trying to hold her. Things were getting out of hand. Goody.

I stared up at Seymour's legs and struggled to my knees. I shoved the derringer into his groin. He froze and stared down at me.

"Don't move, or I'll serve up your balls on a plate," I said.

Ronnie drove her elbow back into Fatty's solar plexus. He bent over a little, hands going to his stomach. She twisted away and kneed him hard in the face. Blood spurted from his nose. He staggered back. She smashed him in the side of the face, getting all her shoulder and upper body into it. He fell down. She had the .22 in her hand.

I fought an urge to yell "Yea Ronnie," but it didn't sound tough enough. We'd do high-fives later. "Tell your friend not to move, Seymour, or I'll pull this trigger."

He swallowed loud enough for me to hear it. "Don't move, Pete, okay?"

Pete just stared at us.

"Ronnie, please get Seymour's gun from him. Thank you."

I was still kneeling in the gravel with the derringer pressed into the man's groin. He let Ronnie take his gun without a fight. Fancy that.

"I've got this one covered, Anita," Ronnie said. I didn't glance at her. She would do her job. I would do mine.

"Seymour, this is a .38 Special, two shots. It can hold a variety of ammunition, .22, .44, or .357 Magnum." This was a lie, the new lightweight version couldn't hold anything higher than .38s, but I was betting Seymour couldn't tell the difference. "Forty-four or .357 and you can kiss the family jewels good-bye. Twenty-two, maybe you'll just be very, very sore. To quote a role model of mine, 'Do you feel lucky today?' "

"What do you want, man, what do you want?" His voice was high and squeaky with fear.

"Who hired you to come after us?"

He shook his head. "No, man, he'll kill us."

"Three-fifty-seven Magnum makes a fucking big hole, Seymour."

"Don't tell her shit," Pete said.

"If he says anything else, Ronnie, shoot his kneecap off," I said.

"My pleasure," Ronnie said. I wondered if she would really do it. I wondered if I'd tell her to do it. Better not to find out.

"Talk to me, Seymour, now, or I pull the trigger." I shoved the gun a little deeper. That must have hurt all on its own. He sort of tried to tippy-toe.

"God, please don't."

"Who hired you?"

"Bruno."

"You asshole, Seymour," Pete said. "He'll kill us."

"Ronnie, please shoot him," I said.

"You said the kneecap, right?"

"Yeah."

"How about an elbow instead?" she asked.

"Your choice," I said.

"You're crazy," Seymour said.

"Yeah," I said, "you remember that. What exactly did Bruno tell you?"

"He said to take you to a building off Grand, on Washington. He said to bring you both, but we could hurt the blonde to get you to come along."

"Give me the address," I said.

Seymour did. I think he would have told me the secret ingredient in the magic sauce if I had asked.

"If you go down there, Bruno will know we told ya," Pete said.

"Ronnie," I said.

"Shoot me now, chickie, it don't matter. You go down there or send the police down there, we are dead."

I glanced at Pete. He seemed very sincere. They were bad guys but . . . "Okay, we won't bust in on him."

"We aren't going to the police?" Ronnie asked.

"No, if we did that, we might as well kill them now. But we don't have to do that, do we, Seymour?"

"No, man, no."

"How much ol' Bruno pay you?"

"Four hundred apiece."

"It wasn't enough," I said.

"You're telling me."

"I'm going to get up now, Seymour, and leave your balls where they are. Don't come near me or Ronnie again, or I'll tell Bruno you sold him out."

"He'd kill us, man. He'd kill us slow."

"That's right, Seymour. We'll just all pretend this never happened, right?" He was nodding vigorously.

"That okay with you, Pete?" I asked.

"I ain't stupid. Bruno'd rip out our hearts and feed them to us. We won't talk." He sounded disgusted.

I got up and stepped carefully away from Seymour. Ronnie covered Pete nice and steady with the Beretta. The .22 was tucked into the waistband of her jogging shorts. "Get out of here," I said.

Seymour's skin was pasty, and a sick sweat beaded his face. "Can I have my gun?" He wasn't very bright.

"Don't get cute," I said.

Pete stood. The blood under his nose had started to dry. "Come on, Seymour. We gotta go now."

They moved on down the street side by side. Seymour looked hunched in upon himself as if he were fighting an urge to clutch his equipment.

Ronnie let out a great whoosh of air and leaned back against the wall. The gun was still clutched in her right hand. "My God," she said.

"Yeah," I said.

She touched my face where Seymour had hit me. It hurt. I winced. "Are you all right?" Ronnie asked.

"Sure," I said. Actually, it felt like the side of my face was one great big ache, but it wouldn't make it hurt any less to say it out loud.

"Are we going down to the building where they were to drop us?"

"No."

"Why not?"

"I know who Bruno is and who gives him orders. I know why they tried to kidnap me. What could I possibly learn that would be worth two lives?"

Ronnie thought about that for a moment. "You're right, I guess. But you aren't going to report the attack to the police?"

"Why should I? I'm okay, you're okay. Seymour and Pete won't be back."

She shrugged. "You didn't really want me to shoot his kneecap off, did you? I mean we were playing good cop, bad cop, right?" She looked at me very steadily as she asked, her solid grey eyes earnest and true.

I looked away. "Let's walk back home. I don't feel much like jogging."

"Me either."

We set off walking down the street. Ronnie untucked her T-shirt and stuck the Beretta in the waistband. The .22 she sort of cupped in her hand. It wasn't very noticeable that way.

"We were pretending, right? Being tough, right?"

Truth. "I don't know."

"Anita!"

"I don't know, that's the truth."

"I couldn't have shot him to pieces just to keep him from talking."

"Good thing you didn't have to then," I said.

"Would you really have pulled the trigger on that man?"

There was a cardinal singing somewhere off in the distance. The song filled the stale heat and made it seem cooler.

"Answer me, Anita. Would you really have pulled the trigger?"

"Yes."

"Yes?" There was a lilt of surprise in her voice.

"Yes."

"Shit." We walked on in silence for a minute or two, then she asked, "What ammo is in the gun today?"

"Thirty-eights."

"It would have killed him."

"Probably," I said.

I saw her look at me sideways as we walked back. There was a look I'd seen before. A mixture of horror and admiration. I'd just never seen it on a friend's face before. That part hurt. But we went out to dinner that night at The Miller's Daughter in Old St. Charles. The atmosphere was pleasant. The food wonderful. As always.

We talked and laughed and had a very good time. Neither of us mentioned what had happened this afternoon. Pretend hard enough and maybe it will go away.

20

At 10:30 that night I was down in the vampire district. Dark blue polo shirt, jeans, red windbreaker. The windbreaker hid the shoulder holster and the Browning Hi-Power. Sweat was pooling in the bends of my arms but it beat the hell out of not having it.

The afternoon fun and games had turned out all right, but that was partly luck. And Seymour losing his temper. And me being able to take a beating and keep on ticking. Ice had kept the swelling down, but the left side of my face was puffy and red, as if some sort of fruit was about to burst out of it. No bruise—yet.

The Laughing Corpse was one of the newest clubs in the District. Vampires are sexy. I'll admit that. But funny? I don't think so. Apparently, I was in the minority. A line stretched away from the club, curling round the block.

It hadn't occurred to me that I'd need a ticket or reservations or whatever just to get in. But, hey, I knew the boss. I walked along the line of people towards the ticket booth. The people were mostly young. The women in dresses, the men in dressy sports wear, with an occasional suit. They were chatting together in excited voices, a lot of casual hand and arm touching. Dates. I remember dates. It's just been a while. Maybe if I wasn't always ass deep in alligators, I'd date more. Maybe.

I cut ahead of a double-date foursome. "Hey," one man said.

"Sorry," I said.

The woman in the ticket booth frowned at me. "You can't just cut in line like that, ma'am."

Ma'am? "I don't want a ticket. I don't want to see the show. I am supposed to meet Jean-Claude here. That's it."

"Well, I don't know. How do I know you're not some reporter?"

Reporter? I took a deep breath. "Just call Jean-Claude and tell him Anita is here. Okay?"

She was still frowning at me.

"Look, just call Jean-Claude. If I'm a nosy reporter, he'll deal with me. If I'm who I say I am, he'll be happy that you called him. You can't lose."

"I don't know."

I fought an urge to scream at her. It probably wouldn't help. Probably. "Just call Jean-Claude, pretty please," I said.

Maybe it was the pretty please. She swiveled on her stool and opened the upper half of a door in the back of the booth. Small booth. I couldn't hear what she said, but she swiveled back around. "Okay, manager says you can go in."

"Great, thanks." I walked up the steps. The entire line of waiting people glared at me. I could feel their hot stares on my back. But I've been stared at by experts, so I was careful not to flinch. No one likes a line jumper.

The club was dim inside, as most clubs are. A guy just inside the door said, "Ticket, please?"

I stared up at him. He wore a white T-shirt that said, "The Laughing Corpse, it's a scream." A caricature of an open-mouthed vampire was drawn very large across his chest. He was large and muscled and had bouncer tattooed across his forehead. "Ticket, please," he repeated.

First the ticket lady, now the ticket man? "The manager said I could come through to see Jean-Claude," I said.

"Willie," the ticket man said, "you send her through?"

I turned around, and there was Willie McCoy. I smiled when I saw him. I was glad to see him. That surprised me. I'm not usually happy to see dead men.

Willie is short, thin, with black hair slicked back from his forehead. I couldn't tell the exact color of his suit in the dimness, but it looked like a dull tomato-red. White button-up shirt, large shiny green tie. I had to look twice before I was sure, but yes, there was a glow-in-the-dark hula girl on his tie. It was the most tasteful outfit I'd ever seen Willie wear.

He grinned, flashing a lot of fang. "Anita, good to see ya."

I nodded. "You, too, Willie."

"Really?"

"Yeah."

He grinned even wider. His canines glistened in the dim light. He hadn't been dead a year yet.

"How long have you been manager here?" I asked.

" 'Bout two weeks."

"Congratulations."

He stepped closer to me. I stepped back. Instinctive. Nothing personal, but a vampire is a vampire. Don't get too close. Willie was new dead, but he was still capable of hypnotizing with his eyes. Okay, maybe no vampire as new as Willie could actually catch me with his eyes, but old habits die hard.

Willie's face fell. A flicker of something in his eyes—hurt? He dropped his voice but didn't try to step next to me. He was a faster study dead than he ever had been alive. "Thanks to me helping you last time, I'm in real good with the boss."

He sounded like an old gangster movie, but that was Willie. "I'm glad Jean-Claude's doing right by you."

"Oh, yeah," Willie said, "this is the best job I ever had. And the boss isn't . . ." He waggled his hands back and forth. "Ya know, mean."

I nodded. I did know. I could bitch and complain about Jean-Claude all I wanted, but compared to most Masters of the City, he was a pussycat. A big, dangerous, carnivorous pussycat, but still, it was an improvement.

"The boss's busy right this minute," Willie said. "He said if you was to come early, to give ya a table near the stage."

Great. Aloud I said, "How long will Jean-Claude be?"

Willie shrugged. "Don't know for sure."

I nodded. "Okay, I'll wait, for a little while."

Willie grinned, fangs flashing. "Ya want me to tell Jean-Claude to hurry it up?"

"Would you?"

He grimaced like he'd swallowed a bug. "Hell no."

"Don't sweat it. If I get tired of waiting, I'll tell him myself."

Willie looked at me sorta sideways. "You'd do it, wouldn't you?"

"Yeah."

He just shook his head and started leading me between the small round tables. Every table was thick with people. Laughing, gasping, drinking, holding hands. The sensation of being surrounded by thick, sweaty life was nearly overwhelming.

I glanced at Willie. Did he feel it? Did the warm press of humanity make his stomach knot with hunger? Did he go home at night and dream of ripping into the loud, roaring crowd? I almost asked him, but I liked Willie as much as I could like a vampire. I did not want to know if the answer was yes.

A table just one row back from the stage was empty. There was a big white cardboard foldy thing that said "Reserved." Willie tried to hold my chair for me, I waved him back. It wasn't women's liberation. I simply never understood what I was supposed to do while the guy shoved my chair in under me. Did I sit there and watch him strain to scoot the chair with me in it? Embarrassing. I usually hovered just above the chair and got it shoved into the backs of my knees. Hell with it.

"Would you like a drink while ya wait?" Willie asked.

"Could I have a Coke?"

"Nuthin' stronger?"

I shook my head.

Willie walked away through the tables and the people. On the stage was a slender man with short, dark hair. He was thin all over, his face almost cadaverous, but he was definitely human. His appearance was more comical than anything, like a long-limbed clown. Beside him, staring blank-faced out at the crowd, was a zombie.

Its pale eyes were still clear, human-looking, but he didn't blink. That familiar frozen stare gazed out at the audience. They were only half listening to the jokes. Most eyes were on the standing deadman. He was just decayed enough around the edges to look scary, but even one row away there was no hint of odor. Nice trick if you could manage it.

"Ernie here is the best roommate I ever had," the comedian said. "He doesn't eat much, doesn't talk my ear off, doesn't bring cute chicks home and lock me out while they have a good time." Nervous laughter from the audience. Eyes glued on ol' Ernie.

"Though there was that pork chop in the fridge that went bad. Ernie seemed to like that a lot."

The zombie turned slowly, almost painfully, to stare at the comedian. The man's eyes flickered to the zombie, then back to the audience, smile in place. The zombie kept staring at him. The man didn't seem to like it much. I didn't blame him. Even the dead don't like to be the butt of jokes.

The jokes weren't that funny anyway. It was a novelty act. The zombie was the act. Pretty inventive, and pretty sick.

Willie came back with my Coke. The manager waiting on my table, la-de-da. Of course, the reserved table was pretty good, too. Willie set the drink down on one of those useless paper lace doilies. "Enjoy," he said. He turned to leave, but I touched his arm. I wish I hadn't.

The arm was solid enough, real enough. But it was like touching wood. It was dead. I don't know what else to call it. There was no feeling of movement. Nothing.

I dropped his arm, slowly, and looked up at him. Meeting his eyes, thanks to Jean-Claude's marks. Those brown eyes held something like sorrow.

I could suddenly hear my heartbeat in my ears, and I had to swallow to calm my own pulse. Shit. I wanted Willie to go away now. I turned away from him and looked very hard at my drink. He left. Maybe it was just the sound of all the laughing, but I couldn't hear Willie walk away.

Willie McCoy was the only vampire I had ever known before he died. I remembered him alive. He had been a small-time hood. An errand boy for bigger fish. Maybe Willie thought being a vampire would make him a big fish. He'd been wrong there. He was just a little undead fish now. Jean-Claude or someone like him would run Willie's "life" for eternity. Poor Willie.

I rubbed the hand that had touched him on my leg. I wanted to forget the feel of his body under the new tomato-red suit, but I couldn't. Jean-Claude's body didn't feel that way. Of course, Jean-Claude could damn near pass for human. Some of the old ones could do that. Willie would learn. God help him.

"Zombies are better than dogs. They'll fetch your slippers and don't need to be walked. Ernie'll even sit at my feet and beg if I tell him to."

The audience laughed. I wasn't sure why. It wasn't that genuine ha-ha laughter. It was that outrageous shocked sound. The I-can't-believe-he-said-that laughter.

The zombie was moving toward the comedian in a sort of slow-motion jerk. Crumbling hands reached outward and my stomach squeezed tight. It was a flashback to last night. Zombies almost always attack by just reaching out. Just like in the movies.

The comedian didn't realize that Ernie had decided he'd had enough. If a zombie is simply raised without any particular orders, he usually reverts to what is normal for him. A good person is a good person until his brain decays, stripping him of personality. Most zombies won't kill without orders, but every once in a while you get lucky and raise one that has homicidal tendencies. The comedian was about to get lucky.

The zombie walked towards him like a bad Frankenstein monster. The comedian finally realized something was wrong. He stopped in mid-joke, turning eyes wide. "Ernie," he said. It was as far as he got. The decaying hands wrapped around his throat and started to squeeze.

For one pleasant second I almost let the zombie do him in. Exploiting the dead is one thing I feel strongly about, but . . . stupidity isn't punishable by death. If it was, there would be a hell of a population drop.

I stood up, glancing around the club to see if they had planned for this eventuality. Willie came running to the stage. He wrapped his arms around the zombie's waist and pulled, lifted the much taller body off its feet, but the hands kept squeezing.

The comedian slipped to his knees, making little argh sounds. His face was going from red to purple. The audience was laughing. They thought it was part of the show. It was a heck of a lot funnier than the act.

I stepped up to the stage and said softly to Willie, "Need some help?"

He stared at me, still clinging to the zombie's waist. With his extraordinary strength Willie could have ripped a finger at a time off the man's neck and probably saved him. But super-vampire strength doesn't help you if you don't think how to use it. Willie never thought. Of course, the zombie might crush the man's windpipe before even a vampire could peel its fingers away. Maybe. Best not to find out.

I thought the comedian was a putz. But I couldn't stand there and watch him die. Really, I couldn't.

"Stop," I said. Low and for the zombie's ears. He stopped squeezing, but his hands were still tight. The comedian was going limp. "Release him."

The zombie let go. The man fell in a near faint on the stage. Willie straightened up from his frantic tugging at the deadman. He smoothed his tomato-red suit back into place. His hair was still perfectly slick. Too much hair goop for a mere zombie wrestling to displace his hairdo.

"Thanks," he whispered. Then he stood to his full five feet four and said, "The Amazing Albert and his pet zombie, ladies and gentlemen." The audience had been a bit uncertain, but the applause began. When the Amazing Albert staggered to his feet, the applause exploded. He croaked into the microphone. "Ernie thinks it's time to go home now. You've been a great audience." The applause was loud and genuine.

The comedian left the stage. The zombie stayed and stared at me. Waiting, waiting for another order. I don't know why everyone can't speak and have zombies obey them. It doesn't even feel like magic to me. There is no tingle of the skin, no breath of power. I speak and the zombies listen. Me and E. F. Hutton.

"Follow Albert and obey his orders until I tell you otherwise." The zombie looked down at me for a second, then turned slowly and shuffled after the man. The zombie wouldn't kill him now. I wouldn't tell the comedian that, though. Let him think his life was in danger. Let him think he had to let me lay the zombie to rest. It was what I wanted. It was probably what the zombie wanted.

Ernie certainly didn't seem to like being the straight man in a comedy routine. Hecklers are one thing. Choking the comic to death is a little extreme.

Willie escorted me back to my table. I sat down and sipped my Coke. He sat down across from me. He looked shaken. His small hands trembled as he sat across from me. He was a vampire, but he was still Willie McCoy. I wondered how many years it would take for the last remnants of his personality to disappear. Ten years, twenty, a century? How long before the monster ate the man?

If it took that long. It wouldn't be my problem. I wouldn't be there to see it. To tell the truth, I didn't want to see it.

"I never liked zombies," Willie said.

I stared at him. "Are you afraid of zombies?"

His eyes flickered to me, then down to the table. "No."

I grinned at him. "You're afraid of zombies. You're phobic."

He leaned across the table. "Don't tell. Please don't tell." There was real fear in his eyes.

"Who would I tell?"

"You know."

I shook my head. "I don't know what you're talking about, Willie."

"The MASTER." You could hear "master" was in all caps.

"Why would I tell Jean-Claude?"

He was whispering now. A new comedian had come up on stage, there was laughter and noise, and still he whispered. "You're his human servant, whether you like it or not. When we speak to you, he tells us we're speaking to him."

We were leaning almost face-to-face now. The gentle brush of his breath smelled like breath mints. Almost all vampires smell like breath mints. I don't know what they did before mints were invented. Had stinky breath, I guess.

"You know I'm not his human servant."

"But he wants you to be."

"Just because Jean-Claude wants something doesn't mean he gets it," I said.

"You don't know what he's like."

"I think I do . . ."

He touched my arm. I didn't jerk back this time. I was too intent on what he was saying. "He's been different since the old master died. He's a lot more powerful than even you know."

This much I had suspected. "So why shouldn't I tell him you're afraid of zombies?"

"He'll use it to punish me."

I stared at him, our eyes inches apart. "You mean he's torturing people to control them."

He nodded.

"Shit."

"You won't tell?"

"I won't tell. Promise," I said.

He looked so relieved, I patted his hand. The hand felt like a hand. His body didn't feel wood hard anymore. Why? I didn't know, and if I asked Willie, he probably wouldn't know either. One of the mysteries of . . . death.

"Thanks."

"I thought you said that Jean-Claude was the kindest master you've ever had."

"He is," Willie said.

Now that was a frightening truth. If being tormented by your darkest fear was the kindest, how much worse had Nikolaos been. Hell, I knew the answer to that one. She'd been psychotic. Jean-Claude wasn't cruel just for the sake of watching people squirm. There was reason to his cruelty. It was a step up.

"I gotta go. Thanks for helping with the zombie." He stood.

"You were brave, you know," I said.

He flashed a grin my way, fangs glinting in the dim light. The smile vanished from his face like someone had turned a switch. "I can't afford to be anything else."

Vampires are a lot like wolf packs. The weak are either dominated or destroyed. Banishment is not an option. Willie was moving up in the ranks. A sign of weakness could stop that rise or worse. I'd often wondered what vampires feared. One of them feared zombies. It would have been funny if I hadn't seen the fear in his eyes.

The comic on stage was a vampire. He was the new dead. Skin chalk-white, eyes like burned holes in paper. His gums were bloodless and receding from canines that would have been the envy of any German shepherd. I had never seen a vampire look so monstrous. They all usually made an effort to appear human. This one wasn't.

I had missed the audience's reaction to his first appearance, but now they were laughing. If I had thought the zombie jokes were bad, these were worse. A woman at the next table laughed so hard, tears spilled down her cheeks.

"I went to New York, tough city. A gang jumped me, but I put the bite on them." People were holding their ribs as if in pain.

I didn't get it. It was genuinely not funny. I gazed around the crowd and found every eye fixed on the stage. They peered up at him with the helpless devotion of the bespelled.

He was using mind tricks. I'd seen vampires seduce, threaten, terrify, all by concentrating. But I had never seen them cause laughter. He was forcing them to laugh.

It wasn't the worst abuse of vampiric powers I'd ever seen. He wasn't trying to hurt them. And this mass hypnosis was harmless, temporary. But it was wrong. Mass mind control was one of the top scary things that most people don't know vampires can do.

I knew, and I didn't like it. He was the fresh dead and even before Jean-Claude's marks, the comic couldn't have touched me. Being an animator gave you partial immunity to vampires. It was one of the reasons that animators are so often vampire slayers. We've got a leg up, so to speak.

I had called Charles earlier, but I still didn't see him. He is not easy to miss in a crowd, sort of like Godzilla going through Tokyo. Where was he? And when would Jean-Claude be ready to see me? It was now after eleven. Trust him to browbeat me into a meeting and then make me wait. He was such an arrogant son of a bitch.

Charles came through the swinging doors that led to the kitchen area. He strode through the tables, heading for the door. He was shaking his head and murmuring to a small Asian man who was having to quick-run to keep up.

I waved, and Charles changed direction towards me. I could hear the smaller man arguing, "I run a very good, clean kitchen."

Charles murmured something that I couldn't hear. The bespelled audience was oblivious. We could have shot off a twenty-one-gun salute, and they wouldn't have flinched. Until the vampire comic was finished, they would hear nothing else.

"What are you, the damn health department?" the smaller man asked. He was dressed in a traditional chef's outfit. He had the big floppy hat wadded up in his hands. His dark uptilted eyes were sparkling with anger.

Charles is only six-one, but he seems bigger. His body is one wide piece from broad shoulders to feet. He seems to have no waist. He is like a moving mountain. Huge. His perfectly brown eyes are the same color as his skin. Wonderfully dark. His hand is big enough to cover my face.

The Asian chef looked like an angry puppy beside Charles. He grabbed Charles's arm. I don't know what he thought he was going to do, but Charles stopped moving. He stared down at the offending hand and said very carefully, voice almost painfully deep, "Do not touch me."

The chef dropped his arm like he'd been burned. He took a step back. Charles was only giving him part of the "look." The full treatment had been known to send would-be muggers screaming for help. Part of the look was enough for one irate chef.

His voice was calm, reasonable when he spoke again, "I run a clean kitchen."

Charles shook his head. "You can't have zombies near the food prep-aration. It's illegal. The health codes forbid corpses near food."

"My assistant is a vampire. He's dead."

Charles rolled his eyes at me. I sympathized. I'd had the same discussion with a chef or two. "Vampires are not considered legally dead anymore, Mr. Kim. Zombies are."

"I don't understand why."

"Zombies rot and carry disease just like any dead body. Just because they move around doesn't mean they aren't a depository for disease."

"I don't . . ."

"Either keep the zombies away from the kitchen or we will close you down. Do you understand that?"

"And you'd have to explain to the owner why his business was not making money," I said, smiling up at both of them.

The chef looked a bit pale. Fancy that. "I . . . I understand. It will be taken care of."

"Good," Charles said.

The chef darted one frightened look at me, then began to thread his way back to the kitchen. It was funny how Jean-Claude was beginning to scare so many people. He'd been one of the more civilized vampires before he became head bloodsucker. Power corrupts.

Charles sat down across from me. He seemed too big for the table. "I got your message. What's going on?"

"I need an escort to the Tenderloin."

It's hard to tell when Charles blushes, but he squirmed in his chair. "Why in the world do you want to go down there?"

"I need to find someone who works down there."

"Who?"

"A prostitute," I said.

He squirmed again. It was like watching an uncomfortable mountain. "Caroline is not going to like this."

"Don't tell her," I said.

"You know Caroline and I don't lie to each other, about anything."

I fought to keep my face neutral. If Charles had to explain his every move to his wife, that was his choice. He didn't have to let Caroline control him. He chose to do it. But it grated on me like having your teeth cleaned.

"Just tell her that you had extra animator business. She won't ask de-tails." Caroline thought that our job was gross. Beheading chickens, raising zombies, how uncouth.

"Why do you need to find this prostitute?"

I ignored the question and answered another one. The less Charles knew about Harold Gaynor, the safer he'd be. "I just need someone to look men-acing. I don't want to have to shoot some poor slob because he made a pass at me. Okay?"

Charles nodded. "I'll come. I'm flattered you asked."

I smiled encouragingly at him. Truth was that Manny was more dangerous and much better backup. But Manny was like me. He didn't look dangerous. Charles did. I needed a good bluff tonight, not firepower.

I glanced at my watch. It was almost midnight. Jean-Claude had kept me waiting an hour. I looked behind me and caught Willie's gaze. He came towards me immediately. I would try to use this power only for good.

He bent close, but not too close. He glanced at Charles, acknowledging him with a nod. Charles nodded back. Mr. Stoic.

"What ya want?" Willie said.

"Is Jean-Claude ready to see me or not?"

"Yeah, I was just coming to get ya. I didn't know you was expecting company tonight." He looked at Charles.

"He's a coworker."

"A zombie raiser?" Willie asked.

Charles said, "Yes." His dark face was impassive. His look was quietly menacing.

Willie seemed impressed. He nodded. "Sure, ya got zombie work after you see Jean-Claude?"

"Yeah," I said. I stood and spoke softly to Charles, though chances were that Willie would hear it. Even the newly dead hear better than most dogs.

"I'll be as quick as I can."

"All right," he said, "but I need to get home soon."

I understood. He was on a short leash. His own fault, but it seemed to bother me more than it bothered Charles. Maybe it was one of the reasons I'm not married. I'm not big on compromise.

21

Willie led me through a door and a short hallway. As soon as the door closed behind us, the noise was muted, distant as a dream. The lights were bright after the dimness of the club. I blinked against it. Willie looked rosy-cheeked in the bright light, not quite alive, but healthy for a deadman. He'd fed tonight on something, or someone. Maybe a willing human, maybe animal. Maybe.

The first door on the left said "Manager's Office." Willie's office? Naw.

Willie opened the door and ushered me in. He didn't come in the office. His eyes flicked towards the desk, then he backed out, shutting the door behind him.

The carpeting was pale beige; the walls eggshell-white. A large black-lacquered desk sat against the far wall. A shiny black lamp seemed to grow out of the desk. There was a blotter perfectly placed in the center of the desk. There were no papers, no paper clips, just Jean-Claude sitting behind the desk.

His long pale hands were folded on the blotter. Soft curling black hair, midnight-blue eyes, white shirt with its strange button-down cuffs. He was perfect sitting there, perfectly still like a painting. Beautiful as a wet dream, but not real. He only looked perfect. I knew better.

There were two brown metal filing cabinets against the left wall. A black leather couch took up the rest of the wall. There was a large oil painting above the couch. It was a scene of St. Louis in the 1700s. Settlers coming downriver in flatboats. The sunlight was autumn thick. Children ran and played. It didn't match anything in the room.

"The picture yours?" I asked.

He gave a slight nod.

"Did you know the painter?"

He smiled then, no hint of fangs, just the beautiful spread of lips. If there had been a vampire GQ, Jean-Claude would have been their cover boy.

"The desk and couch don't match the rest of the decor," I said.

"I am in the midst of remodeling," he said.

He just sat there looking at me. "You asked for this meeting, Jean-Claude. Let's get on with it."

"Are you in a hurry?" His voice had dropped lower, the brush of fur on naked skin.

"Yes, I am. So cut to the chase. What do you want?"

The smile widened, slightly. He actually lowered his eyes for a moment. It was almost coy. "You are my human servant, Anita."

He used my name. Bad sign that. "No," I said, "I'm not."

"You bear two marks, only two more remain." His face still looked pleasant, lovely. The expression didn't match what he was saying.

"So what?"

He sighed. "Anita . . ." He stopped in midsentence and stood. He came around the desk. "Do you know what it means to be Master of the City?" He leaned on the desk, half sitting. His shirt gaped open showing an expanse of pale chest. One nipple showed small and pale and hard. The cross-shaped scar was an insult to such pale perfection.

I had been staring at his bare chest. How embarrassing. I met his gaze and managed not to blush. Bully for me.

"There are other benefits to being my human servant, *ma petite*." His eyes were all pupil, black and drowning deep.

I shook my head. "No."

"No lies, *ma petite,* I can feel your desire." His tongue flicked across his lips. "I can taste it."

Great, just great. How do you argue with someone who can feel what you're feeling? Answer: don't argue, agree. "All right, I lust after you. Does that make you happy?"

He smiled. "Yes." One word, but it flowed through my mind, whispering things that he had not said. Whispers in the dark.

"I lust after a lot of men, but that doesn't mean I have to sleep with them."

His face was almost slack, eyes like drowning pools. "Casual lust is easily defeated," he said. He stood in one smooth motion. "What we have is not casual, *ma petite*. Not lust, but desire." He moved towards me, one pale hand outstretched.

My heart was thudding in my throat. It wasn't fear. I didn't think it was a mind trick. It felt real. Desire, he called it, maybe it was. "Don't," my voice was hoarse, a whisper.

He, of course, did not stop. His fingers traced the edge of my cheek, barely touching. The brush of skin on skin. I stepped away from him, forced to draw a deep shaking breath. I could be as uncool as I wanted, he could feel my discomfort. No sense pretending.

I could feel where he had touched me, a lingering sensation. I looked at the ground while I spoke. "I appreciate the possible fringe benefits, Jean-Claude, really. But I can't. I won't." I met his eyes. His face was a terrible blankness. Nothing. It was the same face of a moment ago, but some spark of humanity, of life, was gone.

My pulse started thudding again. It had nothing to do with sex. Fear. It had a lot to do with fear.

"As you like, my little animator. Whether we are lovers or not, it does not change what you are to me. You are my human servant."

"No," I said.

"You are mine, Anita. Willing or not, you are mine."

"See, Jean-Claude, here's where you lose me. First you try seducing me, which has its pleasant side. When that doesn't work, you resort to threats."

"It is not a threat, *ma petite*. It is the truth."

"No, it isn't. And stop calling me *ma* fucking *petite*."

He smiled at that.

I didn't want him amused by me. Anger replaced fear in a quick warm rush. I liked anger. It made me brave, and stupid. "Fuck you."

"I have already offered that." His voice made something low jerk in my stomach.

I felt the rush of heat as I blushed. "Damn you, Jean-Claude, damn you."

"We need to talk, *ma petite*. Lovers or not, servant or not, we need to talk."

"Then talk. I haven't got all night."

He sighed. "You don't make this easy."

"If it was easy you wanted, you should have picked on someone else."

He nodded. "Very true. Please, be seated." He went back to lean on the desk, arms crossed over his chest.

"I don't have that kind of time," I said.

He frowned slightly. "I thought we agreed to talk this out, *ma petite*."

"We agreed to meet at eleven. You're the one who wasted an hour, not me."

His smile was almost bitter. "Very well. I will give you a . . . condensed version."

I nodded. "Fine with me."

"I am the new Master of the City. But to survive with Nikolaos alive, I had to hide my powers. I did it too well. There are those who think I am not powerful enough to be the Master of all. They are challenging me. One of the things they are using against me is you."

"How?"

"Your disobedience. I cannot even control my own human servant. How can I possibly control all the vampires in the city and surrounding areas?"

"What do you want from me?"

He smiled then, wide and genuine, flashing fangs. "I want you to be my human servant."

"Not in this lifetime, Jean-Claude."

"I can force the third mark on you, Anita." There was no threat as he said it. It was just a fact.

"I would rather die than be your human servant." Master vampires can smell the truth. He would know I meant it.

"Why?"

I opened my mouth to try to explain, but didn't. He would not understand. We stood two feet apart but it might have been miles. Miles across some dark chasm. We could not bridge that gap. He was a walking corpse. Whatever he had been as a living man, it was gone. He was the Master of the City, and that was nothing even close to human.

"If you force this issue, I will kill you," I said.

"You mean that." There was surprise in his voice. It isn't often a girl gets to surprise a centuries-old vampire.

"Yes."

"I do not understand you, *ma petite*."

"I know," I said.

"Could you pretend to be my servant?"

It was an odd question. "What does pretending mean?"

"You come to a few meetings. You stand at my side with your guns and your reputation."

"You want the Executioner at your back." I stared at him for a space of heartbeats. The true horror of what he'd just said floated slowly through my mind. "I thought the two marks were accident. That you panicked. You meant all along to mark me, didn't you?"

He just smiled.

"Answer me, you son of a bitch."

"If the chance arose, I was not averse to it."

"Not averse to it!" I was almost yelling. "You cold-bloodedly chose me to be your human servant! Why?"

"You are the Executioner."

"Damn you, what does that mean?"

"It is impressive to be the vampire who finally caught you."

"You haven't caught me."

"If you would behave yourself, the others would think so. Only you and I need know that it is pretense."

I shook my head. "I won't play your game, Jean-Claude."

"You will not help me?"

"You got it."

"I offer you immortality. Without the compromise of vampirism. I offer you myself. There have been women over the years who would have done anything I asked just for that."

"Sex is sex, Jean-Claude. No one's that good."

He smiled slightly. "Vampires are different, *ma petite*. If you were not so stubborn, you might find out how different."

I had to look away from his eyes. The look was too intimate. Too full of possibilities.

"There's only one thing I want from you," I said.

"And what is that, *ma petite?*"

"All right, two things. First, stop calling me *ma petite;* second, let me go. Wipe these damn marks away."

"You may have the first request, Anita."

"And the second?"

"I cannot, even if I wanted to."

"Which you don't," I said.

"Which I don't."

"Stay away from me, Jean-Claude. Stay the fuck away from me, or I'll kill you."

"Many people have tried through the years."

"How many of them had eighteen kills?"

His eyes widened just a bit. "None. There was this man in Hungary who swore he killed five."

"What happened to him?"

"I tore his throat out."

"You understand this, Jean-Claude. I would rather have my throat torn out. I would rather die trying to kill you than submit to you." I stared at him, trying to see if he understood any of what I said. "Say something."

"I have heard your words. I know you mean them." He was suddenly standing in front of me. I hadn't seen him move, hadn't felt him in my head. He was just suddenly inches in front of me. I think I gasped.

"Could you truly kill me?" His voice was like silk on a wound, gentle with an edge of pain. Like sex. It was like velvet rubbing inside my skull. It felt good, even with fear tearing through my body. Shit. He could still have me. Still take me down. No way.

I looked up into his so-blue eyes and said, "Yes."

I meant it. He blinked once, gracefully, and stepped back. "You are the most stubborn woman I have ever met," he said. There was no play in his voice this time. It was a flat statement.

"That's the nicest compliment you've ever paid me."

He stood in front of me, hands at his sides. He stood very still. Snakes or birds can stand utterly still but even a snake has a sense of aliveness, of action waiting to resume. Jean-Claude stood there with no sense of anything, as if despite what my eyes told me, he had vanished. He was not there at all. The dead make no noise.

"What happened to your face?"

I touched the swollen cheek before I could stop myself. "Nothing," I lied.

"Who hit you?"

"Why, so you can go beat him up?"

"One of the fringe benefits of being my servant is my protection."

"I don't need your protection, Jean-Claude."

"He hurt you."

"And I shoved a gun into his groin and made him tell me everything he knew," I said.

Jean-Claude smiled. "You did what?"

"I shoved a gun into his balls, all right?"

His eyes started to sparkle. Laughter spread across his face and burst out between his lips. He laughed full-throated.

The laugh was like candy: sweet, and infectious. If you could bottle Jean-Claude's laugh, I know it would be fattening. Or orgasmic.

"*Ma petite, ma petite,* you are absolutely marvelous."

I stared at him, letting that wonderful, touchable laugh roll around me. It was time to go. It is very hard to be dignified when someone is laughing uproariously at you. But I managed.

My parting shot made him laugh harder. "Stop calling me *ma petite.*"

22

I stepped back out into the noise of the club. Charles was standing beside the table, not sitting. He looked uncomfortable from a distance. What had gone wrong now?

His big hands were twisted together. Dark face scrunched up into near pain. A kind God had made Charles look big and bad, because inside he was all marshmallow. If I'd had Charles's natural size and strength, I'd have been a guaranteed bad ass. It was sort of sad and unfair.

"What's wrong?" I asked.

"I called Caroline," he said.

"And?"

"The baby-sitter's sick. And Caroline's been called in to the hospital. Someone has to stay with Sam while she goes to work."

"Mm-huh," I said.

He didn't look the least bit tough when he said, "Can going down to the Tenderloin wait until tomorrow?"

I shook my head.

"You're not going to go down there alone," Charles said. "Are you?"

I stared up at the great mountain of a man, and sighed. "I can't wait, Charles."

"But the Tenderloin." He lowered his voice as if just saying the word too loud would bring a cloud of pimps and prostitutes to descend upon us. "You can't go down there alone at night."

"I've gone worse places, Charles. I'll be all right."

"No, I won't let you go alone. Caroline can just get a new sitter or tell the hospital no." He smiled when he said it. Always happy to help a friend. Caroline would give him hell for it. Worst of all, now I didn't want to take Charles with me. You had to do more than look tough.

What if Gaynor got wind of me questioning Wanda? What if he found

Charles and thought he was involved? No. It had been selfish to risk Charles. He had a four-year-old son. And a wife.

Harold Gaynor would eat Charles raw for dinner. I couldn't involve him. He was a big, friendly, eager-to-please bear. A lovable, cuddly bear. I didn't need a teddy bear for backup. I needed someone who would be able to take any heat that Gaynor might send our way.

I had an idea.

"Go home, Charles. I won't go alone. I promise."

He looked uncertain. Like maybe he didn't trust me. Fancy that. "Anita, are you sure? I won't leave you hanging like this."

"Go on, Charles. I'll take backup."

"Who can you get at this hour?"

"No questions. Go home to your son."

He looked uncertain, but relieved. He hadn't really wanted to go to the Tenderloin. Maybe Caroline's short leash was what Charles wanted, needed. An excuse for all the things he really didn't want to do. What a basis for a marriage.

But, hey, if it works, don't fix it.

Charles left with many apologies. But I knew he was glad to go. I would remember that he had been glad to go.

I knocked on the office door. There was a silence, then, "Come in, Anita."

How had he known it was me? I wouldn't ask. I didn't want to know.

Jean-Claude seemed to be checking figures in a large ledger. It looked antique with yellowed pages and fading ink. The ledger looked like something Bob Crachit should have been scribbling in on a cold Christmas Eve.

"What have I done to merit two visits in one night?" he said.

Looking at him now, I felt silly. I spent all this time avoiding him. Now I was going to invite him to accompany me on a bit of sleuthing? But it would kill two bats with one stone. It would please Jean-Claude, and I really didn't want him angry with me, if I could avoid it. And if Gaynor did try to go up against Jean-Claude, I was betting on Jean-Claude.

It was what Jean-Claude had done to me a few weeks ago. He had chosen me as the vampire's champion. Put me up against a monster that had slain three master vampires. And he had bet that I would come out on top against Nikolaos. I had, but just barely.

What was sauce for the goose was sauce for the gander. I smiled sweetly at him. Pleased to be able to return the favor so quickly.

"Would you care to accompany me to the Tenderloin?"

He blinked, surprise covering his face just like a real person. "To what purpose?"

"I need to question a prostitute about a case I'm working on. I need backup."

"Backup?" he asked.

"I need backup that looks more threatening than I do. You fit the bill."

He smiled beatifically. "I would be your bodyguard."

"You've given me enough grief, do something nice for a change."

The smile vanished. "Why this sudden change of heart, *ma petite*?"

"My backup had to go home and baby-sit his kid."

"And if I do not go?"

"I'll go alone," I said.

"Into the Tenderloin?"

"Yep."

He was suddenly standing by the desk, walking towards me. I hadn't seen him rise.

"I wish you'd stop doing that."

"Doing what?"

"Clouding my mind so I can't see you move."

"I do it as often as I can, *ma petite,* just to prove I still can."

"What's that supposed to mean?"

"I gave up much of my power over you when I gave you the marks. I practice what little games are left me." He was standing almost in front of me. "Lest you forget who and what I am."

I stared up into his blue, blue eyes. "I never forget that you are the walking dead, Jean-Claude."

An expression I could not read passed over his face. It might have been pain. "No, I see the knowledge in your eyes of what I am." His voice dropped low, almost a whisper, but it wasn't seductive. It was human. "Your eyes are the clearest mirror I have ever seen, *ma petite*. Whenever I begin to pretend to myself. Whenever I have delusions of life. I have only to look into your face and see the truth."

What did he expect me to say? Sorry, I'll try to ignore the fact that you're a vampire. "So why keep me around?" I asked.

"Perhaps if Nikolaos had had such a mirror, she would not have been such a monster."

I stared at him. He might be right. It made his choice of me as human servant almost noble. Almost. Oh, hell. I would not start feeling sorry for the freaking Master of the City. Not now. Not ever.

We would go down to the Tenderloin. Pimps beware. I was bringing the Master as backup. It was like carrying a thermonuclear device to kill ants. Overkill has always been a specialty of mine.

23

The Tenderloin was originally the red light district on the Riverfront in the 1800s. But the Tenderloin, like so much of St. Louis, moved uptown. Go down Washington past the Fox Theater, where you can see Broadway traveling companies sing bright musicals. Keep driving down Washington to the west edge of downtown St. Louis and you will come to the resurrected carcass of the Tenderloin.

The night streets are neon-coated, sparkling, flashing, pulsing—colors. It looks like some sort of pornographic carnival. All it needs is a Ferris wheel in one of the empty lots. They could sell cotton candy shaped like naked people. The kiddies could play while Daddy went to get his jollies. Mom would never have to know.

Jean-Claude sat beside me in the car. He had been utterly silent on the drive over. I had had to glance at him a time or two just to make sure he was still there. People make noise. I don't mean talking or belching or anything overt. But people, as a rule, can't just sit without making noise. They fidget, the sound of cloth rubbing against the seats; they breathe, the soft intake of air; they wet their lips, wet, quiet, but noise. Jean-Claude didn't do any of these things as we drove. I couldn't even swear he blinked. The living dead, yippee.

I can take silence as good as the next guy, better than most women and a lot of men. Now, I needed to fill the silence. Talk just for the noise. A waste of energy, but I needed it.

"Are you in there, Jean-Claude?"

His neck turned, bringing his head with it. His eyes glittered, reflecting the neon signs like dark glass. Shit.

"You can play human, Jean-Claude, better than almost any vampire I've ever met. What's all this supernatural crap?"

"Crap?" he said, voice soft.

"Yeah, why are you going all spooky on me?"

"Spooky?" he asked, and the sound filled the car. As if the word meant something else entirely.

"Stop that," I said.

"Stop what?"

"Answering every question with a question."

He blinked once. "So sorry, *ma petite,* but I can feel the street."

"Feel the street? What does that mean?"

He settled back against the upholstery, leaning his head and neck into the seat. His hand clasped over his stomach. "There is a great deal of life here."

"Life?" He had me doing it now.

"Yes," he said, "I can feel them running back and forth. Little creatures, desperately seeking love, pain, acceptance, greed. A lot of greed here, too, but mostly pain and love."

"You don't come to a prostitute for love. You come for sex."

He rolled his head so his dark eyes stared at me. "Many people confuse the two."

I stared at the road. The hairs at the back of my neck were standing at attention. "You haven't fed yet tonight, have you?"

"You are the vampire expert. Can you not tell?" His voice had dropped to almost a whisper. Hoarse and thick.

"You know I can never tell with you."

"A compliment to my powers, I'm sure."

"I did not bring you down here to hunt," I said. My voice sounded firm, a tad loud. My heart was loud inside my head.

"Would you forbid me to hunt tonight?" he asked.

I thought about that one for a minute or two. We were going to have to turn around and make another pass to find a parking space. Would I forbid him to hunt tonight? Yes. He knew the answer. This was a trick question. Trouble was I couldn't see the trick.

"I would ask that you not hunt here tonight," I said.

"Give me a reason, Anita."

He had called me Anita without me prompting him. He was definitely after something. "Because I brought you down here. You wouldn't have hunted here, if it hadn't been for me."

"You feel guilt for whomever I might feed on tonight?"

"It is illegal to take unwilling human victims," I said.

"So it is."

"The penalty for doing so is death," I said.

"By your hand."

"If you do it in this state, yes."

"They are just whores, pimps, cheating men. What do they matter to you, Anita?"

I don't think he had ever called me Anita twice in a row. It was a bad sign. A car pulled away not a block from The Grey Cat Club. What luck. I slid my Nova into the slot. Parallel parking is not my best thing, but luckily the car that pulled away was twice the size of my car. There was plenty of room to maneuver, back and forth from the curb.

When the car was lurched nearly onto the curb but safely out of traffic, I cut the engine. Jean-Claude lay back in his seat, staring at me. "I asked you a question, *ma petite,* what do these people mean to you?"

I undid my seat belt and turned to look at him. Some trick of light and shadow had put most of his body in darkness. A band of nearly gold light lay across his face. His high cheekbones were very prominent against his pale skin. The tips of his fangs showed between his lips. His eyes gleamed like blue neon. I looked away and stared at the steering wheel while I talked.

"I have no personal stake in these people, Jean-Claude, but they are people. Good, bad, or indifferent, they are alive, and no one has the right to just arbitrarily snuff them out."

"So it is the sanctity of life you cling to?"

I nodded. "That and the fact that every human being is special. Every death is a loss of something precious and irreplaceable." I looked at him as I finished the last.

"You have killed before, Anita. You have destroyed that which is irreplaceable."

"I'm irreplaceable, too," I said. "No one has the right to kill me, either."

He sat up in one liquid motion, and reality seemed to collect around him. I could almost feel the movement of time in the car, like a sonic boom for the inside of my head, instead of my ear.

Jean-Claude sat there looking entirely human. His pale skin had a certain flush to it. His curling black hair, carefully combed and styled, was rich and touchable. His eyes were just midnight-blue, nothing exceptional but the color. He was human again, in the blink of an eye.

"Jesus," I whispered.

"What is wrong, *ma petite*?"

I shook my head. If I asked how he did it, he'd just smile. "Why all the questions, Jean-Claude? Why the worry about my view of life?"

"You are my human servant." He raised a hand to stop the automatic objection. "I have begun the process of making you my human servant, and I would like to understand you better."

"Can't you just . . . scent my emotions like you can the people on the street?"

"No, *ma petite*. I can feel your desire but little else. I gave that up when I made you my marked servant."

"You can't read me?"

"No."

That was really nice to know. Jean-Claude didn't have to tell me. So why did he? He never gave anything away for free. There were strings attached that I couldn't even see. I shook my head. "You are just to back me up tonight. Don't do anything to anybody unless I say so, okay?"

"Do anything?"

"Don't hurt anyone unless they try to hurt us."

He nodded, face very solemn. Why did I suspect that he was laughing at me in some dark corner of his mind? Giving orders to the Master of the City. I guess it was funny.

The noise level on the sidewalk was intense. Music blared out of every other building. Never the same song, but always loud. The flashing signs proclaimed, "Girls, Girls, Girls. Topless." A pink-edged sign read, "Talk to the Naked Woman of Your Dreams." Eeek.

A tall, thin black woman came up to us. She was wearing purple shorts so short that they looked like a thong bikini. Black fishnet panty hose covered her legs and buttocks. Provocative.

She stopped somewhere between the two of us. Her eyes flicked from one to the other. "Which one of ya does it, and which one of ya watches?"

Jean-Claude and I exchanged glances. He was smiling ever so slightly. "Sorry, we were looking for Wanda," I said.

"A lot of names down here," she said. "I can do anything this Wanda can do and do it better." She stepped very close to Jean-Claude, almost touching. He took her hand in his and lifted it gently to his lips. His eyes watched me as he did it.

"You're the doer," she said. Her voice had gone throaty, sexy. Or maybe that was just the effect Jean-Claude had on women. Maybe.

The woman cuddled in against him. Her skin looked very dark against the white lace of his shirt. Her fingernails were painted a bright pink, like Easter basket grass.

"Sorry to interrupt," I said, "but we don't have all night."

"This is not the one you seek then," he said.

"No," I said.

He gripped her arms just above the elbows and pushed her away. She struggled just a bit to reach him again. Her hands grabbed at his arms, trying to pull herself closer to him. He held her straight-armed, effortlessly. He could have held a semitruck effortlessly.

"I'll do you for free," she said.

"What did you do to her?" I asked.

"Nothing."

I didn't believe him. "Nothing, and she offers to do you for free?" Sarcasm is one of my natural talents. I made sure that Jean-Claude heard it.

"Be still," he said.

"Don't tell me to shut up."

The woman was standing perfectly still. Her hands dropped to her sides, limp. He hadn't been talking to me at all.

Jean-Claude took his hands away from her. She never moved. He stepped around her like she was a crack in the pavement. He took my arm, and I let him. I watched the prostitute, waiting for her to move.

Her straight, nearly naked back shuddered. Her shoulders slumped. She threw back her head and drew a deep trembling breath.

Jean-Claude pulled me gently down the street, his hand on my elbow.

The prostitute turned around, saw us. Her eyes never even hesitated. She didn't know us.

I swallowed hard enough for it to hurt. I pulled free of Jean-Claude's hand. He didn't fight me. Good for him.

I backed up against a storefront window. Jean-Claude stood in front of me, looking down. "What did you do to her?"

"I told you, *ma petite,* nothing."

"Don't call me that. I saw her, Jean-Claude. Don't lie to me."

A pair of men stopped beside us to look in the window. They were holding hands. I glanced in the window and felt color creep up my cheeks. There were whips, leather masks, padded handcuffs, and things I didn't even have a name for. One of the men leaned into the other and whispered. The other man laughed. One of them caught me looking. Our eyes met, and I looked away, fast. Eye contact down here was a dangerous thing.

I was blushing and hating it. The two men walked away, hand in hand.

Jean-Claude was staring in the window like he was out for a Saturday afternoon of window-shopping. Casual.

"What did you do to that woman?"

He stared in the storefront. I couldn't tell exactly what had caught his attention. "It was careless of me, *ma* . . . Anita. My fault entirely."

"What was your fault?"

"My . . . powers are greater when my human servant is with me." He stared at me then. His gaze solid on my face. "With you beside me, my powers are enhanced."

"Wait, you mean like a witch's familiar?"

He cocked his head to one side, a slight smile on his face. "Yes, very close to that. I did not know you knew anything about witchcraft."

"A deprived childhood," I said. I was not going to be diverted from the important topic. "So your ability to bespell people with your eyes is stronger when I'm with you. Strong enough that without trying, you bespelled that prostitute."

He nodded.

I shook my head. "No, I don't believe you."

He shrugged, a graceful gesture on him. "Believe what you like, *ma petite.* It is the truth."

I didn't want to believe it. Because if it were true, then I was in fact his human servant. Not in my actions but by my very presence. With sweat trickling down my spine from the heat, I was cold. "Shit," I said.

"You could say that," he said.

"No, I can't deal with this right now. I can't." I stared up at him. "You keep whatever powers we have between us in check, okay?"

"I will try," he said.

"Don't try, dammit, do it."

He smiled wide enough to flash the tips of his fangs. "Of course, *ma petite.*"

Panic was starting in the pit of my stomach. I gripped my hands into fists at my sides. "If you call me that one more time, I'm going to hit you."

His eyes widened just a bit, his lips flexed. I realized he was trying not to laugh. I hate it when people find my threats amusing.

He was an invasive son of a bitch; and I wanted to hurt him. To hurt him because he scared me. I understand the urge, I've had it before with other people. It's an urge that can lead to violence. I stared up at his softly amused face. He was a condescending bastard, but if it ever came to real violence between us, one of us would die. Chances were good it would be me.

The humor leaked out of his face, leaving it smooth and lovely, and arrogant. "What is it, Anita?" His voice was soft and intimate. Even in the heat and movement of this place, his voice could roll me up and under. It was a gift.

"Don't push me into a corner, Jean-Claude. You don't want to take away all my options."

"I don't know what you mean," he said.

"If it comes down to you or me, I'm going to pick me. You remember that."

He looked at me for a space of heartbeats. Then he blinked and nodded. "I believe you would. But remember, *ma* . . . Anita, if you hurt me, it hurts you. I could survive the strain of your death. The question, *amante de moi,* is could you survive mine?"

Amante de moi? What the hell did that mean? I decided not to ask. "Damn you, Jean-Claude, damn you."

"That, dear Anita, was done long before you met me."

"What does that mean?"

His eyes were as innocent as they ever were. "Why, Anita, your own Catholic Church has declared all vampires as suicides. We are automatically damned."

I shook my head. "I'm Episcopalian, now, but that isn't what you meant."

He laughed then. The sound was like silk brushed across the nape of the neck. It felt smooth and good, but it made you shudder.

I walked away from him. I just left him there in front of the obscene window display. I walked into the crowd of whores, hustlers, customers. There was nobody on this street as dangerous as Jean-Claude. I had brought him down here to protect me. That was laughable. Ridiculous. Obscene.

A young man who couldn't have been more than fifteen stopped me. He was wearing a vest with no shirt and a pair of torn jeans. "You interested?"

He was taller than me by a little. His eyes were blue. Two other boys just behind him were staring at us.

"We don't get many women down here," he said.

"I believe you." He looked incredibly young. "Where can I find Wheel-chair Wanda?"

One of the boys behind him said, "A crip lover, Jesus."

I agreed with him. "Where?" I held up a twenty. It was too much to pay for the information, but maybe if I gave it to him, he could go home sooner. Maybe if he had twenty dollars, he could turn down one of the cars cruising the street. Twenty dollars, it would change his life. Like sticking your finger in a nuclear meltdown.

"She's just outside of The Grey Cat. At the end of the block."

"Thanks." I gave him the twenty. His fingernails had grime embedded in them.

"You sure you don't want some action?" His voice was small and uncertain, like his eyes.

Out of the corner of my eye I saw Jean-Claude moving through the crowd. He was coming for me. To protect me. I turned back to the boy. "I've got more action than I know what to do with," I said.

He frowned, looking puzzled. That was all right. I was puzzled, too. What do you do with a master vampire that won't leave you alone? Good question. Unfortunately, what I needed was a good answer.

24

Wheelchair Wanda was a small woman sitting in one of those sport wheel-chairs that are used for racing. She wore workout gloves, and the muscles in her arms moved under her tanned skin as she pushed herself along. Long brown hair fell in gentle waves around a very pretty face. The makeup was tasteful. She wore a shiny metallic blue shirt and no bra. An ankle-length skirt with at least two layers of multicolored crinoline and a pair of stylish black boots hid her legs.

She was moving towards us at a goodly pace. Most of the prostitutes, male and female, looked ordinary. They weren't dressed outrageously, shorts, midrifts. In this heat who could blame them? I guess if you wear fishnet jumpsuits, the police just naturally get suspicious.

Jean-Claude stood beside me. He glanced up at the sign that proclaimed "The Grey Cat" in a near blinding shade of fuchsia neon. Tasteful.

How does one approach a prostitute, even just to talk? I didn't know. Learn something new every day. I stood in her path and waited for her to come to me. She glanced up and caught me watching her. When I didn't look away, she got eye contact and smiled.

Jean-Claude moved up beside me. Wanda's smile broadened or deepened. It was a definite "come along smile" as my Grandmother Blake used to say.

Jean-Claude whispered, "Is that a prostitute?"

"Yes," I said.

"In a wheelchair?" he asked.

"Yep."

"My," was all he said. I think Jean-Claude was shocked. Nice to know he could be.

She stopped her chair with an expert movement of hands. She smiled, craning to look up at us. The angle looked painful.

"Hi," she said.

"Hi," I said.

She continued to smile. I continued to stare. Why did I suddenly feel awkward? "A friend told me about you," I said.

Wanda nodded.

"You are the one they refer to as Wheelchair Wanda?"

She grinned suddenly, and her face looked real. Behind all those lovely but fake smiles was a real person. "Yeah, that's me."

"Could we talk?"

"Sure," she said. "You got a room?"

Did I have a room? Wasn't she supposed to do that? "No."

She waited.

Oh, hell. "We just want to talk to you for an hour, or two. We'll pay whatever the going rate is."

She told me the going rate.

"Jesus, that's a little steep," I said.

She smiled beatifically at me. "Supply and demand," she said. "You can't get a taste of what I have anywhere else." She smoothed her hands down her legs as she said it. My eyes followed her hands like they were supposed to. This was too weird.

I nodded. "Okay, you got a deal." It was a business expense. Computer paper, ink pens medium point, one prostitute, manila file folders. See, it fit right in.

Bert was going to love this one.

25

We took Wanda back to my apartment. There are no elevators in my building. Two flights of stairs are not exactly wheelchair accessible. Jean-Claude carried her. His stride was even and fluid as he walked ahead of me. Wanda didn't even slow him down. I followed with the wheelchair. It did slow me down.

The only consolation I had was I got to watch Jean-Claude climb the stairs. So sue me. He had a very nice backside for a vampire.

He was waiting for me in the upper hallway, standing with Wanda cuddled in his arms. They both looked at me with a pleasant sort of blankness.

I wheeled the collapsed wheelchair over the carpeting. Jean-Claude followed me. The crinoline in Wanda's skirts crinkled and whispered as he moved.

I leaned the wheelchair against my leg and unlocked the door. I pushed the door all the way back to the wall to give Jean-Claude room. The wheelchair folded inwards like a cloth baby stroller. I struggled to make the metal bars catch, so the chair would be solid again. As I suspected, it was easier to break it than to fix it.

I glanced up from my struggles and found Jean-Claude still standing outside my door. Wanda was staring at him, frowning.

"What's wrong?" I asked.

"I have never been to your apartment."

"So?"

"The great vampire expert . . . come, Anita."

Oh. "You have my permission to enter my home."

He gave a sort of bow from the neck. "I am honored," he said.

The wheelchair snapped into shape again. Jean-Claude set Wanda in her chair. I closed the door. Wanda smoothed her long skirts over her legs.

Jean-Claude stood in the middle of my living room and gazed about. He gazed at the penguin calendar on the wall by the kitchenette. He rifled the pages to see future months, gazing at pictures of chunky flightless birds until he'd seen every picture.

I wanted to tell him to stop, but it was harmless. I didn't write appointments on the calendar. Why did it bother me that he was so damned interested in it?

I turned back to the prostitute in my living room. The night was entirely too weird. "Would you like something to drink?" I asked. When in doubt, be polite.

"Red wine if you have it," Wanda said.

"Sorry, nothing alcoholic in the house. Coffee, soft drinks with real sugar in them, and water, that's about it."

"Soft drink," she said.

I got her a can of Coke out of the fridge. "You want a glass?"

She shook her head.

Jean-Claude was leaning against the wall, staring at me as I moved about the kitchen. "I don't need a glass either," he said softly.

"Don't get cute," I said.

"Too late," he said.

I had to smile.

The smile seemed to please him. Which made me frown. Life was hard around Jean-Claude. He sort of wandered off towards the fish tank. He was giving himself a tour of my apartment. Of course, he would. But at least it would give Wanda and meO some privacy.

"Shit, he's a vampire," Wanda said. She sounded surprised. Which surprised me. I could always tell. Dead was dead to me, no matter how pretty the corpse.

"You didn't know?" I asked.

"No, I'm not coffin-bait," she said. There was a tightness to her face. The flick of her eyes as she followed Jean-Claude's casual movements around the room was new. She was scared.

"What's coffin-bait?" I handed her the soft drink.

"A whore that does vampires."

Coffin-bait, how quaint. "He won't touch you."

She turned brown eyes to me then. Her gaze was very thorough, as if she were trying to read the inside of my head. Was I telling the truth?

How terrifying to go away with strangers to rooms and not know if they will hurt you or not. Desperation, or a death wish.

"So you and I are going to do it?" she asked. Her gaze never left my face.

I blinked at her. It took me a moment to realize what she meant. "No." I shook my head. "No, I said I just wanted to talk. I meant it." I think I was blushing.

Maybe the blush did it. She popped the top on the soda can and took a drink. "You want me to talk about doing it with other people, while you do it with him?" She motioned her head towards the wandering vampire.

Jean-Claude was standing in front of the only picture I had in the room.

It was modern and matched the decor. Grey, white, black, and palest pink. It was one of those designs that the longer you stared at it, the more shapes you could pick out.

"Look, Wanda, we are just going to talk. That's it. Nobody is going to do anything to anybody. Okay?"

She shrugged. "It's your money. We can do what you want."

That one statement made my stomach hurt. She meant it. I'd paid the money. She would do anything I wanted. Anything? It was too awful. That any human being would say "anything" and mean it. Of course, she drew the line at vampires. Even whores have standards.

Wanda was smiling up at me. The change was extraordinary. Her face glowed. She was instantly lovely. Even her eyes glowed. It reminded me of Cicely's soundless laughing face.

Back to business. "I heard you were Harold Gaynor's mistress a while back." No preliminaries, no sweet talk. Off with the clothes.

Wanda's smile faded. The glow of humor died in her eyes, replaced by wariness. "I don't know the name."

"Yeah, you do," I said. I was still standing, forcing her to look up at me in that near painful angle.

She sipped her drink and shook her head without looking up at me.

"Come on, Wanda, I know you were Gaynor's sweetie. Admit you know him, and we'll work from there."

She glanced up at me, then down. "No. I'll do you. I'll let the vamp watch. I'll talk dirty to you both. But I don't know anybody named Gaynor."

I leaned down, putting my hands on the arms of her chair. Our faces were very close. "I'm not a reporter. Gaynor will never know you talked to me unless you tell him."

Her eyes had gotten bigger. I glanced where she was staring. The Windbreaker had fallen forward. My gun was showing, which seemed to upset her. Good.

"Talk to me, Wanda." My voice was soft. Mild. The mildest of voices is often the worst threat.

"Who the hell are you? You're not cops. You're not a reporter. Social workers don't carry guns. Who are you?" That last question had the lilt of fear in it.

Jean-Claude strolled into the room. He'd been in my bedroom. Great, just great. "Trouble, *ma petite*?"

I didn't correct him on the nickname. Wanda didn't need to know there was dissent in the ranks. "She's being stubborn," I said.

I stepped back from her chair. I took off the Windbreaker and laid it over the kitchen counter. Wanda stared at the gun like I knew she would.

I may not be intimidating, but the Browning is.

Jean-Claude walked up behind her. His slender hands touched her shoulders. She jumped like it had hurt. I knew it hadn't hurt. Might be better if it did.

"He'll kill me," Wanda said.

A lot of people seemed to say that about Mr. Gaynor. "He'll never know," I said.

Jean-Claude rubbed his cheek against her hair. His fingers kneading her shoulders, gently. "And, my sweet coquette, he is not here with you to-night." He spoke with his lips against her ear. "We are." He said something else so soft I could not hear. Only his lips moved, soundlessly for me.

Wanda heard him. Her eyes widened, and she started to tremble. Her entire body seemed in the grip of some kind of fit. Tears glittered in her eyes and fell down her cheeks in one graceful curve.

Jesus.

"Please, don't. Please don't let him." Her voice was squeezed small and thin with fear.

I hated Jean-Claude in that moment. And I hated me. I was one of the good guys. It was one of my last illusions. I wasn't willing to give it up, not even if it worked. Wanda would talk or she wouldn't. No torture. "Back off, Jean-Claude," I said.

He gazed up at me. "I can taste her terror like strong wine." His eyes were solid, drowning blue. He looked blind. His face was still lovely as he opened his mouth wide and fangs glistened.

Wanda was still crying and staring at me. If she could have seen the look on Jean-Claude's face, she would have been screaming.

"I thought your control was better than this, Jean-Claude?"

"My control is excellent, but it is not endless." He stood away from her and began to pace the room on the other side of the couch. Like a leopard pacing its cage. Contained violence, waiting for release. I could not see his face. Had the spook act been for Wanda's benefit? Or real?

I shook my head. No way to ask in front of Wanda. Maybe later. Maybe.

I knelt in front of Wanda. She was gripping the soda can so hard, she was denting it. I didn't touch her, just knelt close by. "I won't let him hurt you. Honest. Harold Gaynor is threatening me. That's why I need information."

Wanda was looking at me, but her attention was on the vampire in back of her. There was a watchful tension in her shoulders. She would never relax while Jean-Claude was in the room. The lady had taste.

"Jean-Claude, Jean-Claude."

His face looked as ordinary as it ever did when he turned to face me. A smile crooked his full lips. It was an act. Pretense. Damn him. Was there something in becoming a vampire that made you sadistic?

"Go into the bedroom for a while. Wanda and I need to talk in private."

"Your bedroom." His smile widened. "My pleasure, *ma petite*."

I scowled at him. He was undaunted. As always. But he left the room as I'd asked.

Wanda's shoulders slumped. She drew a shaky breath. "You really aren't going to let him hurt me, are you?"

"No, I'm not."

She started to cry then, soft, shaky tears. I didn't know what to do. I've never known what to do when someone cries. Did I hug her? Pat her hand comfortingly. What?

I finally sat back on the ground in front of her, leaning back on my heels, and did nothing. It took a few moments, but finally the crying stopped. She blinked up at me. The makeup around her eyes had faded, just vanished. It made her look vulnerable, more rather than less attractive. I had the urge to take her in my arms and rock her like a child. Whisper lies, about how everything would be all right.

When she left here tonight, she was still going to be a whore. A crippled whore. How could that be all right? I shook my head more at me than at her.

"You want some Kleenex?"

She nodded.

I got her the box from the kitchen counter. She wiped at her face and blew her nose softly, very ladylike.

"Can we talk now?"

She blinked at me and nodded. She took a shaky sip of pop.

"You know Harold Gaynor, right?"

She just stared at me, dully. Had we broken her? "If he finds out, he will kill me. Maybe I don't want to be coffin-bait, but I sure as hell don't want to die either."

"No one does. Talk to me, Wanda, please."

She let out a shaky sigh. "Okay, I know Harold."

Harold? "Tell me about him."

Wanda stared at me. Her eyes narrowed. There were fine lines around her eyes. It made her older than I had thought. "Has he sent Bruno or Tommy after you yet?"

"Tommy came for a personal meeting."

"What happened?"

"I drew a gun on him."

"That gun?" she asked in a small voice.

"Yes."

"What did you do to make Harold mad?"

Truth or lie? Neither. "I refused to do something for him."

"What?"

I shook my head. "It doesn't matter."

"It can't have been sex. You aren't crippled." She said the last word like it was hard. "He doesn't touch anyone who's whole." The bitterness in her voice was thick enough to taste.

"How did you meet him?" I asked.

"I was in college at Wash U. Gaynor was donating money for something."

"And he asked you out?"

"Yeah." Her voice was so soft, I had to lean forward to hear it.

"What happened?"

"We were both in wheelchairs. He was rich. It was great." She rolled her lips under, like she was smoothing lipstick, then out, and swallowed.

"When did it stop being great?" I asked.

"I moved in with him. Dropped out of college. It was . . . easier than college. Easier than anything. He couldn't get enough of me." She stared down at her lap again. "He started wanting variety in the bedroom. See, his legs are crippled, but he can feel. I can't feel." Wanda's voice had dropped almost to a whisper. I had to lean against her knees to hear. "He liked to do things to my legs, but I couldn't feel it. So at first I thought that was okay, but . . . but he got really sick." She looked at me suddenly, her face only inches from mine. Her eyes were huge, swimming with unshed tears. "He cut me up. I couldn't feel it, but that's not the point, is it?"

"No," I said.

The first tear trailed down her face. I touched her hand. Her fingers wrapped around mine and held on.

"It's all right," I said, "it's all right."

She cried. I held her hand and lied. "It's all right now, Wanda. He can't hurt you anymore."

"Everyone hurts you," she said. "You were going to hurt me." There was accusation in her eyes.

It was a little late to explain good cop, bad cop to her. She wouldn't have believed it anyway.

"Tell me about Gaynor."

"He replaced me with a deaf girl."

"Cicely," I said.

She looked up, surprised. "You've met her?"

"Briefly."

Wanda shook her head. "Cicely is one sick chickie. She likes torturing people. It gets her off." Wanda looked at me as if trying to gauge my reaction. Was I shocked? No.

"Harold slept with both of us at the same time, sometimes. At the end it was always a threesome. It got real rough." Her voice dropped lower and lower, a hoarse whisper. "Cicely likes knives. She's real good at skinning things." She rolled her lips under again in that lipstick-smoothing gesture. "Gaynor would kill me just for telling you his bedroom secrets."

"Do you know any business secrets?"

She shook her head. "No, I swear. He was always very careful to keep me out of that. I thought at first it was so if the police came, I wouldn't be arrested." She looked down at her lap. "Later, I realized it was because he knew I would be replaced. He didn't want me to know anything that could hurt him when he threw me away."

There was no bitterness now, no anger, only a hollow sadness. I wanted her to rant and rave. This quiet despair was aching. A hurt that would never heal. Gaynor had done worse than kill her. He'd left her alive. Alive and as crippled inside as out.

"I can't tell you anything but bedroom talk. It won't help you hurt him."

"Is there any bedroom talk that isn't about sex?" I asked.

"What do you mean?"

"Personal secrets, but not sex. You were his sweetie for nearly two years. He must have talked about something other than sex."

She frowned, thinking. "I . . . I guess he talked about his family."

"What about his family?"

"He was illegitimate. He was obsessed with his real father's family."

"He knew who they were?"

Wanda nodded. "They were rich, old money. His mother was a hooker turned mistress. When she got pregnant, they threw her out."

Like Gaynor did to his women, I thought. Freud is so often at work in our lives. Out loud I said, "What family?"

"He never said. I think he thought I'd blackmail them or go to them with his dirty little secrets. He desperately wants them to regret not welcoming him into the family. I think he only made his money so he could be as rich as they were."

"If he never gave you a name, how do you know he wasn't lying?"

"You wouldn't ask if you could hear him. His voice was so intense. He hates them. And he wants his birthright. Their money is his birthright."

"How does he plan to get their money?" I asked.

"Just before I left him, Harold had found where some of his ancestors were buried. He talked about treasure. Buried treasure, can you believe it?"

"In the graves?"

"No, his father's people got their first fortune from being river pirates. They sailed the Mississippi and robbed people. Gaynor was proud of that and angry about it. He said that the whole bunch of them were descended from thieves and whores. Where did they get off being so high and mighty to him?" She was watching my face as she spoke the last. Maybe she saw the beginnings of an idea.

"How would knowing the graves of his ancestors help him get their treasure?"

"He said he'd find some voodoo priest to raise them. He'd force them to give him their treasure that had been lost for centuries."

"Ah," I said.

"What? Did that help?"

I nodded. My role in Gaynor's little scheme had become clear. Painfully clear. The only question left was why me? Why didn't he go to someone thoroughly disreputable like Dominga Salvador? Someone who would take his money and kill his hornless goat and not lose any sleep over it. Why me, with my reputation for morality?

"Did he ever mention any names of voodoo priests?"

Wanda shook her head. "No, no names. He was always careful about names. There's a look on your face. How could what I have told you just now help you?"

"I think the less you know about that, the better, don't you?"

She stared at me for a long time but finally nodded. "I guess so."

"Is there any place . . ." I let it trail off. I was going to offer her a plane ticket or a bus ticket to anywhere. Anywhere where she wouldn't have to sell herself. Anywhere where she could heal.

Maybe she read it in my face or my silence. She laughed, and it was a rich sound. Shouldn't whores have cynical cackles?

"You are a social worker type after all. You want to save me, don't you?"

"Is it terribly naive to offer you a ticket home or somewhere?"

She nodded. "Terribly. And why should you want to help me? You're not a man. You don't like women. Why should you offer to send me home?"

"Stupidity," I said and stood.

"It's not stupid." She took my hand and squeezed it. "But it wouldn't do any good. I'm a whore. Here at least I know the town, the people. I have regulars." She released my hand and shrugged. "I get by."

"With a little help from your friends," I said.

She smiled, and it wasn't happy. "Whores don't have friends."

"You don't have to be a whore. Gaynor made you a whore, but you don't have to stay one."

There were tears trembling in her eyes for the third time that night. Hell, she wasn't tough enough for the streets. No one was.

"Just call a taxi, okay. I don't want to talk anymore."

What could I do? I called a taxi. I told the driver the fare was in a wheelchair like Wanda told me to. She let Jean-Claude carry her back downstairs because I couldn't do it. But she was very tight and still in his arms. We left her in her chair on the curb.

I watched until the taxi came and took her away. Jean-Claude stood beside me in the golden circle of light just in front of my apartment building. The warm light seemed to leech color from his skin.

"I must leave you now, *ma petite*. It has been very educational, but time grows short."

"You're going to go feed, aren't you?"

"Does it show?"

"A little."

"I should call you *ma vérité*, Anita. You always tell me the truth about myself."

"Is that what *vérité* means? Truth?" I asked.

He nodded.

I felt bad. Itchy, grumpy, restless. I was mad at Harold Gaynor for victimizing Wanda. Mad at Wanda for allowing it. Angry with myself for not being able to do anything about it. I was pissed at the whole world tonight. I'd learned what Gaynor wanted me to do. And it didn't help a damn bit.

"There will always be victims, Anita. Predators and prey, it is the way of the world."

I glared up at him. "I thought you couldn't read me anymore."

"I cannot read your mind or your thoughts, only your face and what I know of you."

I didn't want to know that Jean-Claude knew me that well. That intimately. "Go away, Jean-Claude, just go away."

"As you like, *ma petite*." And just like that he was gone. A rush of wind, then nothing.

"Show-off," I murmured. I was left standing in the dark, tasting the first edge of tears. Why did I want to cry over a whore whom I'd just met? Over the unfairness of the world in general?

Jean-Claude was right. There would always be prey and predator. And I had worked very hard to be one of the predators. I was the Executioner. So why were my sympathies always with the victims? And why did the despair in Wanda's eyes make me hate Gaynor more than anything he'd ever done to me?

Why indeed?

26

The phone rang. I moved nothing but my eyes to glance at the bedside clock: 6:45 A.M. Shit. I lay there waiting, half drifted to sleep again when the answering machine picked up.

"It's Dolph. We found another one. Call my pager . . ."

I scrambled for the phone, dropping the receiver in the process. "H'lo, Dolph. I'm here."

"Late night?"

"Yeah, what's up?"

"Our friend has decided that single family homes are easy pickings." His voice sounded rough with lack of sleep.

"God, not another family."

" 'Fraid so. Can you come out?"

It was a stupid question, but I didn't point that out. My stomach had dropped into my knees. I didn't want a repeat of the Reynolds house. I didn't think my imagination could stand it.

"Give me the address. I'll be there."

He gave me the address.

"St. Peters," I said. "It's close to St. Charles, but still . . ."

"Still what?"

"It's a long way to walk for a single family home. There are lots of houses that fit the bill in St. Charles. Why did it travel so far to feed?"

"You're asking *me*?" he said. There was something almost like laughter in his voice. "Come on out, Ms. Voodoo Expert. See what there is to see."

"Dolph, is it as bad as the Reynolds house?"

"Bad, worse, worst of all," he said. The laughter was still there, but it held an edge of something hard and self-deprecating.

"This isn't your fault," I said.

"Tell that to the top brass. They're screaming for someone's ass."

"Did you get the warrant?"

"It'll come in this afternoon late."

"No one gets warrants on a weekend," I said.

"Special panic-mode dispensation," Dolph said. "Get your ass out here, Anita. Everyone needs to go home." He hung up.

I didn't bother saying bye.

Another murder. Shit, shit, shit. Double shit. It was not the way I wanted to spend Saturday morning. But we were getting our warrant. Yippee. The trouble was I didn't know what to look for. I wasn't really a voodoo expert. I was a preternatural crimes expert. It wasn't the same thing. Maybe I should ask Manny to come along. No, no, I didn't want him near Dominga Salvador in case she decided to cut a deal and give him to the police. There is no statute of limitations on human sacrifice. Manny could still go down for it. It'd be Dominga's style to trade my friend for her life. Making it, in a roundabout way, my fault. Yeah, she'd love that.

The message light on my answering machine was blinking. Why hadn't I noticed it last night? I shrugged. One of life's mysteries. I pressed the playback button.

"Anita Blake, this is John Burke. I got your message. Call me anytime here. I'm eager to hear what you have." He gave the phone number, and that was it.

Great, a murder scene, a trip to the morgue, and a visit to voodoo land, all in one day. It was going to be a busy and unpleasant day. It matched last night perfectly, and the night before. Shit, I was on a roll.

27

There was a patrol cop throwing up his guts into one of those giant, elephant-sized trash cans in front of the house. Bad sign. There was a television news van parked across the street. Worse sign. I didn't know how Dolph had kept zombie massacres out of the news so long. Current events must have been really hopping for the newshounds to ignore such easy headlines. ZOMBIES MASSACRE FAMILY. ZOMBIE SERIAL MURDERER ON LOOSE. Jesus, it was going to be a mess.

The camera crew, complete with microphone-bearing suit, watched me as I walked towards the yellow police tape. When I clipped the official plastic card on my collar, the news crew moved like one animal. The uniform at the police tape held it for me, his eyes on the descending press. I didn't look back. Never look back when the press are gaining on you. They catch you if you do.

The blond in the suit yelled out, "Ms. Blake, Ms. Blake, can you give us a statement?"

Always nice to be recognized, I guess. But I pretended not to hear. I kept walking, head determinedly down.

A crime scene is a crime scene is a crime scene. Except for the unique nightmarish qualities of each one. I was standing in a bedroom of a very nice one-story ranch. There was a white ceiling fan that turned slowly. It made a faint whirring creak, as if it wasn't screwed in tight on one side.

Better to concentrate on the small things. The way the east light fell through the slanting blinds, painting the room in zebra-stripe shadows. Better not to look at what was left on the bed. Didn't want to look. Didn't want to see.

Had to see. Had to look. Might find a clue. Sure, and pigs could fucking fly. But still, maybe, maybe there would be a clue. Maybe. Hope is a lying bitch.

There are roughly two gallons of blood in the human body. As much blood as they put on television and the movies, it's never enough. Try dumping out two full gallons of milk on your bedroom floor. See what a mess it makes, now multiply that by . . . something. There was too much blood for just one person. The carpet squeeched underfoot, and blood came up in little splatters like mud after a rain. My white Nikes were spotted with scarlet before I was halfway to the bed.

Lesson learned: wear black Nikes to murder scenes.

The smell was thick in the room. I was glad for the ceiling fan. The room smelled like a mixture of slaughterhouse and outhouse. Shit and blood. The smell of fresh death, more often than not.

Sheets covered not just the bed, but a lot of the floor around the bed. It looked like giant paper towels thrown over the world's biggest Kool-Aid spill. There had to be pieces all over, under the sheets. The lumps were so small, too small to be a body. There wasn't a single scarlet-soaked bump that was big enough for a human body.

"Please don't make me look," I whispered to the empty room.

"Did you say something?"

I jumped and found Dolph standing just behind me. "Jesus, Dolph, you scared me."

"Wait until you see what's under the sheets. Then you can be scared."

I didn't want to see what was under the army of blood-soaked sheets. Surely, I'd seen enough for one week. My quota of gore had to have been exceeded, night before last. Yeah, I was over my quota.

Dolph stood in the doorway waiting. There were tiny pinched lines by his eyes that I had never noticed. He was pale and needed a shave.

We all needed something. But first I had to look under the sheets. If Dolph could do it, I could do it. Ri-ight.

Dolph stuck his head out in the hallway. "We need some help in here lifting the sheets. After Blake sees the remains we can go home." I think he added that last because no one had moved to help. He wasn't going to get any volunteers. "Zerbrowski, Perry, Merlioni, get your butts in here."

The bags under Zerbrowski's eyes looked like bruises. "Hiya, Blake."

"Hi, Zerbrowski, you look like shit."

He laughed. "And you still look fresh and lovely as a spring morning." He grinned at me.

"Yeah, right," I said.

Detective Perry said, "Ms. Blake, good to see you again."

I had to smile. Perry was the only cop I knew who would be gracious even over the bloody remains. "Nice to see you, too, Detective Perry."

"Can we get on with this," Merlioni said, "or are the two of you planning to elope?" Merlioni was tall, though not as tall as Dolph. But then who was? He had grey curling hair cut short and buzzed on the sides and over his ears. He wore a white dress shirt with the sleeves rolled up to his elbows and a tie at half-mast. His gun stuck out on his left hip like a lumpy wallet.

"You take the first sheet then, Merlioni, if you're in such a damn hurry," Dolph said.

Merlioni sighed. "Yeah, yeah." He stepped to the sheet on the floor. He knelt. "You ready for this, girlie?"

"Better girlie than dago," I said.

He smiled.

"Do it."

"Showtime," Merlioni said. He raised the sheet and it stuck in a wet swatch that pulled up one wet inch at a time.

"Zerbrowski, help him raise the damn thing," Dolph said.

Zerbrowski didn't argue. He must have been tired. The two men lifted the sheet in one wet motion. The morning sunlight streamed through the red sheet and painted the rug even redder than it was, or maybe it didn't make any difference. Blood dripped from the edges of the sheet where the men held it. Wet, heavy drops, like a sink that needed fixing. I'd never seen a sheet saturated with blood before. A morning of firsts.

I stared at the rug and couldn't make sense of it. It was just a pile of lumps, small lumps. I knelt beside them. Blood soaked through the knee of my jeans, it was cold. Better than warm, I guess.

The biggest lump was wet and smooth, about five inches long. It was pink and healthy-looking. It was a scrap of upper intestine. A smaller lump lay just beside it. I stared at the lump but the longer I stared the less it looked like anything. It could have been a hunk of meat from any animal. Hell, the intestine didn't have to be human. But it was, or I wouldn't be here.

I poked the smaller glob with one gloved finger. I had remembered my surgical gloves this time. Goody for me. The glob was wet and heavy and solid. I swallowed hard, but I was no closer to knowing what it was. The two scraps were like morsels dropped from a cat's mouth. Crumbs from the table. Jesus.

I stood. "Next." My voice sounded steady, ordinary. Amazing.

It took all four men lifting from different corners to peel the sheet back from the bed. Merlioni cursed and dropped his corner, "Dammit!"

Blood had run down his arm onto the white shirt. "Did um's get his shirt messy?" Zerbrowski asked.

"Fuck yes. This place is a mess."

"I guess the lady of the house didn't have time to clean up before you came, Merlioni," I said. My eyes flicked down to the bed and the remains of the lady of the house. But I looked back up at Merlioni instead. "Or can't the dago cop take it?"

"I can take anything you can dish out, little lady," he said.

I frowned and shook my head. "Betcha can't."

"I'll take some of that action," Zerbrowski said.

Dolph didn't stop us, tell us this was a crime scene, not a betting parlor. He knew we needed it to stay sane. I could not stare down at the remains and not make jokes. I couldn't. I'd go crazy. Cops have the weirdest sense of humor, because they have to.

"How much you bet?" Merlioni said.

"A dinner for two at Tony's," I said.

Zerbrowski whistled. "Steep, very steep."

"I can afford to foot the bill. Is it a deal?"

Merlioni nodded. "My wife and I haven't been out in ages." He offered his blood-soaked hand. I took it. The cool blood clung to the outside of my surgical gloves. It felt wet, like it had soaked through to the skin, but it hadn't. It was a sensory illusion. I knew that when I took off the gloves my hands would be powder dry. It was still unnerving.

"How we prove who's toughest?" Merlioni asked.

"This scene, here and now," I said.

"Deal."

I turned my attention back to the carnage with renewed determination. I would win the bet. I wouldn't let Merlioni have the satisfaction. It gave me something to concentrate on rather than the mess on the bed.

The left half of a rib cage lay on the bed. A naked breast was still attached to it. The lady of the house? Everything was brilliant scarlet red, like someone had poured buckets of red paint on the bed. It was hard to pick out the pieces. There a left arm, small, female.

I picked up the fingers and they were limp, no rigor mortis. There was a wedding band set on the third finger. I moved the fingers back and forth. "No rigor mortis. What do you think, Merlioni?"

He squinted down at the arm. He couldn't let me outdo him so he fiddled with the hand, turning it at the wrist. "Could be rigor came and went. You know the first rigor doesn't last."

"You really think nearly two days have passed?" I shook my head. "The blood's too fresh for that. Rigor hasn't set in. The crime isn't eight hours old yet."

He nodded. "Not bad, Blake. But what do you make of this?" He poked the rib cage enough to make the breast jiggle.

I swallowed hard. I would win this bet. "I don't know. Let's see. Help me roll it over." I stared into his face while I asked. Did he pale just a bit? Maybe.

"Sure."

The three others were standing at the side of the room, watching the show. Let them. It was a lot more diverting than thinking of this as work.

Merlioni and I moved the rib cage over on its side. I made sure to give him the fleshy parts, so he ended up groping the dead body. Was breast tissue breast tissue? Did it matter that it was bloody and cold? Merlioni looked just a little green. I guess it mattered.

The insides of the rib cage were snatched clean like Mr. Reynolds's rib cage. Clean and bloody smooth. We let the rib cage fall back on the bed. It splattered blood in a faint spray onto us. His white shirt showed it worse than my blue polo shirt did. Point for me.

He grimaced and brushed at the blood specks. He smeared blood from his gloves down the shirt. Merlioni closed his eyes and took a deep breath.

"Are you all right, Merlioni?" I asked. "I wouldn't want you to continue if it's upsetting you."

He glared at me, then smiled. A most unpleasant smile. "You ain't seen it all, girlie. I have."

"But have you touched it all?"

A trickle of sweat slid down his face. "You won't want to touch it all."

I shrugged. "We'll see." There was a leg on the bed, from the hair and the one remaining tennis shoe it looked male. The round, wet mound of the ball socket gleamed out at us. The zombie had just torn the leg off, tearing flesh without tearing bone.

"That must have hurt like a son of a bitch," I said.

"You think he was alive when the leg was pulled off?"

I nodded. "Yeah." I wasn't a hundred percent sure. There was too much blood to tell who had died when, but Merlioni looked a little paler.

The rest of the pieces were just bloody entrails, globs of flesh, bits of bone. Merlioni picked up a handful of entrails. "Catch."

"Jesus, Merlioni, that isn't funny." My stomach was one tight knot.

"No, but the look on your face is," he said.

I glared at him and said, "Throw it or don't, Merlioni, no teasing."

He blinked at me for a minute, then nodded. He tossed the string of entrails. They were awkward to throw but I managed to catch them. They were wet, heavy, flaccid, squeeshy, and altogether disgusting, like touching raw calf's liver but more so.

Dolph made an exasperated sound. "While you two are playing gross out, can you tell me something useful?"

I dropped the flesh back on the bed. "Sure. The zombie came in through the sliding glass door like last time. It chased the man or woman back in here and got them both." I stopped talking. I just froze.

Merlioni was holding up a baby blanket. Some trick had left a corner of it clean. It was edged in satiny pink with tiny balloons and clowns all over it. Blood dripped heavily from the other end of it.

I stared at the tiny balloons and clowns while they danced in useless circles. "You bastard," I whispered.

"Are you referring to me?" Merlioni asked.

I shook my head. I didn't want to touch the blanket. But I reached out for it. Merlioni made sure that the bloody edge slapped my bare arm. "Dago bastard," I said.

"You referring to me, bitch?"

I nodded and tried to smile but didn't really manage it. We had to keep pretending that this was all right. That this was doable. It was obscene. If the bet hadn't held me I'd have run screaming from the room.

I stared at the blanket. "How old?"

"Family portrait out front, I'd guess three, four months."

I was finally on the other side of the bed. There was another sheet-draped spot. It was just as bloody, just as small. There was nothing whole under the sheet. I wanted to call the bet off. If they wouldn't make me look I'd take them all to Tony's. Just don't make me lift that last sheet. Please, please.

But I had to look, bet or no bet, I had to see what there was to see. Might as well see it and win, as run and lose.

I handed the blanket back to Merlioni. He took it and laid it back on the bed, up high so the clean corner would stay clean.

I knelt on one side of the sheet. He knelt on the other. Our eyes met. It was a challenge then, to the gruesome end. We peeled back the sheet.

There were only two things under the sheet. Only two. My stomach contracted so hard I had to swallow vomit. I coughed and almost lost it there, but I held on. I held on.

I'd thought the blood-soaked form was the baby, but it wasn't. It was a doll. So blood-soaked I couldn't tell what color its hair had been, but it was just a doll. A doll too old for a four-month-old baby.

A tiny hand lay on the carpet, covered in gore like everything else, but it was a hand. A tiny hand. The hand of a child, not a baby. I spread my hand just above it to size it. Three, maybe four. About the same age as Benjamin Reynolds. Was that coincidence? Had to be. Zombies weren't that choosy.

"I'm breast-feeding the baby, maybe, when I hear a loud noise. Husband goes to check. Noise wakes the little girl, she comes out of her room to see what's the matter. Husband sees the monster, grabs the child, runs for the bedroom. The zombie takes them here. Kills them all, here." My voice sounded distant, clinical. Bully for me.

I tried to wipe some of the blood off the tiny hand. She was wearing a ring like Mommy. One of those plastic rings you get out of bubble gum machines.

"Did you see the ring, Merlioni?" I asked. I lifted the hand from the carpet and said, "Catch."

"Jesus!" He was on his feet and moving before I could do anything else. Merlioni walked very fast out the door. I wouldn't really have thrown the hand. I wouldn't.

I cradled the tiny hand in my hands. It felt heavy, as if the fingers should curl round my hand. Should ask me to take it for a walk. I dropped the hand on the carpet. It landed with a wet splat.

The room was very hot and spinning ever so slightly. I blinked and stared at Zerbrowski. "Did I win the bet?"

He nodded. "Anita Blake, tough chick. One night of delectable feasting at Tony's on Merlioni's tab. I hear they make great spaghetti."

The mention of food was too much. "Bathroom, where?"

"Down the hall, third door on the left," Dolph said.

I ran for the bathroom. Merlioni was just coming out. I didn't have time to savor my victory. I was too busy tossing my cookies.

28

I knelt with my forehead against the cool linoleum of the bathtub. I was feeling better. Lucky I hadn't taken time to eat breakfast.

There was a tap on the door.

"What?" I said.

"It's Dolph. Can I come in?"

I thought about that for a minute. "Sure."

Dolph came in with a washcloth in his hand. Linen closet, I guessed. He stared at me for a minute or two and shook his head. He rinsed the washrag in the sink and handed it to me. "You know what to do with it."

I did. The rag was cold and felt wonderful on my face and neck. "Did you give Merlioni one, too?" I asked.

"Yeah, he's in the kitchen. You're both assholes, but it was entertaining."

I managed a weak smile.

"Now that you're through grandstanding, any useful observations?" He sat on the closed lid of the stool.

I stayed on the floor. "Did anybody hear anything, this time?"

"Neighbor heard something around dawn, but he went on to work. Said, he didn't want to get involved in a domestic dispute."

I stared up at Dolph. "Had he heard fighting from this house before?"

Dolph shook his head.

"God, if he had just called the police," I said.

"You think it would have made a difference?" Dolph asked.

I thought about that for a minute. "Maybe not to this family, but we might have trapped the zombie."

"Spilled milk," Dolph said.

"Maybe not. The scene is still very fresh. The zombie killed them, then took the time to eat four people. That isn't quick. At dawn the thing was still killing them."

"Your point."

"Seal the area."

"Explain."

"The zombie has to be nearby, within walking distance. It's hiding, waiting for nightfall."

"I thought zombies could go out in daylight," Dolph said.

"They can, but they don't like it. A zombie won't go out in the day unless ordered to."

"So the nearest cemetery," he said.

"Not necessarily. Zombies aren't like vamps or ghouls. It doesn't need to be coffins or even graves. The zombie will just want to get out of the light."

"So where do we look?"

"Sheds, garages, any place that will shield it."

"So he could be in some kid's tree house," Dolph said.

I smiled. Nice to know I still could. "I doubt the zombie would climb if given a choice. Notice that all the houses are one-stories."

"Basements," he said.

"But no one runs down to the basement," I said.

"Would it have helped?"

I shrugged. "Zombies aren't great at climbing, as a rule. This one is faster and more alert but . . . At best the basement might have delayed it. If there were windows, they might have gotten the children out." I rubbed the cloth on the back of my neck. "The zombie picks one-story houses with sliding glass doors. It might rest near one."

"The medical examiner says the corpse is tall, six feet, six-two. Male, white. Immensely strong."

"We knew the last, and the rest doesn't really help."

"You got a better idea?"

"As a matter of fact," I said, "have all the officers about the right height walk the neighborhood for an hour. Then block off that much of the area."

"And search all the sheds and garages," Dolph said.

"And basements, crawl spaces, old refrigerators," I said.

"If we find it?"

"Fry it. Get an exterminator team out here."

"Will the zombie attack during the day?" Dolph asked.

"If disturbed enough, yes. This one's awfully aggressive."

"No joke," he said. "We'd need a dozen exterminator teams or more. The city'll never go for that. Besides, we could walk a pretty damn wide circle. We might search and miss it completely."

"It'll move at dark. If you're ready, you'll find it then."

"Okay. You sound like you're not going to help search."

"I'll be back to help, but John Burke returned my call."

"You taking him to the morgue?"

"Yeah, in time to try to use him against Dominga Salvador. What timing," I said.

"Good. You need anything from me?"

"Just access to the morgue for both of us," I said.

"Sure thing. You think you'll really learn anything from Burke?"

"Don't know till I try," I said.

He smiled. "Give it the old college try, eh?"

"Win one for the Gipper," I said.

"You go visit the morgue and deal with voodoo John. We'll turn this fucking neighborhood upside down."

"Nice to know we've both got our days planned," I said.

"Don't forget this afternoon we check out Salvador's house."

I nodded. "Yeah, and tonight we hunt zombies."

"We're going to end this shit tonight," he said.

"I hope so."

He looked at me, eyes narrowed. "You got a problem with our plans?"

"Just that no plan is perfect."

He was quiet a moment, then stood. "Wish this one was."

"Me, too."

29

The St. Louis County morgue was a large building. It needs to be. Every death not attended by a physician comes to the morgue. Not to mention every murder. In St. Louis that made for some very heavy traffic.

I use to come to the morgue fairly regularly. To stake suspected vampire victims so they wouldn't rise and feast on the morgue attendants. With the new vamp laws, that's murder. You have to wait for the puppies to rise, unless they've left a will strictly forbidding coming back as a vampire. My will says to put me out of my misery if they think I'm coming back with fangs. Hell, my will asks for cremation. I don't want to come back as a zombie either, thank you very much.

John Burke was as I remembered him. Tall, dark, handsome, vaguely villainous. It was the little goatee that did it. No one wears goatees outside of horror movies. You know, the ones with strange cults that worship horned images.

He looked a little faded around the eyes and mouth. Grief will do that to you even if your skin tone is dark. His lips were set in a thin line as we walked into the morgue. He held his shoulders as if something hurt.

"How's it going at your sister-in-law's?" I asked.

"Bleak, very bleak."

I waited for him to elaborate, but he didn't. So I let it go. If he didn't want to talk about it, that was his privilege.

We were walking down a wide empty corridor. Wide enough for three gurneys to wheel abreast. The guard station looked like a WWII bunker, complete with machine guns. In case the dead should rise all at once and make for freedom. It had never happened here in St. Louis, but it had happened as close as Kansas City.

A machine gun will take the starch out of any walking dead. You're only in trouble if there are a lot of them. If there is a crowd, you're pretty much cooked.

I flashed my ID at the guard. "Hi, Fred, long time no see."

"I wish they let you come down here like before. We've had three get up this week and go home. Can you believe that?"

"Vampires?"

"What else? There's going to be more of them than of us someday."

I didn't know what to say, so I said nothing. He was probably right. "We're here to see the personal effects of Peter Burke. Sergeant Rudolph Storr was supposed to clear it."

Fred checked his little book. "Yeah, you're authorized. Take the right corridor, third door on the left. Dr. Saville is waiting for you."

I raised an eyebrow at that. It wasn't often that the chief medical examiner did errands for the police or anybody else. I just nodded as if I had expected royal treatment.

"Thanks, Fred, see you on the way out."

"More and more people do," he said. He didn't sound happy about it.

My Nikes made no sound in the perpetual quiet. John Burke wasn't making any noise either. I hadn't pegged him as a tennis shoe man. I glanced down, and I was right. Soft-soled brown tie-ups, not tennis shoes. But he still moved beside me like a quiet shadow.

The rest of his outfit sort of matched the shoes. A dressy brown sport jacket so dark brown it was almost black, over a pale yellow shirt, brown dress slacks. He only needed a tie, and he could have gone to corporate America. Did he always dress up, or was this just what he had brought for his brother's funeral? No, the suit at the funeral had been perfectly black.

The morgue was always quiet, but on a Saturday morning it was deathly still. Did the ambulances circle like planes until a decent hour on the weekend? I knew the murder count went up on the weekend, yet Saturday and Sunday morning were always quiet. Go figure.

I counted doors on the left-hand side. Knocked on the third door. A faint "Come in," and I opened the door.

Dr. Marian Saville is a small woman with short dark hair bobbed just below her ears, an olive complexion, deeply brown eyes, and fine high cheekbones. She is French and Greek and looks it. Exotic without being intimidating. It always surprised me that Dr. Saville wasn't married. It wasn't for lack of being pretty.

Her only fault was that she smoked, and the smell clung to her like nasty perfume.

She came forward with a smile and an offered hand. "Anita, good to see you again."

I shook her hand, and smiled. "You, too, Dr. Saville."

"Marian, please."

I shrugged. "Marian, are those the personal effects?"

We were in a small examining room. On a lovely stainless-steel table were several plastic bags.

"Yes."

I stared at her, wondering what she wanted. The chief medical examiner didn't do errands. Something else was up, but what? I didn't know her well enough to be blunt, and I didn't want to be barred from the morgue, so I couldn't be rude. Problems, problems.

"This is John Burke, the deceased's brother," I said.

Dr. Saville's eyebrows raised at that. "My condolences, Mr. Burke."

"Thank you." John shook the hand she offered him, but his eyes were all for the plastic bags. There was no room today for attractive doctors or pleasantries. He was going to see his brother's last effects. He was looking for clues to help the police catch his brother's killer. He had taken the notion very seriously.

If he wasn't involved with Dominga Salvador, I would owe him a big apology. But how was I to get him to talk with Dr. Marian hovering around? How was I supposed to ask for privacy? It was her morgue, sort of.

"I have to be here to make sure no evidence is tampered with," she said. "We've had a few very determined reporters lately."

"But I'm not a reporter."

She shrugged. "You're not an official person, Anita. New rules from on high that no nonofficial person is to be allowed to look at murder evidence without someone to watch over them."

"I appreciate it being you, Marian."

She smiled. "I was here anyway. I figured you'd resent my looking over your shoulder less than anyone else."

She was right. What did they think I was going to do, steal a body? If I wanted to, I could empty the damn place and get every corpse to play follow the leader.

Perhaps that was why I needed watching. Perhaps.

"I don't mean to be rude," John said, "but could we get on with this?"

I glanced up at his handsome face. The skin was tight around the mouth and eyes as if it had thinned. Guilt speared me in the side. "Sure, John, we're being thoughtless."

"Your forgiveness, Mr. Burke," Marian said. She handed us both little plastic gloves. She and I slipped into them like pros, but John wasn't used to putting on examining gloves. There is a trick to it—practice. By the time I finished helping him on with his gloves, he was grinning. His whole face changed when he smiled. Brilliant and handsome and not the least villainous.

Dr. Saville popped the seal on the first bag. It was clothing.

"No," John said, "I don't know his clothing. It may be his, and I wouldn't know. Peter and I had . . . hadn't seen each other in two years." The guilt in those last words made me wince.

"Fine, we'll go on to the smaller items," Marian said, and smiled as she said it. Nice and cheery, practicing her bedside manner. She so seldom got to practice.

She opened a much smaller bag and spilled the contents gently on the shiny silver surface. A comb, a dime, two pennies, a movie ticket stub, and a voodoo charm. A gris-gris.

It was woven of black and red thread with human teeth worked into the beading. More bones dangled all the way around it. "Are those human finger bones?" I asked.

"Yes," John said, his voice very still. He looked strange as he stood there, as if some new horror were dawning behind his eyes.

It was an evil piece of work, but I didn't understand the strength of his reaction to it.

I leaned over it, poking it with one finger. There was some dried skin woven in the center of it all. And it wasn't just black thread, it was black hair.

"Human hair, teeth, bones, skin," I said softly.

"Yes," John repeated.

"You're more into voodoo than I am," I said. "What does it mean?"

"Someone died to make this charm."

"Are you sure?"

He glared down at me with withering contempt. "Don't you think if it could be anything else I wouldn't say it? Do you think I enjoy learning my brother took part in human sacrifice?"

"Did Peter have to be there? He couldn't have just bought it afterwards?"

"NO!" It was almost a yell. He turned away from us, pacing to the wall. His breathing was loud and ragged.

I gave him a few moments to collect himself, then asked what had to be asked. "What does the gris-gris do?"

He turned a calm enough face to us, but the strain showed around his eyes. "It enables a less powerful necromancer to raise older dead, to borrow the power of some much greater necromancer."

"How borrow?"

He shrugged. "That charm holds some of the power of the most powerful among us. Peter paid dearly for it, so he could raise more and older dead. Peter, God, how could you?"

"How powerful would you need to be to share your power like this?"

"Very powerful," he said.

"Is there any way to trace it back to the person who made it?"

"You don't understand, Anita. That thing is a piece of someone's power. It is one substance to what soul they have left. It must have been a great need or great greed to do it. Peter could never have afforded it. Never."

"Can it be traced back?"

"Yes, just get it in the room with the person who truly owns it. The thing will crawl back to him. It's a piece of his soul gone missing."

"Would that be proof in court?"

"If you could make the jury understand it, yes, I guess so." He stepped towards me. "You know who did this?"

"Maybe."

"Who, tell me who?"

"I'll do better than that. I'll arrange for you to come on a search of their house."

A grim smile touched his lips. "I'm beginning to like you a great deal, Anita Blake."

"Compliments later."

"What's this mean?" Marian asked. She had turned the charm completely over. There, shining among the hair and bone, was a small charm, like from a charm bracelet. It was in the shape of a musical symbol—a treble clef.

What had Evans said when he touched the grave fragments; they slit her throat, she had a charm bracelet with a musical note on it and little hearts. I stared at the charm and felt the world shift. Everything fell together in one motion. Dominga Salvador hadn't raised the killer zombie. She had helped Peter Burke raise it. But I had to be sure. We only had a few hours until we'd be back at Dominga's door trying to prove a case.

"Are there any women that came in around the same time as Peter Burke?"

"I'm sure there are," Marian said with a smile.

"Women with their throats slit," I said.

She stared at me for a heartbeat. "I'll check the computer."

"Can we take the charm with us?"

"Why?"

"Because if I'm right, she had a charm bracelet with a bow and arrow and little hearts on it, and this came from the bracelet." I held the gold charm up to the light. It sparkled merrily as if it didn't know its owner was dead.

30

Death turns you grey before any other color. Oh, a body that loses a lot of blood will look white or bluish. But once a body starts to decay, not rot, not yet, it looks greyish.

The woman looked grey. Her neck wound had been cleaned and searched. The wound looked puckered like a second giant mouth below her chin.

Dr. Saville pulled her head back casually. "The cut was very deep. It severed the muscles in the neck and the carotid artery. Death was fairly quick."

"Professionally done," I said.

"Well, yes, whoever cut her throat knew what they were doing. There are a dozen different ways to injure the neck that won't kill or won't kill quickly."

John Burke said, "Are you saying that my brother had practice?"

"I don't know," I said. "Do you have her personal effects?"

"Right here." Marian unfastened a much smaller bag and spilled it out on an empty table. The golden charm bracelet sparkled under the fluorescent lights.

I picked the bracelet up in my still gloved hand. A tiny strung bow complete with arrow, a different musical note, two entwined hearts. Everything Evans had said.

"How did you know about the charm and the dead woman?" John Burke asked.

"I took some evidence to a clairvoyant. He saw the woman's death and the bracelet."

"What's that got to do with Peter?"

"I believe a voodoo priestess had Peter raise a zombie. It got away from him. It's been killing people. To hide what she's done, she killed Peter."

"Who did it?"

"I have no proof unless the gris-gris will be proof enough."

"A vision and a gris-gris." John shook his head. "Hard sell to a jury."

"I know. That's why we need more proof."

Dr. Saville just watched us talk, like an eager spectator.

"A name, Anita, give me a name."

"Only if you swear not to go after her until the law has its chance. Only if the law fails, promise me."

"I give you my word."

I studied his face for a minute. The dark eyes stared back, clear and certain. Bet he could lie with a clear conscience. "I don't trust just anybody's word." I stared at him a moment longer. He never flinched. I guess my hard-as-nails look has faded a little. Or maybe he meant to keep his word. It happens sometimes.

"All right, I'll take your word. Don't make me regret it."

"I won't," he said. "Now give me the name."

I turned to Dr. Saville. "Excuse us, Marian. The less you know about all this, the greater your chances of never waking to a zombie crawling through your window." An exaggeration, sort of, but it made my point.

She looked like she wanted to protest but finally nodded. "Very well, but I would dearly love to hear the complete story someday, if it's safe."

"If I can tell it, it's yours," I said.

She nodded again, shut the drawer the Jane Doe lay on, and left. "Yell when you're finished. I've got work to do," she said and the door closed behind her.

She left us with the evidence still clutched in our hands. Guess she trusted me. Or us?

"Dominga Salvador," I said.

He drew a sharp breath. "I know that name. She is a frightening force if all the stories are true."

"They're true," I said.

"You've met her?"

"I've had the misfortune."

There was a look on his face that I didn't much like. "You swore no revenge."

"The police will not get her. She is too crafty for that," he said.

"We can get her legally. I believe that."

"You aren't sure," he said.

What could I say? He was right. "I'm almost sure."

"Almost is not good enough for killing my brother."

"That zombie has killed a lot more people than just your brother. I want her, too. But we're going to get her legally, through the court system."

"There are other ways to get her," he said.

"If the law fails us, feel free to use voodoo. Just don't tell me about it."

He looked amused, puzzled. "No outrage about me using black magic?"

"The woman tried to kill me once. I don't think she'll give up."

"You survived an attack by the Señora?" he asked. He looked amazed.

I didn't like him looking amazed. "I can take care of myself, Mr. Burke."

"I don't doubt that, Ms. Blake." He smiled. "I've bruised your ego. You don't like me being so surprised, do you?"

"Keep your observations to yourself, okay?"

"If you have survived a head-on confrontation with what Dominga Salvador would send to you, then I should have believed some of the stories I heard of you. The Executioner, the animator who can raise anything no matter how old."

"I don't know about that last, but I'm just trying to stay alive, that's all."

"If Dominga Salvador wants you dead that won't be easy."

"Damn near impossible," I said.

"So let us get her first," he said.

"Legally," I said.

"Anita, you are being naive."

"The offer to come on a raid of her house still stands."

"You're sure you can arrange that?"

"I think so."

His eyes had a sort of dark light to them, a sparkling blackness. He smiled, tight-lipped, and very unpleasant, as if he were contemplating tortures for one Dominga Salvador. The private vision seemed to fill him with pleasure.

The skin between my shoulders crept with that look. I hoped John never turned those dark eyes on me. Something told me he would make a bad enemy. Almost as bad as Dominga Salvador. Almost as bad, but not quite.

31

Dominga Salvador sat in her living room smiling. The little girl who had been riding her tricycle on my last trip here was sitting in her grandma's lap. The child was as relaxed and languorous as a kitten. Two older boys sat at Dominga's feet. She was the picture of maternal bliss. I wanted to throw up.

Of course, just because she was the most dangerous voodoo priestess I'd ever met didn't mean she wasn't a grandma, too. People are seldom just one thing. Hitler liked dogs.

"You are more than welcome to search, Sergeant. My house is your house," she said in a candy-coated voice that had already offered us lemonade, or perhaps iced tea.

John Burke and I were standing to one side, letting the police do their job. Dominga was making them feel silly for their suspicions. Just a nice old lady. Right.

Antonio and Enzo were also standing to one side. They didn't quite fit this picture of grandmotherly bliss, but evidently she wanted witnesses. Or maybe a shootout wasn't out of the question.

"Mrs. Salvador, do you understand the possible implications of this search?" Dolph said.

"There are no implications because I have nothing to hide." She smiled sweetly. Damn her.

"Anita, Mr. Burke," Dolph said.

We came forward like props in a magic show. Which wasn't far off. A tall police officer had the video camera ready to go.

"I believe you know Ms. Blake," Dolph said.

"I have had the pleasure," Dominga said.

Butter wouldn't have melted in her lying mouth.

"This is John Burke."

Her eyes widened just a little. The first slip in her perfect camouflage. Had she heard of John Burke? Did the name worry her? I hoped so.

"So glad to meet you at last, Mr. John Burke," she said finally.

"Always good to meet another practitioner of the art," he said.

She bowed her head slightly in acknowledgment. At least she wasn't trying to pretend complete innocence. She admitted to being a voodoo priestess. Progress.

It was obscene for the godmother of voodoo to be playing the innocent.

"Do it, Anita," Dolph said. No preliminaries, no sense of theater, just do it. That was Dolph for you.

I took a plastic bag out of my pocket. Dominga looked puzzled. I pulled out the gris-gris. Her face became very still, like a mask. A funny little smile curled her lips. "What is that?"

"Come now, Señora," John said, "do not play the fool. You know very well what it is."

"I know that it is a charm of some kind, of course. But do the police now threaten old women with voodoo?"

"Whatever works," I said.

"Anita," Dolph said.

"Sorry." I glanced at John, and he nodded. I sat the gris-gris on the carpet about six feet from Dominga Salvador. I had had to take John's word on a lot of this. I had checked some of it over the phone with Manny. If this worked and if we could get it admitted into court, and if we could explain it to the jury, then we might have a case. How many ifs was that?

The gris-gris just sat there for a moment, then the finger bones rippled as if an invisible finger had ruffled them.

Dominga lifted her granddaughter from her lap and shooed the boys over to Enzo. She sat alone on the couch and waited. The strange little smile was still on her face, but it looked sickly now.

The charm began to ooze towards her like a slug, pushing and struggling with muscles it did not have. The hairs on my arms stood to attention.

"You recording this, Bobby?" Dolph asked.

The cop with the video camera said, "I'm getting it. I don't fucking believe it, but I'm getting it."

"Please, do not use such words in front of the children," Dominga said.

The cop said, "Sorry, ma'am."

"You are forgiven." She was still trying to play the perfect hostess while that thing crawled towards her feet. She had nerve. I'd give her that.

Antonio didn't. He broke. He strode forward as if he meant to pluck the thing from the rug.

"Don't touch it," Dolph said.

"You are frightening my grandmother with your tricks," he said.

"Don't touch it," Dolph said again. This time he stood. His bulk seemed to fill the room. Antonio looked suddenly small and frail beside him.

"Please, you are frightening her." But it was his face that was pale and covered with a sheen of sweat. What was ol' Tony in such a fret about? It wasn't his ass going to jail.

"Stand over there," Dolph said, "now, or do we have to cuff you?"

Antonio shook his head. "No, I . . . I will go back." He did, but he glanced at Dominga as he moved. A quick, fearful glance. When she met his eyes, there was nothing but rage in them. Her black eyes glittered with rage. Her face was suddenly contorted with it. What had happened to strip the act away? What was going on?

The gris-gris made its painful way to her. It fawned at her feet like a dog, rolling on the toes of her shoes in abandon like a cat who wants its belly rubbed.

She tried to ignore it, to pretend.

"Would you refuse your returned power?" John asked.

"I don't know what you mean." Her face was under control again. She looked puzzled. Gosh, she was good. "You are a powerful voodoo priest. You are doing this to trap me."

"If you don't want the charm, I will take it," he said. "I will add your magic to mine. I will be the most powerful practitioner in the States." For the first time, John's power flowed across my skin. It was a breath of magic that was frightening. I had begun to think of John as ordinary, or as ordinary as any of us get. My mistake.

She just shook her head.

John strode forward and knelt, reaching for the writhing gris-gris. His power moved with him like an invisible hand.

"No!" She grabbed it, cradling it in her hands.

John smiled up at her. "Do you acknowledge that you made this charm? If not, I can take it and use it as I see fit. It was found in my brother's effects. It's legally mine, correct, Sergeant Storr?"

"Correct," Dolph said.

"No, you cannot."

"I can and I will, unless you look into that camera and admit making it."

She snarled at him. "You will regret this."

"You will regret having killed my brother."

She stared at the video camera. "Very well, I made this charm, but I admit nothing else. I made the charm for your brother, but that is all."

"You performed human sacrifice to make this charm," John said.

She shook her head. "The charm is mine. I made it for your brother, that is all. You have the charm but nothing else."

"Señora, forgive me," Antonio said. He looked pale and shaken and very, very scared.

"Calenta," she said, "shut up!"

"Zerbrowski, take our friend here into the kitchen and take his statement," Dolph said.

Dominga stood at that. "You fool, you miserable fool. Tell them anything more, and I will rot the tongue out of your mouth."

"Get him out of here, Zerbrowski."

Zerbrowski led a nearly weeping Antonio from the room. I had a feeling that ol' Tony had been responsible for getting the charm back. He failed, and he was going to pay the consequences. The police were the least of his problems. If I were him, I'd make damn sure grandma was locked up tonight. I wouldn't want her near her voodoo paraphernalia. Ever.

"We're going to search now, Mrs. Salvador."

"Help yourself, Sergeant. You will find nothing else to help you."

She was very calm when she said it. "Even the stuff behind the doors?" I asked.

"They are gone, Anita. You will find nothing that is not legal and . . . wholesome." She made that last sound like a bad word.

Dolph glanced my way. I shrugged. She seemed awfully sure.

"Okay, boys, take the place apart." Uniforms and detectives moved like they had a purpose. I started to follow Dolph out. He stopped me.

"No, Anita, you and Burke stay up here."

"Why?"

"You're civilians."

A civilian, me? "Was I a civilian when I walked the cemetery for you?"

"If one of my people could have done it, I wouldn't have let you do that either."

"Let me?"

He frowned. "You know what I mean."

"No, I don't think I do."

"You may be a bad ass, you may even be as good as you think you are, but you aren't police. This is a job for cops. You stay in the living room with the civvies just this once. When it's all clear, you can come down and identify the bogeymen for us."

"Don't do me any favors, Dolph."

"I didn't peg you for a pouter, Blake."

"I am not pouting," I said.

"Whining?" he said.

"Cut it out. You've made your point. I'll stay behind, but I don't have to like it."

"Most of the time you're ass deep in alligators. Enjoy being out of the line of fire for once, Anita." With that he led the way towards the basement.

I hadn't really wanted to go down into the darkness again. I certainly didn't want to see the creature that had chased Manny and me up the stairs. And yet . . . I felt left out. Dolph was right. I was pouting. Great.

John Burke and I sat on the couch. Dominga sat in the recliner where she had been since we hit the door. The children had been shooed out to play, with Enzo to watch them. He looked relieved. I almost volunteered to go with them. Anything was better than just sitting here straining to hear the first screams.

If the monster, and that was the only word that matched the noises, was down there, there would be screaming. The police were great with bad guys, but monsters were new to them. It had been simpler, in a way, when all this shit was taken care of by a few experts. A few lone people fighting the good fight. Staking vampires. Turning zombies. Burning witches. Though there is some debate whether I might have ended up on the receiving end of some fire a few years back. Say, the 1950s.

What I did was undeniably magic. Before we got all the bogeymen out in the open, supernatural was supernatural. Destroy it before it destroys you. Simpler times. But now the police were expected to deal with zombies, vampires, the occasional demon. Police were really bad with demons. But then who isn't?

Dominga sat in her chair and stared at me. The two uniforms left in the living room stood like all police stand, blank-faced, bored, but let anyone move and the cops saw it. The boredom was just a mask. Cops always saw everything. Occupational hazard.

Dominga wasn't looking at the police. She wasn't even paying attention to John Burke, who was much closer to her equal. She was staring at little old me.

I met her black gaze and said, "You got a problem?"

The cop's eyes flicked to us. John shifted on the couch. "What's wrong?" he asked.

"She's staring at me."

"I will do a great deal more than stare at you, *chica.*" Her voice crawled low. The hairs at the nape of my neck tried to crawl down my shirt.

"A threat." I smiled. "I don't think you're going to be hurting anybody anymore."

"You mean this." She held out the charm. It writhed in her hand as if thrilled that she had noticed it. She crushed it in her hand. It made futile movements as if pushing against her. Her hand covered it completely. She stared straight at me, as she brought her hand slowly to her chest.

The air was suddenly heavy, hard to breathe. Every hair on my body was creeping down my skin.

"Stop her!" John said. He stood.

The policeman nearest her hesitated for only an instant, but it was enough. When he pried her fingers open, they were empty.

"Sleight of hand, Dominga. I thought better of you than that."

John was pale. "It isn't a trick." His voice was shaky. He sat down heavily on the couch beside me. His dark face looked pale. His power seemed to have shriveled up. He looked tired.

"What is it? What did she do?" I asked.

"You have to bring back the charm, ma'am," the uniform said.

"I cannot," she said.

"John, what the hell did she do?"

"Something she shouldn't have been able to do."

I was beginning to know how Dolph must feel having to depend on me for information. It was like pulling fucking teeth. "What did she do?"

"She absorbed her power back into herself," he said.

"What does that mean?"

"She absorbed the gris-gris into her body. Didn't you feel it?"

I had felt something. The air was clearer now, but it was still heavy. My skin was tingling with the nearness of something. "I felt something, but I still don't understand."

"Without ceremony, without help from the loa, she absorbed it back into her soul. We won't find a trace of it. No evidence."

"So all we have is the tape?"

He nodded.

"If you knew she could do this, why didn't you speak up earlier? We wouldn't have let her hold the thing."

"I didn't know. It's impossible without ceremonial magic."

"But she did it."

"I know, Anita, I know." He sounded scared for the first time. Fear didn't sit well on his darkly handsome face. After the power I'd felt from him, the fear seemed even more out of place. But it was real nonetheless.

I shivered, like someone had walked on my grave. Dominga was staring at me. "What are you staring at?"

"A dead woman," she said softly.

I shook my head. "Talk is cheap, Señora. Threats don't mean squat."

John touched my arm. "Do not taunt her, Anita. If she can do that instantly, there's no telling what else she can do."

The cop had had enough. "She's not doing anything. If you so much as twitch wrong, lady, I'm going to shoot you."

"But I am just an old woman. Would you threaten me?"

"Don't talk either."

The other uniform said, "I knew a witch once who could bespell you with her voice."

Both uniforms had their hands near their guns. Funny how magic changes how people perceive you. They were fine when they thought she needed human sacrifice and ceremony. Let her do one instant trick, and she was suddenly very dangerous. I'd always known she was dangerous.

Dominga sat silently under the watchful eyes of the cops. I had been distracted by her little performance. There were still no screams from downstairs. Nothing. Silence.

Had it gotten them all? That quickly, without a shot fired. Naw. But still, my stomach was tight, sweat trickled down my spine. Are you all right, Dolph? I thought.

"Did you say something?" John asked.

I shook my head. "Just thinking really hard."

He nodded as if that made sense to him.

Dolph came into the living room. I couldn't tell anything by his face. Mr. Stoic.

"Well, what was it?" I asked.

"Nothing," he said.

"What do you mean, nothing?"

"She's cleaned the place out completely. We found the rooms you told me about. One door had been busted from inside, but the room's been scrubbed down and painted." He held up one big hand. It was stained white. "Hell, the paint's still wet."

"It can't all be gone. What about the cement-covered doors?"

"Looks like someone took a jackhammer to them. They're just freshly painted rooms, Anita. The place stinks of pine-scented bleach and wet paint. No corpses, no zombies. Nothing."

I just stared at him. "You've got to be kidding."

He shook his head. "I'm not laughing."

I stood in front of Dominga. "Who warned you?"

She just stared up at me, smiling. I had a great urge to slap that smile off her face. Just to hit her once would feel good. I knew it would.

"Anita," Dolph said, "back off."

Maybe the anger showed on my face, or maybe it was the fact that my hands were balled into fists and I seemed to be shaking. Shaking with anger and the beginnings of something else. If she didn't go to jail, that meant she was free to try to kill me again tonight. And every night after that.

She smiled as if she could read my mind. "You have nothing, *chica*. You have gambled all on a hand with nothing in it."

She was right. "Stay away from me, Dominga."

"I will not come near you, *chica*, I will not need to."

"Your last little surprise didn't work out so well. I'm still here."

"I have done nothing. But I am sure there are worse things that could come to your door, *chica*."

I turned to Dolph. "Dammit, isn't there anything we can do?"

"We got the charm, but that's it."

Something must have showed on my face because he touched my arm. "What is it?"

"She did something to the charm. It's gone."

He took a deep breath and stalked away, then back. "Dammit to hell, how?"

I shrugged. "Let John explain. I still don't understand it." I hate admitting that I don't know something. It's always bothered me to admit ignorance. But hey, a girl can't be an expert on everything. I had worked hard to stay away from voodoo. Work hard and where does it get you? Staring into the black eyes of a voodoo priestess who's plotting your death. A most unpleasant death by the looks of it.

Well, in for a penny, in for a pound. I went back to her. I stood and stared into her dark face and smiled. Her own smile faltered, which made my smile bigger.

"Someone tipped you off and you've been cleaning up this cesspit for two days." I leaned over her, putting my hands on the arms of the chair. It brought our faces close together.

"You had to break down your walls. You had to let out or destroy all your creations. Your inner sanctum, your hougun, is cleaned and whitewashed. All the verve gone. All the animal sacrifices gone. All that slow building of power, line by line, drop by bloody drop, you're going to have to start over, you bitch. You're going to have to rebuild it all.''

The look in those black eyes made me shiver, and I didn't care. "You're getting old to rebuild that much. Did you have to destroy many of your toys? Dig up any graves?''

"Have your joke now, *chica,* but I will send what I have saved to you some dark night.''

"Why wait? Do it now, in daylight. Face me or are you afraid?''

She laughed then, and it was a warm, friendly sound. It startled me so much I stood up straight, almost jumped back.

"Do you think I am foolish enough to attack you with the police all around? You must think me a fool.''

"It was worth a try,'' I said.

"You should have joined with me in my zombie enterprises. We could have been rich together.''

"The only thing we're likely to do together is kill each other,'' I said.

"So be it. Let it be war between us.''

"It always was,'' I said.

She nodded and smiled some more.

Zerbrowski came out of the kitchen. He was grinning from ear to ear. Something good was up.

"The grandson just spilled the beans.''

Everyone in the room stared at him. Dolph said, "Spilled what?''

"Human sacrifice. How he was supposed to get the gris-gris back from Peter Burke after he killed him, on his grandmother's orders, but some joggers came by and he panicked. He's so afraid of her''—he motioned to Dominga—"he wants her behind bars. He's terrified of what she'll do to him for forgetting the charm.''

The charm that we didn't have anymore. But we had the video and now we had Antonio's confession. The day was looking up.

I turned back to Dominga Salvador. She looked tall and proud and terrifying. Her black eyes blazed with some inner light. Standing this close to her, the power crawled over my skin, but a good bonfire would take care of that. They'd fry her in the electric chair, then burn the body and scatter the ashes at a crossroad.

I said softly, "Gotcha.''

She spit at me. It landed on my hand and burned like acid. "Shit!''

"Do that again and we'll shoot you, and save the taxpayers some money,'' Dolph said. He had his gun out.

I went in search of the bathroom to wash her spit off my hand. A blister had formed where it had hit. Second fucking degree burns from her spit. Dear God.

I was glad Antonio had broken. I was glad she was going to be locked away. I was glad she was going to die. Better her than me.

32

Riverridge was a modern housing development. Which meant that there were three models to choose from. You could end up with four identical houses in a row, like cookies on a baking sheet. There was also no river within sight. No ridge either.

The house that was the center of the police search area was identical to its neighbor, except for color. The murder house, which is what the news was calling it, was grey with white shutters. The house that had been passed safely by was blue with white shutters. Neither's shutters worked. They were just for show. Modern architecture is full of perks that are just for show; balcony railings without a balcony, peaked roofs that make it look like you have an extra room that you don't have, porches so narrow that only Santa's elves could sit on them. It makes me nostalgic for Victorian architecture. It might have been overdone, but everything worked.

The entire housing project had been evacuated. Dolph had been forced to give a statement to the press. More's the pity. But you can't evacuate a housing development the size of a small town and keep it quiet. The cat was out of the bag. They were calling them the zombie massacres. Geez.

The sun was going down in a sea of scarlet and orange. It looked like someone had melted two giant crayons and smeared them across the sky. There wasn't a shed, garage, basement, tree house, playhouse, or anything else we could think of that had been left unsearched. Still, we had found nothing.

The newshounds were prowling restlessly at the edge of the search area. If we had evacuated hundreds of people and searched their premises without a warrant and found no zombie . . . we were going to be in deep fucking shit.

But it was here. I knew it was here. All right, I was almost sure it was here.

John Burke was standing next to one of those giant trash cans. Dolph had surprised me by allowing John to come on the zombie hunt. As Dolph said, we needed all the help we could get.

"Where is it, Anita?" Dolph asked.

I wanted to say something brilliant. My God, Holmes, how did you know the zombie was hiding in the flower pot? But I couldn't lie. "I don't know, Dolph. I just don't know."

"If we don't find this thing . . ." He let the thought trail off, but I knew what he meant.

My job was secure if this fell apart. Dolph's was not. Shit. How could I help him? What were we missing? What?

I stared at the quiet street. It was eerily quiet. The windows were all dark. Only the streetlights pushed back the coming dark. Soft halos of light.

Every house had a mailbox on a post near the sidewalk that edged the curb. Some of the mailboxes were unbelievably cute. One had been shaped like a sitting cat. Its paw went up if there was mail in its tummy. The family name was Catt. It was too precious.

Every house had at least one large super duper trash can in front of it. Some of them were bigger than I was. Surely, Sunday couldn't be trash day. Or had today been trash day, and the police line had stopped it?

"Trash cans," I said aloud.

"What?" Dolph asked.

"Trash cans." I grabbed his arm, feeling almost light-headed. "We've stared at those fucking trash cans all day. That's it."

John Burke stood quietly beside me, frowning.

"Are you feeling okay, Blake?" Zerbrowski came up behind us, smoking. The end of his cigarette looked like a bloated firefly.

"The cans are big enough for a large person to hide in."

"Wouldn't your arms and legs fall asleep?" Zerbrowski asked.

"Zombies don't have circulation, not like we do."

Dolph yelled, "Everybody check the trash cans. The zombie is in one of them. Move it!"

Everyone scattered like an anthill stirred with a stick, but we had a purpose now. I ended up with two uniformed officers. Their nameplates said "Ki" and "Roberts." Ki was Asian and male. Roberts was blond and female. A nicely mixed team.

We fell into a rhythm without discussing it. Officer Ki would move up and dump the trash can. Roberts and I would cover him with guns. We were all set to yell like hell if a zombie came tumbling out. It would probably be the right zombie. Life is seldom that cruel.

We'd yell and an exterminator team would come running. At least, they'd better come running. This zombie was entirely too fast, too destructive. It might be more resistant to gunfire. Better not to find out. Just french-fry the sucker and be done with it.

We were the only team working on the street. There was no sound but our footsteps, the rubber crunch of trash cans overturning, the rattle of cans and bottles as the trash spilled. Didn't anybody tie their bags up anymore?

Darkness had fallen in a solid blackness. I knew there were stars and a moon up there somewhere, but you couldn't prove it from where we stood. Clouds as thick and dark as velvet had come in from the west. Only the streetlights made it bearable.

I didn't know how Roberts was doing, but the muscles in my shoulders and neck were screaming. Every time Ki put his hands to the can and pushed, I was ready. Ready to fire, ready to save him before the zombie leapt up and ripped his throat out. A trickle of sweat dripped down his high-cheekboned face. Even in the dim light it glimmered.

Glad to know I wasn't the only one feeling the effort. Of course, I wasn't the one putting my face over the possible hiding place of a berserk zombie. Trouble was, I didn't know how good a shot Ki was, or Roberts either for that matter. I knew I was a good shot. I knew I could slow the thing down until help arrived. I had to stay on shooting detail. It was the best division of labor. Honest.

Screams. To the left. The three of us froze. I whirled towards the screaming. There was nothing to see, nothing but dark houses and pools of streetlight. Nothing moved. But the screams continued high and horrified.

I started running towards the screams. Ki and Roberts were at my back. I ran with the Browning in a two-handed grip pointed up. Easier to run that way. Didn't dare holster the gun. Visions of blood-coated teddy bears, and the screams. The screams sort of faded. Someone was dying up ahead.

There was a sense of movement everywhere in the darkness. Cops running. All of us running but it was too late. We were all too late. The screaming had stopped. No gunshots. Why not? Why hadn't someone gotten off a shot?

We ran down the side yards of four houses when we hit a metal fence. Had to holster the guns. Couldn't climb it with one hand. Dammit. I did my best to vault the fence using my hands for leverage.

I stumbled to my knees in the soft dirt of a flower bed. I was trampling some tall summer flowers. On my knees I was considerably shorter than the flowers. Ki landed beside me. Only Roberts landed on her feet.

Ki stood up without drawing his gun. I drew the Browning while I crouched in the flowers. I could stand up after I was armed.

I had a sense of rushing movement but not clear sight. The flowers obscured my vision. Roberts was suddenly tumbling backwards, screaming.

Ki was drawing his gun, but something hit him, knocked him on top of me. I rolled but was still half under him. He lay still on top of me.

"Ki, move it, dammit!"

He sat up and crawled towards his partner, his gun silhouetted against the streetlight. He was staring down at Roberts. She wasn't moving.

I searched the darkness trying to see something, anything. It had moved more than human fast. Fast as a ghoul. No zombie moved like that. Had I been wrong all along? Was it something else? Something worse? How many lives would my mistake cost tonight? Was Roberts dead?

"Ki, is she alive?" I searched the darkness, fighting the urge to look only at the lighted areas. There was shouting, but it was confusion, "Where is it? Where did it go?" The sounds were getting farther away.

I screamed, "Here, here!" The voices hesitated, then started our way. They were making so much noise, like a herd of arthritic elephants.

"How bad is she hurt?"

"Bad." He'd put his gun down. He was pressing his hands over her neck. Something black and liquid was spreading over his hands. God.

I knelt on the other side of Roberts, gun ready, searching the darkness. Everything was taking forever, yet it was only seconds.

I checked her pulse, one-handed. It was thready, but there. My hand came away covered in blood. I wiped it on my pants. The thing had damn near slit her throat.

Where was it?

Ki's eyes were huge, all pupil. His skin looked leprous in the streetlight. His partner's blood was dripping out between his fingers.

Something moved, too low to the ground to be a man, but about that size. It was just a shape creeping along the back of the house in front of us. Whatever it was had found the deepest shadow and was trying to creep away.

That showed more intelligence than a zombie had. I was wrong. I was wrong. I was fucking wrong. And Roberts was dying because of it.

"Stay with her. Keep her alive."

"Where are you going?" he asked.

"After it." I climbed the fence one-handed. The adrenaline must have been pumping because I made it.

I gained the yard and it was gone. A streaking shape fast as a mouse caught in the kitchen light. A blur of speed, but big, big as a man.

It rounded the corner of the house and I lost sight of it. Dammit. I ran as far from the wall as I could, my stomach tight with anticipation of fingers ripping my throat out. I came round the house gun pointed, two-handed, ready. Nothing. I scanned the darkness, the pools of light. Nothing.

Shouts behind me. The cops had arrived. God, let Roberts live.

There, movement, creeping across the streetlight around the edge of another house. Someone shouted, "Anita!"

I was already running towards the movement. I shouted as I ran, "Bring an exterminator team!" But I didn't stop. I didn't dare stop. I was the only one in sight of it. If I lost it, it was gone.

I ran into the darkness, alone, after something that might not be a zombie at all. Not the brightest thing I've ever done, but it wasn't going to get away. It wasn't.

It was never going to hurt another family. Not if I could stop it. Now. Tonight.

I ran through a pool of light and it made the darkness heavier, blinding me temporarily. I froze in the dark, willing my eyes to adjust faster.

"Perssisstent woman," a voice hissed. It was to my right, so close the hair on my arms stood up.

I froze, straining my peripheral vision. There, a darker shape rising out

of the evergreen shrubs that hugged the edge of the house. It rose to its full
height, but didn't attack. If it wanted me, it could have me before I could
turn and fire. I'd seen it move. I knew I was dead.

"You arrre not like the resst." The voice was sibilant, as if parts of the
mouth were missing, so it put great effort into forming each word. A gentleman's voice decayed by the grave.

I turned towards it, slowly, slowly.

"Put me back."

I had turned my head enough to be able to see some of it. My night
vision is better than most. And the streetlights made it lighter than it should
have been.

The skin was pale, yellowish-white. The skin clung to the bones of his
face like wax that had half-melted. But the eyes, they weren't decayed. They
burned out at me with a glitter that was more than just eyes.

"Put you back where?" I asked.

"My grave," he said. His lips didn't work quite right, there wasn't
enough flesh left on them.

Light blazed into my eyes. The zombie screamed, covering his face. I
couldn't see shit. It crashed into me. I pulled the trigger blind. I thought I
heard a grunt as the bullet hit home. I fired the gun again one-handed, throwing an arm across my neck. Trying to protect myself as I fell half-blind.

When I blinked up into the electric-shot darkness, I was alone. I was
unhurt. Why? Put me back, it had said. In my grave. How had it known
what I was? Most humans couldn't tell. Witches could tell sometimes, and
other animators always spotted me. Other animators. Shit.

Dolph was suddenly there, pulling me to my feet. "God, Blake, are you
hurt?"

I shook my head. "What the hell was that light?"

"A halogen flashlight."

"You damn near blinded me."

"We couldn't see to shoot," he said.

Police had run past us in the darkness. There were shouts of, "There it
is!" Dolph and I and the offending flashlight, bright as day, were left behind
as the chase ran merrily on.

"It spoke to me, Dolph," I said.

"What do you mean, it spoke to you?"

"It asked me to put it back in its grave." I stared up at him as I said it.
I wondered if my face looked like Ki's had, pale, eyes wide and black. Why
wasn't I scared?

"It's old, a century at least. It was a voodoo something in life. That's
what went wrong. That's why Peter Burke couldn't control it."

"How do you know all this? Did it tell you?"

I shook my head. "The way it looked, I could judge the age. It recognized me as someone who could lay it to rest. Only a witch or another
animator could have recognized me for what I am. My money's on an animator."

"Does that change our plan?" he asked.

I stared up at him. "It's killed how many people?" I didn't wait for him to answer. "We kill it. Period."

"You think like a cop, Anita." It was a great compliment from Dolph, and I took it as one.

It didn't matter what it had been in life. So it had been an animator, or rather a voodoo practitioner. So what? It was a killing machine. It hadn't killed me. Hadn't hurt me. I couldn't afford to return the favor.

Shots echoed far away. Some trick of the summer air made them echo. Dolph and I looked at each other.

I still had the Browning in my hand. "Let's do it."

He nodded.

We started running, but he outdistanced me quickly. His legs were as tall as I was. I couldn't match his pace. I might be able to run him into the ground, but I'd never match his speed.

He hesitated, glancing at me.

"Go on, run," I said.

He put on an extra burst of speed and was gone into the darkness. He didn't even look back. If you said you were fine in the dark with a killer zombie on the loose, Dolph would believe you. Or at least he believed me.

It was a compliment but it left me running alone in the dark for the second time tonight. Shouts were coming from two opposite directions. They had lost it. Damn.

I slowed. I had no desire to run into the thing blind. It hadn't hurt me the first time, but I'd put at least one bullet into it. Even a zombie gets pissed about things like that.

I was under the cool darkness of a tree shadow. I was on the edge of the development. A barbed-wire fence cut across the entire back of the subdivision. Farmland stretched as far as I could see. At least the field was planted in beans. The zombie'd have to be lying flat to hide in there. I caught glimpses of policemen with flashlights, searching the darkness, but they were all about fifty yards to either side of me.

They were searching the ground, the shadows, because I'd told them zombies didn't like to climb. But this wasn't any ordinary zombie. The tree rustled over my head. The hair on my neck crawled down my spine. I whirled, looking upwards, gun pointing.

It snarled at me and leapt.

I fired twice before its weight hit me and knocked us both to the ground. Two bullets in the chest, and it wasn't even hurt.

I fired a third time, but I might as well have been hitting a wall.

It snarled in my face, broken teeth with dark stains, breath foul as a new opened grave. I screamed back, wordless, and pulled the trigger again. The bullet hit it in the throat. It paused, trying to swallow. To swallow the bullet?

Those glittering eyes stared down at me. There was someone home, like Dominga's soul-locked zombies. There was someone looking out of those eyes. We froze in one of those illusionary seconds that last years. He was straddling my waist, hands at my throat, but not pressing, not hurting, not yet. I had the gun under his chin. None of the other bullets had hurt him; why would this one?

"Didn't mean to kill," it said softly, "didn't undersstand at firsst. Didn't remember what I wass."

The police were there on either side, hesitating. Dolph screamed, "Hold your fire, hold your fire, dammit!"

"I needed meat, needed it to remember who I wass. Tried not to kill. Tried to walk past all the houssess, but I could not. Too many houssess," he whispered. His hands tensed, stained nails digging in. I fired into his chin. His body jerked backwards, but the hands squeezed my neck.

Pressure, pressure, tighter, tighter. I was beginning to see white star bursts on my vision. The night was fading from black to grey. I pressed the gun just above the bridge of his nose and pulled the trigger again, and again.

My vision faded, but I could still feel my hands, pulling the trigger. Darkness flowed over my eyes and swallowed the world. I couldn't feel my hands anymore.

I woke to screams, horrible screams. The stink of burning flesh and hair was thick and choking on my tongue.

I took a deep shaking breath and it hurt. I coughed and tried to sit up. Dolph was there supporting me. He had my gun in his hand. I drew one ragged breath after another and coughed hard enough to make my throat raw. Or maybe the zombie had done that.

Something the size of a man was rolling over the summer grass. It burned. It flamed with a clean orange light that sent the darkness shattering in fire shadows like the sun on water.

Two exterminators in their fire suits stood by it, covering it in napalm, as if it were a ghoul. The thing screamed high in its throat, over and over, one loud ragged shriek after another.

"Jesus, why won't it die?" Zerbrowski was standing nearby. His face was orange in the firelight.

I didn't say anything. I didn't want to say it out loud. The zombie wouldn't die because it had been an animator when alive. That much I knew about animator zombies. What I hadn't known was that they came out of the grave craving flesh. That they remembered only when they ate flesh.

That I hadn't known. Didn't want to know.

John Burke stumbled into the firelight. He was cradling one arm to his chest. Blood stained his clothing. Had the zombie whispered to John? Did he know why the thing wouldn't die?

The zombie whirled, the fire roaring around it. The body was like the wick of a candle. It took one shaking step towards us. Its flaming hand reached out to me. To me.

Then it fell forward, slowly, into the grass. It fell like a tree in slow motion, fighting for life. If that was the word. The exterminators stayed ready, taking no chances. I didn't blame them.

It had been a necromancer once upon a time. That burning hulk, slowly catching the grass on fire, had been what I was. Would I be a monster if raised from the grave? Would I? Better not to find out. My will said cremation because I didn't want someone raising me just for kicks. Now I had another reason to do it. One had been enough.

I watched the flesh blacken, curl, peel away. Muscles and bone popped in miniature explosions, tiny pops of sparks.

I watched the zombie die and made a promise to myself. I'd see Dominga Salvador burned in hell for what she'd done. There are fires that last for all eternity. Fires that make napalm look like a temporary inconvenience. She'd burn for all eternity, and it wouldn't be half long enough.

33

I was lying on my back in the emergency room. A white curtain hid me from view. The noises on the other side of the curtain were loud and unfriendly. I liked my curtain. The pillow was flat, the examining table was hard. It felt white and clean and wonderful. It hurt to swallow. It even hurt a little bit just to breathe. But breathing was important. It was nice to be able to do it.

I lay there very quietly. Doing what I was told for once. I listened to my breathing, the beating of my own heart. After nearly dying, I am always very interested in my body. I notice all sorts of things that go unnoticed during most of life. I could feel blood coursing through the veins in my arms. I could taste my calm, orderly pulse in my mouth like a piece of candy.

I was alive. The zombie was dead. Dominga Salvador was in jail. Life was good.

Dolph pushed the curtain back. He closed the curtain like you'd close a door to a room. We both pretended we had privacy even though we could see people's feet passing under the hem of the curtain.

I smiled up at him. He smiled back. "Nice to see you up and around."

"I don't know about the up part," I said. My voice had a husky edge to it. I coughed, tried to clear it, but it didn't really help.

"What'd the doc say about your voice?" Dolph asked.

"I'm a temporary tenor." At the look on his face, I added, "It'll pass."

"Good."

"How's Burke?" I asked.

"Stitches, no permanent damage."

I had figured as much after seeing him last night, but it was good to know.

"And Roberts?"

"She'll live."

"But will she be all right?" I had to swallow hard. It hurt to talk.

"She'll be all right. Ki was cut up, too, on the arm. Did you know?"

I shook my head and stopped in mid-motion. That hurt, too. "Didn't see it."

"Just a few stitches. He'll be fine." Dolph plunged his hands in his pants pockets. "We lost three officers. One hurt worse than Roberts, but he'll make it."

I stared up at him. "My fault."

He frowned. "How do you figure that?"

"I should have guessed," I had to swallow, "it wasn't an ordinary zombie."

"It was a zombie, Anita. You were right. You were the one who figured out it was hiding in one of those damn trash cans." He grinned down at me. "And you nearly died killing it. I think you've done your part."

"Didn't kill it. Exterminators killed it." Big words seemed to hurt more than little words.

"Do you remember what happened as you were passing out?"

"No."

"You emptied your clip into its face. Blew its damn brains out the back of its head. You went limp. I thought you were dead. God"—he shook his head—"don't ever do that to me again."

I smiled. "I'll try not to."

"When its brains started leaking out the back of its head, it stood up. You took all the fight out of it."

Zerbrowski pushed into the small space, leaving the curtain gaping behind him. I could see a small boy with a bloody hand crying into a woman's shoulder. Dolph swept the curtain closed. I bet Zerbrowski was one of those people who never shut a drawer.

"They're still digging bullets out of the corpse. And every bullet's yours, Blake."

I just looked at him.

"You are such a bad ass, Blake."

"Somebody has to be with you around, Zerbrow . . ." I couldn't finish his name. It hurt. It figures.

"Are you in pain?" Dolph asked.

I nodded, carefully. "The doc's getting me painkiller. Already got tetanus booster."

"You've got a necklace of bruises blossoming on that pale neck of yours," Zerbrowski said.

"Poetic," I said.

He shrugged.

"I'll check in on the rest of the injured one more time, then I'll have a uniform drive you back to your place," Dolph said.

"Thanks."

"I don't think you're in any condition to drive."

Maybe he was right. I felt like shit, but it was happy shit. We'd done it. We'd solved the crime, and people were going to jail for it. Yippee.

The doctor came back in with the painkillers. He glanced at the two policemen. "Right." He handed me a bottle with three pills in it. "This should see you through the night and into the next day. I'd call in sick if I were you." He glanced at Dolph as he said it. "You hear that, boss?"

Dolph sort of frowned. "I'm not her boss."

"You're the man in charge, right?" the doctor asked.

Dolph nodded.

"Then . . ."

"I'm on loan," I said.

"Loan?"

"You might say we borrowed her from another department," Zerbrowski said.

The doctor nodded. "Then tell her superior to let her off tomorrow. She may not look as hurt as the others, but she's had a nasty shock. She's very lucky there was no permanent damage."

"She doesn't have a superior," Zerbrowski said, "but we'll tell her boss." He grinned at the doctor.

I frowned at Zerbrowski.

"Well, then, you're free to go. Watch those scratches for infection. And that bite on your shoulder." He shook his head. "You cops earn your money." With that parting wisdom, he left.

Zerbrowski laughed. "Wouldn't do for the doc to know we'd let a civvie get messed up."

"She's had a nasty shock," Dolph said.

"Very nasty," Zerbrowski said.

They started laughing.

I sat up carefully, swinging my legs over the edge of the bed. "If you two are through yukking it up, I need a ride home."

They were both laughing so hard that tears were creeping out of their eyes. It hadn't been that funny, but I understood. For tension release laughter beats the hell out of tears. I didn't join them because I suspected strongly that laughing would hurt.

"I'll drive you home," Zerbrowski gasped between giggles.

I had to smile. Seeing Dolph and Zerbrowski giggling was enough to make anyone smile.

"No, no," Dolph said. "You two in a car alone. Only one of you would come out alive."

"And it'd be me," I said.

Zerbrowski nodded. "Ain't it the truth."

Nice to know there was one subject we agreed on.

34

I was half asleep in the back of the squad car when they pulled up in front of my apartment building. The throbbing pain in my throat had slid away on a smooth tide of pain medication. I felt nearly boneless. What had the doctor given me? It felt great, but it was like the world was some sort of movie that had little to do with me. Distant and harmless as a dream.

I'd given Dolph my car keys. He promised to have someone park the car in front of my apartment building before morning. He also said he'd call Bert and tell him I wouldn't be in to work today. I wondered how Bert would take the news. I wondered if I cared. Nope.

One of the uniformed police officers leaned back over the seat and said, "You going to be all right, Miss Blake?"

"Ms.," I corrected automatically.

He gave me a half smile as he held the door for me. No door handles on the inside of a squad car. He had to hold the door for me, but he did it with relish, and said, "You going to be all right, Ms. Blake?"

"Yes, Officer"—I had to blink to read his name tag—"Osborn. Thank you for bringing me home. To your partner, too."

His partner was standing on the other side of the car, leaning his arms on the roof of the car. "It's a kick to finally meet the spook squad's Executioner." He grinned as he said it.

I blinked at him and tried to pull all the pieces together enough to talk and think at the same time. "I was the Executioner long before the spook squad came along."

He spread his hands, still grinning. "No offense."

I was too tired and too drugged to worry about it. I just shook my head. "Thanks again."

I was a touch unsteady going up the stairs. I clutched the railing like it was a lifeline. I'd sleep tonight. I might wake up in the middle of the hallway, but I'd sleep.

It took me two tries to put the key in the door lock. I staggered into my apartment, leaning my forehead against the door to close it. I turned the lock and was safe. I was home. I was alive. The killer zombie was destroyed. I had the urge to giggle, but that was the pain medication. I never giggle on my own.

I stood there leaning the top of my head against the door. I was staring at the toes of my Nikes. They seemed very far away, as if distances had grown since last I looked at my feet. The doc had given me some weird shit. I would not take it tomorrow. It was too reality-altering for my taste.

The toes of black boots stepped up beside my Nikes. Why were there boots in my apartment? I started to turn around. I started to go for my gun. Too late, too slow, too fucking bad.

Strong brown arms laced across my chest, pinning my arms. Pinning me against the door. I tried to struggle now that it was too late. But he had me. I craned my neck backwards trying to fight off the damn medication. I should have been terrified. Adrenaline pumping, but some drugs don't give a shit if you need your body. You belong to the drug until it wears off, period. I was going to hurt the doctor. If I lived through this.

It was Bruno pinning me to the door.

Tommy came up on the right. He had a needle in his hands.

"NO!"

Bruno cupped his hand over my mouth. I tried to bite him, and he slapped me. The slap helped a little but the world was still cotton-coated, distant. Bruno's hand smelled like after-shave. A choking sweetness.

"This is almost too easy," Tommy said.

"Just do it," Bruno said.

I stared at the needle as it came closer to my arm. I would have told them that I was drugged already, if Bruno's hand hadn't been clasped over my mouth. I would have asked what was in the syringe, and whether it would react badly with what I had already taken. I never got the chance.

The needle plunged in. My body stiffened, struggling, but Bruno held me tight. Couldn't move. Couldn't get away. Dammit! Dammit! The adrenaline was finally chasing the cobwebs away, but it was too late. Tommy took the needle out of my arm and said, "Sorry, we don't have any alcohol to swab it off with." He grinned at me.

I hated him. I hated them both. And if the shot didn't kill me, I was going to kill them both. For scaring me. For making me feel helpless. For catching me unaware, drugged, and stupid. If I lived through this mistake, I wouldn't make it again. Please, dear God, let me live through this mistake.

Bruno held me motionless and mute until I could feel the injection taking hold. I was sleepy. With a bad guy holding me against my will, I was sleepy. I tried to fight it, but it didn't work. My eyelids fluttered. I struggled to keep them open. I stopped trying to get away from Bruno and put everything I had into not closing my eyes.

I stared at my door and tried to stay awake. The door swam in dizzying ripples as if I were seeing it through water. My eyelids went down, jerked up, down. I couldn't open my eyes. A small part of me fell screaming into the dark, but the rest of me felt loose and sleepy and strangely safe.

35

I was in that faint edge of wakefulness. Where you know you're not quite asleep, but don't really want to wake up either. My body felt heavy. My head throbbed. And my throat was sore.

The last thought made me open my eyes. I was staring at a white ceiling. Brown water marks traced the paint like spilled coffee. I wasn't home. Where was I?

I remembered Bruno holding me down. The needle. I sat up then. The world swam in clear waves of color. I fell back onto the bed, covering my eyes with my hands. That helped a little. What had they given me?

I had an image in my mind that I wasn't alone. Somewhere in that dizzying swirl of color had been a person. Hadn't there? I opened my eyes slower this time. I was content to stare up at the water-ruined ceiling. I was on a large bed. Two pillows, sheets, a blanket. I turned my head carefully and found myself staring into Harold Gaynor's face. He was sitting beside the bed. It wasn't what I wanted to wake up to.

Behind him, leaning against a battered chest of drawers was Bruno. His shoulder holster cut black lines across his blue short-sleeved dress shirt. There was a matching and equally scarred vanity table near the foot of the bed. The vanity sat between two high windows. They were boarded with new, sweet-smelling lumber. The scent of pine rode the hot, still air.

I started to sweat as soon as I realized that there was no air-conditioning.

"How are you feeling, Ms. Blake?" Gaynor asked. His voice was still that jolly Santa voice with an edge of sibilance. As if he were a very happy snake.

"I've felt better," I said.

"I'm sure you have. You have been asleep for over twenty-four hours. Did you know that?"

Was he lying? Why would he lie about how long I'd been asleep? What would it gain him? Nothing. Truth then, probably.

"What the hell did you give me?"

Bruno eased himself away from the wall. He looked almost embarrassed. "We didn't realize you'd already taken a sedative."

"Painkiller," I said.

He shrugged. "Same difference when you mix it with Thorazine."

"You shot me up with animal tranquilizers?"

"Now, now, Ms. Blake, they use it in mental institutions, as well. Not just animals," Gaynor said.

"Gee," I said, "that makes me feel a lot better."

He smiled broadly. "If you feel good enough to trade witty repartee, then you're well enough to get up."

Witty repartee? But he was probably right. Truthfully, I was surprised I wasn't tied up. Glad of it, but surprised.

I sat up much slower than last time. The room only tilted the tiniest bit, before settling into an upright position. I took a deep breath, and it hurt. I put a hand to my throat. It hurt to touch the skin.

"Who gave you those awful bruises?" Gaynor asked.

Lie or truth? Partial lie. "I was helping the police catch a bad guy. He got a little out of hand."

"What happened to this bad guy?" Bruno asked.

"He's dead now," I said.

Something flickered across Bruno's face. Too quick to read. Respect maybe. Naw.

"You know why I've had you brought here, don't you?"

"To raise a zombie for you," I said.

"To raise a very old zombie for me, yes."

"I've refused your offer twice. What makes you think I'll change my mind?"

He smiled, such a jolly old elf. "Why, Ms. Blake, I'll have Bruno and Tommy persuade you of the error of your ways. I still plan on giving you a million dollars to raise this zombie. The price hasn't changed."

"Tommy offered me a million five last time," I said.

"That was if you came voluntarily. We can't pay full price when you force us to take such chances."

"Like a federal prison term for kidnapping," I said.

"Exactly. Your stubbornness has cost you five hundred thousand dollars. Was it really worth that?"

"I won't kill another human being just so you can go looking for lost treasure."

"Little Wanda has been bearing tales."

"I was just guessing, Gaynor. I read a file on you and it mentioned your obsession with your father's family." It was an outright lie. Only Wanda had known that.

"I'm afraid it's too late. I know Wanda talked to you. She's confessed everything."

Confessed? I stared at him, trying to read his blankly good-humored face. "What do you mean, confessed?"

"I mean I gave her to Tommy for questioning. He's not the artist that Cicely is, but he does leave more behind. I didn't want to kill my little Wanda."

"Where is she now?"

"Do you care what happens to a whore?" His eyes were bright and birdlike as he stared at me. He was judging me, my reactions.

"She doesn't mean anything to me," I said. I hoped my face was as bland as my words. Right now they weren't going to kill her. If they thought they could use her to hurt me, they might.

"Are you sure?"

"Listen, I haven't been sleeping with her. She's just a chippie with a very bent angle."

He smiled at that. "What can we do to convince you to raise this zombie for me?"

"I will not commit murder for you, Gaynor. I don't like you that much," I said.

He sighed. His apple-cheeked face looked like a sad Kewpie doll. "You are going to make this difficult, aren't you, Ms. Blake?"

"I don't know how to make it easy," I said. I put my back to the cracked wooden headboard of the bed. I was comfortable enough, but I still felt a little fuzzy around the edges. But it was as good as it was going to get for a while. It beat the hell out of being unconscious.

"We have not really hurt you yet," Gaynor said. "The reaction of the Thorazine with whatever other medication you had in you was accidental. We did not harm you on purpose."

I could argue with that, but I decided not to. "So where do we go from here?"

"We have both your guns," Gaynor said. "Without a weapon you are a small woman in the care of big, strong men."

I smiled then. "I'm used to being the smallest kid on the block, Harry."

He looked pained. "Harold or Gaynor, never Harry."

I shrugged. "Fine."

"You are not in the least intimidated that we have you completely at our mercy?"

"I could argue that point."

He glanced up at Bruno. "Such confidence, where does she get it?"

Bruno didn't say anything. He just stared at me with those empty doll eyes. Bodyguard eyes, watchful, suspicious, and blank all at the same time.

"Show her we mean business, Bruno."

Bruno smiled, a slow spreading of lips that left his eyes dead as a shark's. He loosened his shoulders, and did a few stretching exercises against the wall. His eyes never left me.

"I take it, I'm going to be the punching bag?" I asked.

"How well you put it," Gaynor said.

Bruno stood away from the wall, limber and eager. Oh, well. I slid off the bed on the opposite side. I had no desire for Gaynor to grab me. Bruno's reach was over twice mine. His legs went on forever. He had to outweigh me by nearly a hundred pounds, and it was all muscle. I was about to get badly hurt. But as long as they didn't tie me up, I'd go down swinging. If I could cause him any serious damage, I'd be satisfied.

I came out from behind the bed, hands loose at my side. I was already in that partial crouch that I used on the judo mat. I doubted seriously if Bruno's fighting skill of choice was judo. I was betting karate or tae kwon do.

Bruno stood in an awkward-looking stance, halfway between an x and a t. It looked like someone had taken his long legs and crumbled them at the knees. But as I moved forward he scooted backwards like a crab, fast and out of reach.

"Jujitsu?" I made it half question.

He raised an eyebrow. "Most people don't recognize it."

"I've seen it," I said.

"You practice?"

"No."

He smiled. "Then I am going to hurt you."

"Even if I knew jujitsu, you'd hurt me," I said.

"It'd be a fair fight."

"If two people are equal in skill, size matters. A good big person will always beat a good small person." I shrugged. "I don't have to like it, but it's the truth."

"You're being awful calm about this," Bruno said.

"Would being hysterical help?"

He shook his head. "Nope."

"Then I'd just as soon take my medicine like, if you'll excuse the expression, a man."

He frowned at that. Bruno was accustomed to people being scared of him. I wasn't scared of him. I'd decided to take the beating. With the decision came a certain amount of calm. I was going to get beat up, not pleasant, but I had made my mind up to take the beating. I could do it. I'd done it before. If my choices were a) getting beat up or b) performing human sacrifice, I'd take the beating.

"Ready or not," Bruno said.

"Here you come," I finished for him. I was getting tired of the bravado. "Either hit me or stand up straight. You look silly crouched down like that."

His fist was a dark blur. I blocked it with my arm. The impact made the arm go numb. His long leg kicked out and connected solidly with my stomach. I doubled over like I was supposed to, all the air gone in one movement. His other foot came up and caught me on the side of the face. It was the same cheek ol' Seymour had smashed. I fell to the floor not sure what part of my body to comfort first.

His foot came for me again. I caught it with both hands. I came up in a rush, hoping to trap his knee between my arms and pop the joint. But he twisted away from me, totally airborne for a moment.

I dropped to the ground and felt the air pass overhead as his legs kicked out where my head had been. I was on the ground again, but by choice. He stood over me, impossibly tall from this angle. I lay on my side, knees drawn up.

He came for me, evidently planning to drag me to my feet. I kicked out with both feet at an angle to his kneecap. Hit it just right above or below and you dislocate it.

The leg buckled, and he screamed. It had worked. Hot damn. I didn't try to wrestle him. I didn't try to grab his gun. I ran for the door.

Gaynor grabbed for me, but I flung open the door and was out in a long hallway before he could maneuver his fancy chair. The hallway was smooth with a handful of doors and two blind corners. And Tommy.

Tommy looked surprised to see me. His hand went for his shoulder holster. I pushed on his shoulder and foot-swept his leg. He fell backwards and grabbed me as he fell. I rode him down, making sure my knee ground into his groin. His grip loosened enough for me to slip out of reach. There were sounds behind me from the room. I didn't look back. If they were going to shoot me, I didn't want to see it.

The hallway took a sharp turn. I was almost to it when the smell slowed me from a run to a walk. The smell of corpses was just around the corner. What had they been doing while I slept?

I glanced back at the men. Tommy was still lying on the floor, cradling himself. Bruno leaned against the wall, gun in hand, but he wasn't pointing it at me. Gaynor was sitting in his chair, smiling.

Something was very wrong.

Around the blind corner came that something that was wrong, very, very wrong. It was no taller than a tall man, maybe six feet. But it was nearly four feet wide. It had two legs, or maybe three, it was hard to tell. The thing was leprously pale like all zombies, but this one had a dozen eyes. A man's face was centered where the neck would have been. Its eyes dark and seeing, and empty of everything sane. A dog's head was growing out of the shoulder. The dog's decaying mouth snapped at me. A woman's leg grew out of the center of the mess, complete with black high-heeled shoe.

The thing shambled towards me. Pulling with three of a dozen arms, dragging itself forward. It left a trail behind it like a snail.

Dominga Salvador stepped around the corner. *"Buenas noches, chica."*

The monster scared me, but the sight of Dominga grinning at me scared me just a little bit more.

The thing had stopped moving forward. It squatted in the hallway, kneeling on its inadequate legs. Its dozens of mouths panted as if it couldn't get enough air.

Or maybe the thing didn't like the way it smelled. I certainly didn't. Covering my mouth and nose with my arm didn't block out much of the smell. The hallway suddenly smelled like bad meat.

Gaynor and his wounded bodyguards had stayed at the end of the hall. Maybe they didn't like being near Dominga's little pet. I know it didn't do much for me. Whatever the reason we were isolated. It was just her and me and the monster.

"How did you get out of jail?" Better to deal with more mundane problems first. The mind-melting ones could wait for later.

"I made my bail," she said.

"This quickly on a murder involving witchcraft?"

"Voodoo is not witchcraft," she said.

"The law sees it as the same thing when it comes to murder."

She shrugged, then smiled beatifically. She was the Mexican grand-mother of my nightmares.

"You've got a judge in your pocket," I said.

"Many people fear me, *chica*. You should be one of them."

"You helped Peter Burke raise the zombie for Gaynor."

She just smiled.

"Why didn't you just raise it yourself?" I asked.

"I didn't want someone as unscrupulous as Gaynor to witness me mur-dering someone. He might use it for blackmail."

"And he didn't realize that you had to kill someone for Peter's gris-gris?"

"Correct," she said.

"You hid all your horrors here?"

"Not all. You forced me to destroy much of my work, but this I saved. You can see why." She caressed a hand down the slimy hide.

I shuddered. Just the thought of touching that monstrosity was enough to make my skin cold. And yet . . .

"How did you make it?" I had to know. It was so obviously a creation of our shared art that I had to know.

"Surely, you can animate bits and pieces of the dead," Dominga said.

I could, but no one else I had ever met could do it. "Yes," I said.

"I found I could take these odds and ends and meld them together."

I stared at the shambling thing. "Meld them?" The thought was too horrible.

"I can create new creatures that have never existed before."

"You make monsters," I said.

"Believe what you will, *chica,* but I am here to persuade you to raise the dead for Gaynor."

"Why don't you do it?"

Gaynor's voice came from just behind us. I whirled, putting the wall at my back so I could watch everybody. What good that would do me, I wasn't sure. "Dominga's power went wrong once. This is my last chance. The last known grave. I won't risk it on her."

Dominga's eyes narrowed, her age-thinned hands forming fists. She didn't like being dismissed out of hand. Couldn't say I blamed her.

"She could do it, Gaynor, easier than I could."

"If I truly believed that, I would kill you because I wouldn't need you anymore."

Hmm, good point. "You've had Bruno rough me up. Now what?"

Gaynor shook his head. "Such a little girl to have taken both my bodyguards down."

"I told you ordinary methods of persuasion will not work on her," Dominga said.

I stared past her at the slathering monster. She called this ordinary?

"What do you propose?" Gaynor asked.

"A spell of compulsion. She will do as I bid, but it takes time to do such a spell for one as powerful as she. If she knew any voodoo to speak of, it would not work at all. But for all her art, she is but a baby in voodoo."

"How long will you need?"

"Two hours, no more."

"This had better work," Gaynor said.

"Do not threaten me," Dominga said.

Oh, goody, maybe the bad guys would fight and kill each other.

"I am paying you enough money to set up your own small country. I should get results for that."

Dominga nodded her head. "You pay well, that is true. I will not fail you. If I can compel Anita to kill another person, then I can compel her to help me in my zombie business. She will help me rebuild what she forced me to destroy. It has a certain irony, no?"

Gaynor smiled like a demented elf. "I like it."

"Well, I don't," I said.

He frowned at me. "You will do as you are told. You have been very naughty."

Naughty? Me?

Bruno had worked himself close to us. He was leaning heavily on the wall, but his gun was very steadily pointed at the center of my chest. "I'd like to kill you now," he said. His voice sounded raw with pain.

"A dislocated knee hurts like hell, doesn't it?" I smiled when I said it. Better dead than a willing servant of the voodoo queen.

I think he ground his teeth. The gun wavered just a little, but I think that was rage, not pain. "I will enjoy killing you."

"You didn't do so good last time. I think the judges would have given the match to me."

"There are no fucking judges here. I am going to kill you."

"Bruno," Gaynor said, "we need her alive and whole."

"After she raises the zombie?" Bruno asked.

"If she is a willing servant of the Señora, then you are not to hurt her. If the compulsion doesn't work, then you may kill her."

Bruno gave a fierce flash of teeth. It was more snarl than smile. "I hope the spell fails."

Gaynor glanced at his bodyguard. "Don't let personal feelings interfere with business, Bruno."

Bruno swallowed hard. "Yes, sir." It didn't sound like a title that came easily to him.

Enzo came around the corner behind Dominga. He stayed near the wall as far from her "creation" as he could get. Antonio had finally lost his job as bodyguard. It was just as well. He was much better suited to stool pigeon.

Tommy came limping down the hall, still sort of scrunched over himself. The big Magnum was in his hands. His face was nearly purple with rage, or maybe pain. "I'm gonna kill you," he hissed.

"Take a number," I said.

"Enzo, you help Bruno and Tommy tie this little girl to a chair in the room. She's a lot more dangerous than she seems," Gaynor said.

Enzo grabbed my arm. I didn't fight him. I figured I was safer in his hands than either of the other two. Tommy and Bruno both looked as if they were looking forward to me trying something. I think they wanted to hurt me.

As Enzo led me past them, I said, "Is it because I'm a woman or are you always this bad at losing?"

"I'm gonna shoot her," Tommy grunted.

"Later," Gaynor said, "later."

I wondered if he really meant that. If Dominga's spell worked, I'd be like a living zombie, obeying her will. If the spell didn't work, then Tommy and Bruno would kill me, a-piece at a time. I hoped there was a third choice.

36

The third choice was being tied to a chair in the room where I woke up. It was the best of the three choices, but that wasn't saying much. I don't like being tied up. It means your options have gone from few to none. Dominga had clipped some of my hair and the tips of my fingernails. Hair and nails for her compulsion spell. Shit.

The chair was old and straight-backed. My wrists were tied to the slats that made up the back of the chair. Ankles tied separately to a leg of the chair. The ropes were tight. I tugged at the ropes, hoping for some slack. There wasn't any.

I had been tied up before, and I always have this Houdini fantasy that this time I'll have enough slack to wiggle free. It never works that way. Once you're tied up, you stay tied up until someone lets you go.

The trouble was when they let me go, they were going to try a nasty little spell on me. I had to get away before then. Somehow, I had to get away. Dear God, please let me get away.

The door opened as if on cue, but it wasn't help.

Bruno entered, carrying Wanda in his arms. Blood had dried down the right side of her face from a cut above the eye. Her left cheek was ripe with a huge bruise. The lower lip had burst in a still bleeding cut. Her eyes were shut. I wasn't even sure she was conscious.

I had an aching line on the left side of my face where Bruno had kicked me, but it was nothing to Wanda's injuries.

"Now what?" I asked Bruno.

"Some company for you. When she wakes up, ask her what else Tommy did to her. See if that will persuade you to raise the zombie."

"I thought Dominga was going to bespell me into helping you."

He shrugged. "Gaynor doesn't put much faith in her since she screwed up so badly."

"He doesn't give second chances, I guess," I said.

"No, he doesn't." He laid Wanda on the floor near me. "You best take his offer, girl. One dead whore and you get a million dollars. Take it."

"You're going to use Wanda for the sacrifice," I said. My voice sounded tired even to me.

"Gaynor don't give second chances."

I nodded. "How's your knee?"

He grimaced. "I put it back in place."

"That must have hurt like hell," I said.

"It did. If you don't help Gaynor, you're going to find out exactly how much it hurt."

"An eye for an eye," I said.

He nodded and stood. He favored his right leg. He caught me looking at the leg.

"Talk to Wanda. Decide what you want to end up as. Gaynor's talking about making you a cripple, then keeping you around as his toy. You don't want that."

"How can you work for him?"

He shrugged. "Pays real well."

"Money isn't everything."

"Spoken by somebody who's never gone hungry."

He had me there. I just looked at him. We stared at each other for a few minutes. There was something human in his eyes at last. I couldn't read it though. Whatever emotion it was, it was nothing I understood.

He turned and left the room.

I stared down at Wanda. She lay on her side without moving. She was wearing another long multicolored skirt. A white blouse with a wide lace collar was half-ripped from one shoulder. The bra she wore was the color of plums. I bet there had been panties to match before Tommy got hold of her.

"Wanda," I said it softly. "Wanda, can you hear me?"

Her head moved slowly, painfully. One eye opened wide and panic-stricken. The other eye was glued shut with dried blood. Wanda pawed at the eye, frantic for a moment. When she could open both eyes, she blinked at me. Her eyes took a moment to focus and really see who it was. What had she expected to see in those first few panicked moments? I didn't want to know.

"Wanda, can you speak?"

"Yes." The voice was soft, but clear.

I wanted to ask if she was all right, but I knew the answer to that. "If you can get over here and free me, I'll get us out of here."

She looked at me like I'd lost my mind. "We can't get out. Harold's gonna kill us." She made that last sound like a statement of pure fact.

"I don't believe in giving up, Wanda. Untie me and I'll think of something."

"He'll hurt me if I help you," she said.

"He's planning on you being the human sacrifice to raise his ancestor. How much more hurt can you get?"

She blinked at me, but her eyes were clearing. It was almost as if panic were a drug, and Wanda was fighting off the influence. Or maybe it was Harold Gaynor who was the drug. Yeah, that made sense. She was a junkie. A Harold Gaynor junkie. Every junkie is willing to die for one more fix. But I wasn't.

"Untie me, Wanda, please. I can get us out of this."

"And if you can't?"

"Then we're no worse off," I said.

She seemed to think about that for a minute. I strained for sounds from the hallway. If Bruno came back while we were in the middle of escaping, it would be very bad.

Wanda propped herself up on her arms. Her legs trailed out behind her under the skirt, dead, no movement at all. She began dragging herself towards me. I thought it would be slow work, but she moved quickly. The muscles in her arms bunched and pushed, working well. She was by the chair in a matter of minutes.

I smiled. "You're very strong."

"My arms are all I have. They have to be strong," Wanda said.

She started picking at the ropes that bound my right wrist. "It's too tight."

"You can do it, Wanda."

She picked at the knot with her fingers, until after what seemed hours, but was probably about five minutes, I felt the rope give. Slack, I had slack. Yea!

"You've almost got it, Wanda." I felt like a cheerleader.

The sound of footsteps clattered down the hall towards us. Wanda's battered face stared up at me, terror in her eyes. "There's not time," she whispered.

"Go back where you were. Do it. We'll finish later," I said.

Wanda hand-walked back to where Bruno had laid her. She had just arranged herself into nearly the same position when the door opened. Wanda was pretending to be unconscious, not a bad idea.

Tommy stood in the doorway. He'd taken off his jacket and the black webbing of the shoulder rig stood out on his white polo shirt. Black jeans emphasized his pinched-in waist. He looked top-heavy from lifting so many weights.

He'd added one new thing to the outfit. A knife. He twirled it in his hand like a baton. It was almost a perfect sheen of light. Manual dexterity. Wowee.

"I didn't know you used a knife, Tommy." My voice sounded calm, normal, amazing.

He grinned. "I have a lot of talents. Gaynor wants to know if you've changed your mind about the zombie raising."

It wasn't exactly a question, but I answered it. "I won't do it."

His grin widened. "I was hoping you'd say that."

"Why?" I was afraid I knew the answer.

"Because he sent me in here to persuade you."

I stared at the glittering knife, I couldn't help myself. "With a knife?"

"With something else long and hard, but not so cold," he said.

"Rape?" I asked. The word sort of hung there in the hot, still air.

He nodded, grinning like a damn Cheshire cat. I wished I could make him disappear except for his smile. I wasn't afraid of his smile. It was the other end I was worried about.

I jerked at the ropes helplessly. The right wrist gave a little more. Had Wanda loosened the rope enough? Had she? Please God, let it be.

Tommy stood over me. I stared up the length of his body and what I saw in his eyes was nothing human. There were all sorts of ways to become a monster. Tommy had found one. There was nothing but an animal hunger in his gaze. Nothing human left.

He put a leg on either side of the chair, straddling me without sitting down. His flat stomach was pressed against my face. His shirt smelled of expensive after-shave. I jerked my head back, trying not to touch him.

He laughed and ran fingers through the tight waves of my hair. I tried to jerk my head out of his reach, but he grabbed a handful of hair and forced my head back.

"I'm going to enjoy this," he said.

I didn't dare jerk at the ropes. If my wrist came free he'd see it. I had to wait, wait until he was distracted enough not to notice. The thought of what I might have to do to distract him, allow him to do to me, made my stomach hurt. But staying alive was the goal. Everything else was gravy. I didn't really believe that, but I tried.

He sat down on me, his weight settling on my legs. His chest was pressed against my face, and there was nothing I could do about it.

He rubbed the flat of the knife across my cheek. "You can stop this anytime. Just say yes, and I'll tell Gaynor." His voice was already growing thick. I could feel him growing hard where he was pressed against my belly.

The thought of Tommy using me like that was almost enough to make me say yes. Almost. I jerked on the ropes and the right one gave a little more. One more hard tug and I could get free. But I'd have just one hand to Tommy's two, and he had a gun and a knife. Not good odds, but it was the best I was going to get tonight.

He kissed me, forcing his tongue in my mouth. I didn't respond, because he wouldn't have believed that. I didn't bite his tongue either because I wanted him close. With only one hand free, I needed him close. I needed to do major damage with one hand. What? What could I do?

He nuzzled my neck, face buried in my hair on the left side. Now or never. I pulled with everything I had and the right wrist popped free. I froze. Surely he'd felt it, but he was too busy sucking on my neck to notice. His free hand massaged my breast.

He had his eyes closed as he kissed to the right side of my neck. His eyes were closed. The knife was loose in his other hand. Nothing I could do about the knife. Had to take the chance. Had to do it.

I caressed the side of his face, and he nuzzled my hand. Then his eyes opened. It had occurred to him that I was supposed to be tied. I plunged my thumb into his open eye. I dug it in, feeling the wet pop as his eye exploded.

He shrieked, rearing back, hand to his eye. I grabbed the wrist with the knife and held on. The screams were going to bring reinforcements. Dammit.

Strong arms wrapped around Tommy's waist and pulled him backwards. I grabbed the knife as he slid to the floor. Wanda was struggling to hold him. The pain was so severe, it hadn't occurred to him to go for his gun. Putting out an eye hurts and panics a lot more than a kick to the groin.

I cut my other hand free and knicked my arm doing it. If I hurried too much, I'd end up slitting my own wrist. I forced myself to be more careful slicing my ankles free.

Tommy had managed to get free of Wanda. He staggered to his feet, one hand still over the eye. Blood and clear liquid trailed down his face. "I'll kill you!" He reached for his gun.

I reversed my grip on the knife and threw it. It thunked into his arm. I'd been aiming for his chest. He screamed again. I picked up the chair and smashed it into his face. Wanda grabbed his ankles, and Tommy went down.

I pounded at his face with the chair until the chair broke apart in my hands. Then I beat him with a chair leg until his face was nothing but a bloody mess.

"He's dead," Wanda said. She was tugging at my pants leg. "He's dead. Let's get out of here."

I dropped the blood-coated chair leg and collapsed to my knees. I couldn't swallow. I couldn't breathe. I was splattered with blood. I'd never beaten someone to death before. It had felt good. I shook my head. Later, I'd worry about it later.

Wanda put an arm over my shoulders. I grabbed her around the waist, and we stood. She weighed a lot less than she should have. I didn't want to see what was under the pretty skirt. It wasn't a full set of legs, but for once that was good. She was easier to move.

I had Tommy's gun in my right hand. "I need this hand free, so hold on tight."

Wanda nodded. Her face was very pale. I could feel her heart pounding against her ribs. "We're going to get out of this," I said.

"Sure," but her voice was shaky. I don't think she believed me. I wasn't sure I believed me.

Wanda opened the door, and out we went.

37

The hallway was just like I remembered it. A long stretch with no cover, then a blind corner at each end.

"Right or left?" I whispered to Wanda.

"I don't know. This house is like a maze. Right I think."

We went right, because at least it was a decision. The worst thing we could do was just stand there waiting for Gaynor to come back.

I heard footsteps behind us. I started to turn, but with Wanda in my arms, I was slow. The gunshot echoed in the hallway. Something hit my left arm, around Wanda's waist. The impact spun me around and sent us both crashing to the floor.

I ended up on my back with my left arm trapped under Wanda's weight. The left arm was totally numb.

Cicely stood at the end of the hallway. She held a small caliber handgun two-handed. Her long, long legs were far apart. She looked like she knew what she was doing.

I raised the .357 and aimed at her, still lying flat on my back on the floor. It was an explosion of sound that left my ears ringing. The recoil thrust my hand skyward, backwards. It was everything I could do not to drop the gun. If I'd needed a second shot I'd have never gotten it off in time. But I didn't need a second shot.

Cicely lay crumpled in the middle of the hallway. Blood was spreading on the front of her blouse. She didn't move, but that didn't mean anything. Her gun was still gripped in one hand. She could be pretending, then when I walked up, she'd shoot me. But I had to know.

"Can you get off my arm, please?" I asked.

Wanda didn't say anything, but she lifted herself to a sitting position, and I could finally see my arm. It was still attached. Goody. Blood was seeping down my arm in a crimson line. A point of icy burning had started to chase away the numbness. I liked the numbness better.

I did my best to ignore the arm as I stood up and walked towards Cicely. I had the Magnum pointed at her. If she so much as twitched, I'd hit her again. Her miniskirt had hiked up her thighs, displaying black garters and matching underwear. How undignified.

I stood over her, staring down. Cicely wasn't going to twitch, not voluntarily. Her silk blouse was soaked with blood. A hole big enough for me to put my fist through took up most of her chest. Dead, very dead.

I kicked the .22 out of her hand, just in case. You can never tell with someone who plays voodoo. I've had people get up before with worse injuries. Cicely just lay there, bleeding.

I was lucky she'd had a ladylike caliber pistol. Anything bigger and I might have lost the arm. I stuck her pistol in the front of my pants, because I couldn't figure out where else to put it. I did click the safety on first.

I'd never been shot before. Bitten, stabbed, beaten, burned, but never shot. It scared me because I wasn't sure how badly I was hurt. I walked back to Wanda. Her face was pale, her brown eyes like islands in her face. "Is she dead?"

I nodded.

"You're bleeding," she said. She tore a strip from her long skirt. "Here, let me wrap it."

I knelt and let her tie the multicolored strip just above the wound. She wiped the blood away with another piece of skirt. It didn't look that bad. It looked almost like a raw, bloody scrape.

"I think the bullet just grazed me," I said. A flesh wound, nothing but a flesh wound. It burned and was almost cold at the same time. Maybe the cold was shock. One little bullet graze and I was going into shock? Surely not.

"Come on, we've got to get out of here. The shots will bring Bruno." It was good that I had pain in the arm. It meant I could feel and I could move the arm. The arm did not want to be wrapped around Wanda's waist again, but it was the only way to move her and keep my right hand free.

"Let's go left. Maybe Cicely came in this way," Wanda said. There was a certain logic to that. We turned and walked past Cicely's body.

She lay there, blue eyes staring impossibly wide. There is never a look of horror on the face of the newly dead, more surprise than anything. As if death had caught them while they weren't looking.

Wanda stared down at the body as we passed it. She whispered, "I never thought she'd die first."

We rounded the corner and came face-to-face with Dominga's monster.

38

The monster stood in the middle of a narrow little hall that seemed to take up most of the back of the house. Many-paned windows lined the wall. And in the middle of those windows was a door. Through the windows I could see black night sky. The door led outside. The only thing standing between us and freedom was the monster.

The only thing, sheesh.

The shambling mound of body parts struggled towards us. Wanda screamed, and I didn't blame her. I raised the Magnum and sighted on the human face in the middle. The shot echoed like captive thunder.

The face exploded in a welter of blood and flesh and bone. The smell was worse. Like rotten fur on the back of my throat. The mouths screamed, an animal howling at its wound. The thing kept coming, but it was hurt. It seemed confused as to what to do now. Had I taken out the dominant brain? Was there a dominant brain? No way to be sure.

I fired three more times, exploding three more heads. The hallway was full of brains and blood and worse. The monster kept coming.

The gun clicked on empty. I threw the gun at it. One clawed hand batted it away. I didn't bother trying the .22. If the Magnum couldn't stop it, the .22 sure as hell couldn't.

We started backing down the hallway. What else could we do? The monster pulled its twisted bulk after us. It was that same sliding sound that had chased Manny and me out of Dominga's basement. I was looking at her caged horror.

The flesh between the different textures of skin, fur, and bone was seamless. No Frankenstein stitches. It was like the different pieces had melted together like wax.

I tripped over Cicely's body, too busy watching the monster to see where my feet were. We sprawled across her body. Wanda screamed.

The monster scrambled forward. Misshapen hands grabbed at my ankles.

I kicked at it, struggling to climb over Cicely's body, away from it. A claw snagged in my jeans and pulled me towards it. It was my turn to scream. What had once been a man's hand and arm wrapped around my ankle.

I grabbed onto Cicely's body. Her flesh was still warm. The monster pulled us both easily. The extra weight didn't slow it down. My hands scrambled at the bare wood floor. Nothing to hold on to.

I stared back at the thing. Eager rotting mouths yawned at me. Broken, discolored teeth, tongues working like putrid snakes in the openings. God!

Wanda grabbed my arm, trying to hold me, but without legs to brace she just succeeded in being pulled closer to the thing. "Let go!" I screamed it at her.

She did, screaming, "Anita!"

I was screaming myself, "No! Stop it! Stop it!" I put everything I had into that yell, not volume, but power. It was just another zombie, that was all. If it wasn't under specific orders, it would listen to me. It was just another zombie. I had to believe that, or die.

"Stop, right now!" My voice broke with the edge of hysteria. I wanted nothing more than just to start screaming and never stop.

The monster froze with my foot halfway to one of its lower mouths. The mismatched eyes stared at me, expectantly.

I swallowed and tried to sound calm, though the zombie wouldn't care. "Release me."

It did.

My heart was threatening to come out my mouth. I lay back on the floor for a second, relearning how to breathe. When I looked up, the monster was still sitting there, waiting. Waiting for orders like a good little zombie.

"Stay here, do not move from this spot," I said.

The eyes just stared at me, obedient as only the dead can be. It would sit there in the hallway until it got specific orders contradicting mine. Thank you, dear God, that a zombie is a zombie is a zombie.

"What's happening?" Wanda asked. Her voice was broken into sobs. She was near hysterics.

I crawled to her. "It's all right. I'll explain later. We have a little time, but we can't waste it. We've got to get out of here."

She nodded, tears sliding down her bruised face.

I helped her up one last time. We limped towards the monster. Wanda shied away from it, pulling on my sore arm.

"It's all right. It won't hurt us, if we hurry." I had no idea how close Dominga was. I didn't want her changing the orders while we were right next to it. We stayed near the wall and squeezed past the thing. Eyes on the back of the body, if it had a back and a front, followed our progress. The smell from the running wounds was nearly overwhelming. But what was a little gagging between friends?

Wanda opened the door to the outside world. Hot summer wind blew our hair into spider silk strands across our faces. It felt wonderful.

Why hadn't Gaynor and the rest come to the rescue? They had to have heard the gunshots and the screaming. The gunshots at least would have brought somebody.

We stumbled down three stone steps to the gravel of a turn around. I stared off into the darkness at hills covered in tall, waving grass and decaying tombstones. The house was the caretaker's house at Burrell Cemetery. I wondered what Gaynor had done to the caretaker.

I started to lead Wanda away from the cemetery towards the distant highway, then stopped. I knew why no one had come now.

The sky was thick and black and so heavy with stars if I'd had a net I could have caught some. There was a high, hot wind blowing against the stars. I couldn't see the moon. Too much starlight. On the hot seeking fingers of the wind I felt it. The pull. Dominga Salvador had completed her spell. I stared off into the rows of headstones and knew I had to go to her. Just as the zombie had had to obey me, I had to obey her. There was no saving throw, no salvaging it. As easy as that I was caught.

39

I stood very still on the gravel. Wanda moved in my arms, turning to look at me. Her face by starlight was incredibly pale. Was mine as pale? Was the shock spread over my face like moonlight? I tried to take a step forward. To carry Wanda to safety. I could not take a step forward. I struggled until my legs were shaking with the effort. I couldn't leave.

"What's the matter? We have to get out of here before Gaynor comes back," Wanda said.

"I know," I said.

"Then what are you doing?"

I swallowed something cold and hard in my throat. My pulse was thudding in my chest. "I can't leave."

"What are you talking about?" There was an edge of hysteria to Wanda's voice.

Hysterics sounded perfect. I promised myself a complete nervous breakdown if we got out of here alive. If I could ever leave. I fought against something that I couldn't see, or touch, but it held me solid. I had to stop or my legs were going to collapse. We had enough problems in that direction already. If I couldn't go forward, maybe, backwards.

I backed up a step, two steps. Yeah, that worked.

"Where are you going?" Wanda asked.

"Into the cemetery," I said.

"Why!"

Good question, but I wasn't sure I could explain it so that Wanda would understand. I didn't understand it myself. How could I explain it to anyone else? I couldn't leave, but did I have to take Wanda back with me? Would the spell allow me to leave her here?

I decided to try. I laid her down on the gravel. Easy, some of my choices were still open.

"Why are you leaving me?" She clutched at me, terrified.

Me, too.

"Make it to the road if you can," I said.

"On my hands?" she asked.

She had a point, but what could I do? "Do you know how to use a gun?"

"No."

Should I leave her the gun, or should I take it with me, and maybe get a chance to kill Dominga? If this worked like ordering a zombie, then I could kill her if she didn't specifically forbid me to do it. Because I still had free will, of a sort. They'd bring me, then send someone back for Wanda. She was to be the sacrifice.

I handed her the .22. I clicked off the safety. "It's loaded and it's ready to fire," I said. "Since you don't know anything about guns, keep it hidden until Enzo or Bruno is right on top of you, then fire point-blank. You can't miss at point-blank range."

"Why are you leaving me?"

"A spell, I think," I said.

Her eyes widened. "What kind of spell?"

"One that allows them to order me to come to them. One that forbids me to leave."

"Oh, God," she said.

"Yeah," I said. I smiled down at her. A reassuring smile that was all lie. "I'll try to come back for you."

She just stared at me, like a kid whose parents left her in the dark before all the monsters were gone.

She clutched the gun in her hands and watched me walk off into the darkness.

The long dry grass hissed against my jeans. The wind blew the grass in pale waves. Tombstones loomed out of the weeds like the backs of small walls, or the humps of sea monsters. I didn't have to think where I was going, my feet seemed to know the way.

Was this how a zombie felt when ordered to come? No, you had to be within hearing distance of a zombie. You couldn't do it from this far away.

Dominga Salvador stood at the crown of a hill. She was highlighted against the moon. It was sinking towards dawn. It was still night, but the end of night. Everything was still velvet, silver, deep pockets of night shadows, but there was the faintest hint of dawn on the hot wind.

If I could delay until dawn, I couldn't raise the zombie. Maybe the compulsion would fade, too. If I was luckier than I deserved.

Dominga was standing inside a dark circle. There was a dead chicken at her feet. She had already made a circle of power. All I had to do was step into it and slaughter a human being. Over my dead body, if necessary.

Harold Gaynor sat in his electric wheelchair on the opposite side of the circle. He was outside of it, safe. Enzo and Bruno stood by him, safe. Only Dominga had risked the circle.

She said, "Where is Wanda?"

I tried to lie, to say she was safe, but truth spilled out of my mouth, "She's down by the house on the gravel."

"Why didn't you bring her?"

"You can only give me one order at a time. You ordered me to come. I came."

"Stubborn, even now, how curious," she said. "Enzo, go fetch the girl. We need her."

Enzo walked away over the dry, rustling grass without a word. I hoped Wanda killed him. I hoped she emptied the gun into him. No, save a few bullets for Bruno.

Dominga had a machete in her right hand. Its edge was black with blood. "Enter the circle, Anita," she said.

I tried to fight it, tried not to do it. I stood there on the verge of the circle, almost swaying. I stepped across. The circle tingled up my spine, but it wasn't closed. I don't know what she'd done to it, but it wasn't closed. The circle looked solid enough but it was still open. Still waiting for the sacrifice.

Shots echoed in the darkness. Dominga jumped. I smiled.

"What was that?"

"I think it was your bodyguard biting the big one," I said.

"What did you do?"

"I gave Wanda a gun."

She slapped me with her empty hand. It wouldn't really have hurt, but she slapped the same cheek Bruno and what's-his-name had hit. I'd been smacked three times in the same place. The bruise was going to be a beaut.

Dominga looked at something behind me and smiled. I knew what it would be before I turned and saw it.

Enzo was carrying Wanda up the hill. Dammit. I'd heard more than one shot. Had she panicked and shot too soon, wasted her ammunition? Damn.

Wanda was screaming and beating her small fists against Enzo's broad back. If we were alive come morning, I would teach Wanda better things to do with her fists. She was crippled, not helpless.

Enzo carried her over the circle. Until it closed everyone could pass over it without breaking the magic. He dropped Wanda to the ground, holding her arms out behind her at a painful angle. She still struggled and screamed. I didn't blame her.

"Get Bruno to hold her still. The death needs to be one blow," I said.

Dominga nodded. "Yes, it does." She motioned for Bruno to enter the circle. He hesitated, but Gaynor told him, "Do what she says."

Bruno didn't hesitate after that. Gaynor was his greenback god. Bruno grabbed one of Wanda's arms. With a man on each arm, and her legs useless, she was still moving too much.

"Kneel and hold her head still," I said.

Enzo dropped first, putting a big hand on the back of Wanda's head. He held her steady. She started to cry. Bruno knelt, putting his free hand on her shoulders to help steady her. It was important for the death to be a single blow.

Dominga was smiling now. She handed me a small brown jar of ointment. It was white and smelled heavily of cloves. I used more rosemary in mine, but cloves were fine.

"How did you know what I needed?"

"I asked Manny to tell me what you used."

"He wouldn't tell you shit."

"He would if I threatened his family." Dominga laughed. "Oh, don't look so sad. He didn't betray you, *chica*. Manuel thought I was merely curious about your powers. I am, you know."

"You'll see soon enough, won't you," I said.

She gave a sort of bow from the neck. "Place the ointment on yourself in the appointed places."

I rubbed ointment on my face. It was cool and waxy. The cloves made it smell like candy. I smeared it on over my heart, under my shirt, both hands. Last the tombstone.

Now all we needed was the sacrifice.

Dominga told me, "Do not move."

I stayed where I was, frozen as if by magic. Was her monster still frozen in the hallway, like I was now?

Dominga laid the machete on the grass near the edge of the circle, then she stepped out of the circle. "Raise the dead, Anita," she said.

"Ask Gaynor one question first, please." That please hurt, but it worked.

She looked at me curiously. "What question?"

"Is this ancestor also a voodoo priest?" I asked.

"What difference does it make?" Gaynor asked.

"You fool," Dominga said. She whirled on him, hands in fists. "That is what went wrong the first time. You made me think it was my powers!"

"What are you babbling about?" he asked.

"When you raise a voodoo priest or an animator, sometimes the magic goes wrong," I said.

"Why?" he asked.

"Your ancestor's magic interfered with my magic," Dominga said. "Are you sure this ancestor had no voodoo?"

"Not to my knowledge," he said.

"Did you know about the first one?" I asked.

"Yes."

"Why didn't you tell me?" Dominga said. Her power blazed around her like a dark nimbus. Would she kill him, or did she want the money more?

"I didn't think it was important."

I think Dominga was grinding her teeth. I didn't blame her. He'd cost her her reputation and a dozen lives. He saw nothing wrong with it. But Dominga didn't strike him dead. Greed wins out.

"Get on with it," Gaynor said. "Or don't you want your money?"

"Do not threaten me!" Dominga said.

Peachy keen, the bad guys were going to fight among themselves.

"I am not threatening you, Señora. I merely will not pay unless this zombie is raised."

Dominga took a deep breath. She literally squared her shoulders and turned back to me. "Do as I ordered, raise the dead."

I opened my mouth to think of some other excuse to delay. Dawn was coming. It had to come.

"No more delays. Raise the dead, Anita, now!" That last word had the tone of a command.

I swallowed hard and walked towards the edge of the circle. I wanted to get out, to leave, but I couldn't. I stood there, leaning against that invisible barrier. It was like beating against a wall that I couldn't feel. I stayed there straining until my entire body trembled. I took a deep shaking breath.

I picked up the machete.

Wanda said, "No, Anita, please, please don't!" She struggled, but she couldn't move. She would be an easy kill. Easier than beheading a chicken with one hand. And I did that almost every night.

I knelt in front of Wanda. Enzo's hand on the back of her head kept her from moving. But she whimpered, a desperate sound low in her throat.

God, help me.

I placed the machete under her neck and told Enzo, "Raise her head up so I can make sure of the kill."

He grabbed a handful of hair and bowed her neck at a painful angle. Her eyes were showing a lot of white. Even by moonlight I could see the pulse in her throat.

I placed the machete back against her neck. Her skin was solid and real under the blade. I raised it just above her flesh, not touching for an instant. I drove the machete straight up into Enzo's throat. The point speared his throat. Blood gushed out in a black wave.

Everyone froze for an instant, but me. I jerked the machete out of Enzo and plunged it into Bruno's gut. His hand with the gun half-drawn fell away. I leaned on the machete and drew it up towards his throat. His insides spilled out in a warm rush.

The smell of fresh death filled the circle. Blood sprayed all over my face, chest, hands, coating me. It was the last step, and the circle closed.

I'd felt a thousand circles close, but nothing like this. The shock of it left me gasping. I couldn't breathe over the rush of power. It was like an electric current was running over my body. My skin ached with it.

Wanda was covered in other people's blood. She was having hysterics in the grass. "Please, please, don't kill me. Don't kill me! Please!"

I didn't have to kill Wanda. Dominga had told me to raise the dead, and I would do just that.

Killing animals never gave me this kind of rush. It felt like my skin was going to crawl off on its own. I shoved the power flowing through me into the ground. But not just into the grave in the circle. I had too much power for just one grave. Too much power for just a handful of graves. I felt the power spreading outward like ripples in a pool. Out and out, until the power was spread thick and clean over the ground. Every grave that I had walked for Dolph. Every grave but the ones with ghosts. Because that was a type of soul magic, and necromancy didn't work around souls.

I felt each grave, each corpse. I felt them coalesce from dust and bone fragments to things that were barely dead at all.

"Arise from your graves all dead within sound of my call. Arise and serve me!" Without naming them all I shouldn't have been able to call a single one from the grave, but the power of two human deaths was too much for the dead to resist.

They rose upward like swimmers through water. The ground rippled underfoot like a horse's skin.

"What are you doing?" Dominga asked.

"Raising the dead," I said. Maybe it showed in my voice. Maybe she felt it. Whatever, she started running towards the circle, but it was too late.

Hands tore through the earth at Dominga's feet. Dead hands grabbed her ankles and sent her sprawling into the long grass. I lost sight of her but I didn't lose control of the zombies. I told them, "Kill her, kill her."

The grass shuddered and surged like water. The sound of muscles pulling away from bone in wet thick pieces filled the night. Bones broke with sharp cracks. Over the sounds of tearing flesh, Dominga shrieked.

There was one last wet sound, thick and full. Dominga's screams broke off abruptly. I felt the dead hands tearing out her throat. Her blood splattered the grass like a black sprinkler.

Her spell shredded on the wind, but I didn't need her urging now. The power had me. I was riding it like a bird on a current of air. It held me, lifted me. It felt solid and insubstantial as air.

The dry sunken earth cracked open over Gaynor's ancestor's grave. A pale hand shot skyward. A second hand came through the crack. The zombie tore the dry earth. I heard other old graves breaking in the still, summer night. It broke its way out of his grave, just like Gaynor had wanted.

Gaynor sat in his wheelchair on the crest of the hill. He was surrounded by the dead. Dozens of zombies in various stages of decay crowded close to him. But I hadn't given the order yet. They wouldn't hurt him unless I told them to.

"Ask him where the treasure is," Gaynor shouted.

I stared at him and every zombie turned with my eyes and stared at him, too. He didn't understand. Gaynor was like a lot of people with money. They mistake money for power. It isn't the same thing at all.

"Kill the man Harold Gaynor." I said it loud enough to carry on the still air.

"I'll give you a million dollars for having raised him. Whether I find the treasure or not," Gaynor said.

"I don't want your money, Gaynor," I said.

The zombies were moving in on every side, slow, hands extended, like every horror movie you've ever seen. Sometimes Hollywood is accurate, whatta ya know.

"Two million, three million!" His voice was breaking with fear. He'd had a better seat for Dominga's death than I had. He knew what was coming. "Four million!"

"Not enough," I said.

"How much?" he shouted. "Name your price!" I couldn't see him now. The zombies hid him from view.

"No money, Gaynor, just you dead, that's enough."

He started screaming, wordlessly. I felt the hands begin to rip at him. Teeth to tear.

Wanda grabbed my legs. "Don't, don't hurt him. Please!"

I just stared at her. I was remembering Benjamin Reynolds's blood-coated teddy bear, the tiny hand with that stupid plastic ring on it, the blood-soaked bedroom, the baby blanket. "He deserves to die," I said. My voice sounded separate from me, distant and echoing. It didn't sound like me at all.

"You can't just murder him," Wanda said.

"Watch me," I said.

She tried to climb my body, but her legs betrayed her and she fell in a heap at my feet, sobbing.

I didn't understand how Wanda could beg for his life after what he had done to her. Love, I suppose. In the end she really did love him. And that, perhaps, was the saddest thing of all.

When Gaynor died, I knew it. When pieces of him stained almost every hand and mouth of the dead, they stopped. They turned to me, waiting for new orders. The power was still buoying me up. I wasn't tired. Was there enough to lay them all to rest? I hoped so.

"Go back, all of you, go back to your graves. Rest in the quiet earth. Go back, go back."

They stirred like a wind had blown through them, then one by one they went back to their graves. They lay down on the hard dry earth and the graves just swallowed them whole. It was like magic quicksand. The earth shuddered underfoot like a sleeper moving to a more comfortable position.

Some of the corpses had been as old as Gaynor's ancestor, which meant that I didn't need a human death to raise one three-hundred-year-old corpse. Bert was going to be pleased. Human deaths seemed to be cumulative. Two human deaths and I had emptied a cemetery. It wasn't possible. But I'd done it anyway. Whatta ya know?

The first light of dawn passed like milk on the eastern sky. The wind died with the light. Wanda knelt in the bloody grass, crying. I knelt beside her.

She jerked back at my touch. I guess I couldn't blame her, but it bothered me anyway.

"We have to get out of here. You need a doctor," I said.

She stared up at me. "What are you?"

Today for the first time I didn't know how to answer that question. Human didn't seem to cover it. "I'm an animator," I said finally.

She just kept staring at me. I wouldn't have believed me either. But she let me help her up. I guess that was something.

But she kept looking at me out of the edge of her eyes. Wanda considered me one of the monsters. She may have been right.

Wanda gasped, eyes wide.

I turned, too slowly. Was it the monster?

Jean-Claude stepped out of the shadows.

I didn't breathe for a moment. It was so unexpected.

"What are you doing here?" I asked.

"Your power called to me, *ma petite.* No dead in the city could fail to feel your power tonight. And I am the city, so I came to investigate."

"How long have you been here?"

"I saw you kill the men. I saw you raise the graveyard."

"Did it ever occur to you to help me?"

"You did not need any help." He smiled, barely visible in the moonlight. "Besides, would it not have been tempting to rend me to pieces, as well?"

"You can't possibly be afraid of me," I said.

He spread his hands wide.

"You're afraid of your human servant? Little ol' *moi*?"

"Not afraid, *ma petite,* but cautious."

He was afraid of me. It almost made some of this shit worthwhile.

I carried Wanda down the hill. She wouldn't let Jean-Claude touch her. A choice of monsters.

40

Dominga Salvador missed her court date. Fancy that. Dolph had searched for me that night, after he discovered that Dominga had made bail. He had found my apartment empty. My answers about where I had gone didn't satisfy him, but he let it go. What else could he do?

They found Gaynor's wheelchair, but no trace of him. It's one of those mysteries to tell around campfires. The empty, blood-coated wheelchair in the middle of the cemetery. They did find body parts in the caretaker's house: animal and human. Only Dominga's power had held the thing together. When she died, it died. Thank goodness. Theory was that the monster got Gaynor. Where the monster came from no one seemed to know. I was called in to explain the body parts, that's how the police knew they'd once been attached.

Irving wanted to know what I really knew about Gaynor's vanishing act. I just smiled and played inscrutable. Irving didn't believe me, but all he had were suspicions. Suspicions aren't a news story.

Wanda is waiting tables downtown. Jean-Claude offered her a job at The Laughing Corpse. She declined, not politely. She'd saved quite a bit of money from her "business." I don't know if she'll make it or not, but with Gaynor gone, she seems free to try. She was a junkie whose drug of choice was dead. It was better than rehab.

By Catherine's wedding the bullet wound was just a bandage on my arm. The bruises on my face and neck had turned that sickly shade of greenish-yellow. It clashed with the pink dress. I gave Catherine the option of me not being in the wedding. The wedding coordinator was all for that, but Catherine wouldn't hear of it. The wedding coordinator applied makeup to the bruises and saved the day.

I have a picture of me standing in that awful dress with Catherine's arm around me. We're both smiling. Friendship is strange stuff.

Jean-Claude sent me a dozen white roses in the hospital. The card read, "Come to the ballet with me. Not as my servant, but as my guest."

I didn't go to the ballet. I had enough problems without dating the Master of the City.

I had performed human sacrifice, and it had felt good. The rush of power was like the memory of painful sex. Part of you wanted to do it again. Maybe Dominga Salvador was right. Maybe power talks to everyone, even me.

I am an animator. I am the Executioner. But now I know I'm something else. The one thing my Grandmother Flores feared most. I am a necromancer. The dead are my specialty.

CIRCUS
OF THE
DAMNED

To Ginjer Buchanan, our editor,
whose faith in Anita and patience with me
has been most appreciated.

Acknowledgments

To the usual suspects: my husband, Gary, and the alternate historians M. C. Sumner, Deborah Millitello, Marella Sands, and Robert K. Sheaff. Good luck in the new house, Bob. We'll miss you much.

1

There was dried chicken blood imbedded under my fingernails. When you raise the dead for a living, you have to spill a little blood. It clung in flaking patches to my face and hands. I'd tried to clean the worst of it off before coming to this meeting, but some things only a shower would fix. I sipped coffee from a personalized mug that said, "Piss me off, pay the consequences," and stared at the two men sitting across from me.

Mr. Jeremy Ruebens was short, dark, and grumpy. I'd never seen him when he wasn't either frowning, or shouting. His small features were clustered in the middle of his face as if some giant hand had mashed them together before the clay had dried. His hands smoothed over the lapel of his coat, the dark blue tie, tie clip, white shirt collar. His hands folded in his lap for a second, then began their dance again, coat, tie, tie clip, collar, lap. I figured I could stand to watch him fidget maybe five more times before I screamed for mercy and promised him anything he wanted.

The second man was Karl Inger. I'd never met him before. He was a few inches over six feet. Standing, he had towered over Ruebens and me. A wavy mass of short-cut red hair graced a large face. He had honest-to-god muttonchop sideburns that grew into one of the fullest mustaches I'd ever seen. Everything was neatly trimmed except for his unruly hair. Maybe he was having a bad hair day.

Ruebens's hands were making their endless dance for the fourth time. Four was my limit.

I wanted to go around the desk, grab his hands, and yell, "Stop that!" But I figured that was a little rude, even for me. "I don't remember you being this twitchy, Ruebens," I said.

He glanced at me. "Twitchy?"

I motioned at his hands, making their endless circuit. He frowned and placed his hands on top of his thighs. They remained there, motionless. Self-control at its best.

"I am not twitchy, Miss Blake."

"It's Ms. Blake. And why are you so nervous, Mr. Ruebens?" I sipped my coffee.

"I am not accustomed to asking help from people like you."

"People like me?" I made it a question.

He cleared his throat sharply. "You know what I mean."

"No, Mr. Ruebens, I don't."

"Well, a zombie queen . . ." He stopped in mid-sentence. I was getting pissed, and it must have shown on my face. "No offense," he said softly.

"If you came here to call me names, get the hell out of my office. If you have real business, state it, then get the hell out of my office."

Ruebens stood up. "I told you she wouldn't help us."

"Help you do what? You haven't told me a damn thing," I said.

"Perhaps we should just tell her why we have come," Inger said. His voice was a deep, rumbling bass, pleasant.

Ruebens drew a deep breath and let it out through his nose. "Very well." He sat back down in his chair. "The last time we met, I was a member of Humans Against Vampires."

I nodded encouragingly and sipped my coffee.

"I have since started a new group, Humans First. We have the same goals as HAV, but our methods are more direct."

I stared at him. HAV's main goal was to make vampires illegal again, so they could be hunted down like animals. It worked for me. I used to be a vampire slayer, hunter, whatever. Now I was a vampire executioner. I had to have a death warrant to kill a specific vampire, or it was murder. To get a warrant, you had to prove the vampire was a danger to society, which meant you had to wait for the vampire to kill people. The lowest kill was five humans, the highest was twenty-three. That was a lot of dead bodies. In the good ol' days you could just kill a vampire on sight.

"What exactly does 'more direct methods' mean?"

"You know what it means," Ruebens said.

"No," I said, "I don't." I thought I did, but he was going to have to say it out loud.

"HAV has failed to discredit vampires through the media or the political machine. Humans First will settle for destroying them all."

I smiled over my coffee mug. "You mean kill every last vampire in the United States?"

"That is the goal," he said.

"It's murder."

"You have slain vampires. Do you really believe it is murder?"

It was my turn to take a deep breath. A few months ago I would have said no. But now, I just didn't know. "I'm not sure anymore, Mr. Ruebens."

"If the new legislation goes through, Ms. Blake, vampires will be able to vote. Doesn't that frighten you?"

"Yes," I said.

"Then help us."

"Quit dancing around, Ruebens; just tell me what you want."

"Very well, then. We want the daytime resting place of the Master Vampire of the City."

I just looked at him for a few seconds. "Are you serious?"

"I am in deadly earnest, Ms. Blake."

I had to smile. "What makes you think I know the Master's daytime retreat?"

It was Inger who answered. "Ms. Blake, come now. If we can admit to advocating murder, then you can admit to knowing the Master." He smiled ever so gently.

"Tell me where you got the information and maybe I'll confirm it, or maybe I won't."

His smile widened just a bit. "Now who's dancing?"

He had a point. "If I say I know the Master, what then?"

"Give us his daytime resting place," Ruebens said. He was leaning forward, an eager, nearly lustful look on his face. I wasn't flattered. It wasn't me getting his rocks off. It was the thought of staking the Master.

"How do you know the Master is a he?"

"There was an article in the *Post-Dispatch*. It was careful to mention no name, but the creature was clearly male," Ruebens said.

I wondered how Jean-Claude would like being referred as a "creature." Better not to find out. "I give you an address and you go in and what, stake him through the heart?"

Ruebens nodded. Inger smiled.

I shook my head. "I don't think so."

"You refuse to help us?" Ruebens asked.

"No, I simply don't know the daytime resting place." I was relieved to be able to tell the truth.

"You are lying to protect him," Ruebens said. His face was growing darker; deep frown wrinkles showed on his forehead.

"I really don't know, Mr. Ruebens, Mr. Inger. If you want a zombie raised, we can talk; otherwise . . ." I let the sentence trail off and gave them my best professional smile. They didn't seem impressed.

"We consented to meeting you at this ungodly hour, and we are paying a handsome fee for the consultation. I would think the least you could do is be polite."

I wanted to say, "You started it," but that would sound childish. "I offered you coffee. You turned it down."

Ruebens's scowl deepened, little anger lines showing around his eyes. "Do you treat all your . . . customers this way?"

"The last time we met, you called me a zombie-loving bitch. I don't owe you anything."

"You took our money."

"My boss did that."

"We met you here at dawn, Ms. Blake. Surely you can meet us half-way."

I hadn't wanted to meet with Ruebens at all, but after Bert took their money, I was sort of stuck with it. I'd set the meeting at dawn, after my night's work, but before I went to bed. This way I could drive home and get eight hours uninterrupted sleep. Let Ruebens's sleep be interrupted.

"Could you find out the location of the Master's retreat?" Inger asked.

"Probably, but if I did, I wouldn't give it to you."

"Why not?" he asked.

"Because she is in league with him," Ruebens said.

"Hush, Jeremy."

Ruebens opened his mouth to protest, but Inger said, "Please, Jeremy, for the cause."

Ruebens struggled visibly to swallow his anger, but he choked it down. Control.

"Why not, Ms. Blake?" Inger's eyes were very serious, the pleasant sparkle seeping away like melting ice.

"I've killed master vampires before, none of them with a stake."

"How then?"

I smiled. "No, Mr. Inger, if you want lessons in vampire slaying, you're going to have to go elsewhere. Just by answering your questions, I could be charged as an accessory to murder."

"Would you tell us if we had a better plan?" Inger said.

I thought about that for a minute. Jean-Claude dead, really dead. It would certainly make my life easier, but . . . but.

"I don't know," I said.

"Why not?"

"Because I think he'll kill you. I don't give humans over to the monsters, Mr. Inger, not even people who hate me."

"We don't hate you Ms. Blake."

I motioned with the coffee mug towards Ruebens. "Maybe you don't, but he does."

Ruebens just glared at me. At least he didn't try to deny it.

"If we come up with a better plan, can we talk to you again?" Inger asked.

I stared at Ruebens's angry little eyes. "Sure, why not?"

Inger stood and offered me his hand. "Thank you, Ms. Blake. You have been most helpful."

His hand enveloped mine. He was a large man, but he didn't try using his size to make me feel small. I appreciated that.

"The next time we meet, Anita Blake, you will be more cooperative," Ruebens said.

"That sounded like a threat, Jerry."

Ruebens smiled, a most unpleasant smile. "Humans First believes the end justifies the means, Anita."

I opened my royal purple suit jacket. Inside was a shoulder holster complete with a Browning Hi-Power 9mm. The purple skirt's thin black belt was just sturdy enough to be looped through the shoulder holster. Executive terrorist chic.

"When it comes to survival, Jerry, I believe that, too."

"We have not offered you violence," Inger said.

"No, but ol' Jerry here is thinking about it. I just want him and the rest of your little group to believe I'm serious. Mess with me, and people are going to die."

"There are dozens of us," Ruebens said, "and only one of you."

"Yeah, but who's going to be first in line?" I said.

"Enough of this, Jeremy, Ms. Blake. We didn't come here to threaten you. We came for your help. We will come up with a better plan and talk to you again."

"Don't bring him," I said.

"Of course," Inger said. "Come along, Jeremy." He opened the door. The soft clack of computer keys came from the outer office. "Good-bye Ms. Blake."

"Good-bye, Mr. Inger, it's been really unpleasant."

Ruebens stopped in the doorway and hissed at me, "You are an abomination before God."

"Jesus loves you, too," I said, smiling. He slammed the door behind them. Childish.

I sat on the edge of my desk and waited to make sure they had left before going outside. I didn't think they'd try anything in the parking lot, but I really didn't want to start shooting people. Oh, I would if I had to, but it was better to avoid it. I had hoped flashing the gun would make Ruebens back off. It had just seemed to enrage him. I rotated my neck, trying to ease some of the tension away. It didn't work.

I could go home, shower, and get eight hours uninterrupted sleep. Glorious. My beeper went off. I jumped like I'd been stung. Nervous, me?

I hit the button, and the number that flashed made me groan. It was the police. To be exact, it was the Regional Preternatural Investigation Team. The Spook Squad. They were responsible for all preternatural crime in Missouri. I was their civilian expert on monsters. Bert liked the retainer I got, but better yet, the good publicity.

The beeper went off again. Same number. "Shit," I said it softly. "I heard you the first time, Dolph." I thought about pretending that I'd already gone home, turned off the beeper, and was now unavailable, but I didn't. If Detective Sergeant Rudolf Storr called me at half-past dawn, he needed my expertise. Damn.

I called the number and through a series of relays finally got Dolph's voice. He sounded tinny and faraway. His wife had gotten him a car phone for his birthday. We must have been near the limit of its range. It still beat the heck out of talking to him on the police radio. That always sounded like an alien language.

"Hi, Dolph, what's up?"

"Murder."

"What sort of murder?"

"The kind that needs your expertise," he said.

"It's too damn early in the morning to play twenty questions. Just tell me what's happened."

"You got up on the wrong side of bed this morning, didn't you?"

"I haven't been to bed yet."

"I sympathize, but get your butt out here. It looks like we have a vampire victim on our hands."

I took a deep breath and let it out slowly. "Shit."

"You could say that."

"Give me the address," I said.

He did. It was over the river and through the woods, way to hell and gone in Arnold. My office was just off Olive Boulevard. I had a forty-five-minute drive ahead of me, one way. Yippee.

"I'll be there as soon as I can."

"We'll be waiting," Dolph said, then hung up.

I didn't bother to say good-bye to the dial tone. A vampire victim. I'd never seen a lone kill. They were like potato chips; once the vamp tasted them, he couldn't stop at just one. The trick was, how many people would die before we caught this one?

I didn't want to think about it. I didn't want to drive to Arnold. I didn't want to stare at dead bodies before breakfast. I wanted to go home. But somehow I didn't think Dolph would understand. Police have very little sense of humor when they're working on a murder case. Come to think of it, neither did I.

2

The man's body lay on its back, pale and naked in the weak morning sunlight. Even limp with death his body was good, a lot of weights, maybe jogging. His longish yellow hair mixed with the still-green lawn. The smooth skin of his neck was punctured twice with neat fang marks. The right arm was pierced at the bend of the elbow, where a doctor draws blood. The skin of the left wrist was shredded, like an animal had gnawed it. White bone gleamed in the fragile light.

I had measured the bite marks with my trusty tape measure. They were different sizes. At least three different vamps, but I would have bet everything I owned that it was five different vampires. A master and his pack, or flock, or whatever the hell you call a group of vampires.

The grass was wet from early morning mist. The moisture soaked through the knees of the coveralls I had put on to protect my suit. Black Nikes and surgical gloves completed my crime-scene kit. I used to wear white Nikes, but they showed blood too easily.

I said a silent apology for what I had to do, then spread the corpse's legs apart. The legs moved easily, no rigor. I was betting that he hadn't been dead eight hours, not enough time for rigor mortis to set in. Semen had dried on his shriveled privates. One last joy before dying. The vamps hadn't cleaned him off. On the inside of his thigh, close to the groin, were more fang marks. They weren't as savage as the wrist wound, but they weren't neat either.

There was no blood on the skin around the wounds, not even the wrist wound. Had they cleaned the blood off? Wherever he was killed, there was a lot of blood. They'd never be able to clean it all up. If we could find where he died, we'd have all sorts of clues. But in the neatly clipped lawn in the middle of a very ordinary neighborhood, there were no clues. I was betting on that. They'd dumped the body in a place as sterile and unhelpful as the dark side of the moon.

Mist floated over the small residential neighborhood like waiting ghosts. The mist was so low to the ground that it was like walking through sheets of drizzling rain. Tiny beads of moisture clung to the body where the mist had condensed. Beads collected in my hair like silver pearls.

I stood in the front yard of a small, lime-green house with white trim. A chain-link fence peeked around one side encircling a roomy backyard. It was October, and the grass was still green. The top of a sugar maple loomed over the house. Its leaves were that brilliant orangey-yellow that is peculiar to sugar maples, as if their leaves were carved from flame. The mist helped the illusion, and the colors seemed to bleed on the wet air.

All down the street were other small houses with autumn-bright trees and bright green lawns. It was still early enough that most people hadn't gone to work yet, or school, or wherever. There was quite a crowd being held back by the uniform officers. They had hammered stakes into the ground to hold the yellow Do-Not-Cross tape. The crowd pressed as close to the tape as they dared. A boy of about twelve had managed to push his way to the front. He stared at the dead man with huge brown eyes, his mouth open in a little "wow" of excitement. God, where were his parents? Probably gawking at the corpse, too.

The corpse was paper-white. Blood always pools to the lowest point of the body. In this case dark, purplish bruising should have set in at buttocks, arms, legs, the entire back of his body. There were no marks. He hadn't had enough blood in him to cause lividity marks. Whoever had murdered him had drained him completely. Good to the last drop? I fought the urge to smile and lost. If you spend a lot of time staring at corpses, you get a peculiar sense of humor. You have to, or you will go stark raving mad.

"What's so funny?" a voice asked.

I jumped and whirled. "God, Zerbrowski, don't sneak up on me like that."

"Is the heap big vampire slayer jumping at shadows?" He grinned at me. His unruly brown hair stuck up in three separate tufts like he'd forgotten to comb it. His tie was at half-mast over a pale blue shirt that looked suspiciously like a pajama top. The brown suit jacket and pants clashed with the top.

"Nice pajamas."

He shrugged. "I've got a pair with little choo-choos on them. Katie thinks they're sexy."

"Your wife got a thing for trains?" I asked.

His grin widened. "If I'm wearing 'em."

I shook my head. "I knew you were perverted, Zerbrowski, but little kids' jammies, that's truly sick."

"Thank you." He glanced down at the body, still smiling. The smile faded. "What do you think of this?" He nodded towards the dead man.

"Where's Dolph?"

"In the house with the lady who found the body." He plunged his hands into the pockets of his pants and rocked on his heels. "She's taking it pretty hard. Probably the first corpse she's seen outside of a funeral."

"That's the way most normal folks see dead people, Zerbrowski."

He rocked forward hard on the balls of his feet, coming to a standstill. "Wouldn't it be nice to be normal?"

"Sometimes," I said.

He grinned. "Yeah, I know what you mean." He got a notebook out of his jacket pocket that looked as if someone had crumbled it in their fist.

"Geez, Zerbrowski."

"Hey, it's still paper." He tried smoothing the notebook flat, but finally gave up. He posed, pen over the wrinkled paper. "Enlighten me, oh preternatural expert."

"Am I going to have to repeat this to Dolph? I'd like to just do this once and go home to bed."

"Hey, me too. Why do you think I'm wearing my jammies?"

"I just thought it was a daring fashion statement." He looked at me. "Mm-huh."

Dolph walked out of the house. The door looked too small to hold him. He's six-nine and built bulky like a wrestler. His black hair was buzzed close to his head, leaving his ears stranded on either side of his face. But Dolph didn't care much for fashion. His tie was tight against the collar of his white dress shirt. He had to have been pulled out of bed just like Zerbrowski, but he looked neat and tidy and businesslike. It never mattered what hour you called Dolph, he was always ready to do his job. A professional cop down to his socks.

So why was Dolph heading up the most unpopular special task force in St. Louis? Punishment for something, that much I was sure of, but I'd never asked what. I probably never would. It was his business. If he wanted me to know, he'd tell me.

The squad had originally been a pacifier for the liberals. See, we're doing something about supernatural crime. But Dolph had taken his job and his men seriously. They had solved more supernatural crime in the last two years than any other group of policemen in the country. He had been invited to give talks to other police forces. They had even been loaned out to neighboring states twice.

"Well, Anita, let's have it."

That's Dolph; no preliminaries. "Gee, Dolph, it's nice to see you too."

He just looked at me.

"Okay, okay." I knelt on the far side of the body so I could point as I talked. Nothing like a visual aid to get your point across. "Just measuring shows that at least three different vampires fed on the man."

"But?" Dolph said.

He's quick. "But I think that every wound is a different vampire."

"Vampires don't hunt in packs."

"Usually they are solitary hunters, but not always."

"What causes them to hunt in packs?" he asked.

"Only two reasons that I've ever come across: first, one is the new dead and an older vampire is teaching the ropes, but that's just two pairs of fangs, not five; second, a master vampire is controlling them, and he's gone rogue."

"Explain."

"A master vampire has nearly absolute control over his or her flock. Some masters use a group kill to solidify the pack, but they wouldn't dump the body here. They'd hide it where the police would never find it."

"But the body's here," Zerbrowski said, "out in plain sight."

"Exactly; only a master that's gone crazy would dump a body like this. Most masters even before vampires were legally alive wouldn't flaunt a kill like this. It attracts attention, usually attention with a stake in one hand and a cross in the other. Even now, if we could trace the kill to the vampires that did it, we could get a warrant and kill them." I shook my head. "Slaughter like this is bad for business, and whatever else vampires are, they're practical. You don't stay alive and hidden for centuries unless you're discreet and ruthless."

"Why ruthless?" Dolph said.

I stared up at him. "It's utterly practical. Someone discovers your secret, you kill them, or make them one of your . . . children. Good business practices, Dolph, nothing more."

"Like the mob," Zerbrowski said.

"Yeah."

"What if they panicked?" Zerbrowski asked. "It was almost dawn."

"When did the woman find the body?"

Dolph checked his notebook. "Five-thirty."

"It's still hours until dawn. They didn't panic."

"If we've got a crazy master vampire, what exactly does that mean?"

"It means they'll kill more people faster. They may need blood every night to support five vampires."

"A fresh body every night?" Zerbrowski made it a question.

I just nodded.

"Jesus," he said.

"Yeah."

Dolph was silent, staring down at the dead man. "What can we do?"

"I should be able to raise the corpse as a zombie."

"I thought you couldn't raise a vampire victim as a zombie," Dolph said.

"If the corpse is going to rise as a vampire, you can't." I shrugged. "The whatever that makes a vampire interferes with a raising. I can't raise a body that is already set to rise as a vamp."

"But this one won't rise," Dolph said, "so you can raise it."

I nodded.

"Why won't this vampire victim rise?"

"He was killed by more than one vampire, in a mass feeding. For a corpse to rise as a vampire, you have to have just one vampire feeding over a space of several days. Three bites ending with death, and you get a vampire.

If every vampire victim could come back, we'd be up to our butts in bloodsuckers.''

"But this victim can come back as a zombie?'' Dolph said.

I nodded.

"When can you do the animating?''

"Three nights from tonight, or really two. Tonight counts as one night.''

"What time?''

"I'll have to check my schedule at work. I'll call you with a time.''

"Just raise the murder victim and ask who killed him. I like it,'' Zerbrowski said.

"It's not that easy,'' I said. "You know how confused witnesses to violent crimes are. Have three people see the same crime and you get three different heights, different hair colors.''

"Yeah, yeah, witness testimony is a bitch,'' Zerbrowski said.

"Go on, Anita,'' Dolph said. It was his way of saying, "Zerbrowski, shut up.'' Zerbrowski shut up.

"A person who died as the victim of a violent crime is more confused. Scared shitless, so that sometimes they don't remember very clearly.''

"But they were there,'' Zerbrowski said. He looked outraged.

"Zerbrowski, let her finish.''

Zerbrowski pantomimed locking his lips with a key and throwing the key away. Dolph frowned. I coughed into my hand to hide the smile. Mustn't encourage Zerbrowski.

"What I'm saying is that I can raise the victim from the dead, but we may not get as much information as you'd expect. The memories we do get will be confused, painful, but it might narrow the field down as to which master vampire led the group.''

"Explain,'' Dolph said.

"There are only supposed to be two master vampires in St. Louis right now. Malcolm, the undead Billy Graham, and the Master of the City. There's always the possibility we've got someone new in town, but the Master of the City should be able to police that.''

"We'll take the head of the Church of Eternal Life,'' Dolph said.

"I'll take the Master,'' I said.

"Take one of us with you for backup.''

I shook my head. "Can't; if he knew I let the cops know who he was, he'd kill us both.''

"How dangerous is it for you to do this?'' Dolph asked.

What was I supposed to say? Very? Or did I tell them the Master had the hots for me, so I'd probably be okay? Neither. "I'll be all right.''

He stared at me, eyes very serious.

"Besides, what choice do we have?'' I motioned at the corpse. "We'll get one of these a night until we find the vampires responsible. One of us has to talk to the Master. He won't talk to police, but he will talk to me.''

Dolph took a deep breath and let it out. He nodded. He knew I was right. "When can you do it?''

"Tomorrow night, if I can talk Bert into giving my zombie appointments to someone else."

"You're that sure the Master will talk to you?"

"Yeah." The problem with Jean-Claude was not getting to see him, it was avoiding him. But Dolph didn't know that, and if he did, he might have insisted on going with me. And gotten us both killed.

"Do it," he said. "Let me know what you find out."

"Will do," I said. I stood up, facing him over the bloodless corpse.

"Watch your back," he said.

"Always."

"If the Master eats you, can I have your nifty coveralls?" Zerbrowski asked.

"Buy your own, you cheap bastard."

"I'd rather have the ones that have enveloped your luscious body."

"Give it a rest, Zerbrowski. I'm not into little choo-choos."

"What the hell do trains have to do with anything?" Dolph asked.

Zerbrowski and I looked at each other. We started giggling and couldn't stop. I could claim sleep deprivation. I'd been on my feet for fourteen straight hours, raising the dead and talking to right-wing fruitcakes. The vampire victim was a perfect end to a perfect night. I had a right to be hysterical with laughter. I don't know what Zerbrowski's excuse was.

3

There are a handful of days in October that are nearly perfect. The sky stretches overhead in a clear blue, so deep and perfect that it makes everything else prettier. The trees along the highway are crimson, gold, rust, burgundy, orange. Every color is neon-bright, pulsing in the heavy golden sunlight. The air is cool but not cold; by noon you can wear just a light jacket. It was weather for taking long walks in the woods with someone you wanted to hold hands with. Since I didn't have anyone like that, I was just hoping for a free weekend to go away by myself. The chances of that were slim and none.

October is a big month for raising the dead. Everyone thinks that Halloween is the perfect season for raising zombies. It isn't. Darkness is the only requirement. But everyone wants an appointment for midnight on Halloween. They think spending All Hallows Eve in a cemetery killing chickens and watching zombies crawl out of the ground is great entertainment. I could probably sell tickets.

I was averaging five zombies a night. It was one more zombie than anyone else was doing in one night. I should never have told Bert that four zombies didn't wipe me out. My own fault for being too damn truthful. Of course, truth was, five didn't wipe me out either, but I was damned if I'd tell Bert.

Speaking of my boss, I had to call him when I got home. He was going to love me asking for the night off. It made me smile just thinking about it. Any day I could yank Bert's chain was a good day.

I pulled into my apartment complex at nearly one in the afternoon. All I wanted was a quick shower and seven hours of sleep. I had given up on eight hours; it was too late in the day for that. I had to see Jean-Claude tonight. Joy. But he was the Master Vampire of the City. If there was another master vampire around, he'd know it. I think they can smell each other. Of course, if Jean-Claude had committed the murder, he wasn't likely to confess.

But I didn't really believe he'd done it. He was much too good a business vampire to get messy. He was the only master vampire I'd ever met who wasn't crazy in some way: psychotic, or sociopath, take your pick.

All right, all right, Malcolm wasn't crazy, but I didn't approve of his methods. He headed up the fastest-growing church in America today. The Church of Eternal Life offered exactly that. No leap of faith, no uncertainty, just a guarantee. You could become a vampire and live forever, unless someone like me killed you, or you got caught in a fire, or hit by a bus. I wasn't sure about the bus part, but I'd always wondered. Surely there must be something massive enough to damage even a vampire beyond healing. I hoped someday to test the theory.

I climbed the stairs slowly. My body felt heavy. My eyes burned with the need to sleep. It was three days before Halloween, and the month couldn't end too soon for me. Business would start dropping off before Thanksgiving. The decline would continue until after New Year's, then it'd start picking up. I prayed for a freak snowstorm. Business drops off if the snow is bad. People seem to think we can't raise the dead in deep snow. We can, but don't tell anyone. I need the break.

The hallway was full of the quiet noises of my day-living neighbors. I was fishing my keys out of my coat pocket when the door opposite mine opened. Mrs. Pringle stepped out. She was tall, slender, thinning with age, white hair done in a small bun at the back of her head. The hair was perfectly white. Mrs. Pringle didn't bother with dyes or makeup. She was over sixty-five and didn't care who knew it.

Custard, her Pomeranian, pranced at the end of his leash. He was a round ball of golden fur with little fox ears. Most cats outweighed him, but he's one of those little dogs with a big-dog attitude. In a past life he was a Great Dane.

"Hello, Anita." Mrs. Pringle smiled as she said it. "You're not just getting in from work, are you?" Her pale eyes were disapproving.

I smiled. "Yeah, I had an . . . emergency come up."

She raised an eyebrow, probably wondering what an animator would have for an emergency, but she was too polite to ask. "You don't take good enough care of yourself, Anita. If you keep burning the candle at both ends, you'll be worn out by the time you're my age."

"Probably," I said.

Custard yapped at me. I did not smile at him. I don't believe in encouraging small, pushy dogs. With that peculiar doggy sense, he knew I didn't like him, and he was determined to win me over.

"I saw the painters were in your apartment last week. Is it all repaired?"

I nodded. "Yeah, all the bullet holes have been patched up and painted over."

"I'm really sorry I wasn't home to offer you my apartment. Mr. Giovoni says you had to go to a hotel."

"Yeah."

"I don't understand why one of the other neighbors didn't offer you a couch for the night."

I smiled. I understood. Two months ago I had slaughtered two killer zombies in my apartment and had a police shootout. The walls and one window had been damaged. Some of the bullets had gone through the walls into other apartments. No one else had been hurt, but none of the neighbors wanted anything to do with me now. I suspected strongly that when my two-year lease was up, I would be asked to leave. I guess I couldn't blame them.

"I heard you were wounded."

I nodded. "Just barely." I didn't bother telling her that the bullet wound hadn't been from the shootout. The mistress of a very bad man had shot me in the right arm. It was healed to a smooth, shiny scar, still a little pink.

"How did your visit with your daughter go?" I asked.

Mrs. Pringle's face went all shiny with a smile. "Oh, wonderful. My last and newest grandchild is perfect. I'll show you pictures later, after you've had some sleep." That disapproving look was back in her eyes. Her teacher face. The one that could make you squirm from ten paces, even if you were innocent. And I hadn't been innocent for years.

I held up my hands. "I give up. I'll go to bed. I promise."

"You see you do," she said. "Come along, Custard, we have to go out for our afternoon stroll." The tiny dog danced at the end of his leash, straining forward like a miniature sled dog.

Mrs. Pringle let three pounds of fluffy fur drag her down the hall. I shook my head. Letting a fuzzball boss you around was not my idea of dog ownership. If I ever had another dog, I'd be boss, or one of us wouldn't survive. It was the principle of the thing.

I opened the door and stepped inside the hush of my apartment. The heater whirred, hot air hissing out of the vents. The aquarium clicked on. The sounds of emptiness. It was wonderful.

The new paint was the same off-white as the old. The carpet was grey; couch and matching chair, white. The kitchenette was pale wood with white and gold linoleum. The two-seater breakfast table in the kitchen was a little darker than the cabinets. A modern print was the only color on the white walls.

The space where most people would have put a full-size kitchen set had the thirty-gallon aquarium against the wall, a stereo catty-corner from it.

Heavy white drapes hid the windows and turned the golden sunlight to a pale twilight. When you sleep during the day, you have to have good curtains.

I flung my coat on the couch, kicked my dress shoes off, and just enjoyed the feeling of my bare feet on the carpet. The panty hose came off next, to lie wrinkled and forlorn by the shoes. Barefoot, I padded over to the fish tank.

The angelfish rose to the surface begging for food. The fish are all wider than my outspread hand. They are the biggest angels I've ever seen outside of the pet store I bought them from. The store had breeding angelfish that were nearly a foot long.

I stripped off the shoulder holster and put the Browning in its second home, a specially made holster in the headboard. If any bad guys snuck up on me, I could pull it and shoot them. That was the idea, anyway. So far it had worked.

When the dry-clean-only suit and blouse were hung neatly in the closet, I flopped down on the bed in my bra and undies, still wearing the silver cross that I wore even in the shower. Never know when a pesky vampire is going to try to take a bite out of you. Always prepared, that was my motto, or was that the Boy Scouts? I shrugged and dialed work. Mary, our daytime secretary, answered on the second ring. "Animators, Incorporated. How may we serve you?"

"Hi, Mary, it's Anita."

"Hi, what's up?"

"I need to talk with Bert."

"He's with a prospective client right now. May I ask what this is pertaining to?"

"Him rescheduling my appointments for tonight."

"Ooh, boy. I'll let you tell him. If he yells at someone, it should be you." She was only half-kidding.

"Fine," I said.

She lowered her voice and whispered, "Client is on her way to the front door. He'll be with you in a jiffy."

"Thanks, Mary."

She put me on hold before I could tell her not to. Muzak seeped out of the phone. It was a butchered version of the Beatles' "Tomorrow." I'd have rather listened to static. Mercifully, Bert came on the line and saved me.

"Anita, what time can you come in today?"

"I can't."

"Can't what?"

"Can't come in today."

"At all?" His voice had risen an octave.

"You got it."

"Why the hell not?" Cursing at me already, a bad sign.

"I got beeped by the police after my morning meeting. I haven't even been to bed yet."

"You can sleep in, don't worry about meeting new clients in the afternoon. Just come in for your appointments tonight."

He was being generous, understanding. Something was wrong.

"I can't make the appointments tonight, either."

"Anita, we're overbooked here. You have five clients tonight. Five!"

"Divide them up among the other animators," I said.

"Everybody is already maxed."

"Listen, Bert, you're the one who said yes to the police. You're the one who put me on retainer to them. You thought it would be great publicity."

"It has been great publicity," he said.

"Yeah, but it's like working two full-time jobs sometimes. I can't do both."

"Then drop the retainer. I had no idea it'd take up this much of your time."

"It's a murder investigation, Bert. I can't drop it."

"Let the police do their own dirty work," he said.

He was a fine one to talk about that. Him with his squeaky-clean fingernails and nice safe office. "They need my expertise and my contacts. Most of the monsters won't talk to the police."

He was quiet on the other end of the phone. His breathing came harsh and angry. "You can't do this to me. We've taken money, signed contracts."

"I asked you to hire extra help months ago."

"I hired John Burke. He's been handling some of your vampire slayings, as well as raising the dead."

"Yeah, John's a big help, but we need more. In fact, I bet he could take at least one of my zombies tonight."

"Raise five in one night?"

"I'm doing it," I said.

"Yes, but John isn't you."

That was almost a compliment. "You have two choices, Bert; either reschedule or delegate them to someone else."

"I am your boss. I could just say come in tonight or you're fired." His voice was firm and matter-of-fact.

I was tired and cold sitting on the bed in my bra and undies. I didn't have time for this. "Fire me."

"You don't mean that," he said.

"Look, Bert, I've been on my feet for over twenty hours. If I don't get some sleep soon, I'm not going to be able to work for anybody."

He was silent for a long time, his breathing soft and regular in my ear. Finally, he said, "All right, you're free for tonight. But you damn well better be back on the job tomorrow."

"I can't promise that, Bert."

"Dammit, Anita, do you want to be fired?"

"This is the best year we've ever had, Bert. Part of that's due to the articles on me in the *Post-Dispatch*."

"They were about zombie rights and that government study you're on. You didn't do them to help promote our business."

"But it worked, didn't it? How many people call up and ask specifically for me? How many people say they've seen me in the paper? How many heard me on the radio? I may be promoting zombie rights, but it's damn good for business. So cut me some slack."

"You don't think I'd do it, do you?" His voice snarled through the phone. He was pissed.

"No, I don't," I said.

His breath was short and harsh. "You damn well better show up tomorrow night, or I'm going to call your bluff.'' He slammed the receiver in my ear. Childish.

I hung up the phone and stared at it. The Resurrection Company in California had made me a handsome offer a few months back. But I really didn't want to move to the west coast, or the east coast for that matter. I liked St. Louis. But Bert was going to have to break down and hire more help. I couldn't keep this schedule up. Sure, it'd get better after October, but I just seemed to be going from one emergency to another for this entire year.

I had been stabbed, beaten, shot, strangled, and vampire-bit in the space of four months. There comes a point where you just have too many things happening too close together. I had battle fatigue.

I left a message on my judo instructor's machine. I went twice a week at four o'clock, but I wasn't going to make it today. Three hours of sleep just wouldn't have been enough.

I dialed the number for Guilty Pleasures. It was a vampire strip joint. Chippendale's with fangs. Jean-Claude owned and managed it. Jean-Claude's voice came over the line, soft as silk, caressing down my spine even though I knew it was a recording. "You have reached Guilty Pleasures. I would love to make your darkest fantasy come true. Leave a message, and I will get back to you.''

I waited for the beep. "Jean-Claude, this is Anita Blake. I need to see you tonight. It's important. Call me back with a time and place.'' I gave him my home number, then hesitated, listening to the tape scratch. "Thanks.'' I hung up, and that was that.

He'd either call back or he wouldn't. He probably would. The question was, did I want him to? No. No, I didn't, but for the police, for all those poor people who would die, I had to try. But for me personally, going to the Master was not a good idea.

Jean-Claude had marked me twice already. Two more marks and I would be his human servant. Did I mention that neither mark was voluntary? His servant for eternity. Didn't sound like a good idea to me. He seemed to lust after my body, too, but that was secondary. I could have handled it if all he wanted was physical, but he was after my soul. That he could not have.

I had managed to avoid him for the last two months. Now I was willingly putting myself within reach again. Stupid. But I remembered the nameless man's hair, soft and mingling with the still-green lawn. The fang marks, the paper-white skin, the fragility of his nude body covered with dew. There would be more bodies to look at, unless we were quick. And quick meant Jean-Claude.

Visions of vampire victims danced in my head. And every one of them was partially my fault, because I was too chickenshit to go see the Master. If I could stop the killings now, with just one dead, I'd risk my soul daily. Guilt is a wonderful motivator.

4

I was swimming in black water, strong smooth strokes. The moon hung huge and shining, making a silver pathway on the lake. There was a black fringe of trees. I was almost to shore. The water was so warm, warm as blood. In that moment I knew why the waters were black. It was blood. I was swimming in a lake of fresh, warm blood.

I woke instantly, gasping for breath. Eyes searching the darkness for . . . what? Something that had caressed my leg just before I woke. Something that lived in blood and darkness.

The phone shrilled, and I had to swallow a scream. I wasn't usually this nervous. It was just a nightmare, dammit. Just a dream.

I fumbled for the receiver and managed, "Yeah."

"Anita?" The voice sounded hesitant, as if its owner might hang up.

"Who is this?"

"It's Willie, Willie McCoy." Even as he said the name, the rhythm of the voice sounded familiar. The phone made it distant and charged with an electric hiss, but I recognized it.

"Willie, how are you?" The minute I said it, I wished I hadn't. Willie was a vampire now; how okay could a dead man be?

"I'm doing real well." His voice had a happy lilt to it. He was pleased that I asked.

I sighed. Truth was, I liked Willie. I wasn't supposed to like vampires. Any vampire, not even if I'd known him when he was alive.

"How ya doing yourself?"

"Okay, what's up?"

"Jean-Claude got your message. He says ta meet him at the Circus of the Damned at eight o'clock tonight."

"The Circus? What's he doing over there?"

"He owns it now. Ya didn't know?"

I shook my head, realized he couldn't see it, and said, "No, I didn't."

"He says to meet 'im in a show that starts at eight."

"Which show?"

"He said you'd know which one."

"Well, isn't that cryptic," I said.

"Hey, Anita, I just do what I'm told. Ya know how it is?"

I did know. Jean-Claude owned Willie lock, stock, and soul. "It's okay, Willie, it's not your fault."

"Thanks, Anita." His voice sounded cheerful, like a puppy who expected a kick and got patted instead.

Why had I comforted him? Why did I care whether a vampire got its feelings hurt, or not? Answer: I didn't think of him as a dead man. He was still Willie McCoy with his penchant for loud primary-colored suits, clashing ties, and small, nervous hands. Being dead hadn't changed him that much. I wished it had.

"Tell Jean-Claude I'll be there."

"I will." He was quiet for a minute, his breath soft over the phone. "Watch your back tonight, Anita."

"Do you know something I should know?"

"No, but . . . I don't know."

"What's up, Willie?"

"Nuthin', nuthin'." His voice was high and frightened.

"Am I walking into a trap, Willie?"

"No, no, nuthin' like that." I could almost see his small hands waving in the air. "I swear, Anita, nobody's gunnin' for you."

I let that go. Nobody he knew of was all he could swear to. "Then what are you afraid of, Willie?"

"It's just that there's more vampires around here than usual. Some of 'em ain't too careful who they hurt. That's all."

"Why are there more vampires, Willie? Where did they come from?"

"I don't know and I don't want to know, ya know? I got ta go, Anita." He hung up before I could ask anything else. There had been real fear in his voice. Fear for me, or for himself? Maybe both.

I glanced at the radio clock on my bedstand: 6:35. I had to hurry if I was going to make the appointment. The covers were toasty warm over my legs. All I really wanted to do was cuddle back under the blankets, maybe with a certain stuffed toy penguin I knew. Yeah, hiding sounded good.

I threw back the covers and walked into the bathroom. I hit the light switch, and glowing white light filled the small room. My hair stuck up in all directions, a mass of tight black curls. That'd teach me not to sleep on it wet. I ran a brush through the curls and they loosened slightly, turning into a frothing mass of waves. The curls went all over the place and there wasn't a damn thing I could do with it except wash it and start over. There wasn't time for that.

The black hair made my pale skin look deathly, or maybe it was the overhead lighting. My eyes were so dark brown they looked black. Two glittering holes in the pastiness of my face. I looked like I felt; great.

What do you wear to meet the Master of the City? I chose black jeans, a black sweater with bright geometric designs, black Nikes with blue swooshes, and a blue-and-black sport bag clipped around my waist. Color coordination at its best.

The Browning went into its shoulder holster. I put an extra ammo clip in the sport bag along with credit cards, driver's license, money, and a small hairbrush. I slipped on the short leather jacket I'd bought last year. It was the first one I'd ever tried on that didn't make me look like a gorilla. Most leather jackets were so long-sleeved, I could never wear them. The jacket was black, so Bert wouldn't let me wear it to work.

I only zipped the jacket halfway up, leaving room so I could go for my gun if I needed to. The silver cross swung on its long chain, a warm, solid weight between my breasts. The cross would be more help against vampires than the gun, even with silver-coated bullets.

I hesitated at the door. I hadn't seen Jean-Claude in months. I didn't want to see him now. My dream came back to me. Something that lived in blood and darkness. Why the nightmare? Was it Jean-Claude interfering in my dreams again? He had promised to stay out of my dreams. But was his word worth anything? No answer to that.

I flicked off the apartment lights and closed the door behind me. I rattled it to make sure it was locked, and I had nothing left to do but drive to the Circus of the Damned. No more excuses. No more delays. My stomach was so tight it hurt. So I was afraid; so what? I had to go, and the sooner I left, the sooner I could come home. If only I believed that Jean-Claude would make things that simple. Nothing was ever simple where he was concerned. If I learned anything about the murders tonight, I'd pay for it, but not in money. Jean-Claude seemed to have plenty of that. No, his coin was more painful, more intimate, more bloody.

And I had volunteered to go see him. Stupid, Anita, very stupid.

5

There was a bouquet of spotlights on the top of the Circus of the Damned. The lights slashed the black night like swords. The multicolored lights that spelled the name seemed dimmer with the huge white lights whirling overhead. Demonic clowns danced around the sign in frozen pantomime.

I walked past the huge cloth signs that covered the walls. One picture showed a man that had no skin; See the Skinless Man. A movie version of a voodoo ceremony covered another banner. Zombies writhed from open graves. The zombie banner had changed since last I'd visited the Circus. I didn't know if that was good or bad; probably neither. I didn't give a damn what they did here, except . . . Except it wasn't right to raise the dead just for entertainment.

Who did they have raising zombies for them? I knew it had to be someone new because I had helped kill their last animator. He had been a serial killer and had nearly killed me twice, the second time by ghoul attack, which was a messy way to die. Of course, the way he died had been messy, too, but I wasn't the one who ripped him open. A vampire had done that. You might say I eased him on his way. A mercy killing. Ri-ight.

It was too cold to be standing outside with my jacket half-unzipped. But if I zipped it all the way, I'd never get to my gun in time. Freeze my butt off, or be able to defend myself. The clowns on the roof had fangs. I decided it wasn't that cold after all.

Heat and noise poured out to meet me at the door. Hundreds of bodies pressed together in an enclosed space. The noise of the crowd was like the ocean, murmurous and large, sound without meaning. A crowd is an elemental thing. A word, a glance, and a crowd becomes a mob. A different being entirely from a group.

There were a lot of families. Mom, Dad, the kiddies. The children had balloons tied to their wrists and cotton candy smeared on their faces and hands. It smelled like a traveling carnival: corn dogs, the cinnamon smell of funnel cakes, snow cones, sweat. The only thing missing was the dust. There was always dust in the air at a summer fair. Dry, choking dust kicked into the air by hundreds of feet. Cars driving over the grass until it is grey-coated with dust.

There was no smell of dirt in the air, but there was something else just as singular. The smell of blood. So faint you'd almost think you dreamed it, but it was there. The sweet copper scent of blood mingled with the smells of cooking food and the sharp smell of a snow cone being made. Who needed dust?

I was hungry, and the corn dogs smelled good. Should I eat first or accuse the Master of the City of murder? Choices, choices.

I didn't get to decide. A man stepped out of the crowd. He was only a little taller than me, with curly blond hair that fell past his shoulders. He was wearing a cornflower-blue shirt with the sleeves rolled up, showing firm, muscular forearms. Jeans no tighter than the skin on a grape showed slender hips. He wore black cowboy boots with blue designs tooled into them. His true-blue eyes matched his shirt.

He smiled, flashing small white teeth. "You're Anita Blake, right?"

I didn't know what to say. It isn't always a good idea to admit who you are.

"Jean-Claude told me to wait for you." His voice was soft, hesitant. There was something about him, an almost childlike appeal. Besides I'm a sucker for a pair of pretty eyes.

"What's your name?" I asked. Always like to know who I'm dealing with.

His smile widened. "Stephen; my name is Stephen." He put out his hand, and I took it. His hand was soft but firm, no manual labor but some weightlifting. Not too much. Enough to firm, not explode. Men my size should not do serious weightlifting. It may look okay in a bathing suit, but in regular clothes you look like a deformed dwarf.

"Follow me, please." He sounded like a waiter, but when he walked into the crowd, I followed him.

He led the way towards a huge blue tent. It was like an old-fashioned circus tent. I'd only seen one in pictures or the movies.

There was a man in a striped coat yelling, "Almost showtime, folks! Present your tickets and come inside! See the world's largest cobra! Watch the fearsome serpent be taken through amazing feats by the beautiful snake charmer Shahar. We guarantee it will be a show you will never forget."

There was a line of people giving their tickets to a young woman. She tore them in half and handed back the stubs.

Stephen walked confidently along the line without waiting. We got some dirty looks, but the girl nodded to us. And in we went.

Tiers of bleachers ran up to the top of the tent. It was huge. Nearly all the seats were full. A sold-out show. Wowee.

There was a blue rail that formed a circle in the middle. A one-ring circus.

Stephen scooted past the knees of about a dozen people to a set of steps. Since we were at the bottom, up was the only way to go. I followed Stephen up the concrete stairs. The tent may have looked like a circus tent, but the bleachers and stairs were permanent. A mini-coliseum.

I have bad knees, which means that I can run on a flat surface but put me on a hill, or stairs, and it hurts. So I didn't try to keep up with Stephen's smooth, running glide. I did watch the way his jeans fit his snug little behind, though. Looking for clues.

I unzipped the leather jacket but didn't take it off. My gun would show. Sweat glided down my spine. I was going to melt.

Stephen glanced over his shoulder to see if I was following, or maybe for encouragement. He flashed a smile that was just lips curling back from teeth, almost a snarl.

I stopped in the middle of the steps, watching his lithe form glide upward. There was an energy to Stephen as if the air boiled invisibly around him. A shapeshifter. Some lycanthropes are better than others at hiding what they are. Stephen wasn't that good. Or maybe he just didn't care if I knew. Possible.

Lycanthropy was a disease, like AIDS. It was prejudice to mistrust someone for an accident. Most people survived attacks to become shapeshifters. It wasn't a choice. So why didn't I like Stephen as well, now that I knew? Prejudiced, *moi*?

He waited at the top of the stairs, still pretty as a picture, but the air of energy contained in too small a space, like his motor was on high idle, shimmered around him. What was Jean-Claude doing with a shapeshifter on his payroll? Maybe I could ask him.

I stepped up beside Stephen. There must have been something in my face, because he said, "What's wrong?"

I shook my head. "Nothing."

I don't think he believed me. But he smiled and led me towards a booth that was mostly glass with heavy curtains on the inside hiding whatever lay behind. It looked for all the world like a miniature broadcast booth.

Stephen went to the curtained door and opened it. He held it for me, motioning me to go first.

"No, you first," I said.

"I'm being a gentleman here," he said.

"I don't need or want doors opened for me. I'm quite capable, thank you."

"A feminist, my, my."

Truthfully, I just didn't want ol' Stephen at my back. But if he wanted to think I was a hard-core feminist, let him. It was closer to the truth than a lot of things.

He walked through the door. I glanced back to the ring. It looked smaller from up here. Muscular men dressed in glittering loincloths pulled a cart in on their bare shoulders. There were two things in the cart: a huge woven basket and a dark-skinned woman. She was dressed in Hollywood's version of a dancing girl's outfit. Her thick black hair fell like a cloak, sweeping to her ankles. Slender arms, small, dark hands swept the air in graceful curves. She danced in front of the cart. The costume was fake, but she wasn't. She knew how to dance, not for seduction, though it was that, but for power. Dancing was originally an invocation to some god or other; most people forget that.

Goosebumps prickled up the back of my neck, creeping into my hair. I shivered while I stood there and sweated in the heat. What was in the basket? The barker outside had said a giant cobra, but there was no snake in the world that needed a basket that big. Not even the anaconda, the world's heaviest snake, needed a container over ten feet tall and twenty feet wide.

Something touched my shoulder. I jumped and spun. Stephen was standing nearly touching me, smiling.

I swallowed my pulse back into my throat and glared at him. I make a big deal about not wanting him at my back, then let him sneak up behind me. Real swift, Anita, real swift. Because he'd scared me, I was mad at him. Illogical, but it was better to be mad than scared.

"Jean-Claude's just inside," he said. He smiled, but there was a very human glint of laughter in his blue eyes.

I scowled at him, knowing I was being childish, and not caring. "After you, fur-face."

The laughter slipped away. He was very serious as he stared at me. "How did you know?" His voice was uncertain, fragile. A lot of lycanthropes pride themselves on being able to pass for human.

"It was easy," I said. Which wasn't entirely true, but I wanted to hurt him. Childish, unattractive, honest.

His face suddenly looked very young. His eyes filled with uncertainty and pain.

Shit.

"Look, I've spent a lot of time around shapeshifters. I just know what to look for, okay?" Why did I want to reassure him? Because I knew what it was like to be the outsider. Raising the dead makes a lot of people class me with the monsters. There are even days when I agree with them.

He was still staring at me, with his hurt feelings like an open wound in his eyes. If he started to cry, I was leaving.

He turned without another word and walked through the open door. I stared at the door for a minute. There were gasps, screams from the crowd. I whirled and saw it. It was a snake, but it wasn't just the world's biggest cobra, it was the biggest freaking snake I'd ever seen. Its body was banded in dull greyish black and off-white. The scales gleamed under the lights. The head was at least a foot and a half wide. No snake was that big. It flared its hood, and it was the size of a satellite dish. The snake hissed, flicking out a tongue that was like a black whip.

I'd had a semester of herpetology in college. If the snake had been a mere eight feet or less, I would have called it a banded Egyptian cobra. I couldn't remember the scientific name to save myself.

The woman dropped to the ground in front of the snake, forehead to the ground. A mark of obedience from her to the snake. To her god. Sweet Jesus.

The woman stood and began to dance, and the cobra watched her. She'd made herself a living flute for the nearsighted creature to follow. I didn't want to see what would happen if she messed up. The poison wouldn't have time to kill her. The fangs were so damn big they'd spear her like swords. She'd die of shock and blood loss long before the poison kicked in.

Something was growing in the middle of that ring. Magic crawled up my spine. Was it magic that kept the snake safe, or magic that called it up, or was it the snake itself? Did it have power all its own? I didn't even know what to call it. It looked like a cobra, perhaps the world's biggest, yet I didn't even have a word for it. God with a little "g" would do, but it wasn't accurate.

I shook my head and turned away. I didn't want to see the show. I didn't want to stand there with its magic flowing soft and cold over my skin. If the snake wasn't safe, Jean-Claude would have had it caged, right? Right.

I turned away from the snake charmer and the world's biggest cobra. I wanted to talk to Jean-Claude and get the hell out of here.

The open door was filled with darkness. Vampires didn't need lights. Did lycanthropes? I didn't know. Gee, so much to learn. My jacket was unzipped all the way, the better for a fast draw. Though truthfully, if I needed a fast draw tonight, I was in deep shit.

I took a deep breath and let it out. No sense putting it off. I walked through the door into the waiting darkness without looking back. I didn't want to see what was happening in the ring. Truth was, I didn't want to see what was behind the darkness. Was there another choice? Probably not.

6

The room was like a closet with drapes all the way around. There was no one in the curtained darkness but me. Where had Stephen gone? If he had been a vampire, I would have believed the vanishing act, but lycanthropes don't just turn into thin air. So, there had to be a second door.

If I had built this room, where would I put an inner door? Answer: opposite the first door. I swept the drapes aside. The door was there. Elementary, my dear Watson.

The door was heavy wood with some flowering vine carved into it. The doorknob was white with tiny pink flowers in the center of it. It was an awfully feminine door. Of course, no rules against men liking flowers. None at all. It was a sexist comment. Forget I thought it.

I did not draw my gun. See, I'm not completely paranoid.

I turned the doorknob and swung the door inward. I kept pushing until it was flush against the wall. No one was hiding behind it. Good.

The wallpaper was off-white with thin silver, gold, and copper designs running through it. The effect was vaguely oriental. The carpeting was black. I didn't even know carpet came in that color. A canopy bed took up most of one side of the room. Black, gauzy curtains covered it. Made the bed indistinct, misty, like a dream. There was someone asleep in a nest of black covers and crimson sheets. A line of bare chest showed it was a man, but a wave of brown hair covered his face like a shroud. It all looked faintly unreal, as if he was waiting for movie cameras to roll.

A black couch was against the far wall, with blood-red pillows thrown along it. A matching love seat was against the last wall. Stephen was curled up on the love seat. Jean-Claude sat on one corner of the couch. He wore black jeans tucked into knee-high leather boots, dyed a deep, almost velvet black. His shirt had a high lace collar pinned at the neck by a thumb-size ruby pendant. His black hair was just long enough to curl around the lace.

The sleeves were loose and billowing, tight at the wrists with lace spilling over his hands until only his fingertips showed.

"Where do you get your shirts?" I asked.

He smiled. "Don't you like it?" His hands caressed down his chest, fingertips hesitating over his nipples. It was an invitation. I could touch that smooth white cloth and see if the lace was as soft as it looked.

I shook my head. Mustn't get distracted. I glanced at Jean-Claude. He was staring at me with those midnight blue eyes. His eyelashes were like black lace.

"She wants you, Master," Stephen said. There was laughter in his voice, derision. "I can smell her desire."

Jean-Claude turned just his head, staring at Stephen. "As can I." The words were innocent, but the feeling behind them wasn't. His voice slithered around the room, low and full of a terrible promise.

"I meant no harm, Master, no harm." Stephen looked scared. I didn't blame him.

Jean-Claude turned back to me as if nothing had happened. His face was still pleasantly handsome, interested, amused.

"I don't need your protection."

"Oh, I think you do."

I whirled and found another vampire standing at my back. I hadn't heard the door open.

She smiled at me, without flashing fang. A trick that the older vampires learn. She was tall and slender with dark skin and long ebony hair that swung around her waist. She wore crimson Lycra bike pants that clung so tight, you knew she wasn't wearing underwear. Her top was red silk, loose and blousy, with thin spaghetti straps holding it in place. It looked like the top to slinky pajamas. Red high-heeled sandals and a thin gold chain set with a single diamond completed the outfit. The word that came to mind was "exotic." She glided towards me, smiling.

"Is that a threat?" I asked.

She stopped in front of me. "Not yet." There was a hint of some other language in her voice. Something darker with rolling, sibilant sounds.

"That is enough," Jean-Claude said.

The dark lady twirled around, black hair like a veil behind her. "I don't think so."

"Yasmeen." The one word was low and dark with warning.

Yasmeen laughed, a harsh sound like breaking glass. She stopped directly in front of me, blocking my view of Jean-Claude. Her hand stretched towards me, and I stepped back, out of reach.

She smiled wide enough to show fangs and reached for me again. I stepped back, and she was suddenly on me, faster than I could blink, faster than I could breathe. Her hand gripped my hair, bending my neck backwards. Her fingertips brushed my skull. Her other hand held my chin, fingers digging in like fleshy metal. My face was immobile between her hands, trapped.

Short of taking my gun out and shooting her, there was nothing I could do. And if her movement was any clue, I'd never get the gun out in time.

"I see why you like her. So pretty, so delicate." She half-turned towards Jean-Claude, nearly giving me her back, but still holding my head immobile.

"I never thought you'd take in a human." She made it sound like I was a stray puppy.

Yasmeen turned back to me. I pressed my 9mm into her chest. No matter how fast she was, she would be hurt if I wanted it. I can feel how old a vampire is inside my head. It's part natural ability, and part practice. Yasmeen was old, older than Jean-Claude. I was betting she was over five hundred. If she had been the new dead, high-tech ammo at point-blank range would have shredded her heart, killed her. But over five hundred and a master vampire, it might not kill her. Or then again, it might.

Something flickered over her face; surprise, and maybe just a touch of fear. Her body was statue-still. If she was breathing, I couldn't tell.

My voice sounded strained from the angle she held my neck, but the words were clear. "Very slowly, take your hands away from my face. Put both hands on top of your head and lace your fingers together."

"Jean-Claude, call off your human."

"I'd do what she says, Yasmeen." His voice was pleased. "How many vampires have you killed now, Anita?"

"Eighteen."

Yasmeen's eyes widened just a bit. "I don't believe you."

"Believe this, bitch: I'll pull this trigger and you can kiss your heart good-bye."

"Bullets cannot harm me."

"Silver-plated can. Move off me, now!"

Yasmeen's hand slid away from my hair and jaw.

"Slowly," I said.

She did what I asked. She stood in front of me with her long-fingered hands clasped across her head. I stepped away from her, gun still pointed at her chest.

"Now what?" Yasmeen asked. A smile still curled her lips. Her dark eyes were amused. I didn't like being laughed at, but when tangling with master vampires you let some things slide.

"You can put your hands down," I said.

Yasmeen did, but she continued to stare at me as if I'd sprouted a second head. "Where did you find her, Jean-Claude? The kitten has teeth."

"Tell Yasmeen what the vampires call you, Anita."

It sounded too much like an order, but this didn't seem the time to bitch at him. "The Executioner."

Yasmeen's eyes widened; then she smiled, flashing a lot of fang. "I thought you'd be taller."

"It disappoints me, too, sometimes," I said.

Yasmeen threw back her head and laughed, wild and brittle, with an edge of hysteria. "I like her, Jean-Claude. She's dangerous, like sleeping with a lion."

She glided towards me. I had the gun up and pointed at her. It didn't even slow her down.

"Jean-Claude, tell her I will shoot her if she doesn't back off."

"I promise not to hurt you, Anita. I will be oh so gentle." She swayed over to me, and I wasn't sure what to do. She was playing with me, sadistic but probably not deadly. Could I shoot her for being a pain in the ass? I didn't think so.

"I can taste the heat of your blood, the warmth of your skin on the air like perfume." Her gliding, hip-swinging walk brought her right in front of me. I pointed the gun at her, and she laughed. She pressed her chest against the tip of my gun.

"So soft, wet, but strong." I wasn't sure who she was talking about, her or me. Neither option sounded pleasant. She rubbed her small breasts against the gun, her nipples caressing the gun barrel. "Dainty, but dangerous." The last word was a whispered hiss that flowed over my skin like ice water. She was the first master I'd ever met who had some of Jean-Claude's voice tricks.

I could see her nipples hardening through the thin material of her shirt. Yikes. I pointed the gun at the floor and stepped away from her. "Jesus, are all vampires over two hundred perverts?"

"I am over two hundred," Jean-Claude said.

"I rest my case."

Yasmeen let a warm trickle of laughter spill out of her mouth. The sound caressed my skin like a warm wind. She stalked towards me. I backed up until I hit the wall. She put a hand on either side of the wall near my shoulders and began to lean in like she was doing a pushup. "I'd like to taste her myself."

I shoved the gun into her ribs, too low for her to rub herself against it. "Nobody lays a fang on me," I said.

"Tough girl." She leaned her face over me, lips brushing my forehead. "I like tough girls."

"Jean-Claude, do something with her before one of us gets killed."

Yasmeen pushed away from me, elbows locked, as far away as she could get without moving her hands. Her tongue flicked over her lips, a hint of fang, but mostly wet lips. She leaned back into me, lips half-parted, but she wasn't going for my neck. She was definitely going for my mouth. She didn't want to *taste* me, she wanted to taste me. I couldn't shoot her, not if she just wanted to kiss me. If she'd been a man, I wouldn't have shot her.

Her hair fell forward over my hands, soft like thick silk. Her face was all I could see. Her eyes were a perfect blackness. Her lips hovered just above my mouth. Her breath was warm, and smelled of breath mints, but under the modern smell was something older: the sweet foulness of blood.

"Your breath smells like old blood," I whispered into her mouth.

She whispered back, lips barely caressing my mouth, "I know." Her lips pressed into mine, a gentle kiss. She smiled with our lips still touching.

The door opened, nearly pinning us to the wall. Yasmeen stood up, but kept her hands around my shoulders. We both looked at the door. A woman with nearly white blond hair looked wildly around the room. Her blue eyes widened as she saw us. She screamed, high and wordless, rage-filled.

"Get off of her!"

I frowned up at Yasmeen. "Is she talking to me?"

"Yes." Yasmeen looked amused.

The woman did not. She ran towards us, hands outstretched, fingers curled into claws. Yasmeen caught her in a blurring moment of pure speed. The woman thrashed and struggled, her hands still reaching for me.

"What the hell is going on?" I asked.

"Marguerite is Yasmeen's human servant," Jean-Claude said. "She thinks you may steal Yasmeen away from her."

"I don't want Yasmeen."

Yasmeen shot me a look of pure anger. Had I hurt her feelings? I hoped so.

"Marguerite, look; she's yours, all right?"

The woman screamed at me, wordless and guttural. What might have been a pretty face was screwed up into something bestial. I'd never seen such instant rage. It was frightening even with a loaded gun in my hand.

Yasmeen had to lift the woman off her feet, holding her struggling in mid-air. "I'm afraid, Jean-Claude, that Marguerite is not going to be satisfied unless she answers the challenge."

"What challenge?" I asked.

"You challenged her claim to me."

"Did not," I said.

Yasmeen smiled. The serpent must have smiled at Eve that way: pleasant, amused, dangerous.

"Jean-Claude, I didn't come here for whatever the hell is going on. I don't want any vampire, let alone a female one," I said.

"If you were my human servant, *ma petite*, there would be no challenge, because once one is bound to a master vampire, it is an unbreakable bond."

"Then what is Marguerite worried about?"

"That Yasmeen may take you as a lover. She does that from time to time to drive Marguerite into jealous rages. For some reason I do not understand, Yasmeen enjoys it."

"Oh, yes, I do enjoy it." Yasmeen turned towards me with the woman still clasped in her arms. She was holding the struggling woman easily, no strain. Of course, vampires can bench press Toyotas. What was one medium-size human to that?

"So what exactly does this mean to me personally?"

Jean-Claude smiled, but there was an edge of tiredness to it. Was he bored? Or angry? Or just tired? "You must fight Marguerite. If you win, then Yasmeen is yours. If you lose, Yasmeen is Marguerite's."

"Wait a minute," I said. "What sort of fight, pistols at dawn?"

"No weapons," Yasmeen said. "My Marguerite is not skilled in weapons. I don't want her hurt."

"Then stop tormenting her," I said.

Yasmeen smiled. "It is part of the fun."

"Sadistic bitch," I said.

"Yes, I am."

Jesus, some people you couldn't even insult. "So you want us to fight bare-handed over Yasmeen?" I couldn't believe I was even asking this question.

"Yes, *ma petite*."

I took a deep breath, looked at my gun, looked back at the screaming woman, then holstered my gun. "Is there any way out of this, besides fighting her?"

"If you admit you are my human servant, then there will be no fight. There will be no need for one." Jean-Claude was watching me, studying my face. His eyes were very still.

"You mean this was a setup," I said. The first warm rumblings of anger chased up my gut.

"A setup, *ma petite*? I had no idea Yasmeen would find you so enticing."

"Bullshit!"

"Admit you are my human servant and all ends here."

"And if I don't?"

"Then you fight Marguerite."

"Fine," I said. "Let's do it."

"What would it cost you to admit what is true, Anita?" Jean-Claude asked.

"I am not your human servant. I will never be your human servant. I wish you'd just accept that and leave me the fuck alone."

He frowned. "*Ma petite*, such language."

"Fuck off."

He smiled then. "As you like, *ma petite*." He sat up on the edge of the couch, maybe so he could see better. "Yasmeen, any time you are ready."

"Wait," I said. I took off my jacket and wasn't sure where to lay it.

The man who had been sleeping on the black-canopied bed reached a hand through the black gauze. "I'll hold it for you," he said.

I stared at him for a minute. He was naked from the waist up. His arms, stomach, chest showed signs of weightlifting, just enough, not too much. He either had a perfect tan or was naturally dark complected. Hair fell in a wavy mass around his shoulders. His eyes were brown and very human. That was nice to see.

I handed him my jacket. He smiled, a quick flash of teeth that chased the last signs of sleep from his face. He sat up with the jacket in one hand, arms encircling his knees that were still hidden under the black and red covers. He laid his cheek on his knees and managed to look winsome.

"Are you quite done, *ma petite*?" Jean-Claude's voice was amused, with an edge of laughter that wasn't humor at all. It was mockery. But whether he was mocking me or himself, I couldn't tell.

"I'm ready, I guess," I said.

"Put her down, Yasmeen. Let us see what happens."

I heard Stephen say, "Twenty on Marguerite."

Yasmeen said, "No fair. I can't bet against my own human servant."

"I'll spot you both twenty that Ms. Blake wins." That came from the man in the bed. I had a second to glance at him, to see him smile at me; then Marguerite was coming.

She slapped at my face, and I blocked it with my forearm. She fought like a girl, all open-handed slaps and fingernails. But she was fast, faster than a human. Maybe she got that from being a human servant, I don't know. Her fingernails raked down my face in a sharp, painful line. That was it: no more Ms. Nice Guy.

I held her off with one hand. She dug her teeth into that hand. I hit her with my right fist as hard as I could, turning my body into it. It was a nice solid hit to the solar plexus.

Marguerite stopped biting my hand and bent over, hands covering her stomach. She was gasping for breath. Good.

My left hand had a bloody imprint of her teeth in it. I touched my left cheek and came away with more blood. Damn, that hurt.

Marguerite knelt on the floor, relearning how to breathe. But she was staring up at me. The look in her blue eyes said the fight wasn't over. As soon as she got her breath back, she would start again.

"Stay down, Marguerite, or I'll hurt you."

She shook her head.

"She can't give up, *ma petite*, or you win Yasmeen's body, if not her heart."

"I don't want her body. I don't want anyone's body."

"Now, that is simply not true, *ma petite*," Jean-Claude said.

"Stop calling me *ma petite*."

"You bear two of my marks, Anita. You are halfway to being my human servant. Admit that, and no one else need suffer tonight."

"Yeah, right," I said.

Marguerite was getting to her feet. I didn't want her on her feet. I moved in before she could stand, and foot-swept her legs out from under her. I forced her shoulders backwards at the same time, and I rode her down. I got her right arm in a joint lock. She tried to get up. I increased the pressure, and she lay back down.

"Give up the fight."

"No." It was only the second coherent thing I'd heard her utter.

"I will break your arm."

"Break it, break it! I don't care." Her face was wild, enraged. God. There was no way to reason with her. Great.

Using the joint lock as a lever, I turned her over on her stomach, increasing the pressure to almost breaking, but not quite. Breaking her arm might not stop the fight. I wanted it over with.

I used my leg and one arm to keep the joint lock on but knelt over her upper body, until my weight would keep her pinned. I took a handful of yellow hair and pulled her neck back. I released her arm and brought my right arm across her neck, with my elbow in front of her Adam's apple and the arm squeezing the arteries on both sides of her neck. I put my right hand on my left wrist and squeezed.

She scratched at my face, but I buried my eyes in her back and she couldn't reach me. She was making small, helpless sounds because she didn't have enough air to make big ones.

Her hands scratched at my right arm, but the sweater was thick. She pushed the sleeve up, exposing my bare arm, and began to shred the skin with her nails. I buried my face deeper into her back and squeezed until my arms shook and I was gritting my teeth. Everything I had was in that one arm, pressing into her slender throat.

Her hands stopped scratching me. They beat against my arm like dying butterflies.

It takes a long time to choke someone into unconsciousness. The movies make it look easy, quick, clean. It isn't easy, it isn't quick, and it sure as hell isn't clean. You can feel the pulse on either side of the neck pounding against your arm while you squeeze the life out of it. The person struggles a lot more than in the movies. And as far as choking someone to death, you better hold on for a long time after they stop moving.

Marguerite went slowly limp, a body part at a time. When she was just dead weight in my arms, I let her go, slowly. She lay on the floor unmoving. I couldn't even see her breathe. Had I squeezed too long?

I touched her neck and found the carotid pulse strong and even. Just out of it, not dead. Good.

I stood and walked back towards the bed.

Yasmeen went to her knees beside Marguerite's still form. "My love, my only one, has she hurt you?"

"She's just unconscious," I said. "She'll come to in a few minutes."

"If you had killed her, I would have torn your throat out."

I shook my head. "Let's not start this shit again. I've had about all the grandstanding I can take for one night."

The man in bed said, "You're bleeding."

Blood was dripping down my right forearm. Marguerite may not have been able to do any real damage, but the scratches were deep enough that some of them might leave scars. Great; I already had a long, thin scar on the underside of my right arm from a knife. Even with the scratches, my right arm had fewer scars than my left. Work-related injuries.

Blood was dripping down my arm rather steadily. The blood didn't show on the black carpeting. A good color if you planned to bleed much in a room.

Yasmeen was helping Marguerite to her feet. The woman had recovered very quickly. Why? Because she was a human servant, of course. Sure.

Yasmeen walked towards the bed, towards me. Her lovely face had thinned until the bones showed through. Her eyes were bright, almost feverish. "Fresh blood, and I haven't fed tonight."

"Control yourself, Yasmeen."

"You have not taught your servant good manners, Jean-Claude," Yasmeen said. She was looking very unkindly at me.

"Leave her alone, Yasmeen." Jean-Claude was standing now.

"Every servant must be tamed, Jean-Claude. You have let it go far too long."

I looked over Yasmeen's shoulder at him. "Tamed?"

"It is an unfortunate stage in the process," he said. His voice was neutral, as if he were talking about taming a horse.

"Damn you." I pulled my gun. I held it two-handed in a teacup grip. Nobody was taming me tonight.

Out of the corner of my eye I saw someone stand up on the other side of the bed. The man was still under the covers. It was a slender woman, her skin the color of coffee with cream. Her black hair was cut very close to her head. She was naked. Where the hell had she come from?

Yasmeen was about a yard from me, tongue playing over her lips, fangs glistening in the overhead light.

"I'll kill you, do you understand that, I'll kill you," I said.

"You'll try."

"Fun and games aren't worth dying for," I said.

"After a few hundred years, that's all that *is* worth dying for."

"Jean-Claude, unless you want to lose her, call her off!" My voice was higher than I wanted it to be, afraid.

At this range the bullet should take out her entire chest. If it worked, there would be no resurrecting her as the undead; her heart would be gone. Of course, she was over five hundred years old. One shot might not do it. Lucky I had more than one bullet.

I caught movement from the corner of my eye. I was half-turned towards it when something flattened me to the ground. The black woman was on top of me. I brought the gun around to fire, not giving a damn if she was human or not. But her hand grabbed my wrists, squeezing. She was going to crush my wrists.

She snarled in my face, all teeth and a low growl. The sound should have had fur around it and pointy teeth. Human faces weren't supposed to look that way.

The woman jerked the Browning out of my hands like taking candy from a baby. She held it wrong, like she didn't know which end of the gun went where.

An arm came around her waist and pulled her backwards off me. It was the man on the bed. The woman turned on him, snarling.

Yasmeen leapt for me. I scooted backwards, putting the wall at my back. She smiled. "Not so tough without your weapon, are you?"

She was suddenly kneeling in front of me. I hadn't seen her come, not even a blur of motion. She appeared beside me like magic.

She had her body up against my knees, pinning me to the wall. Yasmeen dug her fingers into my upper arms and jerked me towards her. Her strength was incredible. She made the black shapeshifter seem fragile.

"Yasmeen, no!" It was Jean-Claude coming to my aid at last. But he was going to be too late. Yasmeen bared her teeth, raised her neck back for the strike, and I couldn't do a damn thing.

She pulled me in tight against her, arms locked behind my back. If I'd been pressed any tighter I'd have come out on the other side.

I screamed, "Jean-Claude!"

Heat; something was burning inside my sweater, over my heart. Yasmeen hesitated. I felt her whole body shudder. What the hell was happening?

A tongue of blue-white flame curled up between us. I screamed and Yasmeen echoed it. We screamed together as we burned.

She fell away from me. Blue-white flame crawled over her shirt. Flames licked around a hole in my sweater. I shrugged out of the shoulder holster and pulled the burning sweater off.

My cross still burned with an intense blue-white flame. I jerked the chain and it snapped. I dropped the cross to the carpet, where the flames smoldered, then died.

There was a perfect cross-shaped burn on my chest, just above my breast, over the beat of my heart. The burn was covered in blisters already. A second-degree burn.

Yasmeen had ripped her own blouse off. She had an identical burn, but lower down between her breasts because she was taller than I was.

I knelt on the floor in just my bra and jeans. Tears were trailing down my face. I had a bigger cross-shaped burn scar on my left forearm. A vampire's human followers had branded me, thinking it was funny. They'd laughed right up to the minute I killed them.

A burn is a bitch. Inch for inch, a burn hurts worse than any other injury.

Jean-Claude stood in front of me. The cross glowed a white-hot light, no flames, but then he wasn't touching it. I looked up to find him shielding his eyes with his arm.

"Put it away, *ma petite*. No one else will harm you tonight, I promise you that."

"Why don't you just back off and let me decide what I'm going to do?"

He sighed. "I was childish to let it get so far out of hand, Anita. Forgive me for my foolishness." It was hard to take the apology seriously while he cowered behind his arm, not daring to look at my glowing cross. But it was an apology. From Jean-Claude, that was a lot.

I picked the cross up by its chain. I had broken the clasp getting it off. I'd need a new chain before it could go around my neck again. I picked my sweater up in my other hand. There was a melted hole bigger than my fist in it. Right over the chest area. The sweater was ruined. No help there. Where do you hide a glowing cross when you aren't wearing a shirt?

The man in the bed handed my leather jacket to me. I met his eyes and saw in them concern, a little fear. His brown eyes were very close to me, and very human. It was comforting, and I wasn't even sure why.

The shoulder holster was flopping down around my waist like suspenders. I shrugged back into the straps. They felt strange next to my bare skin.

The man handed me my gun, butt first. The black shapeshifter stood on the other side of the bed, still naked, glaring at us. I didn't care how he'd gotten my gun from her. I was just glad to have it back.

With the Browning in its holster, I felt safer, though I'd never tried wearing a shoulder holster over bare skin. I suspected it was going to chafe. Oh, well, nothing's perfect.

The man held out a handful of Kleenex to me. The red sheets had slid down, exposing a long nude line of his body to about mid-thigh. The sheet was perilously close to falling off him all together. "Your arm," he said.

I stared down at my right arm. It was still bleeding a little. It hurt so much less than the burn, I had forgotten about it.

I took the Kleenex and wondered what he was doing here. Had he been having sex with the naked woman, the shapeshifter? I hadn't seen her in the bed. Had she been hiding under it?

I cleaned up my arm as best I could; didn't want to bleed too heavily on the leather jacket. I slipped the jacket on, and put the stillglowing cross in my left pocket. Once it was hidden, the glow would stop. The only reason Yasmeen and I had gotten in trouble was that the sweater had a loose weave and her top had left a lot of bare flesh. Vampire flesh touching a blessed cross was always volatile.

Jean-Claude stared down at me, now that the cross was safely hidden. "I am sorry, *ma petite*. I did not mean to frighten you tonight." He held one hand down towards me. The skin was paler than the white lace that covered it.

I ignored his outstretched hand and used the bed to help me stand.

He lowered his hand slowly. His dark blue eyes were very still, looking at me. "It never works as I want it to with you, Anita Blake. Why is that?"

"Maybe you should take the hint, and leave me alone."

He smiled, a bare movement of lips. "I'm afraid it is too late for that."

"What's that supposed to mean?"

The door swung open, banging against the wall and bouncing back. A man stood in the doorway, eyes wide, sweat running down his face. "Jean-Claude . . . the snake." He seemed to be having trouble breathing, as if he had run all the way up the stairs.

"What about the snake?" Jean-Claude asked.

The man swallowed, his breathing slowing. "It's gone crazy."

"What happened?"

The man shook his head. "I don't know. It attacked Shahar, its trainer. She's dead."

"Is it in the crowd?"

"Not yet."

"We will have to finish this discussion later, *ma petite*." He moved for the door, and the rest of the vampires followed at his heels. Stephen went with them. Well trained.

The slender black woman slipped a loose dress, black with red flowers on it, over her head. A pair of red high heels and she was out the door.

The man was out of the bed, naked. There was no time to be embarrassed. He was struggling into a pair of sweats.

This wasn't my problem, but what if the cobra got into the crowd? Not my problem. I zipped the jacket up enough to hide the fact I was shirtless but not so high up I couldn't draw my gun.

I was out the door and into the bright open space of the tent before the nameless man had slipped on his sweat pants. The vampires and shapeshifters were at the edge of the ring, fanning out into a circle around the snake. It filled the small ring with black-and-white coils. The bottom half of a man in a glittering loincloth was disappearing down the cobra's throat. That's what had kept it out of the crowd. It was taking time to feed.

Sweet Jesus.

The man's legs twitched, kicking convulsively. He couldn't be alive. He couldn't be. But the legs twitched as they slid out of sight. Please, God, let it just be a reflex. Don't let him still be alive. The thought was worse than any nightmare I could remember. And I have a lot of material for nightmares.

The monster in the ring wasn't my problem. I didn't have to be the bloody hero this time. People were screaming, running, arms full of children. Popcorn bags and cotton candy were getting crushed underfoot. I waded into the crowd and began pushing my way down. A woman carrying a toddler fell at my feet. A man climbed over them. I dragged the woman to her feet, taking the baby in one arm. People shoved past us. We shuddered just trying to stand still. I felt like a rock in the middle of a raging river.

The woman stared at me, eyes too large for her face. I pushed the toddler into her arms and wedged her between the seats. I grabbed the arms of the nearest large male, sexist that I am, and shouted, "Help them!"

The man's face was startled, as if I had spoken in tongues, but some of the panic faded from his face. He took the woman's arm and began to push his way towards the exit.

I couldn't let the snake get into the crowd. Not if I could stop it. Shit. I was going to play hero, dammit. I started fighting against the tide, to go down when everybody else was coming up and over. An elbow caught me in the mouth and I tasted blood. By the time I fought my way through this mess, it would all be over. God, I hoped so.

7

I stepped out of the crowd like I was flinging aside a curtain. My skin tingled with the memory of shoving bodies, but I stood alone on the last step. The screaming crowd was still up above me, struggling for the exits. But here, just above the ring, there was nothing. The silence lay in thick folds against my face and hands. It was hard to breathe through the thick air. Magic. But whether vampire or cobra, I didn't know.

Stephen stood closest to me, shirtless, slim and somehow elegant. Yasmeen had on his blue shirt, hiding her naked upper body. She had tied the shirt up to expose a tanned expanse of tummy. Marguerite stood beside her. The black woman stood on Stephen's right. She had kicked off her high heels and stood flat-footed in the ring.

Jean-Claude stood on the far side of the circle with two new blond vampires on either side. He turned and stared at me across the distance. I felt his touch inside me where no hand was ever meant to go. My throat tightened; sweat broke on my body. Nothing at that moment would have made me go closer to him. He was trying to tell me something. Something private and too intimate for words.

A hoarse scream brought my attention to the center of the ring. Two men lay broken and bleeding to one side. The cobra reared over them. It was like a moving tower of muscle and scale. It hissed at us. The sound was loud, echoing.

The men lay on the ground at its . . . feet? tail? One of them twitched. Was he alive? My hands squeezed the guardrail until my fingers ached. I was so scared I could taste bile at the back of my throat. My skin was cold with it. You ever have those dreams where snakes are everywhere, so thick on the ground you can't walk unless you step on them? It's almost claustrophobic. The dream always ends with me standing in the middle of the trees with snakes dripping down on me, and all I can do is scream.

Jean-Claude held out one slender hand towards me. The lace covered everything but the tips of his fingers. Everyone else was staring at the snake. Jean-Claude was staring at me.

One of the wounded men moved. A soft moan escaped his lips and seemed to echo in the huge tent. Was it illusion or had the sound really echoed? It didn't matter. He was alive, and we had to keep him that way.

We? What was this "we" stuff? I stared into Jean-Claude's deep blue eyes. His face was utterly blank, wiped clean of any emotion I understood. He couldn't trickme with his eyes. His own marks had seen to that, but mind tricks—if he worked at it—were still possible. He was working at it.

It wasn't words, but a compulsion. I wanted to go to him. To run to him. To feel the smooth, solid grip of his hand. The softness of lace against my skin. I leaned against the railing, dizzy. I gripped it to keep from falling. What the hell were these mind games now? We had other problems, didn't we? Or didn't he care about the snake? Maybe it had all been a trick. Maybe he had told the cobra to run amuck. But why?

Every hair on my body raised, as if some invisible finger had just brushed it. I shivered and couldn't stop.

I was staring down at a pair of very nice black boots, high and soft. I looked up and met Jean-Claude's eyes. He had left his place around the cobra to come to me. It beat the hell out of me going to him.

"Join with me, Anita, and we have enough power to stop the creature."

I shook my head. "I don't know what you're talking about."

He brushed his fingertips down my arm. Even through the leather jacket I could feel his touch like a line of ice, or was it fire?

"How can you be hot and cold at the same time?" I asked.

He smiled, a bare movement of lips. "*Ma petite*, stop fighting me, and we can tame the creature. We can save the men."

He had me there. A moment of personal weakness against the lives of two people. What a choice.

"Once I let you inside my head that far, it'll be easier for you to come in next time. My soul is not up for grabs for anybody's life."

He sighed. "Very well, it is your choice." He started to turn away from me. I grabbed his arm, and it was warm and firm and very, very real.

He turned to me, eyes large and drowning deep, like the bottom of the ocean, and just as deadly. His own power kept me from falling in; alone I would have been lost.

I swallowed hard enough for it to hurt, and pulled my hand away from him. I had the urge to wipe my hand against my pants, as if I had touched something bad. Maybe I had.

"Will silver bullets hurt it?"

He seemed to think about that for a second. "I do not know."

I took a deep breath. "If you stop trying to hijack my mind, I'll help you."

"You'll face it with a gun, rather than with me?" His voice sounded amused.

"You got it."

He stepped away from me and motioned me towards the ring.

I vaulted the rail and landed beside him. I ignored him as much as I was able and started walking towards the creature. I pulled the Browning out. It was nice and solid in my hand. A comforting weight.

"The ancient Egyptians worshipped it as a god, *ma petite*. She was Edjo, the royal serpent. Cared for, sacrificed to, adored."

"It isn't a god, Jean-Claude."

"Are you so sure?"

"I'm a monotheist, remember. It's just another supernatural creepycrawlie to me."

"As you like, *ma petite*."

I turned back to him. "How the hell did you get it past quarantine?"

He shook his head. "Does it matter?"

I glanced back at the thing in the middle of the ring. The snake charmer lay in a bloody heap to one side of the snake. It hadn't eaten her. Was that a sign of respect, affection, dumb luck?

The cobra pushed towards us, belly scales clenching and unclenching. It made a dry, whispering sound against the ring's floor.

He was right; it didn't matter how the thing had gotten into the country. It was here now. "How are we going to stop it?"

He smiled wide enough to flash fangs. Maybe it was the "we." "If you could disable its mouth, I think we could deal with it."

The snake's body was thicker than a telephone pole. I shook my head. "If you say so."

"Can you injure the mouth?"

I nodded. "If silver bullets work on it, yeah."

"My little marksman," he said.

"Can the sarcasm," I said.

He nodded. "If you are going to try to shoot it, I would hurry, *ma petite*. Once it wades into my people, it will be too late." His face was unreadable. I couldn't tell if he wanted me to do it, or not.

I turned and started walking across the ring. The cobra stopped moving forward. It waited, like a swaying tower. It stood there, if something without legs could stand, and waited for me, whiplike tongue flicking out, tasting the air. Tasting me.

Jean-Claude was suddenly beside me. I hadn't heard him come, hadn't felt him come. Just another mind trick. I had other things to worry about right now.

He spoke, low and urgent; I think only I heard. "I will do my best to protect you, *ma petite*."

"You were doing a great job up in your office."

He stopped walking. I didn't.

"I know you are afraid of it, Anita. Your fear crawls through my belly," he called, soft and faint as wind.

I whispered back, not sure he would even be able to hear me. "Stay the fuck out of my mind."

The cobra watched me. I held the Browning in a two-handed grip, pointed at the thing's head. I thought I was out of striking distance, but I wasn't sure. How far away is safe distance from a snake that's bigger than a Mack truck? Two states away, three? I was close enough to see the snake's flat black eyes, empty as a doll's.

Jean-Claude's words blew through my mind like flower petals. I could even have sworn I smelled flowers. His voice had never held the scent of perfume before. "Force it to follow you, and give us its back before you shoot."

The pulse in my neck was beating so hard, it hurt to breathe. My mouth was so dry I couldn't swallow right. I began to move, ever so slowly, away from the vampires and shapeshifters. The snake's head followed me, as it had followed the snake charmer. If it started to strike, I'd shoot it, but if it would just keep moving with me, I'd give Jean-Claude a chance at its back.

Of course, silver bullets might not hurt it. In fact, the thing was so damn big, the ammo I had in the Browning might not do more than irritate it. I felt like I was trapped in one of those monster movies where the giant slime monster keeps coming no matter how much you shoot it. I hoped that was just a Hollywood invention.

If the bullets didn't hurt it, I was going to die. I flashed on the image of the man's legs kicking as they went down. The lump was still visible in the snake's body, like it had fed on a really big rat.

The tongue flicked out and I gasped, swallowing a scream. God, Anita, control yourself. It's just a snake. A giant man-eating cobra snake, but still only a snake. Yeah, right.

Every hair on my body stood at attention. The power that I'd felt the snake charmer calling up was still here. It wasn't enough that the thing was poisonous and had teeth big enough to spear me with. It had to be magic, too. Great, just great.

The smell of flowers was thicker, closer. It hadn't been Jean-Claude at all. The cobra was filling the air with perfume. Snakes don't smell like flowers. They smell musty, and once you know what they smell like, you never forget it. Nothing with fur ever smelled like that. A vampire's coffin smells a bit like snakes.

The cobra turned its giant head with me. "Come on, just a little farther," I was speaking to the snake. Which is pretty stupid, since they're deaf. The smell of flowers was thick and sweet. I shuffled around the ring, and the snake shadowed me. Maybe it was habit. I was small and had long, dark hair, though not nearly as long as the dead snake charmer. Maybe the beastie wanted someone to follow?

"Come on, pretty girl, come to mama," I whispered so low my lips barely moved. Just me and the snake and my voice. I didn't dare look across the ring at Jean-Claude. Nothing mattered but my feet shuffling over the ground, the snake's movements, the gun in my hands. It was like some kind of dance.

The cobra parted its mouth, tongue flicking, giving me a glimpse of scythelike fangs. Cobras have fixed fangs, not retractable like a rattlesnake's. Nice to know I remembered some of my herpetology. Though I bet Dr. Greenburg had never seen anything like this.

I had a horrible impulse to giggle. Instead, I sighted down my arm at the thing's mouth. The scent of flowers was strong enough to touch. I squeezed the trigger.

The snake's head jerked backwards, blood splattering the floor. I fired again and again. The jaws exploded into bits of flesh and bone. The cobra opened its ruined jaws, hissing. I think it was screaming.

Its telephone-pole body slashed the ground, whipping back and forth. Could I kill it? Could just bullets kill it? I fired three more shots into the head. The body turned on itself in a huge wondrous knot. The black and white scales boiled over each other, frenzied, bloodspattered.

A loop of body rolled out and punched my legs out from under me. I came up on knees and one hand, gun in the other hand ready to point. Another coil smashed into me. It was like being hit by a whale. I lay half-stunned under several hundred pounds of snake. One striped coil pinned me to the ground. The beast reared over me, blood and pale drops of poison running down its shattered jaws. If the poison hit my skin, it would kill me. There was too much of it not to.

I lay flat on my back with the snake writhing across me and fired at it. I just kept squeezing the trigger as the head rushed down on me.

Something hit the snake. Something covered in fur dug teeth and claws into the snake's neck. It was a werewolf with furry, man-shaped arms. The cobra reared, pressing me under its weight. The smooth belly scales pushed at my nearly naked upper body like a giant hand, squeezing. It wasn't going to eat me, it was going to crush me to death.

I screamed and fired into the snake's body. The gun clicked empty. Shit!

Jean-Claude appeared over me. His pale, lace-covered hands lifted the coil off me as if it wasn't a thousand pounds of muscle. I scooted backwards on hands and feet. I crab-walked until I hit the edge of the ring, then I popped the empty clip and got the extra out of my sport bag. I didn't remember firing all thirteen rounds, but I must have. I jacked a round into the chamber, and I was ready to rock and roll.

Jean-Claude was elbow deep in snake. He pulled a piece of glistening spine out of the meat, splitting the snake apart.

Yasmeen was tearing at the giant snake like a kid with taffy. Her face and upper body were bathed in blood. She pulled a long piece of snake intestine out and laughed.

I had never really seen vampires use every bit of their inhuman strength. I sat on the edge of the ring with my loaded gun and just watched.

The black shapeshifter was still in human form. She had gotten a knife from somewhere and was happily carving the snake up.

The cobra whipped its head into the ground, sending the werewolf rolling. The snake reared and came smashing down. Its ruined jaws plunged into the black woman's shoulder. She screamed. One fang came out the back of her dress. Poison squirted from the fang, splashing onto the ground. Poison and blood soaked into the back of her dress.

I moved forward, gun ready, but I hesitated. The cobra was flinging its head from side to side, trying to shake the woman off. The fang was too deeply imbedded and the mouth too damaged. The cobra was trapped, and so was the woman.

I wasn't sure I could hit the snake's head without hitting her. The woman was screaming, shrieking. Her hands clawed helplessly at the snake. She'd dropped her knife somewhere.

A blond vampire grabbed the black woman. The snake reared back, lifting the woman in his jaws, worrying her like a dog with a toy. She shrieked.

The werewolf jumped on the snake's neck, riding it like a wild horse. There was no way to shoot without hitting someone now. Dammit. I had to just stand there, watching.

The man from the bed was running across the ring. Had it taken him that long to slip into the grey sweat pants and zippered jacket? The jacket was unzipped and flapped as he ran, exposing most of his tanned chest. He was unarmed as far as I could tell. What the hell did he think he could do? Dammit.

He knelt beside the two men who had been alive when all the shit started. He dragged one of them away from the fight. It was good thinking.

Jean-Claude grabbed the woman. He gripped the fang that speared her shoulder and snapped it off. The crack was loud as a rifle shot. The woman's shoulder stretched away from her body, bones and ligaments snapping. She gave one last shriek and went limp. He carried her towards me, laying her on the ground. Her right arm was hanging by strands of muscle. He had freed her from the snake, and damn near pulled her arm off.

"Help her, *ma petite.*" He left her at my feet, bleeding and unconscious. I knew some first aid, but Jesus. There was no way to put a tourniquet on the wound. I couldn't splint the arm. It wasn't just broken, it was ripped apart.

A breath of wind oozed through the tent. Something tugged at my gut. I gasped and looked up away from the dying girl. Jean-Claude stood beside the snake. All the vampires were tearing at the body, and still it lived. A wind ruffled the lace on his collar, the black waves of his hair. The wind whispered against my face, pulling my heart up into my throat. The only sound I could hear was the thunder of my own blood beating against my ears.

Jean-Claude moved forward almost gently. And I felt something inside me move with him. It was almost like he held an invisible line to my heart, pulse, blood. My pulse was so fast, I couldn't breathe. What was happening?

He was on the snake, hands digging in the flesh just below the mouth. I felt *my* hands dig into the writhing flesh. *My* hands digging at bone, snapping it. *My* hands shoving in almost to the elbow. It was slick, wet, but not warm. Our hands pushed, then pulled, until our shoulders strained with the effort.

The head tore away to land across the ring. The head flopped, mouth snapping at empty air. The body still struggled, but it was dying now.

I had fallen to the ground beside the wounded woman. The Browning was still in my hand, but it wouldn't have helped me. I could hear again, feel again. My hands weren't covered in blood and gore. They had been Jean-Claude's hands, not mine. Dear God, what was happening to me?

I could still feel the blood on my hands. It was an incredibly powerful sensory memory. God!

Something touched my shoulder. I whirled, gun nearly shoved into the man's face. It was the man in the grey sweats. He was kneeling beside me, hands in the air, his eyes staring at the gun in my hands.

"I'm on your side," he said.

My pulse was still thumping in my throat. I didn't trust myself to speak, so I just nodded and stopped pointing the gun at him.

He took off his sweat jacket. "Maybe we can stop some of the blood with this." He wadded the jacket up and shoved it against the wound.

"She's probably in shock," I said. My voice sounded strange, hollow.

"You don't look so good yourself."

I didn't feel so good either. Jean-Claude had entered my mind, my body. It had been like we were one person. I started to shiver and couldn't stop. Maybe it was shock.

"I called the police and an ambulance," he said.

I stared at him. His face was very strong, high cheekbones, square jaw, but his lips were softer, making it a very sympathetic face. His wavy brown hair fell forward like a curtain around his face. I remembered another man with long brown hair. Another human tied to the vampires. He had died badly, and I hadn't been able to save him.

I caught sight of Marguerite on the far side of the ring, watching. Her eyes were wide, her lips half-parted. She was enjoying herself. God.

The werewolf pulled back from the snake. The shapeshifter looked like a very classy version of every wolfman that had ever stalked the streets of London, except it was naked and had genitalia between its legs. Movie wolfmen were always smooth, sexless as a Barbie doll.

The werewolf's fur was a dark honey color. A blond werewolf? Was it Stephen? If it wasn't, then he had disappeared, and I didn't think Jean-Claude would allow that.

A voice yelled, "Everybody freeze!" Across the ring were two patrol cops with their guns out. One of them said, "Jesus Christ!"

I put my gun away while they were staring at the dead snake. The body was still twitching, but it was dead. It just takes longer for a reptile's body to know it's dead than most mammals.

I felt light and empty as air. Everything had a faintly unreal quality. It wasn't the snake. It was whatever Jean-Claude had done to me. I shook my head, trying to clear it, to think. The cops were here. I had things I needed to do.

I fished the little plastic ID card out of my sport bag and clipped it to the collar of my jacket. It identified me as a member of the Regional Preternatural Investigation Team. It was almost as good as a badge.

"Let's go talk to the cops before they start shooting."

"The snake's dead," he said.

The wolfman was tearing at the dead thing with a long pointed muzzle, ripping off chunks of meat. I swallowed hard and looked away. "They may not think the snake is the only monster in the ring."

"Oh." He said it very softly, as if the thought had never occurred to him before. What the hell was he doing with the monsters?

I walked towards the police, smiling. Jean-Claude stood there in the middle of the ring, his white shirt so bloody it clung to him like water, outlining the point of one nipple hard against the cloth. Blood was smeared down one side of his face. His arms were crimson to the elbows. The youngest vampire, a woman, had buried her face in the snake's blood. She was scooping the bloody meat into her mouth and sucking on it. The sounds were wet and seemed louder than they should have been.

"My name's Anita Blake. I work with the Regional Preternatural Investigation Team. I've got ID."

"Who's that with you?" The uniform nodded his head in the man's direction. His gun was still pointed vaguely towards the ring.

I whispered out of the corner of my mouth, "What is your name?"

"Richard Zeeman," he said softly.

Out loud I said, "Richard Zeeman, just an innocent bystander." That last was probably a lie. How innocent could a man be who woke up in a bed surrounded by vampires and shapeshifters?

But the uniform nodded. "What about the rest of them?"

I glanced where he was staring. It didn't look any better. "The manager and some of his people. They waded into the thing to keep it out of the crowd."

"But they ain't human, right?" he said.

"No," I said, "they aren't human."

"Jesus H. Christ, the guys back at the station aren't going to believe this one," his partner said.

He was probably right. I had been here, and I almost didn't believe it. A giant man-eating cobra. Jesus H. Christ indeed.

8

I was sitting in a small hallway that served as the performers' entrance to the big tent. The lighting was permanently dim, as if some of the things rolling through wouldn't like a lot of light. Big surprise there. There were no chairs, and I was getting a little tired of sitting on the floor. I'd given a statement first to a uniform, then to a detective. Then RPIT had arrived and the questioning started all over again. Dolph nodded to me, and Zerbrowski shot at me with his thumb and forefinger. That had been an hour and fifteen minutes ago. I was getting a wee bit tired of being ignored.

Richard Zeeman and Stephen the Werewolf were sitting across from me. Richard's hands were clasped loosely around one knee. He was wearing white Nikes with a blue swoosh, and no socks. Even his ankles were tan. His thick hair brushed the tops of his naked shoulders. His eyes were closed. I could gaze at his muscular upper body as long as I wanted to. His stomach was flat with a triangle of dark hair peeking above the sweat pants. His upper chest was smooth, perfect, no hair at all. I approved.

Stephen was cuddled on the floor, asleep. Bruises blossomed up the left side of his face, black-purple and that raw red color a really bad bruise gets. His left arm was in a sling, but he'd refused to go to the hospital. He was wrapped in a grey blanket that the paramedics had given him. As far as I could tell, it was all he was wearing. I guess he'd lost his clothes when he shapeshifted. The wolfman had been bigger than he was, and the legs had been a very different shape. So the skin-tight jeans and the beautiful cowboy boots were history. Maybe that was why the black shapeshifter had been naked. Had that been why Richard Zeeman was naked, as well? Was he a shapeshifter?

I didn't think so. If he was, he hid it better than anybody I'd ever been around. Besides, if he had been a shapeshifter, why didn't he join the fight against the cobra? He'd done a sensible thing for an unarmed human being; he'd stayed out of the way.

Stephen, who had started out the night looking scrumptious, looked like shit. The long, blond curls clung to his face, wet with sweat. There were dark smudges under his closed eyes. His breathing was rapid and shallow. His eyes were struggling underneath his closed lids. Dream? Nightmare? Do werewolves dream of shapeshifted sheep?

Richard still looked scrumptious, but then a giant cobra hadn't been slamming him into a concrete floor. He opened his eyes, as if he had felt me staring at him. He stared back, brown eyes neutral. We stared at each other without saying anything.

His face was all angles, high-sculpted cheekbones, and firm jaw. A dimple softened the lines of his face and made him a little too perfect for my taste. I've never been comfortable around men that are beautiful. Low self-esteem, maybe. Or maybe Jean-Claude's lovely face had made me appreciate the very human quality of imperfection.

"Is he all right?" I asked.

"Who?"

"Stephen."

He glanced down at the sleeping man. Stephen made a small noise in his sleep, helpless, frightened. Definitely a nightmare.

"Should you wake him?"

"You mean from the dream?" he asked.

I nodded.

He smiled. "Nice thought, but he won't wake up for hours. We could burn the place down around him and he wouldn't move."

"Why not?"

"You really want to know?"

"Sure, I've got nothing better to do right now."

He glanced up the silent hallway. "Good point." He settled back against the wall, bare back searching for a more comfortable piece of wall. He frowned; so much for a comfortable wall.

"Stephen changed back from wolfman to human in less than a two-hour time span." He said it like it explained everything. It didn't.

"So?" I asked.

"Usually a shapeshifter stays in animal form for eight to ten hours, then collapses and changes back to human form. It takes a lot of energy to shapeshift early."

I glanced down at the dreaming shapeshifter. "So this collapse is normal?"

Richard nodded. "He'll be out for the rest of the night."

"Not a great survival method," I said.

"A lot of werewolves bite the dust after collapsing. The human hunters come upon them after they've passed out."

"How do you know so much about lycanthropes?"

"It's my job," he said, "I teach science at a local junior high."

I just stared at him. "You're a junior high science teacher?"

"Yes." He was smiling. "You looked shocked."

I shook my head. "What's a school teacher doing messed up with vampires and werewolves?"

"Just lucky, I guess."

I had to smile. "That doesn't explain how you know about lycanthropes."

"I had a class in college."

I shook my head. "So did I, but I didn't know about shapeshifters collapsing."

"You've got a degree in preternatural biology?" he asked.

"Yep."

"Me, too."

"So how do you know more about lycanthropes than I do?" I said.

Stephen moved in his sleep, flinging his good arm outward. The blanket slid off his shoulder, exposing his stomach and part of a thigh.

Richard drew the blanket back over the sleeping man, covering him, like tucking in a child. "Stephen and I have been friends a long time. I bet you know things about zombies that I never learned in college."

"Probably," I said.

"Stephen's not a teacher, is he?"

"No." He smiled, but it wasn't pleasant. "School boards frown on lycanthropes being teachers."

"Legally, they can't stop you."

"Yeah, right," he said. "They fire-bombed the last teacher who dared to teach their precious children. Lycanthropy isn't contagious while in human form."

"I know that," I said.

He shook his head. "Sorry, it's just a sore topic with me."

My pet project was rights for zombies; why shouldn't Richard have a pet project? Fair hiring practices for the furry. It worked for me.

"You are being tactful, *ma petite*. I would not have thought it of you." Jean-Claude was in the hallway. I hadn't heard him walk up. But I'd been distracted, talking with Richard. Yeah, that was it.

"Could you stamp your feet next time? I'm getting sick of you sneaking up on me."

"I wasn't sneaking, *ma petite*. You were distracted talking to our handsome Mr. Zeeman." His voice was pleasant, mild as honey, and yet there was a threat to it. You could feel it like a cold wind down your spine.

"What's wrong, Jean-Claude?" I asked.

"Wrong? What could possibly be wrong?" Anger and some bitter amusement flowed through his voice.

"Cut it out, Jean-Claude."

"Whatever could be the matter, *ma petite*?"

"You're angry; why?"

"My human servant does not know my every mood. Shameful." He knelt beside me. The blood on his white shirt had dried to a brownish stain that took up most of the shirt front. The lace at his sleeves looked like crumpled brown flowers. "Do you lust after Richard because he's handsome, or because he's human?" His voice was almost a whisper, intimate as if he'd said something entirely different. Jean-Claude whispered better than anyone else I knew.

"I don't lust after him."

"Come, come, *ma petite*. No lies." He leaned towards me, long-fingered hand reaching for my cheek. There was dried blood on his hand.

"You've got blood under your fingernails," I said.

He flinched, his hand squeezing into a fist. Point for my side. "You reject me at every turn. Why do I put up with it?"

"I don't know," I said, truthfully. "I keep hoping you'll get tired of me."

"I am hoping to have you with me forever, *ma petite*. I would not make the offer if I thought I would grow bored."

"I think I would get tired of you," I said.

His eyes widened a bit. I think it was real surprise. "You are trying to taunt me."

I shrugged. "Yes, but it's still the truth. I'm attracted to you, but I don't love you. We don't have stimulating conversations. I don't go through my day saying 'I must remember to share that joke with Jean-Claude, or tell him about what happened at work tonight.' I ignore you when you let me. The only things we have in common are violence and the dead. I don't think that's much to base a relationship on."

"My, aren't we the philosopher tonight." His midnight blue eyes were only inches from mine. The eyelashes looked like black lace.

"Just being honest."

"We wouldn't want you to be less than honest," he said. "I know how you despise lies." He glanced at Richard. "How you despise monsters."

"Why are you angry with Richard?"

"Am I?" he said.

"You know damn well you are."

"Perhaps, Anita, I am realizing that the one thing you want is the one thing I cannot give you."

"And what do I want?"

"Me to be human," he said softly.

I shook my head. "If you think your only shortcoming is being a vampire, you're wrong."

"Really?"

"Yeah. You're an egotistical, overbearing bully."

"A bully?" He sounded genuinely surprised.

"You want me, so you can't believe that I don't want you. Your needs, your desires are more important than anyone else's."

"You are my human servant, *ma petite*. It makes our lives complicated."

"I am not your human servant."

"I have marked you, Anita Blake. You are my human servant."

"No," I said. It was a very firm no, but my stomach was tight with the thought that he was right, and I would never be free of him.

He stared at me. His eyes were as normal as they ever got, dark, blue, lovely. "If you had not been my human servant, I could not have defeated the snake god so easily."

"You mind-raped me, Jean-Claude. I don't care why you did it."

A look of distaste spread across his face. "If you choose the word rape, then you know that I am not guilty of that particular crime. Nikolaos forced herself on you. She tore at your mind, *ma petite*. If you had not carried two of my marks, she would have destroyed you."

Anger was bubbling up from my gut, spreading up my back and into my arms. I had this horrible urge to hit him. "And because of the marks you can enter my mind, take me over. You told me it made mind games harder on me, not easier. Did you lie about that, too?"

"My need was great tonight, Anita. Many people would have died if the creature had not been stopped. I drew power where I could find it."

"From me."

"Yes, you are my human servant. Just by being near me you increase my power. You know that."

I had known that, but I hadn't known he could channel power through me like an amplifier. "I know I'm some sort of witch's familiar for you."

"If you would allow the last two marks, it would be more than that. It would be a marriage of flesh, blood, and spirit."

"I notice you didn't say soul," I said.

He made an exasperated sound low in his throat. "You are insufferable." He sounded genuinely angry. Goody.

"Don't you ever force your way into my mind again."

"Or what?" The words were a challenge, angry, confused.

I was on my knees beside him nearly spitting into his face. I had to stop and take a few deep breaths to keep from screaming at him. I spoke very calmly, low and angry. "If you ever touch me like that again, I will kill you."

"You will try." His face was nearly pressed against mine. As if when he inhaled, he would bring me to him. Our lips would touch. I remembered how soft his lips were. How it felt to be pressed against his chest. The roughness of his cross-shaped burn under my fingers. I jerked back, and felt almost dizzy.

It had only been one kiss, but the memory of it burned along my body like every bad romance novel you'd ever read. "Leave me alone!" I hissed it in his face, hands balled into fists. "Damn you! Damn you!"

The office door opened, and a uniformed officer stuck his head out. "There a problem out here?"

We turned and stared at him. I opened my mouth to tell him exactly what was wrong, but Jean-Claude spoke first. "No problem, officer."

It was a lie, but what was the truth? That I had two vampire marks on me and was losing my soul a piece at a time. Not something I really wanted to be common knowledge. The police sort of frown on people who have close ties with the monsters.

The officer was looking at us, waiting. I shook my head. "Nothing's wrong, officer. It's just late. Could you ask Sergeant Storr if I can go home now?"

"What's the name?"

"Anita Blake."

"Storr's pet animator?"

I sighed. "Yeah, that Anita Blake."

"I'll ask." The uniform stared at the three of us for a minute. "You got anything to add to this?" He was speaking to Richard.

"No."

The uniform nodded. "Okay, but keep whatever isn't happening to a dull roar."

"Of course. Always glad to cooperate with the police," Jean-Claude said.

He nodded his thanks and went back into the office. We were left kneeling in the hallway. The shapeshifter was still asleep on the floor. His breathing made a quiet noise that didn't so much fill the silence as emphasize it. Richard was motionless, dark eyes staring at Jean-Claude. I was suddenly very aware that Jean-Claude and I were only inches apart. I could feel the line of his body like warmth against my skin. His eyes flicked from my face down my body. I was still wearing only a bra underneath the unzipped jacket.

Goosebumps rolled up my arms and down my chest. My nipples hardened as if he had touched them. My stomach clenched with a need that had nothing to do with blood.

"Stop it!"

"I am doing nothing, *ma petite*. It is your own desire that rolls over your skin, not mine."

I swallowed and had to look away from him. Okay, I lusted after him. Great, fine, it didn't mean a thing. Ri-ight. I scooted away from him, putting my back to the wall, not looking at him as I spoke. "I came here tonight for information, not to play footsie with the Master of the City."

Richard was just sitting there, meeting my eyes. There was no embarrassment, just interest, as if he didn't know quite what I was. It wasn't an unfriendly look.

"Footsie," Jean-Claude said. I didn't need to see his face to hear the smile in his voice.

"You know what I mean."

"I've never heard it called 'footsie' before."

"Stop doing that."

"What?"

I glared at him, but his eyes were sparkling with laughter. A slow smile touched his lips. He looked very human just then.

"What did you want to discuss, *ma petite*? It must be something very important to make you come near me voluntarily."

I searched his face for mockery, or anger, or anything, but his face was as smooth and pleasant as carved marble. The smile, the sparkling humor in his eyes, was like a mask. I had no way of telling what lay underneath. I wasn't even sure I wanted to know.

I took a deep breath and let it out slowly through my mouth. "Alright. Where were you last night?" I looked at his face, trying to catch any change of expression.

"Here," he said.

"All night?"

He smiled. "Yes."

"Can you prove it?"

The smile widened. "Do I need to?"

"Maybe," I said.

He shook his head. "Coyness, from you, *ma petite*. It does not become you."

So much for being slick and trying to pull information from the Master. "Are you sure you want this discussed in public?"

"You mean Richard?"

"Yes."

"Richard and I have no secrets from one another, *ma petite*. He is my human hands and eyes, since you refuse to be."

"What's that mean? I thought you could only have one human servant at a time."

"So you admit it." His voice held a slow curl of triumph.

"This isn't a game, Jean-Claude. People died tonight."

"Believe me, *ma petite*, whether you take the last marks and become my servant in more than name is no game to me."

"There was a murder last night," I said. Maybe if I concentrated just on the crime, on my job, I could avoid the verbal pitfalls.

"And?" he prompted.

"It was a vampire victim."

"Ah," he said, "my part in this becomes clear."

"I'm glad you find it funny," I said.

"Dying from vampire bites is only temporarily fatal, *ma petite*. Wait until the third night when the victim rises, then question him." The humor died from his eyes. "What is it that you are not telling me?"

"I found at least five different bite radiuses on the victim."

Something flickered behind his eyes. I wasn't sure what, but it was real emotion. Surprise, fear, guilt? Something.

"So you are looking for a rogue master vampire."

"Yep. Know any?"

He laughed. His whole face lit up from the inside, as if someone had lit a candle behind his skin. In one wild moment he was so beautiful, it made my chest ache. But it wasn't a beauty that made me want to touch it. I remembered a Bengal tiger that I'd seen once in a zoo. It was big enough to ride on like a pony. Its fur was orange, black, cream, oyster-shell white.

Its eyes were gold. The heavy paws wider than my outspread hand paced, paced, back and forth, back and forth, until it had worn a path in the dirt. Some genius had put one barred wall so close to the fence that held back the crowd, I could have reached through and touched the tiger easily. I had to ball my hands into fists and shove them in my pockets to keep from reaching through those bars and petting that tiger. It was so close, so beautiful, so wild, so . . . tempting.

I hugged my knees to my chest, hands clasped tight together. The tiger would have taken my hand off, and yet there was that small part of me that regretted not reaching through the bars. I watched Jean-Claude's face, felt his laughter like velvet running down my spine. Would part of me always wonder what it would have been like if I had just said yes? Probably. But I could live with it.

He was staring at me, the laughter dying from his eyes like the last bit of light seeping from the sky. "What are you thinking, *ma petite?*"

"Can't you read my mind?" I asked.

"You know I cannot."

"I don't know anything about you, Jean-Claude, not a bloody thing."

"You know more about me than anyone else in the city."

"Yasmeen included?"

He lowered his eyes, almost embarrassed. "We are very old friends."

"How old?"

He met my eyes, but his face was empty, blank. "Old enough."

"That's not an answer," I said.

"No," he said, "it is an evasion."

So he wasn't going to answer my question; what else was new? "Are there any other master vampires in town besides you, Malcolm, and Yasmeen?"

He shook his head. "Not to my knowledge."

I frowned. "What's that supposed to mean?"

"Exactly what I said."

"You're the Master of the City. Aren't you supposed to know?"

"Things are a little unsettled, *ma petite.*"

"Explain that."

He shrugged, and even in the bloodstained shirt it looked graceful. "Normally, as Master of the City, all other lesser master vampires would need my permission to stay in the city, but"—he shrugged again—"there are those who think I am not strong enough to hold the city."

"You've been challenged?"

"Let us just say I am expecting to be challenged."

"Why?" I asked.

"The other masters were afraid of Nikolaos," he said.

"And they're not afraid of you." It wasn't a question.

"Unfortunately, no."

"Why not?"

"They are not as easily impressed as you are, *ma petite.*"

I started to say I wasn't impressed, but it wasn't true. Jean-Claude could smell it when I lied, so why bother?

"So there could be another master in the city without your knowledge."

"Yes."

"Wouldn't you sort of sense each other?"

"Perhaps, perhaps not."

"Thanks for clearing that up."

He rubbed fingertips across his forehead as if he had a headache. Did vampires get headaches? "I cannot tell you what I do not know."

"Would the . . ." I groped for a word, and couldn't find one—"more mundane vampires be able to kill someone without your permission?"

"Mundane?"

"Just answer the damn question."

"Yes, they could."

"Would five vampires hunt in a pack without a master vampire to referee?"

He nodded. "Very nice choice of word, *ma petite*, and the answer is no. We are solitary hunters, given a choice."

I nodded. "So either you, Malcolm, Yasmeen, or some mysterious master is behind it."

"Not Yasmeen. She is not strong enough."

"Okay, then you, Malcolm, or a mysterious master."

"Do you really think I have gone rogue?" He was smiling at me, but his eyes held something more serious. Did it matter to him what I thought of him? I hoped not.

"I don't know."

"You would confront me, thinking I might be insane? How indiscreet of you."

"If you don't like the answer, you shouldn't have asked the question," I said.

"Very true."

The office door opened. Dolph came out, notebook in hand. "You can go home, Anita. I'll check the statements with you tomorrow."

I nodded. "Thanks."

"Heh, I know where you live." He smiled.

I smiled back. "Thanks, Dolph." I stood up.

Jean-Claude stood in one smooth motion like he was a puppet pulled up by invisible strings. Richard stood slower, using the wall to stand, as if he were stiff. Standing, Richard was taller than Jean-Claude by at least three inches. Which made Richard six-one. Almost too tall for my taste, but no one was asking me.

"And could we talk to you some more, Jean-Claude?" Dolph said.

Jean-Claude said, "Of course, detective." He walked down the hall. There was a stiffness in the way he moved. Did vampires bruise? Had he been hurt in the fight? Did it matter? No, no, it didn't. In a way Jean-Claude was right; if he had been human, even an egotistical son of a bitch, there might have been possibilities. I'm not prejudiced, but God help me, the man has to at least be alive. Walking corpses, no matter how pretty, are just not my cup of tea.

Dolph held the door for Jean-Claude. Dolph looked back at us. "You're free to go, too, Mr. Zeeman."

"What about my friend Stephen?"

Dolph glanced at the sleeping shapeshifter. "Take him home. Let him sleep it off. I'll talk to him tomorrow." He glanced at his wristwatch. "Make that later today."

"I'll tell Stephen when he wakes up."

Dolph nodded and closed the door. We were alone in the buzzing silence of the hallway. Of course, maybe it was just my own ears buzzing.

"Now what?" Richard said.

"We go home," I said.

"Rashida drove."

I frowned. "Who?"

"The other shapeshifter, the woman whose arm was torn up."

I nodded. "Take Stephen's car."

"Rashida drove us both."

I shook my head. "So you're stranded."

"Looks that way."

"You could call a cab," I said.

"No money." He almost smiled.

"Fine; I'll drive you home."

"And Stephen?"

"And Stephen," I said. I was smiling and I didn't know why, but it was better than crying.

"You don't even know where I live. It could be Kansas City."

"If it's a ten-hour drive, you're on your own," I said. "But if it's reasonable, I'll drive you."

"Is Meramec Heights reasonable?"

"Sure."

"Let me get the rest of my clothes," he asked.

"You look fully dressed to me," I said.

"I've got a coat around here somewhere."

"I'll wait here," I said.

"You'll watch Stephen?" Something like fear crossed his face, filled his eyes.

"What are you afraid of?" I asked.

"Airplanes, guns, large predators, and master vampires."

"I agree with two out of four," I said.

"I'll go get my coat."

I slid down to sit beside the sleeping werewolf. "We'll be waiting."

"Then I'll hurry." He smiled when he said it. He had a very nice smile.

Richard came back wearing a long black coat. It looked like real leather. It flapped like a cape around his bare chest. I liked the way the leather framed his chest. He buttoned the coat and tied the leather belt tight. The black leather went with the long hair and handsome face; the grey sweats and Nikes did not. He knelt and picked Stephen up in his arms, then stood. The leather creaked as his upper arms strained. Stephen was my height and probably didn't weigh twenty pounds more than I did. Petite. Richard carried him like he wasn't heavy.

"My, my, grandmother, what strong arms you have."

"Is my line, 'The better to hold you with'?" He was looking at me very steadily.

I felt heat creeping up my face. I hadn't meant to flirt, not on purpose. "You want a ride, or not?" My voice was rough, angry with embarrassment.

"I want a ride," he said quietly.

"Then can the sarcasm."

"I wasn't being sarcastic."

I stared up at him. His eyes were perfectly brown like chocolate. I didn't know what to say, so I didn't say anything. A tactic I should probably use more often.

I turned and walked away, fishing my car keys out as I moved. Richard followed behind. Stephen snuffled against his chest, pulling the blanket close in his sleep.

"Is your car very far?"

"A few blocks; why?"

"Stephen isn't dressed for the cold."

I frowned at him. "What, you want me to drive the car around and pick you up?"

"That would be very nice," he said.

I opened my mouth to say no, then closed it. The thin blanket wasn't much protection, and some of Stephen's injuries were from saving my life. I could drive the car around.

I satisfied myself with grumbling under my breath, "I can't believe I'm a door-to-door taxi for a werewolf."

Richard either didn't hear me, or chose to ignore it. Smart, handsome, junior high science teacher, degree in preternatural biology, what more could I ask for? Give me a minute and I'd think of something.

9

The car rode in its own tunnel of darkness. The headlights were a moving circle of light. The October night closed behind the car like a door.

Stephen was asleep in the back seat of my Nova. Richard sat in the passenger seat, half-turned in his seat belt to look at me. It was just polite to look at someone when you talk to them. But I felt at a disadvantage because I had to watch the road. All he had to do was stare at me.

"What do you do in your spare time?" Richard asked.

I shook my head. "I don't have spare time."

"Hobbies?"

"I don't think I have any of those, either."

"You must do something besides shoot large snakes in the head," he said.

I smiled and glanced at him. He leaned towards me as much as the seat belt would allow. He was smiling, too, but there was something in his eyes, or his posture, that said he was serious. Interested in what I would say.

"I'm an animator," I said.

He clasped his hands together, left elbow propped on the back of the seat. "Okay, when you're not raising the dead, what do you do?"

"Work on preternatural crimes with the police, mostly murders."

"And?" he said.

"And I execute rogue vampires."

"And?"

"And nothing," I said. I glanced at him again. In the dark I couldn't see his eyes, their color was too dark for that, but I could feel his gaze. Probably imagination. Yeah. I'd been hanging around Jean-Claude too long. The smell of Richard's leather coat mingled with a faint whiff of his cologne. Something expensive and sweet. It went very nicely with the smell of leather.

"I work. I exercise. I go out with friends." I shrugged. "What do you do when you're not teaching?"

"Scuba diving, caving, bird watching, gardening, astronomy." His smile was a dim whiteness in the near dark.

"You must have a lot more free time than I do."

"Actually, the teacher always has more homework than the students," he said.

"Sorry to hear that."

He shrugged, the leather creaked and slithered over his skin. Good leather always moved like it was still alive.

"Do you watch TV?" he asked.

"My television broke two years ago, and I never replaced it."

"You must do something for fun."

I thought about it. "I collect toy penguins." The minute I said it, I wished I hadn't.

He grinned at me. "Now we're getting somewhere. The Executioner collects stuffed toys. I like it."

"Glad to hear it." My voice sounded grumpy even to me.

"What's wrong?" he said.

"I'm not very good at small talk," I said.

"You were doing fine."

No, I wasn't, but I wasn't sure how to explain it to him. I didn't like talking about myself to strangers. Especially strangers with ties to Jean-Claude.

"What do you want from me?" I said.

"I'm just passing the time."

"No, you weren't." His shoulder-length hair had fallen around his face. He was taller, thicker, but the outline was familiar. He looked like Phillip in the shadowed dark. Phillip was the only other human being I'd ever seen with the monsters.

Phillip sagged in the chains. Blood poured in a bright red flood down his chest. It splattered onto the floor, like rain. Torchlight glittered on the wet bone of his spine. Someone had ripped his throat out.

I staggered against the wall as if someone had hit me. I couldn't get enough air. Someone kept whispering, "Oh, God, oh, God," over and over, and it was me. I walked down the steps with my back pressed against the wall. I couldn't take my eyes from him. Couldn't look away. Couldn't breathe. Couldn't cry.

The torchlight reflected in his eyes, giving the illusion of movement. A scream built in my gut and spilled out my throat. "Phillip!"

Something cold slithered up my spine. I was sitting in my car with the ghost of guilty conscience. It hadn't been my fault that Phillip died. I certainly didn't kill him, but . . . but I still felt guilty. Someone should have saved him, and since I was the last one with a chance to do it, it should have been me. Guilt is a many splendored thing.

"What do you want from me, Richard?" I asked.

"I don't want anything," he said.

"Lies are ugly things, Richard."

"What makes you think I'm lying?"

"Finely honed instinct," I said.

"Has it really been that long since a man tried to make polite small talk with you?"

I started to look at him, and decided not to. It had been that long. "The last person who flirted with me was murdered. It makes a girl a little cautious."

He was quiet for a minute. "Fair enough, but I still want to know more about you."

"Why?"

"Why not?"

He had me there. "How do I know Jean-Claude didn't tell you to make friends?"

"Why would he do that?"

I shrugged.

"Okay, let's start over. Pretend we met at the health club."

"Health club?" I said.

He smiled. "Health club. I thought you looked great in your swimsuit."

"Sweats," I said.

He nodded. "You looked cute in your sweats."

"I liked looking great better."

"If I get to imagine you in a swimsuit, you can look great; sweats only get cute."

"Fair enough."

"We made pleasant small talk and I asked you out."

I had to look at him. "Are you asking me out?"

"Yes, I am."

I shook my head and turned back to the road. "I don't think that's a good idea."

"Why not?" he asked.

"I told you."

"Just because one person got killed on you doesn't mean everyone will."

I gripped the steering wheel tight enough to make my hands hurt. "I was eight when my mother died. My father remarried when I was ten." I shook my head. "People go away and they don't come back."

"Sounds scary." His voice was soft and low.

I didn't know what had made me say that. I didn't usually talk about my mother to strangers, or anybody else for that matter. "Scary," I said softly. "You could say that."

"If you never let anyone get close to you, you don't get hurt, is that it?"

"There are also a lot of very jerky men in the twenty-one-to-thirty age group," I said.

He grinned. "I'll give you that. Nice-looking, intelligent, independent women are not exactly plentiful either."

"Stop with the compliments, or you'll have me blushing."

"You don't strike me as someone who blushes easily."

A picture flashed in my mind. Richard Zeeman naked beside the bed, struggling into his sweat pants. It hadn't embarrassed me at the time. It was only now, with him so warm and close in the car, that I thought about it. A warm flush crept up my face. I blushed in the dark, glad he couldn't see. I didn't want him to know I was thinking about what he looked like without his clothes on. I don't usually do that. Of course, I don't usually see a man buck naked before I've even gone out on a date. Come to think of it, I didn't see men naked on dates either.

"We're in the health club, sipping fruit juice, and I ask you out."

I stared very hard at the road. I kept flashing on the smooth line of his thigh and lower things. It was embarrassing, but the harder I tried not to think about it, the clearer the picture seemed to get.

"Movies and dinner?" I said.

"No," he said. "Something unique. Caving."

"You mean crawling around in a cave on a first date?"

"Have you ever been caving?"

"Once."

"Did you enjoy it?"

"We were sneaking up on bad guys at the time. I didn't think much about enjoying it."

"Then you have to give it another chance. I go caving at least twice a month. You get to wear your oldest clothes and get really dirty, and no one tells you not to play in the mud."

"Mud?" I said.

"Too messy for you?"

"I was a bio-lab assistant in college; nothing's too messy for me."

"At least you can say you get to use your degree in your work."

I laughed. "True."

"I use my degree, too, but I went in for educating the munchkins."

"Do you like teaching?"

"Very much." Those two words held a warmth and excitement that you didn't hear much when people talked about their work.

"I like my job, too."

"Even when it forces you to play with vampires and zombies?"

I nodded. "Yeah."

"We're sitting in the juice bar, and I've just asked you out. What do you say?"

"I should say no."

"Why?"

"I don't know."

"You sound suspicious."

"Always," I said.

"Never taking a chance is the worst failure of all, Anita."

"Not dating is a choice, not a failure." I was feeling a wee bit defensive.

"Say you'll go caving this weekend." The leather coat crinkled and moved as he tried to move closer to me than the seat belt would allow. He could have reached out and touched me. Part of me wanted him to, which was sort of embarrassing all on its own.

I started to say no, then realized I wanted to say yes. Which was silly. But I was enjoying sitting in the dark with the smell of leather and cologne. Call it chemistry, instant lust, whatever. I liked Richard. He flipped my switch. It had been a long time since I had liked anybody.

Jean-Claude didn't count. I wasn't sure why, but he didn't. Being dead might have something to do with that.

"Alright, I'll go caving. When and where?"

"Great. Meet in front of my house at, say, ten o'clock on Saturday."

"Ten in the morning?" I said.

"Not a morning person?" he asked.

"Not particularly."

"We have to start early, or we won't get to the end of the cave in one day."

"What do I wear?"

"Your oldest clothes. I'll be dressed in coveralls over jeans."

"I've got coveralls." I didn't mention that I used my coveralls to keep blood off my clothes. Mud sounded a lot more friendly.

"Great. I'll bring the rest of the equipment you need."

"How much more equipment do I need?"

"A hard hat, a light, maybe knee pads."

"Sounds like a boffo first date," I said.

"It will be," he said. His voice was soft, low, and somehow more private than just sitting in my car. It wasn't Jean-Claude's magical voice, but then what was?

"Turn right here," he said, pointing to a side street. "Third house on the right."

I pulled into a short, blacktopped driveway. The house was half brick and some pale color. It was hard to tell in the dark. There were no streetlights to help you see. You forget how dark the night can be without electricity.

Richard unbuckled his seat belt and opened the door. "Thanks for the ride."

"Do you need help getting him inside?" My hand was on the key as I asked.

"No, I got it. Thanks, though."

"Don't mention it."

He stared at me. "Did I do something wrong?"

"Not yet," I said.

He smiled, a quick flash in the darkness. "Good." He unlocked the back door behind him, and got out of the car. He leaned in and scooped Stephen up, holding the blanket close so it didn't slide off. He lifted with his legs more than his back; weightlifting will teach you that. A human body is a lot harder to lift than even free weights. A body just isn't balanced as well as a barbell.

Richard shut the car door with his back. The back door clicked shut, and I unbuckled my seat belt so I could lock the doors. Through the still-open passenger side door Richard was watching me. Over the idling of the car's engine his voice carried, "Locking out the boogeymen?"

"You never know," I said.

He nodded. "Yeah." There was something in that one word that was sad, wistful, innocence lost. It was nice to talk with another person who understood. Dolph and Zerbrowski understood the violence and the nearness of death, but they didn't understand the monsters.

I closed the door and scooted back behind the steering wheel. I buckled my seat belt and put the car in gear. The headlights sparkled over Richard, Stephen's hair like a yellow splash in his arms. Richard was still staring at me. I left him in the dark in front of his house with the singing of autumn crickets the only sound.

10

I pulled up in front of my apartment building at a little after 2:00 A.M. I'd planned to be in bed a long time before this. The new cross-shaped burn was a burning, acid-eating ache. It made my whole chest hurt. My ribs and stomach were sore, stiff. I turned on the dome light in the car and unzipped the leather jacket. In the yellow light bruises were blossoming across my skin. For a minute I couldn't think how I'd gotten hurt; then I remembered the crushing weight of the snake crawling over me. Jesus. I was lucky it was bruises and not broken ribs.

I clicked off the light and zipped the jacket back up. The shoulder straps were chafing on my bare skin, but the burn hurt so much more that the bruises and the chafing seemed pretty darn minor. A good burn will take your mind off everything else.

The light that usually burned over the stairs was out. Not the first time. I'd have to call the office once it opened for the day and report it, though. If you didn't report it, it didn't get fixed.

I was three steps up before I saw the man. He was sitting at the head of the stairs waiting for me. Short blond hair, pale in the darkness. His hands sat on the top of his knees, palms up to show that he didn't have a weapon. Well, that he didn't have a weapon *in his hands*. Edward always had a weapon unless someone had taken it away from him.

Come to think of it, so did I.

"Long time no see, Edward."

"Three months," he said. "Long enough for my broken arm to heal completely."

I nodded. "I got my stitches out about two months ago."

He just sat on the steps looking down at me.

"What do you want, Edward?"

"Couldn't it be a social call?" He was laughing at me, quietly.

"It's two o'clock in the freaking morning; it better not be a social call."

"Would you rather it was business?" His voice was soft, but it carried.

I shook my head. "No, no." I never wanted to be business for Edward. He specialized in killing lycanthropes, vampires, anything that used to be human and wasn't anymore. He'd gotten bored with killing people. Too easy.

"Is it business?" My voice was steady, no tremble. Good for me. I could draw the Browning, but if we ever drew down on each other for real, he'd kill me. Being friends with Edward was like being friends with a tame leopard. You could pet it and it seemed to like you, but you knew deep down that if it ever got hungry enough, or angry enough, it would kill you. Kill you and eat the flesh from your bones.

"Just information tonight, Anita, no problems."

"What sort of information?" I asked.

He smiled again. Friendly ol' Edward. Ri-ight.

"Can we go inside and talk about it? It's freezing out here," he said.

"The last time you were in town you didn't seem to need an invitation to break into my apartment."

"You've got a new lock."

I grinned. "You couldn't pick it, could you?" I was genuinely pleased.

He shrugged; maybe it was the darkness, but if it hadn't been Edward, I'd have said he was embarrassed.

"The locksmith told me it was burglarproof," I said.

"I didn't bring my battering ram with me," he said.

"Come on up. I'll fix coffee." I stepped around him. He stood and followed me. I turned my back on him without worrying. Edward might shoot me someday, but he wouldn't do it in the back after telling me he was just here to talk. Edward wasn't honorable, but he had rules. If he planned to kill me, he'd have announced it. Told me how much people were paying him to off me. Watched the fear slide through my eyes.

Yeah, Edward had rules. He just had fewer of them than most people did. But he never broke a rule, never betrayed his own skewed sense of honor. If he said I was safe for tonight, he meant it. It would have been nice if Jean-Claude had had rules.

The hallway was middle-of-the-night, middle-of-the-week, had-to-get-up-in-the-morning quiet. My day living neighbors were all asnooze in their beds without care. I unlocked the new locks on my door and ushered Edward inside.

"That's a new look for you, isn't it?" he asked.

"What?"

"What happened to your shirt?"

"Oh." Suave comebacks, that's me. I didn't know what to say, or rather, how much to say.

"You've been playing with vampires again," he said.

"What makes you think so?" I asked.

"The cross-shaped burn on your, ah, chest."

Oh, that. Fine. I unzipped the jacket and folded it over the back of the couch. I stood there in my bra and shoulder holster and met his eyes without blushing. Brownie point for me. I undid the belt and slipped out of the shoulder holster, then took it into the kitchen with me. I laid the gun still in its holster on the countertop and got coffee beans out of the freezer, wearing just my bra and jeans. In front of any other male, alive or dead, I would have been embarrassed, but not Edward. There had never been sexual tension between us. We might shoot each other one fine day, but we'd never sleep together. He was more interested in the fresh burn than my breasts.

"How'd it happen?" he asked.

I ground the beans in the little electric spice mill I'd bought for the occasion. Just the smell of freshly ground coffee made me feel better. I put a filter in my Mr. Coffee, poured the coffee in, poured the water in, and pushed the button. This was about as fancy as my cooking skills got.

"I'm going to get a shirt to throw on," I said.

"The burn won't like anything touching it," Edward said.

"I won't button it, then."

"Are you going to tell me how you got burned?"

"Yes." I took my gun and walked into the bedroom. In the back of my closet I had a long-sleeved shirt that had once been purple but had faded to a soft lilac. It was a man's dress shirt and hung down nearly to my knees, but it was comfortable. I rolled the sleeves up to my elbows and buttoned it halfway up. I left it gapping over the burn. I glanced in the mirror and found that most of my cleavage was covered. Perfect.

I hesitated but finally put the Browning Hi-Power in its holster behind the headboard. Edward and I weren't fighting tonight, and anything that came through the door, with its new locks, would have to go through Edward first. I felt pretty safe.

He was sitting on my couch, legs out in front of him crossed at the ankle. He'd sunk down until the top of his shoulders rested on the couch's arm.

"Make yourself at home," I said.

He just smiled. "Are you going to tell me about the vampires?"

"Yes, but I'm having trouble deciding exactly how much to tell you."

The smile widened. "Naturally."

I set out two mugs, sugar, and real cream from the refrigerator. The coffee dripped into the little glass pot. The smell was rich, warm, and thick enough to wrap your arms around.

"How do you like your coffee?"

"Fix it the way you'd fix it for yourself."

I glanced back at him. "No preference?"

He shook his head, still resting against the couch arm.

"Okay." I poured the coffee into the mugs, added three sugars and a lot of cream to each, stirred, and sat them on the two-seater breakfast table.

"You're not going to bring it to me?"

"You don't drink coffee on a white couch," I said.

"Ah." He got up in one smooth motion, all grace and energy. He'd have been very impressive if I hadn't spent most of the night with vampires.

We sat across from each other. His eyes were the color of spring skies, that warm pale blue that still manages to look cold. His face was pleasant, his eyes neutral and watching everything I did.

I told him about Yasmeen and Marguerite. I left out Jean-Claude, the vampire murder, the giant cobra, Stephen the Werewolf, and Rick Zeeman. Which meant it was a very short story.

When I finished Edward sat there, sipping his coffee and staring at me. I sipped coffee and stared back.

"That does explain the burn," he said.

"Great," I said.

"But you left out a lot."

"How do you know?"

"Because I was following you."

I stared at him, choking on my coffee. When I could talk without coughing, I said, "You were what?"

"Following you," he said. His eyes were still neutral, smile still pleasant.

"Why?"

"I've been hired to kill the Master of the City."

"You were hired for that three months ago."

"Nikolaos is dead; the new master isn't."

"You didn't kill Nikolaos," I said. "I did."

"True; you want half the money?"

I shook my head.

"Then what's your complaint? I got my arm broken helping you kill her."

"And I got fourteen stitches, and we both got vampire bit," I said.

"And cleansed ourselves with holy water," Edward said.

"Which burns likes acid," I said.

Edward nodded, sipped his coffee. Something moved behind his eyes, something liquid and dangerous. His expression hadn't changed, I'd swear to it, but it was suddenly all I could do to meet his eyes.

"Why were you following me, Edward?"

"I was told you would be meeting with the new Master tonight."

"Who told you that?"

He shook his head, that inscrutable smile curling his lips. "I was inside the Circus tonight, Anita. I saw who you were with. You played with the vampires, then you went home, so one of them has to be the Master."

I fought to keep my face blank, too blank, so the effort showed, but the panic didn't show. Edward had been following me, and I hadn't known it. He knew all the vampires I had seen tonight. It wasn't that big a list. He'd figure it out.

"Wait a minute," I said. "You let me go up against that snake without helping me?"

"I came in after the crowd ran out. It was almost over by the time I peeked into the tent."

I drank coffee and tried to think of a way to make this better. He had a contract to kill the Master, and I had led him right to him. I had betrayed Jean-Claude. Why did that bother me?

Edward was watching my face as if he would memorize it. He was waiting for my face to betray me. I worked hard at being blank and inscrutable. He smiled that close, canary-eating grin of his. He was enjoying himself. I was not.

"You only saw four vampires tonight: Jean-Claude, the dark exotic one who must be Yasmeen, and the two blonds. You got names for the blonds?"

I shook my head.

His smile widened. "Would you tell me if you had?"

"Maybe."

"The blonds aren't important," he said. "Neither of them were master vamps."

I stared at him, forcing my face to be neutral, pleasant, attentive, blank. Blank is not one of my better expressions, but maybe if I practiced enough . . .

"That leaves Jean-Claude and Yasmeen. Yasmeen's new in town; that just leaves Jean-Claude."

"Do you really think that the Master of the freaking City would show himself like that?" I put all the scorn I could find into my voice. I wasn't the best actor in the world, but maybe I could learn.

Edward stared at me. "It's Jean-Claude, isn't it?"

"Jean-Claude isn't powerful enough to hold the city. You know that. He's, what, a little over two hundred? Not old enough."

He frowned at me. Good. "It's not Yasmeen."

"True."

"You didn't talk to any other vampires tonight?"

"You may have followed me into the Circus, Edward, but you didn't listen at the door when I met the Master. You couldn't have. The vamps or the shapeshifters would have heard you."

He acknowledged it with a nod.

"I saw the Master tonight, but it wasn't anyone who came down to fight the snake."

"The Master let his people risk their lives and didn't help?" His smile was back.

"The Master of the City doesn't have to be physically present to lend his power, you know that."

"No," he said, "I don't."

I shrugged. "Believe it or not." I prayed, please let him believe.

He was frowning. "You're not usually this good a liar."

"I'm not lying." My voice sounded calm, normal, truthful. Honesty-R-Us.

"If Jean-Claude really isn't the Master, then you know who is?"

The question was a trap. I couldn't answer yes to both questions, but hell, I'd been lying; why stop now? "Yes, I know who it is."

"Tell me," he said.

I shook my head. "The Master would kill me if he knew I talked to you."

"We can kill him together like we did the last one." His voice was terribly reasonable.

I thought about it for a minute. I thought about telling him the truth. Humans First might not be up to tangling with the Master, but Edward was. We could kill him together, a team. My life would be a lot simpler. I shook my head and sighed. Shit.

"I can't, Edward."

"Won't," he said.

I nodded. "Won't."

"If I believe you, Anita, it means I need the name of the Master. It means you are the only human who knows that name." The friendly banter seeped out of his face like melting ice. His eyes were as empty and pitiless as a winter sky. There was no one home that I could talk to.

"You don't want to be the only human who knows the name, Anita."

He was right. I didn't, but what could I say? "Take it or leave it, Edward."

"Save yourself a lot of pain, Anita; tell me the name."

He believed. Hot damn. I lowered my eyes to look down into my coffee so he wouldn't see the flash of triumph in my eyes. When I looked back up, I had my face under control. Me and Meryl Streep.

"I don't give in to threats, you know that."

He nodded. He finished his coffee and sat the mug in the middle of the table. "I will do whatever is necessary to finish this job."

"I never doubted that," I said. He was talking about torturing me for information. He sounded almost regretful, but that wouldn't stop him. One of Edward's primary rules was "Always finish a job."

He wouldn't let a little thing like friendship ruin his perfect record.

"You saved my life, and I saved yours," he said. "It doesn't buy you anything now. You understand that?"

I nodded. "I understand."

"Good." He stood up. I stood up. We looked at each other. He shook his head. "I'll find you tonight, and I'll ask again."

"I won't be bullied, Edward." I was finally getting a little mad. He had come in here asking for information; now he was threatening me. I let the anger show. No acting needed.

"You're tough, Anita, but not that tough." His eyes were neutral, but wary, like those of a wolf I'd seen once in California. I'd just walked around a tree and there it had been, standing. I froze. I had never really understood what neutral meant until then. The wolf didn't give a damn if it hurt me or not. My choice. Threaten it, and the shit hit the fan. Give it room to run, and it would run. But the wolf didn't care; it was prepared either way. I was the one with my pulse in my throat, so startled that I'd stopped breathing. I held my breath and wondered what the wolf would decide. It finally loped off through the trees.

I'd relearned how to breathe and gone back down to the campsite. I had been scared, but I could still close my eyes and see the wolf's pale grey eyes. The wonder of staring at a large predator without any cage bars between us. It had been wonderful.

I stared up at Edward now and knew that this, too, was wonderful in its way. Whether I had known the information or not, I wouldn't have told him. No one bullied me. No one. That was one of *my* rules.

"I don't want to have to kill you, Edward."

He smiled then. "You kill me?" He was laughing at me.

"You bet," I said.

The laughter seeped out of his eyes, his lips, his face, until he stared at me with his neutral, predator eyes.

I swallowed and remembered to take slow, even breaths. He would kill me. Maybe. Maybe not.

"Is the Master worth one of us dying?" I asked.

"It's a matter of principle," he said.

I nodded. "Me, too."

"We know where we stand, then," he said.

"Yeah."

He walked towards the door. I followed, and unlocked the door for him. He paused in the doorway. "You've got until full dark tonight."

"The answer will be the same."

"I know," he said. He walked out without even glancing back. I watched him until he disappeared down the stairs. Then I shut the door and locked it. I stood leaning my back against the door and tried to think of a way out.

If I told Jean-Claude, he might be able to kill Edward, but I didn't give humans to the monsters. Not for any reason. I could tell Edward about Jean-Claude. He might even be able to kill the Master. I could even help him.

I tried picturing Jean-Claude's perfect body riddled with bullets, covered in blood. His face blown away by a shotgun. I shook my head. I couldn't do it. I didn't know why exactly, but I couldn't hand Jean-Claude over to Edward.

I couldn't betray either of them. Which left me ass-deep in alligators. So what else was new?

11

I stood on the shore under a black fringe of trees. The black lake lapped and rolled away into the dark. The moon hung huge and silver in the sky. The moonlight made glittering patterns on the water. Jean-Claude rose from the water. Water was streaming in silver lines from his hair and shirt. His short black hair was in tight curls from being wet. The white shirt clung to his body, making his nipples clear and hard against the cloth. He held out his hand to me.

I was wearing a long, dark dress. It was heavy and hung around me like a weight. Something inside the skirt made it stick out to either side like a tiny malformed hoop. A heavy cloak was pushed back over my shoulders. It was autumn, and the moon was harvest-full.

Jean-Claude said, "Come to me."

I stepped off the shore and sank into the water. It filled the skirt, soaking into the cloak. I tore the cloak off, letting it sink out of sight. The water was warm as bath water, warm as blood. I raised my hand to the moonlight, and the liquid that streamed down it was thick and dark and had never been water.

I stood in the shallows in a dress that I had never imagined, by a shore I did not know, and stared at the beautiful monster as he moved towards me, graceful and covered in blood.

I woke gasping for air, hands clutching at the sheets like a lifeline. "You promised to stay out of my dreams, you son of a bitch," I whispered.

The radio clock beside the bed read 2:00 P.M. I'd been asleep for ten hours. I should have felt better, but I didn't. It was as if I'd been running from nightmare to nightmare, and hadn't really gotten to rest. The only dream I remembered was the last one. If they had all been that bad, I didn't want to remember the rest.

Why was Jean-Claude haunting my dreams again? He'd given his word, but maybe his word wasn't worth anything. Maybe.

I stripped in front of the bathroom mirror. My ribs and stomach were covered in deep, nearly purple bruises. My chest was tight when I breathed, but nothing was broken. The burn on my chest was raw, the skin blackened where it wasn't covered in blisters. A burn hurts all the way down, as if the pain burrows from the skin down to the bone. A burn is the only injury where I am convinced I have nerve endings below skin level. How could it hurt so damn bad, otherwise?

I was meeting Ronnie at the health club at three. Ronnie was short for Veronica. She said it helped her get more work as a private detective if people assumed she was male. Sad but true. We would lift weights and jog. I slipped a black sports bra very carefully over the burn. The elastic pressed in on the bruises, but everything else was okay. I rubbed the burn with antiseptic cream and taped a piece of gauze over it. A man's red t-shirt with the sleeves and neck cut out went over everything else. Black biker pants, jogging socks with a thin red stripe, and black Nike Airs completed the outfit.

The t-shirt showed the gauze, but it hid the bruises. Most of the regulars at the health club were accustomed to my coming in bruised or worse. They didn't ask a lot of questions anymore. Ronnie says I was grumpy at them. Fine with me. I like to be left alone.

I had my coat on, gym bag in hand, when the phone rang. I debated but finally picked it up. "Talk to me," I said.

"It's Dolph."

My stomach tightened. Was it another murder? "What's up, Dolph?"

"We got an ID on the John Doe you looked at."

"The vampire victim?"

"Yeah."

I let out the breath I'd been holding. No more murders, and we were making progress; what could be better?

"Calvin Barnabas Rupert, friends called him Cal. Twenty-six years old, married to Denise Smythe Rupert for four years. No children. He was an insurance broker. We haven't been able to turn up any ties with the vampire community."

"Maybe Mr. Rupert was just in the right place at the wrong time."

"Random violence?" He made it a question.

"Maybe."

"If it was random, we got no pattern, nothing to look at."

"So you're wondering if I can find out if Cal Rupert had any ties to the monsters?"

"Yes," he said.

I sighed. "I'll try. Is that it? I'm late for an appointment."

"That's it. Call me if you find out anything." His voice sounded positively grim.

"You'd tell me if you found another body, wouldn't you?"

He gave a snort of laughter. "Make you come down and measure the damn bites, yeah. Why?"

"Your voice sounds grim."

The laughter dribbled out of his voice. "You're the one who said there'd be more bodies. You changed your mind on that?"

I wanted to say, yes, I've changed my mind, but I didn't. "If there is a pack of rogue vampires, we'll be seeing more bodies."

"Can you think of anything else it could be besides vampires?" he asked.

I thought about it for a minute, and shook my head. "Not a damn thing."

"Fine, talk to you later." The phone buzzed dead in my hand before I could say anything. Dolph wasn't much on hello and good-bye.

I had my back-up gun, a Firestar 9mm, in the pocket of my jacket. There was just no way to wear a holster in exercise clothes. The Firestar only held eight bullets to the Browning's thirteen, but the Browning tended to stick out of my pocket and make people stare. Besides, if I couldn't get the bad guys with eight bullets, another five probably wouldn't help. Of course, there was an extra clip in the zipper pocket of my gym bag. A girl couldn't be too cautious in these crime-ridden times.

12

Ronnie and I were doing power circuits at Vic Tanny's. There were two full sets of machines and no waiting at 3:14 on a Thursday afternoon. I was doing the Hip Abduction/Hip Adduction machine. You pulled a lever on the side and the machine went to different positions. The Hip Adduction position looked vaguely obscene, like a gynecological torture device. It was one of the reasons I never wore shorts when we lifted weights. Ronnie either.

I was concentrating on pressing my thighs together without making the weights clink. Weights clinking means you're not controlling the exercise, or it means you're working with too much weight. I was using sixty pounds. It wasn't too heavy.

Ronnie lay on her stomach using the Leg Curl, flexing her calves over her back, heels nearly touching her butt. The muscles under her calves bunched and coiled under her skin. Neither of us is bulky, but we're solid. Think Linda Hamilton in *Terminator 2*.

Ronnie finished before I did and paced around the machines waiting for me. I let the weights ease back with only the slightest clink. It's okay to clink the weights when you're finished.

We eased out from the machines and started running on the oval track. The track was bordered by a glass wall that showed the blue pool. A lone man was doing laps in goggles and a black bathing cap. The other side was bordered by the free weight room and the aerobics studio. The ends of the track were mirrored so you could always see yourself running face on. On bad days I could have done without watching myself; on good days it was kind of fun. A way to make sure your stride was even, arms pumping.

I told Ronnie about the vampire victim as we ran. Which meant we weren't running fast enough. I increased my pace and could still talk. When you routinely do four miles outside in the St. Louis heat, the padded track at Vic Tanny is just not that big a challenge. We did two laps and went back to the machines.

"What did you say the victim's name was again?" She sounded normal, no strain. I increased our pace to a flat-out run. All talking ceased.

Arm machines this time. Regular Pull-over for me, Overhead Press for Ronnie, then two laps of the track, then trade machines.

When I could talk, I answered her question. "Calvin Rupert," I said. I did twelve pull-overs with 100 pounds. Of all the machines, this one is easiest for me. Weird, huh?

"Cal Rupert?" she asked.

"That's what his friends called him," I said, "Why?"

She shook her head. "I know a Cal Rupert."

I watched her and let my body do the exercise without me. I was holding my breath, which is bad. I remembered to breathe and said, "Tell me."

"When I was asking questions around Humans Against Vampires during that rash of vampire deaths. Cal Rupert belonged to HAV."

"Describe him for me."

"Blond, blue or grey eyes, not too tall, well built, attractive."

There might be more than one Cal Rupert in St. Louis, but what were the odds that they'd look that much alike? "I'll have Dolph check it out, but if he was a member of HAV, it might mean the vampire kill was an execution."

"What do you mean?"

"Some of HAV thinks the only good vampire is a dead vampire." I was thinking of Humans First, Mr. Jeremy Ruebens's little group. Had they killed a vampire already? Was this retaliation?

"I need to know if Cal was still a member of HAV or if he'd joined a new, more radical group called Humans First."

"Catchy," Ronnie said.

"Can you find out for me? If I go down there asking questions, they'll burn me at the stake."

"Always glad to help my best friend and the police at the same time. A private detective never knows when having the police owe you one may come in handy."

"True," I said.

I got to wait for Ronnie this time. On leg machines she was faster. Upper body was my area. "I'll call Dolph as soon as we're finished here. Maybe it's a pattern? A hell of a coincidence if it's not."

We started around the track and Ronnie said, "So, have you decided what you're wearing to Catherine's Halloween party?"

I glanced at her, nearly stumbling. "Shit," I said.

"I take that to mean you forgot about the party. You were bitching about it only two days ago."

"I've been a little busy, okay?" I said. But it wasn't all right. Catherine Maison-Gillett was one of my best friends. I'd worn a pink prom dress with puff sleeves in her wedding. It had been humiliating. We'd all told the great lie of all bridesmaids. We could cut the dress short and wear it in normal life. No way. Or I could wear it at the next formal occasion I was invited to. How many formals are you invited to once you graduate college? None. At least none where I'd willingly wear a pink, puff-sleeved, hoop-skirted, reject from *Gone With the Wind*.

Catherine was throwing her very first party since the wedding. The Halloween festivities started long before dark so that I could make an appearance. When someone goes to that much trouble, you have to show up. Dammit.

"I made a date for Saturday," I said.

Ronnie stopped running and stared at me in the mirror. I kept running; if she wanted to ask questions she'd have to catch me first. She caught me.

"Did you say date?"

I nodded, saving my breath for running.

"Talk, Anita." Her voice was vaguely threatening.

I grinned at her and told her an edited version of my meeting with Richard Zeeman. I didn't leave out much, though.

"He was naked in a bed the first time you saw him?" She was cheerfully outraged.

I nodded.

"You do meet men in the most interesting places," she said.

We were jogging on the track again. "When's the last time I met a man?"

"What about John Burke?"

"Other than him." Jerks did not count.

She thought about that for a minute. She shook her head. "Too long."

"Yep," I said.

We were on our last machine, the last two laps, then stretching, showers, and done. I didn't really enjoy exercising. Neither did Ronnie. But we both needed to be in good shape so we could run away from the bad guys, or run them down. Though I hadn't chased after many villains lately. I seemed to do a lot more running away.

We moved over to the open area near the racquetball courts and the tanning rooms. It was the only place with enough room to stretch out. I always stretched before and after exercising. I'd had too many injuries not to be careful.

I started rotating the neck slowly; Ronnie followed me. "I guess I'll have to cancel the date."

"Don't you dare," Ronnie said. "Invite him to the party."

I looked at her. "You've got to be kidding. A first date surrounded by people he doesn't know."

"Who do you know besides Catherine?" she asked.

She had a point there. "I've met her new husband."

"You were in the wedding," Ronnie said.

"Oh, yeah."

Ronnie frowned at me. "Be serious, ask him to the party, make plans for the caving next week."

"Two dates with the same man?" I shook my head. "What if we don't like each other?"

"No excuses," Ronnie said. "This is the closest you've been to a date in months. Don't blow it."

"I don't date because I don't have time to date."

"You don't have time to sleep, either, but you manage it," she said.

"I'll do it, but he may say no to the party. I would rather not go myself."

"Why not?"

I gave her a long look. She looked innocent enough. "I'm an animator, a zombie-queen. Having me at a Halloween party is redundant."

"You don't have to tell people what you do for a living."

"I'm not ashamed of it."

"I didn't say you were," Ronnie said.

I shook my head. "Just forget it. I'll make the counteroffer to Richard, then we'll go from there."

"You'll want a sexy outfit for the party now," she said.

"Do not," I said.

She laughed. "Do too."

"All right, all right, a sexy outfit if I can find one in my size three days before Halloween."

"I'll help you. We'll find something."

She'd help me. We'd find something. It sounded sort of ominous. Predate jitters. Who, me?

13

At *5:15 that* afternoon I was on the phone to Richard Zeeman. "Hi, Richard, this is Anita Blake."

"Nice to hear your voice." His voice was smiling over the phone; I could almost feel it.

"I forgot that I've got a Halloween party to go to Saturday afternoon. They started the party during daylight so I could make an appearance. I can't not show up."

"I understand," he said. His voice was very carefully neutral—neutral cheerful.

"Would you like to be my date for the party? I have to work Halloween night, of course, but the day could be ours."

"And the caving?"

"A rain check," I said.

"Two dates; this could be serious."

"You're laughing at me," I said.

"Never."

"Shit, do you want to go or not?"

"If you promise to go caving a week from Saturday."

"My solemn word," I said.

"It's a deal." He was quiet on the phone for a minute. "I don't have to wear a costume for this party, do I?"

"Unfortunately, yes," I said.

He sighed.

"Backing out?"

"No, but you owe me two dates for humiliating myself in front of strangers."

I grinned and was glad he couldn't see it. I was entirely too pleased. "Deal."

"What costume are you wearing?" he asked.

"I haven't got one yet. I told you I forgot the party; I meant it."

"Hmm," he said. "I think picking out costumes should tell a lot about a person, don't you?"

"This close to Halloween we'll be lucky to find anything in our size."

He laughed. "I might have an ace up my sleeve."

"What?"

He laughed again. "Don't sound so damn suspicious. I've got a friend who's a Civil War buff. He and his wife do re-creations."

"You mean like dress up?"

"Yes."

"Will they have the right sizes?"

"What size dress do you wear?"

That was a personal question for someone who'd never even kissed me. "Seven," I said.

"I would have guessed smaller."

"I'm too chesty for a six, and they don't make six and a halfs."

"Chesty, woo, woo."

"Stop it."

"Sorry, couldn't resist," he said.

My beeper went off. "Damn."

"What's that sound?"

"My beeper," I said. I pressed the button and it flashed the number— the police. "I have to take it. Can I call you back in a few minutes, Richard?"

"I'll wait with bated breath."

"I'm frowning at the phone, I hope you know that."

"Thanks for sharing that. I'll wait here by the phone. Call me when you're done with (sob) work."

"Cut it out, Richard."

"What'd I do?"

"Bye, Richard, talk to you soon."

"I'll be waiting," he said.

"Bye, Richard." I hung up before he could make any more "pitiful me" jokes. The really sad part was I thought it was cute. Gag me with a spoon.

I called Dolph's number. "Anita?"

"Yeah."

"We got another vampire victim. Looks the same as the first one, except it's a woman."

"Damn," I said softly.

"Yeah, we're over here at DeSoto."

"That's farther south than Arnold," I said.

"So?" he said.

"Nothing, just give me the directions."

He did.

"It'll take me at least an hour to get there," I said.

"The stiff's not going anywhere, and neither are we." He sounded discouraged.

"Cheer up, Dolph, I may have found a clue."

"Talk."

"Veronica Sims recognized the name Cal Rupert. Description matches."

"What are you doing talking to a private detective?" He sounded suspicious.

"She's my workout partner, and since she just gave us our first clue, I'd sound a little more grateful, if I were you."

"Yeah, yeah. Hurrah for the private sector. Now talk."

"A Cal Rupert was a member of HAV about two months ago. The description matches."

"Revenge killings?" he asked.

"Maybe."

"Half of me hopes it's a pattern. At least we'd have some place to start looking." He made a sound between a laugh and a snort. "I'll tell Zerbrowski you found a clue. He'll like that."

"All us Dick Tracy Crimebusters speak police lingo," I said.

"Police lingo?" I could feel the grin over the phone. "You find any more clues, you let us know."

"Aye, aye, Sergeant."

"Can the sarcasm," he said.

"Please, I always use fresh sarcasm, never canned."

He groaned. "Just get your butt out here so we can all go home." The phone went dead. I hung up.

Richard Zeeman answered on the second ring. "Hello."

"It's Anita."

"What's up?"

"The message was from the police. They need my expertise."

"A preternatural crime?" he asked.

"Yeah."

"Is it dangerous?"

"To the person who was killed, yeah."

"You know that's not what I meant," he said.

"It's my job, Richard. If you can't deal with it, maybe we shouldn't date at all."

"Hey, don't get defensive. I just wanted to know if you would be in any personal danger." His voice was indignant.

"Fine. I've got to go."

"What about the costumes? Do you want me call my friend?"

"Sure."

"Will you trust me to pick your costume?" he asked.

I thought about that for a few heartbeats. Did I trust him to get me a costume? No. Did I have time to hunt up a costume on my own? Probably not. "Why not?" I said. "Beggars can't be choosers."

"We'll survive the party and then next week we'll go crawl in the mud."

"I can't wait," I said.

He laughed. "Neither can I."

"I've got to go, Richard."

"I'll have the costumes at your apartment for inspection. I'll need directions."

I gave him directions.

"I hope you like your costume."

"Me too. Talk to you later." I hung the receiver on the pay phone's cradle and stared at it. That had been too easy. Too smooth. He'd probably pick out a terrible costume for me. We'd both have a miserable time and be trapped into a second date with each other. Eek!

Ronnie handed me a can of fruit juice and took a sip of her own. She had cranberry and I had ruby red grapefruit. I couldn't stand cranberry.

"What'd cutesie pie say?"

"Please don't call him that," I said.

She shrugged. "Sorry, it just sort of slipped out." She had the grace to look embarrassed.

"I forgive you, this once."

She grinned, and I knew she wasn't repentant. But I'd ribbed her often enough about her dates. Turnabout is fair play. Payback is a bitch.

14

The sun was sinking in a slash of crimson like a fresh, bleeding wound. Purple clouds were piling up to the west. The wind was strong and smelled like rain.

Ruffo Lane was a narrow gravel road. Barely wide enough for two cars to pass each other. The reddish gravel crunched underfoot. Wind rustled the tall, dry weeds in the ditch. The road disappeared over the rise of a hill. Police cars, marked and plain, were lined up along one side of the road as far as I could see. The road disappeared over the rise of a hill. There were a lot of hills in Jefferson County.

I was already dressed in a clean pair of overalls, black Nikes, and surgical gloves when my beeper went off. I had to scramble at the zipper and drag the damn thing out into the dying light. I didn't have to see the number. I knew it was Bert. It was only a half hour until full dark, if that. My boss was wondering where I was, and why I wasn't at work. I wondered if Bert would really fire me. I stared down at the corpse and wasn't sure I cared.

The woman was curled on her side, arms shielding her naked breasts, as if even in death she was modest. Violent death is the ultimate invasion. She would be photographed, videotaped, measured, cut open, sewn back up. No part of her, inside or out, would be left untouched. It was wrong. We should have been able to toss a blanket over her and leave her in peace, but that wouldn't help us prevent the next killing. And there would be a next one; the second body was proof of that.

I glanced around at the police and the ambulance team, waiting to take the body away. Except for the body, I was the only woman. I usually was, but tonight, for some reason, it bothered me. Her waist-length hair spilled out into the weeds in a pale flood. Another blonde. Was that coincidence? Or not? Two was a pretty small sample. If the next victim was blond, then we'd have a trend.

If all the victims were caucasian, blond, and members of Humans

Against Vampires, we'd have our pattern. Patterns helped solve the crime. I was hoping for a pattern.

I held a penlight in my mouth and measured the bite marks. There were no bite marks on the wrists this time. There were rope burns instead. They'd tied her up, maybe hung her from the ceiling like a side of beef. There is no such thing as a good vampire who feeds off humans. Never believe that a vampire will only take a little. That it won't hurt. That's like believing your date will pull out in time. Just trust him. Yeah, right.

There was a neat puncture wound on either side of the neck. There was a bit of flesh missing from her left breast, as if something had taken a bite out of her just above the heart. The bend of her right arm was torn apart. The ball joint was naked in the thin beam of light. Pinkish ligaments strained to hold the arm together.

The last serial murderer that I'd worked on had torn the victims into pieces. I had walked on carpet so drenched with blood that it squelched underfoot. I had held pieces of intestine in my hand, looking for clues. It was the new worst-thing-I'd-ever-seen.

I stared down at the dead woman and was glad she hadn't been torn apart. And it wasn't because I figured it had been an easier death, though I hoped it had. And it wasn't because there were more clues, because there weren't. It was just that I didn't want to see any more slaughtered people. I'd had my quota for the year.

There is an art to holding a penlight in your mouth and measuring wounds without drooling on yourself. I managed. The secret was sucking on the end of the flashlight from time to time.

The thin beam of the flashlight shone on her thighs. I wanted to see if she had a groin wound like the man. I wanted to be sure this was the work of the same killers. It would be a hell of a coincidence if there were two vampire packs hunting separately, but it was possible. I needed to be as sure as I could that we had just one rogue pack. One was plenty, two was a screaming nightmare. Surely, God would not be that unkind, but just in case . . . I wanted to see if she had a groin wound. The man's hands had shown no rope marks. Either the vampires were getting more organized, or it was a different group.

Her arms had been glued over her chest, tied in place by rigor mortis. Nothing short of an axe was going to move her legs, not until final rigor went away, which would be forty-eight hours or so. I couldn't wait two days, but I didn't want to chop the body into pieces either.

I got down on all fours in front of the corpse. I apologized for what I was about to do, but couldn't think of anything better.

The flashlight's thin beam trembled over her thighs, like a tiny spotlight. I touched the line that separated her legs and pushed my fingers in that line, trying to feel by fingertip if there was a wound there.

It must have looked like I was groping the corpse, but I couldn't think of a more dignified way to do it. I glanced up, trying not to feel the solid rubberiness of her skin. The sun was just a splash of crimson in the west like dying coals. True darkness slipped over the sky like a flood of ink. And the woman's legs moved under my hands.

I jumped. Nearly swallowing the flashlight. Nervous, me? The woman's flesh was soft. It hadn't been a moment ago. The woman's lips were half-parted. Hadn't they been closed before?

This was crazy. Even if she had been a vampire, she wouldn't rise until the third night after death. And she'd died from multiple vampire bites in one massive blood feast. She was dead, just dead.

Her skin shimmered white in the darkness. The sky was black; if the moon was up in those black-purple clouds, I couldn't see it. Yet her skin shimmered as if touched by moonlight. She wasn't exactly glowing, but it was close. Her hair glimmered like spider silk spread over the grass. She'd just been dead a minute ago; now she was . . . beautiful.

Dolph loomed over me. At six-nine he loomed even when I was standing up; with me kneeling he was gigantic. I stood up, peeled off one surgical glove, and took the penlight out of my mouth. Never touch anything you're likely to put in your mouth after touching the open wounds of a stranger. AIDS, you know. I shoved the penlight into the breast pocket of the coveralls. I took off the other glove and crumpled them both into a side pocket.

"Well?" Dolph said.

"Does she look different to you?" I asked.

He frowned. "What?"

"The corpse; does it look different to you?"

He stared down at the pale body. "Now that you mention it. It looks like she's asleep." He shook his head. "We're going to have to call an ambulance and have a doctor pronounce her dead."

"She's not breathing."

"Would you want the fact that you weren't breathing to be the only criterion?"

I thought about that for a minute. "No, I guess not."

Dolph leafed through his notebook. "You said a person who dies of multiple vampire bites can't rise from the dead as a vampire." He was reading my own words back at me. I was hoist on my petard.

"That's true in most cases."

He stared down at the woman. "But not in this one."

"Unfortunately no," I said.

"Explain this, Anita." He didn't sound happy. I didn't blame him.

"Sometimes even one bite can make a corpse rise as a vampire. I've only read a couple of articles about it. A very powerful master vamp can sometimes contaminate every corpse it touches."

"Where'd you read the articles?"

"The *Vampire Quarterly*."

"Never heard of it," he said.

I shrugged. "I have a degree in preternatural biology; I must be on someone's list for stuff like that." A thought came to me that wasn't pleasant at all. "Dolph."

"Yeah."

"The man, the first corpse, this is its third night."

"It didn't glow in the dark," Dolph said.

"The woman's corpse didn't look bad until full dark."

"You think the man's going to rise?" he asked.

I nodded.

"Shit," he said.

"Exactly," I said.

He shook his head. "Wait a minute. He can still tell us who killed him."

"He won't come back as a normal vamp," I said. "He died of multiple wounds, Dolph; he'll come back as more animal than human."

"Explain that."

"If they took the body to St. Louis City Hospital, then it's safe behind reinforced steel, but if they listened to me, then it's at the regular morgue. Call the morgue and tell them to evacuate the building."

"You're serious," he said.

"Absolutely."

He didn't even argue with me. I was his preternatural expert, and what I said was pretty much gospel until proven otherwise. Dolph didn't ask for your opinion unless he was prepared to act upon it. He was a good boss.

He slipped into his car, nearest to the murder scene of course, and called the morgue.

He leaned out the open car door. "The body was sent to St. Louis City Hospital, routine for all vampire victims. Even ones our preternatural expert tells us are safe." He smiled at me when he said it.

"Call St. Louis City and make sure they've got the body in the vault room."

"Why would they transport the body to the vampire morgue and not put the body in the vault room?" he asked.

I shook my head. "I don't know. But I'll feel better after you call them."

He took a deep breath and let it go. "Okay." He got back on the phone and dialed the number from memory. Shows what kind of year Dolph's been having.

I stood at the open car door and listened. There wasn't much to hear. No one answered.

Dolph sat there listening to the distant ring of the phone. He stared up at me. His eyes asked the question.

"Somebody should be there," I said.

"Yeah," he said.

"The man will rise like a beast," I said. "It'll slaughter everything in its path unless the master that made it comes back to pick it up, or until it's really dead. They're called animalistic vampires. There's no colloquial term for them. They're too rare for that."

Dolph hung up the phone and surged out of the car, yelling, "Zerbrowski!"

"Here, Sarge." Zerbrowski came at a trot. When Dolph yelled, you came running, or else. "How's it going, Blake?"

What was I supposed to say, terrible? I shrugged and said, "Fine."

My beeper went off again. "Dammit, Bert!"

"Talk to your boss," Dolph said. "Tell him to leave you the fuck alone."

Sounded good to me.

Dolph went off yelling orders. The men scrambled to obey. I slid into Dolph's car and called Bert.

He answered on the first ring; not a good sign. "This better be you, Anita."

"And if it's not?" I said.

"Where the hell are you?"

"Murder scene with a fresh body," I said.

That stopped him for a second. "You're missing your first appointment."

"Yeah."

"But I'm not going to yell."

"You're being reasonable," I said. "What's wrong?"

"Nothing except that the newest member of Animators, Inc., is taking your first two appointments. His name is Lawrence Kirkland. Just meet him at the third appointment, and you can take the last three appointments and show him the ropes."

"You hired someone? How'd you find someone so fast? Animators are pretty rare. Especially one who could do two zombies in one night."

"It's my job to find talent."

Dolph slid into the car, and I slid into the passenger seat.

"Tell your boss you've got to go."

"I've got to go, Bert."

"Wait, you have an emergency vampire staking at St. Louis City Hospital."

My stomach clenched up. "What name?"

He paused, reading the name, "Calvin Rupert."

"Shit."

"What's wrong?" he asked.

"When did the call come in?"

"Around three this afternoon, why?"

"Shit, shit, shit."

"What's wrong, Anita?" Bert asked.

"Why was it marked urgent?" Zerbrowski slipped into the back of the unmarked car. Dolph put the car in gear and hit the sirens and lights. A marked car fell into line behind us, lights strobing into the dark. Lights and sirens, wowee.

"Rupert had one of those dying wills," Bert said. "If he even had one vampire bite, he wanted to be staked."

That was consistent with someone who was a member of HAV. Hell, I had it in my will. "Do we have a court order of execution?"

"You only need that after the guy rises as a vampire. We've got permission from the next of kin; just go stake him."

I grabbed the dashboard as we bounced over the narrow road. Gravel pinged against the underside of the car. I cradled the phone receiver between shoulder and chin and slipped into a seat belt.

"I'm on my way to the morgue now," I said.

"I sent John ahead when I couldn't get you," Bert said.

"How long ago?"

"I called him after you didn't answer your beeper."

"Call him back, tell him not to go."

There must have been something in my voice, because he said, "What's wrong, Anita?"

"We can't get any answer at the morgue, Bert."

"So?"

"The vampire may have already risen and killed everybody, and John's walking right into it."

"I'll call him," Bert said. The connection broke, and I shoved the receiver down as we spilled out onto New Highway 21.

"We can kill the vampire when we get there," I said.

"That's murder," Dolph said.

I shook my head. "Not if Calvin Rupert had a dying will."

"Did he?"

"Yeah."

Zerbrowski slammed his fist into the back of the seat. "Then we'll pop the son of a bitch."

"Yeah," I said.

Dolph just nodded.

Zerbrowski was grinning. He had a shotgun in his hands.

"Does that thing have silver shot in it?" I asked.

Zerbrowski glanced at the gun. "No."

"Please, tell me I'm not the only one in this car with silver bullets."

Zerbrowski grinned. Dolph said, "Silver's more expensive than gold. City doesn't have that kind of money."

I knew that, but I was hoping I was wrong. "What do you do when you're up against vampires and lycanthropes?"

Zerbrowski leaned over the back seat. "Same thing we do when we're up against a gang with Uzi pistols."

"Which is?" I said.

"Be outgunned," he said. He didn't look happy about it. I wasn't too happy about it, either. I was hoping that the morgue attendants had just run, gotten out, but I wasn't counting on it.

15

My vampire kit included a sawed-off shotgun with silver shot, stakes, mallet, and enough crosses and holy water to drown a vampire. Unfortunately, my vampire kit was sitting in my bedroom closet. I used to carry it in the trunk, minus the sawed-off shotgun, which has always been illegal. If I was caught carrying the vampire kit without a court order of execution on me, it was an automatic jail term. The new law had kicked in only weeks before. It was to keep certain overzealous executioners from killing someone and saying, "Gee, sorry." I, by the way, am not one of the overzealous. Honest.

Dolph had cut the sirens about a mile from the hospital. We cruised into the parking lot dark and quiet. The marked car behind us had followed our lead. There was already one marked car waiting for us. The two officers were crouched beside the car, guns in hand.

We all spilled out of the dark cars, guns out. I felt like I'd been shanghaied into a Clint Eastwood movie. I couldn't see John Burke's car. Which meant John checked his beeper more than I did. If the vampire was safely behind metal walls, I promised to answer all beeper messages immediately. Please, just don't let me have cost lives. Amen.

One of the uniforms who had been waiting for us duck-walked to Dolph and said, "Nothing's moved since we got here, Sergeant."

Dolph nodded. "Good. Special forces will be here when they can get to it. We're on the list."

"What do you mean, we're on the list?" I asked.

Dolph looked at me. "Special forces has the silver bullets, and they'll get here as soon as they can."

"We're going to wait for them?" I said.

"No."

"Sergeant, we are supposed to wait for special forces when going into a preternatural situation," the uniform said.

"Not if you're the Regional Preternatural Investigation Team," he said.

"You should have silver bullets," I said.

"I've got a requisition in," Dolph said.

"A requisition, that's real helpful."

"You're a civvie. You get to wait outside. So don't bitch," he said.

"I'm also the legal vampire executioner for the State of Missouri. If I'd answered my beeper instead of ignoring it to irritate Bert, the vampire would be staked already, and we wouldn't be doing this. You can't leave me out of it. It's more my job than it is yours."

Dolph stared at me for a minute or two, then nodded very slowly.

"You should have kept your mouth shut," Zerbrowski said. "And you'd get to wait in the car."

"I don't want to wait in the car."

He just looked at me. "I do."

Dolph started walking towards the doors. Zerbrowski followed. I brought up the rear. I was the police's preternatural expert. If things went badly tonight, I'd earn my retainer.

All vampire victims were brought to the basement of the old St. Louis City Hospital, even those who die in a different county. There just aren't that many morgues equipped to handle freshly risen vampires. They've got a special vault room with a steel reinforced everything and crosses laid on the outside of the door. There's even a feeding tank to take the edge off that first blood lust. Rats, rabbits, guinea pigs. Just a snack to calm the newly risen.

Under normal circumstances the man's body would have been in the vampire room, and there would have been no problem, but I had promised them that he was safe. I was their expert, the one they called to stake the dead. If I said a body was safe, they believed me. And I'd been wrong. God help me, I'd been wrong.

16

St. Louis City Hospital sat like a stubby brick giant in the middle of a combat zone. Walk a few blocks south and you could see Tony Award-winning musicals straight from Broadway. But here we could have been on the dark side of the moon. If the moon had slums.

Broken windows decorated the ground like shattered teeth.

The hospital, like a lot of inner-city hospitals, had lost money, so they had closed it down. But the morgue stayed open because they couldn't afford to move the vampire room.

The room had been designed in the early 1900s when people still thought they could find a cure for vampirism. Lock a vampire in the vault, watch it rise and try to "cure" it. A lot of vamps cooperated because they wanted to be cured. Dr. Henry Mulligan had pioneered the search for a cure. The program was discontinued when one of the patients ate Dr. Mulligan's face.

So much for helping the poor misunderstood vampire.

But the vault room was still used for most vampire victims. Mostly as a precaution, because these days when a vamp rose there was a vampire counsellor waiting to guide the newly risen to civilized vampirehood.

I had forgotten about the vampire counsellor. It was a pioneer program that'd only been in effect a little over a month. Would an older vampire be able to control an animalistic vampire, or would it take a master vampire to control it? I didn't know. I just didn't know.

Dolph had his gun out and ready. Without silver-plated bullets, it was better than spitting at the monster, but barely. Zerbrowski held the shotgun like he knew how to use it. There were four uniformed officers at my back. All with guns, all ready to blast undead ass. So why wasn't I comforted? Because nobody else had any freaking silver bullets, except me.

The double glass doors swooshed open automatically. Seven guns were trained on the door as it moved. My fingers were all cramped up trying not to shoot the damn door.

One of the uniforms swallowed a laugh. Nervous, who us?

"All right," Dolph said, "there are civilians in here. Don't shoot any of them."

One of the uniforms was blond. His partner was black and much older. The other two uniforms were in their twenties: one skinny and tall with a prominent Adam's apple; the other short with pale skin and eyes nearly glassy with fear.

Each policeman had a cross-shaped tie tack. They were the latest style and standard issue for the St. Louis police. The crosses would help, maybe even keep them alive.

I hadn't had time to get my crucifix's chain replaced. I was wearing a charm bracelet that dangled with tiny crosses. I was also wearing an anklet chain, not just because it matched the bracelet, but if anything unusual happened tonight, I wanted to have a backup.

It's sort of a tossup which I'd least like to live without, cross or gun. Better to have both.

"You got any suggestions about how we should do this, Anita?" Dolph asked.

It wasn't too long ago that the police wouldn't have been called in at all. The good ol' days when vampires were left to a handful of dedicated experts. Back when you could just stake a vamp and be done with it. I had been one of the few, the proud, the brave, the Executioner.

"We could form a circle, guns pointing out. It would up our chances of not getting snuck up on."

The blond cop said, "Won't we hear it coming?"

"The undead make no noise," I said.

His eyes widened.

"I'm kidding, officer," I said.

"Hey," he said softly. He sounded offended. I guess I didn't blame him.

"Sorry," I said.

Dolph frowned at me.

"I said I was sorry."

"Don't tease the rookies," Zerbrowski said. "I bet this is his first vampire."

The black cop made a sound between a laugh and a snort. "His first day, period."

"Jesus," I said. "Can he wait out in the car?"

"I can handle myself," the blond said.

"It's not that," I said, "but isn't there some kind of union rule against vampires on the first day?"

"I can take it," he said.

I shook my head. His first fucking day. He should have been out directing traffic somewhere, not playing tag with the walking dead.

"I'll take point," Dolph said. "Anita to my right." He pointed two fingers at the black cop and the blond. "You two on my left." He pointed at the last two uniforms. "Behind Ms. Blake. Zerbrowski, take the back."

"Gee, thanks, Sarge," he muttered.

I almost let it go, but I couldn't. "I'm the only one with silver ammo. I should have point," I said.

"You're a civvie, Anita," Dolph said.

"I haven't been a civvie for years and you know it."

He looked at me for a long second, then nodded. "Take point, but if you get killed, my ass is grass."

I smiled. "I'll try to remember that."

I stepped out in front, a little ahead of the others. They formed a rough circle behind me. Zerbrowski gave me a thumbs-up sign. It made me smile. Dolph gave the barest of nods. It was time to go inside. Time to stalk the monster.

17

The walls were two-tone green. Dark khaki on the bottom, puke green on top. Institutional green, as charming as a sore tooth. Huge steam pipes, higher than my head, covered the walls. The pipes were painted green, too. They narrowed the hallway to a thin passageway.

Electrical conduit pipes were a thinner silver shadow to the steam pipes. Hard to put electricity in a building never designed for it.

The walls were lumpy where they'd been painted over without being scraped first. If you dug at the walls, layer after layer of different color would come up, like the strata in an archaeological dig. Each color had its own history, its own memories of pain.

It was like being in the belly of a great ship. Except instead of the roar of engines, you had the beat of nearly perfect silence. There are some places where silence hangs in heavy folds. St. Louis City Hospital was one of those places.

If I'd been superstitious, which I am not, I would have said the hospital was the perfect place for ghosts. There are different kinds of ghosts. The regular kind are spirits of the dead left behind when they should have gone to Heaven or Hell. Theologians had been arguing over what the existence of ghosts meant for God and the church for centuries. I don't think God is particularly bothered by it, but the church is.

Enough people had died in this place to make it thick with real ghosts, but I'd never seen any personally. Until a ghost wraps its cold arms around me, I'd just as soon not believe in it.

But there is another kind of ghost. Psychic impressions, strong emotions, soak into the walls and floors of a building. It's like an emotional tape recorder. Sometimes with video images, sometimes just sound, sometimes just a shiver down your spine when you walk over a certain spot.

The old hospital was thick with shivery places. I personally had never seen or heard anything, but walking down the hallway you knew somewhere, near at hand, there was something. Something waiting just out of sight, just out of hearing, just out of reach. Tonight it was probably a vampire.

The only sounds were the scrape of feet, the brush of cloth, us moving. There was no other sound. When it's really quiet you start hearing things even if it's just the buzz of your own blood pounding in your ears.

The first corner loomed before me. I was point. I'd volunteered to be point. I had to go around the corner first. Whatever lay around the bend, it was mine. I hate it when I play hero.

I went down on one knee, gun held in both hands, pointing up. It didn't do any good to stick my gun around the corner first. I couldn't shoot what I couldn't see. There are a variety of ways to go around blind corners, none of them foolproof. It mostly matters whether you're more afraid of getting shot or getting grabbed. Since this was a vampire I was more worried about being grabbed and having my throat ripped out.

I pressed my right shoulder against the wall, took a deep breath, and threw myself forward. I didn't do a neat shoulder roll into the hallway. I just sort of fell on my left side with the gun held two-handed out in front of me. Trust me, this is the fastest way to be able to aim around a corner. I wouldn't necessarily advise it if the monsters were shooting back.

I lay in the hallway, heart pounding in my ears. The good news was there was no vampire. The bad news was that there was a body.

I came up to one knee, still searching the shadowed hallway for hints of movement. Sometimes with a vampire you don't see anything, you don't even hear it, you feel it in your shoulders and back, the fine hairs on the back of your neck. Your body responds to rhythms older than thought. In fact, thinking instead of doing can get you dead.

"It's clear," I said. I was still kneeling in the middle of the hallway, gun out, ready for bear.

"You through rolling around on the floor?" Dolph asked.

I glanced at him, then back to the hallway. There was nothing there. It was all right. Really.

The body was wearing a pale blue uniform. A gold and black patch on the sleeve said "Security." The man's hair was white. Heavy jowls, a thick nose, his eyelashes like grey lace against his pale cheeks. His throat was just so much raw meat. The spine glistened wetly in the overhead lights. Blood splashed the green walls like a macabre Christmas card.

There was a gun in the man's right hand. I put my back to the left-hand wall and watched the corridor to either side until the corners cut my view. Let the police investigate the body. My job tonight was to keep us alive.

Dolph crouched beside the body. He leaned forward, doing a sort of push-up to bring his face close to the gun. "It's been fired."

"I don't smell any powder near the body," I said. I didn't look at Dolph when I said it. I was too busy watching the corridor for movement.

"The gun's been fired," he said. His voice sounded rough, clogged.

I glanced down at him. His shoulders were stiff, his body rigid with some kind of pain.

"You know him, don't you?" I said.

Dolph nodded. "Jimmy Dugan. He was my partner for a few months when I was younger than you are. He retired and couldn't make it on the pension, so he got a job here." Dolph shook his head. "Shit."

What could I say? "I'm sorry" didn't cut it. "I'm sorry as hell" was a little better but it still wasn't enough. Nothing I could think of to say was adequate. Nothing I could do would make it better. So I stood there in the blood-spattered hall and did nothing, said nothing.

Zerbrowski knelt beside Dolph. He put a hand on his arm. Dolph looked up. There was a flash of some strong emotion in his eyes; anger, pain, sadness. All the above, none of the above. I stared down at the dead man, gun still clasped tight in his hand, and thought of something useful to say.

"Do they give the guards here silver bullets?"

Dolph glanced up at me. No guessing this time; it was anger. "Why?"

"The guards should have silver bullets. One of you take it, and we'll have two guns with silver bullets."

Dolph just stared at the gun. "Zerbrowski."

Zerbrowski took the gun gently, as if afraid of waking the man. But this vampire victim wasn't going to rise. His head lolled to one side, muscles and tendons snapped. It looked like somebody had scooped out the meat and skin around his spine with a big spoon.

Zerbrowski checked the cylinder. "Silver." He rolled the cylinder into the revolver and stood up, gun in his right hand. The shotgun he held loosely in his left hand.

"Extra ammo?" I asked.

Zerbrowski started to kneel back down, but Dolph shook his head. He searched the dead man. His hands were candy-coated in blood when he was done. He tried to wipe the drying blood onto a white handkerchief but the blood stained the lines in his hands, gathered around his fingernails. Only soap and scrubbing would get it off.

He said, softly, "Sorry, Jimmy." He still didn't cry. I would have cried. But then, women have more chemicals in their tear ducts. It makes us tear up easier than men. Honest.

"No extra ammo. Guess Jimmy thought five'd be enough for some dumb-ass security job." His voice was warm with anger. Anger was better than crying. If you can manage it.

I kept checking the corridor, but my eyes kept going to the dead man. He was dead because I hadn't done my job. If I hadn't told the ambulance drivers that the body was safe, they'd have put him in the vault, and Jimmy Dugan wouldn't have died.

I hate it when things are my fault.

"Go," Dolph said.

I took the lead. There was another corner. I did my little kneel-and-roll routine again. I lay half on my side, gun pointed two-handed down the hallway. Nothing moved in the long, green hallway. There was something lying in the floor. I saw the lower part of the guard first. Legs in pale blue, blood-drenched pants. A head with a long brown ponytail lay to one side of the body like a forgotten lump of meat.

I got to my feet, gun still hovering, looking for something to aim at. Nothing moved except the blood that was still dripping down the walls. The blood dripped slowly like rain at the end of the day, thickening, congealing as it moved.

"Jesus!" I wasn't sure which uniform said it, but I agreed.

The upper body had been ripped apart as if the vampire had plunged both hands into her chest and pulled. Her spine had shattered like Tinkertoys. Gobbets of flesh, blood, and bone sprinkled the hallway like gruesome flower petals.

I could taste bile at the back of my throat. I breathed through my mouth in deep, even breaths. Mistake. The air tasted like blood—thick, warm, faintly salty. There was an underlying sourness where the upper intestine and stomach had been broken open. Fresh death smells like a cross between a slaughterhouse and an outhouse. Shit and blood is what death smells like.

Zerbrowski was scanning the hallway, borrowed gun in hand. He had four bullets. I had thirteen, plus an extra clip in my sport bag. Where was the second guard's gun?

"Where's her gun?" I asked.

Zerbrowski's eyes flicked to me, then to the corpse, then back to scanning the hallway. "I don't see it."

I'd never met a vampire that used a gun, but there was always a first time. "Dolph, where's the guard's gun?"

Dolph knelt in the blood and tried to search the body. He moved the bloody flesh and pieces of cloth around, like you'd stir it with a spoon. Once the sight would have made me lose my lunch, but it didn't anymore. Was it a bad sign that I didn't throw up on the corpses anymore? Maybe.

"Spread out, look for the gun," Dolph said.

The four uniforms spread out and searched. The blond was pasty and swallowed convulsively, but he was making it. Good for him. It was the tall one with the prominent Adam's apple that broke first. He slid on a piece of meat that set him down hard on his butt in a pool of congealed blood. He scrambled to his knees and vomited against the wall.

I was breathing quick, shallow breaths. The blood and carnage hadn't been enough, but the sound of someone else throwing up just might be.

I pressed my shoulders into the wall and moved towards the next corner. I will not throw up. I will not throw up. Oh, God, please don't let me throw up. Have you ever tried to aim a gun while throwing your guts up? It's damn near impossible. You're helpless until you're finished. After seeing the guards, I didn't want to be helpless.

The blond cop was leaning against the wall. His face was shiny with a sick sweat. He looked at me and I could read it in his eyes. "Don't," I whispered, "please don't."

The rookie fell to his knees and that was it. I lost everything I'd eaten that day. At least I didn't throw up on the corpse. I'd done that once, and

Zerbrowski had never let me live it down. On that particular case, the complaint was that I'd tampered with evidence.

If I'd been the vampire, I would have come then while half of us were vomiting our guts out. But nothing slithered around the corner. Nothing came screaming out of the darkness. Lucky us.

"If you're all done," Dolph said, "we need to find her gun and what did this."

I wiped my mouth on the sleeve of my coveralls. I was sweating, but there hadn't been time to take them off. My black Nikes stuck to the floor with little squeech sounds. There was blood on the bottom of my shoes. Maybe the coverall wasn't such a bad idea.

What I wanted was a cool cloth. What I got was to continue down the green hallway, making little bloody footprints behind me. I scanned the floor and there it was, footprints going away from the body, back down the hall towards the first guard.

"Dolph?"

"I see them," he said.

The faint footprints walked through the carnage and down the corner, away from us. Away sounded good, but I knew better. We were here to get up close and personal. Dammit.

Dolph knelt by the largest piece of the body. "Anita."

I walked over to him, avoiding the bloody footprints. Never step on clues. The police don't like it.

Dolph pointed at a blackened piece of cloth. I knelt carefully, glad that I was still in my overalls. I could kneel in all the blood I wanted without messing my clothes. Always prepared, like a good Boy Scout.

The woman's shirt was charred and blackened. Dolph touched the material with the tip of his pencil. The cloth flaked in heavy layers, cracking like stale bread. Dolph poked a hole through one of the layers. It crumbled. A burst of ash and a sharp acrid smell came up from the body.

"What the hell happened to her?" Dolph asked.

I swallowed, still tasting vomit at the back of my throat. This wasn't helping. "It's not cloth."

"What is it, then?"

"Flesh."

Dolph just looked at me. He held the pencil like it might break. "You're serious."

"Third-degree burn," I said.

"What caused this?"

"Can I borrow your pencil?" I asked.

He handed it to me without a word.

I dug at what was left of her chest. The flesh was so badly fried that her shirt melted into it. I pushed the layers aside, digging downward with the pencil. The body felt horribly light, and crisp like the burned skin of a chicken. When I'd plunged half the length of the pencil into the burn, I touched something solid. I used the pencil to pry it upward. When it was almost at the surface I put fingers inside the hole and pulled a lump of twisted metal from the burned flesh.

"What is it?" Dolph asked.

"It's what's left of her cross."

"No," he said.

The lump of melted silver glinted through the black ash. "This was her cross, Dolph. It melted into her chest, caught her clothing on fire. What I don't understand is why the vampire kept contact with the burning metal. The vampire should be nearly as burned as she is, but it's not here."

"Explain that," he said.

"Animalistic vampires are like PCP addicts. They don't feel pain. I think the vampire crushed her to his chest, the cross touched him, burst into flames, and the vampire stayed against her, tearing her apart while they burned. Against any normal vampire, she would have been safe."

"So crosses can't stop this one," he said.

I stared at the lump of metal. "Apparently not."

The four uniforms were looking at the dim hallway, a little frantically. They hadn't bargained on the crosses not working. Neither had I. The bit about not feeling pain had been a small footnote to one article. No one had theorized that that would mean crosses didn't protect you. If I survived, I'd have to work up a little article for the *Vampire Quarterly*. Crosses melting into flesh, wowee.

Dolph stood up. "Keep together, people."

"The crosses don't work," one uniform said. "We gotta go back and wait for special teams."

Dolph just looked at him. "You can go back if you want to." He glanced down at the dead guard. "It's volunteer only. The rest of you go back outside and wait for special teams."

The tall one nodded and touched his partner's arm. His partner swallowed hard, his eyes flicking to Dolph, then to the guard's crispy-crittered body. He let his partner drag him away down the hall. Back to safety and sanity. Wouldn't it have been nice if we all could have gone? But we couldn't let something like this escape. Even if I hadn't had an order of execution, we would have had to kill it, rather than take the risk of letting it get outside.

"What about you and the rookie?" Dolph asked the black cop.

"I've never run from the monsters. He's free to go back with the others."

The blond shook his head, gun in hand, fingers mottled with tension. "I'm staying."

The black cop gave him a smile that meant more than words. He'd made a man's choice. Or would that be a mature person's choice? Whatever, he was staying.

"One more corner and the vault should be in sight," I said.

Dolph glanced at the last corner. His eyes met mine and I shrugged. I didn't know what was going to be around the corner. This vampire was doing things that I would have said were impossible. The rules had been changed, and not in our favor.

I hesitated on the wall farthest from the corner. I pushed my back into the wall and slid slowly into sight, around the corner. I was staring down a short, straight hallway. There was a gun lying in the middle of the floor. The second guard's gun? Maybe. On the left-hand wall there should have been a big steel door with crosses hanging on it. The steel had exploded outward in a twisted silver mess. They'd put the body in the vault after all. I hadn't gotten the guards killed. They should have been safe. Nothing moved. There was no light in the vault. It was just a blasted darkness. If there was a vampire waiting in the room, I couldn't see it. Of course, I wasn't all that close, either. Close did not seem to be a good idea.

"Clear, as far as I can see," I said.

"You don't sound sure," Dolph said.

"I'm not," I said. "Peek around the corner at what's left of the vault."

He didn't peek, but he looked. He let out a soft whistle. Zerbrowski said, "Je-sus."

I nodded. "Yeah."

"Is it in there?" Dolph asked.

"I think so."

"You're our expert. Why don't you sound sure?" Dolph asked.

"If you would have asked me if a vampire could plow through five feet of silver-steel with crosses hung all over the damn place, I'd have said no way." I stared into the black hole. "But there it is."

"Does this mean you're as confused as we are?" Zerbrowski asked.

"Yep."

"Then we're in deep shit," he said.

Unfortunately, I agreed.

18

The vault loomed up before us. Pitch black with a crazy vampire waiting inside; just my cup of tea. Ri-ight.

"I'll take point now," Dolph said. He had the second guard's gun in his hands. His own gun was tucked out of sight. He had silver bullets now; he'd go first. Dolph was good about that. He'd never order one of his men to do something he wouldn't do himself. Wish Bert was like that. Bert was more likely to promise your first-born child, then ask if it was all right with you.

Dolph hesitated at the open mouth of the vault. The darkness was thick enough to cut. It was the absolute darkness of a cave. The kind where you can touch your eyeballs with your fingers and not blink.

He motioned us forward with the gun, but he went past the darkness, farther down the hallway. The bloody footprints entered the darkness and came back out. Bloody footprints going down the hall, around the corner. I was getting tired of corners.

Zerbrowski and I moved up to stand on either side of Dolph. The tension slid along my neck, shoulders. I took a deep breath and let it out, slowly. Better. Look, my hand's not even shaking.

Dolph didn't roll around on the floor to clear the corner. He just went around back to the wall, two-handed aim, ready for bear.

A voice said, "Don't shoot, I'm not dead."

I knew the voice.

"It's John Burke. He's with me."

Dolph glanced back at me. "I remember him."

I shrugged; better safe then sorry. I trusted Dolph not to shoot John by accident, but there were two cops here I'd never met. Always err on the side of caution when it comes to firearms. Words to survive by.

John was tall, slender, dark complected. His short hair was perfectly black with a broad white streak in front. It was a startling combination. He'd always been handsome, but now that he'd shaved off his beard, he looked less like a Hollywood villain and more like a leading man. Tall, dark, and handsome, and knew how to kill vampires. What more could you ask for? Plenty, but that's another story.

John came around the corner smiling. He had a gun out, and better yet, he had his vampire kit in one hand. "I came ahead to make sure the vampire didn't get loose while you were en route."

"Thanks, John," I said.

He shrugged. "Just protecting the public welfare."

It was my turn to shrug. "Anything you say."

"Where's the vampire?" Dolph asked.

"I was tracking it," John said.

"How?" I asked.

"Bloody bare footprints."

Bare footprints. Sweet Jesus. The corpse didn't have shoes, but John did. I turned towards the vault. Too late, too slow, too damn bad.

The vampire came out of the darkness, moving too fast to see. It was just a blur that smashed into the rookie, driving him into the wall. He screamed, gun pressed to the vampire's chest. The gun was loud in the hallway, echoing in the pipes. The bullets came out the back of the vampire like they'd hit mist. Magic.

I moved forward, trying to aim without hitting the rookie. He was screaming, one continuous sound. Blood sprayed in a warm rain. I shot at the thing's head but it moved, incredibly fast, tossing the man against the other wall, tearing at him. There was a lot of yelling and movement, but it all seemed far away, slowed down. It would all be over in a matter of moments. I was the only one close enough with silver bullets. I stepped in, body brushing the vampire, and put the barrel to the back of its skull. A normal vampire wouldn't have let me do it. I pulled the trigger, but the vampire whirled, lifting the man off his feet, throwing him into me. The bullet went wide and we crashed to the floor. The air was knocked out of me for a second with the weight of two adult males on my chest. The rookie was on top of me, screaming, bleeding, dying.

I wedged the gun against the back of the vamp's skull and fired. The back of the head exploded outward in a fine spray of blood, bone, and heavier, wetter things. The vampire kept digging at the man's throat. It should have been dead, but it wasn't.

The vampire reared back, blood-clotted teeth straining. It had paused like a man breathing between swallows. I shoved the barrel in its mouth. The teeth grated on the metal. The face exploded from the upper lip to the top of the head. The lower teeth mouthed the air but couldn't get a bite. The headless body raised up on its hands, as if trying to get up. I touched the gun to its chest and pulled the trigger. At this distance I might be able to take out its heart. I'd never actually tried to take out a vampire using just a pistol. I wondered if it would work. I wondered what would happen to me if it didn't.

A shudder ran through the thing's body. It breathed outward in a long, wordless sigh.

Dolph and Zerbrowski were there dragging the thing backwards. I think it was dead already, but just in case, the help was appreciated. John splashed the vampire with holy water. The liquid bubbled and fizzed on the dying vampire. It was dying. It really was.

The rookie wasn't moving. His partner dragged him off me, cradling him against his chest like a child. Blood plastered the blond hair to his face. The pale eyes were wide open, staring at nothing. The dead are always blind, one way or another.

He'd been brave, a good kid, though he wasn't that much younger than me. But I felt about a million years old staring into his pale, dead face. He was dead, just like that. Being brave doesn't save you from the monsters. It just ups your chances.

Dolph and Zerbrowski had taken the vampire to the floor. John was actually straddling the body with a stake and mallet in hand. I hadn't used a stake in years. Shotgun was my choice. But then, I was a progressive vampire slayer.

The vampire was dead. It didn't need to be staked, but I just sat against the wall and watched. Better safe than sorry. The stake went in easier than normal because I'd made a hole for it. My gun was still in my hand. No need to put it up yet. The vault was still an empty blackness; where there was one vampire there were often more. I'd keep the gun out.

Dolph and Zerbrowski went to the ruined vault, guns out. I should have gotten up and gone with them, but it seemed very important right now just to breathe. I could feel the blood pumping through my veins; every pulse in my body was loud. It was good to be alive; too bad I hadn't been able to save the kid. Yeah, too bad.

John knelt beside me. "You all right?"

I nodded. "Sure."

He looked at me like he didn't believe it, but he let it go. Smart man.

The light flashed on in the vault. Rich, yellow light, warm as a summer's day. "Je-sus," Zerbrowski said.

I stood up, and nearly fell; my legs were shaky. John caught my arm, and I stared at him until he let go. He gave a half-smile. "Still a hard case."

"Always," I said.

There had been two dates between us. Mistake. It made working together more awkward, and he couldn't cope with me being a female version of him. He had this old southern idea of what a lady should be. A lady should not carry a gun and spend most of her time covered in blood and corpses. I had two words for that attitude. Yeah, those are the words.

There was a large fish tank smashed against one wall. It had held guinea pigs, or rats, or rabbits. All it held now were bright splashes of blood and bits of fur. Vampires don't eat meat, but if you put small animals in a glass container, then throw it against the wall, you get diced small animals. There wasn't enough left to scoop up with a spoon.

There was a head near the glass mess, probably male, judging from the short hair and style. I didn't go any closer to check. I didn't want to see the face. I'd have been brave tonight. I had nothing left to prove.

The body was in one piece, barely. It looked like the vampire had shoved both hands into the chest, grabbed a handful of ribs and pulled. The chest was nearly torn in two, but a band of pink muscle tissue and intestine held it together.

"The head's got fangs," Zerbrowski said.

"It's the vampire counsellor," I said.

"What happened?"

I shrugged. "At a guess, the counsellor was leaning over the vamp when it rose. It killed him, quick and messy."

"Why'd it kill the vampire counsellor?" Dolph asked.

I shrugged. "It was more animal than human, Dolph. It woke up in a strange place with a strange vampire leaning over it. It reacted like any trapped animal and protected itself."

"Why couldn't the counsellor control it? That's what he was here for."

"The only person who can control an animalistic vampire is the master who made it. The counsellor wasn't powerful enough to control it."

"Now what?" John asked. He'd put up his gun. I still hadn't. I felt better with it out for some reason.

"Now I go make my third animation appointment of the evening."

"Just like that?"

I looked up at him, ready to be angry at somebody. "What do you want me to do, John? Fall into a screaming fit? That wouldn't bring back the dead, and it would annoy the hell out of me."

He sighed. "If you only matched your packaging."

I put my gun back in the shoulder holster, smiled at him, and said, "Fuck you."

Yeah, those are the words.

19

I had washed most of the blood off my face and hands in the bathroom at the morgue. The bloodstained coveralls were in my trunk. I was clean and presentable, or as presentable as I was going to get tonight. Bert had said to meet the new guy at my third appointment for the night. Oakglen Cemetery, ten o'clock. The theory was that the new man already raised two zombies and would just watch me raise the third one. Fine with me.

It was 10:35 before I pulled into Oakglen Cemetery. Late. Dammit. It'd make a great impression on the new animator, not to mention my client. Mrs. Doughal was a recent widow. Like five days recent. Her dearly departed husband had left no will. He'd always meant to get around to it, but you know how it is, just kept putting it off. I was to raise Mr. Doughal in front of two lawyers, two witnesses, the Doughals' three grown children, and a partridge in a pear tree. They'd made a ruling just last month that the newly dead, a week or less, could be raised and verbally order a will. It would save the Doughals half their inheritance. Minus lawyer fees, of course.

There was a line of cars pulled over to the side of the narrow gravel road. The tires were playing hell with the grass, but if you didn't park off to one side, nobody could use the road. Of course, how many people needed to use a cemetery road at 10:30 at night? Animators, voodoo priests, pot-smoking teenagers, necrophiliacs, satanists. You had to be a member of a legitimate religion and have a permit to worship in a cemetery after dark. Or be an animator. We didn't need a permit. Mainly because we didn't have a reputation for human sacrifice. A few bad apples have really given voodooists a bad name. Being Christian, I sort of frown on satanism. I mean, they are, after all, the bad guys. Right?

As soon as my foot hit the road, I felt it. Magic. Someone was trying to raise the dead, and they were very near at hand.

The new guy had already raised two zombies. Could he do a third?

Charles and Jamison could only do two a night. Where had Bert found someone this powerful on such short notice?

I walked past five cars, not counting my own. There were nearly a dozen people pressed around the grave. The women were in skirt-suits; the men all wore ties. It was amazing how many people dressed up to come to the graveyard. The only reason most people come to the graveyard is for a funeral. A lot of clients dress for one, semi-formal, basic black.

It was a man's voice leading the mourners in rising calls of, "Andrew Doughal, arise. Come to us, Andrew Doughal, come to us."

The magic built on the air until it pressed against me like a weight. It was hard to get a full breath. His magic rode the air, and it was strong, but uncertain. I could feel his hesitation like a touch of cold air. He would be powerful, but he was young. His magic tasted untried, undisciplined. If he wasn't under twenty-one, I'd eat my hat.

That's how Bert had found him. He was a baby, a powerful baby. And he was raising his third zombie of the night. Hot damn.

I stayed in the shadows under the tall trees. He was short, maybe an inch or two taller than me, which made him five-four at best. He wore a white dress shirt and dark slacks. Blood had dried on the shirt in nearly black stains. I'd have to teach him how to dress, as Manny had taught me. Animating is still on an informal apprenticeship. There are no college courses to teach you how to raise the dead.

He was very earnest as he stood there calling Andrew Doughal from the grave. The crowd of lawyers and relatives huddled at the foot of the grave. There was no family member inside the blood circle with the new animator. Normally, you put a family member behind the tombstone so he or she could control the zombie. This way, only the animator could control it. But it wasn't an oversight, it was the law. The dead could be raised to request and dictate a will but only if the animator, or some neutral party, had control of it.

The mound of flowers shuddered and a pale hand shot upward, grabbing at the air. Two hands, the top of a head. The zombie spilled from the grave like it was being pulled by strings.

The new animator stumbled. He fell to his knees in the soft dirt and dying flowers. The magic stuttered, wavering. He'd bitten off one zombie more than he could finish. The dead man was still struggling from the grave. Still trying to get its legs free, but there was no one controlling it. Lawrence Kirkland had raised the zombie, but he couldn't control it. The zombie would be on its own with no one to make it mind. Uncontrolled zombies give animators a bad name.

One of the lawyers was saying, "Are you all right?"

Lawrence Kirkland nodded his head, but he was too exhausted to speak. Did he even now realize what he'd done? I didn't think so. He wasn't scared enough.

I walked up to the huddled group. "Ms. Blake, we missed you," the lawyer said. "Your . . . associate seems to be ill."

I gave them my best professional smile. See nothing wrong. A zombie isn't about to go amuck. Trust me.

I walked to the edge of the blood circle. I could feel it like a wind pushing me back. The circle was shut, and I was on the outside. I couldn't get in unless Lawrence asked me in.

He was on all fours, hands lost in the flowers of the grave. His head hung down, as if he was too tired to raise it. He probably was.

"Lawrence," I said softly, "Lawrence Kirkland."

He turned his head in slow motion. Even in the dark I could see the exhaustion in his pale eyes. His arms were trembling. God, help us.

I leaned in close so the audience couldn't hear what I said. We'd try to keep the illusion that this was just business as usual, as long as I could. If we were lucky, the zombie would just wander away. If we weren't lucky, it would hurt someone. The dead are usually pretty forgiving of the living, but not always. If Andrew Doughal hated one of his relatives, it would be a long night.

"Lawrence, you have to break the circle and let me in," I said.

He just stared at me, eyes dull, no glimmer of understanding. Shit.

"Break the circle, Lawrence, now."

The zombie was free to its knees. Its white dress shirt gleamed against the darkness of the burial suit. Uncomfortable for all eternity. Doughal looked pretty good for the walking dead. He was pale with thick grey hair. The skin was wavy, pale, but there were no signs of rot. The kid had done a good job for the third zombie of the night. Now if only I could control it, we were home free.

"Lawrence, break the circle, please!"

He said something, too low for me to hear. I leaned as close as the blood would let me get and said, "What?"

"Larry, name's Larry."

I smiled, it was too ridiculous. He was worried about me calling him Lawrence instead of Larry with a rogue zombie climbing out of the dirt. Maybe he'd snapped under the pressure. Naw.

"Open the circle, Larry," I said.

He crawled forward, nearly falling face first into the flowers. He scraped his hand across the line of blood. The magic snapped. The circle of power was gone, just like that. Now it was just me.

"Where's your knife?"

He tried to look back over his shoulder but couldn't manage it. I saw the blade gleam in the moonlight on the other side of the grave.

"Just rest," I said. "I'll take care of it."

He collapsed into a little ball, hugging his arms around himself, as if he was cold. I let him go, for now. The first order of business had to be the zombie.

The knife was lying beside the gutted chicken he'd used to call the zombie. I grabbed the knife and faced the zombie over the grave. Andrew Doughal was leaning against his own tombstone, trying to orient himself.

It's hard on a person, being dead; it takes a few minutes to wake up the dead brain cells. The mind doesn't quite believe that it should work. But it will, eventually.

I pushed back the sleeve of my leather jacket and took a deep breath. It was the only way, but I didn't have to like it. I drew the blade across my wrist. A thin, dark line appeared. The skin split and blood trickled out, nearly black in the moonlight. The pain was sharp, stinging. Small wounds always felt worse than big ones . . . at first.

The wound was small and wouldn't leave a scar. Short of slitting my wrist, or someone else's, I couldn't remake the blood circle. It was too late in the ceremony to get another chicken and start over. I had to salvage this ceremony, or the zombie would be free with no boss. Zombies without bosses tended to eat people.

The zombie was still sitting on its tombstone. It stared at nothing with empty eyes. If Larry had been strong enough, Andrew Doughal might have been able to talk, to reason on his own. Now he was just a corpse waiting for orders, or a stray thought.

I climbed onto the mound of gladioluses, chrysanthemums, carnations. The perfume of flowers mixed with the stale smell of the corpse. I stood knee-deep in dying flowers and waved my bleeding wrist in front of the zombie's face.

The pale eyes followed my hand, flat and dead as day-old fish. Andrew Doughal was not home, but something was, something that smelled blood and knew its worth.

I know that zombies don't have souls. In fact, I can only raise the dead after three days. It takes that long for the soul to leave. Incidentally, the same amount of time it takes for vampires to rise. Fancy that.

But if it isn't the soul reanimating the corpse, then what is it? Magic, my magic, or Larry's. Maybe. But there was something in the corpse. If the soul was gone, something filled the void. In an animation that worked, magic filled it. Now? Now I didn't know. I wasn't even sure I wanted to know. What did it matter as long as I pulled the fat out of the fire? Yeah. Maybe if I kept repeating that, I'd even believe it.

I offered the corpse my bleeding wrist. The thing hesitated for a second. If it refused, I was out of options.

The zombie stared at me. I dropped the knife and squeezed the skin around the wound. Blood welled out, thick and viscous. The zombie snatched at my hand. Its pale hands were cold and strong. Its head bowed over the wound, mouth sucking. It fed at my wrist, jaws working convulsively, swallowing as hard and as fast as it could. I was going to have the world's worst hickey. But at least it hurt.

I tried to draw my hand away, but the zombie just sucked harder. It didn't want to let go. Great.

"Larry, can you stand?" I asked softly. We were still trying to pretend that nothing had gone wrong. The zombie had accepted blood. I controlled it now, if I could get it to let go.

Larry looked up at me in slow motion. "Sure," he said. He got to his feet using the burial mound for support. When he was standing, he asked, "What now?"

Good question. "Help me get it loose." I tried to pull my wrist free, but the thing hung on for dear life.

Larry wrapped his arms around the corpse and pulled. It didn't help.

"Try the head," I said.

He tried pulling back on the corpse's hair, but zombies don't feel pain. Larry pried a finger along the corpse's mouth, breaking the suction with a little pop. Larry looked like he was going to be sick. Poor him; it was my arm.

He wiped his finger on his dress slacks, as if he had touched something slimy. I wasn't sympathetic.

The knife wound was already red. It would be a hell of a bruise tomorrow.

The zombie stood on top of its grave, staring at me. There was life in the eyes; someone was home. The trick was, was it the right someone?

"Are you Andrew Doughal?" I asked.

He licked his lips and said, "I am." It was a rough voice. A voice for ordering people about. I wasn't impressed. It was my blood that gave him the voice. The dead really are mute, really do forget who and what they are, until they taste fresh blood. Homer was right; makes you wonder what else was true in the *Iliad*.

I put pressure on the knife wound with my other hand and stepped back, off the grave. "He'll answer your questions now," I said. "But keep them simple. He's been mostly dead all day."

The lawyers didn't smile. I guess I didn't blame them. I waved them forward. They hung back. Squeamish lawyers? Surely not.

Mrs. Doughal poked her lawyer in the arm. "Get on with it. This is costing a fortune."

I started to say we don't charge by the minute, but for all I knew Bert had arranged for the longer the corpse was up, the more expensive it was. That actually was a good idea. Andrew Doughal was fine tonight. He answered questions in his cultured, articulate voice. If you ignored the way his skin glistened in the moonlight, he looked alive. But give it a few days, or weeks. He'd rot; they all rotted. If Bert had figured out a way to make clients put the dead back in their graves before pieces started to fall off, so much the better.

There were few things as sad as the family bringing dear old mom back to the cemetery with expensive perfume covering up the smell of decay. The worst was the client who had bathed her husband before bringing him back. She had to bring most of his flesh in a plastic garbage sack. The meat had just slid off the bone in the warm water.

Larry moved back, stumbling over a flowerpot. I caught him, and he fell against me, still unsteady.

He smiled. "Thanks . . . for everything." He stared at me, our faces inches apart. A trickle of sweat oozed down his face in the cold October night.

"You got a coat?"

"In my car."

"Get it and put it on. You'll catch your death sweating in this cold."

His smile flashed into a grin. "Anything you say, boss." His eyes were bigger than they should have been, a lot of white showing. "You pulled me back from the edge. I won't forget."

"Gratitude is great, kid, but go get your coat. You can't work if you're home sick with the flu."

Larry nodded and started slowly towards the cars. He was still unsteady, but he was moving. The flow of blood had almost stopped on my wrist. I wondered if I had a Band-Aid in my car big enough to cover it. I shrugged and started to follow Larry towards the cars. The lawyers' deep, courtroom voices filled the October dark. Words echoing against the trees. Who the hell were they trying to impress? The corpse didn't care.

20

Larry and I sat on the cool autumn grass watching the lawyers draw up the will. "They're so serious," he said.

"It's their job to be serious," I said.

"Being a lawyer means you can't have a sense of humor?"

"Absolutely," I said.

He grinned. His short, curly hair was a red so bright, it was nearly orange. His eyes were blue and soft as a spring sky. I'd seen both hair and eyes in the dome light from our cars. Back in the dark he looked grey-eyed and brown-haired. I'd hate to have to give a witness description of someone I only saw in the dark.

Larry Kirkland had that milk-pale complexion of some redheads. A thick sprinkling of golden freckles completed the look. He looked like an over-grown Howdy Doody puppet. I mean that in a cute way. Being short, really short for a man, I was sure he wouldn't like being called cute. It was one of my least favorite endearments. I think if all short people could vote, the word "cute" would be stricken from the English language. I know it would get my vote.

"How long have you been an animator?" I asked.

He glanced at the luminous dial of his watch. "About eight hours."

I stared at him. "This is your first job, anywhere?"

He nodded. "Didn't Mr. Vaughn tell you about me?"

"Bert just said he'd hired another animator named Lawrence Kirkland."

"I'm in my senior year at Washington University, and this is my se-mester of job co-op."

"How old are you?"

"Twenty; why?"

"You're not even legal," I said.

"So I can't drink or go in porno theaters. No big loss, unless the job takes us to places like that." He looked at me and leaned in. "Does the job take us to porno theaters?'' His face was neutrally pleasant, and I couldn't tell if he was teasing or not. I gambled that he was kidding.

"Twenty is fine." I shook my head.

"You don't look like twenty's fine," he said.

"It's not your age that bothers me," I said.

"But something bothers you."

I wasn't sure how to put it into words, but there was something pleasant and humorous in his face. It was a face that laughed more often than it cried. He looked bright and clean as a new penny, and I didn't want that to change. I didn't want to be the one who forced him to get down in the dirt and roll.

"Have you ever lost someone close to you? Family, I mean?"

The humor slipped away from his face. He looked like a solemn little boy. "You're serious."

"Deadly," I said.

He shook his head. "I don't understand."

"Just answer the question. Have you ever lost someone close to you?"

He shook his head. "I've even got all my grandparents."

"Have you ever seen violence up close and personal?"

"I got into fights in high school."

"Why?"

He grinned. "They thought short meant weak."

I had to smile. "And you showed them different."

"Hell, no; they beat the crap out of me for four years." He smiled.

"You ever win a fight?"

"Sometimes," he said.

"But the winning's not the important part," I said.

He looked very steadily at me, eyes serious. "No, it's not."

There was a moment of nearly perfect understanding between us. A shared history of being the smallest kid in class. Years of being the last picked for sports. Being the automatic victim for bullies. Being short can make you mean. I was sure that we understood each other but, being female, I had to verbalize it. Men do a lot of this mind-reading shit, but sometimes you're wrong. I needed to know.

"The important part is taking the beating and not giving up," I said.

He nodded. "Takes a beating and keeps on ticking."

Now that I'd spoiled our first moment of perfect understanding by making us both verbalize, I was happy. "Other than school fights, you've never seen violence?"

"I go to rock concerts."

I shook my head. "Not the same."

"You got a point to make?" he asked.

"You should never have tried to raise a third zombie."

"I did it, didn't I?" He sounded defensive, but I pressed on. When I have a point to make, I may not be graceful, but I'm relentless.

"You raised and lost control of it. If I hadn't come along, the zombie would have broken free and hurt someone."

"It's just a zombie. They don't attack people."

I stared at him, trying to see if he was kidding. He wasn't. Shit. "You really don't know, do you?"

"Know what?"

I covered my face with my hands and counted to ten, slowly. It wasn't Larry I was mad at, it was Bert, but Larry was so convenient for yelling. I'd have to wait until tomorrow to yell at Bert, but Larry was right here. How lucky.

"The zombie had broken free of your control, Larry. If I hadn't come along and fed it blood, it would have found blood on its own. Do you understand?"

"I don't think so."

I sighed. "The zombie would have attacked someone. Taken a bite out of someone."

"Zombies attacking humans is just superstition, ghost stories."

"Is that what they're teaching in college now?" I asked.

"Yes."

"I'll loan you some back copies of *The Animator*. Trust me, Larry, zombies do attack people. I've seen people killed by them."

"You're just trying to scare me," he said.

"Scared would be better than stupid."

"I raised it. What do you want from me?" He looked completely baffled.

"I want you to understand what nearly happened here tonight. I want you to understand that what we do isn't a game. It's not parlor tricks. It's real, and it can be dangerous."

"All right," he said. He'd given in too easily. He didn't really believe. He was humoring me. But there are some things you can't tell someone. He, or she, has to learn some things in person. I wished I could wrap Larry up in cellophane and keep him on a shelf, all safe and secure and untouched, but life didn't work that way. If he stayed in this business long enough, the new would wear off. But you can't tell someone who's reached twenty and never been touched by death. They don't believe in the boogeyman.

At twenty I'd believed in everything. I suddenly felt old.

Larry pulled a pack of cigarettes out of his coat pocket.

"Please tell me you don't smoke," I said.

He looked up at me, eyes sort of wide and startled. "You don't smoke?"

"No."

"You don't like people to smoke around you?" He made it a question.

"No," I said.

"Look, I feel pretty awful right now. I need the cigarette, okay?"

"Need it?"

"Yeah, need it." He had one slender white cigarette between two fingers of his right hand. The pack had disappeared back into his pocket. A disposable lighter had appeared. He looked at me very steadily. His hands were shaking just a bit.

Shit. He'd raised three zombies on his first night out, and I was going to be talking to Bert about the wisdom of sending Larry out on his own.

Besides, we were outside. "Go ahead."

"Thanks."

He lit the cigarette and drew a deep breath of nicotine and tar. Smoke curled out of his mouth and nose, like pale ghosts. "Feel better already," he said.

I shrugged. "Just so you don't smoke in the car with me."

"No problem," he said. The tip of his cigarette pulsed orange in the dark as he sucked on it. He looked past me, letting smoke curl from his lips as he said, "We're being paged."

I turned and, sure enough, the lawyers were waving at us. I felt like a janitor being called in to clean up the messy necessities. I stood up, and Larry followed me.

"You sure you feel well enough for this?" I asked.

"I couldn't raise a dead ant, but I think I'm up to watching you do it."

There were bruises under his eyes and the skin was too tight around his mouth, but if he wanted to play macho man who was I to stop him? "Great; let's do it."

I got salt out of my trunk. It was perfectly legal to carry zombie-raising supplies. I suppose the machete that I used for beheading chickens could be used as a weapon, but the rest of the stuff was considered harmless. Shows you what the legal system knows about zombies.

Andrew Doughal had recovered himself. He still looked a little waxy, but his face was serious, concerned, alive. He smoothed a hand down the stylish lapel of his suit coat. He looked down at me, not just because he was taller but because he was good at looking down. Some people have a real talent for being condescending.

"Do you know what's happening, Mr. Doughal?" I asked the zombie.

He looked down his narrow patrician nose. "I am going home with my wife."

I sighed. I hated it when zombies didn't realize they were dead. They acted so . . . human.

"Mr. Doughal, do you know why you're in a cemetery?"

What's happening?" one of the lawyers asked.

"He's forgotten that he's dead," I said softly.

The zombie stared at me, perfectly arrogant. He must have been a real pain in the ass when he was alive, but even assholes are piteous once in a while.

"I don't know what you are babbling about," the zombie said. "You obviously are suffering from some delusion."

"Can you explain why you are here in a cemetery?" I asked.

"I don't have to explain anything to you."

"Do you remember how you got to the cemetery?"

"We . . . we drove, of course." The first hint of unease wavered through his voice.

"You're guessing, Mr. Doughal. You don't really remember driving to the cemetery, do you?"

"I . . . I . . ." He looked at his wife, his grown children, but they were walking to their cars. No one even looked back. He was dead, no getting around that, but most families didn't just walk away. They might be horrified, or saddened, or even sickened, but they were never neutral. The Doughals had gotten the will signed, and they were leaving. They had their inheritance. Let good ol' dad crawl back into his grave.

He called, "Emily?"

She hesitated, stiffening, but one of her sons grabbed her arm and hurried her toward the cars. Was he embarrassed, or scared?

"I want to go home," he yelled after them. The arrogance had leaked away, and all that was left was that sickening fear, the desperate need not to believe. He felt so alive. How could he possibly be dead?

His wife half-turned. "Andrew, I'm sorry." Her grown children hustled her into the nearest car. You would have thought they were the getaway drivers for a bank robbery, they peeled out so fast.

The lawyers and secretaries left as fast as was decent. Everybody had what they'd come for. They were done with the corpse. The trouble was that the "corpse" was staring after them like a child who was left in the dark.

Why couldn't he have stayed an arrogant SOB?

"Why are they leaving me?" he asked.

"You died, Mr. Doughal, nearly a week ago."

"No, it's not true."

Larry moved up beside me. "You really are dead, Mr. Doughal. I raised you from the dead myself."

He stared from one to the other of us. He was beginning to run out of excuses. "I don't feel dead."

"Trust us, Mr. Doughal, you are dead," I said.

"Will it hurt?"

A lot of zombies asked that; will it hurt to go back into the grave? "No, Mr. Doughal, it doesn't hurt. I promise."

He took a deep, shaking breath and nodded. "I'm dead, really dead?"

"Yes."

"Then put me back, please." He had rallied and found his dignity. It was nightmarish when the zombie refused to believe. You could still lay them to rest, but the clients had to hold them down on the grave while they screamed. I'd only had that happen twice, but I remembered each time as if it had happened last night. Some things don't dim with time.

I threw salt against his chest. It sounded like sleet hitting a roof. "With salt I bind you to your grave."

I had the still-bloody knife in my hand. I wiped the gelling blood across his lips. He didn't jerk away. He believed. "With blood and steel I bind you to your grave, Andrew Doughal. Be at peace, and walk no more."

The zombie laid full length on the mound of flowers. The flowers seemed to flow over him like quicksand, and just like that he was swallowed back into the grave.

We stood there a minute in the empty graveyard. The only sounds were the wind sighing high up in the trees and the melancholy song of the year's last crickets. In *Charlotte's Web*, the crickets sang, "Summer is over and gone. Over and gone, over and gone. Summer is dying, dying." The first hard frost, and the crickets would be dying. They were like Chicken Little, who told everyone the sky was falling; except in this case, the crickets were right.

The crickets stopped suddenly like someone had turned a switch. I held my breath, straining to hear. There was nothing but the wind, and yet . . . My shoulders were so tight they hurt. "Larry?"

He turned innocent eyes to me. "What?"

There, three trees to our left, a man's figure was silhouetted against the moonlight. I caught movement out of the corner of my eye, on the right side. More than one. The darkness felt alive with eyes. More than two.

I used Larry's body to shield me from the eyes, drawing my gun, holding it along my leg so it wouldn't be obvious.

Larry's eyes widened. "Jesus, what's wrong?" His voice was a hoarse whisper. He didn't give us away. Good for him. I started herding him towards the cars, slowly, just your friendly neighborhood animators finished with their night's work and going home to a well-deserved rest.

"There are people out here."

"After us?"

"After me, more likely," I said.

"Why?"

I shook my head. "No time for explanations. When I say run, run like hell for the cars."

"How do you know they mean to hurt us?" His eyes were flashing a lot of white. He saw them now, too. Shadows moving closer, people out in the dark.

"How do you know they don't mean to hurt us?" I asked.

"Good point," he said. His breathing was fast and shallow. We were maybe twenty feet from the cars.

"Run," I said.

"What?" his voice sounded startled.

I grabbed his arm and dragged him into a run for the cars. I pointed the gun at the ground, still hoping whoever it was wouldn't be prepared for a gun.

Larry was running on his own, puffing a little from fear, smoking, and maybe he didn't run four miles every other day.

A man stepped in front of the cars. He brought up a large revolver. The Browning was already moving. It fired before my aim was steady. The muzzle flashed brilliant in the dark. The man jumped, not used to being shot at. His shot whined into the darkness to our left. He froze for the seconds it took me to aim and fire again. Then he crumpled to the ground and didn't get up again.

"Shit." Larry breathed it like a sigh.

A voice yelled, "She's got a gun."

"Where's Martin?"

"She shot him."

I guess Martin was the one with the gun. He still wasn't moving. I didn't know if I killed him or not. I wasn't sure I cared, as long as he didn't get up and shoot at us again.

My car was closer. I shoved car keys into Larry's hands. "Open the door, open the passenger side door, then start the car. Do you understand me?"

He nodded, freckles standing out in the pale circle of his face. I had to trust that he wouldn't panic and take off without me. He wouldn't do it out of malice, just fear.

Figures were converging from all directions. There had to be a dozen or more. The sound of running feet whispering on grass came over the wind.

Larry stepped over the body. I kicked a .45 away from the limp hand. The gun slid out of sight under the car. If I hadn't been pressed for time, I'd have checked his pulse. I always like to know if I've killed someone. Makes the police report go so much smoother.

Larry had the car door open and was leaning over to unlock the passenger side door. I aimed at one of the running figures and pulled the trigger. The figure stumbled, fell, and started screaming. The others hesitated. They weren't used to being shot at. Poor babies.

I slid into the car and yelled, "Drive, drive, drive!"

Larry peeled out in a spray of gravel. The car fishtailed, headlights swaying crazily. "Don't wrap us around a tree, Larry."

His eyes flicked to me. "Sorry." The car slowed from stomach-turning speed to grab-the-door-handle-and-hold-on speed. We were staying between the trees; that was something.

The headlights bounced off trees; tombstones flashed white. The car skidded around a curve, gravel spitting. A man stood framed in the middle of the road. Jeremy Ruebens of Humans First stood pale and shining in the lights. He stood in the middle of a flat stretch of road. If we could make the turn beyond him, we'd be out on the highway and safe.

The car was slowing down.

"What are you doing?" I asked.

"I can't just hit him," Larry said.

"The hell you can't."

"I can't!" His voice wasn't outraged, it was scared.

"He's just playing chicken with us, Larry. He'll move."

"Are you sure?" A little boy's voice asking if there really was a monster in the closet.

"I'm sure; now floor it and get us out of here."

He pressed down on the accelerator. The car jumped forward, rushing toward the small, straight figure of Jeremy Ruebens.

"He's not moving," Larry said.

"He'll move," I said.

"Are you sure?"

"Trust me."

His eyes flicked to me, then back to the road. "You better be right," he whispered.

I believed Ruebens would move. Honest. But even if he wasn't bluffing, the only way out was either past him or through him. It was Ruebens's choice.

The headlights bathed him in glaring white light. His small, dark features glared at us. He wasn't moving.

"He isn't moving," Larry said.

"He'll move," I said.

"Shit," Larry said. I couldn't have agreed more.

The headlights roared up onto Jeremy Ruebens, and he threw himself to one side. There was the sound of brushing cloth as his coat slid along the car's side. Close, damn close.

Larry picked up speed and swung us around the last corner and into the last straight stretch. We spilled out onto the highway in a shower of gravel and spinning tires. But we were out of the cemetery. We'd made it. Thank you, God.

Larry's hands were white on the steering wheel. "You can ease down now," I said. "We're safe."

He swallowed hard enough for me to hear it, then nodded. The car started gradually approaching the speed limit. His face was beaded with sweat that had nothing to do with the cool October evening.

"You all right?"

"I don't know." His voice sounded sort of hollow. Shock.

"You did good back there."

"I thought I was going to run over him. I thought I was going to kill him with the car."

"He thought so, too, or he wouldn't have moved," I said.

He looked at me. "What if he hadn't moved?"

"He did move."

"But what if he hadn't?"

"Then we would have gone over him, and we'd still be on the highway, safe."

"You would have let me run him down, wouldn't you?"

"Survival is the name of the game, Larry. If you can't deal with that, find another business to be in."

"Animators don't get shot at."

"Those were members of Humans First, a right-wing fanatic group that hates anything to do with the supernatural." So I was leaving out about the personal visit from Jeremy Ruebens. What the kid didn't know might not hurt him.

I stared at his pale face. He looked hollow-eyed. He'd met the dragon, a little dragon as dragons go, but once you've seen violence, you're never the same again. The first time you have to decide, live or die, us or them, it changes you forever. No going back. I stared at Larry's shocked face and wished it could have been different. I wished I could have kept him shining, new, and hopeful. But as my Grandmother Blake used to say, "If wishes were horses, we'd all ride."

Larry had had his first taste of my world. The only question was, would he want a second dose, or would he run? Run or go, stay or fight, age-old questions. I wasn't sure which way I wanted Larry to choose. He might live longer if he got the hell away from me, but then again maybe he wouldn't. Heads they win, tails you lose.

21

"What about my car?" Larry asked.

I shrugged. "You've got insurance, right?"

"Yes, but . . ."

"Since they couldn't trash us, they may decide to trash your car."

He looked at me as if he wasn't sure whether I was kidding. I wasn't.

There was a bicycle in front of us suddenly, out of the dark. A child's pale face flashed in the headlights. "Watch out!"

Larry's eyes flicked back to the road in time to see the kid's wide, startled eyes. The brakes squealed, and the child vanished from the narrow arch of lights. There was a crunch and a bump before the car skidded to a stop. Larry was breathing heavy; I wasn't breathing at all.

The cemetery was just on our right. We were too close to stop, but . . . but, shit, it was a kid.

I stared out the back window. The bicycle was a crumpled mess. The child lay in a very still heap. God, please don't let him be dead.

I didn't think Humans First had enough imagination to have a child in reserve as bait. If it was a trap, it was a good one, because I couldn't leave the tiny figure crumpled by the road.

Larry was gripping the steering wheel so hard his arms shook. If I thought he'd been pale before, I'd been wrong. He looked like a sick ghost.

"Is he . . . hurt?" His voice squeezed out deep and rough with something like tears. It wasn't hurt he'd wanted to say. He just couldn't bring himself to use the big "D" word. Not yet, not if he could help it.

"Stay in the car," I said.

Larry didn't answer. He just sat there staring at his hands. He wouldn't look at me. But, dammit, this wasn't my fault. The fact that he'd lost his cherry tonight was not my fault. So why did it feel like it was?

I got out of the car, Browning ready in case the crazies decided to chase us onto the road. They could have gotten the .45 and be coming to shoot us.

The child hadn't moved. I was just too far away to see the chest rise and fall. Yeah, that was it. I was maybe a yard away.

Please be alive.

The child lay sprawled on its stomach, one arm trapped underneath, probably broken. I scanned the dark cemetery as I knelt by the child. No right-wing crazies came swarming out of the darkness. The child was dressed in the proverbial little boy's outfit of striped shirt, shorts, and tiny running shoes. Who had sent him out dressed for summer on this cold night? His mother. Had some woman dressed him, loved him, sent him out to die?

His curly brown hair was silken, baby-fine. The skin of his neck was cool to the touch. Shock? It was too soon to be cold from death. I waited for the big pulse in his neck, but nothing happened. Dead. Please, God, please.

His head raised up, and a soft sound came out of his mouth. Alive. Thank you, God.

He tried to roll over but fell back against the road. He cried out.

Larry was out of the car, coming towards us. "Is he all right?"

"He's alive," I said.

The boy was determined to roll over, so I grabbed his shoulders and helped. I tried to keep his right arm in against his body. I had a glimpse of huge brown eyes, round baby face, and in his right hand was a knife bigger than he was. He whispered, "Tell him to come help move me." Tiny little fangs showed between baby lips. The knife pressed against my stomach over the sport bag. The point slid underneath the leather jacket to touch the shirt underneath. I had one of those frozen moments when time stretches out in slow-mo nightmare. I had all the time in the world to decide whether to betray Larry, or die. Never give anyone to the monsters; it's a rule. I opened my mouth and screamed, "Run!"

The vampire didn't stab me. He just froze. He wanted me alive; that's why the knife and not fangs. I stood up, and the vampire just stared up at me. He didn't have a backup plan. Great.

The car stood, open doors spilling light out into the darkness. The head-lights made a wide theatrical swash. Larry was just standing there, frozen, undecided. I yelled, "Get in the car!"

He moved towards the open car door. A woman was standing in the glare of the headlights. She was dressed in a long white coat open over the cream and tan of a very nice pants suit. She opened her mouth and snarled into the light, fangs glistening.

I was running, screaming, "Behind you!"

Larry stared at me; his gaze went past me. His eyes widened. I could hear the patter of little feet behind me. Terror spread across Larry's face. Was this the first vampire he'd ever seen?

I drew my gun, but was still running. You can't hit shit when you're running. I had a vampire in front and behind. Coin toss.

The female vampire bounded onto the hood of the car and propelled herself in a long, graceful leap that carried her into Larry and sent them tumbling across the road.

I couldn't shoot her without risking Larry. I whirled at the last second and put the gun point-blank into the child-vampire's face.

His eyes widened. I squeezed the trigger. Something hit me from behind. The shot went wild and I was on the road, flat on my stomach with something bigger than a bread box on top of me.

The air was knocked out of me. But I turned, trying to point the gun back at the thing on my back. If I didn't do something now, I might never have to worry about breathing again.

The boy came up on me, knife flashing downward. The gun was turning, but too slowly. I would have screamed if I'd had air. The knife buried into the sleeve of my jacket. I felt the blade bite into the road underneath. My arm was pinned. I squeezed the trigger and the shot went harmlessly off into the dark.

I twisted my neck to try to see who, or what, was straddling me. It was a what. In the red glow of the rear car lights his face was all flat, high cheekbones with narrow, almost slanted eyes and long, straight hair. If he'd been any more ethnic, he'd have been carved in stone, surrounded by snakes and Aztec gods.

He reached over me and encircled my right hand, the one that was pinned, the one that was still holding the gun. He pressed the bones of my hand into the metal. His voice was deep and soft. "Drop the gun or I'll crush your hand." He squeezed until I gasped.

Larry screamed, high and mournful.

Screaming was for when you didn't have anything better to do. I scraped my left sleeve against the road, baring my watch and the charm bracelet. The three tiny crosses glinted in the moonlight. The vampire hissed but didn't let go of my gun hand. I dragged the bracelet across his hand. A sharp smell of burning flesh; then he used his free hand to drag at my left sleeve. Holding onto just the sleeve, he held my left hand back, so I couldn't touch him with the crosses.

If he'd been the new dead, just the sight of the crosses would have sent him screaming; but he wasn't just old dead, he was ancient. It was going to take more than blessed crosses to get him off my back.

Larry screamed again.

I screamed, too, because I couldn't do anything else, except hold onto the gun and make him crush my hand. Not productive. They didn't want me dead, but hurt, hurt was okay. He could crush my hand into bloody pulp. I gave up my gun, screaming, tugging at the knife that held my arm pinned, trying to jerk my left sleeve free of his hand so I could plunge the crosses into his flesh.

A shot exploded above our heads. We all froze and stared back at the cemetery. Jeremy Ruebens and company had recovered their gun and were shooting at us. Did they think we were in cahoots with the monsters? Did they care who they shot?

A woman screamed, "Alejandro, help me!" The scream was from behind us. The vampire on my back was suddenly gone. I didn't know why, and I didn't care. I was left with the child-monster looming over me, staring at me with large dark eyes.

"Doesn't it hurt?" he asked.

It was such an unexpected question that I answered it. "No."

He looked disappointed. He squatted down beside me, hands on his small thighs. "I meant to cut you so I could lick the blood." His voice was still a little boy's voice, would always be a little boy's voice, but the knowledge in his eyes beat down on my skin like heat. He was older than Jean-Claude, much older.

A bullet smashed into the rear light of my car, just above the boy's head. He turned towards the fanatics with a very unchildlike snarl. I tried to pull the knife out of the road, but it was imbedded. I couldn't budge it.

The boy crawled into the darkness, vanishing with a backwash of wind. He was going for the fanatics. God help them.

I looked back over my shoulder. Larry was on the ground with a woman with long, waving brown hair on top of him. The man who'd been on top of me, Alejandro, and another woman were struggling with the vampire on Larry. She wanted to kill him, and they were trying to stop her. It seemed like a good plan to me.

Another bullet whined towards us. It didn't come close. A half-strangled scream, and then no more gunshots. Had the boy gotten him? Was Larry hurt? And what the hell could I do to help him, and me?

The vampires seemed to have their hands full. Whatever I was going to do, now was the time. I tried unzipping the leather jacket left-handed, but it stuck halfway down. Great. I bit the side of the jacket, using my teeth in place of the trapped hand. Unzipped; now what?

I pulled the sleeve off my left hand with my teeth, then put the sleeve under my hip and wiggled out of it. Slipping my right hand free of the pinned sleeve was the easy part.

Alejandro picked up the brown-haired woman and threw her over the car. She sailed into the darkness, but I didn't hear her hit the ground. Maybe she could fly. If she could, I didn't want to know.

Larry was nearly lost to sight behind a curtain of pale hair. The second female was bending over him like a prince about to bestow the magic kiss. Alejandro got a handful of that long, long hair and jerked her to her feet. He flung her into the side of the car. She staggered but didn't go down, snapping at him like a dog on a leash.

I went wide around them, holding the crosses out in front like every old movie you've ever seen. Except I'd never seen a vampire hunter with a charm bracelet.

Larry was on his hands and knees, swaying ever so slightly. His voice was high, nearly hysterical. He just kept repeating, "I'm bleeding, I'm bleeding."

I touched his arm, and he jumped like I'd bit him. His eyes flashed white.

Blood was welling down his neck, black in the moonlight. She'd bit him, Jesus help us, she'd bit him.

The pale female was still fighting to get to Larry. "Can't you smell the blood?" It was a plea.

"Control yourself, or I'll do it for you." Alejandro's voice was a low scream. The anger in his voice cut and sliced. The pale woman went very still.

"I'm all right now." Her voice held fear. I'd never heard one vampire be scared to . . . death of another. Let them fight it out. I had better things to do. Like figuring out how to get us past the remaining vampires and into the car.

Alejandro had the female shoved against the car with one hand. My gun was in his left hand. I unsnapped the anklet with its matching crosses. You can't sneak up on a vampire. Even the new dead are jumpier than a long-tailed cat in a room full of rocking chairs. Since I had no chance of sneaking up on him, I tried the direct approach.

"She bit him, you son of a bitch. She bit him!" I pulled the back of his shirt as if to get his attention. I dropped the crosses down his back.

He screamed.

I brushed the bracelet crosses across his hand. He dropped the gun. I caught it. A tongue of blue flame licked up his back. He clawed and scrambled, but he couldn't reach the crosses. Burn, baby, burn.

He whirled, shrieking. His open hand caught me on the side of the head. I was airborne. I slammed back-first into the road. I tried to take as much of the impact as I could with my arms, but my head rocked back, slamming into the road.

The world swam with black spots. When my vision cleared, I was staring up into a pale face; long, yellow-white hair the color of corn silk traced over my cheek as the vampire knelt to feed.

I still had the Browning in my right hand. I pulled the trigger. Her body jerked backwards like someone had shoved her. She fell back onto the road, blood pouring out of a hole in her stomach that was nothing compared to the wound in her back. I hoped I'd shattered her spine.

I staggered to my feet.

The male vampire, Alejandro, tore off his shirt. The crosses fell to the road in a little pool of molten blue fire. His back was burned black, with blisters here and there to add color. He whirled on me, and I shot him once in the chest. The shot was rushed, and he didn't go down.

Larry grabbed the vampire's ankle. Still Alejandro kept coming, dragging Larry across the blacktop like a child. He grabbed Larry's arm, jerking him to his feet. Larry threw a chain over the vampire's head. The heavy silver cross burst into flame. Alejandro screamed.

I yelled, "Get in the car, now!"

Larry slid into the driver's seat and kept sliding until he was in the passenger seat. He slammed the passenger side door shut and locked it, for what good it would do. The vampire tore the chain and threw the cross end over end into the roadside trees. The cross winked out of sight like a falling star.

I slid into the car, slamming the door and locking it. I clicked the safety on the Browning and shoved it between my legs.

The vampire, Alejandro, was huddled around his pain, too hurt to give chase right that second. Goodie.

I shoved the car in gear and gunned it. The car fishtailed. I slowed to the speed of light, and the car straightened out on the road. We poured down the dark tunnel in a circle of flickering light and tree shadows. And down at the end of our tunnel was a figure in white with long, brown hair spilling in the wind. It was the vampire that had jumped Larry. She was just standing there in the middle of the road. Just standing there. We were about to find out if vampires played chicken. I was about to take my own advice. I put the gas pedal to the floorboards. The car lurched forward. The vampire just stood there while we barreled down at her.

At the last second I realized she wasn't going to move, and I didn't have time to. We were about to test my theory about cars and vampiric flesh. Where's a silver car when you need one?

22

The headlights flashed on the vampire like a spotlight. I had an image of pale face, brown hair, fangs stretched wide. We hit her going sixty. The car shuddered. She rolled in painful slow motion up over the hood, and yet it was happening too fast for me to do anything. She hit the windshield with a sharp, crackling sound. Metal screamed.

The windshield crumbled into a mass of spiderweb cracks. I was suddenly trying to see through the wrong end of a smashed prism. The safety glass had done its job. It hadn't shattered and cut us to ribbons. It had just cracked all to hell, and I couldn't see to drive. I stamped down on the brakes.

An arm shot through the glass, raining glittering shards down on Larry. He screamed. The hand closed on his shirt, pulling him into the broken teeth of the windshield.

I turned the wheel to the left as hard as I could. The car spun out and all I could do was let off the gas, not touch the brake, and ride.

Larry had a death grip on the door arm and the headrest. He was screaming, fighting not to be pulled through the jagged glass. I said a quick prayer and let go of the wheel. The car spun helplessly. I shoved a cross against the hand. It smoked and bubbled. The hand let go of Larry and vanished through the hole in the crumbled glass.

I grabbed at the steering wheel, but it was too little too late. The car careened off the road into the ditch. Metal screamed as something under the car broke, something large. I was slammed into the driver's side door. Larry was suddenly on top of me; then we were both tumbling to the other side. Then it was over. The silence was startling. It was as if I'd gone deaf. There was a great roaring whiteness in my ears.

Someone said, "Thank God," and it was me.

The passenger side door peeled open like the shell of a nut. I scrambled back away from the opening. Larry was left stranded and staring. He was jerked out of the car. I slid into the front floorboard, aiming where Larry had vanished.

I was staring up at Larry's body with a dark hand clamped so tight on his throat, I didn't know if he could breathe. I stared down the barrel of my gun at the dark face of the vampire, Alejandro. His face was unreadable as he said, "I will tear his throat out."

"I'll blow your head off," I said. A hand came fishing through the broken windshield. "Back off or you lose that pretty face."

"He will die first," the vampire said. But the hand vanished back through the hole. There was the sound of some other language in the vampire's English. Emotion gave him an accent.

Larry's eyes were too wide, showing too much white. He was breathing, shallow and too fast. He'd hyperventilate, if he lived that long.

"Decide," the vampire said. His voice was flat, empty of everything. Larry's terror-filled eyes were eloquent enough for both of them.

I hit the safety on the gun and handed it butt-first to his outstretched hand. It was a mistake, I knew that, but I also knew I couldn't sit here and watch Larry's throat be ripped out. There are some things that are more important than physical survival. You gotta be able to look at yourself in the mirror. I gave up my gun for the same reason I'd stopped for the child. There was no choice. I was one of the good guys. Good guys were self-sacrificing. It was a rule somewhere.

23

Larry's face was a bloody mask. No single cut seemed to be serious, but nothing bleeds like a shallow scalp wound. Safety glass was not designed to be vampire-proof. Maybe I could write in and suggest it.

Blood trickled over Alejandro's hand, still gripping Larry's throat. The vampire had stuffed my gun in the back of his pants. He handled the gun like he knew how to use one. Pity. Some vampires were technophobes. It gave you an edge, sometimes.

Larry's blood flowed over the vampire's hand. Sticky and warm like barely solid Jell-O. The vampire didn't react to the blood. Iron self-control. I stared into his nearly black eyes and felt the pull of centuries like monstrous wings unfolding in his eyes. The world swam. The inside of my head was sinking, expanding. I reached out to touch something, anything to keep from falling. A hand gripped mine. The skin was cool and smooth. I jerked back, falling against the car.

"Don't touch me! Don't ever touch me!"

The vampire stood uncertainly, Larry's throat gripped in one blood-streaked hand, holding his other hand out towards me. It was a very human gesture. Larry's eyes were bugging out.

"You're choking him," I said.

"Sorry," the vampire said. He released him.

Larry fell to his knees, gasping. His first breath was a hissing scream for air.

I wanted to ask Larry how he was, but I didn't. My job was to get us out of here alive, if possible. Besides, I had an idea how Larry felt. Hurt. No need to ask stupid questions.

Well, maybe one stupid question. "What do you want?" I asked.

Alejandro looked at me, and I fought the urge to look at his face while I talked to him. It was hard. I ended up staring at the hole my bullet had made in the side of his chest. It was a very small hole, and had already stopped bleeding. Was he healing that fast? Shit. I stared at the wound as hard as I could. To fight the urge for eye contact. It's hard to be tough when you're staring at someone's chest. But I'd had years of practice before Jean-Claude decided to share his "gift" with me. Practice makes . . . well, you know.

The vampire hadn't answered me, so I asked again, voice steady and low. I didn't sound like someone who was afraid. Bully for me. "What do you want?"

I felt the vampire look at me, almost as if he'd run a finger down my body. I shivered and couldn't stop. Larry crawled to me, head hanging, dripping blood as he moved.

I knelt beside him. And before I could stop myself, the stupid question popped out. "Are you all right?"

His eyes raised to me through a mask of blood. He finally said, "Nothing a few stitches wouldn't cure." He was trying to make a joke. I wanted to hug him and promise the worst was over. Never make promises you can't keep.

The vampire didn't exactly move, but something brought my attention back to him. He stood knee-deep in autumn weeds. My eyes were on a level with his belt buckle, which made him about my height. Short for a man. A white, Anglo-Saxon, twentieth-century man. The belt buckle glinted gold and was carved into a blocky, stylized human figure. The carving, like the vampire's face, was straight out of an Aztec calendar.

The urge to look upward and meet his eyes crawled over my skin. My chin had actually risen an inch or so before I realized what I was doing. Shit. The vamp was messing with my mind, and I couldn't feel it. Even now, knowing he had to be doing something to me, I couldn't sense it. I was blind and deaf just like every other tourist.

Well, maybe not every tourist. I hadn't been munched on yet, which probably meant they wanted something more than just blood. I'd be dead otherwise, and so would Larry. Of course, I was still wearing blessed crosses. What could this creature do once I was stripped of crosses? I did not want to find out.

We were alive. It meant they wanted something that we couldn't give them dead. But what?

"What in the hell do you want?"

His hand came into view. He was offering his hand to help me stand. I stood without help, putting myself a little in front of Larry.

"Tell me who your master is, girl, and I won't hurt you."

"Who else will, then?" I asked.

"Clever, but I swear you will leave here in safety if you give me the name."

"First of all, I don't have a master. I'm not even sure I have an equal." I fought the urge to glance at his face, see if he got the joke. Jean-Claude would have gotten it.

"You stand before me, making jokes?" His voice sounded surprised, nearly outraged. Good, I think.

"I don't have a master," I said. Master vampires can smell truth or lies.

"If you truly believe that, you are deluding yourself. You bear two master signs. Give me the name and I will destroy him for you. I will free you of this . . . problem."

I hesitated. He was older than Jean-Claude. A lot older. He might be able to kill the Master of the City. Of course, that would leave this master vampire in control of the city. He and his three helpers. Four vampires, one less than were killing people, but I was willing to bet there was a fifth vamp around here somewhere. You couldn't have that many rogue master vampires running around one medium-size city.

Any master that was slaughtering civilians would be a bad thing to have in charge of all the vampires in the area. Just call it a feeling.

I shook my head. "I can't."

"You want free of him, do you not?"

"Very much."

"Let me free you, Ms. Blake. Let me help you."

"Like you helped the man and woman you murdered?"

"I did not murder them," he said. His voice sounded very reasonable. His eyes were powerful enough to drown in but the voice wasn't as good. There was no magic to the voice. Jean-Claude's was better. Or Yasmeen's, for that matter. Nice to know that not every talent came equally with time. Ancient wasn't everything.

"So you didn't strike the fatal blow. So what? Your flunkies do your will, not their own."

"You'd be surprised how much free will we have."

"Stop it," I said.

"What?"

"Sounding so damn reasonable."

There was laughter in his voice. "You would rather I rant and rave?"

Yes, actually, but I didn't say it out loud. "I won't give you the name. Now what?"

There was a rush of wind at my back. I tried to turn, to face the wind. The woman in white rushed at me. Fangs straining, hands clawing, spattered with other people's blood, the vampire smashed into me. We fell backwards into the weeds with her on top. She darted towards my neck like a snake. I shoved my left wrist into her face. One cross brushed her lips. A flash of light, the stench of burning flesh, and the vampire was gone, screaming into the darkness. I had never seen any vampire move that fast. Had it been mind-magic? Had she tricked me that badly even with a blessed cross? How many over-five-hundred-year-old vamps can you have in one pack? Two, I hoped. Any more than that and they'd have us outnumbered.

I scrambled to my feet. The master vampire was on his hands and knees beside the remains of my car. Larry was nowhere in sight. A flutter of panic clawed at my chest; then I realized Larry had crawled underneath the car so the vampire couldn't make him a hostage again. When all else fails, hide. It works for rabbits.

The vampire's blistered back was bent at a painful angle as he tried to pull Larry out from under the car. "I will pull this arm out of its socket, if you do not come here!"

"You sound like you've got a kitten under the bed," I said.

Alejandro whirled around. He flinched, like it hurt. Great.

I felt something move behind me. I didn't argue with the sensation. Say it was nerves; I turned, crosses ready. Two vampires behind me. One was the pale-haired female. I guess the shot had missed her spine; pity. The other vampire could have been her male twin. They both hissed and cowered from the crosses. Nice to see someone was bothered.

The master came at me from the back, but I heard him. Either the burn was making him clumsy, or the crosses were helping me. I stood halfway between the three vampires, crosses sort of pointed at both groups. The blonds peered over their arms, but the crosses had them well and truly scared. The master never hesitated. He came in a rushing burst of speed. I backpedaled, tried to keep the crosses between us, but he grabbed my left forearm. With the crosses dangling inches from his flesh, he held on.

I pulled, getting as much distance from him as I could, then hit him in the solar plexus with everything I had. He made an "umph" sound, then flicked his hand at my face. I rocked back and tasted blood. He'd barely touched me, but he'd proven his point. If I wanted to exchange blows, he'd beat the crap out of me.

I hit him in the throat. He gagged and looked surprised. Beaten to snot was still a hell of a lot better than being bitten. I'd rather be dead than have pointy teeth.

His fist closed over my right fist, squeezing just enough to let me feel his strength. He was still trying to warn me off rather than hurt me. Bully for him.

He raised both his arms, drawing me closer into his body. I didn't want closer, but there didn't seem to be a hell of a lot I could do about it. Unless, of course, vampires had testicles. The throat shot had hurt. I glanced at his face, almost close enough to kiss. I leaned into him, getting as much room as I could. He just kept drawing me closer. His own momentum helped.

My knee hit him hard, and I ground it up and into him. It was not a glancing blow. He crumpled forward but didn't let go of my hands. I wasn't loose, but it was a start, and I'd answered an age-old question. Vampires did have balls.

He jerked my hands behind my back, pinning me between his arms and his body. His body felt wooden, stiff, and unyielding as stone. It had been warm and soft and hurtable only a second before. What had happened?

"Take the things off her wrist," he said. He wasn't talking to me.

I tried to crane my head around to see what was coming up behind me. I couldn't see anything. The two pale vampires were still huddled in the face of the naked crosses.

Something touched my wrist. I jerked, but he held me still. "If you struggle, he will cut you."

I turned my head as far back as I could, and was staring into the round eyes of the boy vampire. He'd recovered his knife and was using it to poke at the bracelet.

The master vampire's hands squeezed my arms until I thought they'd pop from the pressure like shaken soda pop. I must have made some sound, because he said, "I did not mean to hurt you tonight." His mouth was pressed against my ear, lost in my hair. "This was your choice."

The bracelet broke with a small snap. I felt it fall away into the weeds. The master vampire drew a deep breath, as if it were easier to breathe now. He was only an inch or two taller than I was, but he held both my wrists in one small hand, fingers squeezing to make the grip tight. It hurt, and I fought not to make small, helpless noises.

He stroked his free hand through my hair, then grabbed a handful and pulled my head backwards so he could see my eyes. His eyes were solid, absolute black; the whites had drowned. "I will have his name, Anita, one way or another."

I spit in his face.

He screamed, tightening his grip on my wrists until I cried out. "I could have made this pleasant, but now I think I want you to hurt. Look into my eyes, mortal, and despair. Taste of my eyes, and there will be no secrets between us." His voice dropped to the barest of whispers. "Perhaps I will drink your mind like others drink blood, and leave nothing behind but your mindless husk."

I stared into the darkness that was his eyes and felt myself fall, forward, impossibly forward, and down, down into a blackness that was pure and total, and had never known light.

24

I was staring up into a face I didn't know. The face was holding a bloody handkerchief to its forehead. Short hair, pale eyes, freckles. "Hi, Larry," I said. My voice sounded distant and strange. I couldn't remember why.

It was still dark. Larry's face had been cleaned up a little, but the wound was still bleeding. I couldn't have been out that long. Out? Where had I been out to? All I could remember was eyes, black eyes. I sat up too fast. Larry caught my arm or I would have fallen.

"Where are the . . ."

"Vampires," he finished for me.

I leaned into his arm and whispered, "Yeah."

There were people all around us in the dark, huddled in little whispering groups. The lights of a police car strobed the darkness. Two uniforms were standing quietly next to the car, talking with a man whose name wouldn't come to me.

"Karl," I said.

"What?" Larry asked.

"Karl Inger, the tall man talking to the police."

Larry nodded. "That's right."

A small, dark man knelt beside us. Jeremy Ruebens of Humans First, who last I knew had been shooting at us. What the hell was going on?

Jeremy smiled at me. It looked genuine.

"What makes you my friend all of a sudden?"

His smile broadened. "We saved you."

I pushed away from Larry to sit on my own. A moment of dizziness and I was fine. Yeah, right. "Talk to me, Larry."

He glanced at Jeremy Ruebens, then back to me. "They saved us."

"How?"

"They threw holy water on the one who bit me." He touched his throat with his free hand, an unconscious gesture, but he noticed me watching. "Is she going to have control over me?"

"Did she enter your mind at the same time as she bit you?"

"I don't know," he said. "How can you tell?"

I opened my mouth to explain, then closed it. How to explain the unexplainable? "If Alejandro, the master vampire, had bitten me at the same time he rolled my mind, I'd be under his power now."

"Alejandro?"

"That's what the other vampires called the master."

I shook my head, but the world swam in black waves and I had to swallow hard not to vomit. What had he done to me? I'd had mind games played on me before, but I'd never had a reaction like this.

"There's an ambulance coming," Larry said.

"I don't need one."

"You've been unconscious for over an hour, Ms. Blake," Ruebens said. "We had the police call an ambulance when we couldn't wake you."

Ruebens was close enough for me to reach out and touch him. He looked friendly, positively radiant, like a bride on her big day. Why was I suddenly his favorite person? "So they threw holy water on the vamp that bit you; what then?" I asked Larry.

"They drove the rest of them off with crosses and charms."

"Charms?"

Ruebens pulled out a chain with two miniature metalfaced books hanging on it. Both books would have fit in the palm of my hand with room to spare. "They aren't charms, Larry. They're tiny Jewish Holy Books."

"I thought a Star of David."

"The star doesn't work, because it's a racial symbol, not really a religious symbol."

"So it's like miniature Bibles?"

I raised my eyebrows. "The Torah contains the Old Testament, so yeah, it's like miniature Bibles."

"Would the Bible work for us Christians?"

"I don't know. Probably, I've just never been attacked by vampires while carrying a Bible." That was probably my fault. In fact, when was the last time I'd read the Bible? Was I becoming a Sunday Christian? I'd worry about my soul later, after my body felt a little better.

"Cancel the ambulance; I'm fine."

"You are not fine," Ruebens said. He reached out as if to touch me. I looked at him. He stopped in mid-motion. "Let us help you, Ms. Blake. We share common enemies."

The police were walking towards us over the dark grass. Karl Inger was coming, too, talking softly to the police as they moved.

"Do the police know you were shooting at us first?"

Something passed over Ruebens's face.

"They don't know, do they?"

"We saved you, Ms. Blake, from a fate worse than death. I was wrong

to try and hurt you. You raise the dead, but if you are truly enemies with
the vampires, then we are allies.''

"The enemy of my enemy is my friend, huh?''

He nodded.

The police were almost here, almost within earshot. "All right, but you
ever point a gun at me again and I'll forget you saved me.''

"It will never happen again, Ms. Blake; you have my word.''

I wanted to say something disparaging, but the police were there. They'd
hear. I wasn't going to tell on Ruebens and Humans First, so I had to save
my smart alec comebacks for later use. Knowing Ruebens, I'd get another
chance.

I lied to the police about what Humans First had done, and I lied about
what Alejandro had wanted from me. It was just another of those mindless
attacks that had happened twice already. Later, to Dolph and Zerbrowski,
I'd tell the truth, but right now I just didn't feel like explaining the entire
mess to strangers. I wasn't even sure Dolph would get the whole story. Like
the fact that I was almost assuredly Jean-Claude's human servant.

Nope, no need to mention that.

25

Larry's car was a late-model Mazda. The vampires had kept Humans First so busy they hadn't had time to trash the car. Lucky for us, since my car was totaled. Oh, I'd have to go through the insurance company and let them tell me the car was totaled, but there was something large broken underneath the car; fluids darker than blood were leaking out. The front end looked like we'd hit an elephant. I knew totaled when I saw it.

We'd spent the last several hours at the emergency room. The ambulance attendants insisted I see a doctor, and Larry needed three small stitches in his forehead. His orangey hair fell forward and hid the wound. His first scar. The first of many if he stayed in this business and hung around me.

"You've been on the job, what, fourteen hours? What do you think so far?" I asked.

He glanced at me sideways, then back to the road. He smiled, but it didn't look funny. "I don't know."

"Do you want to be an animator when you graduate?"

"I thought I did," he said.

Honesty; a rare talent. "Not sure now?"

"Not really."

I let it rest there. My instinct was to talk him out of it. To tell him to go into some sane, normal business. But I knew that raising the dead wasn't just a job choice. If your "talent" was strong enough, you had to raise the dead or risk the power coming out at odd moments. Does the term roadkill mean anything to you? It meant something to my stepmother Judith. Of course, she wasn't pleased with my job. She thought it was gruesome. What could I say? She was right.

"There are other job choices for a preternatural biology degree."

"What? A zoo, exterminator?"

"Teacher," I said, "park ranger, naturalist, field biologist, researcher."

"And which of those jobs can make you this kind of money?" he asked.

"Is money the only reason you want to be an animator?" I was disappointed.

"I want to do something to help people. What better than using my specialized skills to rid the world of dangerous undead?"

I stared at him. All I could see was his profile in the darkened car, face underlit from the dashboard. "You want to be a vampire executioner, not an animator." I didn't try to keep the surprise out of my voice.

"My ultimate goal, yes."

"Why?"

"Why do you do it?"

I shook my head. "Answer the question, Larry."

"I want to help people."

"Then be a policeman; they need people on the force who know preternatural creatures."

"I thought I did pretty good tonight."

"You did."

"Then what's wrong?"

I tried to think how to phrase it in fifty convincing words or less. "What happened tonight was awful, but it gets worse."

"Olive's coming up; which way do I turn?"

"Left."

The car took the exit and slid into the turning lane. We sat at the light with the turn signal blinking in the dark.

"You don't know what you're getting into," I said.

"Then tell me," he said.

"I'll do better than that. I'll show you."

"What's that supposed to mean?"

"Turn right at the third light."

We rolled into the parking lot. "First building on the right."

Larry slid into the only open space he could find. My parking space. My poor little Nova wouldn't be coming back to it.

I took off my jacket in the darkness of the car. "Hit the overhead light," I said.

He did as he was told. He was better at following orders than I was. Which, since he'd be following my orders, was fine.

I showed him the scars on my arms. "The cross-shaped burn is from human servants who thought it was funny. The mound of scar tissue at the bend of my arm is where a vampire tore my arm to pieces. Physical therapist says it's a miracle that I got full use of my arm back. Fourteen stitches from a human servant, and that's just my arms."

"There's more?" His face looked pale and strange in the dome light.

"A vampire shoved the broken end of a stake in my back."

He winced.

"And my collarbone was broken at the same time my arm got chewed up."

"You're trying to scare me."

"You bet," I said.

"I won't be scared off."

Tonight should have scared him off without my showing him my scars. But it hadn't. Dammit, he'd stick, if he didn't get killed first. "All right, you're staying for the rest of the semester, great, but promise me you won't go hunting vampires without me."

"But Mr. Burke . . ."

"He helps execute vampires, but he doesn't hunt them alone."

"What's the difference between an execution and a hunt?"

"An execution just means a body that needs staking, or a vampire that's all nice and chained up waiting for the final stroke."

"Then what's a hunt?" he asked.

"When I go back out after the vampires that nearly killed us tonight, that's a hunt."

"And you don't trust Mr. Burke to teach me to hunt?"

"I don't trust Mr. Burke to keep you alive."

Larry's eyes widened.

"I don't mean he'd deliberately hurt you. I mean I don't trust anybody but me with your life."

"You think it'll come down to that?"

"It damn near did."

He was quiet for a handful of minutes. He stared down at his hands that were smoothing back and forth over the steering wheel. "I promise not to go vampire hunting with anybody but you." He stared at me, blue, blue eyes studying my face. "Not even Mr. Rodriguez? Mr. Vaughn said he taught you."

"Manny did teach me, but he doesn't hunt vampires anymore."

"Why not?"

I met his true-blue eyes and said, "His wife's too afraid, and he's got four kids."

"You and Mr. Burke aren't married and don't have kids."

"That's right."

"Neither do I," he said.

I had to smile. Had I ever been this eager? Naw. "No one likes a smart alec, Larry."

He grinned, and it made him look about thirteen. Jesus, why wasn't he running for cover after tonight? Why wasn't I? No answers, at least none that made sense. Why did I do it? Because I was good at it, came the answer. Maybe Larry could be good at it, too. Maybe, or maybe he'd just get dead.

I got out of the car and leaned back in the open door. "Go straight home, and if you don't have an extra cross, buy one tomorrow."

"Okay," he said.

I shut the door on his solemn, earnest face. I walked up the stairs and didn't look back. I didn't watch him drive away, still alive, still eager after his first brush with the monsters. I was only four years older than he was. Four years. It felt like centuries. I had never been that green. My mother's death when I was eight saw to that. It takes the edge off the shiny brightness to lose a parent early.

I was still going to try to talk Larry out of being a vampire executioner, but if all else failed, I'd work with him. There are only two kinds of vampire hunters: good ones and dead ones. Maybe I could make Larry one of the good ones. It beat the hell out of the alternative.

26

It was 3:34, Friday morning. It had been a long week. Of course, when hadn't it been a long week this year? I had told Bert to hire more help. He hired Larry. Why didn't that make me happy? Because Larry was just another victim waiting for the right monster. Please keep him safe, God, please. I'd had about as many innocents die on me as I thought I could handle.

The hallway had that middle-of-the-night feel to it. The only sounds were the hush of the heating vents, the muffled sound of my Nike Airs on the carpeting. It was too late for my day-living neighbors to stay up, and too early for them to get up. Two hours before dawn, you get privacy.

I opened my brand-new burglarproof lock and stepped into the darkness of my apartment. I hit the lights and flooded the white walls, carpet, couch, and chair with bright light. No matter how good your night vision is, everyone likes light. We're creatures of the daylight, no matter what we do for a living.

I threw my jacket on the kitchen counter. It was too dirty to toss on the white couch. I had mud and bits of weed plastered all over me. But very little blood; the night had turned out all right.

I was slipping out of the shoulder holster when I felt it. The air currents had moved, as if something had moved through them. Just like that I knew I wasn't alone.

My hand was on the gun butt when Edward's voice came out of the darkness of my bedroom. "Don't, Anita."

I hesitated, fingers touching the gun. "And if I do?"

"I'll shoot you. You know I'll do it." His voice was that soft, sure predatory sound. I'd seen him use flamethrowers when his voice sounded like that. Smooth and calm as the road to Hell.

I eased away from my gun. Edward would shoot me if I forced him to. Better not to force it, not yet. Not yet.

I clasped my hands on top of my head without waiting for him to tell me. Maybe I'd get brownie points for being a cooperative prisoner. Naw.

Edward stepped out of the darkness like a blond ghost. He was dressed all in black except for his short hair and pale face. His black-gloved hands held a Beretta 9mm pointed very steadily at my chest.

"New gun?" I asked.

The ghost of a smile curled his lips. "Yes, like it?"

"Beretta's a nice gun, but you know me."

"A Browning fan," he said.

I smiled at him. Just two ol' buddies talking shop.

He pressed the gun barrel against my body while he took the Browning from me. "Lean and spread it."

I leaned on the back of the couch while he patted me down. There was nothing to find, but Edward didn't know that. He was never careless. That was one of the reasons he was still alive. That, and the fact that he was very, very good.

"You said you couldn't pick my lock," I said.

"I brought better tools," he said.

"So it's not burglarproof."

"It would be to most people."

"But not to you."

He stared at me, his eyes as empty and dead as winter's sky. "I am not most people."

I had to smile. "You can say that again."

He frowned at me. "Give me the master's name, and we don't have to do this." The gun never wavered. My Browning stuck out of the front of his belt. I hoped he'd remembered the safety. Or maybe I didn't.

I opened my mouth, closed it, and just looked at him. I couldn't give Jean-Claude over to Edward. I was the Executioner, but the vampires called Edward Death. He'd earned the name.

"I thought you'd be following me tonight."

"I went home after watching you raise the zombie. Guess I should have stayed around. Who bloodied your mouth?"

"I'm not going to tell you a bloody thing. You know that."

"Everyone breaks, Anita, everyone."

"Even you?"

That ghost of a smile was back again. "Even me."

"Someone got the better of Death? Tell, tell."

The smile widened. "Some other time."

"Nice to know there'll be another time," I said.

"I'm not here to kill you."

"Just to frighten or torture me into revealing the master's name, right?"

"Right," he said, voice soft and low.

"I was hoping you'd say wrong."

He almost shrugged. "Give me the Master of the City, Anita, and I'll go away."

"You know I can't do that."

"I know you have to, or it's going to be a very long night."

"Then it's going to be a long night, because I'm not going to give you shit."

"You won't be bullied," he said.

"Nope."

He shook his head. "Turn around, lean your waist up against the couch, and put your hands behind your back."

"Why?"

"Just do it."

"So you can tie my hands?"

"Do it, now."

"I don't think so."

The frown was back. "Do you want me to shoot you?"

"No, but I'm not going to just stand here while you tie me up, either."

"The tying up doesn't hurt."

"It's what comes after that I'm worried about."

"You knew what I'd do if you didn't help me."

"Then do it," I said.

"You're not cooperating."

"So sorry."

"Anita."

"I just don't believe in helping people who are going to torture me. Though I don't see any bamboo slivers. How can you possibly torture someone without bamboo slivers?"

"Stop it." He sounded angry.

"Stop what?" I widened my eyes and tried to look innocent and harmless, me and Kermit the Frog.

Edward laughed, a soft chuckle that rolled and expanded until he squatted on the floor, gun loose in his hands, staring up at me. His eyes were shiny.

"How can I torture you when you keep making me laugh?"

"You can't; that was the plan."

He shook his head. "No, it wasn't. You were just being a smartass. You're always a smartass."

"Nice of you to notice."

He held up his hand. "No more, please."

"I'll make you laugh until you beg for mercy."

"Just tell me the damn name. Please, Anita. Help me." The laughter drained from his eyes like the sun slipping out of the sky. I watched the humor, the humanity, slip away, until his eyes were as cold and empty as a doll's. "Don't make me hurt you," he said.

I think I was Edward's only friend, but that wouldn't stop him from hurting me. Edward had one rule: do whatever it takes to get the job done. If I forced him to torture me, he would, but he didn't want to.

"Now that you've asked nicely, try the first question again," I said.

His eyes narrowed, then he said, "Who hit you in the mouth?"

"A master vampire," I said softly.

"Tell me what happened." It was too much like an order for my taste, but he did have both the guns.

I told him everything that had happened. All about Alejandro. Alejandro who felt so old inside my head, it made my bones ache. I added one tiny lie, lost in all that truth. I told him Alejandro was Master of the City. One of my better ideas, heh?

"You really don't know where his daytime resting place is, do you?"

I shook my head. "I'd give it to you if I had it."

"Why this change of heart?"

"He tried to kill me tonight. All bets are off."

"I don't believe that."

It was too good a lie to waste, so I tried salvaging it. "He's also gone rogue. It's him and his flunkies that have been killing innocent citizens."

Edward smirked at the innocent, but he let it go. "An altruistic motive, that I believe. If you weren't such a damn bleeding heart, you'd be dangerous."

"I kill my share, Edward."

His empty, blue eyes stared at me; then he nodded, slowly. "True."

He handed me back my gun, butt first. A tight, clenched ball in my stomach unrolled. I could breathe deep, long sighs of relief.

"If I find out where this Alejandro stays, you want in on it?"

I thought about that for a minute. Did I want to go after five rogue vampires, two of them over five hundred years old? I did not. Did I want to send even Edward after them alone? No, I did not. Which meant . . .

"Yeah, I want a piece of them."

Edward smiled, broad and shining. "I love my work."

I smiled back. "Me, too."

27

Jean-Claude lay in the middle of a white canopied bed. His skin was only slightly less white than the sheets. He was dressed in a nightshirt. Lace fell down the low collar, forming a lace window around his chest. Lace flowed from the sleeves, nearly hiding his hands. It should have looked feminine, but Jean-Claude made it utterly masculine. How could any man wear a white lace gown and not look silly? Of course, he wasn't a man. That must be it.

His black hair curled in the lace collar. Touchable. I shook my head. Not even in my dreams. I was dressed in something long and silky. It was a shade of blue almost as dark as his eyes. My arms looked very white against it. Jean-Claude got to his knees and reached his hand out to me. An invitation.

I shook my head.

"It is only a dream, *ma petite*. Will you not come to me even here?"

"It's never just a dream with you. It always means more."

His hand fell to the sheets, fingertips caressing the cloth.

"What are you trying to do to me, Jean-Claude?"

He looked very steadily at me. "Seduce you, of course."

Of course. Silly me.

The phone beside the bed rang. It was one of those white princess phones with lots of gold on it. There hadn't been a telephone a second before. It rang again, and the dream fell to shreds. I came awake grabbing for the phone.

"Hello."

"Hey, did I wake you?" Irving Griswold asked.

I blinked at the phone. "Yeah, what time is it?"

"It's ten o'clock. I know better than to call early."

"What do you want, Irving?"

"Grouchy."

"I got in late. Can we skip the sarcasm?"

"I, your true-blue reporter friend, will forgive you that grumpy hello, if you answer a few questions."

"Questions?" I sat up, hugging the phone to me. "What are you talking about?"

"Is it true that Humans First saved you last night, as they're claiming?"

"Claiming? Can you talk in complete sentences, Irving?"

"The morning news had Jeremy Ruebens on it. Channel five. He claimed that he and Humans First saved your life last night. Saved you from the Master Vampire of the City."

"Oh, he did not."

"May I quote you?"

I thought about that for a minute. "No."

"I need a quote for the paper. I'm trying to give a chance for a rebuttal."

"A rebuttal?"

"Hey, I was an English major."

"That explains so much."

"Can you give me your side of the story, or not?"

I thought about that for a minute. Irving was a friend and a good reporter. If Ruebens was already on the morning news with the story, I needed to get my side out. "Can you give me fifteen minutes to make coffee and get dressed?"

"For an exclusive, you bet."

"Talk to you then." I hung up and went straight for the coffeemaker. I was wearing jogging socks, jeans, and the oversized t-shirt I'd slept in when Irving called back. I had a steaming cup of coffee on the bedside table beside the phone. Cinnamon hazelnut coffee from V. J.'s Tea and Spice Shop over on Olive. Mornings didn't get much better than this.

"Okay, spill it," he said.

"Gee, Irving, no foreplay?"

"Get to it, Blake, I've got a deadline."

I told him everything. I had to admit that Humans First had saved my cookies. Darn. "I can't confirm that the vampire they ran off was the Master of the City."

"Hey, I know Jean-Claude is the master. I interviewed him, remember?"

"I remember."

"I know this Indian guy was not Jean-Claude."

"But Humans First doesn't know that."

"A double exclusive, wowee."

"No, don't say that Alejandro isn't the master."

"Why not?"

"I'd clear it with Jean-Claude first, if I were you."

He cleared his throat. "Yeah, not a bad idea." He sounded nervous.

"Is Jean-Claude giving you trouble?"

"No, why do you ask?"

"For a reporter you lie badly."

"Jean-Claude and I got business just between us. It doesn't concern The Executioner."

"Fine; just watch your back, okay?"

"I'm flattered that you're worried about me, Anita, but trust me, I can handle it."

I didn't argue with that. I must have been in a good mood. "Anything you say, Irving."

He let it go, so I did, too. No one could handle Jean-Claude, but it wasn't my business. Irving had been the one hot for the interview. So there were strings attached; not a big surprise, and not my business. Really.

"This'll be on the front page of the morning paper. I'll check with Jean-Claude about whether to mention this new vamp isn't the master."

"I'd really appreciate it if you could hold off on that."

"Why?" He sounded suspicious.

"Maybe it wouldn't be such a bad idea for Humans First to believe Alejandro is the master."

"Why?"

"So they don't kill Jean-Claude," I said.

"Oh," he said.

"Yeah," I said.

"I'll bear that in mind," he said.

"You do that."

"Gotta go; deadline calls."

"Okay, Irving, talk to you later."

"Bye, Anita, thanks." He hung up.

I sipped the still-steaming coffee, slowly. The first cup of the day should never be rushed. If I could get Humans First to believe the same lie Edward bought, then no one would be hunting Jean-Claude. They'd be hunting Alejandro. The master that was slaughtering humans. Put the police on the case, and we had the rogue vamps outnumbered. Yeah, I liked it.

The trick was, would everyone buy it? Never know until you try.

28

I had finished a pot of coffee and managed to get dressed when the phone rang again. One of those mornings.

"Yeah," I said.

"Ms. Blake?" the voice sounded very uncertain.

"Speaking."

"This is Karl Inger."

"Sorry if I sounded abrupt. What's up, Mr. Inger?"

"You said you'd speak to me again if we had a better plan. I have a better plan," he said.

"For killing the Master of the City?" I made it a question.

"Yes."

I took a deep breath and let it out slow, away from the phone. Didn't want him to think I was heavy breathing at him. "Mr. Inger . . ."

"Please, hear me out. We saved your life last night. That must be worth something."

He had me there. "What's your plan, Mr. Inger?"

"I'd rather tell you in person."

"I'm not going to my office for some hours yet."

"Could I come to your home?"

"No." It was automatic.

"You don't bring business home?"

"Not when I can help it," I said.

"Suspicious of you."

"Always," I said.

"Can we meet somewhere else? There's someone I want you to meet."

"Who, and why?"

"The name won't mean anything to you."

"Try me."

"Mr. Oliver."

"First name?"

"I don't know it."

"Okay, then why should I meet him?"

"He has a good plan for killing the Master of the City."

"What?"

"No, I think it will be better if Mr. Oliver explains it in person. He's much more persuasive than I am."

"You're doing okay," I said.

"Then you'll meet me?"

"Sure, why not?"

"That's wonderful. Do you know where Arnold is?"

"Yes."

"There's a pay fishing lake just outside of Arnold on Tesson Ferry Road. Do you know it?"

I had an impression that I had driven by it on the way to two murders. All roads led to Arnold. "I can find it."

"How soon can you meet me there?" he asked.

"An hour."

"Great; I'll be waiting."

"Is this Mr. Oliver going to be at the lake?"

"No, I'll drive you from there."

"Why all the secrecy?"

"Not secrecy," he said, his voice dropped, embarrassed. "I'm just not very good at giving directions. It'll be easier if I just take you."

"I can follow you in my car."

"Why, Ms. Blake, I don't think you entirely trust me."

"I don't entirely trust anybody, Mr. Inger, nothing personal."

"Not even people who save your life?"

"Not even."

He let that drop, probably for the best, and said, "I'll meet you at the lake in an hour."

"Sure."

"Thank you for coming, Ms. Blake."

"I owe you. You've made sure I'm aware of that."

"You sound defensive, Ms. Blake. I did not mean to offend you."

I sighed. "I'm not offended, Mr. Inger. I just don't like owing people."

"Visiting Mr. Oliver today will clear the slate between us. I promise that."

"I'll hold you to that, Inger."

"I'll meet you in an hour," he said.

"I'll be there," I said.

We hung up. "Damn." I'd forgotten I hadn't gotten to eat yet today. If I'd remembered, I'd have said two hours. Now I'd have to literally grab something on the way. I hated eating in the car. But, heh, what's a little mess between friends? Or even between people who've saved your life? Why did it bother me so much that I owed Inger?

Because he was a right-wing fruitcake. A zealot. I didn't like doing business with zealots. And I certainly didn't like owing my life to one.

Ah, well; I'd meet him, then we'd be square. He had said so. Why didn't I believe it?

29

Chip-Away Lake was about half an acre of man-made water and thin, raised man-made bank. There was a little shed that sold bait and food. It was surrounded by a flat gravel parking lot. A late-model car sat near the road with a sign that read, "For Sale." A pay fishing lake and a used car lot combined; how clever.

An expanse of grass spread out to the right of the parking lot. A small, ramshackle shed and what looked like the remains of some large industrial barbecue. A fringe of woods edged the grass, rising higher into a wooded hill. The Meramec River edged the left side of the lake. It seemed funny to have free-flowing water so close to the man-made lake.

There were only three cars in the parking lot this cool autumn afternoon. Beside a shiny burgundy Chrysler Le Baron stood Inger. A handful of fishermen had bundled up and put poles in the water. Fishing must be good to get people out in the cold.

I parked beside Inger's car. He strode towards me smiling, hand out like a real estate salesman who was happy I'd come to see the property. Whatever he was selling, I didn't want. I was almost sure of that.

"Ms. Blake, so glad you came." He clasped my hand with both of his, hearty, good-natured, insincere.

"What do you want, Mr. Inger?"

His smile faded around the edges. "I don't know what you mean, Ms. Blake."

"Yes, you do."

"No, I really don't."

I stared into his puzzled face. Maybe I spent too much time with slimeballs. After a while you forget that not everyone in the world is a slimeball. It just saves so much time to assume the worst.

"I'm sorry, Mr. Inger. I . . . I've been spending too much time looking for criminals. It makes you cynical."

He still looked puzzled.

"Never mind, Mr. Inger; just take me to see this Oliver."

"Mr. Oliver," he said.

"Sure."

"Shall we take my car?" He motioned towards his car.

"I'll follow you in mine."

"You don't trust me." He looked hurt. I guess most people aren't used to being suspected of wrongdoing before they've done anything wrong. The law says innocent until proven guilty, but the truth is, if you see enough pain and death, it's guilty until proven innocent.

"All right, you drive."

He looked very pleased. Heartwarming.

Besides I was carrying two knives, three crosses, and a gun. Innocent or guilty, I was prepared. I didn't expect to need the weaponry with Mr. Oliver, but later, I might need it later. It was time to go armed to the teeth, ready for bear, or dragon, or vampire.

30

Inger drove down Old Highway 21 to East Rock Creek. Rock Creek was a narrow, winding road barely wide enough for two cars to pass. Inger drove slow enough for the curves, but fast enough so you didn't get bored.

There were farmhouses that had stood for years and new houses in subdivisions where the earth was raw and red as a wound. Inger turned into one of those new subdivisions. It was full of large, expensive-looking houses, very modern. Thin, spindly trees were tied to stakes along the gravel road. The pitiful trees trembled in the autumn wind, a few surprised leaves still clinging to the spider-thin limbs. This area had been a forest before they bulldozed it. Why do developers destroy all the mature trees, then plant new trees that won't look good for decades?

We pulled up in front of a fake log cabin that was bigger than any real cabin had ever been. Too much glass, the yard naked dirt the color of rust. The white gravel that made up the driveway had to have been brought in from miles away. All the native gravel was as red as the dirt.

Inger started to go around the car, to open my door I think. I opened my own door. Inger seemed a little lost, but he'd get over it. I'd never seen the sense in perfectly healthy people not opening their own doors. Especially car doors where the man had to walk all the way around the car, and the woman just waited like a . . . a lump.

Inger led the way up the porch steps. It was a nice porch, wide enough to sit on come summer evenings. Right now it was all bare wood and a huge picture window with closed drapes in a barn-red design with wagon wheels drawn all over it. Very rustic.

He knocked on the carved wooden door. A pane of leaded glass decorated the center of the door, high up and sparkling, more for decoration than for seeing through. He didn't wait for the door to be opened, but used a key and walked in. He didn't seem to expect an answer, so why knock?

The house was in a thick twilight of really nice drapes, all closed against the syrup-heavy sunlight. The polished wood floors were utterly bare. The mantel of the heavy fireplace was naked, the fireplace cold. The place smelled new and unused, like new toys on Christmas. Inger never hesitated. I followed his broad back into the wooden hallway. He didn't look behind to see if I was keeping up. Apparently when I'd decided not to let him open my door for me, he seemed to have decided that no further courtesy was necessary.

Fine with me.

There were doors at widely spaced intervals along the hallway. Inger knocked at the third door on the left. A voice said, "Enter."

Inger opened the door and went inside. He held the door for me, standing very straight by the door. It wasn't courtesy. He stood like a soldier at attention. Who was in the room to make Inger toe the line? One way to find out.

I went into the room.

There was a bank of windows to the north with heavy drapes pulled across them. A thin line of sunlight cut across the room, bisecting a large, clean desk. A man sat in a large chair behind the desk.

He was a small man, almost a midget or a dwarf. I wanted to say dwarf, but he didn't have the jaw or the shortened arms. He looked well formed under his tailored suit. He had almost no chin and a sloping forehead, which drew attention to the wide nose and the prominent eyebrow ridge. There was something familiar about his face, as if I'd seen it somewhere else before. Yet I knew I'd never met a person who looked just like him. It was a very singular face.

I was staring at him. I was embarrassed and didn't like it. I met his eyes; they were perfectly brown and smiling. His dark hair was cut one hair at a time, expensive and blow-dried. He sat in his chair behind the clean polished desk and smiled at me.

"Mr. Oliver, this is Anita Blake," Inger said, still standing stiffly by the door.

He got out of his chair and came around the desk to offer me his small, well-formed hand. He was four feet tall, not an inch more. His handshake was firm and much stronger than he looked. A brief squeeze, and I could feel the strength in his small frame. He didn't look musclebound, but that easy strength was there, in his face, hand, stance.

He was small, but he didn't think it was a defect. I liked that. I felt the same way.

He gave a close-lipped smile and sat back down in his big chair. Inger brought a chair from the corner and put it facing the desk. I took the chair. Inger remained standing by the now-closed door. He was definitely at attention. He respected the man in the chair. I was willing to like him. That was a first for me. I'm more likely to instantly mistrust than like someone.

I realized that I was smiling. I felt warm and comfortable facing him, like he was a favorite and trusted uncle. I frowned at him; what the hell was happening to me?

"What's going on?" I said.

He smiled, his eyes sparkling warmly at me. "Whatever do you mean, Ms. Blake?"

His voice was soft, low, rich, like cream in coffee. You could almost taste it. A comforting warmth to your ears. I only knew one other voice that could do similar things.

I stared at the thin band of sunlight only inches from Oliver's arm. It was broad daylight. He couldn't be. Could he?

I stared at his very alive face. There was no trace of that otherness that vampires gave off. And yet, his voice, this warm cosy feeling, none of it was natural. I'd never liked and trusted anyone instantly. I wasn't about to start now.

"You're good," I said. "Very good."

"Whatever do you mean, Ms. Blake?" You could have cuddled into the warm fuzziness of his voice like a favorite blanket.

"Stop it."

He looked quizzically at me, as if confused. The act was perfect, and I realized why; it wasn't an act. I'd been around ancient vampires, but never one that had been able to pass for human, not like this. You could have taken him anywhere and no one would have known. Well, almost no one.

"Believe me, Ms. Blake, I'm not trying to do anything."

I swallowed hard. Was that true? Was he so damn powerful that the mind tricks and the voice were automatic? No; if Jean-Claude could control it, this thing could, too.

"Cut the mind tricks, and curb the voice, okay? If you want to talk business, talk, but cut the games."

His smile widened, still not enough to show fangs. After a few hundred years, you must get really good at smiling like that.

He laughed then; it was wonderful, like warm water falling from a great height. You could have jumped into it and bathed, and felt good.

"Stop it, stop it!"

Fangs flashed as he finished chuckling at me. "It isn't the vampire marks that allowed you to see through my, as you call them, games. It is natural talent, isn't it?"

I nodded. "Most animators have it."

"But not to the degree you do, Ms. Blake. You have power, too. It crawls along my skin. You are a necromancer."

I started to deny it, but stopped. Lying to something like this was useless. He was older than anything I'd ever dreamed of, older than any nightmare I'd ever had. But he didn't make my bones ache; he felt good, better than Jean-Claude, better than anything.

"I could be a necromancer. I choose not to be."

"No, Ms. Blake, the dead respond to you, all the dead. Even I feel the pull."

"You mean I have a sort of power over vampires, too?"

"If you could learn to harness your talents, Ms. Blake, yes, you have a certain power over all the dead, in their many guises."

I wanted to ask how to do that, but stopped myself. A master vampire wasn't likely to help me gain power over his followers. "You're taunting me."

"I assure you, Ms. Blake, that I am very serious. It is your potential power that has drawn the Master of the City to you. He wants to control that emerging power, for fear it will be turned against him."

"How do you know that?"

"I can taste him through the marks he has laid upon you."

I just stared at him. He could taste Jean-Claude. Shit.

"What do you want from me?"

"Very direct; I like that. Human lives are too short to waste in trivialities."

Was that a threat? Staring into his smiling face, I couldn't tell. His eyes were still sparkling, and I was still feeling very warm and fuzzy towards him. Eye contact. I knew better than that. I stared at the top of his desk and felt better, or worse. I could be scared now.

"Inger said you had a plan for taking out the Master of the City. What is it?" I spoke staring at his desk. My skin crawled with the desire to look up. To meet his eyes, to let the warmth and comfort wash over me. Make all the decisions easy.

I shook my head. "Stay out of my mind or this interview is over."

He laughed again, warm and real. It raised goose bumps on my arms. "You really are good. I haven't met a human in centuries that rivaled you. A necromancer; do you realize how rare that talent is?"

Really I didn't, but I said, "Yes."

"Lies, Ms. Blake, to me, please don't bother."

"We're not here to talk about me. Either state your plan or I'm leaving."

"I am the plan, Ms. Blake. You can feel my powers, the ebb and flow of more centuries than your little master has ever dreamed of. I am older than time itself."

That I didn't believe, but I let it go. He was old enough; I wasn't going to argue with him, not if I could help it.

"Give me your master and I will free you of his marks."

I glanced up, then quickly down. He was still smiling at me, but the smile didn't look real anymore. It was an act like everything else. It was just a very good act.

"If you can taste my master in the marks, can't you just find him yourself?"

"I can taste his power, judge how worthy a foe he would be, but not his name and not where he lies; that is hidden." His voice was very serious now, not trying to trick me. Or at least I didn't think it was; maybe that was a trick, too.

"What do you want from me?"

"His name and his daytime resting place."

"I don't know the daytime resting place." I was glad it was the truth, because he would smell a lie.

"Then his name, give me his name."

"Why should I?"

"Because I wish to be Master of the City, Ms. Blake."

"Why?"

"So many questions. Is it not enough that I would free you from his power?"

I shook my head. "No."

"Why should you care about what happens to the other vampires?"

"I don't, but before I hand you the power to control every vampire in the immediate area, I'd like to know what you intend to do with all that power."

He laughed again. This time it was just a laugh. He was trying.

"You are the most stubborn human I have met in a very long time. I like stubborn people; they get things done."

"Answer my question."

"I think it is wrong to have vampires as legal citizens. I wish to put things back as they were."

"Why should you want vampires to be hunted again?"

"They are too powerful to be allowed to spread unchecked. They will take over the human race much quicker through legislation and voting rights than they ever could through violence."

I remembered the Church of Eternal Life, the fastest-growing denomination in the country. "Say you're right; how would you stop it?"

"By forbidding the vampires to vote, or take part in any legislation."

"There are other master vampires in town."

"You mean Malcolm, the head of the Church of Eternal Life."

"Yes."

"I have observed him. He will not be able to continue his one-man crusade to make vampires legitimate. I shall forbid it and dismantle his church. Surely you see the church as the larger danger, as I do."

I did, but I hated agreeing with an ancient master vampire. It seemed wrong somehow.

"St. Louis is a hotbed of political activity and entrepreneurial vampires. They must be stopped. We are predators, Ms. Blake; nothing we do can change that. We must go back to being hunted or the human race is doomed. Surely you see that."

I did see that. I believed that. "Why would you care if the human race is doomed? You're not part of it anymore."

"As the oldest living vampire, it is my duty to keep us in check, Ms. Blake. These new rights are getting out of hand and must be stopped. We are too powerful to be allowed such freedom. Humans have their right to be human. In the olden days only the strongest, smartest, or luckiest vampires survived. The human vampire hunters weeded out the stupid, the careless, the violent. Without that check-and-balance system, I fear what will happen in a few decades.''

I agreed, wholeheartedly; it was sorta scary. I agreed with the oldest living thing I'd ever met. He was right. Could I give him Jean-Claude? Should I give him Jean-Claude?

''I agree with you, Mr. Oliver, but I can't just give him up, just like that. I don't know why really, but I can't.''

''Loyalty; I admire that. Think upon it, Ms. Blake, but do not take too long. I need to put my plan into action as soon as possible.''

I nodded. ''I understand. I . . . I'll give you an answer within a couple of days. How do I reach you?''

''Inger will give you a card with a number on it. You may safely speak to him as to me.''

I turned and looked at Inger, still standing at attention beside the door. ''You're his human servant, aren't you?''

''I have that honor.''

I shook my head. ''I need to leave now.''

''Do not feel badly that you could not recognize Inger as my human servant. It is not a mark which shows; otherwise how could they be our human ears and eyes and hands, if everyone knew they were ours?''

He had a point. He had a lot of points. I stood up. He stood up, too. He offered me his hand.

''I'm sorry, but I know that touching makes the mind games easier.''

The hand dropped back to his side. ''I do not need to touch you to play mind games, Ms. Blake.'' The voice was wonderful, shining and bright as Christmas morning. My throat was tight, and the warmth of tears filled my eyes. Shit, shit, shit, shit.

I backed for the door, and Inger opened it for me. They were just going to let me leave. He wasn't going to mind-rape me and get the name. He was really going to let me walk away. That did more to prove him a good guy than anything else. Because he could have squeezed my mind dry. But he let me go.

Inger closed the door behind us, slowly, reverently.

''How old is he?'' I asked.

''You couldn't tell?''

I shook my head. ''How old?''

Inger smiled. ''I am over seven hundred years old. Mr. Oliver was ancient when I met him.''

''He's older than a thousand years.''

''Why do you say that?''

''I've met a vampire that was a little over a thousand. She was scary, but she didn't have that kind of power.''

He smiled. ''If you wish to know his true age, then you must ask him yourself.''

I stared up at Inger's smiling face for a minute. I remembered where I'd seen a face like Oliver's. I'd had one anthropology class in college. There'd been a drawing that looked just like Oliver. It had been a reconstruction of a *Homo erectus* skull. Which made Oliver about a million years old.

"My God," I said.

"What's wrong, Ms. Blake?"

I shook my head. "He can't be that old."

"How old is that?"

I didn't want to say it out loud, as if that would make it real. A million years. How powerful would a vampire grow in a million years?

A woman walked up the hallway towards us, coming from deeper in the house. She swayed on bare feet, toenails painted a bright scarlet that matched her fingernails. The belted dress she wore matched the nail polish. Her legs were long and pale, but it was that kind of paleness that promised to tan if it ever got enough sunlight. Her hair fell past her waist, thick and absolute black. Her makeup was perfect, her lips scarlet. She smiled at me; fangs showed below her lips.

But she wasn't a vampire. I didn't know what the hell she was, but I knew what she wasn't. I glanced at Inger. He didn't look happy.

"Shouldn't we be going?" I said.

"Yes," he said. He backed towards the front door and I backed behind him. Neither of us took our eyes off the fanged beauty slinking down the hall towards us.

She moved in a liquid run that was almost too fast to follow. Lycanthropes could move like that, but that wasn't what she was, either.

She was around Inger and coming for me. I gave up being cool and sort of ran backwards towards the front door. But she was too fast for me, too fast for any human.

She grabbed my right forearm. She looked puzzled. She could feel the knife sheath on my arm. She didn't seem to know what it was. Bully for me.

"What are you?" My voice was steady. Not afraid. Heap big vampire slayer. Yeah, right.

She opened her mouth wider, tongue caressing the fangs. The fangs were longer than a vampire's; she'd never be able to close her mouth around them.

"Where do the fangs go when you close your mouth?" I said.

She blinked at me, the smile slipping away from her face. She ran her tongue over them, then they folded back into the roof of her mouth.

"Retractable fangs. Cool," I said.

Her face was very solemn. "I'm glad you enjoyed the show, but there's so much more to see." The fangs unfolded again. She widened her jaws, almost a yawn, flashing the fangs nicely in the dim beams of sunlight that got around the drapes.

"Mr. Oliver will not like you threatening her," Inger said.

"He grows weak, sentimental." Her fingers dug into my arm stronger than she should have been.

She was holding my right arm, so I couldn't go for the gun. The knives were out for similar reasons. Maybe I should wear more guns.

She hissed at me, a violent explosion of air that no human throat ever made. The tongue that flicked out was forked.

"Sweet Jesus, what are you?"

She laughed, but it didn't sound right now; maybe the split tongue. Her pupils had narrowed to slits, her irises turned a golden yellow while I watched.

I tugged on my arm but her fingers were like steel. I dropped to the floor. She lowered my arm but didn't let go.

I leaned back on my left side, drew my legs up under me, and kicked her right kneecap with everything I had. The leg crumpled. She screamed and fell to the floor, but she let my arm go.

Something was happening to her legs. They seemed to be growing together, the skin spreading. I'd never seen anything like it, and I didn't want to now.

"Melanie, what are you doing?" The voice was behind us. Oliver stood in the hallway just short of the brighter light of the living room. His voice was the sound of rocks falling, trees breaking. A storm that was just words but seemed to cut and slash.

The thing on the floor cringed from the voice. Her lower body was becoming serpentine. A snake of some kind. Jesus.

"She's a lamia," I said softly. I backed away, putting the outside door to my back, hand on the door knob. "I thought they were extinct."

"She is the last one," Oliver said. "I keep her with me because I fear what she would do left to her own desires."

"Your creature that you can call, what is it?" I asked.

He sighed, and I felt the years of sadness in that one sound. A regret too deep for words. "Snakes, I can call snakes."

I nodded my head. "Sure." I opened the door and backed out onto the sunny porch. No one tried to stop me.

The door shut behind me and after a few minutes Inger came out. He was stiff with anger. "We most humbly apologize for her. She is an animal."

"Oliver needs to keep her on a tighter leash."

"He tries."

I nodded. I knew about trying. Doing your best, but anything that could control a lamia could play mind games with me all day, and I might never know it. How much of my trust and good wishes was real and how much of it was manufactured by Oliver?

"I'll drive you back."

"Please."

And away we went. I'd met my first lamia and perhaps the oldest living creature in the world. A red-fucking-letter day.

31

The phone was ringing as I unlocked the apartment door. I shoved the door open with my shoulder and ran for the phone. I got it on the fifth ring and nearly yelled, "Hello."

"Anita?" Ronnie made it a question.

"Yeah, it's me."

"You sound out of breath."

"I had to run for the phone. What's up?"

"I remembered where I knew Cal Rupert from."

It took me a minute to remember who she was talking about. The first vampire victim. I'd forgotten, just for a moment, that there was a murder investigation going on. I was a little ashamed of that. "Talk to me, Ronnie."

"I was doing some work for a local law firm last year. One of the lawyers specialized in drawing up dying wills."

"I know that Rupert had a dying will. That's how I could stake him without waiting for an order of execution."

"But did you also know that Reba Baker had a dying will with the same lawyer?"

"Who's Reba Baker?"

"It may be the female victim."

My stomach tightened. A clue, a real live clue. "What makes you think so?"

"Reba Baker was young, blond, and missed an appointment. She doesn't answer her phone. They called her at work, and she hasn't been in for two days."

"The length of time she'd have been dead," I said.

"Exactly."

"Call Sergeant Rudolf Storr. Tell him what you just told me. Use my name to get to him."

"You don't want to check it out ourselves?"

"Not on your life. This is police business. They're good at it. Let 'em earn their paychecks."

"Shucks, you're no fun."

"Ronnie, call Dolph. Give it to the police. I've met the vampires that are killing these people. We don't want to make ourselves targets."

"You what!"

I sighed. I'd forgotten that Ronnie didn't know. I told her the shortest version that would make any sense. "I'll fill you in on everything Saturday morning when we work out."

"You going to be all right?"

"So far, so good."

"Watch your back, okay?"

"Always; you too."

"I never seem to have as many people after my back as you do."

"Be thankful," I said.

"I am." She hung up.

We had a clue. Maybe a pattern, except for the attack on me. I didn't fit any pattern. They'd come after me to get Jean-Claude. Everybody wanted Jean-Claude's job. The trouble was, you couldn't abdicate; you could only die. I liked what Oliver had had to say. I agreed with him, but could I sacrifice Jean-Claude on the altar of good sense? Dammit.

I just didn't know.

32.

Bert's office was small and painted pale blue. He thought it was soothing to the clients. I thought it was cold, but that fit Bert, too. He was six feet tall with the broad shoulders and build of an ex-college football player. His stomach was moving a little south with too much food and not enough exercise, but he carried it well in his seven-hundred-dollar suits. For that kind of money, the suits should have carried the Taj Mahal.

He was tanned, grey-eyed, with a buzz haircut that was nearly white. Not age, his natural hair color.

I was sitting across from his desk in work clothes. A red skirt, matching jacket, and a blouse that was so close to scarlet I'd had to put on a little makeup so that my face didn't seem ghostly. The jacket was tailored so that my shoulder holster didn't show.

Larry sat in the chair beside me in a blue suit, white shirt, and blue-on-blue tie. The skin around his stitches had blossomed into a multicolored bruise across his forehead. His short red hair couldn't hide it. It looked like someone had hit him in the head with a baseball bat.

"You could have gotten him killed, Bert," I said.

"He wasn't in any danger until you showed up. The vampires wanted you, not him."

He was right, and I didn't like it. "He tried to raise a third zombie."

Bert's cold little eyes lit up. "You can do three in a night?"

Larry had the grace to look embarrassed. "Almost."

Bert frowned. "What's 'almost' mean?"

"It means he raised it, but lost control of it. If I hadn't been there to fix things, we'd have had a rampaging zombie on our hands."

He leaned forward, hands folded on his desk, small eyes very serious. "Is this true, Larry?"

"I'm afraid so, Mr. Vaughn."

"That could have been very serious, Larry. You understand that?"

"Serious?" I said. "It would have been a bloody disaster. The zombie could have eaten one of our clients!"

"Now, Anita, no reason to frighten the boy."

I stood up. "Yes, there is."

Bert frowned at me. "If you hadn't been late, he wouldn't have tried to raise the last zombie."

"No, Bert. You are not making this all my fault. You sent him out on his first night alone. Alone, Bert."

"And he handled himself well," Bert said.

I fought the urge to scream, because it wouldn't help. "Bert, he's a twenty-year-old college student. This is a freaking seminar for him. If you get him killed, it's gonna look sorta bad."

"May I say something?" Larry asked.

I said, "No."

Bert said, "Certainly."

"I'm a big boy. I can take care of myself."

I wanted to argue that, but looking into his true-blue eyes I couldn't say it. He was twenty. I remembered twenty. I'd known everything at twenty. It took me another year to realize I knew nothing. I was still hoping to learn something before I hit thirty, but I wasn't holding my breath.

"How old were you when you started working for me?" Bert said.

"What?"

"How old were you?"

"Twenty-one; I'd just graduated college."

"When will you turn twenty-one, Larry?" Bert asked.

"March."

"See, Anita, he's just a few months younger. He's the same age you were."

"That was different."

"Why?" Bert said.

I couldn't put it into words. Larry still had all his grandparents. He'd never seen death and violence up close and personal. I had. He was an innocent, and I hadn't been innocent for years. But how to explain that to Bert without hurting Larry's feelings? No twenty-year-old man likes to hear that a woman knows more about the world than he does. Some cultural fables die hard.

"You sent me out with Manny, not alone."

"He was supposed to go out with you, but you had police business to handle."

"That's not fair, Bert, and you know it."

He shrugged. "If you'd been doing your job, he wouldn't have been alone."

"There've been two murders. What am I supposed to do? Say sorry, folks, I've got to babysit a new animator. Sorry about the murders."

"Nobody has to babysit me," Larry said.

We both ignored him.

"You have a full time job here with Animators, Inc."

"We've had this argument before, Bert."

"Too many times," he said.

"You're my boss, Bert. Do what you think best."

"Don't tempt me."

"Hey, guys," Larry said, "I'm getting the feeling that you're using me for an excuse to fight. Don't get carried away, okay?"

We both glared at him. He didn't back down, just stared at us. Point for him.

"If you don't like the way I do my job, Bert, fire me, but stop yanking my chain."

Bert stood up, slowly, like a leviathan rising from the waves. "Anita . . ."

The phone rang. We all stared at it for a minute. Bert finally picked it up and growled, "Yeah, what is it?"

He listened for a minute, then glared at me. "It's for you." His voice was incredibly mild as he said it. "Detective Sergeant Storr, police business."

Bert's face was smiling, butter wouldn't have melted in his mouth.

I held out my hand for the phone without another word. He handed me the receiver. He was still smiling, his tiny grey eyes warm and sparkling. It was a bad sign.

"Hi, Dolph, what's up?"

"We're at the lawyer's office that your friend Veronica Sims gave us. Nice that she called you first and not us."

"She called you second, didn't she?"

"Yeah."

"What have you found out?" I didn't bother to keep my voice down. If you're careful, one side of a conversation isn't very enlightening.

"Reba Baker is the dead woman. They identified her from morgue photos."

"Pleasant way to end the work week," I said.

Dolph ignored that. "Both victims were clients with dying wills. If they died by vampire bite, they wanted to be staked, then cremated."

"Sounds like a pattern to me," I said.

"But how did the vampires find out that they had dying wills?"

"Is this a trick question, Dolph? Someone told them."

"I know that," he said. He sounded disgusted.

I was missing something. "What do you want from me, Dolph?"

"I've questioned everyone, and I'd swear they were all telling the truth. Could someone have been giving the information and not remember?"

"You mean could the vampire have played mind games, so that the traitor wouldn't know afterwards?"

"Yeah," he said.

"Sure," I said.

"Could you tell which one the vampire got to if you were here?"

I glanced at my boss's face. If I missed another night during our busiest season, he might fire me. There were days when I didn't think I'd care. This wasn't one of them. "Look for memory losses; hours, or even entire nights."

"Anything else?"

"If someone has been feeding info to the vampires, they may not remember it, but a good hypnotist will be able to raise the memory."

"The lawyer is screaming about rights and warrants. We've only got a warrant for the files, not for their minds."

"Ask him if he wants to be responsible for tonight's murder victim, one of his own clients?"

"She; the lawyer's a woman," he said.

How embarrassing and how sexist of me. "Ask her if she's willing to explain to her client's family why she obstructed your investigation."

"The clients won't know unless we let it out," he said.

"That's true," I said.

"Why, that would be blackmail, Ms. Blake."

"Isn't it, though?" I said.

"You had to be a cop in a past life," he said. "You're too devious not to be."

"Thanks for the compliment."

"Any hypnotists you'd recommend?"

"Alvin Thormund. Wait a sec and I'll get his number for you." I got out my thin business card holder. I tried to only keep cards I wanted to refer to from time to time. We'd used Alvin for several cases of vampire victims with amnesia. I gave Dolph the number.

"Thanks, Anita."

"Let me know what you find out. I might be able to identify the vampire involved."

"You want to be there when we put them under?"

I glanced at Bert. His face was still relaxed, pleasant. Bert at his most dangerous.

"I don't think so. Just make a recording of the session. If I need to, I'll listen to it later."

"Later may mean another body," he said. "Your boss giving you trouble again?"

"Yeah," I said.

"You want me to talk to him?" Dolph asked.

"I don't think so."

"He being a real bastard about it?"

"The usual."

"Okay, I'll call this Thormund and record the sessions. I'll let you know if we find out anything."

"Beep me."

"You got it." He hung up. I didn't bother to say good-bye. Dolph never did.

I handed the phone back to Bert. He hung it up still staring at me with his pleasant, threatening eyes. "You have to go out for the police tonight?"

"No."

"How did we merit this honor?"

"Cut the sarcasm, Bert." I turned to Larry. "You ready to go, kid?"

"How old are you?" he asked.

Bert grinned.

"What difference does it make?" I asked.

"Just answer the question, okay?"

I shrugged. "Twenty-four."

"You're only four years older than me. Don't call me kid."

I had to smile. "Deal, but we better be going. We have dead to raise, money to make." I glanced at Bert.

He was leaning back in his chair, blunt-fingered hands clasped over his belly. He was grinning.

I wanted to wipe the grin off his face with a fist. I resisted the urge. Who says I have no self-control?

33

It was an hour before dawn. When all the Whos down in Whoville were asnooze in their beds without care. Sorry, wrong book. If I get to stay awake until dawn, I get just a tad slaphappy. I'd been up all night teaching Larry how to be a good, law-abiding animator. I wasn't sure Bert would appreciate the last, but I knew I would.

The cemetery was small. A family plot with pretensions. A narrow two-lane road rounded a hill, and suddenly there it was, a swathe of gravel beside the road. You had seconds to decide to turn in, that this was it. Tombstones climbed up the hill. The angle was so steep, it looked like the coffins should have slid downhill.

We stood in the dark with a canopy of trees whispering overhead. The woods were thick on either side of the road. The little plot was just a narrow space beside the road, but it was well cared for. There were still-living family members to see to the upkeep. I didn't even want to imagine how they mowed the hillside. Maybe a rope-and-pulley system to make sure the mower didn't roll over and add another corpse.

Our last clients of the night had just driven away back to civilization. I'd raised five zombies. Larry had raised one. Yeah, he could have raised two, but we just ran out of darkness. It doesn't take that long to raise a zombie, at least for me, but there's travel time included. In four years I'd only had two zombies in the same cemetery on the same night. Most of the time you were driving like a maniac to make all the appointments.

My poor car had been towed to a service station, but the insurance people hadn't seen it yet. It would take days or weeks for them to tell me it was totaled. There hadn't been time to rent a car for the night, so Larry was driving. He'd have been with me even if I'd had the car. I was the one bitching about not having enough help, so I got to train him. It was only fair, I guessed.

The wind rushed through the trees. Dry leaves scurried across the road.

The night was full of small, hurried noises. Rushing, rushing, towards . . . what? All Hallows Eve. You could feel Halloween on the air.

"I love nights like this," Larry said.

I glanced over at him. We were both standing with our hands in our pockets staring out into the darkness. Enjoying the evening. We were also both covered in dried chicken blood. Just a nice, normal night.

My beeper went off. The high-pitched beep sounded very wrong in the quiet, windswept night. I hit the button. Mercifully, the noise stopped. The little light flashed a phone number at me. I didn't recognize the number. I hoped it wasn't Dolph, because an unfamiliar number this late at night, or early in the morning, meant another murder. Another body.

"Come on, we gotta get to a phone."

"Who is it?"

"I'm not sure." I started down the hill.

He followed me and asked, "Who do you think it is?"

"Maybe the police."

"The murders you're working on?"

I glanced back at him and rammed my knee into a tombstone. I stood there for a few seconds, holding my breath while the pain ran through me. "Shiiit!" I said softly and with feeling.

"Are you all right?" Larry touched my arm.

I drew away from his hand, and he let his hand drop. I wasn't much into casual touching. "I'm fine." Truth was, it still hurt, but what the hell? I needed to get to a phone, and the pain would get better the more I walked on it. Honest.

I stared carefully ahead to avoid other hard objects. "What do you know about the murders?"

"Just that you're helping the police on a preternatural crime, and that it's taking you away from your animating jobs."

"Bert told you that."

"Mr. Vaughn, yes."

We were at the car. "Look, Larry, if you're going to work for Animators, Inc., you've got to drop all this Mr. and Ms. stuff. We aren't your professors. We're coworkers."

He smiled, a flash of white in the dark. "All right, Ms. . . . Anita."

"That's better. Now let's go find a phone."

We drove into Chesterfield on the theory that, as the closest town, it would have the closest phone. We ended up at a bank of pay phones in the parking lot of a closed service station. The station glowed softly in the dark, but a halogen streetlight beamed over the pay phones, turning night into day. Insects and moths danced around the light. The swift, flitting shapes of bats swam in and out of the light, eating the insects.

I dialed the number while Larry waited in the car. Give him a point for discretion. The phone rang twice; then a voice said, "Anita, is that you?"

It was Irving Griswold, reporter and friend. "Irving, what in blazes are you doing paging me at this hour?"

"Jean-Claude wants to see you tonight, now." His voice sounded rushed and uncertain.

"Why are you delivering the message?" I was afraid I wasn't going to like the answer.

"I'm a werewolf," he said.

"What's that got to do with anything?"

"You didn't know." He sounded surprised.

"Know what?" I was getting angry. I hate twenty questions.

"Jean-Claude's animal is a wolf."

That explained Stephen the Werewolf and the black woman. "Why weren't you there the other night, Irving? Did he let you off your leash?"

"That's not fair."

He was right. It wasn't. "I'm sorry, Irving. I'm just feeling guilty because I introduced the two of you."

"I wanted to interview the Master of the City. I got my interview."

"Was it worth the price?" I said.

"No comment."

"That's my line."

He laughed. "Can you come to the Circus of the Damned? Jean-Claude has some information on the master vampire that jumped you."

"Alejandro?"

"That's the one."

"We'll be there as soon as we can, but it's going to be damn close to dawn before we can get to the Riverfront."

"Who's we?"

"A new animator I'm breaking in. He's driving." I hesitated. "Tell Jean-Claude no rough stuff tonight."

"Tell him yourself."

"Coward."

"Yes, ma'am. See you as soon as you can get here. Bye."

"Bye, Irving." I held the buzzing receiver for a few seconds, then hung up. Irving was Jean-Claude's creature. Jean-Claude could call wolves the way Mr. Oliver called snakes. The way Nikolaos had called rats, and wererats. They were all monsters. It was just a choice of flavors.

I slid back into the car. "You wanted more experience with vampires, right?" I buckled the seat belt.

"Of course," Larry said.

"Well, you're going to get it tonight."

"What do you mean?"

"I'll explain while you drive. We don't have much time before dawn."

Larry threw the car in gear and peeled out of the parking lot. He looked eager in the dim glow of the dashboard. Eager and very, very young.

34

The Circus of the Damned had closed down for the night, or would that be morning? It was still dark, but there was a wash of lightness to the east as we parked in front of the warehouse. An hour earlier, and there wouldn't have been a parking place even close to the Circus. But the tourists leave as the vampires fold down for the night.

I glanced at Larry. His face was smeared with dried blood. So was mine. It hadn't occurred to me until just now to find some place to clean up first. I glanced up at the eastern sky and shook my head. There was no time. Dawn was coming.

The toothed clowns still glowed and twirled atop the marquee, but it was a tired dance. Or maybe I was the one who was tired.

"Follow my lead in here, Larry. Never forget that they are monsters; no matter how human they look, they aren't. Don't take off your cross, don't let them touch you, and don't stare directly into their eyes."

"I know that from class. I had two semesters of Vampire Studies."

I shook my head. "Class is nothing, Larry. This is the real thing. Reading about it doesn't prepare you for it."

"We had guest speakers. Some of them were vampires."

I sighed and let it go. He'd have to learn on his own. Like everybody else did. Like I had.

The big doors were locked. I knocked. The door opened a moment later. Irving stood there. He wasn't smiling. He looked like a chubby cherub with soft, curling hair in a fringe over his ears, and a big bald spot in the middle. Round, wire-framed glasses perched on a round little nose. His eyes widened a little as we stepped inside. The blood looked like what it was in the light.

"What have you been doing tonight?" he asked.

"Raising the dead," I said.

"This the new animator?"

"Larry Kirkland, Irving Griswold. He's a reporter, so everything you say can be used against you."

"Hey, Blake, I've never quoted you when you said not to. Give me that."

I nodded. "Given."

"He's waiting for you downstairs," Irving said.

"Downstairs?" I said.

"It is almost dawn. He needs to be underground."

Ah. "Sure," I said, but my stomach clenched tight. The last time I'd gone downstairs at the Circus, it had been to kill Nikolaos. There had been a lot of killing that morning. A lot of blood. Some of it mine.

Irving led the way through the silent midway. Someone had hit the switch, and the lights were dull. The fronts of the games had been shut and locked down, covers thrown over the stuffed animals. The scent of corn dogs and cotton candy hung on the air like aromatic ghosts, but the smells were dim and tired.

We passed the haunted house with its life-size witch on top, standing silent and staring with bulging eyes. She was green and had a wart on her nose. I'd never met a witch that looked anything but normal. They certainly weren't green, and warts could always be surgically removed.

The glass house was next. The darkened Ferris wheel towered over everything. "I feel like one, / Who treads alone / Some banquet hall deserted, / Whose lights are fled, / Whose garlands dead, / And all but he departed," I said.

Irving glanced back to me. "Thomas Moore, *Oft in the Stilly Night.*"

I smiled. "I couldn't remember the title to save myself. I'll just have to agree with you."

"Double major, journalism and English literature."

"I bet that last comes in handy as a reporter," I said.

"Hey, I slip a little culture in when I can." He sounded offended, but I knew he was pretending. It made me feel better to have Irving joking with me. It was nice and normal. I needed all the nice I could get tonight.

It was an hour until dawn. What harm could Jean-Claude do in an hour? Better not to ask.

The door in the wall was heavy and wooden with a sign reading, "Authorized Personnel Only Beyond This Point." For once I wished I wasn't authorized.

The little room beyond was just a small storage room with a bare light bulb hanging from the ceiling. A second door led down the stairs. The stairs were almost wide enough for the three of us to walk abreast, but not quite. Irving walked ahead of us, as if we still needed leading. There was nowhere to go but down. Prophetic, that.

There was a sharp bend to the stairs. There was a brush of cloth, the sensation of movement. I had my gun out and ready. No thought necessary, just lots and lots of practice.

"You won't need that," Irving said.

"Says you."

"I thought the Master was a friend of yours," Larry said.

"Vampires don't have friends."

"How about junior high science teachers?" Richard Zeeman walked around the corner. He was wearing a forest-green sweater with a lighter green and brown forest woven into it. The sweater hung down nearly to his knees. On me it would have been a dress. The sleeves were pushed back over his forearms. Jeans and the same pair of white Nikes completed the outfit. "Jean-Claude sent me up to wait for you."

"Why?" I asked.

He shrugged. "He seems nervous. I didn't ask questions."

"Smart man," I said.

"Let's keep moving," Irving said.

"You sound nervous, too, Irving."

"He calls and I obey, Anita. I'm his animal."

I reached out to touch Irving's arm, but he moved away. "I thought I could play human, but he's shown me that I'm an animal. Just an animal."

"Don't let him do that to you," I said.

He stared at me, his eyes filled with tears. "I can't stop him."

"We better get moving. It's almost dawn," Richard said.

I glared at him for saying it.

He shrugged. "It'll be better if we don't keep the master waiting. You know that."

I did know that. I nodded. "You're right. I don't have any right to get mad at you."

"Thanks."

I shook my head. "Let's do it."

"You can put the gun up," he said.

I stared at the Browning. I liked having it out. For security it beat the hell out of a teddy bear. I put the gun away. I could always get it out again later.

At the end of the stairs there was one last door—smaller, rounded with a heavy iron lock. Irving took out a huge black key and slipped it into the door. The lock gave a well-oiled click, and he pushed it forward. Irving was trusted with the key to below the stairs. How deep was he in, and could I get him out?

"Wait a minute," I said.

Everyone turned to me. I was the center of attention. Great. "I don't want Larry to meet the Master, or even know who he is."

"Anita . . ." Larry started.

"No, Larry, I've been attacked twice for the information. It is definitely on a need-to-know basis. You don't need to know."

"I don't need you to protect me," he said.

"Listen to her," Irving said. "She told me to stay away from the Master. I said I could handle myself. I was wrong, real wrong."

Larry crossed his arms over his chest, a stubborn set to his bloodstained cheeks. "I can take care of myself."

"Irving, Richard, I want a promise on this. The less he knows, the safer he'll be."

They both nodded.

"Doesn't anyone care what I think?" Larry asked.

"No," I said.

"Dammit, I'm not a child."

"You two can fight later," Irving said. "The Master's waiting."

Larry started to say something; I raised my hand. "Lesson number one; never keep a nervous master vampire waiting."

Larry opened his mouth to argue, then stopped. "Okay, we'll argue later."

I wasn't looking forward to later, but arguing with Larry over whether I was being overprotective beat the hell out of what lay beyond the door. I knew that. Larry didn't, but he was about to learn, and there wasn't a damn thing I could do to stop it.

35

The ceiling stretched upward into the darkness. Huge drapes of silky material fell in white and black, forming cloth walls. Minimalist chairs in black and silver formed a small conversation group. A glass and dark wood coffee table took up the center of the room. A black vase with a bouquet of white lilies was the only decoration. The room looked half-finished, as if it needed paintings hung on the walls. But how do you hang paintings on cloth walls? I was sure Jean-Claude would figure it out eventually.

I knew the rest of the room was a huge cavernous warehouse made of stone, but the only thing left of that was the high ceiling. There was even black carpeting on the floor, soft and cushioned.

Jean-Claude sat in one of the black chairs. He was slumped in the chair, ankles crossed, hands clasped across his stomach. His white shirt was plain, just a simple dress shirt except for the fact that the front sides were sheer. The line of buttons, cuffs, and collar was solid, but the chest was laid bare through a film of gauze. His cross-shaped burn was brown and clear against the pale skin.

Marguerite sat at his feet, head laid on his knee like an obedient dog. Her blond hair and pale pink pants suit seemed out of place in the black-and-white room.

"You've redecorated," I said.

"A few comforts," Jean-Claude said.

"I'm ready to meet the Master of the City," I said.

His eyes widened, a question forming on his face.

"I don't want my new coworker to meet the Master. It seems to be dangerous information right now."

Jean-Claude never moved. He just stared at me, one hand absently rubbing Marguerite's hair. Where was Yasmeen? In a coffin somewhere, tucked safely away from the coming dawn.

"I will take you alone to meet ... the Master," he said at last. His voice was neutral, but I could detect a hint of laughter underneath the words. It wasn't the first time Jean-Claude had found me funny, and it probably wouldn't be the last.

He stood in one graceful movement, leaving Marguerite kneeling beside the empty chair. She looked displeased. I smiled at her, and she glared at me. Baiting Marguerite was childish, but it made me feel better. Everyone needs a hobby.

Jean-Claude swept the curtains aside to show darkness. I realized then that there was discreet electric light in the room, indirect lighting set in the walls themselves. There was nothing but the flicker of torches beyond the curtains. It was like that one piece of cloth held back the modern world with all its comforts. Beyond lay stone and fire and secrets best whispered in the dark.

"Anita?" Larry called after me. He looked uncertain, maybe even scared. But I was taking the most dangerous thing in the room with me. He'd be safe with Irving and Richard. I didn't think Marguerite was a danger without Yasmeen to hold her leash.

"Stay here, Larry, please. I'll be back as soon as I can."

"Be careful," he said.

I smiled. "Always."

He grinned. "Yeah, sure."

Jean-Claude motioned me through and I went, following the sweep of his pale hand. The curtain fell behind us, cutting off the light. Darkness closed around us like a fist. Torches sparked against the far wall but couldn't touch the swelling dark.

Jean-Claude led the way into the dark. "We wouldn't want your co-worker to overhear us." His voice whispered in the dark, growing like a wind to beat against the curtains.

My heart hammered against my rib cage. How the hell did he do that? "Save the dramatics for someone you can impress."

"Brave words, *ma petite*, but I taste your heartbeat in my mouth." The last word breathed over my skin as if his lips had passed just over the nape of my neck. Goosebumps marched down my arms.

"If you want to play games until after dawn, that's fine with me, but Irving told me that you had information on the master vampire that attacked me. Do you, or was it a lie?"

"I have never lied to you, *ma petite*."

"Oh, come on."

"Partial truths are not the same thing as lies."

"I guess that depends on where you're sitting," I said.

He acknowledged that with a nod. "Shall we sit against the far wall, out of hearing range?"

"Sure."

He knelt in the thin circle of a torch's light. The light was for my benefit, and I appreciated it. But no sense telling him that.

I sat across from him, back to the wall. "So, what do you know about Alejandro?"

He was staring at me, a peculiar look on his face.

"What?" I asked.

"Tell me everything that happened last night, *ma petite*, everything about Alejandro."

It was too much like an order for my tastes, but there was something in his eyes, his face; uneasiness, almost fear. Which was silly. What did Jean-Claude have to fear from Alejandro? What indeed? I told him everything I remembered.

His face went carefully blank, beautiful and unreal like a painting. The colors were still there, but the life, the movement, had fled. He put one finger between his lips and slowly slid it out of sight. The finger came glistening back to the light. He extended that wet finger towards me. I scooted away from him.

"What are you trying to do?"

"Wash the blood off of your cheek. Nothing more."

"I don't think so."

He sighed, the barest of sounds, but it slithered over my skin like air. "You make everything so difficult."

"Glad you noticed."

"I need to touch you, *ma petite*. I believe Alejandro has done something to you."

"What?"

He shook his head. "Something impossible."

"No riddles, Jean-Claude."

"I believe he has marked you."

I stared at him. "What do you mean?"

"Marked you, Anita Blake, marked you with the first mark, just as I have."

I shook my head. "That's not possible. Two vampires can't have the same human servant."

"Exactly," he said. He moved towards me. "Let me test the theory, *ma petite*, please."

"What does testing the theory mean?"

He said something soft and harsh in French. I'd never heard him curse before. "It is after dawn and I am tired. Your questions will make something simple last all bloody day." There was real anger in his voice, but under that was tiredness and that thread of fear. The fear scared me. He was supposed to be some untouchable monster. Monsters weren't afraid of other monsters.

I sighed. Was it better to just get it over with, like a shot? Maybe. "All right, in the interest of time. But give me some idea of what to expect. You know I don't like surprises."

"I must touch you to search first for my marks, then for his. You should not have fallen so easily into his eyes. That should not have happened."

"Get it over with," I said.

"Is my touch so repulsive that you must prepare yourself as for pain?"

Since that was almost exactly what I was doing, I wasn't sure what to say. "Just do it, Jean-Claude, before I change my mind."

He slid his finger between his lips again.

"Do you have to do it that way?"

"*Ma petite*, please."

I squirmed against the cool stone wall. "All right, no more interruptions."

"Good." He knelt in front of me. His fingertip traced my right cheek, leaving a line of wetness down my skin. The dried blood was gritty under his touch. He leaned into me, as if he was going to kiss me. I put my hands on his chest to keep him from touching me. His skin was hard and smooth under the gauze of his shirt.

I jerked away and hit my head against the wall. "Dammit."

He smiled. His eyes glinted blue in the torchlight. "Trust me." He moved in, lips hovering over my mouth. "I won't hurt you." The words whispered into my mouth, a soft push of air.

"Yeah, right," I said, but the words came out soft and uncertain.

His lips brushed mine, then pressed gently against my mouth. The kiss moved from my lips to my cheek. His lips were soft as silk, gentle as marigold petals, hot as the noonday sun. They worked down my skin until his mouth hovered over the pulse in my neck.

"Jean-Claude?"

"Alejandro was alive when the Aztec empire was just a dream." He whispered it against my skin. "He was there to greet the Spaniards and watch the Aztecs fall. He has survived when others have died or gone mad." His tongue flicked out, hot and wet.

"Stop it." I pushed against him. His heart beat against my hands. I pushed my hands upward to his throat. The big pulse in his throat fluttered against my skin. I placed a thumb over the smoothness of one of his eyelids. "Move it or lose it," I said. My voice was breathy with panic, and something worse . . . desire.

The feel of his body against me, under my hands, his lips touching me— some hidden part of me wanted it. Wanted him. So I lusted after the Master; so what? Nothing new. His eyeball trembled under my thumb, and I wondered if I could do it. Could I blank out one of those midnight-blue orbs? Could I blind him?

His lips moved against my skin. Teeth brushed my skin, the hard brush of fangs rubbed against my throat. And the answer was, suddenly, yes. I tensed to press inward, and he was gone like a dream, or a nightmare.

He stood in front of me, looking down, his eyes all dark, no white showing. His lips had drawn back from his teeth to expose glistening fangs. His skin was marble-white and seemed to glow from inside, and still he was beautiful.

"Alejandro has given you the first mark, *ma petite*. We share you. I do not know how, but we do. Two more marks and you are mine. Three more and you are his. Would it not be better to be mine?''

He knelt in front of me again, but was careful not to touch me. ''You desire me as a woman desires a man. Is that not better than some stranger taking you by force?''

''You didn't ask my permission for the first two marks. They weren't by choice.''

''I am asking permission now. Let me share with you the third mark.''

''No.''

''You would rather serve Alejandro?''

''I'm not going to serve anyone,'' I said.

''This is a war, Anita. You cannot be neutral.''

''Why not?''

He stood up and paced a tight circle. ''Don't you understand? The killings are a challenge to my authority, and his marking you is another challenge. He will take you from me if he can.''

''I don't belong to you, or to him.''

''What I have tried to get you to believe, to accept, he will shove down your throat.''

''So I'm in the middle of an undead turf war because of your marks.''

He blinked, opened his mouth, then closed it. Finally, ''Yes.''

I stood up. ''Thanks a lot.'' I walked past him. ''If you have any more info on Alejandro, send me a letter.''

''This will not go away just because you wish it to.''

I stopped in front of the curtain. ''Hell, I knew that. I've wished hard enough for you to leave me alone.''

''You would miss me if I were not here.''

''Don't flatter yourself.''

''And do not lie to yourself, *ma petite*. I would give you a partnership. He will give you slavery.''

''If you really believed this partnership crap, you wouldn't have forced the first two marks on me. You would have asked. For all I know, the third mark can't be given without my cooperation.'' I stared at him. ''That's it, isn't it? You need my help or something for the third mark. It's different from the first two. You son of a bitch.''

''The third mark without your . . . help would be like rape to making love. You would hate me for all eternity if I took you by force.''

I turned my back on him and grabbed the curtain. ''You got that right.''

''Alejandro will not care if you hate him. He wants only to hurt me. He will not ask your permission. He will simply take you.''

''I can take care of myself.''

''Like you took care last night?''

Alejandro had rolled me under and over and I hadn't even known it. What protection did I have against something like that? I shook my head and jerked back the curtain. The light was so bright, I was blind. I stood in the glare waiting for my eyes to adjust. The cool darkness blew against my back. The light was hot and intrusive after the darkness, but anything was better than whispers in the night. Blinded by the light or blinded by darkness; I'd take light every time.

36

Larry was lying on the floor, head cradled in Yasmeen's lap. She held his wrists. Marguerite had pinned his body under her own. She was licking the blood off his face with long, lingering strokes of her tongue. Richard lay in a crumpled heap, blood running down his face. There was something on the floor. It writhed and moved. Grey fur flowed over it like water. A hand reached skyward, then shrank like a dying flower, bones glistening, shoving upward through the flesh. The fingers shrank, flesh rolling over the nubs of raw flesh. All that raw meat and no blood. The bones slid in and out with wet, sucking noises. Drops of clear fluid spattered the black rug. But no blood.

I drew the Browning and moved so I could point it somewhere between Yasmeen and the thing on the floor. I had my back to the curtain but moved away from it. Too easy for something to reach through.

"Let him go, now."

"We haven't hurt him," Yasmeen said.

Marguerite leaned into Larry's body; one hand cupped his groin, massaging.

"Anita!" His eyes were wide, skin pale; freckles stood out like ink spots.

I fired a shot inches from Yasmeen's head. The sound was sharp and echoed. Yasmeen snarled at me. "I can rip his throat out before you squeeze that trigger again."

I aimed for Marguerite's head, right over one blue eye. "You kill him, I kill Marguerite. You willing to make the trade?"

"Yasmeen, what are you doing?" Jean-Claude came in at my back. My eyes flicked to him, then back to Marguerite. Jean-Claude wasn't the danger, not now.

The thing on the floor rose on four shaky legs and shook itself like a dog after a bath. It was a huge wolf. Thick grey-brown fur covered the animal, fluffy and dry as if the wolf had been freshly washed and blow-dried. Liquid formed a thick puddle on the carpet. Bits of clothing were scattered around. The wolf had emerged from the mess newly formed, re-born.

A pair of round wire-framed glasses sat on the glass and black coffee table, neatly folded.

"Irving?"

The wolf gave a small half-growl, half-bark. Was that a yes?

I had always known that Irving was a werewolf, but seeing it was something else entirely. Until just that moment I hadn't really believed, not really. Staring into the wolf's pale brown eyes, I believed.

Marguerite lay on the ground behind Larry now. Her arms wrapped around his chest, legs wrapping his waist. Most of her was hidden behind him, shielded.

I had spent too much time gazing at Irving. I couldn't shoot Marguerite without risking Larry. Yasmeen was kneeling beside them, one hand gripping a handful of Larry's hair. "I will snap his neck."

"You will not harm him, Yasmeen," Jean-Claude said. He stood beside the coffee table. The wolf moved up beside him, growling softly. His fingers brushed the top of the wolf's head.

"Call off your dogs, Jean-Claude, or this one dies." She stretched Larry's throat into one straining pale line to emphasize her point. The Band-Aid that had been hiding his vampire bite had been removed. Marguerite's tongue flicked out, touching the straining flesh.

I was betting that I could shoot Marguerite in the forehead while she licked Larry's neck, but Yasmeen could, and might, break his neck. I couldn't take the chance.

"Do something, Jean-Claude," I said. "You're the Master of the City. She's supposed to take your orders."

"Yes, Jean-Claude, order me."

"What's going on here, Jean-Claude?" I asked.

"She is testing me."

"Why?"

"Yasmeen wants to be Master of the City. But she isn't strong enough."

"I was strong enough to keep you and your servant from hearing this one's screams. Richard called your name, and you heard nothing because I kept you from it."

Richard stood just behind Jean-Claude. Blood was smeared from the corner of his mouth. There was a small cut on his right cheek that trickled blood down his face. "I tried to stop her."

"You did not try hard enough," Jean-Claude said.

"Argue amongst yourselves later," I said. "Right now, we have a problem."

Yasmeen laughed. The sound wriggled down my spine like someone had spilled a can of worms. I shuddered, and decided then and there that I'd shoot Yasmeen first. We'd find out if a master vampire was really faster than a speeding bullet.

She released Larry with a laugh and stood. Marguerite still clung to him. He got to his hands and knees with the woman riding him like a horse, arms and legs still clamped around him. She was laughing, kissing his neck.

I kicked her in the face as hard as I could. She slid off Larry and lay dazed on the floor. Yasmeen started forward and I fired at her chest. Jean-Claude hit my arm, and the shot went wide.

"I need her alive, Anita."

I jerked away from him. "She's crazy."

"But he needs my assistance to combat the other masters," Yasmeen said.

"She'll betray you if she can," I said.

"But I still need her."

"If you can't control Yasmeen, then how in the hell are you going to fight Alejandro?"

"I don't know," he said. "Is that what you wanted to hear? I do not know."

Larry was still huddled by our feet.

"Can you get up?"

He looked up at me, eyes shiny with unshed tears. He used one of the chairs to brace himself and almost fell. I grabbed his arm, gun still in my right hand. "Come on, Larry, we're getting out of here."

"Sounds great to me." His voice was incredibly breathless, straining not to cry.

We worked our way towards the door, me helping Larry walk, gun still out pointed vaguely at everything in the room.

"Go with them, Richard. See them safely to their car. And do not fail me again like you did today."

Richard ignored the threat and walked around us to hold the door open. We walked through without turning our backs on the vampires or the were-wolf. When the door closed, I let out a breath I hadn't even known I was holding.

"I can walk now," Larry said.

I let go of his arm. He put a hand against the wall but otherwise seemed okay. The first slow tear trailed down his cheek. "Get me out of here."

I put my gun up. It wouldn't help now. Richard and I both pretended not to notice Larry's tears. They were very quiet. If you hadn't been looking directly at him, you wouldn't have known he was crying.

I tried to think of something to say, anything. But what could I say? He had seen the monsters, and they had scared the shit out of him. They scared the shit out of me. They scared the shit out of everybody. Now Larry knew that. Maybe it was worth the pain. Maybe not.

37

Early-morning light lay heavy and golden on the street outside. The air was cool and misty. You couldn't see the river from here, but you could feel it; that sense of water on the air that made every breath fresher, cleaner.

Larry got out his car keys.

"You okay to drive?" I asked.

He nodded. The tears had dried in thin tracks down his face. He hadn't bothered to wipe them away. He wasn't crying anymore. He was as grim-faced as you could be and still look like an overgrown Howdy Doody. He opened his door and got in, sliding across to unlock the passenger side.

Richard stood there. The cool wind blew his hair across his face. He ran fingers through it to keep it from his face. The gesture was achingly familiar. Phillip had always been doing that. Richard smiled at me, and it wasn't Phillip's smile. It was bright and open, and there was nothing hidden in his brown eyes.

Blood had started to dry at the corner of his mouth, and on his cheek.

"Get out while you still can, Richard."

"Out from what?"

"There's going to be an undead war. You don't want to be caught in the middle."

"I don't think Jean-Claude would let me walk away," he said. He wasn't smiling when he said it. I couldn't decide whether he was handsomer smiling or solemn.

"Humans don't do too well in the middle of the monsters, Richard. Get out if you can."

"You're human."

I shrugged. "Some people would argue that."

"Not me." He reached out to touch me. I stood my ground and didn't move away. His fingertips brushed the side of my face, warm and very alive.

"See you at three o'clock this afternoon, unless you're going to be too tired."

I shook my head, and his hand dropped away from my face. "Wouldn't miss it," I said.

He smiled again. His hair blew in a tangle across his face. I kept the front of my own hair cut short enough so that it stayed out of my eyes, most of the time. Layering was a wonderful thing.

I opened the passenger side door. "I'll see you this afternoon."

"I'll bring your costume with me."

"What am I going to be dressed as?"

"A Civil War bride," he said.

"Does that mean a hoop skirt?"

"Probably."

I frowned. "And what are you going to be?"

"A Confederate officer."

"You get to wear pants," I said.

"I don't think the dress would fit me."

I sighed. "It's not that I'm not grateful, Richard, but . . ."

"Hoop skirts aren't your style?"

"Not hardly."

"My offer was grubbies and all the mud we could crawl in. The party was your idea."

"I'd get out of it if I could."

"It might be worth all the trouble just to see you dressed up. I get the feeling it's a rarity."

Larry leaned across the seat, and said, "Can we get a move on? I need a cigarette and some sleep."

"I'll be right there." I turned back to Richard but suddenly didn't know what to say. "See you later."

He nodded. "Later."

I got in the car, and Larry pulled away before I got my seat belt fastened. "What's the rush?"

"I want to get as far away from this place as I can."

I looked at him. He still looked pale.

"You all right?"

"No, I'm not all right." He looked at me, blue eyes bright with anger. "How can you be so casual after what just happened?"

"You were calm after last night. You got bitten last night."

"But that was different," he said. "That woman sucked on the bite. She . . ." His hands clenched the steering wheel so tightly his hands shook.

"You were hurt worse last night; what makes this tougher?"

"Last night was violent, but it wasn't . . . perverted. The vampires last night wanted something. The name of the Master. The ones tonight didn't want anything, they were just being . . ."

"Cruel," I offered.

"Yes, cruel."

"They're vampires, Larry. They aren't human. They don't have the same rules."

"She would have killed me tonight on a whim."

"Yes, she would have," I said.

"How can you bear to be around them?"

I shrugged. "It's my job."

"And my job, too."

"It doesn't have to be, Larry. Just refuse to work on vampire cases. Most of the rest of the animators do."

He shook his head. "No, I won't give up."

"Why not?" I asked.

He didn't say anything for a minute. He pulled onto 270 headed south. "How could you talk about a date this afternoon after what just happened?"

"You have to have a life, Larry. If you let this business eat you alive, you'll never make it." I studied his face. "And you never answered my question."

"What question?"

"Why won't you give up the idea of being a vampire executioner?"

Larry hesitated, concentrating on driving. He suddenly seemed very interested in passing cars. We drove under a railroad bridge, warehouses on either side. Many of the windows were broken or missing. Rust dripped down the bridge overpass.

"Nice section of town," he said.

"You're avoiding the question. Why?"

"I don't want to talk about it."

"I asked about your family; you said they were all alive. What about friends? You lose a friend to the vamps?"

He glanced at me. "Why ask that?"

"I know the signs, Larry. You're determined to kill the monsters because you've got a grudge, don't you?"

He hunched his shoulders and stared straight ahead. The muscles in his jaws clenched and unclenched.

"Talk to me, Larry," I said.

"The town I come from is small, fifteen hundred people. While I was away at college my freshman year, twelve people were murdered by a pack of vampires. I didn't know them, any of them, really. I knew them to say hi to, but that was it."

"Go on."

He glanced at me. "I went to the funerals over Christmas break. All those coffins, all those families. My dad was a doctor, but he couldn't help them. Nobody could help them."

"I remember the case," I said. "Elbert, Wisconsin, three years ago, right?"

"Yes, how did you know?"

"Twelve people is a lot for a single vampire kill. It made the papers. Brett Colby was the vampire hunter they got for the job."

"I never met him, but my parents told me about him. They made him sound like a cowboy riding into town to take down the bad guys. He found and killed five vampires. He helped the town when nobody else could."

"If you just want to help people, Larry, be a social worker, or a doctor."

"I'm an animator; I've got a built-in resistance to vampires. I think God meant for me to hunt them."

"Geez Louise, Larry, don't go on a holy crusade, you'll end up dead."

"You can teach me."

I shook my head. "Larry, this isn't personal. It can't be personal. If you let your emotions get in the way, you'll either get killed or go stark raving mad."

"I'll learn, Anita."

I stared at his profile. He looked so stubborn. "Larry . . ." I stopped. What could I say? What brought any of us into this business? Maybe his reasons were as good as my own, maybe better. It wasn't just love of killing, like with Edward. And heaven knew I needed help. There were getting to be too many vampires for just little ol' me.

"All right, I'll teach you, but you do what I say, when I say it. No arguments."

"Anything you say, boss." He grinned at me briefly, then turned back to the road. He looked determined and relieved, and young.

But we were all young once. It passes, like innocence and a sense of fair play. The only thing left in the end is a good instinct for survival. Could I teach Larry that? Could I teach him how to survive? Please, God, let me teach him, and don't let him die on me.

38

Larry dropped me off in front of my apartment building at 9:05. It was way past my bedtime. I got my gym bag out of the back seat. Didn't want to leave my animating equipment behind. I locked and shut the door, then leaned in the passenger side door. "I'll see you tonight at five o'clock back here, Larry. You're designated driver until I get a new car."

He nodded.

"If I'm late getting home, don't let Bert send you out alone, okay?"

He looked at me then. His face was full of some deep thought that I couldn't read. "You think I can't handle myself?"

I knew he couldn't handle himself, but I didn't say that out loud. "It's only your second night on the job. Give yourself and me a break. I'll teach you how to hunt vampires, but our primary job is raising the dead. Try to remember that."

He nodded.

"Larry, if you have bad dreams, don't worry. I have them too sometimes."

"Sure," he said. He put the car in gear, and I had to close the door. Guess he didn't want to talk anymore. Nothing we'd seen yet would give me nightmares, but I wanted Larry to be prepared, if mere words could prepare anyone for what we do.

A family was loading up a grey van with coolers and a picnic hamper. The man smiled. "I don't think we'll get many more days like this."

"I think you're right." It was that pleasant small talk that you use with people whose names you don't know but whose faces you keep seeing. We were neighbors, so we said hello and good-bye to each other, but nothing else. That was the way I liked it. When I came home, I didn't want someone coming over to borrow a cup of sugar.

The only exception I made was Mrs. Pringle, and she understood my need for privacy.

The apartment was warm and quiet inside. I locked the door and leaned against it. Home, ah. I tossed the leather jacket on the back of the couch and smelled perfume. It was flowery and delicate with a powdery undertaste that only the really expensive ones have. It wasn't my brand.

I pulled the Browning and put my back to the door. A man stepped around the corner from the dining room area. He was tall, thin, with black hair cut short in front, long in back, the latest style. He just stood there, leaning against the wall, arms crossed over his chest, smiling at me.

A second man came up from behind the couch, shorter, more muscular, blond, smiling. He sat on the couch, hands where I could see them. Nobody had any weapons, or none that I could see.

"Who the hell are you?"

A tall black man came out of the bedroom. He had a neat mustache, and dark sunglasses hid his eyes.

The lamia stepped out beside him. She was in human form, in the same red dress as yesterday. She wore scarlet high heels today, but nothing else had changed.

"We've been waiting for you, Ms. Blake."

"Who are the men?"

"My harem."

"I don't understand."

"They belong to me." She trailed red nails down the black man's hand hard enough to leave a thin line of blood. He just smiled.

"What do you want?"

"Mr. Oliver wants to see you. He sent us to fetch you."

"I know where the house is. I can drive there on my own."

"Oh, no, we've had to move," she said, swaying into the room. "Some nasty bounty hunter tried to kill Oliver yesterday."

"What bounty hunter?" Had it been Edward?

She waved a hand. "We were never formally introduced. Oliver wouldn't let me kill him, so he escaped, and we had to move."

It sounded reasonable, but . . . "Where is he now?"

"We'll take you to him. We've got a car waiting outside."

"Why didn't Inger come for me?"

She shrugged. "Oliver gives orders and I follow them." A look passed over her lovely face—hatred.

"How long has he been your master?"

"Too long," she said.

I stared at them all, gun still out but not pointed at anyone. They hadn't offered to hurt me. So why didn't I want to put the gun up? Because I'd seen what the lamia changed into, and it had scared me.

"Why does Oliver need to see me so soon?"

"He wants your answer."

"I haven't decided yet whether to give him the Master of the City."

"All I know is that I was told to bring you. If I don't, he'll be angry. I don't want to be punished, Ms. Blake; please come with us."

How do you punish a lamia? Only one way to find out. "How does he punish you?"

The lamia stared at me. "That is a very personal question."

"I didn't mean it to be."

"Forget it." She swayed towards me. "Shall we go?" She had stopped just in front of me, close enough to touch.

I was beginning to feel silly with the gun out, so I put it up. Nobody was threatening me. A novel approach.

Normally, I still would have offered to follow them in my car, but my car was dead. So . . . if I wanted to meet Oliver, I had to go with them.

I wanted to meet Oliver. I wasn't willing to give him Jean-Claude, but I was willing to give him Alejandro. Or at least enlist his aid against Alejandro. I also wanted to know if it was Edward who had tried to kill him. There weren't that many of us in the business. Who else could it be?

"All right, let's go," I said. I got my leather jacket from the couch and opened the door. I motioned them all out the door. The men went without a word, the lamia last.

I locked the door behind us. They waited politely out in the hall for me. The lamia took the tall black man's arm. She smiled. "Boys, one of you offer the lady your arm."

Blondie and black-hair turned to look at me. Black-hair smiled. I hadn't been with this many smiling people since I bought my last used car.

They both offered me their arms, like in some late movie. "Sorry, guys, I don't need an escort."

"I've trained them to be gentlemen, Ms. Blake; take advantage of it. There are precious few gentlemen around these days."

I couldn't argue with that, but I also didn't need help down the stairs. "I appreciate it, but I'm fine."

"As you like, Ms. Blake." She turned to the two men. "You two are to take special care of Ms. Blake." She turned back to me. "A woman should always have more than one man."

I fought the urge to shrug. "Anything you say."

She gave a brilliant smile and strutted down the hall on her man's arm. The two men sort of fell in beside me. The lamia spoke back over her shoulder, "Ronald here is my special beau. I don't share him; sorry."

I had to smile. "That's fine, I'm not greedy."

She laughed, a high-pitched delighted sound with an edge of giggle to it. "Not greedy; oh, that's very good, Ms. Blake, or may I call you Anita?"

"Anita's fine."

"Then you must call me Melanie."

"Sure," I said. I followed her and Ronald down the hall. Blondie and Smiley hovered on either side of me, lest I trip and stub my toe. We'd never get down the stairs without one of us falling.

I turned to Blondie. "I believe I will take your arm." I smiled back at Smiley. "Could we have a little room here?"

He frowned, but he stepped back. I slipped my left hand through Blondie's waiting arm. His forearm swelled under my hand. I couldn't tell if he was flexing or was just that musclebound. But we all made it down the stairs safely with lonely Smiley bringing up the rear.

The lamia and Ronald were waiting by a large black Lincoln Continental. Ronald held the door for the lamia, then slid into the driver's seat.

Smiley rushed forward to open the door for me. How had I known he would? Usually I complain about things like that, but the whole thing was too strange. If the worst thing that happened to me today was having over-zealous men open doors for me, I'd be doing fine.

Blondie slid into the seat next to me, sliding me to the middle of the seat. The other one had run around and was getting in the other side. I was going to end up sandwiched between them. No big surprise.

The lamia named Melanie turned around in her seat, propping her chin on her arm. "Feel free to make out on the way. They're both very good."

I stared into her cheerful eyes. She seemed to be serious. Smiley put his arm across the back of the seat, brushing my shoulders. Blondie tried to take my hand, but I eluded him. He settled for touching my knee. Not an improvement.

"I'm really not into public sex," I said. I moved Blondie's hand back to his own lap.

Smiley's hand slid around my shoulder. I moved up in the seat away from both of them. "Call them off," I said.

"Boys, she's not interested."

The men scooted back from me, as close to their sides of the car as they could get. Their legs still gently touched mine, but at least nothing else was touching.

"Thank you," I said.

"If you change your mind during the drive, just tell them. They love taking orders, don't you, boys?"

The two men nodded, smiling. My, weren't we a happy little bunch? "I don't think I'll change my mind."

The lamia shrugged. "As you like, Anita, but the boys will be sorely disappointed if you don't at least give them a good-bye kiss."

This was getting weird; cancel that, weirder. "I never kiss on the first date."

She laughed. "Oh, I like it. Don't we, boys?" All three men made appreciative sounds. I had the feeling they'd have sat up and begged if she'd told them to. Arf, arf. Gag me with a spoon.

39

We drove south on 270. Steep, grassy ditches and small trees lined the road. Identical houses sat up on the hills, fences separating the small yards from the next small yard. Tall trees took up many yards. Two-seventy was the major highway that ran through St. Louis, but there was almost always a feeling of green nature, open spaces; the gentle roll of the land was never completely lost.

We took 70 West heading towards St. Charles. The land opened up on either side to long, flat fields. Corn stretched tall and golden, ready to be harvested. Behind the field was a modern glass building that advertised pianos and an indoor golf range. An abandoned SAM's Wholesale and a used-car lot led up to the Blanchette bridge.

The left side of the road was crisscrossed by water-filled dikes to keep the land from flooding. Industry had moved in with tall glass buildings. An Omni Hotel complete with fountain was nearest the road.

A stand of woods that still flooded too often to be torn down and turned into buildings bordered the left-hand side of the road until the trees met the Missouri River. Trees continued on the other bank as we entered St. Charles.

St. Charles didn't flood, so there were apartment buildings, strip malls, a deluxe pet supermarket, a movie theater, Drug Emporium, Old Country Buffet, and Appleby's. The land vanished behind billboards and Red Roof Inns. It was hard to remember that the Missouri River was just behind you, and this had once been forest. Hard to see the land for the buildings.

Sitting in the warm car with only the sound of wheels on pavement and the murmur of voices from the front seat, I realized how tired I was. Even stuck between the two men, I was ready for a nap. I yawned.

"How much farther?" I asked.

The lamia turned in her seat. "Bored?"

"I haven't been to sleep yet. I just want to know how much longer the ride is going to take."

"So sorry to inconvenience you," she said. "It isn't much farther, is it, Ronald?"

He shook his head. He hadn't said a word since I'd met him. Could he talk?

"Exactly where are we going?" They didn't seem to want to answer the question, but maybe if I phrased it differently.

"About forty-five minutes outside of St. Peters."

"Near Wentzville?" I asked.

She nodded.

An hour to get there and nearly two hours back. Which would make it around 1:00 when I got home. Two hours of sleep. Great.

We left St. Charles behind, and the land reappeared—fields on either side behind well-tended barbed-wire fences. Cattle grazed on the low, rolling hills. The only sign of civilization was a gas station close to the highway. There was a large house set far back from the road with a perfect expanse of grass stretching to the road. Horses moved gracefully over the grass. I kept waiting for us to pull into one of the gracious estates, but we passed them all by.

We finally turned onto a narrow road with a street sign that was so rusted and bent, that I couldn't read it. The road was narrow and instant rustic. Ditches crowded in on either side. Grass, weeds, the year's last goldenrod, grew head-high and gave the road a wild look. A field of beans gone dry and yellow waited to be harvested. Narrow gravel driveways appeared out of the weeds with rusted mailboxes that showed that there were houses. But most of the houses were just glimpses through the trees. Barn swallows dipped and dived over the road. The pavement ended abruptly, spilling the car onto gravel.

Gravel pinged and clattered under the car. Wooded hills crowded the gravel road. There was still an occasional house, but they were getting few and far between. Where were we going?

The gravel ended, and the road was only bare reddish dirt with large reddish rocks studded in it. Deep ruts swallowed the car's tires. The car bounced and fought its way down the dirt. It was their car. If they wanted to ruin it driving over wagon tracks, that was their business.

Finally, even the dirt road ended in a rough circle of rock. Some of the rocks were nearly as big as the car. The car stopped. I was relieved that there were some things even Ronald wouldn't drive a car over.

The lamia turned around to face me. She was smiling, positively beaming. She was too damn cheerful. Something was wrong. Nobody was this cheery unless they wanted something. Something big. What did the lamia want? What did Oliver want?

She got out of the car. The men followed her like well-trained dogs. I hesitated, but I'd come this far; might as well see what Oliver wanted. I could always say no.

The lamia took Ronald's arm again. In high heels on the rocky ground, it was a sensible precaution. I in my little Nikes didn't need help. Blondie and Smiley offered an arm apiece; I ignored them. Enough of this play-acting. I was tired and didn't like being dragged to the edge of the world. Even Jean-Claude had never dragged me to some forsaken backwoods area. He was a city boy. Of course, Oliver had struck me as a city boy, too. Shows that you can't judge a vampire by one meeting.

The rocky ground led up to a hillside. More boulders had crashed down the side of the hill to lie in crumbled, broken heaps. Ronald actually picked Melanie up and carried her over the worst of the ground.

I stopped the men before they could offer. "I can make it myself; thanks anyway."

They looked disappointed. The blond said, "Melanie has told us to look after you. If you trip and fall in the rocks, she'll be unhappy with us."

The brunette nodded.

"I'll be fine, boys, really." I went ahead of them, not waiting to see what they'd do. The ground was treacherous with small rocks. I scrambled over a rock bigger than I was. The men were right behind me, hands extended ready to catch me if I fell. I'd never even had a date who was this paranoid.

Someone cursed, and I turned to see the brunette sprawled on the ground. I had to smile. I didn't wait for them to catch up. I'd had enough nurse-maiding, and the thought of getting no sleep today had put me in a bad mood. Our biggest night of the year, and I was going to be wasted. Oliver better have something important to say.

Around a tall pile of rubble was a slash of black opening, a cave. Ronald carried the lamia inside without waiting for me. A cave? Oliver had moved to a cave? Somehow it didn't fit my picture of him in his modern, sunlit study.

Light hovered at the entrance to the cave, but a few feet in the darkness was thick. I waited at the edge of the light, unsure what to do. My two caretakers came in behind me. They pulled small penlights out of their pockets. The beams seemed pitifully small against the darkness.

Blondie took the lead; Smiley brought up the rear. I walked in the middle of their thin strings of light. A faint pool followed my feet and kept me from tripping over stray bits of rock, but most of the tunnel was smooth and perfect. A thin trickle of water took up the center of the floor, working its patient way through the stone. I stared up at the ceiling lost in darkness. All this had been done by water. Impressive.

The air was cool and moist against my face. I was glad I had the leather jacket on. It'd never get warm here, but it'd never get really cold either. That's why our ancestors lived in caves. Year-round temperature control.

A wide passage branched to the left. The deep sound of water gurgled and bumped in the darkness. A lot of water. Blondie ran his light over a stream that filled most of the left passage. It was black, and looked deep and cold.

"I didn't bring my wading boots," I said.

"We follow the main passage," Smiley said. "Don't tease her. The mistress will not like it." His face looked very serious in the half-light.

The blond shrugged, then moved his light straight ahead. The trickle of water spread in a thin fan pattern on the rock but there was still plenty of dry rock on either side. I wasn't going to have to get my feet wet, yet.

We took the left-hand side of the wall. I touched it to keep my balance and jerked away. The walls were slimy with water and melting minerals.

Smiley laughed at me. I guess laughing was allowed.

I glanced back at him, frowning, then put my hand back on the wall. It wasn't that icky. It had just surprised me. I'd touched worse.

The sound of water thundering from a great height filled the darkness. There was a waterfall up ahead; I didn't need my eyes to tell me that.

"How tall do you think the waterfall is?" Blondie asked.

The thundering filled the darkness. Surrounded us. I shrugged. "Ten, twenty feet, maybe more."

He shone his light on a trickle of water that fell about five inches. The tiny waterfall was what fed the thin stream. "The cave magnifies the sound and makes it sound like thunder," he said.

"Neat trick," I said.

A wide shelf of rock led in a series of tiny waterfalls up to a wide base of stone. The lamia sat on the edge of the shelf, high-heeled feet dangling over the edge. Maybe a rise of eight feet, but the ceiling soared overhead into blackness. That was what made the water echo.

Ronald stood at her back, like a good bodyguard, hands clasped in front of him. There was a wide opening near them that led farther into the cave towards the source of the little stream.

Blondie climbed up and offered me a hand.

"Where's Oliver?"

"Just ahead," the lamia said. There was an edge of laughter to her voice, as if there was some joke I wasn't getting. It was probably going to be at my expense.

I ignored Blondie's hand and made it up to the shelf by myself. My hands were covered with a thin coat of pale brown mud and water, a perfect recipe for slime. I fought the urge to wipe them on my jeans and knelt by the small pool of water that fed the waterfalls. The water was ice-cold, but I washed my hands in it and felt better. I dried them on my jeans.

The lamia sat with her men grouped around her as if they were posing for a family photo. They were waiting on someone. Oliver. Where was he?

"Where's Oliver?"

"I'm afraid he won't be coming." The voice came from ahead of me farther into the cave. I stepped back but couldn't go far without stepping off the edge.

The two flashlights turned on the opening like tiny spotlights. Alejandro stepped into the thin beam of lights. "You won't be meeting Oliver tonight, Ms. Blake."

I went for my gun before anything else could happen. The lights went out, and I was left in the absolute dark with a master vampire, a lamia, and three hostile men. Not one of my better days.

40

I dropped to my knees, gun ready, close to my body. The darkness was thick as velvet. I couldn't see my hand in front of my face. I closed my eyes, trying to concentrate on hearing. There; the scrape of shoes on stone. The movement of air as someone moved closer to me. I had thirteen silver bullets. We were about to find out if silver would hurt a lamia. Alejandro had already taken a silver bullet in the chest and didn't look much the worse for it.

I was in very deep shit.

The footsteps were almost on top of me. I could feel the body close to me. I opened my eyes. It was like looking inside a ball of ebonite, utterly black. But I could feel someone standing over me. I raised the gun to gut or lower chest level and fired still on my knees.

The flashes were like lightning in the darkness, blue-flame lightning. Smiley fell backwards in the flash of light. I heard him fall over the edge, then nothing. Nothing but darkness.

Hands grabbed my forearms, and I hadn't heard a thing. It was Alejandro. I screamed as he dragged me to my feet.

"Your little gun cannot hurt me," he said. His voice was soft and close. He hadn't taken my gun away. He wasn't afraid of it. He should have been.

"I have offered Melanie her freedom once Oliver and the city's Master are dead. I offer you eternal life, eternal youth, and you may live."

"You did give me the first mark."

"Tonight I will give you the second," he said. His voice was soft and ordinary compared to Jean-Claude's, but the intimacy of the dark and his hands on me made the words more than they should have been.

"And if I don't want to be your human servant?"

"Then I will take you anyway, Anita. Your loss will damage the Master. It will lose him followers, confidence. Oh, yes, Anita, I will have you. Join with me willingly, and it will be pleasure. Fight me, and it will be agony."

I used his voice to aim the gun at his throat. If I could sever his spine, a thousand years and more old or not, he might die. Might. Please, God.

I fired. The bullet took him in the throat. He jerked backwards but didn't let go of my arms. Two more bullets into his throat, one into his jaw, and he threw me away from him, shrieking.

I ended on my back in the ice-cold water.

A flashlight cut through the dark. Blondie stood there, a perfect target. I fired at it and the light went out, but there was no scream. I'd rushed the shot and missed. Damn.

I couldn't climb down the rock in the dark. I'd fall and break a leg. So the only way left was deeper into the cave, if I could get there.

Alejandro was still screaming, wordless, rage-filled. The screams echoed and bounced on the rock walls until I was deaf as well as blind.

I scrambled through the water, putting a wall at my back. If I couldn't hear them, maybe they couldn't hear me.

"Get that gun away from her," the lamia said. She had moved and seemed to be beside the wounded vampire.

I waited in the dark for some clue that they were coming for me. There was a rush of cool air against my face. It wasn't them moving. Was I that close to the opening that led deeper into the cave? Could I just slip away? In the dark, not knowing if there were pits, or water deep enough to drown in? Didn't sound like a good idea. Maybe I could just kill them all here. Fat chance.

Through the echoes of Alejandro's shrieks was another sound, a high-pitched hissing, like that of a giant snake. The lamia was shapechanging. I had to get away before she finished. Water splashed almost on top of me. I looked up, and there was nothing to see, just the solid blackness.

I couldn't feel anything, but the water splashed again. I pointed up and fired. The flash of light revealed Ronald's face. The dark glasses were gone. His eyes were yellow with slitted pupils. I saw all that in the lightning flash of the gun. I fired twice more into that slit-eyed face. He screamed, and fangs showed below his teeth. God. What was he?

Whatever Ronald was, he fell backwards. I heard him hit the water in a splash that was much too loud for the shallow pool. I didn't hear him move after he fell. Was he dead?

Alejandro's screams had stopped. Was he dead, too? Was he creeping closer? Was he even now almost on top of me? I held the gun out in front of me and tried to feel something, anything, in the darkness.

Something heavy dragged across the rock. My stomach clenched tight. The lamia. Shit.

That was it. I eased my shoulder around the corner into the opening. I crept along on knees and one hand. I didn't want to run if I didn't have to. I'd brain myself on a stalactite or drop into some bottomless pit. Alright, maybe not bottomless, but if I fell thirty feet or so, it wouldn't have to be bottomless. Dead is dead.

Icy water soaked through my jeans and shoes. The rock was slick under my hand. I crawled as fast as I could, hand searching for some drop-off, some danger that my eyes couldn't see.

The heavy, sliding sound filled the blackness. It was the lamia. She'd already changed. Would her scales be quicker over the slick rocks, or would I be quicker? I wanted to get up and run. Run as far and as fast as I could. My shoulders tightened with the need to get away.

A loud splash announced she'd entered the water. She could move faster than I could crawl; I was betting on that. And if I ran . . . and fell or knocked myself silly? Well, better to have tried than to be caught crawling in the cold like a mouse.

I scrambled to my feet and started to run. I kept my left hand out in front of me to protect my face, but the rest I left to chance. I couldn't see shit. I was running full out, blind as a bat, my stomach tight with anticipation of some pit opening up under my feet.

The sounds of sliding scales was getting farther away. I was outrunning her. Great.

A piece of rock slammed into my right shoulder. The impact spun me into the other wall. My arm was numb from shoulder to fingertips. I'd dropped the gun. Three bullets left, but that had been better than nothing. I leaned into the wall, cradling my arm, waiting for the feeling to return, wondering if I could find my gun in the dark, wondering if I had time.

A light bobbed towards me down the tunnel. Blondie was coming; risking himself, if I'd had my gun. But I didn't have my gun. I could have broken my arm ramming into that ledge. The feeling was coming back in a painful wash of prickles and a throbbing ache where the rock had hit me. I needed a flashlight. What if I hid and got Blondie's light? I had two knives. As far as I knew, Blondie wasn't armed. It had possibilities.

The light was going slowly, sweeping from side to side. I had time, maybe. I got to my feet and felt for the rock that had nearly taken my arm off. It was a shelf with an opening behind it. Cool air blew against my face. It was a small tunnel. It was shoulder level to me, which made it about face level for Blondie. Perfect.

I placed my hands palm down and pushed up. My right arm protested, but it was doable. I crawled into the tunnel, hands out in front searching for stalactites or more rock shelves. Nothing but small, empty space. If I'd been much bigger, I wouldn't have fit at all. Hurray for being petite.

I got out the knife for my left hand. The right was still trembling. I was better right-handed, like most right-handed people, but I practiced left-handed, too—ever since a vampire broke my right arm and using my left had been the only thing that saved me. Nothing like near death to get you to practice.

I crouched on my knees in the tunnel, knife gripped, using my right hand for balance. I would only get one chance at this. I had no illusions about my chances against an athletic man who outweighed me by at least a hundred pounds. If the first rush didn't work, he'd beat me to a pulp or give me to the lamia. I'd rather be beaten.

I waited in the dark with my knife and prepared to slit someone's throat. Not pretty when you think of it that way. But necessary, wasn't it?

He was almost here. The thin penlight looked bright after the darkness. If he shone the light in the direction of my hiding place before he got beside it, I was sunk. Or if he passed close to the left-hand side of the tunnel, and not under me . . . Stop it. The light was almost underneath me. I heard his feet wade through the water, coming closer. He was hugging the right-hand side of the wall, just like I wanted him to.

His pale hair came into sight nearly even with my knees. I moved forward and he turned. His mouth made a little "O" of surprise; then the blade plunged into the side of his neck. Fangs flicked from behind his teeth. The blade snicked on his spine. I grabbed his long hair in my right hand, bowing his neck, and tore the knife out the front of his throat. Blood splashed outward in a surprised shower. The knife and my left hand were slick with it.

He fell to the tunnel floor with a loud splash. I scrambled off the ledge and landed beside his body. The light had rolled into the water, still glowing. I fished it out. Lying almost under Blondie's hand was the Browning. It was wet, but that didn't matter. You could shoot most modern guns underwater and they worked fine. That was one of the things that made terrorism so easy.

Blood turned the stream dark. I shone the light back down the tunnel. The lamia was framed in the small light. Her long black hair spilled over her pale upper body. Her breasts were high and prominent with deep, nearly reddish nipples. From the waist down she was ivory-white with zigzags of pale gold. The long belly scales were white speckled with black. She reared on that long, hard tail and flicked her forked tongue at me.

Alejandro stood up behind her, covered in blood but walking, moving. I wanted to shout, "Why don't you die" but it wouldn't help; maybe nothing would help.

The lamia pushed onward down the tunnel. The gun had killed her men with their fangs, Ronald with his snake eyes. I hadn't tried it on her yet. What did I have to lose?

I kept the light on her pale chest and raised the gun.

"I am immortal. Your little bullets will not harm me."

"Come a little closer and let's test the theory," I said.

She slid towards me, arms moving as if in time with legs. Her whole body moved with the muscular thrusts of the tail. It looked curiously natural.

Alejandro stayed leaning against the wall. He was hurt. Yippee.

I let her get within ten feet; close enough to hit her, far enough away to run like hell if it didn't work.

The first bullet took her just above the left breast. She staggered. It hit her, but the hole closed like water, smooth and unblemished. She smiled.

I raised the gun, just a little, and fired just above the bridge of her perfect nose. Again she staggered, but the hole didn't even bleed. It just healed. Normal bullets had about as much effect on vampires.

I put the gun in the shoulder holster, turned, and ran.

A wide crack led off from the main tunnel. I'd have to take off my jacket to squeeze through. The last thing I wanted was to get stuck with the lamia able to work her way through to me. I stayed with the main tunnel.

The tunnel was smooth and straight as far as I could see. Shelves projected out at angles, some with water trickling out of them, but crawling on my belly with a snake after me wasn't my idea of a good time.

I could run faster than she could move. Snakes, even giant snakes, just weren't that fast. As long as I didn't hit a dead end, I'd be fine. God, I wished I believed that.

The stream was ankle-deep now. The water was so cold, I had trouble feeling my feet. Running helped. Concentrating on my body, moving, running, trying not to fall, trying not to think about what was behind me. The real trick would be, was there another way out? If I couldn't kill them and couldn't get past them and there was only one way out, I was going to lose.

I kept running. I did four miles three times a week, plus a little extra. I could keep running. Besides, what choice did I have?

The water was filling the passageway and growing deeper. I was knee-deep in water. It was slowing me down. Could she move faster in water than I could? I didn't know. I just didn't know.

A rush of air blew against my back. I turned, and there was nothing there. The air was warm and smelled faintly of flowers. Was it the lamia? Did she have other ways of catching me besides just chasing? No; lamias could perform illusions only on men. That was their power. I wasn't male, so I was safe.

The wind touched my face, gently, warm and fragrant with a rich, green smell like freshly dug roots. What was happening?

"Anita."

I whirled, but there was no one there. The circle of light showed only tunnel and water. There was no sound but the lapping of water. Yet . . . the warm wind blew against my cheek, and the smell of flowers was growing stronger.

Suddenly, I knew what it was. I remembered being chased up the stairs by a wind that couldn't have been there, the glow of blue fire like free-floating eyes. The second mark.

It had been different, no smell of flowers, but I knew that was it. Alejandro didn't have to touch me to give me the mark, no more than Jean-Claude had.

I slipped on the slick stones and fell neck-deep in water. I scrambled to my feet, thigh-deep in water. My jeans were soaked and heavy. I sloshed forward, trying to run, but the water was too deep for running. It'd be quicker to swim.

I dove into the water, flashlight grasped in one hand. The leather jacket dragged at me, slowed me down. I stood up and stripped it off and let it float with the current. I hated to lose the jacket, but if I survived, I could buy more.

I was glad I was wearing a long-sleeved shirt and not a sweater. It was too damn cold to strip down anymore. It was faster swimming. The warm wind tickled down my face, hot after the chill of the water.

I don't know what made me look behind me, just a feeling. Two pinpoints of blackness were floating towards me in the air. If blackness could burn, then that's what it was: black flame coming for me on the warm, flower-scented breeze.

A rock wall loomed ahead. The stream ran under it. I held onto the wall and found there was maybe an inch of air space between the water and the roof of the tunnel. It looked like a good way to drown.

I treaded water and shone the flashlight around the passage. There; a narrow shelf of rock to climb out on, and blessed be, another tunnel. A dry one.

I pulled myself up on the shelf, but the wind hit me like a warm hand. It felt good and safe, and it was a lie.

I turned, and the black flames hovered over me like demonic fireflies. "Anita, accept it."

"Go to hell!" I pressed my back to the wall, surrounded by the warm tropical wind. "Please, don't do this," but it was a whisper.

The flames descended slowly. I hit at them. The flames passed through my hands like ghosts. The smell of flowers was almost chokingly sweet. The flames passed into my eyes, and for an instant I could see the world through bits of colored flame and a blackness that was a kind of light.

Then nothing. My vision was my own. The warm breeze died slowly away. The scent of flowers clung to me like some expensive perfume.

There was the sound of something large moving in the dark. I brought the flashlight up slowly into the dark-skinned face of a nightmare.

Straight, black hair was cut short and smooth around a thin face. Golden eyes with pupils like slits stared at me unblinking, immobile. His slender upper body dragged his useless lower body closer to me.

From the waist down he was all translucent skin. You could still see his legs and genitals, but they were all blending together to form a rough snake-like shape. Where do little lamias come from when there are no male lamias? I stared at what had once been a human being and screamed.

He opened his mouth, and fangs flicked into sight. He hissed, and spit dribbled down his chin. There was nothing human left in those slitted eyes. The lamia was more human than he was, but if I was changing into a snake maybe I'd be crazy, too. Maybe crazy was a blessing.

I drew the Browning and fired point-blank into his mouth. He jerked back, shrieking, but no blood, no dying. Dammit.

There was a scream from farther away, echoing towards us. "Raju!" The lamia was screaming for her mate, or warning him.

"Anita, don't hurt him." This from Alejandro. At least he had to yell. He couldn't whisper in my mind anymore.

The thing pulled itself towards me, mouth gaping, fangs straining.

"Tell him not to hurt me!" I yelled back.

The Browning was safely in its holster, and I was out of bullets anyway.

Flashlight in one hand, knife in the other, I waited. If they got here in time to call him off, fine. I didn't have much faith in silver knives if silver bullets didn't harm him, but I wasn't going down without a fight.

His hands were bloody from dragging his body over the rocks. I never thought I'd see anything that was worse than being changed into a vampire, but there it was, crawling towards me.

It was between me and the dry tunnel, but it was moving agonizingly slowly. I pressed my back to the wall and got to my feet. He—it—moved faster, definitely after me. I ran past it, but a hand closed on my ankle, yanked me to the ground.

The creature grabbed my legs and started to pull me towards it. I sat up and plunged the knife into its shoulder. It screamed, blood spilling down its arm. The knife stuck in the bone, and the monster jerked it out of my hand.

Then it reared back and struck my calf, fangs sinking in. I screamed and drew the second knife.

It raised its face, blood trickling down its mouth, heavy yellow drops clinging to its fangs.

I plunged the blade into one golden eye. The creature shrieked, drowning us in echoes. It rolled onto its back, lower body thrashing, hands clawing. I rolled with it and pushed the knife in with everything I had.

I felt the tip of the knife scrape on its skull. The monster continued to thrash and fight, but it was as hurt as I could make it. I left the knife in its eye but jerked the one free of its shoulder.

"Raju, no!"

I flashed the light on the lamia. Her pale upper body gleamed wet in the light. Alejandro was beside her. He looked nearly healed. I'd never seen a vampire that could heal that fast.

"I will kill you for their deaths," the lamia said.

"No, the girl is mine."

"She has killed my mate. She must die!"

"I will give her the third mark tonight. She will be my servant. That is revenge enough."

"No!" she screamed.

I was waiting for the poison to start working, but so far the bite just hurt, no burning, no nothing. I stared at the dry tunnel, but they'd just follow me and I couldn't kill them, not like this, not today. But there'd be other days.

I slipped back into the stream. There was still only an inch of air space. Risk drowning, or stay, and either be killed by a lamia or enslaved by a vampire. Choices, choices.

I slipped into the tunnel, mouth pressed near the wet roof. I could breathe. I might survive the day. Miracles do happen.

Small waves began to slosh through the tunnel. A wave washed over my face, and I swallowed water. I treaded water as gently as I could. It was my movements that were making the waves. I was going to drown myself.

I stayed very still until the water calmed, then took a deep breath, hyperventilating to expand the lungs and take in as much air as I could. I dunked under the water and kicked. It was too narrow for anything but a scissor kick. My chest was tight, throat aching with the need to breathe. I surfaced and kissed rock. There wasn't even an inch of air. Water splashed into my nose and I coughed, swallowing more water. I pressed as close to the ceiling as I could, taking small shallow breaths, then under again, kicking, kicking for all I was worth. If the tunnel filled completely before I was through it, I was going to die.

What if the tunnel didn't end? What if it was all water? I panicked, kicking furiously, flashlight bouncing crazily off the walls, hovering in the water like a prayer.

Please, God, please, don't let me die here like this.

My chest burned, throat bursting with the need to breathe. The light was dimming, and I realized it was my eyes that were losing the light. I was going to pass out and drown. I pushed for the surface and my hands touched empty air.

I took a gasping breath that hurt all the way down. There was a rocky shore and one bright line of sunlight. There was a hole up in the wall. The sunlight formed a misty haze in the air. I crawled onto the rock, coughing and relearning how to breathe.

I still had the flashlight and knife in my hands. I didn't remember holding onto them. The rock was covered in a thin sheet of grey mud. I crawled through it towards the rockslide that had opened the hole in the wall.

If I could make it through the tunnel, maybe they could, too. I didn't wait to feel better. I put the knife back in its sheath, slid the flashlight in my pocket, and started crawling.

I was covered in mud, hands scraped raw, but I was at the opening. It was a thin crack, but through it I could see trees and a hill. God, it looked good.

Something surfaced behind me.

I turned.

Alejandro rose from the water into the sunlight. His skin burst into flame, and he shrieked, diving into the water away from the burning sun.

"Burn, you son of bitch, burn."

The lamia surfaced.

I slipped into the crack and stuck. I pulled with my hands and pushed with my feet, but the mud slid and I couldn't get through.

"I will kill you."

I wrenched my back and put everything I had into wriggling free of that damn hole. The rock scraped along my back and I knew I was bleeding. I fell out onto the hill and rolled until a tree stopped me.

The lamia came to the crack. Sunlight didn't hurt her. She struggled to get through, tearing at the rock, but her ample chest wasn't going to fit. Her snake body might be narrowable, but the human part wasn't.

But just in case, I got to my feet and started down the hill. It was steep enough that I had to walk from tree to tree, trying not to fall down the hill. The whoosh of cars was just ahead. A road; a busy one by the sound of it.

I started to run, letting the momentum of the hill take me faster and faster towards the sounds of cars. I could glimpse the road through the trees.

I stumbled out onto the edge of the road, covered in grey mud, slimy, wet to the bone, shivering in the autumn air. I'd never felt better. Two cars wheezed by, ignoring my waving arms. Maybe it was the gun in the shoulder holster.

A green Mazda pulled up and stopped. The driver leaned across and opened the passenger side door. "Hop in."

It was Edward.

I stared into his blue eyes, and his face was as blank and unreadable as a cat's, and just as self-satisfied. I didn't give a damn. I slid into the seat and locked the door behind me.

"Where to?" he asked.

"Home."

"You don't need a hospital?"

I shook my head. "You were following me again."

He smiled. "I lost you in the woods."

"City boy," I said.

His smile widened. "No name-calling. You look like you flunked your Girl Scout exam."

I started to say something, then stopped. He was right, and I was too tired to argue.

41

I was sitting on the edge of my bathtub in nothing but a large beach towel. I had showered and shampooed and washed the mud and blood down the drain. Except for the blood that was still seeping out of the deep scrape on my back. Edward held a smaller towel to the cut, putting pressure on it.

"When the bleeding stops, I'll bandage it up for you," he said.

"Thanks."

"I seem to always be patching you up."

I glanced over my shoulder at him and winced. "I've returned the favor."

He smiled. "True."

The cuts on my hands had already been bandaged. I looked like a tan version of the mummy's hand.

He touched the fang marks on my calf gently. "This worries me."

"Me, too."

"There's no discoloration." He looked up at me. "No pain?"

"None. It wasn't a full lamia, maybe it wasn't that poisonous. Besides, you think anywhere in St. Louis is going to have lamia antivenom? They've been listed extinct for over two hundred years."

Edward palpated the wound. "I can't feel any swelling."

"It's been over an hour, Edward. If poison was going to kick in, it would have by now."

"Yeah." He stared at the bite. "Just keep an eye on it."

"I didn't know you cared," I said.

His face was blank, empty. "It would be a lot less interesting world without you in it." The voice was flat, unemotional. It was like he wasn't there at all. Yet it was a compliment. From Edward, it was a huge compliment.

"Gee whiz, Edward, contain your excitement."

He gave a small smile that left his eyes blue and distant as winter skies.

We were friends of a sort, good friends, but I would never really understand him. There was too much of Edward that you couldn't touch, or even see.

I used to believe that if it came to it, he'd kill me, if it were necessary. Now, I wasn't sure. How could you be friends with someone who you suspected might kill you? Another mystery of life.

"The bleeding's stopped," he said. He smeared antiseptic on the wound, then started taping bandages in place. The doorbell rang.

"What time is it?" I asked.

"Three o'clock."

"Shit."

"What is it?"

"I have a date coming over."

"You? Have a date?"

I frowned at him. "It's not that big a deal."

Edward was grinning like the proverbial cat. He stood up. "You're all fixed up. I'll go let him in."

"Edward, be nice."

"Me, nice?"

"All right, just don't shoot him."

"I think I can manage that." Edward walked out of the bathroom to let Richard in.

What would Richard think being met at the door by another man? Edward certainly wasn't going to help matters. He'd probably offer him a seat without explaining who he was. I wasn't even sure I could explain that.

"This is my friend the assassin." Nope. A fellow vampire slayer, maybe.

The bedroom door was closed so I could get dressed in privacy. I tried to put on a bra and found that my back hurt a lot. No bra. That limited what I could wear, unless I wanted to give Richard more of a look-see than I had planned on. I also wanted to keep an eye on the bite wound. So pants were out.

Most of the time I slept in oversize t-shirts, and slipping on a pair of jeans was my idea of a robe. But I did own one real robe. It was comfortable, a nice solid black, silky to the touch and absolutely not see-through.

A black silk teddy went with it, but I decided that was a little friendlier than I wanted to be; besides, the teddy wasn't comfortable. Lingerie seldom is.

I pulled the robe out of the back of my closet and slipped it on. It was smooth and wonderful next to my skin. I crossed the front so the bordered edge was high up on my chest and tied the black belt tight in place. Didn't want any slippage.

I listened at the door for a second and heard nothing. No talking, no moving around, nothing. I opened the door and walked out.

Richard was sitting on the couch with an armful of costumes hung over the back. Edward was making coffee in the kitchen like he owned the place.

Richard turned at my entrance. His eyes widened just a little. The hair still damp from the shower, and the slinky robe—what was he thinking?

"Nice robe," Edward said.

"It was a present from an overly optimistic date."

"I like it," Richard said.

"No smart remarks or you can just leave."

His eyes flicked to Edward. "Did I interrupt something?"

"He's a coworker, nothing more." I frowned at Edward, daring him to say anything. He smiled and poured coffee for all three of us.

"Let's sit at the table," I said. "I don't drink coffee on a white couch."

Edward sat the mugs on the small table. He leaned against the cabinets, leaving the two chairs for us.

Richard left his coat on the couch and sat down across from me. He was wearing a bluish-green sweater with darker blue designs worked across the chest. The color brought out the perfect brown of his eyes. His cheekbones seemed higher. A small Band-Aid marred his right cheek. His hair had gentle auburn highlights. Wondrous what the right color can do for a person.

The fact that I looked great in black had not escaped my notice. From the look on Richard's face, he was noticing, but his eyes kept slipping back to Edward.

"Edward and I were out hunting down the vampires that have been doing the killings."

His eyes widened. "Did you find out anything?"

I looked at Edward.

He shrugged. It was my call.

Richard hung around with Jean-Claude. Was he Jean-Claude's creature? I didn't think so, but then again . . . Caution is always better. If I was wrong, I'd apologize later. If I was right, I'd be disappointed in Richard but glad I hadn't told.

"Let's just say we lost today."

"You're alive," Edward said.

He had a point.

"Did you almost die today?" Richard's voice was outraged.

What could I say? "It's been a rough day."

He glanced at Edward, then back to me. "How bad was it?"

I motioned my bandaged hands at him. "Scrapes and cuts; nothing much."

Edward hid a smile in his coffee mug.

"Tell me the truth, Anita," Richard said.

"I don't owe you any explanations." My voice sounded just a tad defensive.

Richard stared down at his hands, then looked up at me. There was a look in his eyes that made my throat tight. "You're right. You don't owe me anything."

I found an explanation slipping out of my mouth. "You might say I went caving without you."

"What do you mean?"

"I ended up going through a water-filled tunnel to escape the bad guys."

"How water-filled?"

"All the way to the top."

"You could have drowned." He touched my hand with his fingertips.

I sipped coffee and moved my hand away from his, but I could feel where he had touched me like a lingering smell. "But I didn't drown."

"That's not the point," he said.

"Yes," I said, "it is. If you're going to date me, you have to get used to the way I work."

He nodded. "You're right, you're right." His voice was soft. "It just caught me off guard. You nearly died today and you're sitting there drinking coffee like it's ordinary."

"For me, it is, Richard. If you can't deal with that, maybe we shouldn't even try." I caught Edward's expression. "What are you grinning at?"

"Your suave and debonair way with men."

"If you're not going to be helpful, then leave."

He put his mug down on the counter. "I'll leave you two lovebirds alone."

"Edward," I said.

"I'm going."

I walked him to the door. "Thanks again for being there, even if you were following me."

He pulled out a plain white business card with a phone number done in black on it. That was all, no name, no logo; but what would have been appropriate, a bloody dagger, or maybe a smoking gun? "If you need me, call this number."

Edward had never given me a number before. He was like the phantom—there when he wanted to be, or not there, as he chose. A number could be traced. He was trusting me a lot with the number. Maybe he wouldn't kill me.

"Thank you, Edward."

"One bit of advice. People in our line of work don't make good significant others."

"I know that."

"What's he do for a living?"

"He's a junior high science teacher," I said.

Edward just shook his head. "Good luck." With that parting shot, he left.

I slipped the business card into the robe pocket and went back to Richard. He was a science teacher, but he also hung out with the monsters. He'd seen it get messy, and it hadn't fazed him, much. Could he handle it? Could I? One date and I was already borrowing trouble that might never come up. We might dislike each other after only one evening together. I'd had it happen before.

I stared at the back of Richard's head and wondered if the curls could be as soft as they looked. Instant lust; embarrassing, but not that uncommon. All right, it was uncommon for me.

A sharp pain ran up my leg. The leg that the lamia-thing had bitten. Please, no. I leaned against the counter divider. Richard was watching me, puzzled.

I swept the robe aside. The leg was swelling and turning purplish. How had I not noticed it? "Did I mention I got bitten by a lamia today?"

"You're joking," he said.

I shook my head. "I think you're going to have to take me to the hospital."

He stood up and saw my leg. "God! Sit down."

I was starting to sweat. It wasn't hot in the apartment.

Richard helped me to the couch. "Anita, lamias have been extinct for two hundred years. No one's going to have any antivenom."

I stared at him. "I guess we're not going to get that date."

"No dammit, I won't sit here and watch you die. Lycanthropes can't be poisoned."

"You mean you want to rush me to Stephen and let him bite me?"

"Something like that."

"I'd rather die."

Something flickered through his eyes, something I couldn't read; pain, maybe. "You mean that?"

"Yes." A rush of nausea flowed over me like a wave. "I'm going to be sick." I tried to get up and go for the bathroom but collapsed on the white carpet and vomited blood. Red and bright and fresh. I was bleeding to death inside.

Richard's hand was cool on my forehead, his arm around my waist. I vomited until I was empty and exhausted. Richard lifted me to the couch. There was a narrow tunnel of light edged by darkness. The darkness was eating the light, and I couldn't stop it. I could feel myself begin to float away. It didn't hurt. I wasn't even scared.

The last thing I heard was Richard's voice. "I won't let you die."

It was a nice thought.

42

The dream began. I was sitting in the middle of a huge canopied bed. The drapes were heavy blue velvet, the color of midnight skies. The velvet bedspread was soft under my hands. I was wearing a long white gown with lace at the collar and sleeves. I'd never owned anything like it. No one had in this century.

The walls were blue and gold wallpaper. A huge fireplace blazed, sending shadows dancing around the room. Jean-Claude stood in the corner of the room, bathed in orange and black shadows. He was wearing the same shirt I'd last seen him in, the one with the peekaboo front.

He walked towards me, fire-shadows shining in his hair, on his face, glittering in his eyes.

"Why don't you ever dress me in anything normal in these dreams?"

He hesitated. "You don't like the gown?"

"Hell, no."

He gave a slight smile. "You always did have a way with words, *ma petite*."

"Stop calling me that, dammit."

"As you like, Anita." There was something in the way he said my name that I didn't like at all.

"What are you up to, Jean-Claude?"

He stood beside the bed and unbuttoned the first button of his shirt.

"What are you doing?"

Another button, and another, then he was pulling the shirt out of his pants and letting it slide to the floor. His bare chest was only a little less white than my gown. His nipples were pale and hard. The strand of dark hair that started low on his belly and disappeared into his pants fascinated me.

He crawled up on the bed.

I backed away, clutching the white gown to me like some heroine in a bad Victorian novel. "I don't seduce this easy."

"I can taste your lust on the back of my tongue, Anita. You want to know what my skin feels like next to your naked body."

I scrambled off the bed. "Leave me the fuck alone. I mean it."

"It's just a dream. Can't you even let yourself lust in a dream?"

"It's never just a dream with you."

He was suddenly standing in front of me. I hadn't seen him move. His arms locked behind my back, and we were on the floor in front of the fire. Fire-shadows danced on the naked skin of his shoulders. His skin was fragile, smooth, and unblemished—so soft I wanted to touch it forever. He was on top of me, his weight pressing against me, pushing me into the floor. I could feel the line of his body molded against mine.

"One kiss and I'll let you up."

I stared into his midnight-blue eyes from inches away. I couldn't talk. I turned my face away so I wouldn't have to look into the perfection of his face. "One kiss?"

"My word," he whispered.

I turned back to him. "Your word isn't worth shit."

His face leaned over mine, lips almost touching. "One kiss."

His lips were soft, gentle. He kissed my cheek, lips brushing down the line of my cheek, touching my neck. His hair brushed my face. I thought that all curly hair was coarse, but his was baby fine, silken soft. "One kiss," he whispered against the skin of my throat, tongue tasting the pulse in my neck.

"Stop it."

"You want it."

"Stop it, now!"

He grabbed a handful of hair, forcing my neck backwards. His lips had thinned back, exposing fangs. His eyes were drowning blue without any white at all.

"NO!"

"I will have you, *ma petite*, even if it is to save your life." His head came downward, striking like a snake. I woke up staring at a ceiling I didn't recognize.

Black and white drapes were suspended from the ceiling in a soft fan. The bed was black satin with too many pillows thrown all over the place. The pillows were all black or white. I was wearing a black gown with spaghetti straps. It felt like a real silk and fit me perfectly.

The floor was ankle-deep white carpet. A black lacquer vanity and chest of drawers were placed at far corners of the room. I sat up and could see myself in the mirror. My neck was smooth, no bite marks. Just a dream, just a dream, but I knew better. The bedroom had the unmistakable touch of Jean-Claude.

I had been dying of poison. How had I gotten here? Was I underneath the Circus of the Damned, or somewhere else altogether? My right wrist hurt.

There was a white swathe of bandages around my wrist. I didn't remember hurting it in the cave.

I stared at myself in the vanity mirror. In the black negligee my skin was white, my hair long and black as the gown. I laughed. I matched the decor. I matched the damn decor.

A door opened behind a white curtain. I got a glimpse of stone walls behind the drapes. He was wearing nothing but the silky bottoms of men's pajamas. He padded towards me on bare feet. His bare chest looked like it had in my dream, except for the cross-shaped scar; it hadn't been there in the dream. It marred the marble perfection of him, made him seem more real somehow.

"Hell," I said. "Definitely Hell."

"What, *ma petite*?"

"I was wondering where I was. If you're here, it has to be Hell."

He smiled. He looked entirely too satisfied, like a snake that had been well-fed.

"How did I get here?"

"Richard brought you."

"So I really was poisoned. That wasn't part of the dream?"

He sat on the far edge of the bed, as far away from me as he could get and still sit down. There were no other places to sit. "I'm afraid the poison was very real."

"Not that I'm complaining, but why aren't I dead?"

He hugged his knees to his chest, a strangely vulnerable gesture. "I saved you."

"Explain that."

"You know."

I shook my head. "Say it."

"The third mark."

"I don't have any bite marks."

"But your wrist is cut and bandaged."

"You bastard."

"I saved your life."

"You drank my blood while I was unconscious."

He gave the slightest nod.

"You son of a bitch."

The door opened again, and it was Richard. "You bastard, how could you give me to him?"

"She doesn't seem very grateful to us, Richard."

"You said you'd rather die than be a lycanthrope."

"I'd rather die than be a vampire."

"He didn't bite you. You're not going to be a vampire."

"I'll be his slave for eternity; great choice."

"It's only the third mark, Anita. You aren't his servant yet."

"That's not the point." I stared at him. "Don't you understand? I'd rather you let me die than have done this."

"It is hardly a fate worse than death," Jean-Claude said.

"You were bleeding from your nose and eyes. You were bleeding to death in my arms." Richard took a few steps towards the bed, then stopped. "I couldn't just let you die." His hands reached outward in a helpless gesture.

I stood up in the silky gown and stared at them both. "Maybe Richard didn't know any better, but you knew how I felt, Jean-Claude. You don't have any excuses."

"Perhaps I could not stand to watch you die, either. Have you thought of that?"

I shook my head. "What does the third mark mean? What extra powers does it give you over me?"

"I can whisper in your mind outside of dreams now. And you have gained power as well, *ma petite*. You are very hard to kill now. Poison won't work at all."

I kept shaking my head. "I don't want to hear it. I won't forgive you for this, Jean-Claude."

"I did not think you would," he said. He seemed wistful.

"I need clothes and a ride home. I've got to work tonight."

"Anita, you've almost died twice today. How can you . . ."

"Can it, Richard. I need to go to work tonight. I need something that's mine and not his. You invasive bastard."

"Find her some clothes and take her home, Richard. She needs time to adjust to this new change."

I stared at Jean-Claude still huddled on the corner of the bed. He looked adorable, and if I'd had a gun, I'd have shot him on the spot. Fear was a hard, cold lump in my gut. He meant to make me his servant, whether I liked it or not. I could scream and protest, and he'd ignore it.

"Come near me again, Jean-Claude, for any reason, and I'll kill you."

"Three marks bind us now. It would harm you, too."

I laughed, and it was bitter. "Do you really think I give a damn?"

He stared at me, face calm, unreadable, lovely. "No." He turned his back on us both and said, "Take her home, Richard. Though I do not envy you the ride there." He glanced back with a smile. "She can be quite vocal when she's angry."

I wanted to spit at him, but that wouldn't have been enough. I couldn't kill him, not right then and there, so I let it go. Grace under pressure. I followed Richard out the door and didn't look back. I didn't want to see his perfect profile in the vanity mirror.

Vampires weren't supposed to have reflections, or souls. He had one. Did he have the other? Did it matter? No, I decided, it didn't matter at all. I was going to give Jean-Claude to Oliver. I was going to give the city to Mr. Oliver. I was going to set the Master of the City up for assassination. One more mark and I'd be his forever. No way. I'd see him dead first, even if it meant I died with him. No one forced me into anything, not even eternity.

43

I ended up wearing one of those dresses with the waist that hit you about at the hips. The fact that the dress was about three sizes too big didn't help matters. The shoes fit even if they were high heels. It was better than going barefoot. Richard turned up the heat in the car because I'd refused his coat.

We were fighting, and we hadn't even had one date. That was a record even for me.

"You're alive," he said for the seventieth time.

"But at what price?"

"I believe that all life is precious. Don't you?"

"Don't go all philosophical on me, Richard. You handed me over to the monsters, and they used me. Don't you understand that Jean-Claude has been looking for an excuse to do this to me?"

"He saved your life."

That seemed to be the extent of his argument. "But he didn't do it to save my life. He did it because he wants me as his slave."

"A human servant isn't a slave. It's almost the opposite. He'll have almost no power over you."

"But he'll be able to talk inside my head, invade my dreams." I shook my head. "Don't let him sucker you."

"You're being unreasonable," he said.

That was it. "I'm the one with my wrist slit open where the Master of the City fed. He drank my blood, Richard."

"I know."

There was something about the way he said it. "You watched, you sick son of a bitch."

"No, it wasn't like that."

"How was it?" I sat with my arms crossed over my stomach, glaring at him. So that was the hold Jean-Claude had on him. Richard was a voyeur.

"I wanted to make sure he only did enough to save your life."

"What else could he have done? He drank my blood, dammit."

Richard concentrated on the road suddenly, not looking at me. "He could have raped you."

"I was bleeding from my eyes and nose, you said. Doesn't sound very romantic to me."

"All the blood, it seemed to excite him."

I stared at him. "You're serious?"

He nodded.

I sat there feeling cold down to my toes. "What made you think he was going to rape me?"

"You woke up on a black bedspread. The first one was white. He laid you on it and started to strip down. He took your robe off. There was blood everywhere. He smeared his face in it, tasted it. Another vampire handed him a small gold knife."

"There were more vamps there?"

"It was like a ritual. The audience seemed to be important. He slit your wrist and drank at it, but his hands . . . he was touching your breasts. I told him that I had brought you so you could live, not so he could rape you."

"That must have gone over real big."

Richard was very quiet all of a sudden.

"What?"

He shook his head.

"Tell me, Richard. I mean it."

"Jean-Claude looked up with blood all over his face and said, 'I have not waited this long to take what I want her to give freely. It is a temptation.' Then he looked down at you, and there was something in his face, Anita. It was scary as hell. He really believes you'll come around. That you'll . . . love him."

"Vampires don't love."

"Are you sure?"

I glanced at him, then away. I stared at the window at the daylight that was just now beginning to fade. "Vampires don't love. They can't."

"How do you know that?"

"Jean-Claude does not love me."

"Maybe he does, as much as he can."

I shook my head. "He bathed in my blood. He slit my wrist. That isn't my idea of love."

"Maybe it's his."

"Then it's too damn weird for me."

"Fine, but admit that he may love you, as much as he's able."

"No."

"It scares you to think that he loves you, doesn't it?"

I stared out the window as hard as I could. I didn't want to be talking about this. I wanted to undo this whole damn day.

"Or is it something else that you're afraid of?"

"I don't know what you're talking about."

"Yes, you do." He sounded so sure of himself. He didn't know me well enough to be that certain.

"Say it out loud, Anita. Say it just once and it won't seem so scary."

"I don't have anything to say."

"You're telling me that no part of you wants him. Not a piece of you might love him back."

"I don't love him; that much I'm sure of."

"But?"

"You are persistent," I said.

"Yes," he said.

"All right, I'm attracted to him. Is that what you wanted to hear?"

"How attracted?"

"That's none of your damn business."

"Jean-Claude warned me to stay away from you. I just want to know if I'm really interfering. If you're attracted to him, maybe I should stay out of it."

"He's a monster, Richard. You've seen him. I can't love a monster."

"If he was human?"

"He's an egotistical, controlling bastard."

"But if he was human?"

I sighed. "If he was human, we might work something out, but even alive, Jean-Claude can be such an SOB. I don't think it would work."

"But you're not even going to try because he's a monster."

"He's dead, Richard, a walking corpse. It doesn't matter how pretty he is, or how compelling, he's still dead. I don't date corpses. A girl's got to have some standards."

"So no corpses," he said.

"No corpses."

"What about lycanthropes?"

"Why? You thinking of fixing me up with your friend?"

"Just curious about where you draw the line."

"Lycanthropy is a disease. The person's already survived a vicious attack. It'd be like blaming the rape victim."

"You ever date a shapeshifter?"

"It's never come up."

"What else wouldn't you date?"

"Things that were never human to begin with, I guess. I really haven't thought about it. Why the interest?"

He shook his head. "Just curious."

"Why aren't I still pissed at you?"

"Maybe because you're glad to be alive, no matter what the cost."

He pulled into the parking lot of my apartment building. Larry's car was idling in my parking space. "Maybe I am glad to be alive, but I'll let you know about the cost when I find out what it really is."

"You don't believe Jean-Claude?"

"I wouldn't believe Jean-Claude if he told me moonlight was silver."

Richard smiled. "Sorry about the date."

"Maybe we can try again sometime."

"I'd like that," he said.

I opened the door and stood shivering in the cool air. "Whatever happens, Richard, thanks for watching out for me." I hesitated, then said, "And whatever hold Jean-Claude's got on you, break it. Get away from him. He'll get you killed."

He just nodded. "Good advice."

"Which you're not going to take," I said.

"I would if I could, Anita. Please believe that."

"What does he have on you, Richard?"

He shook his head. "He ordered me not to tell you."

"He ordered you not to date me, too."

He shrugged. "You better get going. You're going to be late for work."

I smiled. "Besides, I'm freezing my butt off."

He smiled. "You do have a way with words."

"I spend too much time hanging around with cops."

He put the car in gear. "Have a safe night at work."

"I'll do my best."

He nodded. I closed the door. Richard didn't seem to want to talk about what Jean-Claude had on him. Well, no rule said we had to play honesty on the first date. Besides, he was right. I was going to be late for work.

I tapped on Larry's window. "I've got to change, then I'll be right back down."

"Who was that dropping you off?"

"A date." I left it at that. It was a much easier explanation than the truth. Besides, it was almost true.

44

This is the only night of the year that Bert allows us to wear black to work. He thinks the color is too harsh for normal business hours. I had black jeans and a Halloween sweater with huge grinning jack o' lanterns in a stomach-high line. I topped it off with a black zipper sweatshirt and black Nikes. Even my shoulder holster and the Browning matched. I had my backup gun in an inner pants holster. I also had two extra clips in my sport bag. I had replaced the knife I'd had to leave in the cave. There was a derringer in my jacket pocket and two extra knives, one down the spine, the other in an ankle holster. Don't laugh. I left the shotgun home.

If Jean-Claude found out I'd betrayed him, he'd kill me. Would I know when he died? Would I feel it? Something told me that I would.

I took the card that Karl Inger had given me and called the number. If it had to be done, it best be done quickly.

"Hello?"

"Is this Karl Inger?"

"Yes, it is. Who is this?"

"It's Anita Blake. I need to speak with Oliver."

"Have you decided to give us the Master of the City?"

"Yes."

"If you'll hold for a moment, I'll fetch Mr. Oliver." He laid the receiver down. I heard him walking away until there was nothing but silence on the phone. Better than Muzak.

Footsteps coming back, then: "Hello, Ms. Blake, so good of you to call."

I swallowed, and it hurt. "The Master of the City is Jean-Claude."

"I had discounted him. He isn't very powerful."

"He hides his powers. Trust me, he's a lot more than he seems."

"Why the change of heart, Ms. Blake?"

"He gave me the third mark. I want free of him."

"Ms. Blake, to be bound thrice to a vampire, and then have that vampire die, can be quite a shock to the system. It could kill you."

"I want free of him, Mr. Oliver."

"Even if you die?" he said.

"Even if I die."

"I would have liked to have met you under different circumstances, Anita Blake. You are a remarkable person."

"No, I've just seen too much. I won't let him have me."

"I will not fail you, Ms. Blake. I will see him dead."

"If I didn't believe that, I wouldn't have told you."

"I appreciate your confidence."

"One other thing you should know. The lamia tried to betray you today. She's in league with another master named Alejandro."

"Really?" His voice sounded amused. "What did he offer her?"

"Her freedom."

"Yes, that would tempt Melanie. I keep her on such a short rein."

"She's been trying to breed. Did you know that?"

"What do you mean?"

I told him about the men, especially the last one that had been nearly changed.

He was quiet for a moment. "I have been most inattentive. I will deal with Melanie and Alejandro."

"Fine. I'd appreciate a call tomorrow to let me know how things went."

"To be sure he's dead," Oliver said.

"Yes," I said.

"You'll get a call from Karl or myself. But first, where can we find Jean-Claude?"

"The Circus of the Damned."

"How appropriate."

"That's all I can tell you."

"Thank you, Ms. Blake, and Happy Halloween."

I had to laugh. "It's going to be a hell of a night."

He chuckled softly. "Indeed. Good-bye, Ms. Blake." The phone went dead in my hand.

I stared at the phone. I'd had to do it. Had to. So why did my stomach feel tight? Why did I have the urge to call Jean-Claude and warn him? Was it the marks, or was Richard right? Did I love Jean-Claude in some strange, twisted way? God help me, I hoped not.

45

It was full dark on All Hallows Eve. Larry and I had made two appointments. He'd raised one, and I'd raised the other. He had one more to go, and I had three. A nice normal night.

What Larry was wearing was not normal. Bert had encouraged us to wear something fitting for the holiday. I'd chosen the sweater. Larry had chosen a costume. He was wearing blue denim overalls, a white dress shirt with the sleeves rolled up, a straw hat, and work boots. When asked, he'd said, "I'm Huck Finn. Don't I fit the part?"

With his red hair and freckles, he did fit the part. There was blood on the shirt now, but it was Halloween. There were a lot of people out with fake blood on them. We fitted right in tonight.

My beeper went off. I checked the number, and it was Dolph. Damn.

"Who is it?" Larry asked.

"The police. We've got to find a phone."

He glanced at the dashboard clock. "We're ahead of schedule. How about the McDonald's just off the highway?"

"Great." I prayed that it wasn't another murder. I needed a nice normal night. At the back of my head like a bit of remembered song, two sentences kept playing: "Jean-Claude is going to die tonight. You set him up."

It seemed wrong to kill him from a safe distance. To not look him in the eyes and pull the trigger myself, to not give him a chance to kill me first. Fair play and all that. Fuck fair play; it was him or me. Wasn't it?

Larry parked in the McDonald's lot. "I'm gonna get a Coke while you call in. You want something?"

I shook my head.

"You all right?"

"Sure. I'm just hoping it's not another murder."

"Jesus, I hadn't thought of that."

We got out of the car. Larry went into the dining room. I stayed in the little entrance area with the pay phone.

Dolph picked up on the third ring. "Sergeant Storr."

"It's Anita. What's up?"

"We finally broke the paralegal that was feeding information to the vampires."

"Great; I thought it might be another murder."

"Not tonight; the vamp's got more important business."

"What's that supposed to mean?"

"He's planning on getting every vampire in the city to slaughter humans for Halloween."

"He can't. Only the Master of the City could do that, and then only if he was incredibly powerful."

"That's what I thought. Could be the vampire's crazy."

I had a thought, an awful thought. "You got a description of the vampire?"

"Vampires," he said.

"Read it to me."

I heard paper rustling, then: "Short, dark, very polite. Saw one other vampire twice with the boss vamp. He was medium height, Indian or Mexican, longish black hair."

I clutched the phone so tight my hand trembled. "Did the vampire say why he was going to slaughter humans?"

"Wanted to discredit legalized vampirism. Now isn't that a weird motive for a vampire?"

"Yeah," I said. "Dolph, this could happen."

"What are you saying?"

"If this master vampire could kill the Master of the City and take over before dawn, he might pull it off."

"What can we do?"

I hesitated, almost telling him to protect Jean-Claude, but it wasn't a matter for the police. They had to worry about laws and police brutality. There was no way to take something like Oliver alive. Whatever was going to happen tonight had to be permanent.

"Talk to me, Anita."

"I've gotta go, Dolph."

"You know something; tell me."

I hung up. I also turned off my beeper. I dialed Circus of the Damned. A pleasant-voiced woman answered, "Circus of the Damned, where all your nightmares come true."

"I need to speak to Jean-Claude. It's an emergency."

"He's busy right now. May I take a message?"

I swallowed hard, tried not to yell. "This is Anita Blake, Jean-Claude's human servant. Tell him to get his ass to the phone now."

"I . . ."

"People are going to die if I don't talk to him."

"Okay, okay." She put me on hold with a butchered version of "High Flying" by Tom Petty.

Larry came out with his Coke. "What's up?"

I shook my head. I fought the urge to jump up and down, but that wouldn't get Jean-Claude to the phone any sooner. I stood very still, hugging one arm across my stomach. What had I done? Please don't let it be too late.

"*Ma petite?*"

"Thank God."

"What has happened?"

"Just listen. There's a master vampire on his way to the Circus. I gave him your name and your resting place. His name is Mr. Oliver and he's older than anything. He's older than Alejandro. In fact, I think he's Alejandro's master. It's all been a plan to get me to betray the city to him, and I fell for it."

He was quiet so long that I asked, "Did you hear me?"

"You really meant to kill me."

"I told you I would."

"But now you warn me. Why?"

"Oliver wants control of the city so he can send all the vampires out to slaughter humans. He wants it back to the old days when vampires were hunted. He said legalized vampirism was spreading too fast. I agree, but I didn't know what he meant to do."

"So to save your precious humans you will betray Oliver now."

"It isn't like that. Dammit, Jean-Claude, concentrate on the important thing here. They're on their way. They may be there already. You've got to protect yourself."

"To keep the humans safe."

"To keep your vampires safe, too. Do you really want them under Oliver's control?"

"No. I will take steps, *ma petite*. We will at least give him a fight." He hung up.

Larry was staring at me with wide eyes. "What the hell is happening, Anita?"

"Not now, Larry." I fished Edward's card out of my bag. I didn't have another quarter. "Do you have a quarter?"

"Sure." He handed it to me without any more questions. Good man.

I dialed the number. "Please, be there. Please, be there."

He answered on the seventh ring.

"Edward, it's Anita."

"What's happened?"

"How would you like to take on two master vampires older than Nikolaos?"

I heard him swallow. "I always have so much fun when you're around. Where should we meet?"

"The Circus of the Damned. You got an extra shotgun?"

"Not with me."

"Shit. Meet me out front ASAP. The shit's going to really hit the fan tonight, Edward."

"Sounds like a great way to spend Halloween."

"See you there."

"Bye, and thanks for inviting me." He meant it. Edward had started out as a normal assassin, but humans had been too easy, so he went for vamps and shapeshifters. He hadn't met anything he couldn't kill, and what was life without a little challenge?

I looked at Larry. "I need to borrow your car."

"You're not going anywhere without me. I've heard just your side of the conversations, and I'm not getting left out."

I started to argue, but there wasn't time. "Okay, let's do it."

He grinned. He was pleased. He didn't know what was going to happen tonight, what we were up against. I did. And I wasn't happy at all.

46

I stood just inside the door of the Circus staring at the wave of costumes and glittering humanity. I'd never seen the place so crowded. Edward stood beside me in a long black cloak with a death's-head mask. Death dressed up as death; funny, huh? He also had a flamethrower strapped to his back, an Uzi pistol, and heaven knew how many other weapons secreted about his person. Larry looked pale but determined. He had my derringer in his pocket. He knew nothing about guns. The derringer was an emergency measure only, but he wouldn't stay in the car. Next week, if we were still alive, I'd take him out to the shooting range.

A woman in a bird costume passed us in a scent of feathers and perfume. I had to look twice to make sure that it was just a costume. Tonight was the night when all shapeshifters could be out and people would just say, "Neat costume."

It was Halloween night at the Circus of the Damned. Anything was possible.

A slender black woman stepped up to us wearing nothing but a bikini and an elaborate mask. She had to step close to me to be heard over the murmur of the crowd. "Jean-Claude sent me to bring you."

"Who are you?"

"Rashida."

I shook my head. "Rashida had her arm torn off two days ago." I stared at the perfect flesh of her arm. "You can't be her."

She raised her mask so I could see her face, then smiled. "We heal fast."

I had known lycanthropes healed fast, but not that fast, not that much damage. Live and learn.

We followed her swaying hips into the crowd. I grabbed hold of Larry's hand with my left hand. "Stay right with me tonight."

He nodded. I threaded through the crowd holding his hand like a child or a lover. I couldn't stand the thought of him getting hurt. No, that wasn't true. I couldn't stand the thought of him getting killed. Death was the big boogeyman tonight.

Edward followed at our heels. Silent as his namesake, trusting that he'd get to kill something soon.

Rashida led us towards the big, striped circus tent. Back to Jean-Claude's office, I supposed. A man in a straw hat and striped coat said, "Sorry, the show's sold out."

"It's me, Perry. These are the ones the Master's been waiting for." She hiked her thumb in our direction.

The man drew aside the tent flap and motioned us through. There was a line of sweat on his upper lip. It was warm, but I had the feeling it wasn't that kind of sweat. What was happening inside the tent? It couldn't be too bad if they were letting the crowd in to watch. Could it?

The lights were bright and hot. I started to sweat under the sweatshirt, but if I took it off, people would stare at my gun. I hated that.

Circular curtains had been rigged to the ceiling, creating two curtained-off areas in the large circus ring. Spotlights surrounded the two hidden areas. The curtains were like prisms. With every step we took, the colors changed and flowed over the cloth. I wasn't sure if it was the cloth or some trick of the lights. Whatever, it was a nifty effect.

Rashida stopped just short of the rail that kept the crowd back. "Jean-Claude wanted everybody to be in costume, but we're out of time." She pulled at my sweater. "Lose the jacket and it'll have to do."

I pulled my sweater out of her hand. "What are you talking about, costumes?"

"You're holding up the show. Drop the jacket and come on." She did a long, lazy leap over the railing and strode barefoot and beautiful across the white floor. She looked back at us, motioning for us to follow.

I stayed where I was. I wasn't going anywhere until somebody explained things. Larry and Edward waited with me. The audience near us was staring intently, waiting for us to do something interesting.

We stood there.

Rashida disappeared into one of the curtained circles. "Anita."

I turned, but Larry was staring at the ring. "Did you say something?"

He shook his head.

"Anita?"

I glanced at Edward, but it hadn't been his voice. I whispered, "Jean-Claude?"

"Yes, *ma petite*, it is I."

"Where are you?"

"Behind the curtain where Rashida went."

I shook my head. His voice had resonance, a slight echo, but otherwise it was as normal as his voice ever got. I could probably talk to him without moving my lips, but if so, I didn't want to know. I whispered, "What's going on?"

"Mr. Oliver and I have a gentleman's agreement."

"I don't understand."

"Who are you talking to?" Edward asked.

I shook my head. "I'll explain later."

"Come into my circle, Anita, and I will explain everything to you at the same time I explain it to our audience."

"What have you done?"

"I have done the best I could to spare lives, *ma petite*, but some will die tonight. But it will be in the circle with only the soldiers called to task. No innocents will die tonight, whoever wins. We have given our words."

"You're going to fight it out in the ring like a show?"

"It was the best I could do on such short notice. If you had warned me days ago, perhaps something else could have been arranged."

I ignored that. Besides, I was feeling guilty.

I took off the sweatshirt and laid it across the railing. There were gasps from the people near enough to see my gun.

"The fight's going to take place out in the ring."

"In front of the audience?" Edward said.

"Yep."

"I don't get it," Larry said.

"I want you to stay here, Larry."

"No way."

I took a deep breath and let it out slowly. "Larry, you don't have any weapons. You don't know how to use a gun. You're just cannon fodder until you get some training. Stay here."

He shook his head.

I touched his arm. "Please, Larry."

Maybe it was the please, or the look in my eyes—whatever, he nodded.

I could breathe a little easier. Whatever happened tonight, Larry wouldn't die because I'd brought him into it. It wouldn't be my fault.

I climbed over the railing and dropped to the ring. Edward followed me with a swish of black cape. I glanced back once. Larry stood gripping the rail. There was something forlorn about him standing there alone, but he was safe; that was what counted.

I touched the shimmering curtain, and it was the lights. The cloth was white up close. I lifted it to one side, and entered, Edward at my back.

There was a multilayered dais complete with throne in the center of the circle. Rashida stood with Stephen near the foot of the dais. I recognized Richard's hair and his naked chest before he lifted the mask off his face. It was a white mask with a blue star on one cheek. He was wearing glittering blue harem pants with a matching vest and shoes. Everyone was in costume but me.

"I was hoping you wouldn't make it in time," Richard said.

"What, and miss the Halloween blowout of all time?"

"Who's that with you?" Stephen asked.

"Death," I said.

Edward bowed.

"Trust you to bring death to the ball, *ma petite*."

I looked up the dais, to the very top. Jean-Claude stood in front of the throne. He was finally wearing what his shirts hinted at, but this was the real thing. The real French courtier. I didn't know what to call half of the costume. The coat was black with tasteful silver here and there. A short half-cloak was worn over one shoulder only. The pants were billowy and tucked into calf-high boots. Lace edged the foldover tops of the boots. A wide white collar lay at his throat. Lace spilled out of the coat sleeves. It was topped off by a wide, almost floppy hat with a curving arch of black and white feathers.

The costumed throng moved to either side, clearing the stairs up to the throne for me. I somehow didn't want to go. There were sounds outside the curtains. Heavy things being moved around. More scenery and props being moved up.

I glanced at Edward. He was staring at the crowd, eyes taking in everything. Hunting for victims, or for familiar faces?

Everyone was in costume, but very few people were actually wearing masks. Yasmeen and Marguerite stood about halfway up the stairs. Yasmeen was in a scarlet sari, all veils and sequins. Her dark face looked very natural in the red silk. Marguerite was in a long dress with puffed sleeves and a wide lace collar. The dress was of some dark blue cloth. It was simple, unadorned. Her blond hair was in complicated curls with one large mass over each ear and a small bun atop her head. Hers, like Jean-Claude's, looked less like a costume and more like antique clothing.

I walked up the stairs towards them. Yasmeen dropped her veils enough to expose the cross-shaped scar I'd given her. "Someone will pay you back for this tonight."

"Not you personally?" I asked.

"Not yet."

"You don't care who wins, do you?"

She smiled. "I am loyal to Jean-Claude, of course."

"Like hell."

"As loyal as you were, *ma petite*." She drew out each syllable, biting each sound off.

I left her to laugh at my back. I guess I wasn't the one to complain about loyalties.

There were a pair of wolves sitting at Jean-Claude's feet. They stared at me with strange pale eyes. There was nothing human in the gaze. Real wolves. Where had he gotten real wolves?

I stood two steps down from him and his pet wolves. His face was unreadable, empty and perfect.

"You look like something out of *The Three Musketeers*," I said.

"Accurate, *ma petite*."

"Is it your original century?"

He smiled a smile that could have meant anything, or nothing.

"What's going to happen tonight, Jean-Claude?"

"Come, stand beside me, where my human servant belongs." He extended a pale hand.

I ignored the hand and stepped up. He'd talked inside my head. It was getting silly to argue. Arguing didn't make it not true.

One of the wolves growled low in its chest. I hesitated.

"They will not harm you. They are my creatures."

Like me, I thought.

Jean-Claude put his hand down towards the wolf. It cringed and licked his hand. I stepped carefully around the wolf. But it ignored me, all its attention on Jean-Claude. It was sorry it had growled at me. It would do anything to make up for it. It groveled like a dog.

I stood at his right side, a little behind the wolf.

"I had picked out a lovely costume for you."

"If it was anything that would have matched yours, I wouldn't have worn it."

He laughed, soft and low. The sound tugged at something low in my gut. "Stay here by the throne with the wolves while I make my speech."

"We really are going to fight in front of the crowd."

He stood. "Of course. This is the Circus of the Damned, and tonight is Halloween. We will show them a spectacle the likes of which they have never seen."

"This is crazy."

"Probably, but it keeps Oliver from bringing the building down around us."

"Could he do that?"

"That and much more, *ma petite*, if we had not agreed to limit our use of such powers."

"Could you bring the building down?"

He smiled, and for once gave me a straight answer. "No, but Oliver does not know that."

I had to smile.

He draped himself over the throne, one leg thrown over a chair arm. He tucked his hat low until all I could see was his mouth. "I still cannot believe that you betrayed me, Anita."

"You gave me no choice."

"You would really see me dead rather than have the fourth mark."

"Yep."

He whispered, "Showtime, Anita."

The lights suddenly went off. There were screams from the audience as it sat in the sudden dark. The curtain pulled back on either side. I was suddenly on the edge of the spotlight. The light shone like a star in the dark. Jean-Claude and his wolves were bathed in a soft light. I had to agree that my pumpkin sweater didn't exactly fit the motif.

Jean-Claude stood in one boneless movement. He swept his hat off and gave a low, sweeping bow. "Ladies and gentlemen, tonight you will witness a great battle." He began to move slowly down the steps. The spotlight moved with him. He kept the hat off, using it for emphasis in his hand. "The battle for the soul of this city."

He stopped, and the light spread wider to include two blond vampires. The two women were dressed as 1920s flappers, one in blue, the other in red. The women flashed fangs, and there were gasps from the audience. "Tonight you will see vampires, werewolves, gods, devils." He filled each word with something. When he said "vampires," there was a ruffling at your neck. "Werewolves" slashed from the dark, and there were screams. "Gods" breathed along the skin. "Devils" were a hot wind that scalded your face.

Gasps and stifled screams filled the dark.

"Some of what you see tonight will be real, some illusion; which is which will be for you to decide." "Illusion" echoed in the mind like a vision through glass, repeating over and over. The last sound died away with a whisper that sounded like a different word altogether. "Real," the voice whispered.

"The monsters of this city fight for control of it this Halloween. If we win, then all goes peaceful as before. If our enemies win . . ." A second spotlight picked out the top of a second dais. There was no throne. Oliver stood at the top with the lamia in full serpent glory. Oliver was dressed in a baggy white jump suit with large polka dots on it. His face was white with a sad smile drawn on it. One heavily lined eye dropped a sparkling tear. A tiny pointed hat with a bright blue pom-pom topped his head.

A clown? He had chosen to be a clown? It wasn't what I had pictured him in. But the lamia was impressive with her striped coils curled around him, her naked breasts caressed by his gloved hand.

"If our enemies win, then tomorrow night will see a bloodbath such as no city in the world has ever seen. They will feed upon the flesh and blood of this city until it is drained dry and lifeless." He had stopped about halfway down. Now he began to come back up the stairs. "We fight for your lives, your very souls. Pray that we win, dear humans; pray very, very hard."

He sat in the throne. One of the wolves put a paw on his leg. He stroked its head absently.

"Death comes to all humans," Oliver said.

The spotlight died on Jean-Claude, leaving Oliver as the only light in the darkness. Symbolism at its best.

"You will all die someday. In some small accident, or long disease. Pain and agony await you." The audience rustled uneasily in their seats.

"Are you protecting me from his voice?" I asked.

"The marks are," Jean-Claude said.

"What is the audience feeling?"

"A sharp pain over the heart. Age slowing their bodies. The quick horror of some remembered accident."

Gasps, screams, cries filled the dark as Oliver's words sought out each person and made them feel their mortality.

It was obscene. Something that had seen a million years was reminding mere humans how very fragile life was.

"If you must die, would it not be better to die in our glorious embrace?" The lamia crawled around the dais to show herself to all the audience. "She could take you, oh, so sweetly, soft, gentle into that dark night. We make death a celebration, a joyful passing. No lingering doubts. You will want her hands upon you in the end. She will show you joys that few mortals ever dream of. Is death such a high price to pay, when you will die anyway? Wouldn't it be better to die with our lips upon your skin than by time's slowly ticking clock?"

There were a few cries of "Yes ... Please ..."

"Stop him," I said.

"This is his moment, *ma petite*. I cannot stop him."

"I offer you all your darkest dreams come true in our arms, my friends. Come to us now."

The darkness rustled with movement. The lights came up, and there were people coming out of the seats. People climbing over the railing. People coming to embrace death.

They all froze in the light. They stared around like sleepers waking from a dream. Some looked embarrassed, but one man close to the rail looked near tears, as if some bright vision had been ripped away. He collapsed to his knees, shoulders shaking. He was sobbing. What had he seen in Oliver's words? What had he felt in the air? God, save us from it.

With the lights I could see what they had moved in while we waited behind the curtains. It looked like a marble altar with steps leading up to it. It sat between the two daises, waiting. For what? I turned to ask Jean-Claude, but something was happening.

Rashida walked away from the dais, putting herself close to the railing, and the people. Stephen, wearing what looked like a thong bathing suit, stalked to the other side of the ring. His nearly naked body was just as smooth and flawless as Rashida's. "We heal fast," she'd said.

"Ladies and gentlemen, we will give you a few moments to recover yourselves from the first magic of the evening. Then we will show you some of our secrets."

The crowd settled back into their seats. An usher helped the crying man back to his seat. A hush fell over the people. I had never heard so large a crowd be so silent. You could have dropped a pin.

"Vampires are able to call animals to their aid. My animal is the wolf." He walked around the top of the dais displaying the wolves. I stood there in the spotlight and wasn't sure what to do. I wasn't on display. I was just visible.

"But I can also call the wolf's human cousin. The werewolf." He made a wide, sweeping gesture with his arm. Music began. Soft and low at first, then rising in a shimmering crescendo.

Stephen fell to his knees. I turned, and Rashida was on the ground as well. They were going to change right here in front of the crowd. I'd never seen a shapeshifter shift before. I had to admit a certain . . . curiosity.

Stephen was on all fours. His bare back was bowed with pain. His long yellow hair trailed on the ground. The skin on his back rippled like water, his spine standing like a ridge in the middle. He stretched out his hands as if he were bowing, face pressed to the ground. Bones broke through his hands. He groaned. Things moved under his skin like crawling animals. His spine bowed upward as if rising like a tent all on its own. Fur started to flow out of the skin on his back, spreading impossibly fast like a timelapse photo. Bones and some heavy, clear liquid poured out of his skin. Shapes strained and ripped through his skin. Muscles writhed like snakes. Heavy, wet sounds came as bone shifted in and out of flesh. It was as if the wolf's shape was punching its way out of the man's body. Fur flowed fast and faster, the color of dark honey. The fur hid some of the changes, and I was glad.

Something between a howl and a scream tore from his throat. Finally, there was that same manwolf form as the night we fought the giant cobra. The wolfman threw his muzzle skyward and howled. The sound raised the hairs on my body.

A second howl echoed from the other side. I whirled, and there was a second wolfman form, but this one was as black as pitch. Rashida?

The audience applauded wildly, stamping and shouting.

The werewolves crept back to the dais. They crouched at the bottom, one on each side.

"I have nothing so showy to offer you." The lights were back on Oliver. "The snake is my creature." The lamia twined around him, hissing loud enough to carry to the audience. She flicked a forked tongue to lick his whitecoated ear.

He motioned to the foot of the dais. Two black-cloaked figures stood on either side, hoods hiding their faces. "These are my creatures, but let us keep them for a surprise." He looked across at us. "Let it begin."

The lights went out again. I fought the urge to reach for Jean-Claude in the thick dark. "What's happening?"

"The battle begins," he said.

"How?"

"We have not planned the rest of the evening, Anita. It will be like every battle, chaotic, violent, bloody."

The lights came up gradually until the tent was bathed in a dim glow, like dusk or twilight. "It begins," Jean-Claude whispered.

The lamia flowed down the steps, and each side ran for the other. It wasn't a battle. It was a free-for-all, more like a bar brawl than a war.

The cloaked things ran forward. I had a glimpse of something vaguely snakelike but not. A spatter of machine-gun fire and the thing staggered back. Edward.

I started down the steps, gun in hand. Jean-Claude never moved. "Aren't you coming down?"

"The real battle will happen up here, *ma petite*. Do what you can, but in the end it will come down to Oliver's power and mine."

"He's a million years old. You can't beat him."

"I know."

We stared at each other for a moment. "I'm sorry," I said.

"So am I, *ma petite*, Anita, so am I."

I ran down the steps to join the fight. The snake-thing had collapsed, bisected by the machine-gun fire. Edward was standing back to back with Richard, who had a revolver in his hands. He was shooting it into one of the cloaked things and wasn't even slowing it down. I sighted down my arm and fired at the cloaked head. The thing stumbled and turned towards me. The hood fell backwards, revealing a cobra's head the size of a horse's. From the neck down it was a woman, but from the neck up . . . Neither my shot nor Richard's had made a dent. The thing came up the steps towards me. I didn't know what it was, or how to stop it. Happy Halloween.

47

The thing rushed towards me. I dropped the Browning and had one of the knives halfway out when it hit me. I was on the steps with the thing on top of me. It reared back to strike. I got the knife free. It plunged its fangs into my shoulder. I screamed and shoved the knife into its body. The knife went in, but no blood, no pain. It gnawed on my shoulder, pumping poison in, and the knife did nothing.

I screamed again. Jean-Claude's voice sounded in my head, ''Poison cannot harm you now.''

It hurt like hell, but I wasn't going to die from it. I plunged the knife into its throat, screaming, not knowing what else to do. It gagged. Blood ran down my hand. I hit it again, and it reared back, blood on its fangs. It gave a frantic hiss and pushed itself off me. But I understood now. The weak spot was where the snake part met human flesh.

I groped for the Browning left-handed; my right shoulder was torn up. I squeezed and watched blood spurt from the thing's neck. It turned and ran, and I let it go.

I lay on the steps holding my right arm against my body. I didn't think anything was broken, but it hurt like hell. It wasn't even bleeding as badly as it should have been. I glanced up at Jean-Claude. He was standing motionless, but something moved, like a shimmer of heat. Oliver was just as motionless on his dais. That was the real battle; the dying down here didn't mean much except to the people who were going to die.

I cradled my arm against my stomach and walked down the steps towards Edward and Richard. By the time I was at the bottom of the steps, the arm felt better. Good enough to change the gun to my right hand. I stared at the bite wound, and damned if it wasn't healing. The third mark. I was healing like a shapeshifter.

''Are you all right?'' Richard asked.

''I seem to be.''

Edward was staring at me. "You should be dying."

"Explanations later," I said.

The cobra thing lay at the foot of the dais, its head bisected by machine-gun fire. Edward caught on quick.

There was a scream, high and piercing. Alejandro had Yasmeen twisted around in his arms, one arm behind her back, his other arm pinning her shoulders to his chest. It was Marguerite who had screamed. She was struggling in Karl Inger's arms. She was outmatched. Apparently, so was Yasmeen.

Alejandro tore into her throat. She screamed. He snapped her spine with his teeth, blood splattering his face. She sagged in his arms. Movement, and his hand came out through the other side of her chest, the heart crushed to a bloody pulp.

Marguerite shrieked over and over again. Karl let her go, but she didn't seem to notice. She scratched fingernails down her cheeks until blood ran. She collapsed to her knees, still clawing at her face.

"Jesus," I said, "stop her."

Karl stared across at me. I raised the Browning, but he ducked behind Oliver's dais. I went towards Marguerite. Alejandro stepped between us.

"Do you want to help her?"

"Yes."

"Let me lay the last two marks upon you, and I will get out of your way."

I shook my head. "The city for one crazy human servant? I don't think so."

"Anita, down!" I dropped flat to the floor, and Edward shot a jet of flame over my head. I could feel the wash of heat bubbling overhead.

Alejandro shrieked. I raised my eyes only enough to see him burning. He motioned outward with one burning hand, and I felt something wash over me back towards . . . Edward.

I rolled over, and Edward was on his back, struggling to his feet. The nozzle of the flamethrower was pointed this way again. I dropped without being told.

Alejandro motioned, and the flame peeled backwards, flowing towards Edward.

He rolled frantically to put out the flames on his cloak. He threw the burning death's-head mask onto the ground. The flamethrower's tank was on fire. Richard helped him struggle out of it, and they ran. I hugged the ground, hands over my head. The explosion shook the ground. When I looked up, tiny burning pieces were raining down, but that was all. Richard and Edward were peering around the other side of the dais.

Alejandro stood there with his clothes charred, his skin blistered. He began walking towards me.

I scrambled to my feet, pointing my gun at him. Of course, the gun hadn't done a whole lot of good before. I backed up until I bumped the steps.

I started shooting. The bullets went in. He even bled, but he didn't stop. The gun clicked on empty. I turned and ran.

Something hit me in the back, slamming me to the ground. Alejandro was suddenly on my back, one hand in my hair, bending my neck backwards.

"Put down the machine gun or I'll break her neck."

"Shoot him!" I screamed.

But Edward threw the machine gun on the floor. Dammit. He got out a pistol and took careful aim. Alejandro's body jerked, then he laughed. "You can't kill me with silver bullets."

He put a knee in my back to hold me down; then a knife flashed in his hand.

"No," Richard said, "he won't kill her."

"I'll slit her throat if you interfere, but if you leave us alone, I won't harm her."

"Edward, kill him!"

A vampire jumped Edward, riding him to the ground. Richard tried to pull her off him, but a tiny vampire leaped on his back. It was the woman and the little boy from that first night.

"Now that your friends are busy, we will finish our business."

"NO!"

The knife just nicked the surface, sharp, painful, but such a little cut. He leaned over me. "It won't hurt, I promise."

I screamed.

His lips touched the cut, locked on it, sucking. He was wrong. It did hurt. Then the smell of flowers surrounded me. I was drowning in perfume. I couldn't see. The world was warm and sweet-scented.

When I could see again, think again, I was lying on my back, staring up at the tent roof. Arms drew me upward, cradled me. Alejandro held me close. He'd cut a line of blood on his chest, just above the nipple. "Drink."

I put my hands flat against him, fighting him. His hand squeezed the back of my neck, forcing me closer to the wound.

"NO!"

I drew the other knife and plunged it into his chest, searching for the heart. He grunted and grabbed my hand, squeezed until I dropped the knife. "Silver is not the way. I am past silver."

He pushed my face towards the wound, and I couldn't fight him. I just wasn't strong enough. He could have crushed my skull in one hand, but all he did was press my face to the cut on his chest.

I struggled, but he kept my mouth pressed to the wound. The blood was salty sweet, vaguely metallic. It was only blood.

"Anita!" Jean-Claude screamed my name. I wasn't sure if it was aloud or in my head.

"Blood of my blood, flesh of my flesh, the two shall be as one. One flesh, one blood, one soul." Somewhere deep inside me, something broke. I could feel it. A wave of liquid warmth rushed up and over me. My skin danced with it. My fingertips tingled. My spine spasmed, and I jerked upright. Strong arms caught me, held me, rocked me.

A hand smoothed my hair from my face. I opened my eyes to see Alejandro. I wasn't afraid of him anymore. I was calm and floating.

"Anita?" It was Edward. I turned towards the sound, slowly.

"Edward."

"What did he do to you?"

I tried to think how to explain it, but my mind wouldn't bring up the words. I sat up, pushing gently away from Alejandro.

There was a pile of dead vampires around Edward's feet. Maybe silver didn't hurt Alejandro, but it had hurt his people.

"We will make more," Alejandro said. "Can you not read this in my mind?"

And I could, now that I thought about it, but it wasn't like telepathy. Not words. I—knew he was thinking about the power I'd just given him. He felt no regret about the vampires that had died.

The crowd screamed.

Alejandro looked up. I followed his gaze. Jean-Claude was on his knees, blood pouring down his side. Alejandro envied Oliver the ability to draw blood from a distance. When I became Alejandro's servant, Jean-Claude had been weakened. Oliver had him.

That had been the plan all along.

Alejandro held me close, and I didn't try to stop him. He whispered against my cheek, "You are a necromancer, Anita. You have power over the dead. That is why Jean-Claude wanted you as his servant. Oliver thinks to control you through controlling me, but I know that you are a necromancer. Even as a servant, you have free will. You do not have to obey as the others do. As a human servant, you are yourself a weapon. You can strike one of us and draw blood."

"What are you saying?"

"They have arranged that the loser be stretched over the altar and staked by you."

"What . . ."

"Jean-Claude, as affirmation of his power. Oliver, as a gesture to show how well he controlled what once belonged to Jean-Claude."

There was a gasp from the crowd. Oliver was levitating ever so slowly. He floated to the ground. Then he raised his arms, and Jean-Claude floated upward.

"Shit," I said.

Jean-Claude hung nearly unconscious in empty, shining air. Oliver laid him gently on the ground, and fresh blood splattered the white floor.

Karl Inger came into sight. He picked Jean-Claude up under the arms.

Where was everybody? I looked around for some help. The black werewolf was torn apart, parts still twitching. I didn't think even a lycanthrope could heal the mess. The blond werewolf wasn't much better, but Stephen was dragging himself towards the altar. With one leg completely ripped away, he was trying.

Karl laid Jean-Claude on the marble altar. Blood began to seep down the side. He held him lightly at the shoulder. Jean-Claude could bench press a car. How could Karl hold him down?

"He shares Oliver's strength."

"Quit doing that," I said.

"What?"

"Answering questions I haven't asked yet."

He smiled. "It saves so much time."

Oliver picked up a white, polished stake and a padded hammer. He held them out towards me. "It's time."

Alejandro tried to help me stand, but I pushed him away. Fourth mark or no fourth mark, I could stand on my own.

Richard screamed, "No!" He ran past us towards the altar. It all seemed to happen in slow motion. He jumped at Oliver, and the little man grabbed him by the throat and tore his windpipe out.

"Richard!" I was running, but it was too late. He lay bleeding on the ground, still trying to breathe when he didn't have anything to breathe with.

I knelt by him, tried to stop the flow of blood. His eyes were wide and panic-filled. Edward was with me. "There's nothing you can do. Nothing any of us can do."

"No."

"Anita." He pulled me away from Richard. "It's too late."

I was crying and hadn't known it.

"Come, Anita; destroy your old master, as you wanted me to." Oliver was holding the hammer and stake out towards me.

I shook my head.

Alejandro helped me stand. I reached for Edward, but it was too late. Edward couldn't help. No one could help me. There was no way to take back the fourth mark, or heal Richard, or save Jean-Claude. But at least I wouldn't put the stake through Jean-Claude. That I could stop. That I would not do.

Alejandro was leading me towards the altar.

Marguerite had crawled to one side of the dais. She was kneeling, rocking gently back and fourth. Her face was a bloody mask. She'd clawed her eyes out.

Oliver held the stake and mallet out to me with his white-gloved hands, still wet with Richard's blood. I shook my head.

"You will take it. You will do as I say." His little clown face was frowning at me.

"Fuck you," I said.

"Alejandro, you control her now."

"She is my servant, master, yes."

Oliver held the stake out towards me. "Then have her finish him."

"I cannot force her, master." Alejandro smiled as he said it.

"Why not?"

"She is a necromancer. I told you she would have free will."

"I will not have my grand gesture spoiled by one stubborn woman."

He tried to roll my mind. I felt him rush over me like a wind inside my head, but it rolled off and away. I was a full human servant; vampire tricks didn't work on me, not even Oliver's.

I laughed, and he slapped me. I tasted fresh blood in my mouth. He stood beside me, and I could feel him tremble. He was so angry. I was ruining his moment.

Alejandro was pleased. I could feel his pleasure like a warm hand in my stomach.

"Finish him, or I promise you I'll beat you to a bloody pulp. You don't die easily now. I can hurt you worse than you can imagine, and you'll heal. But it will still hurt just as badly. Do you understand me?"

I stared down at Jean-Claude. He was staring at me. His dark blue eyes were as lovely as ever.

"I won't do it," I said.

"You still care about him? After all he has done to you?"

I nodded.

"Do him, now, or I will kill him slowly. I will pick pieces of flesh from his bones but never kill him. As long as his heart and head are intact, he won't die, no matter what I do to him."

I looked at Jean-Claude. I couldn't stand by and let Oliver torture him, not if I could help it. Wasn't a clean death better? Wasn't it?

I took the stake from Oliver. "I'll do it."

Oliver smiled. "You've made a wise decision. Jean-Claude would thank you if he could."

I stared down at Jean-Claude, stake in one hand. I touched his chest just over the burn scar. My hand came away smeared with blood.

"Do it, now!" Oliver said.

I turned to Oliver, reaching my left hand out for the hammer. As he handed it to me, I shoved the ash stake through his chest.

Karl screamed. Blood poured out of Oliver's mouth. He seemed frozen, as if he couldn't move with the stake in his heart, but he wasn't dead, not yet. My fingers tore into the meat of his throat and pulled, pulled great gobbets of flesh, until I saw spine, glistening and wet. I wrapped my hand around his spine and jerked it free. His head lolled to one side, held by a few strips of meat. I jerked his head clear and tossed it across the ring.

Karl Inger was lying beside the altar. I knelt by him and tried to find a pulse, but there wasn't one. Oliver's death had killed him too.

Alejandro came to stand by me. "You've done it, Anita. I knew you could kill him. I knew you could."

I stared up at him. "Now you kill Jean-Claude, and we rule the city together."

"Yes."

I shoved upward before I could think about it, before he could read my mind. I shoved my hands into his chest. Ribs cracked and scraped my skin. I grabbed his beating heart and crushed it.

I couldn't breathe. My chest was tight, and it hurt. I pulled his heart out of the hole. He fell, eyes wide and surprised. I fell with him.

I was gasping for air. Couldn't breathe, couldn't breathe. I lay on top of my master and felt my heart beating for both of us. He wouldn't die. I laid my fingers against his throat and started to dig. I put my hands around his throat and squeezed. I felt my hands dig into flesh, but the pain was overwhelming. I was choking on blood, our blood.

My hands went numb. I couldn't tell if I was still squeezing or not. I couldn't feel anything except the pain. Then even that slipped away, and I was falling, falling into a darkness that had never known light, and never would.

48

I woke up staring into an off-white ceiling. I blinked at the ceiling for a minute. Sunlight lay in warm squares across the blanket. There were metal rails on the bed. An IV dripped to my arm.

A hospital—then I wasn't dead. Surprise, surprise.

There were flowers and a bunch of shiny balloons on a small bedside table. I lay there a moment, enjoying the fact that I wasn't dead.

The door opened, and all I could see was a huge bunch of flowers. Then the flowers lowered, and it was Richard.

I think I stopped breathing. I could feel all the blood rushing through my skin. There was a soft roaring in my head. No. I wasn't going to faint. I never fainted. I finally managed to say, "You're dead."

His smile faded. "I'm not dead."

"I saw Oliver tear out your throat." I could see it in front of me like an overlay in my mind. I saw him gasping, dying. I found I could sit up. I braced myself, and the IV needle moved under my skin, the tape pulling. It was real. Nothing else seemed real.

He raised a hand towards his throat, then stopped himself. He swallowed hard enough for me to hear it. "You saw Oliver tear out my throat, but it didn't kill me."

I stared at him. There was no bandage on his cheek. The circle cut had healed. "No human being could survive that," I said softly.

"I know." He looked incredibly sad as he said it.

Panic filled my throat until I could barely breathe. "What are you?"

"I'm a lycanthrope."

I shook my head. "I know what a lycanthrope feels like, moves like. You aren't one."

"Yes, I am."

I kept shaking my head. "No."

He came to stand beside the bed. He held the flowers awkwardly, as if he didn't know what to do with them. "I'm next in line to be pack leader. I can pass for human, Anita. I'm good at it."

"You lied to me."

He shook his head. "I didn't want to."

"Then why did you?"

"Jean-Claude ordered me not to tell you."

"Why?"

He shrugged. "I think because he knew you'd hate it. You don't forgive deceit. He knows that."

Would Jean-Claude deliberately try to ruin a potential relationship between Richard and me? Yep.

"You asked what hold Jean-Claude had on me. That was it. My pack leader loaned me to Jean-Claude on the condition that no one find out what I was."

"Why are you a special case?"

"They won't let lycanthropes teach kids, or anybody else for that matter."

"You're a werewolf."

"Isn't that better than being dead?"

I stared up at him. His eyes were still the same perfect brown. His hair fell forward around his face. I wanted to ask him to sit down, to let me run my fingers through his hair, to keep it from that wonderful face.

"Yeah, it's better than being dead."

He let out a breath, as if he'd been holding it. He smiled and held the flowers out to me.

I took them because I didn't know what else to do. They were red carnations with enough baby's breath to form a white mist over the red. The carnations smelled like sweet cloves. Richard was a werewolf. Next in line for pack leader. He could pass for human. I stared up at him. I held out my hand to him. He took it, and his hand was warm and solid, and alive.

"Now that we've established why you're not dead, why aren't I dead?"

"Edward did CPR on you until the ambulances came. The doctors don't know what caused your heart to stop, but there's no permanent damage."

"What did you tell the police about all the bodies?"

"What bodies?"

"Come off it, Richard."

"By the time the ambulance got there, there were no extra bodies."

"The audience saw it all."

"But what was real and what was illusion? The police got a hundred different versions from the audience. They're suspicious, but they can't prove anything. The Circus has been shut down until the authorities can be sure it's safe."

"Safe?" I laughed.

He shrugged. "As safe as it ever was."

I slipped my hand out of Richard's grasp, using both hands to smell the flowers again. "Is Jean-Claude . . . alive?"

"Yes."

A great sense of relief washed over me. I didn't want him dead. I didn't want Jean-Claude dead. Shit. "He's still Master of the City, then. And I'm still bound to him."

"No," Richard said, "Jean-Claude told me to tell you. You're free. Alejandro's marks sort of canceled his out. You can't serve two masters, he said."

Free? I was free? I stared at Richard. "It can't be that easy."

Richard laughed. "You call this easy?"

I looked up. I had to smile. "All right, it wasn't easy, but I didn't think anything short of death would get Jean-Claude off my back."

"Are you happy the marks are gone?"

I started to say, "Of course," then stopped myself. There was something very serious in Richard's face. He knew what it was to be offered power. To be one with the monsters. It could be horrible, and wonderful.

Finally I said "Yes."

"Really?"

I nodded.

"You don't seem too enthused," he said.

"I know I should be jumping for joy, or something, but I just feel empty."

"You've been through a lot the last few days. You're entitled to be a little numb."

Why wasn't I happier to be rid of Jean-Claude? Why wasn't I relieved to be no one's human servant? Because I'd miss him? Stupid. Ridiculous. True.

When something gets too hard to think about, think about something else. "So now everyone knows you're a werewolf."

"No."

"You were hospitalized, and you've already healed. I think they'll guess."

"Jean-Claude had me hidden away until I healed. This is my first day up and around."

"How long have I been out?"

"A week."

"You're joking."

"You were in a coma for three days. The doctors still don't know what made you start breathing on your own."

I had come that close to the great beyond. I couldn't remember any tunnel of light, or soothing voices. I felt cheated. "I don't remember."

"You were unconscious; you're not supposed to remember."

"Sit down, before I get a crick looking up at you."

He pulled up a chair and sat down by the bed, smiling at me. It was a nice smile.

"So you're a werewolf."

He nodded.

"How did it happen?"

He stared down at the floor, then up. His face looked so solemn, I was sorry I'd asked. I was expecting some great tale of a savage attack survived. "I got a bad batch of lycanthropy serum."

"You what?"

"You heard me." He seemed embarrassed.

"You got a bad shot?"

"Yes."

My smile got wider and wider.

"It's not funny," he said.

I shook my head. "Not at all." I knew my eyes were shiny, and it was all I could do not to laugh out loud. "You've got to admit it's nicely ironic."

He sighed. "You're going to hurt yourself. Go ahead and laugh."

I did. I laughed until it hurt, and Richard joined in. Laughter is contagious, too.

49

A *dozen white* roses came later that day with a note from Jean-Claude. The note read, ''You are free of me, if you choose. But I hope you want to see me as much as I want to see you. It is your choice. Jean-Claude.''

I stared at the flowers for a long time. I finally had a nurse give them to someone else, or throw them away, or whatever the hell she wanted to do with them. I just wanted them out of my sight. So I was still attracted to Jean-Claude. I might even, in some dark corner, love him a little. It didn't matter. Loving the monsters always ends badly for the human. It's a rule.

That brought me to Richard. He was one of the monsters, but he was alive. That was an improvement over Jean-Claude. And was he any less human than I was: zombie queen, vampire slayer, necromancer? Who was I to complain?

I don't know where they put all the body parts, but no police ever came asking. Whether I'd saved the city or not, it was still murder. Legally, Oliver had done nothing to deserve death.

I got out of the hospital and went back to work. Larry stayed on. He's learning how to hunt vampires, God save him.

The lamia was truly immortal. Which I guess means lamias can't have been extinct. They just must always have been rare. Jean-Claude got the lamia a green card and gave her a job at the Circus of the Damned. I don't know if he's letting her breed, or not. I haven't been near the Circus since I got out of the hospital.

Richard and I finally had that first date. We went for something fairly traditional: dinner and a movie. We're going caving next week. He promised no underwater tunnels. His lips are the softest I've ever kissed. So he gets furry once a month. No one's perfect.

Jean-Claude hasn't given up. He keeps sending me gifts. I keep refusing them. I have to keep saying no until he gives up, or until hell freezes over, whichever comes first.

Most women complain that there are no single, straight men left. I'd just like to meet one who's human.